I0741417

THE PRESIDENTIAL PRETENDER©

Also by Jay Lumbert

The Alchemist Conspiracy
The Varicose Vigilantes
The Varicose Vigilantes II - Hedge Money
Working HR For Private Business
Retirement Planning Simplified By Jay
Retirement Plans Simplified By Jay

THE
PRESIDENTIAL PRETENDER

Jay Lumbert

Shaksper Books

Shaksper Books
USA

THE PRESIDENTIAL PRETENDER

Copyright © 2010 by E. Jay Lumbert

All rights reserved. No part of this book may be used or reproduced by any means, graphic, electronic, or mechanical, including photocopying, recording, taping or by any information storage retrieval system without the written permission of the publisher except in the case of brief quotations embodied in critical articles and reviews.

All Shaksper Books titles may be ordered through booksellers everywhere, or by contacting:

Shaksper Books

www.shaksperbooks.com   admin@shaksperbooks.com
1-800-469-0935

ISBN -13:978-0-9800501-7-2   (pbk)

ISBN -13:978-0-9800501-8-9   (lg prt pbk)

ISBN -13:978-0-9800501-9-6   (ebk)

ISBN -10: 0-9800501-7-0   (pbk)

ISBN -10:0-9800501-8-9   (lg prt pbk)

ISBN -10:0-9800501-9-7   (ebk)

Printed in the United States of America

This is a work of fiction. All names, characters and events are a product of the author's imagination or are used fictitiously. Any resemblance to actual persons, businesses, events or places is purely coincidental.

This book is dedicated to Christi, Sabrina, Allyssa, Billy & Katrina.
You are my greatest joy.

Author's Note:

The Presidential Pretender began as my Master's Thesis at Wesleyan University. A few years ago, I began assembling the many pieces of this novel, stitching it together like a quilt. I studied politics and religion. I studied cosmology and technology. I studied personal and international warfare. I studied punishment and forgiveness.

What evolved was a book is about the human experience in its most glorious and heinous forms, a story of love and hate, goodness and evil, all woven into today's complicated world of politics and terrorism. The book explores the innate character of mankind and how far we can justify abhorrent behavior as normal. It explores the depths to which a good man or woman can fall, crawling deep within in the darkness to find where that bottom might be. It also celebrates mankind's extraordinary capacity to forgive.

Set within Jack Trance's incredible world of wealth, mystery, legacy and duty, this book will lead you on a journey that (I hope) will take you to places you rarely get to go—where the adrenaline rushes and the mind flows freely, where the emotions of love and hate combine with concepts like duty, forgiveness and country—perhaps into Sammantha's spinning world.

I hope this book will move you. It will certainly make you think. Where the book ultimately takes you, will depend on your experience with life. I hope it is a good place, because we all deserve one.

There are many people that helped with this book. As always, I must thank my extraordinary wife, Deb. Without her, none of this would exist. I must also thank my family for providing me the emotional support to bring such a project to completion. This isn't easy and I thank you for your sacrifices.

Thanks must go to Dianne Eaton, Matt Gross, Pat Hull, Paul Corrigan, Stan Alexander and Alicemarie Adams, independent readers, who gave suggestions on the manuscript.

As always, I express my profound thanks to all of the men and women who (daily) volunteer to trade their lives for my freedom. Without you, and the patriots who came before you, I would not have the great opportunity to share my stories. America is an extraordinary experiment that owes its sustenance to you.

I hope this book is as enjoyable for you to read as it was for me to write.

Beyond a doubt truth bears the same relation to falsehood as light to darkness. There are three classes of people: those who see, those who see when they are shown, those who do not see.

Who sows virtue reaps honor.

Leonardo da Vinci

A man that studieth revenge keeps his own wounds green.

God hangs the greatest weights upon the smallest wires.

In taking revenge, a man is but even with his enemy; but in passing it over, he is superior.

Sir Francis Bacon

Like the physical, the psychical is not necessarily in reality what it appears to us to be.

Illusions commend themselves to us because they save us pain and allow us to enjoy pleasure instead. We must therefore accept it without complaint when they sometimes collide with a bit of reality against which they are dashed to pieces.

Sigmund Freud

A man who has not passed through the inferno of his passions has never overcome them.

Great talents are the most lovely and often the most dangerous fruits on the tree of humanity. They hang upon the most slender twigs that are easily snapped off.

Knowledge rests not upon truth alone, but upon error also.

The most intense conflicts, if overcome, leave behind a sense of security and calm that is not easily disturbed. It is just these intense conflicts and their conflagration which are needed to produce valuable and lasting results.

Your vision will become clear only when you can look into your own heart. Who looks outside, dreams; who looks inside, awakes.

Carl Jung

CHAPTER 1
_____________PP_____________

In the center of the room, on a splintered wooden floor, with knees clenched against her chest, Sammantha Starodubov began to rock. Back and forth like a baby's cradle. The rocking never faltered, never slowed. For minute after minute she just kept rocking, ticking with the precision of a slow moving metronome. Sammantha's breath trailed white in the fetid, frigid air, slipping out in vague plumes from under the coarse woolen blanket draped over her head. An hour passed. The seat of her jeans was wearing thin but she didn't notice. Her mind was elsewhere.

Sammantha thought of blood. Blood on her feet, on her hands, and blood on her lips. She thought of sunlight, pouring through the windows like a searchlight onto the bodies of her parents as they lay dead on the kitchen floor. She thought of twenty-five years of being alone.

Another hour passed. Sammantha saw her mother in the summer sunlight. Her face was serene, as if feeling love or the afterglow of sex. Her father was smiling, tossing her high against the sky so she could splash down into their backyard pool. She saw her puppy, Boris, as he licked the blood off her hands.

She didn't know who killed her parents or why. She knew only what she had been told. It was *The Americans*. The American government had forced her to be carried off like a circus animal and perform like one. Never again. Sammantha's nostrils swelled with the sweet, sickly smell of death. Her eyes were closed, but she saw her father's hand stretched out, almost touching the face of her mother. A quarter century of pain. She remembered it as if it were yesterday.

"Never again," she said.

 She'd repay them. She'd repay them all.

Blood spread from her father's head, across the floor to Sammantha's feet. The odor reached up into her nose like dead fingers. She reached down to shake her mother's head. Wake up! There was blood on her hands, her mother's blood. Blood she could never wash away.

Sammantha could feel the anger bubbling deep within her belly. It felt hot and frothy and powerful. She could feel it pressing against her, like a tidal surge, the pressure building, threatening to breach the wall she had built against its strength, leaping up and over and onto the floor in steaming chunks. She would have to break this wall, if she were to survive. It would have to be soon. For now, she took her other defense against it. Sammantha began to cry. "I have not forgotten," she said softly. "Never have I forgotten."

Sammantha rocked harder. She remembered the shoes. Black, thick-soled work shoes with heavy brown, poorly cuffed pants draped across the laces.

"They killed your parents," he'd said. He spoke Russian, her native tongue. "The Americans killed them, your mother and father. Do you understand?"

Twelve years old, she had nodded wordlessly. Then she'd let that man take her into his arms. Those hairy, smelly arms. And he did things…unspeakable things while she wept.

Sammantha took a long, steady breath and looked to her watch. Three hours gone. Just three hours more. She shook her head and looked to the water-streaked ceiling and sobered. *God, give me strength.*

Sammantha wiped her tears and tried to stand. Her legs quivered; and she sat back down. Only then did she feel the pain, the physical pain. She looked to her jeans and saw a wet stain spreading along the fabric. Blood. New blood. Fresh blood from rocking on the splintered floor. Her body was bleeding, her nerves raw and open to the world.

Sammantha narrowed her eyes. She pressed her arms against the floor and willed herself to her feet. She stretched her oxygen-starved legs until she steadied. She frowned, as she looked at the darkness seeping along her thighs. She couldn't worry about minor body aches. Not today. Today was a day of triumph. *Today you begin repayment*, she thought. Repayment to the few who had helped her. Retribution for the others, that sordid series of users and abusers who had discarded her like a dirty paper towel.

Sammantha leaned down and pressed her palms against the floor. She wrapped her hands around her ankles and pulled her face to her knees. She held there, like a dancer, until she felt herself loosen and relax. Taking a deep, measured breath she stood erect. She gazed around the room and shook her head slowly. A grim smile spread across her lips. Age, smoke and dust had turned the wallpaper into the color of sun-faded newsprint. Crude pictures and desperate cries for recognition were scrawled across the wall with crayons and spray paint—in obnoxious shades of purple and red, fluorescent orange and puke green. Jesus Saves...God is dead...Free Mandela...Obama is king…Crips die…Bloods suck…The Nightriders...I did it with Gina... Bobby and Carmen forever…

The dregs of America, thought Sammantha. *The discarded souls of America…I've lived here like them...as one of them. I paid the price. But not after today. Never again. Never again.*

Sammantha took the morning newspaper and crumpled it into a group of tight balls. She thrust the balls into a small, rusty cast iron stove that sat against the wall. She took her last three meager sticks of firewood and dropped them inside. She lit a match and watched the paper catch fire. *Burn baby burn.*

Sammantha began to walk slowly around the room. She traced her right index finger along the wallpaper and thought of how much it was like *her*—torn in countless places, with ragged pieces pulling away at the corners, scribbled upon, barfed on, ripped and forced to wear obscenities like a badge. She stopped beside what had once been two fine brass lamps built into the wall, amazed they were still there at all. They might have fetched a full dollar or two from the local scrap vulture. The lamps were dented and scratched. They were surrounded by holes made by errant fists and crowbars. The wall around them was a mosaic of air vents and rats' nests, with the two broken-down lamps serving like drunken sentries. They came out at night, the rats. She'd often sat on the floor in the darkness, picking them off with a pellet gun. It was good training and it soothed her mind. She liked rats; they were like soul mates.

A flash of childhood tried to sneak back into her consciousness. She fought it off by walking to the far end of the room, to the part her landlord referred to as "the kitchen."

She flipped on the single working unit of a two-burner stove, poured water into a chipped teapot from a plastic jug and set the pot down to heat.

"Today you die, too, Sandra," she said. Her lips tightened into a grim smile. "I'll almost miss this place." Sandra Smith. Not her real name, just the one she had been using for the past six months. It had served her well. She and Sandra had reached a place she had only dreamed she could attain. She was on the brink of something great.

Sammantha looked to her hands—skilled hands, surgeon's hands, avenger's hands. That was what they would be today, if all went right. Sammantha studied the thin leather gloves that covered those fingers. Protected, they looked sleek and benign.

Sammantha's mind was dragged back again, kicking and screaming across the Virginia countryside—to the white Colonial with its black shutters, its stained-glass windows and its broad green lawns. Twenty-five acres, three horses, the below-ground swimming pool and two green Buicks in the circular driveway. Her American nightmare. She sees her bedroom. It is painted yellow and it houses a world full of dolls. Cabbage Patch and Barbie. Raggedy Ann and Andy. She leaves these dolls behind, all of them orphans, just like her. There is a birthday party. Her birthday, with young, innocent, happy girls. They sing karaoke. It is a new thing, something none of them have tried before. It is something foreign and rare and exciting. They eat cake and ice cream at the dining room table. She helps her mother clean up in the kitchen. She walks across that very same floor, the one covered just a week later with the debris of death.

The kitchen, she thought. She sees her mother staring at the ceiling, her hair twisted, some of it clotted black, a swatch of it still gleaming red in the sunlight. She sees her butterfly cup, shattered beside her mother's ear. She was so excited, bursting through the door to tell her mother the news. Straight A's again. Five dollars for each and another year of riding lessons earned. Life is a cup full of promise. Then she falls to her knees beside her mother, her tongue so thick in her throat that it feels like a dry sponge. She fights for air.

"Momma? Daddy?"

And then...the shoes. Those black shoes.

"They killed your parents…The Americans killed them, your mother and father. Do you understand? They are dead because they came to America."

"I understand. I will never forget. Never."

The teapot whistled. Sammantha glanced at her watch and began to wring her hands. Ten minutes. Instant coffee. A nervous need. Then she'd begin to prepare for the reception. The British Embassy. The beginning.

Sammantha reached into the cupboard high above the stove for her cup, her single cup, her special cup. The cupboard had no door, just strips of splintered wood where the screws had been ripped away. She felt the cup through her gloves. She smiled as she pulled it into the light, her cup, with colorful butterflies flying happily in the faded sunshine. It was glued together in so many places that it resembled an archaeological ruin more than a functioning coffee cup. That's what it was, the one priceless ruin of her aborted childhood.

Sammantha's mind veered again, like a car skidding on a patch of ice, leaving her powerless to steer or stop. It was all she could do to hold on. Her mind stops at the horse corral behind her parent's home. It sees the small pond where she and her father go fishing, and out beyond the pond to the wooded paths where she likes to ride. She sees the great bay windows of the kitchen, where she sits looking out while her mother hums happily as she makes hot cocoa and pours it into Sammantha's butterfly cup.

"Mama...dear Mama..."

Sammantha swiped at an escaped tear that was dripping along her cheek. She carried her cup carefully, with two hands like a child, to the solitary chair in the dusty room. The chair was puffy and brown, tattered and torn, with thick white clumps of stuffing peeking out through its exposed springs. Sammantha lowered herself carefully into the seat and winced when the metal clawed at the rawness of her ragged skin.

Mother, she thought. *Mother was always there when I had a bump or bruise.* "I'll see that they pay, mother. Today we'll begin to exact our price."

Minutes later, her coffee drained, Sammantha walked to the far edge of the room to a free-standing sink. Beside the sink sat a dingy porcelain bathtub that smelled faintly of urine no matter how many times she cleaned it. Across from the tub, a cracked and blotchy mirror stretched from the floor to eye height. Sammantha undressed before the mirror, watching intently as each piece of clothing fell away from her body, until she stood there naked, except for her gloves, her thin satin slippers and her hair net.

Sammantha could have been a Broadway dancer. She was long and lean, her edges taut but rounded. Her muscles were smooth but dense with strength. With proper training she might have been a gymnast or an Olympic skater. Her caretakers had deemed other training more useful. Sammantha could kill a man with the flick of a wrist, and deliver a lethal injection that could not be traced. She raised computer viruses like a mother nurtures children, and she could cut a brain as naturally as a housewife sliced carrots. In the next few months she would use that training. Her life would come full circle. She would repay the ones who had damned her to hell. She would take them there with her, every last one of them.

Sammantha studied what she saw in the mirror, the intense face with the thoughtful, tortured eyes. Her hair was the color of corn silk. It was thick, straight and smooth. It would fall several inches below her shoulders, framing a Slavic face that had sharp, angular cheeks, a high forehead and rounded sensuous lips. Her lips parted to reveal an orthodontist's vision of the ideal mouth, with straight front teeth bleached to perfection.

It was her eyes that made her unique. One was green, the other blue. They were like shades of the ocean. Like the ocean, they moved without stop, changing colors with her movements and her moods.

With a flash of her teeth and a crinkle of her nose, Sammantha could transform a deathly, calculating stare into the warmth of sunshine. This gave her power over men. With a subtle glance she could spin a man into her web. She could reach inside him and shudder his loins, fill him with desire—and the thought that he, and he alone, was the one man who could satisfy her.

Sammantha stuffed her clothes into a small canvas suitcase. This was all that was left of Sandra Smith. Everything else had been burned the night before. She had cleaned the room of stray hairs and fingerprints. Only the mattress on the floor, the lousy tea kettle and the smelly brown chair remained. She'd leave her door open and it would all be gone by morning.

Sammantha spread her legs and sneered at herself in the mirror. "That's what they've always wanted, isn't it? They didn't care about your mind. They didn't worry about what you might *feel*, what *needs* you had, what *pain* you felt." Sammantha ran her fingers through her pubic hairs. "I'll give you what you want, my princess, now just spread your legs and everything will be fine..." Sammantha closed her eyes and bit her lip. She saw her dead mother's face and shook it off. "But you didn't kill me, did you? None of you had me. Not really. None of you. You hear!"

Sammantha stepped toward the mirror and stopped only inches away. "I got something from you, every last one of you. I salvaged my life. I earned my education, I made my money...My..." She closed her eyes. After several moments she whispered, "And now it's time for revenge—on all of you, every single last one of you."

Sammantha cleaned herself, then began to apply her makeup. After thirty minutes she smiled, pleased with her looks. She reached down and dabbed a finger into a jar of black powder. She massaged the powder under her eyes until they were both surrounded by pronounced, well-darkened, raccoon circles. She painted small, nearly invisible brown stripes around her lips and eyes to give her the subtle, saddened look of a clown. She viewed herself again and smiled slyly.

"Much better." No one would look at her now. She inserted two brown contact lenses into her eyes and examined them closely. Even better.

Sammantha had looked this way the day she had applied for her job at the British Embassy. She had looked this way every day since. No one at the Embassy had seen the sensuous beauty that could turn a strong man's knees to jelly. They knew the dour but efficient Miss Smith—with muddy-brown hair tied in a tight bun behind a stern, worn-out face.

Sammantha wrapped her hair into a thin rubber cap and fit it tightly against her head. She covered the cap with her Miss Smith wig. With the wig securely in place, Sammantha reached into the cupboard under the basin. From inside she pulled a brown paper bag. in it were a servant's uniform and a pair of white, rubber-soled shoes. She dressed quickly, and within moments the transformation was complete.

The Sandra Smith standing in the mirror bore no resemblance to the Sammantha Starodubov underneath. She was a dull-witted, slow-moving, plain-faced twit, lumbering through world in an ignorant fog. She was sweet, kind, gentle, and boring—not the tortured, provocative genius that suffered inside.

Just two things left, thought Sammantha. She walked to the pitiful kitchen and dropped to her knees. She reached into a tilting wooden cupboard. It was dusty with cobwebs and guarded inside by three rusty rat traps spaced on the outer edge of the bottom. Sammantha reached over the traps for a wooden pointer that she'd left inside. She took the pointer within her gloved fingers and used it to touch beneath a small plastic vial that was resting in the jaws of a fourth trap, a bear trap, with jagged, rusty fangs. There was a loud *crack* as the pointer snapped in two. Only then did Sammantha reach for the container and grasp it with her hand. As she pulled back her arm, it scraped against a rough piece of veneer, just a tiny tweak that Sammantha noticed, but ignored.

Sammantha stood up. With effort, she twisted the heel off her right shoe. She held the shoe toward the light. A hollow space had been expertly carved inside the heel to match the vial. Sammantha snapped the vial into place and fit the heel back onto her shoe.

"How I have waited for this," she said softly.

Sammantha took her butterfly cup from the counter. She wrapped it in a dishtowel and placed it gently into her suitcase. She took one last look at the room, threw the key onto the counter, and walked out.

CHAPTER 2
_____________PP_____________

Jason "Jock" Tilson sat down at the foot of a king-sized bed with an ornate, 19th century canopy. He leaned back on his muscular arms, gazing across the room as a woman pulled a cream colored silk evening dress over a plain white camisole.

"Nice view, Kiki," said Jock.

"Keep your eyes to yourself." The woman leaned over to straighten the folds of her dress. Her breasts bulged above the top of the dress and Jock angled for a better look.

"Even better," he said. Jock swung his feet off the bed and walked slowly toward Kiki.

"You take another step toward me and I'll scream." Kiki backed away. Jock didn't stop. "If you don't keep your hands off me—" Kiki turned away and giggled.

Jock touched Kiki's shoulders and ran his lips along the back of her neck. He inhaled the damp sweetness of her clean skin and rocked her gently in his arms. He ran his broad fingers down along her slim frame until she grabbed his hand.

"I'm warning you," Kiki said sharply.

"Do you know how much I love you?"

"No."

Jock pouted. "I am deeply offended."

Kiki sighed and let her gown drop to the floor. "Don't say I didn't warn you." She took a long, resigned breath and pulled herself against her husband's bare chest.

"That's better," he said.

"I really wanted to make a good impression," Kiki said. She twirled an errant wisp of her husband's hair before cradling his face with her hands. She kissed him gently, lovingly. "And now look what we're doing."

"We're supposed to be late."

Kiki chuckled. "You? Late?"

"Really. I think we should be late."

"Why don't you just say it," she said.

"Say what?"

"You know."

"No, I don't."

"Yes, you do."

"I'm not scared." Jock lifted a spotless crystal ash tray off one of the end tables and turned it over in his hands. He peered at it as if it were something odd and unusual.

"Yes, you are scared."

"Of what?"

"You know."

"I won't fail."

"No, you won't."

"Where'd this ash tray come from?"

"It's historic. Sit on the bed."

Jock put down the ash tray and sat beside his wife. She took his hands and looked at him intently, almost motherly.

"Remember that eight year old boy?"

"No."

"Yes, you do."

"What about him?"

"You remember that day? Down on his knees, with flowers in his hands."

"He was young and stupid."

"And so sure of himself. You proposed to me when you were eight years old, Jock."

"Children say lots of silly things."

Kiki laughed. "You told me that we would be married. You said you would be president. You said we would live happily ever after."

The president frowned. "Yeah, well—"

As the first lady lay back upon the bed, her breasts spread flat across her chest, making her look like a teasing nymph in a Rubens painting. She smiled. "And you were right."

"But—"

The first lady held up her hand. "Stop. In all this time, never once have I doubted you."

"But, Jesus, Kiki. This isn't some childhood fantasy. We're *here*. *Now*. I'm not eight years old. I've learned things since then."

"This is what you have worked for your entire life."

Jock Tilson closed his eyes. "They say, be careful what you wish for…"

"…for you may get that wish," finished the first lady.

"What if I fail?"

Kiki laughed. "And when have you failed?"

Jock stood suddenly, his back stiff. "Failed?" He began to pace and his lips turned into a pouting frown. "You know damned well when I failed. The Yale game."

"Not that again."

"The Ivy championship on the line—"

"That was over twenty years ago."

"I struck out."

"That's baseball, Jock."

"The bottom of the ninth and I struck out."

"Copley was on fire that day. Two others struck out in that same inning. He struck out eighteen in the game."

"But they're not president."

Kiki laughed. "I ask you when you've failed and you talk about baseball. A boy's game. Half a lifetime ago." Kiki tried to stand but the president pressed her back against the bed.

"Have I told you that I love you today?"

Kiki sighed. "Yes. Twice."

"Oh…Well, I love you. And it's a *man's* game."

"Boy's game. You're all boys. Go get dressed, so we can get to work on time."

"First things first." Jock drew the straps of Kiki's dress across her shoulders and began to slip it down her back.

"Darling," she said. "You've never doubted me, have you?"

Jock smiled and shook his head.

"Of course you haven't," she continued. "You've made me the happiest grandmother in the world." She hesitated. "I left my diaphragm at Camp David yesterday. Since you're not clipped and I'm not on the pill…Unless you want to be changing diapers for your second year in office, I suggest you get your butt over to your side of the room and put on your clothes."

Jock groaned good-naturedly. "I'll send Kelley out for condoms."

"He's the vice president, not an errand boy."

"It'll give him something to do. He needs something to stay busy."

Kiki looked at Jock, waiting for him to crack. She waited for half a minute, her eyes never blinking, until they both erupted in laughter.

"Wouldn't the press have a field day?" Kiki said between tears. "You think they were hard on Quayle and Biden…"

"We could—"

"Not on your life."

"I'll send the—"

"Get dressed! I love you, but get dressed."

Jock pinched Kiki's thigh. She gave a muffled shout, then slapped her husband's bare bottom. She pushed him off the bed. "Just remember who's boss."

"Yes, ma'am."

"As much as I'd love to, at forty-six, I'm just too old to be lugging another child on my hip."

"As usual, you're right," said the president.

It was the middle of winter, only weeks since Jock Tilson had been sworn to the presidency. Tonight was one of his first official acts. The Washington temperature hovered around zero. A biting wind was blowing down the Potomac, an arctic chill on the heels of snow.

"You'd think the British would wait until it was warm," said Kiki, as she straightened her dress.

Jock smiled as he pulled a starched white shirt up over one arm. "It's the international hierarchy, dear. We couldn't very well attend a reception at the Italian embassy until we've first been hosted by the British, the Germans and so on. The world's a global village, remember? With all of the usual sibling rivalries."

"Don't they know you're leaving tonight?"

Jock thought about his secret meeting with the new king of Saudi Arabia. Arab tensions were high and OPEC members were grumbling, as usual. He needed to discuss oil policy with the king, far outside the glare of public opinion. He would be spending the night upon Air Force One. While America was starting breakfast, he would be seated on a ceremonial pillow drinking coffee and eating goat's eyes with the king.

"That's all hush, hush. Not a word to anyone."

"You'll be leaving right after the reception?"

"Have to."

"Good. I'm tired. I can use some rest."

Jock finished buttoning his shirt, then began to rub Kiki's shoulders. "You sure you don't want to come along? Maybe join the mile high club?"

"Not tonight, dear." Kiki turned and pulled her husband's chest close to her face. "Have I told you that I love you today?"

"Twice."

"Well, I love you today."

"You make me very happy."

"You still can't have sex."

CHAPTER 3
_____________PP_____________

Jack Trance stared at his reflection in a full length mirror that was built into the wall. His tuxedo was expertly cut to his hardened frame. His shirt was the color of cream, expensively smooth and rich. His brown hair was expertly cut and stylishly long in the back. His brown eyes seemed to radiate strength and intelligence. There were other things behind that focused stare. There was a quiet confidence, but there was also a kind of Weltschmerz, a hollow, longing sadness borne from seeing far too much of the world's darker sides. Trance's cheeks were high and chiseled. In normal times he would have looked sleek and elegant. Now there was a gaunt, haunting shadow surrounding him, like the life had been carved out of him by a hidden disease.

Trance frowned as he fumbled impatiently with a black, silk bow tie. He glanced across the room to a woman seated at a blue marble vanity. The woman was primping her hair, working her way ever-closer to declaring sartorial success. The woman was in her mid thirties, athletically slim, with sensitive walnut eyes, and tawny auburn hair that flowed smoothly down her shoulders.

Trance said, "I really don't want to do this. Let's go to St. Croix."

The woman ignored him. She reached for a tube of mascara and began touching up her eyelashes. "Remember last year, how the president asked you to be nice to his successor?"

"That doesn't mean I have to go to Tilson's parties. I hate these things."

"The president asked you here as a personal favor."

"I've never met the man. Can't be too personal."

"Jack—"

They had been discussing this for days. The last place Trance wanted to be was Washington. Things happened to him here. Bad things. But, as the nation's most accomplished operative, as well as one of its richest men, the new president had called personally to ask for a private meeting at the British Embassy.

"This is a free country, you know. We don't *have* to do anything." Trance pulled fruitlessly at his tie and groaned. He looked at his fingers, still trembling from drug withdrawal. "Damn this tie. Can't we go somewhere else?"

Lauren Haverford continued looking into the mirror, calmly plucking her eyebrows. "I think you should give the guy a break. He's new. He's got a lot to learn."

"He doesn't need me, Lauren. There will be plenty of people clamoring over themselves to brown their noses on his butt. He's got no use for a small town lawyer." Trance gave up on the tie. He focused on his French cuffs. He managed to slip his cufflinks on without a problem. "Besides," he continued. "I told Miller I was out."

Lauren smiled but didn't speak. Out of the corner of her eye she noticed Trance begin to fumble again with his tie.

"You told that to Miller years ago," said Lauren sweetly. "Since then you've been anything but retired."

Trance's eyes darted toward Lauren, but he held back comment. Instead, he strode to a phone and punched for room service.

"How may I help you, Mr. Trance?" said the concierge.

"Clive, could you please bring me a black clip-on bow tie? A formal one?"

Lauren stifled a laugh as Trance dropped the receiver back into place. "I heard that," he said.

"Get over here, hotshot. I'll tie that thing."

"But—"

"Get your butt over here."

"Yes, sir!"

Lauren motioned for Trance to take a seat at the vanity. She settled him upon the wide, thickly cushioned bench and patted his shoulders.

"Honey," she said. "This is a party, a social engagement, not a crisis." Lauren pulled Trance's aborted knot apart and began tying a new one.

"It doesn't feel right."

"It's been nearly a month since your kidnapping. So, you were tortured and hooked on drugs. Big deal. You need to move on. Get back in the game."

"I don't want the game."

"The game wants you. It needs you."

Trance closed his eyes. "Lauren, you know what happens. The president will get to know me. Miller will shoot his mouth off. The next thing you know, I'll be in some Godforsaken place fighting for who knows what…"

"Just tell him *no*."

"Good idea. Let's go see Wilson in Austria. I hear the skiing is fantastiche."

"I thought you wanted warmth?"

"Okay. We'll visit Stick in Fiji."

"Who says your friends want to see you?"

Lauren looked at Trance. She felt like a girl staring into a store window, coveting a priceless doll she could never afford. She wished that things were different, that she could ease his fear. Perhaps if she hadn't pursued her career, if she'd married him when he had asked…maybe then, things would be different. But now?

Lauren thought of that day—the darkest day of her life. She sees herself dressed in a pink chiffon gown, holding a bouquet of spring flowers, staring blankly forward as the words drone on. Trance's young bride stands trembling beside her. *She's pretty*, Lauren thinks. *She'll make him a good wife*. Lauren wipes at tears she can't hide. She looks across the aisle to the groom. Trance fiddles nervously with his cufflinks and shifts his weight from one foot to the other and back. Lauren looks to him and they lock eyes. *What is he thinking?* she wonders. Finally, someone will make him happy. She aches to be that woman, but it will never be. If only she could go back and change the past.

"And do you, Janice, take this man…"

Trance's eyes glance toward Lauren. He smiles, as if fortified by her strength.

It should have been me, she thinks. *If I'd only said yes.*

"…'till death do you part?"

"I do," whispered Lauren. Her heart jumped, as Trance's touch brought her back to their suite at the Ritz-Carlton on 22nd Street, N.W..

"You do what?" Trance asked.

Lauren blushed. She brought her hand up to gently caress Trance's face.

"I…" She hesitated. "…I was just remembering your wedding day." Lauren felt Trance's jaw tighten. "I was remembering Janice, and how I wished you both a life of happiness. I was also remembering how much I wished it had been me."

Trance shook his head. "No, Lauren."

"Jack—"

"No."

"Jack, it's been over six years." She let the words hang and continued, "You've got to move on."

"Lauren—"

Trance sat down on the bed and slumped his shoulders. He drew a deep breath through his nose and exhaled slowly. Lauren stood beside him and cradled his head against her hip. She could feel him shudder.

"I love you," she said. "I always have. I always will. You know that."

"I can't let it happen again," he said firmly.

"It wasn't your fault."

"My fault?" Trance got to his feet and began to pace the room. "Of course it was my fault."

"She was a fine woman, Jack," said Lauren softly. "We both loved her. But she knew what she was getting into."

Trance stopped abruptly and laughed. "She had no goddamn clue. Only I knew what she was getting into and I should have stopped it."

"Bullshit." Lauren took hold of Trance's shoulders and squeezed them. She shook him gently. "Listen to me, Jack. It was terrorists that killed Janice, not you. Not Miller. Not anyone else. So let it go. It's not…your…fault. It won't happen again. It won't."

Lauren relaxed her grip and sank back against the bed. She grabbed a feather pillow from beside the wooden headboard and laid it over her face.

Trance looked at her, feeling helpless. His eyes glazed, and he began to look aimlessly about the large suite, as he remembered the day he'd learned of his wife's death.

***

The office is not overly large, but it reeks of money and influence. Along the walls hang faded pictures of the Miller family mansions, including the Newport monstrosity on Bellevue Avenue, just down the street from a home owned by Trance's uncle. There are pictures of sailboats docked at private harbors. There are large family portraits with no one smiling. The floor is covered with a thick oriental carpet. The furniture is from seventeenth and eighteenth century European royalty.

"She's dead, Jack," says Miller, only seconds after Trance has been shown into his office.

"Don't play me, Jake."

"It happened nearly a month ago. You couldn't be contacted."

"Couldn't be contacted? My wife is dead and you can't call me in?"

"We couldn't jeopardize the mission."

Trance smiles angrily. "Ah, yes, the mission. Of course, we couldn't sacrifice the mission." He hesitates, staring across the ten feet that separates the two men. "You *had* her killed."

"Jack—"

"You had her killed so I wouldn't quit."

Trance takes two quick steps toward Miller. He grabs him by the collar and pushes him against the wall. He lifts Miller up with one hand. Miller's feet are dangling off the floor and he is wiggling like a captured squirrel.

"Who did it?"

Miller sputters, "It…was…terrorists—"

Trance presses his free palm against Miller's throat. Miller begins to choke and his legs begin to flail against the wall. His shoes make a rhythmic *thump, thump, thump,* but no one rushes in to see what is wrong. No one dares.

"It was you, wasn't it?" says Trance.

Miller shakes his head. Spit begins to drool down his chin. His eyes begin to bulge until he looks like a bloated fish. Trance lets him hang there for several more seconds. Then he slowly lets him down. Trance turns and sinks into a Queen Anne chair. He covers his face with his hands and begins to moan. *Like a frigging child*, thinks Miller. A child at the helm of the Starship Enterprise. Miller hunches over and coughs. He rubs at his swollen red neck until his breathing returns to normal. Then he puts his crimson face against Trance's nose.

"I had orders to send her out," Miller croaks. "She had orders to go."

"She was quitting the CIA. You knew that."

Miller shrugs. "She was ours until the orders came through. You know the drill."

"She was two months pregnant. Asshole."

Miller closes his eyes. "I'm sorry, Jack. I didn't know. I had my orders." Miller walks to his desk and reaches into the second drawer on the right. He withdraws a Beretta nine millimeter pistol and points it at Trance. He smiles and places the gun upon the desk. He reaches back into the drawer. He withdraws a large bottle of pink Pepto Bismol. He unscrews the cap and takes several large swallows. Without looking at Trance he screws the cap back on the bottle and returns it to the drawer, smacking his lips like it was his last meal. Miller looks up from the desk toward Trance. Trance hasn't moved from the chair, except to raise his chin.

"I could kill you now," says Miller.

"Fine with me. Do it."

Miller lifts the pistol off the top of the desk. He holds it with familiar, practiced fingers and walks toward Trance. He stops three feet from the chair and aims the gun between Trance's eyes. He holds it there for several long seconds. Trance doesn't move. Then Miller flips the gun into the air, catches it by the barrel, and offers it to Trance.

"It's unmarked," he says. "You can kill me and walk out of here a free man. If you're going to do it, do it now. Because I can't tell you who gave those orders. And we're never going to talk about this again."

Miller holds out the gun for more than a minute before letting it drop to the floor.

"We all do our duty," Miller says.

***

"Duty," whispered Trance.

"Duty?" said Lauren. "Did I hear you say 'duty'?"

Trance's head snapped toward Lauren. It took him a moment to return through the years. He shook his head slowly, as he cleared the cobwebs.

"Miller's behind our invitation to this party. He wants to torture me."

"I'm sure the president just wants to meet you." Lauren's tears had stopped. She ventured a glance in the mirror. Her makeup had smudged on her cheeks but she ignored it. She looped Trance's tie a final time and pulled it snugly against his collar.

"Any new president would need to meet with you, Jack. Tilson is getting it done early."

Trance thought of Miller again. A CIA lifer, he had been Trance's liaison for the secret, covert operations team known as T-Force. T-Force had been created to diffuse international events before they occurred. Their prime objective was to keep the world free and in peace—a tall order in an ever-more-complicated world. T-Force had made its mark, although no one outside a small group of patriots ever knew. Like all efforts involving the government, things grew out of hand. Their orders grew blacker and wetter. Operations began to include the assassination of foreign government officials and international blackmail, behaviors that mimicked the very acts they were pledged to terminate. Trance tried to quit, but they wouldn't let him. When Janice became pregnant, Trance had made his decision to terminate. This time for good. Regardless of the cost, even if it meant his life.

One day, as Miller was briefing him on a mission to Central America, Trance reached the tipping point. "I can't do this anymore, Jacob."

Miller sighed. "Lost your nerve, Trance?"

"Screw you."

"It's her, isn't it? Your new little wifey?"

"No, Miller. I don't like what you stand for, what *we* stand for, not anymore."

"You'll do this one for us? We're counting on you, Jack. You can quit after this one. I'll even help you get out. I'll cover your ass so they won't kill you."

"Awfully nice of you, Jake."

When Trance had returned, his wife was dead. They'd had him on a string ever since.

Trance turned his head toward Lauren. "Miller's an ass."

Lauren laughed and pointed in the mirror. "How do you like your tie?"

"Almost as good as a clip-on."

Lauren lightly slapped the side of Trance's head. "Go to hell."

Trance stood and kissed Lauren gently on the forehead. "Already been there. I'll wear this tie, just for you."

"Undt you vill like it," replied Lauren, with her best fake German accent.

CHAPTER 4

_______________PP_______________

The wind swirled plumes of crystallized snow high into the air, making Washington's Massachusetts Avenue look more like the arctic tundra than a busy city street. Sammantha Starodubov bent her head against the sting and marched like a soldier along the salted, but slippery sidewalk. Sammantha wore a short, thin coat over her Embassy uniform. It was barely long enough to cover her knees. She felt strangely warm, knowing that each step brought her closer to the revenge she had been planning for most of her life. She could almost feel its sweetness on her tongue.

Sammantha blinked against the icy air as it stabbed at her contact lenses. Unwanted tears swelled in her eyes. She dabbed at them lightly, trying not to disturb the carefully created aura of darkness around them. The eyes were brown, not green and blue. The contacts made Sandra Smith myopic, not Sammantha's hawk-like 20/15 vision. The awkward lenses made it easier for Sammantha to maintain Sandra's clumsy, blind-dog demeanor, but they made it far more challenging to walk on this unholy night.

Sammantha gazed upward and wondered how long she'd been walking. The night was deathly dark, brightened only by the snowy glow of streetlamps and the occasional headlights of the sparse Washington traffic. She squinted and caught her bearings. Only six more blocks. Embassy Row. Land of gold. Six more blocks to the money, power and privilege—people far too insulated against the kind of pain she had been forced to endure. Technocrats and bureaucrats, Perrier and caviar, sailboats and Sunday brunches—Alice in Washingtonland. People thinking backwards, kings and queens and mad hatters, all of them living an illusion.

"They'll pay," she murmured in Russian. "Tonight they will begin to pay."

CHAPTER 5
______PP______

The mood was holiday festive inside the British Embassy. A stringed quartet played Mozart from a square wooden stage erected in a secluded corner. Light sparkled off the radiant chandeliers, the freshly cleaned silver, the Baccarat crystal, and the polished teeth of the arriving guests. To Sammantha, the men looked like manicured penguins in their pressed tuxedos, all squawking about the stock market and the upcoming Super Bowl. The women looked like stiff mannequins, adorned in long silk evening gowns that seemed to hold both their controlled emotions and liposuctioned thighs in check.

The British Ambassador held court off to the side of the room near the entryway. A semi-circle of early arrivals had gathered around him to pay respect and score political points.

Sammantha's Sandra carried an oval Reed and Barton silver tray, propped with champagne flutes sitting on top of dainty white napkins. She milled about, keeping the guests well quenched. Now and then an annoyed-looking penguin would motion to her from across the room and she would deftly negotiate the crowd until, smiling, she offered her tray. *Here you go, piggy, piggy.* Then she would curtsey and move on. Sammantha went about her job efficiently. When her tray emptied she began grabbing empty glasses off of end tables, coffee tables and high boys. She lifted three glasses off the black Steinway grand piano. *Slobs.* She rubbed the wet circles dry with a towel that she'd stuck into a pocket in her apron. She carried the tray back into the kitchen and refilled it with a new set of sparkling glasses and a fresh stack of napkins. A few minutes later she repeated the process. Then again. Six months of living like this she thought, all so that she could kill the American government. A small price to pay for the glory, the revenge and the righteous retribution.

Sammantha noticed one of the penguins brazenly waving his watch like a holiday flag. She glanced at it as she headed back toward the kitchen. It was a Patek-Phillipe. A forty thousand dollar waste, she thought, on a boor like that. Then she smiled. That watch would melt someday soon, along with its owner. But first things first.

It was only minutes before the president and first lady were scheduled to arrive. Sammantha's Sandra walked nervously into the kitchen. Baxter Whitley gave her a smile. Whitley had been the chef for the Embassy for over twenty years. He was a heavyset man with round rosy cheeks and downy tufts of hair that made him look like a cherub in a Renaissance painting, despite his fifty plus years. He was busily pouring champagne.

"Thirsty crowd tonight," he said with his clipped, but robust British voice.

"Must be the weather," said Sandra. She met Whitley's gaze with a glazed, hollow stare.

Poor girl, thought Whitley. *So nice, but so dull.* "I hear you're leaving us? Somebody told me, after this evening?"

Sandra shrugged and smiled shyly. She looked like a schoolgirl begging for acceptance by the class prima donna. "I am, sir. Thank you for noticing."

"Well, it's been bloody nice having you here, miss. You've been a diligent worker, kept to yourself, always on time. And dependable, always dependable. I suppose I never told you that?"

"Thank you very much, sir."

"Who will have you're services now?"

Sandra seemed to blush, with color on her face almost seeping through her dark shadow makeup. She scraped a shoe against the floor and blinked, doe-eyed at the chef.

"Speak up, girl," said Whitley with a friendly smile. "Did somebody say Australia? You came to us out of their embassy, didn't you?"

Sandra nodded. "I... I'm not very pretty, Mr. Whitley. And I don't got... don't...have much schooling. But I... there's a man...he's asked me to marry him. I'll be leaving tomorrow. God willing."

"You?" asked Whitley. "Getting married?" He never would have guessed it. Whitley laughed heartily. "Well bloody me bloomers...Sandra Smith getting married..." Whitley drained the champagne bottle. He dropped it into a recycling bin and ran a set of stubby fingers though his feathery white hair. "Why that's bloody wonderful." Whitley pressed a glass of champagne into Sandra's hand and took another for himself. "We must have a toast!" He lifted his glass into the air. The other workers in the embassy kitchen were too busy to pay attention, so the two of them drank alone. Whitley bellowed, "To Sandra Smith, may she live happily ever after!" Whitley downed the contents of his glass in three quick gulps. He held the glass upside down in front of his eyes until a single drop of champagne could be seen clinging to the rim. He slurped it with a satisfied grin. "The best part," he said. His face turned serious. "What's this chap's name?"

"Jones, sir."

"Is he good to you, child?"

"Yes, sir."

"To the future Mrs. Jones, then!" Whitley reached a meaty hand around Sandra's shoulder and peered at her with his bloodshot eyes. He voice cracked as he said, "I'll miss you, Sandra. You make this place seem normal. Please, leave us a forwarding address, will you?"

"I will, Mr. Whitley."

Sammantha's Sandra headed back to work. Whitley returned to his pouring, muttering, "I wish people would tell me these things..."

Before she reached the door, Sammantha stopped. She turned back to face the rotund chef. "Thank you," she said. "You've been nicer to me than any man I've known..." She walked back and gave Whitley a quick, nervous hug. Then she kissed his cheek. "I'll never forget you." Sammantha broke out of Whitley's embrace. "I must get ready. President Tilson should be arriving soon."

"Talley ho for the president." Whitley emptied another glass of champagne and burped with half-inebriated satisfaction. He adjusted his ample belt and returned to his pouring, humming as he worked.

Sammantha glided into the reception hall and glanced about the room. Still no president. Her eyes were drawn to a man ushering a woman toward the British Ambassador. Sammantha froze, feeling a tingle run along her neck. She felt an involuntary shiver and began flitting like a hummingbird for empty glasses. She maneuvered closer to the Ambassador, who was speaking to this man, the man she hated above all others.

"Ah, Mr. Trance," she heard the Ambassador say. "So good of you to join us again...This must be Miss Lauren Haverford..." The Ambassador took Lauren's proffered hand and gave it an exaggerated, but perfunctory kiss.

"Your name is spoken of highly in international banking circles," he said to her softly.

Lauren blushed with obvious surprise. "Thank you, Mr. Ambassador."

Deford Brighton had been a diplomat with the British Foreign Service for nearly thirty-five years. He was the second son of a Duke, schooled at Eton and Oxford. He was marvelously well-bred and he looked it. Unfortunately for Brighton, he'd been left no money and no title, a deadly combination for a man of his stature and breeding. His salary couldn't quite match his expensive tastes, or those of his third wife, even with his MI6 stipend. To make ends meet, he'd made a slight concession to his country's honor and joined the CIA payroll. A hundred grand a year for verifying information the Yanks already knew. Plus, of course, his job of facilitating meetings like this. They were allies, after all. Not enemies.

He was an essential cog in British American cooperation.

Brighton leaned toward Trance as he shook his hand. "Perhaps, when all of this early hubbub is over, we might chat privately. Catch up on old times?"

"Sure," said Trance. There would be a meeting with the president, just as he had feared.

As Trance led Lauren away from the Ambassador, he said, "Didn't I tell you?"

"He just wants to talk, that's all."

Trance and Lauren stood still for a moment, both of them looking out over the crowd. It was an impressive gathering that included the nominees for secretary of state and defense, several Supreme Court justices, a former president and his first lady.

"Is it true that no one can leave here before the president?" asked Lauren.

"No," said Trance, grinning. "One can always leave before the guest of honor. It's just considered bad protocol. A good way to get on the Washington shitlist."

"Even if I had an emergency?"

"Even if you were dying. In Washington protocol, some things are more important than emergencies, more important than life. Did you want to leave? I'm ready."

Lauren saw the amusement in Trance's eyes. She knew he was only half serious. Half.

"You'd like that, wouldn't you? A good reason never to be invited to Washington again? 'He can't be invited to the reception, Mr. Ambassador. He left the British embassy last year before the guest of honor…He's a terrible boor…'"

A brief hush spread across the room as the president and first lady glided through the main embassy doors. The room grew silent, like the skip of a heartbeat, the noise stopping for one hesitating instant, before resuming to the incessant drone of subdued voices.

Sammantha's heart began thumping in her chest. Her temples burned and throbbed, especially during that brief, silent acknowledgment of the honored guests. Sammantha actually *felt* Tilson's presence before she saw him. She fought off a wave of nausea. Sweat began to slick up her palms, so much that she was afraid to carry her tray. She heaved a heavy breath. Could she really do this? Sammantha walked back toward the kitchen. She held her tray high as she pushed with her hip against the swinging door. She set the silver tray down and excused herself. She walked to the servants' ladies room and locked the door. She pressed her ear against the door and listened. No one was there. She pulled off her shoe, then tapped the heel against the sink until it came loose. She took off the heel cup and removed the plastic vial. She unscrewed its cap and withdrew an eye dropper from inside. She slipped the dropper into her apron pocket. She screwed the top back onto the vial and returned it to her shoe. She walked back into the kitchen and stood beside Whitley.

"Are you ready, girl?" he said.

"I'm so happy you chose me," said Sammantha's Sandra. Her voice sounded soft and reverent, more like she was speaking to the Dalai Lama than to a drunken cook. "You don't know how much this means to me. This is the most important moment in my life."

Whitley looked like a father watching his daughter walk down the wedding aisle. His eyes were beaming and misting with emotion. He was glad that he had chosen this plain, shy girl to serve the president of the United States. He pulled a fresh bottle of Taittinger from an iced, stainless steel bucket. He popped the cork and poured two glasses. He matched each one with a silk doily before setting them on a silver tray that was adorned with white, monogrammed linen.

"There you go, now," he said. "Don't spill anything."

"Oh, I won't, Mr. Whitley."

"Good girl." Whitley held the tray while Sandra steadied it in her hands. "Some day maybe you'll tell your grandchildren about tonight," he said.

You poor man, thought Sammantha. *If you only knew.* Sammantha wheeled around and headed toward the door. She appeared to stumble. As she did, her right hand reached out over the glasses and squeezed two drops of liquid into one glass. She righted herself and continued out into the room, while pocketing the eye dropper.

Sammantha positioned herself at a discreet distance behind the president and first lady. She watched for a sign from Brighton, who was chatting with them pleasantly. The ambassador nodded and Sammantha stepped forward.

"May I offer you and the first lady a glass of champagne?" said Brighton.

Sammantha felt a lump form in her throat. It felt like she had swallowed a walnut. This was the moment. The moment of a lifetime.

"I'd love some," the first lady said. She turned to her husband. "How about you, dear?"

The president nodded. The first lady swiped the two glasses off of Sammantha's tray before she could react.

"Thank you," said the first lady. She gave Sammantha a warm, genuine smile.

Bitch, thought Sammantha. *I know what you're really thinking. You think I'm nothing. You were supposed to wait and take the glass that was offered you. That was the plan. Now you've gone and screwed up everything.* Sammantha barely controlled the instinct to slap the first lady across the face. She'd waited a quarter century for this. She'd put up with the pawing and panting, the sour breath, the sweat and the false cries of love. All for this chance, this one chance. *Don't you blow it for me now.*

"I'm honored," Sandra said.

Kiki turned and offered a glass to her husband. Sammantha tried to follow her movements, but Brighton stepped in front of her and blocked her way.

"That will be all, my dear." The ambassador pressed his palm against Sammantha's back and gently pushed her away.

Which glass had the president taken? Damn that woman! All the years of planning. All of the promises made and the billions invested. *That hick slut could ruin it all.* There would be no second chance.

The first lady raised her glass to toast her husband and the British Ambassador.

"To our two great nations. May they work effectively together to bring a lasting peace to the world."

"Hear, hear!" said both men.

As the Tilsons raised their glasses to their lips, Sammantha knew that one of them would be dead by morning. She just hoped it was the right one.

The Ambassador found Trance and Lauren seated alone in a quiet corner of the main reception room. Lauren was gulping shrimp and recounting anecdotes from a recent business trip to Japan. Trance was clutching his sides in laughter, his cheeks actually damp from tears.

"I'm not kidding," cried Lauren. "It really happened that way. What would you expect me to do, eat it?"

"There you are!" shouted the Ambassador above the din. Brighton wore a broad, plastic smile. His eyes were calculating. "I've been looking all over for you two." He tossed his head toward one end of the room. "I thought we might have our chat now." The Ambassador grabbed Trance by the forearm. "Please, step this way, Jack."

Brighton turned without waiting for a reply and sped off across the room.

"He's pleasantly rude," said Lauren.

Trance winked. "A gentle rebuke. We're supposed to mingle, not sit in a corner and have fun. Would you like to leave now? It's your last chance."

"You really want to go?"

Trance nodded. His eyes looked playful, but also serious. "Absolutely. We're not trapped. C'mon. You want to ski or swim?"

"Not so fast, Trance. You've got to have your meeting with Mr. Big. I didn't fly all the way to Washington to get on some Capitol blacklist." Lauren glanced out over the crowd. "I think I'll do some mingling. Maybe I can pick up some deposits for the bank."

Trance touched Lauren's cheek and smiled. Then he followed the Ambassador's trail through the mass of milling penguins. They stopped at the entrance to a private room on the second floor at the far end of the Embassy.

The Ambassador twisted a skeleton key into the lock of a thick oak door. He turned the brass knob, pressed the door slightly ajar, took a brief look at Trance, winked and walked away. Trance stood alone, staring forward through the half-opened door at the president. Tilson was chatting pleasantly with another man. His feet were propped over a cherry coffee table. An unlit briar pipe dangled loosely from his teeth. There was a delicate tea set on the table. Two partially filled cups held what looked to be black coffee. After several seconds the president looked toward Trance and waived him in.

"Ah, Mr. Trance. Please, join us."

Tilson stood and offered his hand. He gripped Trance's fist and shook it with a firm one, two, three. He held Trance's hand as if measuring him by the feel. Satisfied, he relaxed.

"You've got a good grip," Tilson said. He turned Trance's palm over in his hand and looked along the outer edge. "Is that a callous?"

"Yes, sir."

Tilson's eyes looked surprised and confused. "Goddamn strange place for a callous. It feels more like steer horn."

Trance laughed. "I spent years pounding boards for my Masters. Too many. I don't do it anymore, but some of the scars remain."

Trance looked to the president's other guest. The man was standing with his arms rigidly by his side. His hands were clenched and his face was sickly pale. Their eyes locked.

"We were beginning to think you might not show," said Tilson. The president could almost feel the hate between his two guests, could almost hear sparks crackling in the air. It made him think of the air after a thunderstorm, when its electric charge hung like an invisible mist. "I believe you know Mr. Miller?"

Trance nodded. His lips pressed into a thin, white line. "Unfortunately."

"Ah, yes, well...Mr. Miller has informed me that you and he are 'reluctant allies'."

Trance's lips stretched into a smile. "We were, but not anymore. I'm retired."

From the corner of his eye, Trance could see Miller twitch. He noticed two slight bulges under the lapels of Miller's expensive Tuxedo. The left lapel likely hid Miller's Beretta. He'd lay odds that the other held a hip flask filled with Pepto Bismol.

"Care for a drink?" said Tilson amiably, studying Trance's face through his confident, pale-blue eyes.

Trance ignored him.

"Miller did tell you that I've retired, didn't he?"

The president sat back down on the couch and motioned for Trance to join him. "I wouldn't dream of asking you to do anything against your will, Mr. Trance, particularly for something as meaningless as your country." Tilson saw Trance flinch. *Good*, he thought. *I've got him*. He propped his feet back on the coffee table and leaned back comfortably. "No...I would just like to schedule a few sessions with you. That's all. You can fill me in on some things, particularly your past dealings with my predecessors. Mr. Miller thought you might be a bit...ah...reluctant to do so. So, he offered to be here. To facilitate."

Trance peered at Miller. "Awfully nice of you, Jake." Then Trance looked squarely at the president. "I can assure you this; it will not help you to have Miller here."

The president looked from Trance to Miller, and then to his folded hands. "Hmm." Tilson lifted his feet off the table and reached for a file that was lying on the table's corner.

"Miller and I have been going over your history." He thumbed through the contents of the folder. "Quite impressive."

Trance grimaced. He looked questioningly at Miller. Miller shook his head, almost imperceptibly, in warning.

"That's what it is, sir, history. Something seen through the bias of someone else. Nothing more."

"I'm a student of history, Jack. May I call you Jack? I like history, not for the details, but for the big picture." Tilson laughed. "I've got your history boiled down to one page."

The president opened the folder and pulled out a single sheet of white paper. On top of it was a yellow tab with the letters *SCI* printed on it with bold black type. He stood and offered the paper to Trance.

"It's only fair you should see it."

Trance took the paper and glanced through it quickly.

ULTRA SECRET UMBRA

Re: Jack Trance

Considered a national treasure by three presidents. Should be approached with caution.

Parents: His father General John Trance—early member OSS, later CIA. John was son of Japanese mother and American father. His mother Patricia Hopewell. (American Royalty. Sister of Senator Winthrop Hopewell, dec.) Jack Trance only child.

Personal History: Black belt Aikido age nine. Currently ninth degree (highest in the Western hemisphere). World champion: Form, Knives, Sword. Black belts four other disciplines. Victor in competition sponsored by Robert Yang (See Restricted FBI/CIA/Homeland Files). Lived in nine countries as child. Fluent eleven languages, including Russian and Mandarin Chinese. Speaks and writes (at least) six others. Photographic memory. Perfect Navy GTC score. Annapolis, third in class. Reportedly failed final chemistry exam to allow classmate to graduate higher. Instructor, Navy War Games. Genius. Strategic prowess praised by superiors. Weapons expert, all. Sharpshooter. SEAL, Search and Rescue. Captured during mission in Iran. Prisoner, six weeks. Will not divulge or discuss treatment. Possible emotional damage, memory loss. Not confirmed. Severe physical damage. (See Jerome Freeman) Reportedly healed. Highly decorated. Congressional Medal of Honor. Self-funded rogue insurgents in Nepal against Chinese. Court marshal considered but not implemented, as official military discharge (honorable) had been granted. Recruited by Winthrop Hopewell (dec. Senator) to form T-Force, elite secret arm of CIA. (Ultra-classified. See.) Mission Statement to "diffuse international crises prior to public knowledge." Successful, numerous occasions. Wife assassinated, by (suspected) Arab jihadists. Not confirmed. Resigned T-Force under psychological duress (death of spouse?). Became paid consultant—primarily to U.S. Govt. (Ultra-classified. See) Payments to date exceed $30,000,000 to offshore accounts. Refused substantial ($5-$10 billion) inheritance at death of parents. Accepted second inheritance. (See Hopewell, von Hoffenburg.) Known accounts in Switzerland, Austria, France, Luxembourg, Grand Cayman and United States total $11 billion cash and gold bullion. Rumors of far more. Sole owner Hopewell Industries. 65 known subsidiaries, U.S. Large foreign operations & presence. Personal U.S. income taxes, approximately $2 billion annually, due to distribution from LLCs. Led team to avert world war between U.S., China & Russia. Did not. Repeat. Did not have government authorization. (Files stored in maximum security archives. Available only with approval.) Graduate of Naval Academy, Harvard School of Law. Legal practice in Vermont. Fees donated to charities. Closest known friends: Lauren Haverford, banker. Res. Boston. Believed to be stable and reliable. "Stick" Granger, mercenary. Res. South Pacific. "Spike" Jackson, auto dealer. Res. New York (Southampton). Jesse Tompkin, T-Force. Res. McLean, VA.

Emotional Profile:

Complex. Considered overly idealistic, unpredictable, and irreplaceable. Answers to self rather than authority. Caution advised. Extreme patriot. Can be manipulated into action.

END SUMMARY

Trance looked up from the paper and let it fall to the table.

"I told you, I'm retired."

"Humor me, Jack. I can call you Jack?"

Trance laughed. "Call me anything, Mr. President. Just don't call me."

The president nodded grimly. "Call me Jock." The president lit his pipe and drew several deep puffs. "I'm new at this, you know."

"No shit. It gets easier. That's your responsibility, sir. You campaigned for the job. I didn't."

The president motioned for Miller to leave. Miller stood his ground. "I wouldn't advise this—"

"You wouldn't advise what, Mr. Miller?" interrupted Tilson.

"Him…being alone with him."

"Listen, Miller…. From here on out, let's get one thing straight. I may be new, but I am the president. That means I give the orders, doesn't it?"

Miller's face seemed to flatten, his cheeks flushing red. His lips began to tremble. His eyes took on the focused look of a sniper, just as he was about to pull the trigger.

"I suppose you do give the orders, sir."

"Suppose you get your ass out of here."

When the door had closed behind Miller, the president sucked on his pipe. He sat in quiet contemplation, before saying, "He is a bit of an asshole, isn't he?"

When Trance looked at the president, his eyes made Tilson think of a concentration camp survivor. Trance's eyes looked drained of life, staring at him through something that was not really there, as if his life had been left behind in some far off place. "He killed my wife, my uncle and my fiancée."

"That sucks."

Trance's eyes focused back on the president with a visible, almost audible snap. "It was all *in the line…*" Trance drew a slow breath through his nose, as he pieced his thoughts on Miller. He exhaled softly and said, "In all fairness, Jock, he does his job well. You could do far worse. It takes an imperfect man to head the CIA effectively. He fills the mold. He probably is the best man for the job."

"That's what I wanted to know. I'll tell him you said that."

"I'll deny every word."

The president gazed at Trance for several long moments. He met the younger man's warning stare with one of his own. The president started to say something but hesitated. Then he said, "You can't forgive him?"

"I'd kill him if I thought it would do any good."

The president whistled. "Care to talk about it?"

"Nothing to say. He had my wife killed. I watched him shoot both my uncle and my fiancée."

"I read about your wife." Tilson shifted uncomfortably in his chair. "Miller was ordered to send her." Tilson leaned back and propped his feet back up on the table. "You know, Jack, I'll admit that I am a babe in the woods when it comes to Washington. Spent most of my life in northern Maine. Grew up there, practiced law there. Governed there. That's a far cry from the world you've known. So, all this stuff about espionage, subterfuge and behind the scenes politics…"

"What are you getting at, sir?"

Tilson reached inside his coat and pulled out a stack of three by five note cards. "Every new president gets lists, dozens of lists. Lists that tell him more crap than he'd ever want or need to know."

Tilson thumbed though his pile of cards. "I've got lists on which members of Congress cheat on their wives, which of them have drinking problems, trans-gender issues, drug addictions." He began to systematically toss the cards onto the coffee table. "I now know where half the skeletons in this city lie. And who's getting paid to keep them quiet. Sordid town, this one. Worse than I ever dreamed."

"Welcome to the land of Oz."

The president handed one of the cards to Trance.

"I make these cards from the computer printouts they give me. This one's got the name of New York's best bagel bakery. Love bagels with freshly ground peanut butter, maybe a banana on top. It's the best."

Trance glanced to the company name on top, *Emil Radler Bagels*. He read several other unfamiliar company names below it.

"Bagels?" said Trance.

"Bagels," said the president. "Emil makes my bagels. The next company makes pastries. There's bacon from a small farm in Virginia, Polish sausage from Pennsylvania, and flowers for my wife. Commit that card to memory, Trance. Then destroy it. I've got a spare."

"State secrets, sir?"

The president chuckled. His humor was infectious. Trance found himself laughing with him.

"Good to see you lighten up, Trance." Tilson's manner sobered quickly. He reached inside his tuxedo and withdrew a black leather, wallet-sized folder. "Then I have the lists that really matter." He fingered through the folder and pulled out several cards. "When I was first elected I requested lists of potential candidates for every major position in this administration. I had my secretary enter them into my personal database. Then I did some analyzing of my own. I'm a firm believer in doing my own homework, you see."

Tilson tossed several of the cards onto the table.

"Know what I found?"

Trance appeared uninterested, but the president waited patiently. Finally, Trance said, "Incompetence?"

The president's lips curled into a grin.

"Yeah, that too. I ran a cross-check of names that surfaced on more than one list. Your name came up a surprising number of times. More than anyone else, in fact."

"Some of the incompetents work for you, I see."

Tilson's eyes searched Trance's face for several seconds. "Always so modest?" he asked softly.

"You'll find many people who can do a better job than I can, on just about everything. I'm just a country lawyer."

Tilson shuffled through the lists. "You came up as a potential candidate for Secretary of the Army, the Navy, Secretary of State, Secretary of Defense, the head of JAG…"

Trance chuckled softly. "You'd be in deep shit with me on your team, sir."

The president ignored him. "…Attorney General, Ambassador to wherever, and director of the CIA."

"What are you asking, sir?"

"I thought you were the underachieving son of wealthy parents."

Trance laughed. "Money is no measure of a man, sir. And me…I'm just trying not to rock the boat.

I've got personal issues to deal with before I start helping guys like you."

"My predecessor told me about the kidnapping…that drug dealer in Miami."

"So much for confidentiality. Did he tell you how they tortured me, and then hooked me on just about every drug known to man?"

"He did."

"That was less than a month ago, Jock. That's not my biggest problem, though. I've got other things to worry about."

"So, you won't help me?"

"I'm just a small-town lawyer, sir. Not a very good one at that…There's not much I can do about the problems of this country."

"That's not what I've heard."

"What are you asking, sir?"

"You keep saying that."

"And you keep evading me. I'd like to know where we stand."

"I want your help, that's all."

Trance sighed. "I'm retired, sir. Can't you just leave me alone? All of you?"

Trance gazed at Tilson with pleading eyes. He liked this president. He seemed like a good, moral man. The cynic in Trance wondered how long it would take him to change. The optimist in Trance gave him hope.

The president remained silent, an effective tactic he'd learned as a boy, one he still used often.

Finally, Trance continued, "Do you want some advice, sir?"

"That's why you're here."

"There's going to be a vacancy on the Federal Reserve Board in about a year..."

"I'm already looking—"

Trance held up his hand. Tilson took a breath and let his large frame sink further back into his seat. "I'm listening."

"There's a banker with me at this party who ought to be on that board."

"Lauren Haverford."

Trance grinned. The president *had* done his homework. "She's brilliant. She's dedicated. There is no one on the board from her district. You couldn't make a better choice."

"She's on my short list. You do know that most members of the Federal Reserve Board are economists, not bankers?"

Trance replied, "By definition, the members of the board are supposed to be a *'fair representation of the financial, agricultural, industrial, and commercial interests and geographical divisions of the country,'* sir. She's not Feldstein or Friedman or Laffer. But she knows her stuff cold. She's a global, creative thinker, far more than most of the myopics on that board. Besides, with all your issues, you need another banker on the board. And a woman might go well with the voters. You can do both at once."

"I'll make a deal with you."

"No deals," said Trance. "She deserves this on her own."

Tilson mused for a moment, tapping his right index finger against his teeth. Finally, he stood and reached out his hand. "When the time comes, I'll nominate her. No strings attached."

"You won't regret it."

"I hope not." Tilson gripped Trance's hand, looking slightly down on him from his six-foot-three inch frame. "I hope to hear from you again, soon."

Trance shook his head and laughed. "I can see why they like you, sir." He paused, still not willing to be trapped. "It was nice meeting you, Mr. Pres—"

"Jock."

"Jock." Trance let go of Tilson's hand and said, "I would offer to help you, but I'm not much of a Company man anymore."

Trance walked to the heavy wooden door and pulled it open. Then he turned back toward Tilson. "Sir?"

"Yes, Jack?"

"For what it's worth, I did vote for you. I think you might make a damned fine leader. Don't let them drag you down."

Tilson looked surprised, then pleased.

"Thank you, Jack. I appreciate that. I will welcome your help…When you're ready."

"I'll think about it, sir."

"Tell Lauren to call my appointment secretary. For what it's worth, Jack, I don't want Company men. I just want *good* men and women."

Trance leaned against the door, speaking softly, "That's a good start, sir."

When Trance returned to the reception he found Lauren cornered by the French Foreign Minister. He had her trapped beneath his outstretched arm. He was whispering to her in a low voice. "Perhaps we should discuss this over dinner sometime..."

Trance hovered within earshot, curious how Lauren would escape. He didn't venture forward.

Lauren wiggled out from beneath the Frenchman's arm and smiled. "That's a most attractive offer, Ambassador Francoise. While I enjoy your esteemed company, I must politely decline dinner. Perhaps you would care to schedule an appointment with me at the bank?" At that moment Lauren caught sight of Trance, laughing at her. She looked like a child who just saw the neighborhood ice cream truck turn the corner onto her own street.

"Oh, there you are!" she cried. Lauren motioned toward Trance.

Trance turned and began to walk away. He stopped slowly, then looked back at Lauren and laughed.

"Darling," he said. "Where have you been? I've been looking all over for you."

Lauren grasped Trance's hand and turned to introduce him to the French minister. But the minister was already gone.

"Men," she said.

"Any new deposits?"

"A couple nice offers."

"I heard."

"How was your chat?"

"Oh, fine," said Trance. "Turns out he didn't want to talk about me at all."

"I told you so." Lauren listened to her own words and shook her head. "What do you mean?"

"He asked me about you."

"Right."

"Nothing important, really."

"Of course not."

"Something to do with some board position. I don't know. Federal something…Didn't pay much attention."

Lauren gripped Trance's shoulders and turned him toward her.

"What board position?"

"I forget. Reserve something, I think."

"Don't tease me. Not about this." Lauren dug her fingernails playfully into Trance's skin until he pulled away.

"My, God," he said. "You're as bad as the French. Maybe he said *Federal Reserve Board.* Is that a board? They have a vacancy coming up or something? Tilson was reference checking, I think…Don't worry… I told him you were too busy to be joining any more boards."

"Not interested? Jack, if you…Not interested? If you're talking about the Federal Reserve Board…Do you know how many people have been angling for that vacancy?"

"Guess I blew it then."

"Don't play with me, Jack. Not about this."

"You're to call his appointment secretary."

Lauren gasped. "No."

"Yes."

"Yes? No joke? The president wants to see me?"

"You've got the appointment."

"Don't kid with me, Jackie. Not about this…Anything but this." She looked into Trance's eyes. "You're serious, aren't you?"

Trance nodded. "Yep."

"You cut some kind of deal, didn't you?"

"He said you were on his short list. He asked me what I thought about you. I might have said something nice. It was the least I could do."

"What did you say?"

"I said I'd kill him if he didn't appoint you. Wasn't sure if that would go over too well. I guess he took me seriously."

"The FRB. It's a fourteen year term, you know. He'll never do it."

"It's a done deal, Lauren. Believe me. Now, can we get out of here? I need some sleep."

Lauren put her arms around Trance and hugged him. She kissed him on the cheek. Then she hugged him again. "After Tilson leaves, dear. Not a moment before."

CHAPTER 6
______________PP______________

The Ritz-Carlton hotel buzzed with a palpable undercurrent of power. Groups of men had gathered in the lobby, important diplomats returning from the British Embassy reception not far away. A group of women had also clustered. Their jewels sparkled voluptuously in the soft light. Their laughter sounded loud and forced. Half a dozen South American trade ministers stood arguing in a corner. They had not been present at the embassy, but were scheduled to meet with the vice president in the morning. Hands waved everywhere and points were scored on their running mental tote boards.

Silence suddenly snuffed the room, as a solitary woman glided across the lobby. She was dressed in a gown of red silk, with a wrap of flowing black Sable draped across her broad shoulders. The woman calmly made her way to the concierge. She paid no attention to the lustful stares she drew from throughout the room, stares from men bored with mere beauty, naturally drawn to her like moths to light. The woman stood over six feet tall in her red spike heels. Blond hair cascaded beyond the end of her wrap and danced lightly across her bare back. The smooth, almost translucent gown hugged the woman's thighs, molding around her taut muscles like a second skin as she moved. This would have been blatantly sexual, had she shown even a passing interest in her admirers. Instead, the woman oozed class. She didn't give a damn what anyone else thought. She was a world to herself.

"You have a reservation for Sammantha Starodubov," the woman said coolly. A command, not a question. She froze the hotel clerk with a shot from her multi-colored eyes. Then she thawed him with a bright, white smile.

The clerk wiped imaginary dust off his lapel, then nervously curled the thin hairs of his graying mustache.

"Ah...of course..." The clerk glanced at the woman's left hand to see if she wore a ring. No ring. He smiled. "…Ms. Starodubov."

"I want a split of Dom Pérignon delivered to my suite in thirty minutes, along with two ounces of Beluga caviar. Make sure both are chilled appropriately. I want a *Post* brought to me first thing in the morning, please."

"But of course, m...madam. Anything else?"

Sammantha glanced back through the edge of her fur collar, toward the men in the lobby. They had already resumed their animated conversations, speaking as if she didn't exist. *Self-possessed assholes*, she thought.

The concierge coughed nervously. Sammantha jerked her head back toward him and smiled warmly.

"A key card?" she asked.

"Oh, but of course." The man unlocked a drawer and withdrew a plastic room card.

"Any valuables you wish placed in our safe?"

Sammantha shook her head.

"Someone to carry your bags?" The concierge looked out over his desk to the Hermes's luggage sitting on the floor behind Sammantha.

Of course, you dumb shit, she thought. "Yes, thank you." Sammantha gave the man a brief smile, turned, and started walking toward the elevators. Three bellhops scurried forward like roaches to fight for her luggage. There was a brief exchange, an assertion of dominance, before one peeled away and two of them followed Sammantha to the elevator.

The elevator door swung open. Sammantha stepped inside, gazing briefly at her reflection in the shiny elevator wall. That's where she saw him, reflected off the gleaming metal, just before the doors snapped shut.

Jack Trance was walking through the hotel lobby with Lauren Haverford's arm curled around the crook of his elbow. They had just finished a brandy in the 9th floor lounge. Lauren was picking up a FedEx letter, before she and Trance retired to the Residences section of the complex.

"Well," said Trance. "Guess it's back to the real fantasy world."

The concierge scurried forward, smiling obsequiously.

"Good evening, Mr. Trance. And to you, Miss Haverford." The concierge handed Lauren her overnight letter. "Will you be needing anything else?"

"No, thanks. We're fine," said Trance. He shook the man's hand. The concierge turned quickly away.

"He's rather fawning," said Lauren, once the man was out of earshot.

"Might have something to do with my hundred-dollar tips, plus the occasional five hundred."

"You don't?"

"I still do."

"Whatever for?"

Trance ignored Lauren's question. He stared back out across the lobby as if searching for someone he was afraid of finding.

Lauren squeezed Trance's arm. She leaned over and whispered into his ear. "It's spy shit, isn't it?"

Trance nodded. "He helped me once, back when this was just a simple hotel."

Lauren stared at the people in the lobby, imagining that some of them were spies, like in a James Bond film. Trance pulled her by the elbow and led her onward toward the Residence elevators.

When they were out of earshot, Trance said, "He's not a spy. Just observant. That's all."

The elevator doors opened and they walked inside. After the door closed behind them Lauren looked at Trance accusingly.

"You say you're retired, but you still make payoffs."

"That's not a payoff. It's a tip, a reasonable tip."

"Ten bucks is a reasonable tip. You're making payoffs."

Trance shrugged his shoulders. "It's like playing professional football, Lauren. You're out of the game, but old injuries never go away. The scars, the broken bones, the torn up cartilage—"

"What are you saying? That you've got injuries?"

"I'm saying that once you've played in the game of espionage, it never leaves you. It stays with you for life."

"The scars will heal. You'll see."

"They'll never get the chance. Tilson will find a reason to call me. You wait."

"But you told him—"

"He'll find a cause, sweetheart. Some last great cause. They always do."

The elevator stopped on Trance's floor. As they walked toward his suite, Trance put his hand against Lauren's lips to keep her silent. Only once they were inside the suite did Trance continue. "I feel something here, in this hotel."

"You need to relax."

"I felt it at the British Embassy, too. Something's going down. Something bad, something worse than bad."

"You're just uptight." Lauren began to massage Trance's shoulders. "By morning everything will be fine."

"Don't think so. The president had a shadow of death in his eyes."

"You and that Eastern, sixth sense crap."

Trance smiled. "You know I'm right, Lauren."

"He is going to need you, isn't he?"

"Yeah." The life in Trance's eyes suddenly seemed far away, like its force had sunk back into his brain, leaving nothing but empty glass.

"Tell him to take a flying leap."

"Sure," mumbled Trance. "I always do."

Lauren hung her coat in the closet. Trance threw his jacket onto the bed and trekked toward the toilet. When he returned, Lauren was seated before the suite's broad picture window overlooking the Washington skyline. She had two champagne flutes in hand.

"Why won't you marry me?" she said.

"Lauren, let's not—" Trance tried to look at Lauren, but he couldn't force his eyes to face her.

"I won't die," she said.

"We all die."

"You know what I mean." Lauren took Trance's hand. "I won't die because of you. That was before, Jack. This is now. You've carried your cross. Put it down."

"I can't. You know that."

"Don't be silly. Life is full of chances. Let *me* take the chance. Let *us* have the chance."

"You're better off alone."

"Don't give me that crap, Jack Trance. We're both on the back side of thirty. I've never loved anyone but you, and I'm not about to start. And you…you need me."

Trance slowly looked toward Lauren. He fought the pressure of tears that lurked close to the surface, like wary crocodiles. He tried to speak. All he could do was shake his head. Finally, he murmured, "I would if I could. But I can't let you die. I love you too much."

Lauren pulled Trance against her chest.

"It's all right," she said. "I'll take what I can get. How about a warm bath, some tender foreplay, and some good raw sex?"

They both began to laugh.

Trance said, "As much as I might want marriage…I just can't take the chance…can't take the chance of losing you…of having you killed…like Janice and Gretel."

Lauren closed her eyes. "It's different now, Jack. Someday you'll see. Lauren took him by the hand. "Come on, I'll scrub your back."

***

It was well after midnight when Kiki Tilson settled into bed. She felt tired and increasingly sick, like the flu was settling into her muscles for a nice long stay. All she wanted was to drift into sleep. Instead, she picked up the phone and dialed Air Force One, for the second time that night.

"Hello, sweetheart," she said, when Tilson answered the phone. "I hope I didn't wake you."

"Just catching a nap. You all right?"

"It's just a flu, I think."

"I'll send for a doctor."

"No," said Kiki. "I'll be fine. I'm just tired, that's all. I'll feel great by morning."

"I wish I were there."

"I'd just keep you awake." Kiki laughed. "Just as I am now."

Kiki knew that her husband needed rest for his meetings. But she felt a strong urge, no, a craving *need* to talk with him, like it was her last act on earth.

"Jock?"

"Yes, sweetheart?"

"Have I told you that I love you today?"

"Three times."

"That was yesterday."

"Oh, yeah."

"I love you today. Goodnight."

"You get some sleep."

After his wife hung up the phone, Tilson turned to his secretary. "Make sure that Kiki isn't disturbed tomorrow morning, will you?"

"Of course, Mr. President."

When Jock Tilson, the President of the United States, awoke half way around the world, his wife was dead.

CHAPTER 7
PP

Sammantha Starodubov squirmed as consciousness began to swell around her like a blister. She buried her face into her pillow and groaned. *Another frigging day to get through.* Sammantha rolled over and peered with one eye at the bedside clock. Five thirty A.M. Still dark. The traffic beneath her hotel window was muffled by the rare blanket of fresh Washington snow. She could barely hear it through the thick hotel glass. But it was enough to send her mind wandering back to that day when she was twelve, when her life had been split apart like a fractured coconut. Yes, while other people were embracing the day, Sammantha braced *for* it. Another day to get through. Another day made bearable only by its goal. She began it as she always did. She remembered.

Summer vacation has arrived. Twelve-year-old Sammantha sits in the back seat of an air conditioned Volvo station wagon. Beside her sits Sandra Smith, her neighbor and closest friend. They are whispering excitedly about how Katie, about how she had kissed a boy... *on the lips*! Sandra's mother drives them home from their last day of private day school.

The car swings into the circular driveway of the Starodubov estate. It skids to a stop on a bed of small white stones. Sammantha swings the door open. Then she leans over to hug her friend.

"Have a great time in New Hampshire," she says. "I'll miss you all summer!"

"You should come," says Sandra.

"Yes," says Sandra's mother, turning around from the front seat. "It gets so stifling down here. I'm sure your parents will let you come for a visit, maybe even the summer."

Sammantha smiles. "I would, but this is going to be the best summer ever. Mom and I bought a colt at last week's auction. We'll be training him together. I'm going to ride him in the shows."

"Another horse?" asks Sandra.

"This one's special. He's the best."

"What's his name?"

"Starr. We picked him up yesterday."

The car begins to roll away. Sammantha runs alongside, holding onto Sandra's outstretched hand. Finally, when she can hold on no longer, Sammantha stops and starts waving. "See you! I'll miss you!"

Sammantha runs into the house, leaving the front door ajar; she is so excited.

"Mom. I'm home!" Sammantha wonders what kind of cookies her mother has for her today. Every afternoon they eat them with a glass of milk, in the kitchen alcove looking out over the stables and the pond. Oreos are her favorite. She loves to split them apart and make the double stuff.

Sammantha runs through the dining room, slowing just enough to negotiate the turn into the kitchen. She comes to the doorway laughing, her eyes searching the table where her mother will be waiting. She slips and falls to the floor.

Sammantha's jaw twitches. She struggles to comprehend what she sees. Slowly, she stands up and stares. She stares at the black trails of crusting blood. She looks to the bodies lying motionless on the floor, throats cut, eyes wide open. They look almost alive. She reaches out to touch the face of her mother. "Mama?" She pauses. "You must be tired, Mama."

Sammantha feels a strange calm spread through her, a rising shadow that spills up her neck and over her head like warm foam. She glides to the alcove, her eyes unfocused and staring blankly. There are two tall stacks of Oreo cookies and two glasses of milk. She sees her cup, her butterfly cup. Sammantha sits down and eats both stacks of cookies. They taste funny, so she drinks the milk. The milk tastes bad, too. Like blood. Sammantha looks to her hands. She has to wash it away. The blood. On her hands, in her mouth. She starts for the sink and her cup falls to the floor. It shatters into a scattering of small, jagged pieces. Sammantha stands over the cup, staring at the remains of her life. She feels her stomach rumble and the cookies pour out of her mouth like chunky soup.

Sammantha sits down between the pieces of her cup and the vomit. She begins to rock. She rocks, back and forth, like the metronome she uses when playing the piano. Her young Bulldog puppy, Boris, comes up and sits beside her. He flops down and licks up the cookies. Then he stands, shaking and whining and licking the blood off her fingers.

Sammantha isn't sure how long she remains that way. She remembers the knocking. It is dark by then. There are knuckles tapping against the back door, gently at first, like a small tree branch in the wind, then with increasing force. She walks dazedly to the door and opens it. She sees the feet first, the pair of heavy black work shoes framed by those brown cuffless pants. She looks up and sees a tall man with a paunchy looking face. He has smoke-stained teeth and sour, vodka tainted breath.

"Excuse me, child," he says in Russian. "I have an appointment with your father." The man glances beyond Sammantha into the kitchen. After a moment his eyes narrow and he bares his yellow teeth. His eyes harden and he looks at her sternly.

"So, they have come," he says. "I'm sorry…" He hesitates. "…my dear."

Sammantha stares at this stranger for several long moments. She follows his eyes to her parents' bodies on the floor.

"Why are they dead?" she asks in Russian.

"They loved you very much."

Sammantha nods and she sinks back to the floor. She feels a tear and then another. She begins to crawl toward her parents' outstretched bodies. "They can't be dead. We're training my new horse today. We have to train him and ride him in the shows—" Sammantha slides through the blood and draws herself beside her mother's face. "Mama?" She touches her mother's cheek. Nothing. Then, as if pinched into a tight emotional fissure, Sammantha begins to feel numb. Her world looks like distorted, filmy pictures taken through a foggy lens.

The man takes her into his arms. She reaches her arms around his neck as he lifts her. She smells that stale mustiness. Somehow, she feels comforted.

"It's the Americans," he says after a long moment. "Your father called me. He was afraid of them. The American government. That is why I am here. You must come with me, my child, or they will kill you, too. We must go, now."

"I need my cup...I can't leave without my cup...And my dog...we can't just leave my dog..."

Sammantha goes with him, the aide to the Soviet Ambassador. She lives with him for a month, crying during the day and lying frozen beside him at night. He touches her in places she has never been touched, doesn't want to be touched. Places that make her feel sick and make her moan with fear and rage. She can't move; he is all she has. She lets it happen. She has to. Night after night, escaping deep within herself, rocking, where no one can find her. There is nowhere else to go.

Then one day, without warning, she is on her way to Russia. Sammantha Starodubov's family becomes a memory, a string of black letters arranged in the obituary section of the *Washington Post*.

Sammantha heard the newspaper drop outside her hotel door. She threw down the bedcovers and let the coldness sweep across her naked body. She tossed on a terrycloth bathrobe and walked across the expansive suite to the door. She held her breath, opened the door and reached for the *Post*. Nothing. The front page said nothing about the president or his wife. Nothing. "I have not worked this hard to fail," she said. Perhaps she had. She didn't think so. Someone was dead. She could feel it.

Sammantha turned on the television and skipped through the news channels. Nothing. She turned off the television. She hung her head for a moment. Then she walked to a corner of the room, sat down on the floor, and began to rock.

CHAPTER 8
PP

Kiki Tilson's secretary, Darlene Hamilton, paced the floor of her White House office. It was after eight o'clock. The first lady had a full day's schedule, beginning half an hour ago. Hamilton had been advised by the president's own secretary that Kiki wasn't well. No one had told her what appointments to keep, or which ones to break. There were twelve eagle scouts from California waiting in the lobby. They would soon be joined by four nationally honored high school teachers, a marching band from Georgia, the ten year old grower of the world's largest rutabaga, and a Las Vegas juggling duo. Then it would be off to the Watergate Hotel, where the first lady was to speak before a PTO luncheon. And after that—

The phone rang. Hamilton snatched it quickly.

"Yes?"

"Darlene, this is Jock."

"Good morning, Mr. President."

"Could I speak with Kiki, please?"

"She isn't here yet, sir. I was told not to disturb her."

"I understand what you were told, Darlene. She's not answering her wireless." Tilson paused. "Would you do me a favor and check on her?"

"Of course, Mr. President."

"I'll call you back in fifteen minutes."

The phone went dead. Hamilton dropped the receiver back into its cradle. She looked at her watch and started moving. She smiled at the eagle scouts who were seated outside her office, waiting expectantly for their visit with the first lady and their White House tour. "I'm sorry. The first lady is still detained. I've ordered some pastries up from the kitchen, along with sodas, milk and juice. They should be here momentarily. Please be patient. I'll be right back."

At the stairway, Hamilton was joined by a marine escort. They climbed the two flights of stairs to the president's living quarters, where Hamilton knocked upon the bedroom door. There was no answer.

"Shoot," she said. She knocked again. "Kiki?" Hamilton tried the door but it was locked. She motioned to the two guards who were stationed at the top of the stairs. "Has the first lady left her room this morning?"

"No, Miss Hamilton."

"Has anyone been inside?"

"No, ma'am."

"The president has asked me to speak to her. She wasn't feeling well. I'd like you to open her door, please."

The two guards looked at each other, silently processing their conflicting duties.

"You know I have authorization to enter this room at any time," said Darlene sharply. "Open it. Now."

One of the guards pressed a series of numbers into a keypad. He swiped a plastic card and nodded. "It's open, Miss Hamilton."

Hamilton hesitantly opened the first lady's bedroom door. She relaxed when she saw her friend sleeping peacefully. Then she shivered. The room was frigid, well below sixty degrees. She motioned for the guards to wait by the door and walked inside. "Kiki?" she said. "Kiki, Jock is worried about you. He asked me to—" The first lady didn't move. "Kiki?" Hamilton stepped beside the bed and shook the first lady's shoulder. Her skin was cold. "Kiki, for Christ's sake—" Hamilton pressed her palm against the first lady's forehead. "Oh, my God." She turned to the guards. "Get a doctor! Fast!"

CHAPTER **9**
___________PP___________

Sammantha Starodubov weaved her black BMW through the heavy traffic on the New Jersey Turnpike. As strains of Wagner pulsed through the car's custom speakers, Sammantha jerked her head from side to side with the dramatic thrusts of the music.

This was a spectacular day. A perfect day. News of the first lady's "illness" was everywhere. How many times had she thought of doing something like this? Every waking hour of her life. This was just the first part of her plan, just a detail that had to be dealt with before she put her end game in play. After a quarter century of hating, after decades of plotting revenge, her goal was within her grasp. It would be glorious. The worst disaster the country…no…the worst disaster the *world* had ever seen.

Sammantha reached between her legs and pressed her hands into the throbbing dampness. She had hoped it would be like this. She wished it could go on forever, the revenge so sweet. This was nearly as sweet as love.

Would he be waiting for her? she wondered. The crucial cog in her wheel of salvation? Would Brandon Copley be there?

Sammantha thought back to how she'd lured Copley into her life.

She remembered his picture on that cheap billboard off Broadway. There was something in those sad, mocking eyes, the eyes of an actor long since fallen, the eyes of a man with just enough left inside him to get from one performance to the next. How often had she seen that look in her own sad mirror? It was fitting that he was the one man who could help her.

***

It is the opening night of *Murders in the Dark*. Brandon Copley, IV is playing the leading role. The theater is barely half filled, but Sammantha sits in the back. She is dressed in a low cut black dress, with high silver pumps. Her makeup is minimal, a touch of eye shadow and faint pink lip gloss. Her jewelry is plain though elegant, a pair of two carat diamond earrings and a three carat drop necklace—gifts from an Arab prince for services rendered. She wears no rings. Her wrists are bare.

After the play, Sammantha goes back stage. She has visions of people running around shouting and screaming after the show, of having to charm protective security guards to get to Copley. Instead, she finds herself unmolested, unnoticed in fact. There is no mob, only a stage crew hurriedly putting away the props. Sammantha steps in front of one of the young men. He stops and smiles, while his eyes grope lewdly along Sammantha's shapely frame.

"Can you tell me where I might find Brandon Copley?"

The young man gives her a final, approving nod and points down a hall. "Should be the second door on your right…When he can't give you what you need, do come back to me, darling."

"Not on your life, pig."

The man grins and walks away, whistling.

When Sammantha enters the dressing room she expects something far different than the whirling free-for-all that she sees. Actors are climbing over each other for space, wielding elbows like blunt swords. Most of the actors are half naked. She feels strangely vulnerable and assaulted by their immodesty.

"I'm looking for Brandon Copley," Sammantha says to a short, dark-haired woman.

"In the back," says the woman. She points over her shoulder toward a half-opened door.

Sammantha walks to the door and inches her head inside the dressing room. The area is small and cluttered. Copley sits before a large mirror, swabbing at his face with a cotton ball. Beside him sits his co-star, doing the same. Both of them are in underwear. The co-star is naked to the waist.

"Excuse me," says Sammantha. She turns away when Copley stands.

"Yes?" says Copley, smiling. "May we help you?"

Sammantha forces herself to look at Copley. She keeps her eyes above his briefs.

"I…I wanted to meet you."

"Me?" he says. Copley glances at his co-star, who rolls her eyes. "You wanted me?"

"I saw your picture...on the billboard."

"The billboard?"

"Yes. I enjoyed the play."

Copley laughs. "The play stinks and we all know it. The picture on the billboard is ten years old. I'm not the man I used to be. I'm not sure I ever was."

"The play was…odd. I thought *you* were quite good. You haven't aged much really, Mr. Copley."

Copley's co-star raises her eyebrows. She mumbles, "Your lucky day, Brandon," and keeps swabbing her face. An amused glow spreads across her lips. She begins to hum the show tune *I'm a Big Girl Now*.

Copley laughs again. "You must be new to New York."

"Well, no. Not really."

"You liked my performance?"

"Yes. Yes, I did."

"And you thought you were over the hill," murmurs Copley's co-star.

"Well, then," Copley says, preening and winking at his co-star. He looks at Sammantha. "That entitles you to a late dinner on the town, wherever you choose. The Copley despotism still has its privileges."

What can she possibly want from me? he wonders. No matter. She is *hot*, and he hasn't known lukewarm in years.

Later that night, Sammantha waited inside a yellow taxi, just outside the entrance to the Tavern on the Green. Copley emerged from the restaurant smiling.

"We're in," he said. Copley paid the taxi fare and gave the driver a twenty dollar tip. He opened the rear cab door. Sammantha slid out of the seat, allowing her dress to ride high along her sensuous thighs. The ploy wasn't lost on Copley. He licked his lips like a dog seeing a ham bone.

"Good that we're late," he said. "I was able to secure us a table. A fine one at that."

Copley extended an elbow. Sammantha gracefully wrapped her arm within it and allowed him to strut her to a quiet table in the corner of the restaurant.

Sammantha guided the conversation toward Copley's life in the theater. She watched him closely, as he finished his first, then his second bottle of cabernet. His handsome, doughboy face began to sag. His blue eyes grew out of focus. His lips began to twitch, like he was using them for some version of Morse code. Copley's shoulders became progressively hunched, as if he were cowering from some unknown fear. He talked loudly, too volubly, as if the words fortified his confidence. Sammantha could see his self esteem drip to the floor, until it lay in a sad, lonely puddle, like blood.

Sammantha seamlessly moved the conversation from the theater to Copley's personal history. He talked glibly through the wine, as if he were reciting lines he had memorized for life.

"I was supposed to be the family savior," he said. "I was the one who would restore the family to its historic preeminence in New York business and social circles. My parents died when I was young. By the time I came of age and received my trust, half the money was gone. I failed miserably when I tried to make more. Oh, I made several stabs at business. I found it depressing. Did some time on Wall Street, swimming with the sharks, outside the cage. They taught me the grand game, how to systematically transfer a client's money into your own pocket with as little loss to the client as possible. While I played that subtle game of craft, I managed to trade away nearly everything I had. I got addicted to options trading. Yeah, I'm a recovering options junkie; can't go near the stuff without breaking into a cold sweat. I got smart and traded down for an addiction to alcohol. Far safer. On Wall Street, I was a man I didn't like or respect. I was an actor, showing a fake face to the world, caring little for those around me. I had to act to survive, in that cutthroat world.

"One day, at the age of twenty-five, I realized that, wherever I was, my life would be spent as an actor. It fell around me like parade confetti, the sudden realization that I would get paid according to how well I pulled it off, the acting. I chose the *stage* over the *street*. At least on stage, people *knew* I was acting. Truth be known, I'm quite good, when I stay sober. That's my problem, you see. I like to drink. Quit options trading cold turkey. But alcohol? Alcohol is the life blood of an actor. The nectar of the muse. At least that's what we like to tell ourselves."

Copley grew somber and gulped his glass empty. "Waiter!" he cried loudly, motioning across the room with the empty wine bottle. The waiter nodded. Copley grunted, then burped. He smiled; then he grew somber. "Now, child," he said. "Tell me a little about you."

Sammantha stared at the man across the table. Should she tell him how she had been schooled in Russia? That she had graduated Harvard College at age nineteen, how she'd followed that with a quick trip through Harvard Medical School and a residency at Johns Hopkins? That she had spent her childhood immersed in books to escape what they did to her at night? Should she tell him about her work, how she practiced her craft in rogue countries, particularly in Asia, the Middle East and Africa? That her work was most prized by terrorists who prayed daily for the end of America? Should she tell him how she was raped on the day her parents were killed, at the brittle age of twelve, how she had been abused so many times, that if each time were a brick, she would be surrounded by an impregnable tower? Should she tell him how she focused her rage on America—that her greatest goal in life was to see his country in ashes?

"I'm a nurse," she said. "I care for select private patients when they need me." She paused, wanting to say more, something that might lead him to the truth. Instead, she lied, "I grew up in the Midwest on a small wheat farm. I studied nursing because my parents wanted me to help others." She laughed. "They expected a veterinarian."

"You speak of your parents as if they were dead."

This time Sammantha didn't lie. She closed her eyes and nodded. "They are."

"I'm sorry."

"Yeah," she said. "So am I." She looked into Copley's increasingly vacant eyes.

Copley gave a half smile. "My parents were older when I was born. They're long since gone. We're orphans, you and me."

We are, thought Sammantha. Like soul mates. You, me, and the rats.

Murders in the Dark was a second-rate play. Its run, if it could be called that, lasted only four days. By the time the sets were broken down and the IOUs were issued to the unpaid actors, Sammantha Starodubov had become the new matriarch of Copley Manor.

***

The tires on the BMW squealed as Sammantha yanked it off Park Avenue and aimed it toward Gramercy Park. She drove around the small square twice, looking through the iron fence, hoping to find him there. He liked to sit on his wooden bench in the afternoons, reciting Shakespeare, as if he were a king. It was his escape. Brandon Copley was comfortable in this place, this quiet enclave of the city. He was most comfortable playing four-hundred-year-old-roles. He was a fish out of water in any other part of his native city. Here, he ruled.

Copley wasn't in the park, so Sammantha pulled the car into the narrow driveway beside his residence. Copley lived in a square, red brick building with tarnished copper trim. It was old. But it was elegant and stately, like its former owners. Even in its disheveled state, the six-story home would fetch an enormous sum, were it to come on the market.

Sammantha grabbed two suitcases out of the BMW's trunk and hefted them to the front of the building. After climbing the eight stairs to the main door she looked up. The Copley family crest was chiseled deeply into the weathered marble overhang. There was no color to the crest, the paint having long since worn away. But the clean solid lines of the shield and the sword remained, as if the family would endure forever.

Clyde, the doorman, started toward Sammantha as she poked her head through the entrance. Sammantha waved him off. "I've got 'em, Clyde." Sammantha held the heavy door with her hip while dragging her bags over the threshold.

The doorman hobbled toward Sammantha. Clyde's back was rounded like a whale. His shoes made a kind of *swish thump* as he dragged his left leg behind him like a club. His head drifted from side to side as if he were speaking to himself, some sort of nervous degeneration or shell shock from one of the wars. "Are you sure, Miss Sammantha? I could..."

Sammantha shook her head. "Really, Clyde..." Hurt rose in the old man's eyes. Sammantha paused, then held out a bag. "Could you carry this?"

Clyde acknowledged her with a thankful smile. "I know I'm not much good 'round here anymore, Miss Sammantha." Clyde half carried and half dragged Sammantha's bag, huffing as if he were pulling a stalled car.

"Nonsense." Sammantha looked at Clyde's pale skin. It looked like the surface of a mushroom, with rumpled brown age spots sprouting everywhere like coin-sized freckles. His hair was like beach sand, bleached white and silky smooth. His eyebrows were fat and tufted like cheese puffs. "You've worked here for almost fifty years, Clyde. You are part of the family, more than you could ever know." It was true. Clyde had been Mr. Everything to the Copley's for over half a century. At one time he'd been the majordomo to a staff of forty. He'd supervised the properties, the family gardeners, the maids, the secretaries and the cooks. He had seen that Brandon received proper care from his nursemaids, and later from his tutors. He was the one who had taught Copley how to throw a baseball.

Sammantha carried her bag to the elevator and rested it on the worn hall carpet. She waited patiently as Clyde shuffled up behind her with the other. "What women want these days, Clyde, isn't servitude. They want comfort. You bring comfort, honest comfort. Do you understand?"

When Clyde reached Sammantha he was wheezing. He put his hands on his knees and sucked in air like he'd nearly drowned. Sammantha patted his shoulder. "You make us all feel good, sir Clyde."

Clyde bowed his head for a brief moment. Then he peered at Sammantha through his blinking rheumy eyes, watching her closely, like a dog waiting for her to throw a stick or a ball.

"Have you seen Brandon, Clyde?"

"Ain't seen 'im all day, Miss." Clyde looked to his feet.

"Thank you, Clyde. I understand."

Sammantha pretended to search for something in her purse. "How are things with your family, Clyde?" she said, as she fingered through the large leather bag.

"Oh, Miss Sammantha, they're jus' fine."

"And your great grandchildren?" Sammantha still didn't look at Clyde, avoiding eye contact. Clyde wore pain and pleasure on his sleeve. Sometimes...sometimes, that was just too much for Sammantha to see.

Clyde's eyes grew animated and he grinned. His back straightened like it had been snapped in place by an invisible chiropractor's hand. This time Sammantha looked at him and smiled.

"The great grand children, they're *real* fine."

"And Howard, our future surgeon?"

Clyde's eyes grew sad and he shook his head. It was a look Sammantha had seen reflected in her own dark days. It was the sadness of unanswered prayers, of lost hope.

"Aw, he's fine, Miss. He's got himself two jobs. Someday he hopes to go back to college."

"I thought he was doing well at Columbia?"

Sammantha leaned against the wall and waited for Clyde to process the question. It was as if he had to do math in his head before responding to her in his quiet, respectful voice.

"He was, Miss Sammantha. An' doin' real well." Clyde hesitated. "He has to help his momma now, with the bills. She lost her job, you see. Bad economy, they say." Clyde wheezed again. "God bless that boy."

Sammantha closed her eyes. She remembered her own helpless struggle. It was like being stranded on a lonely island, watching ships pass by in the distance, without them ever getting close enough to hail. "Don't worry," she said. "If he wants it bad enough—" Her words trailed off. Howard couldn't screw his way to an education like she had. He had a mother to care for. Lucky man.

"I suppose so." Sparkling liquid brimmed around the deep-set folds of Clyde's cloudy eyes. "I suppose so."

Sammantha grasped Clyde's hands and squeezed them tightly. She looked at him solemnly, silently, as if waiting for wisdom and hope that refused to come. "If I could help you, I would." She couldn't help him now, not without giving herself away and jeopardizing everything she'd worked for.

Clyde squeezed back on her fingers. "No matter, Miss Sammantha. The Lord gives us what the Lord gives us. We're all part of His great plan."

"Yes...yes. I guess so." *What kind of God does this? What kind of God would cause what I've endured?*

Sammantha picked up her bags and stepped inside the elevator. She closed the outside metal grate and then the brass door. She pressed a handle, which set the ancient elevator into its anguished climb, clicking and creaking as it moved slowly upward.

"Amazed this damn thing still works," she said quietly. Sammantha kept her hand near the red button labeled "Emergency Stop," just in case the elevator finally did die. She tapped her foot nervously, as she always did, looking through the glass side door at the greasy insides of the elevator shaft. "I could crawl up this shaft faster than this old crate," she mumbled.

Sammantha was always in a hurry. She had too many things to do. Everything had a purpose, including the next few minutes, especially the next few minutes.

The elevator shuddered and stopped when it reached the sixth floor. Sammantha pulled the brass lever to one side to open the door. Then she opened the outside grate. She carried her bags down the hallway until she came to the parlor where Copley spent most of his time. "I'm home!" she yelled. "Baby, I'm home!"

Sammantha pushed an ancient black button on the wall. The lights snapped on. "Brandon?" She dropped her bags and listened for sound—nothing, except the muted noise of the New York streets, seventy feet below.

If he's been out carousing again. "Brandon!"

"Wh... what?" Sammantha heard Copley cry from the far end of the hall. She also heard a muffled *thump*. She walked across the parlor floor to the hallway that she called the "great hall of fame," the rows of family portraits—Copley's all. Each picture sported the required Copley sneer, with each portrait framed in gold leaf and set exactly three and a half feet from the next. Between the portraits hung other "family" photographs, each with stilted poses and forced smiles.

Copley was in the library, with his body slung across a purple eighteenth century velvet ottoman. His face had a scraggly, three or four day beard. His white silk shirt was torn. His pants were unzipped but still on. Beside him lay three empty bottles of Jack Daniels. A fourth was on the floor and nearly gone. The cap was unscrewed and the bottle rested next to a half-empty glass.

"H… hello, Samm," said Copley. His voice was hoarse and unsteady, his eyes bleary and unfocused.

"Hello, Brandon," Sammantha said curtly. She averted her eyes, looking instead to the fireplace behind Copley. Like many things in the old home, there was a story behind that fireplace. It was a gift of thanks from the government of France. An early Copley had teamed with Junius Morgan to lend fifty million dollars to France in 1870, to help finance the Franco-Prussian war. France had lost, but Copley's support had not gone forgotten or unrewarded. The Copleys had made many millions trading with the French after that, as had the Morgans. *What a difference the generations can make*, Sammantha thought disdainfully. She thought of her task and wondered if she could accomplish it with this shell of a man.

"Are you all right, Brandon, dear?"

Copley smiled sheepishly. Sammantha winced when she saw his mossy green teeth.

"We had quite the bender, I see."

"I missed you," said Copley. "What am I supposed to do when you vanish? For weeks on end, you are gone. What am I supposed to do?"

"Practice your acting. You're an actor, aren't you?"

"You could have called."

"You're right. I *should* have called." Sammantha's voice softened. "I missed you so. And I knew that if I called you, all I would do was cry."

Copley's head began to clear. With stiff effort, he sat up and wrung his face with his hands. "What day is it?"

"The twenty-first, dear."

Copley looked toward the ceiling as he tried to think.

"The twenty-first... the twenty-first.... Sunday?"

"Yes, Sunday."

"Guess I better take a shower."

"How long have you been like this, Brandon?"

"Since Thursday, I think...Maybe Wednesday."

Sammantha touched Copley on the cheek like a compassionate, loving wife. "Come along, dear. I'll help you with a bath. Then I've got something to tell you. Something that will make you very, very happy."

CHAPTER **10**
PP

Jacob Miller was holding court in his office. He was sitting with practiced nonchalance behind his elegant, teak sea-captain's desk. His Donald Trump hair was flipped back over his ears and stylishly coiffed on top. His hands cradled the back of his neck, with his elbows stuck out like bat wings. Tortoise shell glasses were drooping down the end of his nose. He held his chin high, peering down at the man standing before him. His prey was Budd Doheny, Director of the Presidential Protection Division of the Secret Service. Doheny was a square jawed man with dark Irish eyes. His nose was broad and flattened, as ex-boxer's noses often are. His body was thick and rounded, as solid as an outdoor postal box. Beside Doheny stood Steve Cramm. Cramm was a chief inspector with the FBI. He was gawky thin and a willowy intellectual, with an ectomorphic frailty that made him look like he could break under a hard exhale of breath. Beside Cramm and Doheny stood two of Cramm's assistants. Each was a mirror of the other—hair closely cropped, cleanly shaven, their bodies hard and trim, their manner precise. They were ex-Marines, gone to the softer side.

Doheny's face crunched into a repugnant scowl, while Miller played with him like a cat with an injured mouse, pawing him from side-to-side with his words.

"We've been ordered to request your help," said Doheny. Doheny looked beyond Miller's fluffy hair, never meeting his eyes, just staring at the wall. He took a deep breath and sighed. "As you know, I'm not in favor of this—"

Miller interrupted. "You've got your ass in a sling because it was your team that was penetrated." Miller grinned like a fortune-telling gypsy stealing a client's money, his eyes glowing with schadenfreude, an almost guilty pleasure at Doheny's misery. Almost. He began to gloat. "I know the story. You screwed up. So Tilson figured you'd have motivation to see this thing through, enough impetus to direct all your worthless cretins to find the truth. So, rather than have the FBI run this thing, as they normally would, and should, he chose you to ride point. That's a big chunk of salt on your wounds." Miller looked from Doheny to Cramm, and then from Cramm to his two assistants. "Right so far?"

Doheny nodded.

Miller continued. "Tilson insisted you work closely with the FBI, so you brought Cramm in to help save your butt." He glanced toward Cramm. "A good choice, I might add. At least he'll give you a fighting chance. The FBI's got resources you could never dream of having." Miller paused. Then his lips widened into a grin. "Oh, that's right, Doheny. You used to do this sort of thing for the FBI, until you got scared and soft and joined the SS."

A thin smile skipped across Doheny's lips, like a brief fleck of sunlight sparkling off water, then vanishing in the clouds. The Secret Service had some of the toughest bastards alive, men ready to step in front of a bullet at any time. Doheny didn't take the bait. He nodded and glanced at Cramm. Then he shrugged. "For what good they've done me so far."

You wimp, thought Miller, *taking it out on your own team rather than me.* "I assume Tilson wants his wife's killer even more than he wants the presidency?" said Miller.

"You could say that."

"If he doesn't find his killer, you'll be the whipping boy?"

Doheny winced, but whispered, "Right, sir."

Miller smiled. "Kinda like having your nuts in a vice, isn't it?" Miller reached into the side drawer of his desk, removed a large, pink bottle of Pepto Bismol and tipped it into his mouth. "I'd be a fool to get involved."

For the first time, Doheny looked directly at Miller. "I'd be a fool to want you." Doheny spread out his hands in a weary, helpless gesture. "Unfortunately, we both have no choice."

Miller took two more swigs of Pepto and replaced the cap. "Presidential order?"

Doheny nodded. "Yeah."

"Perhaps you'd like to tell me where we stand?"

Doheny looked at Cramm. Cramm looked at Doheny. They locked eyes and subtly signaled each other. Then Doheny continued, "The last thing we wanted was to bring the CIA into this quagmire."

Doheny thought back to his morning meeting with the president's national security advisor, Jeremiah Pincenogle, and grimaced.

Doheny and Pincenogle were seated at the president's cherry conference table in a rounded corner of the Oval Office. The table looked like an old piece of dining room furniture, which it was. Kiki had brought it with them from Maine. It was covered with hundreds of scratch marks and strings of writing indentations. It also had deep pockmarks where things like forks and metal toys had crash landed. Kiki had liked to surround Tilson with things that reminded him of home and his family, to keep him grounded as he ruled the world. Now it just made him feel empty.

The president was still hosting a security briefing below the White House. He was expected back shortly, but he had ordered Pincenogle to brief Doheny on the rules for the investigation into his wife's assassination.

Pincenogle was a big, bulky man with sharp beak of a nose and a fat neck that hung in round rolls over the tight collars of his crisp white dress shirts. He looked like a snapping turtle squeezed into a business suit. His movements seemed deliberately slow and his face was pinched, making him look like he was fighting off the urge to take a big dump.

"The president wanted me to lay the new ground rules."

"Ground rules? That's bullshit," barked Doheny. "What in hell does he know about investigating a murder?"

"He knows what he wants."

"Like shit, he does. He doesn't know diddlysquat about intelligence and you know it. What sort of punk-assed ideas are you feeding him, Jeremiah?"

"He wants you to bring in the CIA."

"Yeah, that's just what we need." Doheny snorted. "We should keep this investigation as tight as a virgin, or every half-assed terrorist group from here to China is going to be taking credit and gunning for the president." Doheny stood up from the table and leaned against it with both hands, pressing his face within inches of the president's chief security advisor.

Pincenogle looked Doheny squarely in the eye and pondered his statement. His head seemed to bob in and out of his turtle shell with each successive breath. Finally, he scratched at the gray, two-day stubble on his chin and stared off across the room.

Pincenogle said, "Well, then. I guess your job is to see that doesn't happen, isn't it Budd? I'll hold you personally accountable for every threat we receive and don't repel."

"Screw you."

Pincenogle chuckled. His body vibrated like jelly and his seat groaned with the motion. "At least you care."

"Look, sir," said Doheny. "Let us see this through, without CIA interference. We're making headway and we don't need infighting."

"You've had time, Doheny, and what have you got? Bupkiss."

Doheny bit his lip. His fists clenched, then opened and clenched again. He seemed to measure his words carefully, but when he spoke, the words came in a rapid, uncontrolled jumble. "We've had three frigging days, sir. That's all! Things take time and you know it. I've got to get a court order before I can investigate any suspect or take them in for questioning. I've got a goddamn Congressional committee breathing down my frigging neck saying I can't violate anyone's civil rights in searching for clues or answers. They want me to tell them everything I do or think. You know what that's like, Jeremiah? We've been so friggin' emasculated that I can't do my job. If we open up the investigation...It's hard enough to keep a lid on this thing...but with others involved, I don't know what the hell they might say."

"The first lady is dead, Doheny. You got that? The truth's coming out soon. She's got no double. The woman is *dead*."

Pincenogle let the silence hang for several long moments. Doheny's eyes narrowed and he finally said, "Then you're setting yourself up, sir, and the president, too. If someone can come in and knock off the first lady, only weeks after the start of this administration, and not get caught, you'll have every penny ante terrorist gunning for glory. You've got to confirm her death on the day you arrest her killers, Jeremiah. Because, if you don't, you're going to look like the Keystone cops."

"No, Doheny. That will be *you* and *your* boys looking incompetent," said Pincenogle. "You see, you've already screwed up. I'm just an observer here."

Doheny closed his eyes. He understood it now. Everyone in this administration was new. Each of them was jockeying for power, but there was no *leadership*. No one would take the lead. A long feather would go to the man who solved this mystery. Wasn't that one of the reasons he wanted to keep the investigation to himself in the first place? Didn't he see this as his ticket to the career express elevator?

Pincenogle pursed his turtle beak. He raised his turtle head and said, "You need the CIA because they can do things you can't, Doheny. Your hands are tied. You know that. We know that. Miller doesn't have to follow those same rules. He can fly under the radar and do the things you can only dream of. He's got the black and wet ops teams that you need. Let him be your eyes and ears. He can interrogate for information and get a private oo-rah. Or, he can hire a consultant to do it, far outside the glare of politics. If you so much as fart in front of a suspect, you'll go to jail. You work with Miller, and that's that."

So, here he was now, standing across from Jacob Miller, inviting the CIA to hog the glory and kick his ass.

Doheny drew a deep breath. He glanced toward Miller, then to his partner, Cramm. He looked back at Miller and let out air in a low gush. "All right, asshole. There's not much to go on. The first lady turns up dead in her sleep. The forensics are called in. They carve her six ways to Sunday and call more experts to look at the parts. Blood work gets processed by Washington CSI...the CDC...the EPA and JHU..."

"JHU?" interrupted Miller.

"Johns Hopkins University."

"Don't patronize me, Doheny, or I'll have you sent to Alaska in a New York minute. Or, maybe I'll have one part sent to Alaska and another brought to Afghanistan."

Doheny's face tinged red. He clenched and unclenched his fists but he kept his mouth shut. It would be like Miller to do something extreme. By Alaska, did Miller mean a reassignment? He knew what the two parts meant; two parts meant dead.

"What they came up with is this: She was poisoned. Nerve compounds." Doheny looked at Cramm. This was his area.

Cramm said, "She ingested toxins that paralyzed her muscles. We found traces of Hemlock and botulism—basic shit, but powerful. That might have killed her, but probably not. We think they were red herrings, because we also found two other compounds, of which the formulas are, as of yet, unidentified. Some sort of synthetic, designer crap that we haven't seen. We nearly missed them, 'cause they were breaking down in her fast. Hemlock normally begins to take effect after several hours, botulism several hours after that. Either could kill you, but the other stuff, we think that sealed the deal. This is a sophisticated kill. Very professional."

"Poisoned?" asked Miller.

Doheny frowned. "What are you, deaf? It probably happened at the Embassy dinner." Doheny paused. "I believe you were there?"

"Who told you I was there?"

"I know everything that goes on around the president."

Miller returned the grin. "You wish you did. No chance of suicide?"

Doheny clenched his fists again. "I'll forget you mentioned that. Kiki Tilson had the all-American dream. She loved her life."

Miller sucked in through his teeth and took another absentminded sip of his Pepto shake. There was just a smidgeon left, so Miller tipped the bottle to drain the final drops. Then he said, "Lots of people suffocate under the all-American dream, Doheny."

"You must be one constipated dude, Miller…Drinking all that crap."

Miller ignored him. "Seems like a simple matter of tracing the poisons to the killer, Doheny. Shouldn't be more than a few suspects who could produce exotic nerve compounds. What do you need me for?"

"We don't. But we all know it could take months, or years, to track the trail of those compounds."

Miller snickered. "That's why they're making you come to me. Because you can't do the job."

"Personally, I want your butt out of this."

Miller slowly grinned. He looked almost happy as he raised his index finger and ticked it from side to side. "What if I *want* to help?"

"You'll get nothing from us," said Cramm. "You might even get *gone*." Cramm's hand moved imperceptivity toward his pistol.

Miller began to laugh. He was enjoying this conversation, like he might a tennis match with a man he hated, one who was nowhere near his equal on the court. "Good one, Cramm."

Doheny said, "We *do* want you to *appear* to take an interest. If you play nice, we'll leave you be."

Miller sucked more air through his teeth and pulled an imaginary hair off his custom Savile Row suit. Without looking up he said, softly, "Boys shouldn't make threats to men, boys."

"So don't make one."

Miller leveled his eyes at Doheny. "You, sir, are one stupid shit. With a simple phone call I could have you neutered before you leave this office and be no worse for wear. You are little piss-ant players in this game. You've got no frigging clue what is going on in the real world."

The two men stared at each other for close to a minute. Ever since 9/11, the U.S. security agencies had been engaging in the new spirit of cooperation brought about by that day. This was about as cordial as it came.

"All right, boys," Miller lied. "I'll stay as clear as I can." He reached into his desk and removed a pocket flask with a new supply of antacid. He took a gulp and said, "Be warned. If you screw up, I'll kick your asses, butt naked, from one side of this town to the other, with your heads stuck up inside them. Understood?"

Doheny looked at Cramm. Cramm looked at Doheny. Then both men looked at Miller. They each made a slight, deferential bow.

"Guess we have a deal, then," said Doheny.

The two men and their assistants walked out of Miller's office.

Miller leaned onto the back legs of his chair. How could he work this to his advantage? What was best for the president, and what was best for the country? He dialed his assistant's extension and barked into his wireless headset.

"Get me the White House."

A few moments later Miller's phone buzzed. He punched the speaker button. "Talk to me."

"The president's chief of staff is on the line, sir."

Miller lifted the corded receiver and spoke to his old friend, "Hey, Geoff. How's he doing?"

"He's lost it, Jake. Kiki was his backbone. Without her he's a goddamned jellyfish. This was a man that would run through walls just a week ago. Now he's afraid of his shadow…Ya gotta help me here."

Miller wiped the sheen off his brow and flicked the sweat onto his pants. It never stopped. He was like a babysitter, and the country was some big blubbering child who couldn't stay out of trouble.

"Tilson's going to forward your nomination as CIA Director, Jake, provided you haven't got nanny problems. And provided he hasn't resigned, or we haven't had to commit him before then."

"It's that bad?"

"All he can think about is payback."

Revenge, thought Miller. Nothing more wasteful than thoughts of revenge. "That's not good, Geoff."

"It's freaking pathetic, if you ask me."

This made Miller think about Jack Trance. Trance had wanted payback, too. He had come up dry. Always dry. His wife's killers had vanished into oblivion, leaving Trance with a hole in him the size of Pennsylvania. He was still effective, all right. He looked good, had all the skills, but the essence that had made him special was getting harder to find. He was like a race car that had trouble shifting into its top gear. Miller couldn't let this happen to the president. It wasn't good for him; it wasn't good for the country. Then, of course, there was his own little issue…Miller flushed that thought from his mind and took another drink of antacid. Fuck them. Fuck them all, he thought.

Miller said, "Give him some slack, Geoff. Losing a wife really sucks. I've seen what it does, felt what it does. It'll take some time before he adjusts. We've just got to bring this thing full circle, and do it fast."

A few moments later, Jock Tilson came on the line.

Miller said, "I was so sorry to hear about your wife, Mr. President. Doheny and Cramm were just here."

"Can you help them?"

"I'll try, sir. But if I may, sir, I would like to offer some words of advice."

Tilson waited while Miller summoned the words, words he, himself, needed to hear.

"We do need to find who did this, for the sake of the country…But for your sake, sir, I hope you can move beyond revenge. Feelings like this work like acid, sir, burning deep into your gut until it consumes your every waking moment."

Miller heard Tilson laugh. "Never thought I'd hear such words from *you*, Miller. Seeing how you wear pain on your chest like a medal. Let's find Kiki's killers. Then we'll deal with the aftermath. Put your best men on it, Jake. Spare no expense. Get this done."

"You've already got good talent, Mr. President. Doheny and Cramm are the best you've got."

"I want Trance."

Oh, shit. Miller inhaled deeply and closed his eyes. He'd known this was coming. "I don't think Trance is right for the job, sir. This same thing happened to him…So, I'm not sure he'll keep the right kind of perspective, the objectivity he'll need. Besides, I can't order him, sir. You know that. He's a free man."

"Why don't you try asking him? As a favor, to me." Tilson's voice was pleading, like Geoff had said. He was whining like a child who had lost his binky.

"I will call him, Mr. President. I will. But I make no promises."

"Tell him I need him."

CHAPTER 11
PP

Jack Trance was seated in his small Vermont law office, attempting to mitigate a divorce between a local land developer and his vengeful wife. Unwittingly, he had been hired by both, the wife using her maiden name as she paid his retainer. Now, neither would relinquish claim to the services of the local crackerjack lawyer, who also happened to be the only decent lawyer in town.

Trance was trapped behind his desk as the dueling couple stood before him, preparing for combat like gladiators. Behind them, Trance's door lay open, with the edge of his assistant's desk just visible. His assistant was looking back through the doorway, laughing at Trance.

"My wife tells me you're her attorney," said the developer, his eyes darting toward his estranged spouse and back to Trance.

"Yes, Bill. I am."

"But you're *my* lawyer."

"That is true. However, I think it best that I represent only one of you. Unless you two want to compromise."

Bill Moffet thrust back his shoulders and bellowed toward the ceiling, "Larissa may get half of every goddamn thing that I own, but she's sure as hell not going to screw me out of my own goddamn attorney!"

"Screw you out of your attorney?" shouted Larissa. "The only thing you'll ever get screwed out of is this marriage. And it was your own screwing that caused it!"

Moffet held out his hands. There was a pleading in his eyes. They reminded Trance of the eyes of a Basset Hound, his lower lids droopy and moist. "I didn't touch her. I swear I didn't touch her." Moffett looked toward Trance. "Help me here, Jack. Will you?"

"Listen to him," spat Larissa. "He says he didn't touch her. Well, I know better. I read the emails."

"Is that what this thing is about?" asked Trance. "Emails?"

Larissa slammed her purse against Trance's desk. "Yes, that's what it's about. I read the emails."

"*She* sent the emails. Not me. *She* said she loved *me*. *I* never said that to *her*, and nothing happened."

Trance's phone began to sound, while his clients squared off like they were in a ring, the Pit Bull and the Basset Hound. Trance leaned back in his chair, listening for his assistant's voice to come through the opened door. He frowned, as he watched his clients stand nose against nose, accusation against accusation. What the hell was he doing here? he wondered. Did he really need this? Yes, he did. This was the only place he felt normal, where he didn't have to carry the expectations on his shoulders, the burdens of country and family and mankind. This was where all the problems of the world could become obfuscated by a simple argument between Bill and Larissa Moffett. Trance cocked an ear so he could hear his assistant answer the phone.

"Law office. Judy speaking....Ah, he's in a conference right now...No, I can't disturb him...for president Tilson? A favor for the president? He doesn't like to be disturbed, Mr. Miller…"

"I'll take that, Judy," said Trance, over his clients' screaming. He needed a break, and this could be something important.

"Excuse me," he said to his clients. "I must take a call."

Trance rose from his desk. His clients ignored him and fought on. Trance walked into the reception area and took the phone from Judy. He touched her on the shoulder. "Would you go get us some donuts from Dot's, please?"

"Aw," said Judy. "I was hoping to listen."

"Please, Judy."

"Wait 'til I tell everyone about this…The president—"

"Don't say a word."

Judy hunched her shoulders and grinned playfully. "You know I wouldn't."

Judy stepped out of Trance's office and ambled through the hard-packed snow toward Dot's Diner to get Trance his donuts.

"What's up, Jake?" said Trance.

"Who's that bimbo you've got working for you, Trance?"

"Easy, Miller. She's better educated than you or me, and far more efficient. What's your problem?"

"First, I must advise you that I am taping this conversation."

"No shit."

"I've got a job for you."

"Not interested." Trance looked around his office, making sure no one was listening.

"You may want to hear about this. It's for—"

Trance spoke firmly into the phone, interrupting Miller with a cool, level voice. "No, Jake. I've had enough of your kind of business. I don't care what kind of guilt trip you lay on me. I'm trying to live my life, not lose it. Let someone else do it. I'm tired of the game. You've got a hundred men who can do the job better than I can."

"You don't even want to listen?" Trance could almost feel Miller smiling on the other end of the line. He'd been baited but he wouldn't bite.

"The story always sounds compelling, Jake. Call someone else. Please."

"Suit yourself."

Miller hung up the phone and laughed out loud. He'd just driven one mucho grande spike between Trance and the president. A true master stroke. This could only strengthen him and weaken Trance with Tilson. Rarely did he get a gift like this. This deserved a special drink. He walked to his small refrigerator and pulled out a tray of ice. He removed a single cube and dropped it into a glass. He poured three fingers of Pepto Bismol into the glass, gave it a splash of lime and gulped it down, smacking his lips when he was done.

Miller called the president. "Trance says he's not up to it, sir."

"He won't help me?" *How could Trance be so insensitive? After the same thing happened to him? He has to know what it's like.*

"He says we have others who can do a better job. He's right, you know. We can handle this without him. It's not like he's Superman or something."

"I see. Thank you for trying, Miller."

The phone went dead.

Tilson called for Mandy Potempkin, his secretary.

"Mandy, cancel my meeting with Lauren Haverford for tomorrow. Don't reschedule." *Life's a two-way street, Trance, and I'm the traffic cop.*

Miller placed his phone back in its receiver. He sat down in his chair and leaned back to enjoy the moment. This had become a very fine day, indeed. Even his stomach settled into a smooth comfortable purr.

***

When Judy sauntered into Trance's reception area, carrying a brown paper bag, Trance was avoiding the divorce battle by reading an old copy of *Harvard Law Review*. As Judy closed the door behind her, Trance looked to her and smiled. Judy was exceedingly bright but surprisingly uncomplicated. She was well-rounded mentally and physically, with many varied interests. If she had a flaw, one glaring anomaly in her healthy, disciplined life, it was donuts from Dot's. She would run an extra three miles today, just so she could eat them sans guilt. She was already chewing the remains of a cream-filled cruller as the door clicked behind her. A ring of powdered sugar circled her lips.

"Done already?" she said. Her voice almost whined with disappointment. "I was hoping to talk to the president."

Trance looked puzzled. "The president?"

"Mr. Miller said that the president wanted to talk with you. And I was hoping—"

"Miller told you that? He is an evil, conniving little man. I didn't talk to the president." Had Miller offered Trance's services to the president? Was that what the call was about? Goddamned Miller.

Trance grabbed the donut bag and carried it into his office. After two steps he stopped. Bill Moffet and his wife were caught in a love-lock that would make a Vegas dancer blush. Trance stood in mid-stride, gaping as the two of them kissed and groped. He turned away as the developer slipped his hand along his wife's back side and then deep down her skirt."

"Ah hem," interrupted Trance.

"Oh, Jack!" said Larissa.

"I seemed to have missed something?"

Larissa reached around her husband's neck and pulled his head down to give him noogies with her knuckles. "You missed this big lug apologizing for the first time in his life. He did give me the passwords to his email accounts. Not the sign of a guilty man."

"Does this mean you won't need my services?"

"You bet," said Moffet. "Thanks to you. You're as good as they say you are, Trance."

Trance walked to his desk and pulled a manila folder from a wire stand.

"I'll give you back your deposits."

"No, no," said Moffet. "You earned every penny."

Trance laughed. "I did nothing. Take back your three grand."

"Give it to charity. Everybody knows that's what you do." Moffet took his wife by the hand and began to lead her out of the office. Then he stopped and looked at Trance. He held out his hand and the two men shook. "They call you 'The Miracle Worker,' you know. Now I see why."

"I did nothing."

"And you did it just right."

Trance scribbled his signature onto the back of the two checks and carried them to Judy, along with the bag of uneaten donuts. He smiled as the Moffets walked arm in arm out the door of his office.

"Bring these checks to Jimbo at the woman's shelter, will you? Then take the rest of the day off. I'm going skiing."

"Sure," said Judy, with no hint of surprise in her voice. She was used to this. She took the bag and the checks, polished off the last of a jelly donut and walked to a closet against the wall. She pulled a pair of dark blue ski pants, a white turtleneck, and a blue fleece jacket from the shelves and threw them into Trance's open arms.

"Anything else, boss?"

"Go have fun." Judy would go back home to her husband, a budding architect. He would probably meet her at the door with a kiss. They would grab some lunch, perhaps make love. Then they would be off to Killington for the rest of the day.

"Sure, Jack. You, too." Judy doubted Trance would have fun. She knew where he was going. He was going to visit his past.

Soon Trance was speeding along the narrow, snow-covered Vermont country roads in his white Porsche 959. The low slung supercar moved like a cruise missile, tightly hugging the rugged ground as Trance wound out the engine. He accelerated into the corners, urging his car to the limits of its lower gears, then easing the throttle as his speed topped a hundred and seventy kilometers per hour along the slim straight-aways.

The air was cold. The sun had broken through the clouds to bathe the snowy mountains to a near blinding whiteness. Trance had the top down on his convertible, and the air ripped at his hair and face like icicle claws. He pulled a pair of Randolph Engineering aviator sunglasses out of his glove box. As he wrapped the glasses around his ears he caught movement in the corner of his eye, a blue splash in his rearview mirror, as another car wound through the tight curves behind him. Trance accelerated and never looked back.

CHAPTER 12
_____________PP_____________

Steam rolled out over the top of the shower door, fogging the mirrors like smoky glass. The air was moist and hot, dripping like a sultry, Georgia summer night. Sammantha struggled to pull Brandon Copley's pants over his uncooperative feet, dragging him halfway across the bedroom before his pants finally tore free. She grabbed Copley by the shoulders and pulled him into the bathroom toward the shower. His underwear slipped down around his ankles and pooled like a lump of spent candle wax. Copley tried to stand, but he caught his toes in the webbing of his jockey shorts and tumbled forward, nearly dumping himself to the floor. Sammantha steadied him as he wobbled, supporting him until the fluttering ceased.

"For God's sakes, Brandon, quit acting like a drunken baby."

Copley stared at Sammantha and blinked. Then he smiled. "Maybe a drink would help me regain my coordination."

"Hold still." Sammantha lifted Copley's feet one at a time and removed his reeking socks. "You're barely awake as it is. You don't need another drink." Sammantha shook her head. "Sometimes," she said softly. She took hold of the bottom of her sweater and pulled it up over her head in one quick motion. She was naked underneath. Copley vaguely followed the bounce of her firm, rounded breasts. He gazed laconically as she unzipped her jeans, his eyes hollow as they followed the descent of her hand. He looked to her face and she slowly drew her tongue across the front of her teeth.

"Are...are you seducing me?" he said. Copley pulled in his bulging stomach and thrust out his chin, making him look like an out-of-shape fighter preparing to enter the ring against a man half his age, like Jack Black taking on *Rocky* in his prime.

"I don't want to get these clothes wet," she said. "That's all."

Copley's eyes began to focus as Sammantha wriggled out of her tight jeans. His eyes darted toward the red silk thong that clung around her hips. With a single finger Sammantha drew it down, slowly, seductively, until she stood naked before him, looking like a Playboy pinup. "I missed you," she said huskily, from the back of her throat. The words came slowly, with feeling. She almost meant it. Almost, but not quite. Not yet.

Brandon felt a tiny twitter between his legs. Through the fog in his brain he recognized the feeling, like an old toy found in the dusty attic of his mind. He began to rise.

"Take me right now," purred Sammantha, her voice soft and low. "Right here. Give it to me. Right here. Everything you have." Sammantha put her hands on her hips and widened her stance. Her body glistened, as the mist settled against her skin like sweet dew.

Copley moved toward her unsteadily.

"I've missed you so," said Sammantha. She tossed her hair and arched her back as Copley began to stroke her nipples with his trembling hands. She closed her eyes, parted her lips, and pushed her hips forward against Copley's growing penis. "Brandon."

Copley felt himself respond. His hands slid down behind her. He cupped her tight bottom and pulled her up against him. "Do you mean that?"

God, he stinks, thought Sammantha. "Please, Brandon, please." Sammantha pushed Copley to the floor and pulled him on top of her. She reached between her legs and pulled slick wetness from inside her. She guided Copley out of his haze, into her body, and within her control. Copley gasped. She felt him shudder as he slipped inside. She wrapped her arms around his hips, pulled him forward and rocked him, like a baby.

"Oh, I missed you so," said Copley. "Why do you leave me?"

"Oh, darling," said Sammantha, looking at her watch. "Don't think of that now. Just love me. Fill me with your love. Fill me up inside, until I overflow. Give it to me, Brandon, give it to me..."

Moments later it was over. Copley lay above her, panting like an overheated dog. Sammantha stroked his back softly, waiting for the best time to begin. How many years had she been waiting for the next five minutes? "Do you love me, Brandon?"

"More than anything." Copley's breath still came in shallow, rapid gasps. His face was pink and dripping with steam and sweat, his hair looking like he had just run through the jungle.

"Those are just words."

"It's true."

"More than anything?"

"Yes, anything."

"Even your acting?"

"What do you mean, 'even my acting'? Acting is what I do. It's who I am."

"I know," said Sammantha softly. "I know."

After a long shower, Sammantha led Copley by the hand into the bedroom. She tossed her towel to the floor and settled down into the bed. She looked up at Copley and smiled. Her eyes drifted behind him to the walls, to the all-too-familiar faces of long deceased Copleys—Copleys that all seemed to look down their noses at her. She smiled toward these dead scions of a long-lost empire, knowing that the last in their steely line was like soft clay in her hands. "I've got a present for you," she said.

"I don't deserve presents."

Copley walked to his dresser and rummaged vainly for his hair brush. He frowned and began to scratch the back of his scalp. "I could have sworn…"

"Looking for your brush?" asked Sammantha playfully.

Copley turned. Sammantha was smiling. It made him think of Broadway Klieg lights. *How odd*, he thought, *how the mind can slip off course so quickly.*

"I threw it out," she said.

"You what? That brush belonged to my great grandfather. You can't just throw my things out, Samm—"

"You have a new brush..." Sammantha walked to her handbag and withdrew a felt bag. "…with a matching comb."

"I don't want a new brush."

"Ah," said Sammantha. "But this one is special. It's just like the president's brush."

Copley pouted as Sammantha pressed the soft bag into his hands.

"It's a very special brush, you know. Made with the finest boar bristles and the smoothest African Ivory. There are only two of these in the world. One is in the White House. The other is here," she lied. There was only one; it was a one-of-a-kind.

Copley pulled the brush from the bag and turned it over in his hands. He peered at it and grunted. The back of it had a grouping of elaborate hand carvings. It felt balanced in his hands, like an expensive, hand-crafted pistol. "It does look nice."

"President Tilson received the other as a gift, from the president of Nigeria. Maybe someday your grandson will cherish this, as you did yours."

Copley laughed. "Grandson? I have no children and probably never will. My one brief marriage ended with my wife speedballing to death while I was working...Never try that again...marriage, I mean."

He laughed. "Me? Never done drugs. Always preferred stock options or alcohol. Now it's just the booze. It's far more benign."

"I'm not on the pill."

Copley's lips twitched, like they did when he was deep in thought, which was rare these days. He sat silently for nearly a minute, before looking up toward Sammantha through his reddened eyes.

"What do you see in me?" he whispered.

Sammantha stroked Copley's face like she might her Sable fur, running her fingers along it slowly in long, gentle trails.

"I see a very wonderful man, a brilliant actor. I see someone who deserves to be recognized as one of this country's finest individuals."

Copley snorted. "You see a middle-aged drunk who can't keep a job. A washed out actor who has to beg for second rate parts on the outskirts of the outskirts of Broadway. You see the last remaining heir of a once-distinguished family who's lost nearly every dime they had. A man who's brought nothing but shame to his name."

Sammantha took the brush from Copley's palm and began to stroke his hair.

"Have you ever thought about what it would be like to be president?" she asked.

"Be a pain in the royal ass, if you ask me."

"It would certainly restore the grandeur of your family."

"You're dreaming." Copley envisioned himself on the international stage, being the president.

"I think you look like him. Like Tilson."

Copley chuckled. "Maybe if I were forty pounds lighter and spent a few years in the gym."

"There'd be a lot of acting."

Copley looked inward as he imagined himself playing the part. "It's the greatest role in the world. He's always on stage."

"Yes, he is..." Sammantha said quietly, thinking of Tilson.

After she was dressed, Sammantha locked herself in the bathroom. She took a chrome pill box from her purse and shook a tiny white tablet into her palm. She flushed the toilet, ran the sink water for several seconds, unfastened the top button on her blouse and returned to the bedroom. When Copley looked her way, she paused, giving him her best Penthouse pose, leaning against the door jam, fluffing her hair around her pouting lips.

"Can I get you something to drink, Brandon darling?"

"You don't mind?" Copley looked puzzled.

"No." Sammantha smiled. "Not after what you just did for me."

Copley grinned, not with a smile, but with the greedy, aching eyes of an addict about to get his next fix. "A glass of Jack, then? No ice."

Sammantha walked across the room to a battered wooden high boy table that was loaded with liquor bottles, an assortment of glasses, packets of drink mixes, a shaker, and a melted bucket of ice. She cracked a fresh bottle of Jack Daniels and turned her back to Copley as she dropped the white tablet into his glass. She poured two inches of whiskey and swished it around. She dropped three cubes of ice into a second glass, filled it with water and a package of sour mix, then stirred it well, taking her time until the pill had fully dissolved in Copley's drink.

Copley walked to the window overlooking Gramercy Park and stared at the New York skyline. "Nice night," he said.

Without speaking, Sammantha carried the drinks to the window. She handed one to Copley, then raised the other and said, "To the future president."

"Whoever he might be."

Sammantha refused to drink. "To President Brandon Copley." Sammantha glared at Copley, looking like a nun who'd heard a boy burp loudly in church. There was no forgiveness or understanding in her eyes. Just accusation.

Copley saw her anger and looked to his shaking hand. He had no will to argue. "Sure, babe." He lifted his glass, watching out of the corner of his eye as Sammantha did the same. "To President Brandon Copley. And to oblivion—may it come early, often, and someday remain eternal."

"Eternal oblivion. Of course," said Sammantha, smiling to herself. That was her goal, wasn't it? Oblivion? No, not oblivion. Destruction. She wanted complete and total destruction.

Copley drained his glass in several quick gulps. Then he looked hopefully at Sammantha for more.

"That will be enough."

"Sammantha…"

"You promised me before I left, Brandon. No more drinking."

Copley looked back out the window and laughed. "So I lied. Drunks lie, you must know that."

"You said you wouldn't drink anymore. As a gift to me."

"But you're letting me have one now."

The street outside appeared to blur before Copley's eyes, as if he were looking through gauze into a kaleidoscope. His eyelids began to droop and he smiled crookedly, looking more like a crack house addict than the president of the United States.

"I let you have a drink because I love you."

"Then love me more. Just one more."

Sammantha took hold of Copley's arm. "I need you to do something first."

Sammantha led Copley to a maroon leather couch and helped him sit. Beside the couch stood a mahogany end table. Sammantha unfolded a paper from her back pocket and placed it on the table. She pressed a pen into Copley's hand and said, "Sign this while I fix you another drink." Copley smiled. Without reading the words, he signed his life away.

Moments later, Copley's eyes slowly closed. He fell sideways onto the couch and began to snore.

"Well Brandon," Sammantha said. "Our time has come."

***

Sammantha Starodubov thought back to that day in Russia, when everything had grown so clear. It was a cloudy, gloomy Moscow morning. Her fiancé was long since dead, and she was living the Moscow estate he'd left her. The television was on, broadcasting a speech by Senator Jason Tilson, as he announced his intention to run for the U.S. presidency.

As the television cameras zoomed in on his face, Sammantha's house manager, Katarina, said, "I held him, when he was a baby. Tilson. His mother worked with me in America."

Sammantha ignored Katarina as she focused on the political implications of this man's candidacy, and what it would mean to her plan.

"He has a twin," Katarina said. "But that is a secret. A secret that only I know."

It was then that Sammantha turned her full attention to Katarina. "Really? Tell me."

That was when she had learned that the future American president had a twin; one that nobody knew was alive. She learned how their young mother had worked as a maid on a Bar Harbor estate. How their father, their real father, that bastard Copley, had raped that sixteen year old servant girl and stolen one of her sons.

Yes. Her plan had come into view then, a sweeping panorama as big as the Virginia sky. All she had to do was wait. That, of course, and help Tilson win the presidency. Using the Obama strategy of small, non-traceable Internet donations with pre-paid credit cards, she had pumped more than $200 million into Tilson's campaign, all without his knowledge. She learned everything there was to know about both men, Copley and Tilson, until she knew each of them better than herself. They were so different, yet they were identical, spawned by the same malicious seed and a loving egg.

As Sammantha looked at the drugged-out Copley lying prone on his living room couch, she remembered his washed-out face on the New York City billboard. She thought back to Tilson's clear-eyed, smiling face after he'd won his party's nomination. They looked nothing alike. There was a resemblance to the knowing eye, with one a mere shadow of the other. Their lives had been so different that even genetics could not shape them alike. Copley was smoky rooms and barroom stools. Tilson was country air and five mile runs. Tilson was hard and lean, Copley was soft and wasted. Tilson's eyes were alert and expressive, while Copley's were drunk and unfocused. Tilson had grown up outdoors, playing all kinds of sports. Copley had spent his childhood playing the piano and studying Mozart. Copley's one sport was baseball. Introduced to it by Clyde, his father's butler, it had been nurtured by private coaches. Tilson had played pickup games in the neighborhood schoolyard with groups of friends. Copley had no friends.

Jock Tilson was the son of a poor mother who mucked cows at 4 A.M. Brandon Copley, IV had simply appeared one day, held in the arms of his fifty-year-old mother and sequestered in a mansion overlooking Gramercy Park.

Sammantha looked at Copley as he snored. She could almost see him being served with tea and crumpets while listening to his grandfather tell stories of how his father, Vanderbilt and Morgan had helped to shape America. Brandon Copley had bored her time and again, repeatedly telling how the Copley family had owned vast interests in railroads, steel, and heavy manufacturing. How they had always numbered among Lady Astor's select "four hundred," the ones invited to her balls. Those memories had grooved a pathway so deep into Copley's mind, preaching how it was up to him to continue the great family legacy, that if his brain ever jumped the track there would be no jumping back on.

From what she'd learned, Brandon had been a model child, always doing what he was told, even after his parents had shipped him off to Fessenden and Deerfield, demanding nothing less than an A in every course. He did it because it was expected. He'd found drama during his freshman year at Deerfield. It was here that he finally felt free. It was here that he could remove the expectations of his family and become someone else, if only for a night. That, of course, was why his parents forbid him from ever acting again. Then baseball became his savior.

Copley's father greased his way into Yale, where he was supposed to prepare for law. His life was following its demanded destiny like a trail of crumbs, when, one day, his life finally did leave the tracks. Copley's parents were killed by a rogue lion, while on an African safari. He changed his major from history to drama and a star was almost born. He still played baseball, and helped Yale win the Ivy League title against Harvard, by striking out their most feared hitter, Jock Tilson, with the bases loaded to end the game.

Without his parents to push him, though, Copley's ambition withered like tomatoes on a dry September vine. With no sense of purpose, no rules laid down by parents, no common sense and no sense of restraint, Copley's his life began its slow death spiral, ending where he now lay on a couch, drunk and snoring, after signing away everything he had left.

Sammantha twirled Copley's wet hair with one finger. Then she traced along his cheek with the back of a fingernail. It wasn't all his fault. She knew how destiny could turn in an unexpected moment, how it could take someone's fire and snuff it out with one simple stroke. She had felt that stroke, hadn't she? And so had Copley.

Copley's twin had all the advantages. Jock Tilson had been raised on a simple farm, rolling out of bed each morning long before the sun rose into the sky. He would feed the chickens and gather the eggs. He would milk the cows and muck the stalls. By the time he walked off to school, Tilson had already put in hours of concentrated labor. Tilson never complained, because his single mother worked even harder. When he walked into the barns, long before daylight, she was already there—her face smudged with dirt or cow dung, her hair askew, her lips smiling, her eyes ablaze with affection and zest for the day.

"Hello, darling," she would say. "It's another great day, isn't it?" She would give her son a big hug. "And you are the best thing about it…I love you so."

Tilson earned his way to Harvard College, then Harvard Law. After a couple years slaving in a big Boston law firm, he had moved back to Maine and married his childhood sweetheart. The rest was history—a small legal practice, assistant district attorney, district attorney, U.S. senator and finally, the presidency.

Now Kiki was dead, and Jock Tilson was becoming more like his brother every day. In a few more months, no one would be able to tell them apart. It was almost as if some unseen hand were guiding her, clearing the path for her to make things right, to even the score. If she believed in God, she might have felt His hand. But she didn't believe in God, not anymore. This was something else. This was justice.

CHAPTER 13

_______________PP_______________

President Jock Tilson's fingers drummed loudly against the top of the Resolute desk. *Thump. thump, thump*. The shades were drawn in the Oval Office and no lights were on. The sunlight was fading outside. Inside, the room was beginning to match the president's own dark mood. The men standing before him looked like shadows, waiting motionless for the president to speak. Tilson crossed his legs, leaned back in his chair and ordered his reports.

"Speak."

Doheny was the first to talk. His voice had a tinny, whiny quality making him sound like a fourth grade schoolgirl who'd just been hit by the class bully. "We haven't had enough time. Not yet. We're not totally sure what *caused* her death. We certainly don't know who killed her, Mr. President."

Doheny and Cramm stood at attention in the gloom, waiting for the onslaught they knew would come.

"You men are paid for solutions, not excuses. You were supposed to be the best." said Tilson. "I chose you over the FBI, Doheny, because you've got investigative experience with the FBI, and with the Financial Crimes Division of the Secret Service. The director of Homeland insisted that you were one of the few who might see the whole picture—the criminal trail and the money trail. Obviously, he was wrong."

"We've only had six days, sir."

"Israel won a goddamned war in six days. You've had six frigging days and you still can't say *what* killed my wife. Let alone who."

"Israel didn't have to follow our laws, sir."

"No excuse."

"They still don't know who shot Kennedy, sir," mumbled Doheny.

The moment the words left his mouth, Doheny knew he had made a mistake. A big mistake. As Tilson stared at him, Doheny felt like wax in a lava lamp, his insides turning into a burning, bubbling liquid as he stood. He blurted, "Okay, so most think it was E. Howard Hunt, since he admitted to it on his deathbed. Of course, he fingered Hoover, the mob and the CIA…so no one would believe him…No one could…Of course, I'm sure that Kiki wasn't killed by our people…Okay, I think I better just shut up."

Tilson ignored Doheny. He ran his hands through his hair. It hadn't been washed in days, and his fingers couldn't smooth the errant clumps that stuck out in every direction like matted dog fur. Tilson looked like a disheveled, preoccupied professor who couldn't find his car keys when they were hanging on his belt. His temper was growing increasingly volatile. He was licking his lips between every word, cracking and chapping them like a man stranded in the desert, a man wandering in dazed circles just before he died. He was about to throw a tantrum when Jacob Miller slipped in through the Oval Office door.

"Excuse me, Mr. President," said Miller.

"It's about time," cried Tilson.

Miller stopped in place and stared into Tilson's hollow eyes. He briefly closed his own eyes, then motioned for Cramm and Doheny to leave the room. The two men slunk out gratefully.

"Begging your pardon, Mr. President," said Miller calmly, after the two men had left. "I, too, haven't had much sleep. My secretary is bitching like he's got PMS. Now you're losing it, big time. I suggest you remember your position. You are the fucking president…just in case you've forgotten."

Tilson looked at Miller for a stunned moment. Then he laughed. He walked over to Miller, towering above him. Then he engulfed him with a big brotherly arm.

"I deserved that, Jacob. Seems like we're all a bit edgy." Tilson guided Miller toward his conference table at the far end of the office. "Is it true…" he asked, "…that you're worth over forty million?"

"Don't know, sir. Something like that, I guess. Who knows, these days?"

Tilson pressed his hands together. "Do you mind if I ask you something?"

Miller blinked. "Does it matter?"

"I want to know why you do it."

"Do it, sir? You mean the job?"

"Yeah. I want to know why men with your wealth gravitate to Washington. Is it the power?"

Miller smiled. "Guess I just got misdirected somewhere along the way, sir."

"And Trance…He's worth a thousand times that, isn't he?"

Miller laughed. "We're a couple of losers, aren't we?"

"It's eating you up inside, isn't it?"

"Sir?"

"You drink Mylanta like its water."

"Pepto Bismol."

The president grew solemn. "Miller…" He laid his palms flat upon his desk. "…The difference between us is that I have always enjoyed what I've done. You do it because of some warped sense of duty, or some sick need that you have to serve." Miller began to protest but Tilson held up his hand. "I'm not criticizing, just observing."

Miller ruffled his shoulders and said, "Well then, you haven't a goddamn clue, Mr. President. Truth is, I find great pleasure in helping our country. Deep pleasure." Miller reached into his coat and withdrew his silver hip flask. "And the rest…" He shrugged. So what if he had a few hang-ups?

Tilson pondered Miller's words and answered softly, "I always had my wife, Kiki. Together we made it fun." Tilson closed his eyes and bit his lower lip. "It's not fun anymore."

"Now you know why I drink the Pepto. I lost my wife, too, you see." Miller's lips tightened into a thin white line. For the briefest of moments, he looked like he was about to cry. "It's not the same without a good woman, is it? A woman you love so much that it makes you ache, a woman that puts this whole crazy world into its rightful place. Believe me, I *know* where you are. You have to go on, sir. That's *all* you can do."

"You punish yourself, don't you?"

Miller said nothing. Tilson waved a hand. "I don't care about your reasons. Not really." He smiled. "Did you know that I first proposed to Kiki when we were eight years old?"

"You used to be very sure of yourself, Mr. President."

Tilson ran the back of his hand across his eyes. He turned away and wiped the wetness on his pants. "When you've been together for that long, it's hard to go on alone."

"It is your duty."

"Yeah." Tilson stood and stretched. "Have you been able to get Trance to help out?"

"He wants no part of government work."

"Government work?" Tilson laughed. "Even when it's a personal favor and of national interest?"

"That's what he tells me, sir." *Well*, thought Miller. *That's not really what he says, but it's close enough. For my purposes.*

"Selfish bastard."

Miller spread out his hands. *Yes, I am.* "It eats *him* up more than it does you or me, sir. Because he *can* blame himself. I did all I could to get him, but it isn't going to happen."

Tilson pressed his hands together. He looked closely into Miller's eyes. "I wonder how hard you tried." He drew a resigned breath. "I suppose we ought to get back at it."

Miller retrieved Cramm and Doheny from the hallway. When they entered the Oval Office, Tilson seemed more like his usual self. The men took seats around the conference table, while Tilson remained standing. "Well, boys. Let's roll up our sleeves and dig in. Anybody want a drink?"

They all declined.

"Good. Never trust a man who drinks on the job."

Tilson pressed his knuckles on the table and leaned forward. "Doheny, tell me *everything* you've got."

Doheny fumbled with his notes and spread them across the table.

"Although the first lady's death is still, officially, due to 'natural causes,' we've got slews of terrorist groups taking credit for her assassination. We expected that. We're running down each lead. We're also receiving a marked increase in the number of threats upon your life, sir. There's a lot of chatter—"

"Tell me something worth knowing." Tilson slouched into a chair.

"Well, sir. As you know, your wife's... the first lady's... body showed traces of hemlock, a toxin known to cause paralysis, and in some cases, loss of breathing. We don't think the level found in her blood was enough to kill her. But there may have been enough to keep her immobile."

"You're sure she was poisoned?"

"Definitely, sir." Doheny scratched his head. He pressed his fingers against the bridge of his nose, closing his eyes as if he were in pain. Then he opened his eyes and looked at the president. "The ultimate cause of death might actually have been botulism."

"Botulism?"

"Like what you might get in a bad clam, or tainted soup."

"A clam," said the president softly. "You think my wife was murdered by clam? She didn't even like clams."

Doheny ignored Tilson. "There were also those two other compounds that we have yet to identify. We don't think the poison was binary. We do think it was administered at the British Embassy." He opened a brown, calf-grain leather briefcase and pulled out several photos.

"Not a British plot?" asked Tilson.

"Not a British plot, sir. Their ambassador has answered our questions freely. He is as outraged as we are."

"The prime minister didn't seem contrite when she called with condolences."

Doheny shook his head. "She was not aware that we suspect the embassy."

Tilson nodded. "Go on."

"Well, sir, it's like trying to read Braille with rubber gloves. We don't have much, beyond the disappearance of a member of the embassy staff." Doheny passed around a black and white photo of Sandra Smith. "She said she was getting married."

"Poor guy," said Tilson. The photo looked nothing like Sammantha Starodubov. It looked more like some cartoon caricature in a Tim Burton film, like *Nightmare in Washington.*

"Now she has vanished."

"She was reportedly bound for Sidney, Australia," said Cramm.

"There's no record of her having left the country," continued Doheny. "No video anywhere."

"You searched her home?" asked Tilson.

"As if she never existed, sir. Not a fingerprint or a hair in the place."

"Motive?" Tilson began to walk slowly around the table, mumbling to himself. He pinched his eyebrows together with his thumb and forefinger and closed his eyes, as if this was some magic cure to their blindness. "Can't think of why someone would want to kill my wife…"

"No motive yet, sir," said Doheny, watching as the president came toward him. "But Ms. Smith did serve champagne to you and your wife."

Tilson stopped pacing when he reached Doheny's chair. He placed a hand upon his shoulder. "Were you ever in a fraternity?"

"Sir?"

"Do you know what it's like to be blackballed?"

"Ah, no. My college didn't have frats."

Tilson lowered his voice. "Come up blank on this case and you will know what it's like. No, you'll know what it's like to have a White House blackball. That's a stain you'll wear for the rest of your life."

"There are dead-ends everywhere, Mr. President," said Miller. "Smith's trail leads nowhere. Her Social Security number was taken from a woman whose last known address was a cardboard box beneath a bridge in New York City. That was two years ago. It gets worse with her references."

"That's not possible," said Tilson. "You and I both know the scrutiny given to embassy staffs."

"I haven't finished, sir."

Miller drew a folder from a titanium Halliburton case.

"She was referred to the Brits by the attaché to the Australian embassy, a Mr. Robert Fallon. Because of his strong referral, Smith received less than exhaustive scrutiny. A few phone calls, a driver's license check." A drop of sweat began trickling down Miller's forehead. He flicked at it with his right index finger, stopped, and took a centering breath, before continuing. "Fallon is a person of interest to U.S. security. Of course the Brits had no way of knowing this. We knew nothing of the referral."

"But we're getting somewhere, right?" Tilson sat back down into his seat. "We talking terrorists?"

"I wouldn't blame terrorists yet, sir," said Miller.

Doheny and Cramm exchanged furtive looks. Miller was doing exactly what they had warned him against. He was taking over.

"Fallon disappeared Sunday night."

The president turned to Cramm. "And your men? Have they done *anything* worthwhile? Anything?"

"We've questioned dozens of suspects, sir. It's kinda hard though, with them having more rights than citizens, and lawyers from the ACLU standing at the ready."

"You question them, damn it! And do it right."

"You may recall that we are no longer allowed to interrogate, sir. Technically, that's a function of your office, sir, although even your hands are tied. We've asked for questioning leeway. We even got permission to say 'please.' That's about as far as they let us go, before we have to let them go. No probable cause, you see. I've got three hundred agents looking for more. But we're still shooting ghosts in the dark."

Tilson pulled a handkerchief from his back pocket and blew his nose. He blew it again and then stuffed the handkerchief in his pocket. "Listen," he said, looking at all three men. "I've always considered myself to be a patient man, a reasonable man. So I will be reasonable. I won't fire your asses right now. But from this moment forward, as long as I am president, you men will do nothing else but look for my wife's killers. You don't see your families, you don't shit, you don't even sleep. Is that clear?"

The three men exchanged glances, a fact not lost on Tilson. They all spoke, in unison, "Yes, sir."

"Now, get out of here."

CHAPTER 14

_______________PP_______________

Dry, hardened snow crunched underneath the down-filled boots of Nikolai Ogarkov as he walked the path toward his expansive woodpile. Behind him rose his decadent dacha, a thirty-thousand square foot monument built with whole trees and huge hunks of rough-cut stone during the "People's" Communist regime. The home stretched majestically along the edge of a large lake. The lake was frozen solid from the bitter, mountainous Russian air. Tufts of light snow danced across it like pixies. A thin trickle of smoke wafted from one of the six brick chimneys poking through the dacha's roof. The smoke trail was barely visible as it melted into the slate-gray, predawn sky. There was no sign of animal life—no reindeer, not even a squirrel. There were a few hearty birds flittering about for food, but that was all. Nor were there any of the Russian president's guards. They were not allowed within two hundred yards of the retreat, just like the animals.

The air had a biting, bone numbing chill, even though it had already warmed to a balmy five degrees below zero, Fahrenheit. This was the kind of weather Ogarkov enjoyed the most. He had grown up in the seaport city of Tiksi, far above the Arctic Circle by the Laptev Sea. His father had been the leading Party official. It was there that he had learned to cope with the elements, just as he now managed his opposition within the fractious Russian leadership.

As Ogarkov pulled four round logs off the pile, he thought of his unlikely rise to power. He thought of his early days, when communism had reigned. He had accepted communism for what it was—an ill-conceived but well-intentioned attempt at equality. He abhorred the abuses of its power. He had embraced the economic tide of Gorbachev's Glasnost and Perestroika. He had straddled the divide caused by Putin and his enforcers. He had been as surprised as anyone, when he was anointed by the press and propelled to unprecedented popularity within Russia.

Except for Putin, Ogarkov's recent predecessors had stumbled politically, with each succumbing to the many warring factions within the government. Capitalism had taken hold, weakly. But it was an unwieldy snake with many dangerous heads. How could he appease them all?

Ogarkov had become a folk hero. He was credited with pulling Russia out of its long economic malaise. Trade with the Americans and Western Europe was rising steadily. Russian exports were even beginning to lose their stigma of being cheaply made replicas of foreign goods.

Yes, thought Ogarkov, _we've come a long, long way. But I have little to do with it...I am at the mercy of the Oligarchs. I float where they blow me. There is still so far to go and I must try to do my part. I cannot, will not, rest until there is a durable peace. Perhaps that is the one thing I can control._

Ogarkov dropped the wood into the snow. _Peace_, he thought. _But at what price?_

With his black-gloved fingers, Ogarkov reached for a shaft of smooth wood that was peeking up through a blanket of snow. The well-worn, oak axe handle felt good in his hands, with its promise of physical pleasure and pain. He dislodged the axe from its base, a weathered, flattened tree stump nearly four feet across. He brushed the snow off the top of the stump and set one of the logs lengthwise on its level surface. He drew the axe high above his head, grasping the wooden handle with both hands. Then, with a practiced, fluid stroke, he swung unerringly down upon the log and split it in two. Just one single swipe. How he wished it were so easy to govern.

Ogarkov was a strong man with a chest like a workhorse and squat, sturdy legs. His arms bulged like a weightlifter's, built by his endless childhood hours spent removing stones from his father's poor wheat-growing land. His imposing physical bulk made him look taller than his modest six feet.

Ogarkov had a long, sloping forehead that crested with a dark, bushy unibrow. This single eyebrow framed forceful looking eyes that were known for their intensity. His gaze was so powerful that it could cause an adversary to shrink and stutter. His eyes looked like clear glass balls filled with liquid light, eyes that could channel some inner, mind-bending force against anyone who dared to oppose him. The reality was, his eyes held only truth and fairness, rather powerful poison against most politicians.

Ogarkov swung the axe again and again. With broad powerful strokes, he split each of the remaining three logs with a single slash. He grabbed four more. Sweat began to seep from his brow. It ran down the outside edges of his eyes, where it met the dimpled cleft of his whiskered chin before turning to ice.

Ogarkov continued chopping and his sweat came harder. Icicles formed on his chin, before cracking with his movement and falling into the snow. In an hour he had a solid, neatly stacked pile of fresh firewood for the day.

Ogarkov stopped to catch his breath. His chest heaved. He bent forward, wearily leaning his axe against the stump that he'd used for cutting. *I'm too old for this*, he thought. Perhaps his time *had* passed. He pricked his ears, as he heard the far-off sound of an automobile engine roaring through the virgin woods. Soon he could hear the tinkle of chains clanking against the snow-covered roads. His guests were arriving. In fifteen minutes they would emerge from their treacherous ride along the narrow, ice-covered drive and come shivering into his cozy country home. He was ready for them. He swung his axe into the stump and turned toward the dacha.

They're all decadent, he thought. Decadent and drunk with power. That was the problem. He didn't trust them. Neither should his country.

Ogarkov placed a squat tin coffee pot on the back burner of his stone, wood-powered stove and tossed three fresh logs into its mouth. He plopped a huge iron skillet onto the stone surface. Into it he tossed two pounds of Oscar Mayer bacon, carefully separating the pieces as they began to sizzle. He emptied two dozen eggs into another iron pan. He poured in some milk and scrambled the eggs with a whisk as they began to cook. Ogarkov was laying crisp strips of bacon onto neat rows of paper towels when a black Jeep Cherokee rolled into sight through the kitchen window. There was a knock on the door, just as Ogarkov was spooning immense piles of eggs onto four heated plates.

"Come in!" he yelled in Russian. "The door is open."

His guests entered single file into the kitchen. There were four of them. Three were influential Russian leaders, although only two of them had been expected. The fourth was a woman with stunning beauty. Ogarkov had never met this woman, although her reputation was almost legendary. She was the one who made men grow weak in the knees. She made men loose with their senses and free with their money. She also had the rare power to heal.

The first man in line stopped and the guests crunched into each other like an accordion. Ogarkov smiled inwardly, as he noticed their surprise at his meal. He hoped that his suspicions were not so apparent, as he looked at his uninvited guest.

"Thought you might be hungry," he said cheerfully. "Come. Sit and eat. I'll set one more place."

Ogarkov gestured toward a crude, lopsided farmers table that was neatly set for four. The men walked across the rough pine floor, each stopping behind a wooden chair. They waited as Ogarkov grabbed a fifth chair from across the kitchen and set it down for the woman. Only after she was seated did the other men sit.

Ogarkov dropped a bacon-filled wicker basket onto the center of the table. Beside it he placed a second basket, this one mounded with thick brown toast. He motioned toward several jars of jelly and a pot of freshly whipped butter.

"Eat," he said. "Before it gets cold." He paused and then looked at the woman. "You must be Sammantha Starodubov, no?"

Sammantha dipped her head. "I am."

Ogarkov grunted and sat down. Without another word he began to eat. Ogarkov's guests looked furtively at one another, and then stared silently, sullenly at their food while their host dug in like a recently-rescued island castaway.

Ogarkov ate in the same manner that he worked. It was an all-out effort, as if he needed to replace, in mere moments, the enormous energy he had consumed cutting wood. After a minute he said, "This is the American president's favorite breakfast." He inhaled a bacon strip with two quick bites and then frowned. "Except for the bagels he has delivered daily." He smiled. "The frozen bagels that I ordered from Emil Radler seem to be lost somewhere in Moscow." *Probably stolen by one of you*, he thought. After another forkful of eggs he continued. "Good, yes?"

His guests began to eat, looking warily at their president, while waiting for him to begin the meeting he had called on such short notice. Slowly, like a train just leaving the rail yard, their eating began to assume growing speed.

When his guests appeared relaxed, Ogarkov said, "We can never be truly secure until the world is free of nuclear weapons. I think we should disarm."

Ogarkov's statement floated through the air like a large soap bubble. His guests all stopped in mid-bite and turned toward him, staring, as if waiting for the bubble to pop.

Ogarkov looked at his guests and smiled.

"Don't all talk at once…Well? Does anyone disagree?" He turned to one of the men. "Ivan Petrovski, what do you think?"

"Yes…" stammered Petrovski. "…The issue bears thought. But it must be given a great deal of study. A great deal."

"Come now, Ivan. Tell me that you wouldn't feel more comfortable if the world were free of nuclear weapons."

The Russian Prime Minister regained his composure. He thought for a moment, then replied, "Unlike you, Nikolai, I suffered because of the Great War. I was a babe as Hitler began his march on our beloved Leningrad, but I saw death. I saw people kill to keep from being killed." He paused. "I know the horror of war, Nikolai. My mother nearly starved to death, choosing to give her children food as she wasted into nothing…She never recovered, not really…I heard her cry, as countless others died, including my own father…" He hesitated. "…So I know about war." Petrovski poured himself a second cup of coffee and took a thoughtful sip. "Now, you ask me if I would want to see the world free of nuclear weapons. Do you take me for a fool? I would like nothing more than to see the world live in lasting peace. But I don't have such a simplistic view of the world, as you and your followers."

Petrovski stared into the eyes of Ogarkov, as if waiting for an argument. Ogarkov stared back, with a look of understanding, almost kindness rounding his face. Petrovski took a breath and continued.

"In the Great War, we could have avoided the pain of the Germans if we had simply laid down our arms and surrendered. But we didn't, did we? And why not? Because we had to preserve our way of life. We didn't want a world dominated by capitalist pigs and fascist dictators."

Petrovski sneaked a look at the other guests. Would the others support him? Their faces looked like lifeless sponges, showing no trace of emotion, no register of support or disdain, just absorbing his words like a spill.

Before Petrovski could continue, Ogarkov began to clap his hands. "But now *we* are the capitalist pigs."

"You doubt my loyalty?"

Ogarkov sobered. "Nobody doubts your loyalties to Russia, Ivan," he said softly. "You and I would be the last to put into jeopardy the system that has brought us so many fine things." Ogarkov looked around at the walls of his dacha, then to the men beside him. They were all clad in expensive suits of the finest cloth, with new L.L. Bean boots. Their shirts and ties were made of fine Indian silks. He looked at his own blue Levis and his bright, customized Nike running shoes. He looked to the diamond-studded Rolex President watch he wore on his wrist. Ogarkov motioned toward the other men.

"We agree that the sanctity of the Motherland must come above all else?"

Everyone nodded.

"Suppose that I were to come to an agreement with the Americans that leaves us with an equal hand, but also sets into motion a process that will rid the world of nuclear weapons? To this, what would you say?"

Vasily Nabokov, chief of the Russian Armed Forces, frowned. "We've already emasculated ourselves on the European Continent. Our nuclear threat is the only sword that defends us."

"Come, come," said Ogarkov. "You and I both know that our reduction treaties with the West were simply cost cutting measures disguised as compromise. How else could we get away with taking billions in foreign aid? We had to show good faith, so we destroyed some old tanks, outdated ships and a few inoperable nuclear missiles. What we gave was meaningless. We are still secure with our offensive threat, just like our neighbors. As always, we remain in a stand-off, where the devastation to the victor would also make him a loser.

"That is the problem. What I am seeking is full-scale nuclear disarmament. This will bring, not a brief respite to the danger, but a true and lasting peace. Then we can devote our energies to such matters as putting bread into the mouths of our people."

Nabokov grunted noisily. "We maintained the largest free-standing army in the world for good reason," he said. "It may have weakened our economy, but it kept us safe."

"It devastated our economy," said Ogarkov. "Still does. And it has kept us on the ever-present edge of destruction." He lifted a coffee cup to his lips and looked closely into the eyes of the other three men at the table. He didn't look at Sammantha. Not yet. "The world is different today. We have less to fear, militarily, at least."

"We have far more to fear!" cried Nabokov. "They whittle away at our power, slowly, like mice chewing into a cereal box. Then they build nests inside and piss everywhere. Soon, even our advantage in space will be overcome. Then what will we have?"

"The war today, *Comrade*," replied Ogarkov, sarcastically with a weary sigh, "is being waged economically. Unless we—"

"We should strike while we still can."

Ogarkov looked stunned.

Nabokov's eyes suddenly took on the wildness of a hunted man—stabbing from side to side, rounding into two large, owl-like circles. "We can conquer the world and take losses of no more than thirty percent."

"You would kill fifty million of our own people?" Ogarkov said slowly.

"We could save those who are most important. Then we would have lasting peace…A peace we can *control*, Comrade."

"Comrade, my ass." Ogarkov could not understand the concept of peace through war, despite its effectiveness. But he was used to it. He'd fought it all his life. He knew that he could never change the minds of such men. He could only keep their power in check. "We will have lasting peace…" he said disdainfully, "…but it must be without destruction. When we invest the money that our military wastes, we will again become one of the world's greatest economic powers." His voice softened. "We can have it all." Ogarkov looked to the other men. "If only we have faith." Again, he didn't look at Sammantha.

Nabokov bit his lip. He knew it was senseless to argue with a man like Ogarkov. So he studied his options, his opportunities. If the West disarmed…fat chance that would happen…But, if it did, and he could accrue his own nuclear arsenal, the West would bow to *his* feet. Orchestrated correctly, Russian hegemony could be almost guaranteed.

Nabokov settled into a more comfortable position. *Yes, this is worth considering*, he thought. "Are you going to make a proposal?"

"Would I have your support?"

Nabokov was the most powerful member of the old guard, still battling Ogarkov for power on an increasingly unlevel playing field. Nabokov had been unable to stop the bloodless, but anemic Russian economic revolution. But he could block such a radical proposal as nuclear disarmament. Peace? There could be no real peace. Not among men. Ever.

After a long silence, Nabokov said, "If you can deliver a guarantee that the rest of the world will disarm, I will support it."

Ogarkov exhaled deeply, with visible relief. He leaned back in his chair and looked to the ceiling, as if counting the hundreds of wooden pegs that held the insides of the great dacha together. He said, "My predecessors did much to advance the motherland. I hope to continue this work. Perhaps one day we may all live in peace, free from the ever-present threat of nuclear annihilation." Ogarkov pressed his palms together in front of his nose. "One last question." He looked to Nabokov. "What is your price?"

"My price?"

"Your price."

"I wish only to help." Nabokov's eyes gave away none of his anger. How dare the president question his loyalty? How dare he accuse him of putting himself above country? "Should you convince the West to destroy their nuclear arsenals, I shall personally oversee the destruction of ours."

Ogarkov thought he understood immediately. If Nabokov could not stop him, he would join him, at the price of being elevated to a national hero. This vain and vile man would share in the glory, maybe even take it all. No matter. Ogarkov didn't care about glory, only the result.

"You shall be given full control then," said the Russian president. Ogarkov extended his hand. As Nabokov grasped it, Ogarkov squeezed down on the military leader's fingers, pressing them together like he might a soft tube of toothpaste. He watched Nabokov's face redden, as if somehow his constricted hand had pumped all his blood into his head. Ogarkov released his grip, then turned toward Sammantha Starodubov.

"I believe this lady has a proposal."

The other men looked at Sammantha. Surprise spread across their faces, their sense of order marred, the lines of their faces flattening and seeming to melt into their skin. They had assumed Sammantha was there for sexual favors, not as an equal, or as a leader. A proposal?

Sammantha cleared her throat. "Thank you, Mr. President." She took a small sip of coffee and looked from face to face. "I can make the American president do anything you wish."

Nabokov's eyes narrowed, but he didn't dispute her. He had heard of her powers, legends really. How she had appeared out of heaven, or was it hell, at the age of twelve. She had been kept by a series of brutal Oligarchs—every one of them meeting death at the hands of a competitor. Each man had left her a small tribute. Until the last, who had left her everything. She had graduated Phys Mat at fifteen. Then it was college and medical school in America. She had returned a doctor, with exceptional skills, and set up shop as "surgeon to the stars." Terrorist stars. Al Qaeda, HAMAS, Hezbollah, the Iranian government. The list was long. She had saved many men. But, oh, she had also broken men. How many marriages had she ruined? More than a few, he knew. She was a viper with very lethal fangs. Or an angel with a touch as soft as a cloud.

Nabokov shrugged. "How will you do this?"

"President Ogarkov will offer to visit the new American leader in his own country. It will be great for Tilson's face—but it will put him under pressure to perform. Then I will do my part to…to influence him, to relieve his pressure." Sammantha smiled. No one doubted what she meant.

Nabokov drummed his fingers upon the table, while chewing noisily on his last piece of bacon. After several moments he spoke. "Unfortunately, it is not the Americans I fear. It is our neighbors in Northern Africa, and Eastern Asia."

"They pose no threat to us."

"But they do," said Nabokov curtly. "At least four Muslim countries are producing nuclear weapons, albeit on a limited scale. It doesn't take much to destroy a city though, does it? As we've found out with our own nuclear meltdowns. If they gain the capability to deliver their warheads accurately, which they will because we've *sold* them the missiles, we have more to fear from Muslims than we do the Americans."

"They will fall in line, Vasily," said Ogarkov, after a moment of thoughtful silence. He reached into his shirt pocket and withdrew a box of Marlboro cigarettes. He tapped the top of the pack against the rough table with several quick snaps of his wrist, then flipped back the top. "You see," he said. "We've already taken measures against that possibility."

Nabokov's ears tinged red. He did his best to appear calm, waiting a few seconds before responding coldly. "Is there something you have not told me?"

The Russian president smiled. "Many things, my friend." He stood from the table and signaled that the meeting was over. Nothing more was said. The men began to collect their coats and gather by the door.

"Miss Starodubov will stay here with me." Ogarkov put a hand on her shoulder and waved the others out into the cold.

When the three men were back in the Jeep, Nabokov turned toward the third man in the group— the one who had not been invited to this encounter with the Russian president.

"And what does our esteemed member of the FSB think of Ogarkov's proposal?"

Boris Trotski pondered his answer, before responding in a soft, reflective voice. "Nuclear disarmament is just a simplistic, idealistic dream of a senile old man. The American president won't waste time on this. His nation is far more concerned with the planet's temperature two hundred years from now than its actual safety. And the rest of the world? There is no chance they will disarm their nukes. I wonder what that bitch has promised to deliver. Her usual favors, perhaps? More importantly, what does our great leader keep hidden from us?"

"Certainly no more than we have hidden from him."

"He is dangerous."

"He won't be in power much longer."

The men remained silent, each thinking much the same about the man beside him.

As the Jeep descended down the snowy mountain road, slowly slipping out of sight, Ogarkov turned toward Sammantha. "Is it true? Is it true that you engineered the first lady's assassination?"

Sammantha's eyes widened in mock surprise. "I have heard the rumors, but I would never do such a thing. I save lives; I don't take them. Now that she is dead, however, I can gain control of the American presidency…provided I have your support."

The Russian president stared at Sammantha, weighing her words. He pondered what sort of woman could assassinate another in cold blood. What kind of woman could harbor such ambition or rage? "Can you do it, Miss Starodubov? Can you really get Tilson to help me disarm the world?"

Sammantha widened her stance and threw back her hair. Ogarkov couldn't help but feel aroused. He wanted her, like no woman he had wanted before. He had thought he was well past the age of caring for sex. But Starodubov rekindled something inside him that he'd thought was long-since dead. Perhaps she could do the same with Tilson. "Yes," he mused. "I suppose you can." Ogarkov waited for Sammantha to speak. She said nothing. She seemed to be somewhere far away, drifting in some other long-lost world. He waved his hand in front of her face. She didn't blink. Her eyes weren't even there.

"Miss Starodubov…What is it you want?"

Sammantha's eyes came back into focus. She smiled and said, "Nothing for myself, but much for the cause."

"What are your reasons?"

"My reasons are personal."

Ogarkov laughed. "Perhaps you just want to screw the American president?"

Sammantha's eyes widened. Then, with a sudden, almost invisible flash of her fist, she hit Ogarkov in the nose.

"I am not a whore!" she yelled. Sammantha began breathing heavily, like a tired, but wounded bull, with the tip of a matador's sword hovering just above her heart, and every last fiber of her being ready to fight it. "I know you look at me that way. You all do. What would you have done if someone had murdered your parents when you were a child? What would you have done, if the only men who would protect you were the same men who wanted to climb on top of you and rut with you like a chained lamb…slobber all over your breasts and grunt and groan like some hungry pig?" Sammantha let the question hang in the air. "I am *not* a whore. I am not."

Suddenly, Ogarkov saw Sammantha as a wounded sparrow, not the preying eagle he had thought she was. "My God," he said. "How they must have hurt you…"

Sammantha sniffed and sneered. "You have no idea." She drew a breath and steadied herself. Ogarkov could give her much of what she still needed. The rest she could raise in the Middle and Far East. "I have already spent the billions left to me by my fiancé. I want one billion dollars from you, in U.S. bearer bonds or gold bullion. Within two days. For that you will get your peace."

Ogarkov studied Sammantha's face and nodded. He had made his decision. "You will have your money. First, tell me your plan."

Sammantha relaxed. She had what she wanted. Ogarkov would get more than he paid for. He didn't need to know that. Not now. He wanted to believe that he could buy peace. So let him.

"Jock Tilson likes to go boating on Moosehead Lake with his mother. I have purchased more than a million acres of land by that lake, as part of a business deal I made with the pitiful heir to a failing fortune. I am building a compound there, from which I will execute my plan. A plan that will not fail. Tragically, the American president will have an accident on Moosehead lake. And when he wakes up…" Sammantha paused. "…he will do anything I wish. That is all you need know."

Ogarkov nodded slowly. "You demand a great deal of money."

"I have already spent as much. I may need even more from you. Remember, there were five presidential hopefuls on each side. It narrowed to just four when the primaries kicked in. I had to plan for each one. Fortunately, the right man won his nomination and then the election." Sammantha paused. "Perhaps, in part to the two hundred million I funneled to his campaign. There is much more left to do. That will take cash, lots of it."

Ogarkov peered into the eyes of Sammantha Starodubov, trying to look beyond her beauty into her dark, tortured soul. He couldn't see a thing. The window to that secret place was long-since shuttered, like an abandoned building. Ogarkov sighed and shrugged his shoulders. "Peace is never cheap. I will have the funds delivered here tomorrow morning."

Sammantha closed her eyes. She knew what was coming, what they always demanded. They demanded *her*. It was a small price to pay for revenge. She would close her eyes and dream of destruction, a great mushroom cloud filling the air, the sudden rush of wind, the great sucking sound and the blow. It would be a glorious end to her life. A release.

Ogarkov touched her lightly. She didn't recoil, but her body was as rigid as a tree trunk. "I am not like the others," he said. "I will ask nothing more from you. I wish only a chance at peace. But if you need someone, Sammantha, someone to talk to, or someone to help you, I can be a good listener, and a good partner."

Sammantha Starodubov looked into the gentle but forceful eyes of the Russian leader. She wanted to cry. She felt the strength flow out of her knees like cracking ice, and she dropped to the wooden floor. She began to rock. Back and forth, like always. "I can do this, I can do this alone," she mumbled. "I always have and I always will." Rock, rock.

Ogarkov placed his hand upon Sammantha's shoulder and patted it softly. "Poor child. Oh, how they must have hurt you."

CHAPTER **15**
_______________PP_______________

Chuck Boggs enjoyed many things. But there were two things in life that he truly loved. He loved reading western novels, and he loved smoking Cuban cigars. That's why he liked his job. It allowed him to enjoy both with few complaints or restraints.

There was an odd smell that rose around Boggs. It was the smell of stale smoke mingling with even staler body odor, forming an almost visible cloud around him, following behind him like a faithful puppy. Boggs chewed at the ends of his cigars until they broke apart in his darkly stained teeth. If he stood in one place for long, there was usually a scattered litter of tobacco shreds and spit puddling somewhere around his feet.

At 520 First Avenue though, it wasn't the smell of his body, the half eaten cigars on the floor, or even the forbidden-but-tolerated heavy blue smoke that hung low in his office that was disconcerting. No, it was the smell of death, the faint stench of formaldehyde squirming into every body pore. It was also the clean, ordered neatness of everything else in the Office of the Chief Medical Examiner. Everything except for Boggs's personal swirling cloud.

Chuck Boggs owned the dark. He worked at night, only at night. He was better and faster than any other Level II pathologist, so they let him be. Despite his odd quirks, Chuck Boggs was an intensely organized man. No one could cut and bag a body faster than he could, or piece the truth from the divergent data with such quickness and accuracy. He could slice and dice like a Benihana chef, and around the NYPD he was respectfully known as *La Machine*. Despite his speed, he usually found things that most others would surely miss.

Michael Baden might be better known, but at the coroner's office, Boggs's word was gospel. It was the only place he earned such respect. Respect wasn't the reason he worked so fast and so well, though. He raced through his loose quota so he could get back to his books. Sometimes he could read for hours, while the rest of the city slept. That was the best, like a perfect lover.

It was two o'clock in the morning and there was a skin-frosting wind beating down on the city. New York had been enduring a cold snap for over a week. All anyone could talk about was the weather. As usual, Boggs hadn't noticed. He was in Cheyenne, Wyoming a hundred and twenty years ago, just about to shoot the bad guys at the corral, when the phone rang.

Boggs let it ring until he had killed his final hombre. With a bow-legged swagger and a jutting chin, he picked up the phone and answered, using his best John Wayne. "Howdy, pardner. What can I do for ya?"

"That you, Boggs?"

"Yeah, it's me. What is it? I'm busy."

Boggs heard the caller laugh. "We've got a floater with your name on it, Boggsy. It's all pulpy and fresh, like Charlie the Tuna."

Boggs leaned back in his chair and swore. He hated floaters. "Aw, shit. Can't you save it for someone else? I've got a lot of work to catch up on."

"I want you on this one."

Boggs smiled grimly, cursing his skills. "Where'd it surface?"

"Hudson."

Boggs looked forlornly toward his overturned book. "You know how much I hate floaters, Reilly.

Can't this wait 'til morning? You'll want fresh eyes on this one, won't you? Please say yes."

The police detective laughed again. "No can do. Besides, this one's a beaut. I put your name on him the moment I saw him there in the ice. I'm sending him in. Don't do anything to him 'til I get there, okay?"

"Yeah," said Boggs. There was obviously no way out of this one. He'd have to kiss the rescued cowgirl later.

"I'll be an hour. Maybe two."

Then again, maybe he'd get to kiss the girl after all. Boggs lifted his eyebrows in surprise. It was two o'clock in the morning. This one couldn't wait for sleep, but Reilly would still take an hour or two to come in. "Workin' long and late, I see."

"It's been a bad night, Boggsy. We had to bust a prostitution ring. It was some kind of ugly."

"You didn't take down the governor or the mayor, did you?"

"Not tonight."

"I used to think you were a good man, Reilly. Now I think you're just a twisted pervert, upsetting life's balance in any way you can."

Reilly laughed. "Takes a pervert to know one."

"Got that right. You sound tired, Reilly, like you've cracked or something. You crackin' up, Reilly?"

"The day I crack, Boggsy, is the day I die."

"When you do, I'll cut you up good. That'll make my year." Boggs paused. "What are you and your boys really doing down by the river at this time of night? Surely not busting whores and Johns and governors?"

The detective's voice hardened, as if Boggs' words had carved into his flesh and hit his bones. "Just doing our jobs, man. Now it's time you do yours."

The phone went dead. Boggs shrugged. Reilly must be tired, he thought. Fighting New York crime did that to you real fast. Those guys were all either saints or masochists, sometimes both.

CHAPTER **16**
PP

Jock Tilson stared at the letter in his hand. It was handwritten with elegant English calligraphy, the letters so well crafted they looked like they had been drawn by an artist. It was the fifth time he'd read the note since morning, yet it still sent goose bumps running down his spine.

It was nearly seven A.M. Tilson was expecting his national security advisor, the secretary of state and his defense secretary at any moment. His eyes moved slowly from word to word again. This was an extraordinary opportunity, if it were real.

... I send you my deep regrets for the death of your wife. I believe I know how you feel, for I lost my own wife three years ago, to cancer. After my wife's death, nothing seemed to matter, not even the pressing problems of my beloved country. In time, I realized that I could never have her back, and that the only sensible thing for me to do was to go on. It will never be the same for you either, no?

I relieved much of the pain by immersing myself into the affairs of my country. Eventually, this became the only thing that mattered—making a better Russia, and a better, safer world.

When I was elected president, I had visions of a world in peace. I wanted a safer planet. I suspect that you shared these same visions when you first took office. Perhaps it doesn't seem as important now, with the loss of your wife. For me, such was the case, especially in the beginning. Time is a great healer. You will see.

Perhaps this is an awkward time for me to raise such a subject, but the affairs of the world do not stop for the tragedies of one man, or even those of a nation. I offer to meet with you in your country, so that we can begin a serious discussion as to how we can eliminate the specter of nuclear war in our time.

I suggest the month of July, if that is convenient for you. I have prepared a proposed agenda, which you will find with this letter. Modify it if you must, but please, let us move forward. I ask you to destroy this letter. It is of a personal nature and meant only for your eyes. The agenda you may keep.

I hope to meet with you soon, so that we may become friends.
Respectfully Yours,
Nikolai Ogarkov.

Tilson's "body man," Josh Stone, knocked on the Oval Office door and announced his visitors.

"Just a moment," Tilson said. For an instant he thought of keeping the letter. What a piece of history it would be—he could see it resting prominently in the Tilson Presidential Library. Tilson fed the letter to his shredder anyway, watching it emerge as jumbled strings of dust particles. He pushed a button underneath his desk that unbolted the Oval Office door and said, "Send them in."

Tilson stood up and walked to greet his four guests. The first to grab his extended hand was Kenneth "Boxer" Henning.

"Boxer," said Tilson.

"Mr. President."

Henning was a veteran of three administrations. A navy pilot during the Vietnam War, he was one kill short of becoming an ace when his craft was downed by a stray frag. He'd endured two days of floating in heavy seas with a severely broken right leg. He still walked with a well-disguised limp. Henning was a hardened man, determined to see that America never had to face war again. As a retired, but still powerful admiral, he had run against Tilson for the presidential nomination. He'd received enough primary delegates to trade them for his position as secretary of defense. At six-foot-one Henning was nearly as tall as the president, even with rounded shoulders and a slight stoop. His hair was gray and his tanned face appeared leathery and wrinkled, especially when seen up close. Like an ex-ballplayer, he carried around a ceramic coffee cup into which he spit the juice from Skoal Bandits that he sucked nonstop.

Garrett Sloan was the second man to greet the president. Sloan was of average height and exceedingly slim. Now fifty-five, he ran six miles every day and kept himself in top physical condition. He did the same with his mind. He exercised it regularly by reading books on anything and everything. Sloan was never without a crossword puzzle. He filled them in, unerringly, with a gold ink pen. He was a walking encyclopedia and there was no one better qualified for his position as secretary of state. Sloan was also a Washington veteran, having held positions for both the Republican and Democratic parties. Harvard bred, with doctorates in political science and sociology, he had taught graduate studies in Cambridge, before being plucked for government service by a former president. After serving as undersecretary of agriculture, ambassador to Great Britain, and treasury secretary, he'd accepted a stint as CEO of a major brokerage firm, resisting all other offers, until Tilson finally coaxed him back into government service. Sloan shook Tilson's hand, then stood at relaxed attention beside Henning.

Tilson next shook the hand of his Secretary of Commerce, Harry Hatfield. Hatfield had grown up an army brat. The son of a general, he had earned two stars himself before joining the private sector and starting, then selling, one of the world's largest security agencies, based in Atlanta. Hatfield's well publicized affairs with Hollywood starlets had vaulted him into the public eye. His Q rating had remained famously high ever since. He was a burly man with reddish, wavy hair and an ever-present smile showing the whitest, bleached teeth in Washington. As the president's designated golfer, Hatfield spent much of his time on the links entertaining various government leaders. His deeply tanned skin made him look like a young George Hamilton.

The final man into the room, as always, was Jeremiah Pincenogle, the president's turtle-like national security advisor, waddling behind the others with a soft *huffing* noise.

"Sit down, men," said Tilson with a half smile. He motioned toward his conference table. "I've had a summit proposal from Ogarkov."

"It's a bit early to be summiting, don't you think?" said Sloan. "What's the target date?"

"July."

Henning whistled softly. "He's baiting you, sir."

Tilson turned toward Sloan. "What do you think?"

Sloan thought for a moment before speaking. He pressed his thin fingers against the front of his lips and began tapping them softly. "Boxer could be right. He made the proposal directly to you? Not through intermediaries?"

Tilson nodded. "To me."

"Most unusual. You've got a draft?"

Tilson handed Sloan the sheet of paper that had come with the destroyed letter. Sloan took it. When he read its contents, he laughed.

"Yes. He's screwing with you."

Sloan handed the paper to Henning. Henning snorted and handed it to Hatfield who did the same.

"Looks like bullshit to me," said Hatfield. He glanced at his watch. Tilson wondered if he was late for a tee time. None of the men seemed to see Ogarkov's proposal as anything but propaganda.

Tilson retrieved the paper and read the proposed agenda out loud.

"Eliminate all nuclear weapons from every country in the world."

Sloan smiled. "Well, he has certainly simplified what, for the past half century, has been a most complex issue." He angled his head toward the paper. "You think this is for real?"

Tilson nodded. "Hand-delivered in a sealed pouch by Andropov last night."

"The Russian Ambassador comes down off his hill and delivers a piece of paper with nine…ten words on it... and we're supposed to act on it like he means it?" said Henning. "I'd call that suicidal bullshit for any president, sir."

"I agree," said Pincenogle, speaking for the first time. He settled down onto his chair, relaxing like a turtle getting ready to sun himself on a rock.

Tilson made no mention of the accompanying letter. To them it never existed. To him, it was already beginning to seem like an old dream.

After a long silence, Henning waved a tanned hand and continued, "Look, Mr. President. I know you're real green here in Washington, so I'll help you out. Things sort of follow a certain protocol, know what I mean? Except for the trenches in Congress, Washington is a bunch of photo ops and PR. Say the right things and everyone goes home looking good. We've all got a lot of other things to get squared away in this country before we start going global or attempting the impossible with this kind of shit."

Tilson nodded and said, "How can a meeting with the Russian president be untimely?"

Henning looked at Sloan, then at Pincenogle, then back to the president. "Well, besides the screwup in protocol, the Russians would want nothing more than to make you look bad. Disarm our nuclear forces? You are one idealistic son-of-a-bitch, I'll give you that. The Russians'd run roughshod all over our asses if we disarmed our nukes. Do you think, for one single minute, that they'll disarm? You think Iran's going to disarm? Or Israel? Pakistan? Or China? Even if they say they will, it will take years to produce any sort of mutual verification program. You want political suicide, this is it on the fast track."

Tilson turned toward his secretary of state.

"Your thoughts, Garrett?"

Sloan liked to pause before speaking, a habit that annoyed most of his egotistical colleagues. He found it often kept him from setting his foot in his mouth, in a world that loved to make people eat their shoes.

"It's a big world, Mr. President. The admiral has a point. There is no foolproof way to verify any treaty. Who's to say that other nations of the world will follow your lead?"

Henning interjected. "Yeah. What about those towel-head terrorists in the Middle East? Who's going to tell Iran they can't have nukes? Russia? Give me a friggin' break."

Sloan patiently waited until Henning was through. When the defense secretary finished spouting, Sloan continued, "Even today, the Russians could probably make short order of Europe with conventional forces, Mr. President. No matter what anyone else tells you."

"That's exactly what I mean!" shouted Henning. "Any elimination of nuclear weapons would leave our allies essentially defenseless. The only thing really keeping the Russians out of Paris is France's nuclear presence." Henning paused, then smiled. "This could be a way to get rid of the French, though, once and for all. Is that your plan?"

Tilson laughed. "A united Germany might want a piece of France, too."

Henning blurted, "You're wrong, Mr. President. Germany's got saggy tits for an army. With NATO in shambles and the U.N. just a social organization…"

Sloan gently grabbed Henning's shoulder, but his eyes delivered a harsh rebuke. Henning drew a breath and whispered, "Sorry."

Sloan spoke again. "Any significant reduction in nuclear arms would have to be accompanied by a balancing in conventional forces."

"Exactly what I was saying," cried Henning. "And don't forget China!"

"Shut your mouth, Boxer." Sloan returned his attention to the president. He briefly glanced at Pincenogle, the national security advisor, who had remained strangely silent during Henning's tirade. Pincenogle was looking out the window, as if bored. The reasoned professor in Sloan said, "Both sides will want to keep a few nukes in their arsenals—to be used as a deterrent to a conventional attack, or to counter actions by terrorists…"

Henning slammed his fist upon the table. "We've got to keep our nukes! At least let us keep the neutron warheads. Ten of those are cleaner than any *one* of the coal plants going up in China."

Sloan glanced at Henning but continued speaking. "…We'll need at least twelve months to prepare for a Summit, not three or four. Let's face it, sir. You haven't been exactly on your game lately."

"And you, Admiral?" Tilson turned toward Henning.

"I say we put a real Star Wars defense system in place before we negotiate reductions. We should build some big-assed pulse weapons and laser cannons that we can shoot from space. Ain't nothin' like bein' in the position of strength, the big dog on the block…"

The president's desk clock ticked loudly as Tilson sat quietly in thought. Boxer Henning began chewing on the end of his pen. Sloan appeared to calmly ponder some interesting intellectual problem, maybe a crossword in his head. Hatfield glanced at his watch again.

"Ever play sports, admiral?" said Tilson, suddenly looking at Henning.

"Yeah. What of it?"

"One thing I've learned from sports is that the best physical player or the strongest team does not always win. There are intangibles—exhaustive preparation, mental toughness, physical discipline and heart. The team that is best prepared has a leg up on their foe. The man or team that wants victory the most can often find a way to win, despite any odds. Finesse over strength."

"Or sometimes, just plain dumb luck," mumbled Henning.

Tilson signaled that the debate was over. "Gentlemen, I'm going to host a summit in July. It will be here, at Camp David. And by God, we'll put together a framework that will bring lasting peace…and freedom from nuclear weaponry."

"Make it December, sir," said Sloan. "We've got far too much to do."

Tilson shook his head. "August. That's as long as I'll wait."

Sloan sighed. "Never let it be said that the ol' Sloanster ever stood in the way of peace, even if he thought his president was acting like an idealistic college freshman."

Tilson grinned. "I'll take that as a compliment." He rose from his chair, signaling that the meeting was over. He looked toward Sloan, as if preparing to speak. But Boxer Henning stepped between them.

"Mr. President?" said Henning. "May I say something?"

Tilson looked at the secretary of defense with a patronizing glance. "Yes?"

"The Russians will never hold those meetings here, sir."

"And if they did?"

"I'd say you'd used up your share of miracles," interrupted Sloan. "He's right. They'd never have them here, not with a rookie."

Tilson sighed deeply. "I appreciate your candor, gentlemen, but I am disappointed by your pessimism. Optimism breeds success. I will approach it that way. Good night." Tilson led them all toward the door.

"Blind optimism gets you killed," mumbled Henning.

"Duly noted."

CHAPTER **17**
PP

Chuck Boggs was back reading his Louis L'Amour classic when his intercom buzzed.

"Boggs," he heard his someone say. "Your floater's here." Boggs could swear he heard the caller chuckling as he rang off.

Boggs set his book down and reached for his coffee cup. He'd need a hot cup, probably more. A floater. God, how he hated floaters. As he poured the remains of his dead brew into the sink, and filled his cup with a fresh supply, he thought of his first floater. It had been over twenty years since old Marley had drawn him aside during his first week on the job. In all that time, not a single thing about them had changed. Except that he didn't puke when he saw one, at least not often.

"Son," Marley had said. "There's one thing you'll never get used to in this business, and that's a floater. I'm going to tell you why. A floater's a body that's been in the water for too long. The body sinks to the bottom at death, until it begins to decompose. Then the gasses, mostly methane, hydrogen sulfide and carbon dioxide made by the bacteria, cause the body to rise like a balloon and float.

"During the winter, like now, it could take weeks, or even months, before a body floats. The cold water acts like a refrigerator, making the bacteria chew more slowly. Bodies can get trapped under ice and only rise in the spring. Those are the worst. Smell like a sonofabitch.

"They hardly look like people, floaters, 'cause so many things happen to screw 'em up. The worst, maybe, is the swelling. Bodies become bloated, almost unrecognizable, except for prominent body features like a dick or something. I've even seen the gasses make a man look like Johnny Wad."

It was at that moment that Marley had drawn back the sheet to expose him to his first floater. Boggs had barfed on the spot, with big chunks of a Whopper and fries sliding over his shoes. Now he felt the bile rise in his throat as he prepared himself for the one coming in. You just never got used to floaters. Not really.

Ten minutes later, men from Unit Two wheeled in a body that was sloshing inside a zippered black bag.

"This one is fresh, Boggs," said one of men. "Just like you like them."

Boggs sneered at the young kid and said, "Screw you."

Boggs carefully removed the body from the bag and began cutting the clothes off the puffed and bloated limbs. The skin was pale and bleached from its days in the water. The eyes were swollen shut. When the body was finally naked, Boggs covered it with a white sheet and shoved it into a refrigerated compartment.

"You sleep for a while," he said to the corpse. "I've got to go take a leak, drink some more coffee and wait for Reilly, you sorry bastard."

A few minutes later, Boggs's phone rang.

"What?" he said testily.

"Reilly, here."

"Where are you? I want to be done with this."

"I'm tied up."

"That's your problem. Or maybe your pleasure?"

"Wait for me."

"No chance. I've got a schedule to keep, and I've got a frigging floater to slice into."

Boggs heard Reilly cover his end of the phone and swear at something or someone.

Boggs softened. "Hard night, huh?"

"Yeah."

"I'll wait, then. No hurry."

"Thanks, bud."

It was just after nine A.M. when Detective Reilly shuffled into Boggs's office. He found the doctor asleep in his chair, his face drooping against a book that was lying flat upon his desk. Reilly quietly took a seat and motioned to a man who came in behind him. His companion looked old, with long, thin white hair, sad tired eyes, an unshaven face and a clean, starched, faded blue uniform.

"Ahem," said Reilly.

Boggs stirred. "What?" He looked up. "Oh, shit. I was hoping you wouldn't show."

"Doctor Boggs," said Reilly, turning toward the old man. "This is Clyde Davis. He's here to identify our floater."

Boggs reached into his desk, pulled out a fresh cigar, unwrapped it and jammed it into his mouth. "I found no I.D. You got a name for this sorry sucker, Reilly?"

Reilly removed a soggy wallet from a plastic baggie and handed it to Boggs. "This was in his pants pocket. Says his name was Copley. Brandon Copley, IV. This man..." Reilly motioned toward Clyde. "...has worked for the Copleys for over fifty years. Says his boss disappeared about two weeks ago."

"You a relative?" asked Boggs.

"He has no relatives left, sir," replied Clyde

Clyde thought back to the sunny day, forty-six years before, when Henrietta Copley had brought the young baby home. What a surprise it had been, her not being pregnant and all. He had loved that babe like his own. Now, to have to do this? Brandon had asked him to lie in his letter. So he would, not that he wanted to.

"That's verified," said Reilly. "No relatives."

Boggs shrugged. "Follow me, boys." He led the two men through a whitish hallway to the storage lockers. As they walked inside, Clyde caught his breath, as the stiff odor assaulted his lungs and his eyes.

"Sort of gets to you, don't it?" said Boggs. "I don't even smell it anymore." He reached for one of the drawer handles and pulled the body out from the wall. "That Copley?" he said.

Clyde hesitated for the briefest of moments. Then he said, "Yes, sir. That's him, all right." *Lord save me*, he thought. *I do this only because I love you.*

"I want to know what killed him," said Reilly.

"No problem," said Boggs, as he slammed the drawer shut. "Get to it first thing tonight, after a good day's sleep." Boggs spat a piece of tobacco into a waste basket by the wall and walked out of the room. Without turning he said, "Nice to meet you, Mr. Clyde."

Reilly touched Clyde on the shoulder and nudged him toward the door. "This way," he said.

"He's not too friendly like, is he?" said Clyde. His eyes followed Boggs as he vanished down the hall. Then he looked down to his shoes, as if they could give him comfort.

"Boggs?" said Reilly, laughing. "Don't mind him. He's full of crap. But he's a good guy, once you get to know him."

"Somehow," said Clyde slowly. "I don't think mister Boggs likes or trusts nobody."

Reilly frowned, feeling a strange but familiar tweak in his stomach—that piece of gut intuition that sometimes directed his emotions like road signs. "Why in the hell would you think that?"

Clyde shook his head. "No reason, sir." He stopped walking. He looked at Reilly, as if he were about to say something. He blinked several times, his eyes looking oddly pained, then he hobbled onward, silent as a dead bird.

CHAPTER **18**

_________PP_________

The surface of the Maine Turnpike looked like a jet runway in the night. The reflective highway lane dividers stretched out to the horizon. They clicked by like shooting stars as Sammantha flew north like a goose in the spring, focused forward, wings flapping unerringly toward her goal. There was a single, fuzzy red glow of tail lights far in the distance, blinking in and out of sight as Sammantha's rental car moved up and down the long rolling hills. From behind her, several dim sets of headlights intermittently bounced against her rear view mirror, softly lighting the shadows on her face. Sammantha was alone. She liked it that way.

Sammantha fiddled with the tuner to the car's cheap stereo, as the country station she had been listening to since Boston faded into static. "C'mon," she said, as she impatiently worked to find another. Finally she came upon the clear signal of WXLF, *The Wolf.* A fitting name, she thought. She was about to create a wolf in sheep's clothing.

Sammantha thought of how she both liked and hated country music. Her stomach twisted stupidly with songs of faded love and blue eyes crying in the rain. Her throat, in it's overly sentimental weakness, grew taut when they sang of families and love that would always be true. Love could never be true, she thought. There is no love. Love is dead.

The clear strains of a steel guitar and a singer's pure country voice came through the speakers. Here it was again, that stupid song by Jaime Crandall.

You said that you needed your freedom,
And I let you go willingly,
'Cause a bird that is caged,
Can never be happy,
And a woman possessed,
Never free...

Damned right, thought Sammantha. No one would possess her again. It wouldn't be long now, before she would fly free from the cage they had trapped her in. Soon, she would be free. She would put America in that cage and trap it there for decades.

"Let's see how you like it," she whispered to the night.

CHAPTER 19
___________PP___________

The waiting area looked like almost every other dentist's office across America. There were old copies of *Sports Illustrated, Time* and *Golf Digest* tossed carelessly on top of three low wooden tables. Beside each table was a grouping of steel and plastic chairs. There was a glass partition along the far wall, with more chairs along each of the other three sides of the room. Hung along the walls were half a dozen plastic-framed pictures of snow-capped mountains and tree-rimmed lakes. It was enough to make Sammantha gag. They looked like pictures torn out of the *National Geographic* and hung up like worthless trophies announcing prowess and success.

When Sammantha walked into the reception area, she saw a young boy connecting the dots in a *Highlights* magazine, while his mother studied the latest antics of British Royalty in *People.* Neither the boy nor the mother looked up. Sammantha rang a small chrome bell at the glass partition and waited. She was greeted by a plump, middle-aged nurse who looked like a pumpkin squeezed into a dress. Her face was an unnatural, tanning tube orange, with wrinkled ridges carving deep crevasses in her face as she smiled. The woman handed Sammantha a new patient questionnaire, which was clipped to a legal sized backing made of pressed board. "Here you go, dearie. Just fill this in and the doctor will see you, soon."

When Sammantha returned her questionnaire, the receptionist checked the form with a perfunctory glance. Then she opened the door to the inner sanctum. A white-clad hygienist stood waiting. She smiled at Sammantha and motioned for her to follow. "This way, Ms. Smith. The doctor will see you in just a few minutes." Her voice was soft and comforting, an oft-practiced and valuable art in an office like this.

Doctor Keenan was a general practitioner who handled everything from checkups and cleanings to cosmetic oral surgery and root canals. He was seated in his office, struggling with a foot-high mound of paperwork when Sammantha was led inside by the hygienist.

"Good morning," said Keenan. "You called with an emergency last night? What seems to be the problem…" He looked down to her file. "…Miss Smith?"

"I've got this *throbbing* in my gums." Sammantha's voice was gentle but husky. When Sammantha emphasized the word throbbing, she said it with a breathless, almost sexual sigh. She looked straight into Keenan's eyes. "I'm so glad you agreed to see me this morning…my being from out of town and all."

Keenan waved her off. "It's my job, Miss Smith. I love to help people."

Sammantha lowered her eyes. "I suppose I should also have a regular checkup and a cleaning while I'm here. That is, if you can *squeeze* me in."

Keenan's face rounded into a toothy smile. "Doesn't sound too difficult for an old country doc." Keenan stood and walked into the doorway. He pointed toward his hygienist, who was at the end of the hallway. Wearing polyisoprene surgical gloves, the woman was taking fistfuls of dental utensils out of a stainless steel sanitizer and wrapping them with sterilized plastic. "See my hygienist and nurse over there? Her name is Chelsea. She'll see that you're comfortable. I'll be with you shortly."

Dr. Timothy Keenan had a large and successful dental practice. He was proud that he still worked with people, rather than teeth and dollars. Not that he didn't like his money. He lived in a ponderous mansion that had been built by one of Maine's old logging barons. He kept himself tanned by escaping south to the islands whenever he could. He was sixty years old and dyed his hair Asian-girl black. He kept in condition by running daily and working out in his home gym three times a week. Though he wasn't tall, he was lean and still ruggedly handsome.

As Sammantha followed Chelsea, she marveled at how easy this was. *Try to do this in New York*, she thought, as Keenan's hygienist led her into small operating room and guided her into a leather dentist's chair.

When Sammantha sat down her body remained rigidly in place. It stayed frozen, even as Chelsea wrapped the end of a dentist's bib around her neck and pulled a tray of tools to her side.

"Relax, honey," Chelsea said. "This won't hurt. Doctor Keenan is as gentle as they come. You want heat?"

"Excuse me?"

"Our chairs are heated. Helps some people relax. You want me to warm up your chair?"

"Oh. No, thanks. I'll be okay." Sammantha already felt sweat puddling under her arms and running down her back.

"You know, we normally don't do this for call-ins. Dr. Keenan must like you."

Chelsea began working with unhurried precision and the same thoroughness that her boss had taught her thirty years before. She scraped the tartar between Sammantha's teeth with a series of instruments, dropping each one onto the white padded tray by her side when she was done. Every once in a while she said, "Open," and squirted a stream of water into Sammantha's open mouth

After all the picking and scraping, she pressed a motorized cleaning disk into Sammantha's mouth, gently massaging her teeth and gums. It was then that she finally began talking, in a folksy way that told Sammantha that she'd been waiting to gossip all along. "Name's Chelsea," she said. "In case Dr. Keenan didn't tell you, although he usually does, I'm chief cook and bottle washer around here. I do all the things the doctor won't do. He's so big into the *people* side of the business that he wouldn't get around to doing any actual work unless someone pushed him into the room with all the instruments ready." Chelsea took a deep, concentrated breath, and then began again. "I know that I talk a lot but I just find that I have so much to say, you know how that can be when the words just need to come out and you just don't have the strength or the discipline to shut up, you have wonderful teeth."

"Thank you," mumbled Sammantha. "You have a wonderful chair side manner."

Chelsea brightened and her eyes glowed warmly. Bright, friendly, intelligent, sharp eyes.

"Your dental work is very unusual."

Sammantha frowned. This wasn't good.

"These look like steel fillings. Are you from…like… Eastern Europe or something?"

"I've traveled a lot," Sammantha said after rinsing her mouth. "I've had work done in Europe. Seems I always need dental work when I'm on vacation."

Keenan's hygienist stuck a small mirror inside Sammantha's mouth and peered at her teeth more closely. "Not bad, considering. Your teeth are really quite beautiful."

"Thank you."

After one last perusal, Keenan's hygienist continued with her polishing. When she finished, Chelsea pulled the brush off the polishing wand and leaned across Sammantha to slide the motorized handle back into its resting place. As she let go of the handle she brushed back against Sammantha's hand.

"Ouch!" Chelsea felt a stinging prick in her forearm. She looked around for the cause but saw nothing.

"Oh, I'm so sorry!" said Sammantha. "It must be this stupid ring again." She held up her hand, revealing a four pronged ring setting without the center stone. "Second time that diamond has fallen out." She laughed. "The ring's about as reliable as the man who gave it to me. Neither can stay in the same place for long. You're not hurt, are you?"

Chelsea held up her arm. There was a thin line of blood snaking along her skin. "That ring's a damned weapon," she said, but laughed it off. "I'll be fine."

Sure, thought Sammantha. *After a couple days of hell, you will.* "Will you help me look for the stone when we're done? I lost the guy. I'd hate to lose the stone, too. My little revenge, you see."

"Sure, honey. Been there." Chelsea searched the floor and found the two carat diamond. "Now, that's a doozie," she said, as she placed the stone into Sammantha's palm.

After the cleaning and several sets of unneeded X-rays, Dr. Keenan walked cheerfully into the room.

"What brings you to Bangor, Miss Smith?" Keenan pressed the X-rays against a backlit screen and studied them while he talked.

"Escaping the City for a few days. You know, New York. Claustrophobic."

"Most people go south this time of year."

Sammantha chuckled. "That's why I go north." She paused and smiled demurely, with her sparkling teeth at Keenan. "I ski."

"Ah. Of course." Keenan looked over Sammantha's patient report and raised his eyebrows. "I see you're a doctor, too?"

"I am," she sighed. "Sometimes I think I would have been happier working as a hygienist for someone like you." Sammantha lifted her green and blue eyes toward Keenan and fluttered her eyelids. *Gag me*, she thought. But it worked.

Keenan was almost sure that Sammantha was flirting. He felt a tingle between his legs. Oh, yes. Got to be flirting.

"You could be my hygienist any day," he said. Wincing, he turned slightly red. Then he pretended to write notes. This was going to get interesting; he just knew it.

CHAPTER **20**
PP

Trance and Lauren were seated in the large, airy Palm Court of the Plaza Hotel in New York. Trance was dressed in a custom-tailored blue pin-stripe suit, with a pink shirt and an open collar. Lauren wore a full-length silk dress, a one-of-a-kind design that Trance had given her before their night at the opera.

It was 6:45 A.M. on Sunday. The city was already gurgling with traffic. Cabbies maneuvered like race car drivers to advance a few yards ahead of the competition. Occasionally, the horn of an irate driver would honk. The hotel walls and the stained glass windows muffled most of the noise. Inside, they just heard the muted conversation of a few other diners, along with the occasional tinkling of silverware. The sidewalk traffic was still sparse, but it was already showing signs of picking up, particularly around the Pulitzer fountain.

"I really don't think I like the opera," said Trance, as he spread a slab of cream cheese over an onion bagel.

"Uh-hmm," said Lauren. She sliced several fresh strawberries onto a stack of waffles and doused it all with maple syrup. *There's another two miles of running*, she thought. "Right."

"They get too emotional."

"Is that why you cried?" Lauren grinned but kept her eyes on her food.

"I didn't cry," said Trance quickly. He flicked a piece of nonexistent dust off his jacket.

"Yeah, you did. I saw you trying to hide your tears. I kept waiting for you to break out sobbing like that lady behind me."

"I—" Trance shut his mouth and grinned sheepishly. "I still don't like opera. I only go to brush up on my German."

"This was in Italian."

"Oh, yeah. Italian, too."

Lauren drove a spoon into half a grapefruit. Juice spurted across the table into Trance's face.

Lauren giggled, "Sorry!"

"Can't take you anywhere, can I?" Trance reached across the table and patted Lauren's hand. Then he took her spoon. "No weapons allowed in here, dear."

"I surrender."

Trance looked closely at the spoon. Then he handed it back to Lauren. "It's okay now. I disarmed the firing mechanism." He leaned back in his chair and closed his eyes.

"You're such a whiz with weapons, Jack." Lauren looked closely at Trance. "You tired?"

"Exhausted."

"Could have fooled me. After the opera, I was ready to call it a night. But you…you had to go to 21 and pig out. Then you dragged me to that jazz club, to listen to that noise until two in the morning."

"How was I to know that we'd run into Jackson?"

"Spike wasn't the problem. After he left, *you* had to spend two hours baring your soul like some condemned convict."

"You're a good listener."

"It was more like a marathon than a date."

"It wasn't me who insisted upon walking through Central Park. It's dangerous out there."

"I wasn't tired."

"Well, neither was I," said Trance.

Lauren reached out and stroked Trance's hand. "I had a wonderful time."

Trance opened his eyes and took a sip of coffee. He took a long, deep breath and then closed his eyes again.

"Something bothering you?" asked Lauren.

Trance put his elbows on the table and let his chin fall into his palms. "Yeah."

"Don't be a mime, Trance. Tell me."

"I'm upset that Tilson yanked your nomination to the FRB."

Lauren shrugged. "I'm sure he had his reasons. It was a long shot anyway."

"Long shot, my tail. You're the best man for the job."

Lauren smiled. "Thanks. It is pretty much a man's club. They've got Liz. That's probably all the estrogen they can stand." Lauren reached across the table and ran her fingers through Trance's hair. "Would you still love me if I had a sex change?"

"Not quite the same way, darling."

"Chauvinist."

"I'd still respect you in the morning, though."

"That's very reassuring."

There was a young boy walking through the lobby, politely selling newspapers while making no eye contact with the well-heeled guests. The boy had the threadbare look of a street kid living on his own. Trance motioned and the boy swooped toward him like a hawk on a field mouse. As the boy approached, Trance continued his conversation. "It's not a matter of gender, Lauren. You've got better qualifications than half the men serving on the board right now. I'm afraid it's a case of the president sending me a message."

When the boy reached their table, Trance looked at the boy's eyes and waited until he looked back. "What's your name, son?"

"Who's asking?" The boy's eyes flared. Trance could see the boil of free floating anger bubbling just below the surface.

"You on your own?"

The boy's eyes narrowed. "What's it to you?"

"How old are you?"

"Fourteen."

"That means twelve."

The boy couldn't help but smile. "Close enough."

Trance narrowed his own eyes. He looked at the boy from head to foot. "You go to school?"

"You some do-good white boy?"

"Yeah. I want you to grow up to be president."

The boy smiled again. "Just buy the paper, man."

Trance reached into his pocket and pulled out a gold money clip. He flipped off five one hundred dollar bills and laid them into the boy's open palm.

"Thanks." The boy turned to leave.

"Hold it," said Trance. "You don't get five C notes without answering some questions. What's your name?"

The boy laid the paper in front of Trance and said, "Jabar. And yeah. My mom died, and my dad…well…"

"Ever know your dad?"

Jabar shook his head. "I'm not sure."

"Tough break." Trance reached into his pocket and pulled out a card. He scribbled a phone number on the back and said, "This is my wireless number. I've got a foundation that sends kids like you to the finest schools. You want that?"

"You are some kinda stupid, mister."

Trance held out the card. "Take it, Jabar. You'll have to work like hell, but it will be worth it."

The boy wiped his hands on his pants. He looked like he wanted to reach for the card. "No shit?"

"Word." Trance wiggled the card. "Ever heard of Spike Jackson?"

"Action Jackson Auto Man? The car guy?"

"Yeah. He's the biggest car dealer on the east coast."

"So what?"

"I gave him *his* start. Maybe I can do the same for you one day. You call me. Or call Jackson at his office in Hauppauge. Tell him Trance sent you. Where you go from there is up to you. I like your style. You're working before seven on a Sunday. I'm offering you a chance at a reward." Trance paused. "One thing, though. You should look people in the eye, Jabar. That way people know that you're somebody. You want to be somebody, believe me."

The boy stared at Trance for a long moment. He took the card and walked slowly away.

"You think he'll call?" said Lauren.

"Maybe. I hope so." Trance watched as Jabar made his way slowly out of the hotel, staring at the card.

"Bleeding heart," said Lauren.

Trance grinned. "People deserve opportunity, Lauren. Second chances. We all screw up. Sometimes, things screw up on us. God gave me money; I recirculate it. Where were we?"

"The Federal Reserve."

"Right. I think it's my fault that the president withdrew his offer."

"I thought you had nothing to do with it?"

"I didn't, really. But Tilson did ask a favor, which I think I later refused."

"You think?"

"Miller."

"I see."

"I don't think you do."

Lauren's lower lip quivered, ever-so-slightly. Heat seemed to rise around the top edges of her cheeks until she looked like she was ready to melt.

"I'm sorry," said Trance.

Lauren tossed her head to the side and laughed. "I thought Tilson was a bigger man than that—putting on the squeeze."

"He lost his wife. That does something to you." Trance picked at a loose cuticle on his left hand. Without looking up, he said, "Maybe I'll call him."

"Not on your life!" Lauren's shouting broke the quiet calm of the opulent dining area. A few heads turned, but the quiet quickly regained control. She whispered, "You'll not do a damn thing for my sake."

"Why not?"

Light began to sparkle around the edges of Lauren's dampening eyes. She hid her face by looking out across the restaurant. She sniffed, then reached over and touched Trance on the hand. "I really didn't want it anyway. Not really."

"And I don't like ice cream."

Beneath the table Lauren twisted her napkin. She squeezed it until her fingers began to burn. She forced a smile and looked at the newspaper, "Give me the business section, will you?"

Trance reached for the paper, his eye caught the headline.

LAST COPLEY HEIR DEAD. FOUND IN RIVER.

Trance sifted through the *Times* until he found the business section. He handed it across the table, then peeled off the front section and began reading the article about Brandon Copley. "Let's learn why a rich man might end up in a river." Trance skimmed through the article.

Brandon Copley IV, the son of Brandon and Henrietta Copley, was found dead on Friday in the Hudson River. He was the last heir to a once-powerful family that helped to shape the growth of America, with its once-vast family fortune.

Copley reportedly signed a typed suicide note, and left it in his opulent residence in Gramercy Park. He has no living relatives. The fate of his estate is unknown. Copley was best known as the playboy actor who reportedly squandered half a billion dollars after the death of his parents. In recent years, he has reportedly been living off a trust set up for him by his paternal grandfather.

Copley was widely regarded as an actor with much talent and training, with little ambition. Once considered a rising star on Broadway, he has been all but invisible in New York theater since his acclaimed portrayal of Hamlet nearly fifteen years ago.

The body was identified by a long-time employee of the family, a Mr. Clyde Davis. In an interview with this reporter, Mr. Davis said, "He's dead, all right. He's all bloated up and dead."

Trance set the paper aside. "What makes someone do such a thing?"

Lauren lifted her head out of the paper. "What, dear?"

Trance tossed the front section to Lauren and she read it quickly.

Shrugging her shoulders, Lauren said, "Beats me."

"Doesn't sound right to me. Does it sound right to you?"

"Nothing surprises me anymore, Jack. You, of all people, should know that."

CHAPTER 21
PP

Dr. Timothy Keenan pressed the tips of his fingers against Sammantha's gums. "Does that hurt?"
Sammantha shook her head.
Keenan moved his fingers farther back in her mouth and pressed again. "How about that?"
"It *throbs*."
Keenan's eyebrows creased to form a single line meeting at the bridge of his nose. He moved his fingers along the outside bone of Sammantha's jaw, almost as if he were giving a massage. After several moments he stood straight, peeled off his latex gloves, and pulled a pen out of his pocket. After making several marks on a diagram of the human mouth, he began to explain.

Pointing toward the diagram he said, "I don't think you've got anything to worry about, Ms. Smith."
"Please, call me Sadie."
Keenan's eyes flicked toward Sammantha, then back to the diagram. "Sadie, you've got some god-awful old dental work in there. Steel fillings. Probably the source of your pain. Where'd you have this work done, Russia?"
"Romania. I lived there when I was a girl," Sammantha lied.
"Those fillings ought to be replaced with some composite resins." Keenan bent over his diagram and inked dots on several teeth. "These are the ones. Shouldn't be a problem. See your dentist when you get the chance." He handed her the paper.
Sammantha frowned. "Couldn't you do it?"
Keenan shook his head. "It's better that you see your regular dentist. I'm booked weeks in advance. I saw you today because I thought you might have an emergency." He held up Sammantha's folder and tapped it against his free hand. "All you need right now is a little aspirin or Advil. You'll be fine."
Disappointment seemed to spread across Sammantha's face. "I see." She stood up from her chair, adjusted her tight-fitting skirt, and laughed. "Wouldn't you know it? I find the only dentist I feel comfortable with and he lives five hundred miles away."
Keenan studied Sammantha closely, looking into those multi-colored eyes, as if he could find a blueprint or roadmap into her thoughts. Why did he have the feeling that he was being manipulated? "Is this some sort of mental blackmail?"
Purple blotches erupted across Sammantha's cheeks, spreading rapidly, like grape juice spilled on a napkin. "Blackmail? Heavens no."
Keenan's eyes seemed to be laughing. "It's emotional blackmail, all right. If I don't fix your fillings, I'll feel guilty all week, at least until I forget you."
"Forget me?" Sammantha playfully touched Keenan's arm. "I would never let you do that, doctor."
Keenan stiffened, in several places. He ran a hand through his dyed black hair and began fiddling with some operating tools so Sammantha wouldn't see the bulge forming in his pants. "I think, maybe, I could fit in you...I'm sorry...fit you in tomorrow, if you come in early. And then..." He hesitated, licking his rapidly drying lips. "...then, perhaps you might join me for dinner?"
Sammantha leaned back against the wall of Keenan's office. She angled her face slightly to the side, so the outside light would fall softly across her skin. She lifted her chin and gave Keenan her best *you can screw me* look. "I think we understand each other well, doctor."
Keenan led Sammantha back to the reception area. He dropped her file into the lap of a middle-aged

woman with flabby skin, frizzy blond hair, darkened roots and perfect teeth. "Will you process this, Karen? Ms. Smith will be back tomorrow for some urgent care."

Keenan hovered over his appointment secretary's shoulder and glanced at the following day's schedule. Sammantha trailed behind him like a shadow.

"Reschedule tomorrow's seven thirty appointment with Mrs. Daley," Keenan said. "She won't mind. Ms. Smith needs immediate attention."

"Yes, doctor."

Keenan bowed slightly toward Sammantha, then walked back into his office out of sight. As the receptionist began to move Mrs. Daley in her computer calendar, Sammantha took a quick glance around to make sure that Chelsea, Keenan, or anyone else on Keenan's staff wasn't watching. Then, while the secretary was typing, she dropped a small white pill into her coffee cup.

"We will see you tomorrow, then," said Keenan's secretary, with a wide, toothy smile.

"I'm sure you will." *Fat chance.*

Sammantha walked cheerfully out of Keenan's office. As she closed the door behind her, she began to laugh. There would be no need to break into the doctor's office tonight. Tomorrow, she would be able to calmly copy everything she came for.

***

Sammantha glanced at her watch as she pulled open the door to Keenan's office. She was ten minutes early, as planned. If everything else was on schedule, she should find bedlam on the inside. She wasn't disappointed. Keenan's face seemed to have aged a decade overnight. He looked more like a hung over carnival worker than a relaxed and respected oral surgeon. If he were a cartoon character there might have been a rain cloud hovering over his head.

"Doctor Keenan," said Sammantha, showing a look of deep concern and surprise. "Is something the matter?"

Keenan was pacing across the reception area, mumbling to himself. "Huh? Oh, yeah, well… First my receptionist calls in sick. Then I get a call from Chelsea, saying her stomach's in knots and that she can't get away from the bathroom. My other hygienist is skiing this week, in Banff, Canada." Keenan paced some more. "I haven't had anyone miss work in years. Now two in one day? I've got a full schedule through eight tonight, and I don't know what to do."

"Must be all this cold weather we're having. Can't you call a temp agency? That's what we do in New York. Or, maybe you can get through the day on your own?"

Keenan threw out his hands, looking like an exasperated golfer who had just plunked a ball into the water. "Never had to worry about it," he said with a sigh. "When I was younger, my wife would fill in." He paused, his eyes rounded, looking tired and lonely. "She died a couple years back. Since then, I've always had at least one hygienist here, usually two. I was hoping to have my office manager handle the front desk, but I can't get her on the phone. I can reschedule today's cleanings and get by without Chelsea, but I can't handle the appointments and the phones too." Keenan began walking toward his suite of rooms. With a swing of his arm he said, "We better get started, Sadie. This is going to be a day from hell."

Sammantha reclined hesitantly into the heated leather chair. As Keenan began to place the bib around her neck, Sammantha sat upright and said, "Why don't you let me help?"

"What? Oh, I couldn't do that."

"Why not? You think I can't do this? When I went solo I had to do it all, just like you and your wife. Show me where you keep your files. I'll take care of those. I can work the phones, too. Your Nortel system looks much like mine. And, if you need an assistant for surgery…" Sammantha shrugged. "…you've got a board certified surgeon at your side. Although I'll admit, I'm far better with brains and spines and hearts than I'd be with a tooth. Teeth scare the devil out of me."

Keenan thought for a moment. Then he cocked his head. "Why on earth would you do this?"

Sammantha touched Keenan lightly on the hand. "Call it professional courtesy." She squeezed his fingers and smiled. "Besides, I *like* you."

Later that morning, a man dressed in a brown UPS uniform delivered a bogus package to Keenan's office. Sammantha handed him a thick, sealed manila envelope, which he quietly tucked under his arm.

"Have them back in two hours," she whispered. Then she raised her voice. "Have a nice day!" *What can Brown do for you?* she thought. *Help you kill off the American government, that's what.*

Sammantha watched her man walk out the front door, she sat back in her chair, while locking her fingers together and resting her head against them. One more piece of her plan was almost complete. Jock Tilson's personal dentist for over thirty-five years, Dr. Timothy Keenan, had just given her complete copies of the president's dental records.

CHAPTER 22

______________PP______________

The sun was just threatening to lift over the eclectic skyline, where new office buildings hovered between the ancient, pointed minarets of the city. All movement seemed to stop, as the wailing call for Fajr, the dawn prayer, began drifting down from somewhere above. Inside the palace, all Muslim subjects, Allah's chosen, fell to their knees to face Mecca. The palace grew silent, save for the low hum of the forced air heaters and the mumbles of quiet prayer.

In his office, General Mu'annar Abu Hussein al-Talid pressed his forehead against the floor. His lips moved silently, as he recited a long passage of the Qur'an from memory. His white robe draped gracefully from his shoulders, gathering at his waist where it billowed over a twist of black rope. A black and white head cloth fell over his shoulders, held in place by a band of shiny, silver-colored fabric. Talid's palms and elbows lay flat against his hand-woven prayer rug, his body motionless except for his ever-moving lips. His eyes remained closed for several minutes. He opened them only after his prayers were completed.

The city snapped awake. The palace began to move with a blur of bodies, despite the early hour. Talid stood and absentmindedly brushed at the bottom of his robe, where his knees had rested upon his prayer rug. He turned to Yussef al-Karkhabi, his faithful lieutenant. He touched Karkhabi on the shoulder and Karkhabi bowed toward him.

Karkhabi said, "Who but you, oh Great One, would have had the foresight to prepare a heathen woman for such a plan?"

Talid removed his headdress and replaced it with a military cap. He walked to a gold-framed mirror hanging on the wall, so he could adjust it to the proper angle. As he tipped his cap to the side, Talid fingered the vestige of a scar running down the back of his skull. He tried in vain to feel the smooth, thin line that he knew was underneath his hair, the scar caused by a bullet, and made insignificant by the life-saving surgery that Sammantha Starodubov had performed. It had been five years. Aside from the occasional bout of violent temper, he had recovered fully. Talid smiled.

"It was not my idea, Yussef. It was hers."

"But in your wisdom—"

"I owe her my life."

"But she is a woman—"

"Of many skills," interrupted Talid.

Karkhabi bit his lip. He pressed his palms together, and bowed toward his ruler. "Then you have taught her well."

The lines around Talid's eyes grew deep as he smiled. Leathered by too many years in the sun and sand, thick furrows were dug across his skin like corn rows. Looking at Talid, Karkhabi thought of how his leader's face made him look far older than his fifty-one years. Talid's eyes though…his eyes were as wild and dangerous as they'd been during their all-too-brief childhood.

Talid gripped Karkhabi by the shoulder. "You needn't flatter me, my friend. Your job is secure. Who but you has been with me since the beginning? We were mere boys in rags, stealing garbage to survive, when our bonds were forged."

Karkhabi looked to the ground, humbled by his master's compliments. It was true. They had been together since childhood. This didn't matter. He knew, that although he was Talid's closest friend, perhaps his only friend, despite the fact that he was the orchestrator of Talid's terrorist network throughout the world, he was just one impulse away from death. Talid ruled with absolute power. To keep that power, to keep his enemies at bay, Talid must show that he was willing to sacrifice anything to keep it. So, occasionally, he did so. What better example than to kill his closest friend? Karkhabi never forgot the time he had watched Talid put a pistol to his youngest son's head and pull the trigger. This image festered in his brain like a boil, how Talid had kicked his son's lifeless body out of his way like a dead dog.

In spite of the compliments, Yussef Karkhabi remained on his guard. He could never understand or predict his leader. Because his leader's core was as solid as the ever-shifting sands blowing in the desert.

"The woman," said Karkhabi, brushing aside Talid's compliment, "You are using her?"

Without looking at Karkhabi, Talid replied. "Do not be fooled by her, my friend. She uses us as we use her. Never think, for one single moment, that Miss Starodubov is under our sandals." Talid plucked a date off a silver tray and bit it in half. Chewing thoughtfully, he continued, "She will do as we ask." He lay the remaining half of the date on his tongue. "So long as it suits her purpose."

"But it is we who supply her money."

"She has others who give her money, my friend."

"But our contacts—"

"Merely a convenience to her." Talid laughed. Then he sighed wearily. "Believe what you will..." As Talid spoke, he turned toward his friend. With an unseen hand he reached under his robe. He lifted the cover off a jewel-encrusted scabbard. With a swift and almost invisible motion, he stepped forward and raised the knife. Before Karkhabi could react, Talid pulled Karkhabi's head against his chest and laid the four-inch dagger blade against his Adam's apple. Talid pressed the steel against his friend's skin until a trickle of blood ran down the blade and onto his fingers. Karkhabi breathed in shallow, short bursts. He fought to remain motionless, knowing any sign of resistance could cause Talid to strike like a startled snake.

"What did I do?" Karkhabi croaked.

Talid let go; then he laughed. Karkhabi's shoulders slumped and he reached for his neck.

"You see, my dear friend," said Talid. "You cannot trust even your closest brother." He began to wash his dagger's blade in a delicately carved wooden bowl of water resting on the edge of his desk. "Sammantha Starodubov cannot be trusted." Without warning, Talid took hold of Karkhabi again. "See!" This time Talid pressed the blade to Karkhabi's tongue. He pressed it back into his open throat until it tickled the skin of his epiglottis. Karkhabi fought off the urge to gag. Any motion forward would cause the razor edge of the dagger to slice through his throat and cut into his neck, bones and all. He could almost hear the dagger tearing through the joints and the gristle. Oh yes, having witnessed this tactic too many times before.

"This is the way *she* will be, if we are not careful." Talid paused. "We must watch her at every moment, my dear friend. Because, some day, she may try to betray us..." Talid withdrew the knife. Then he nicked Karkhabi's neck again for fun. The flow of blood intensified. It began to drip to the floor, puddling into a weaving trail. "If she betrays us, I will use you as an example of what happens to the people who fail me. Do you understand?"

"I will not let her betray you," whispered Karkhabi.

Talid let him go. "Good."

Karkhabi covered the wounds on his neck with both hands. His eyes followed Talid without blinking. They stared fixedly at the dagger, as Talid wiped the blade on his own discarded headdress and then slipped it back into its scabbard. Only when Talid closed the flap and hooked it under his robe, did Karkhabi let his shoulders slump and his hands come down.

Talid pulled a white silk handkerchief from somewhere inside his robe and tossed it toward his friend. "You do understand me, then?"

"Yes, general. I understand." Karkhabi dabbed at his neck. He was relieved to find that his wounds stopped bleeding quickly, despite all the early flow.

Talid walked to the edge of the room and picked up a pitcher of fresh water. "Good," he said. Talid took the handkerchief from Karkhabi. He dipped it into the water and began wiping his friend's neck with surprisingly gentle strokes. "Tell me," Talid softly said, "Now that the first lady is dead, how goes the rest of our plan?"

Karkhabi winced as Talid suddenly pressed hard into his wound, as if demanding the right answer. "Our…laboratory preparations are progressing well. We have spared no expense. To date we have spent—"

"I care not what we have spent," interrupted Talid. "She has already saved us more than we could ever spend. She has brought us to places we have never dreamed of reaching. The first lady is dead…" Talid shook his head, as if in awe.

"You asked for an update."

Talid waived weakly with one hand and sighed. "Proceed."

"We have invested over five hundred million dollars with Miss Starodubov. More than half our estimated budget, and—"

Talid interrupted. "She gets everything she demands." He stared at Karkhabi, while Karkhabi remained mute, waiting for Talid's great wisdom. "God is great. Our cause is just. And remember, she and Allah saved my life."

Karkhabi grew more animated, now that he knew his bleeding neck wouldn't kill him. "To protect our interests, she should be under surveillance." He hesitated. "I offer to send my son to watch her."

Karkhabi thought of his son, his greatest source of pride. He was graduated with honors from Princeton, with a Masters in engineering from the Cal Poly and a doctorate in nuclear science from MIT. He was a highly sought consultant to Middle Eastern nations, as well as many major U.S. corporations in the region.

"Your son is *not* qualified to do this, my friend. He will only be in the way."

"I offer him as a sign of my commitment." Karkhabi felt a brief flush of hope. Perhaps Talid would not make him sacrifice his son after all.

"As you wish," said Talid. He turned toward his office desk, which was piled high with an unruly hill of papers. "As you see, I am busy. Tell your son that I will call for him shortly. That is all."

Karkhabi left the office. As the door closed, Talid walked toward a side door leading to a small anti-chamber. He opened the chamber door and looked toward its sole occupant, who was seated cross-legged on a fluffed up floor cushion.

"Did you hear what my dear, close friend and advisor has said about you?"

Sammantha Starodubov stood like a graceful, long-legged gazelle. "Tell me."

"Karkhabi says I pay you too much."

Sammantha scoffed. She spread her hands submissively out from her sides. "What do *you* think?"

Talid's eyes grew focused. He stared at Sammantha's cleavage, watching as it slowly rose and fell with her breathing.

"The death of the first lady was payment enough for my small tokens. If you deliver the American president, as you promise, Allah will bless you a thousand times."

"Will I have seventy virgins, Talid, like you promise your jihadists?"

"At least that many, my sweet."

"I prefer a man with experience." She paused. "I will do more than deliver Tilson to you, Talid. Much more. More than you could ever dream."

Talid smiled and he slithered toward Sammantha. "I certainly do know what you can deliver," he said in a lowered, husky voice.

Sammantha reached her hand into Talid's robe. She ran her hand up his naked thighs. Talid groaned. He let his head fall back, his face lifting toward the heavens, thanking Allah for all his blessings. Then Sammantha ripped Talid's dagger from its scabbard, and pressed it hard against his neck.

"I'm not your whore, Talid. And you know what I can do with a knife."

Talid began to laugh. It was a deep throaty sound that started somewhere far inside his belly. "You do know how to please a man. Oh, Miss Sammantha," he said. "I am rock hard and await your every command. If you slit my throat, so be it. I will die a happy man."

"Not today, Talid. You don't die today. Nor will you enjoy my favors. Not anymore. I am done with that."

Talid frowned. "Don't I please you?"

"I…I've found someone."

Talid shrugged. "My, my." He fluffed his robe back into place and pulled the dagger from Sammantha's hand. "Very well. Deliver on your promises. Or you die."

This time Sammantha laughed. "I know what you really want, Talid. Both of us know that. And I *always* deliver."

"I am going to help you."

"No. You won't. I must do this myself."

Talid ran the sharp edge of his knife against his open palm until a red line of blood began to crawl along his hand like a worm. "You cut me deeply, Sammantha. You started the bloodshed with your assassination. Surely you didn't think that I would ignore Allah's sign that it is time to implement my own agenda?"

"You must wait."

I cannot; I must help. So, tell me, who is *your* greatest enemy? Who is it that could stop your plan? Tell me."

Sammantha's face grew pale. She felt a gurgle in her gut, like a shepherd's lamb stew boiling over a fire, all hot and greasy and dripping with fat. Her skin took on a sickly, paste-like hue. It was so pallid that Talid looked almost concerned, if only for a moment. Sammantha nearly retched. She managed to control her breathing and her stomach. But she couldn't settle her mind. If Talid began his own crusade against America, it could ruin her plan. Talid wanted to destroy America, just as she did. His idea of destruction was to incite fear, with random suicide bombings on busses and trains, maybe shoot a few planes out of the sky. That was penny ante shit when compared to her grand scheme. She was going to level all of Washington, every last bit of ground. She was going to take down the president and every congressman, senator and supreme court justice in sight, all in one single, glorious ball of fire.

September 11th would be a mere candle when compared to the inferno she would unleash. Of course, Talid did not know this. None of them did. This was her own, secret war. Her war-within-the-war, something she had dreamed of since *The Americans* had stolen her childhood, her family and her life. She couldn't tell Talid her plan. But she would have to give him something.

"Trust me, Talid. You don't want to do this."

Talid's face reddened, but his teeth eked out an eerie smile. He looked with focused concentration into Sammantha's eyes. When Sammantha stared back, she saw a razor glint inside Talid's heart, with a deathly sharp edge that would rip away everything in its way. It already had.

"I trust no one," he said.

Sammantha closed her eyes. She did not need this, but she knew she couldn't stop it. Talid was a terrorist of the worst kind, with hundreds of sleeper cells spread across the West. He had thousands of mind-numbed zealots that would follow his every command. Any one of them would strap on a suicide pack of C4 as calmly as brushing teeth. They were embedded in America like dust mites in an old, woolen rug. Nothing short of ethnic cleansing could remove them all. That would never happen, not in America. Too many of them *were* America now, solid tax-paying citizens generations deep, mixing into the blended melting pot of American life, protected by a Constitution that was as solid as a diamond and as flexible as mercury. There was no way to tell the difference between the outraged or the outrageous. And the U.S. Constitution would protect the rights of the innocent, even if it meant that terrorists killed freely in the streets. Better that a hundred guilty men go free than one innocent man be jailed. America would never be able to fight them. It didn't have the will.

"Believe me when I say this, Talid. You don't want to fuck with me, or my plan."

Talid pondered Sammantha's words. He looked into her eyes and strolled through them, like they were a brick path leading to a park bench in Sammantha's mind. He sat himself there, feeling each beat of her heart like it were his own, sensing, knowing the veracity of her words. Talid smiled. His teeth had the radiant whiteness of polished ivory against his sun-darkened skin. Sammantha could almost feel them biting into her like the fangs of a rabid fox.

"I will try to stop my people until you are through, Miss Starodubov. But my men are like sharks. They smell the blood in the water, they sense the kill, they attack. The death of the first lady, at the hands of someone they know is one of their own? It drives them into frenzy. A feeding frenzy. We must give them more people to kill."

"Then kill some of *them*. Remind them of their lowly place. Have some balls, Talid. Be a *man*."

Talid's hand reached for his dagger. He lunged toward Sammantha with such speed, and such rage that she was caught off guard. She didn't want to, but she had to defend herself. With a calm, practiced hand she forced Talid's strike to go wide with the outside of her hand. With Talid's head exposed, Sammantha knew that she could take him down instantly and kill him on the spot. That would make her a target around the world, for people that would stop at nothing to see her dead. She could take the knife. That would emasculate Talid. He'd call out his dogs, do anything to save face. She could fight *him*, but not his entire palace guard.

"Mercy!" cried Sammantha. She crossed her arms and raised them into the air above her head. She knelt down, pretending to plead for her life. "You are my master. I meant no disrespect. I just have passion for our cause. There is one...one man that needs to be killed. His name is Trance. Jack Trance. You can kill *him*. You *must* kill him." *He killed my fiancé. I killed his wife. You kill him and the circle is complete.*

Talid straightened. He looked down his nose at Sammantha and smirked. No woman could attack him like this and live. Then again, no other woman had ever pulled a bullet out of his skull. "So, you want me to be a man?" Talid slashed at Sammantha's slacks with his dagger. He caught them at the waist and ripped them clear to the knee of one leg. Sammantha's pants flapped open like a banana peel. Talid stood there, staring at the tiny red thong that Sammantha wore like a flower. Sammantha subtly turned toward him to give him a better look, spreading her legs as if to invite him. After a long while, Talid snorted and walked away.

"You are still a whore," he said, without looking back toward her. "I know this Trance. He is not easy to kill. But he *will* die, even if I have to do it myself. Then I will take you to my bed and you will not resist."

Talid picked up his phone and said, "Send in the boy."

A few moments later, Karkhabi's son hesitantly knocked on the office door.

Talid looked at Sammantha. She was standing half naked in her tiny red thong. He grinned. "Come in, Omar."

Omar Karkhabi stopped in mid stride as he entered the office. He looked at Sammantha Starodubov, gaping like a teenage boy who has just seen his first female breast. He bowed his head quickly and looked to Sammantha's feet. His eyes tried to wander up her legs, to that pulsing red thong. Instead, he shifted them sideways to Talid's bleeding hand. Slowly, he looked up into Talid's eyes.

Sammantha smiled, showing no sign that anything was unusual. She was to work with this boy, so she studied him closely. He was a shade over six feet tall, with a face of smooth olive skin. He was lean, but not muscular, like someone who had grown up too quickly and hadn't quite filled into his frame. His hair was oil black. It was combed straight back over his head. He had a small tuft of black fuzz on his chin. It had the makings of a beard, but it still looked more like darkened chick down than real whiskers. His eyes were alert, but they looked clueless and bewildered.

"I don't believe you two have met," said Talid. He gestured toward Sammantha and then to Omar. "Omar, this is Sammantha Starodubov. Your father has told you about her, no?"

Omar nodded. "She is a doctor…a surgeon. I am to return with her to America."

Talid looked at Sammantha. "This is Omar Karkhabi. He is the son of my closest friend and advisor. You are to take him with you. Feel free to use his talents. He has a doctorate from MIT."

"He doesn't look more than eighteen."

"I am twenty-one," interrupted Omar.

Talid slapped Omar across the face. "Show respect, Omar. Do not interrupt your elders, even a woman."

Sammantha laughed out loud. She thought of what it must look like to Omar. With her torn slacks draped around her ankles, her lacy red thong and the dried blood from Talid's hand spread across her thighs. *A doctorate at twenty-one. Perhaps I will find a good use for his talents.*

Talid continued. "Omar has studied math, mechanical engineering and the nuclear sciences. I have been trying to convince him to work with his people, to help process the spent fuel from our two nuclear reactors, to build weapons to help us protect ourselves. So far, he has refused me." Talid shrugged. "If he were not my friend's son, he would be an example, perhaps a dead one." He smiled. "Instead of death, I am sending him with you." Talid motioned for them both to leave. "There will be a time when I *tell* him what to do. Until then, Miss Starodubov, do what you do best."

Omar's eyes narrowed. He looked from Sammantha to Talid and back. Sammantha looked at Omar with growing respect. Omar was making a statement against his nation's absolute leader, a statement that Sammantha already surmised might one day cost him his life.

"Now leave my home. Do not fail. Either of you."

CHAPTER 23
______________PP______________

It was late afternoon and a hazy sun was beginning to wander into the clouds out over the horizon. The light seemed filtered, giving the surrounding countryside the tint of unpolished silver. Jack Trance mushed his way through thick clusters of bare branches, breaking a fresh trail in the woods with his cross country skis. His arms and legs flailed rapidly as he pushed through the crusted snow for every ounce of speed and power. Sweat dripped down his forehead and steam rose out of his windbreaker, surrounding him with a kind of opaque mist in the cold, still air.

Trance had been skiing hard for over two hours, ignoring his aching lungs and the bloodied slashes made by tree branches along his cheeks. Though not skiing there directly, he knew where he would stop—at a place surrounded by two hundred acres of wilderness. He had bought the land years before, far away from the beat of traffic, miles along a dirt logging road that was unreachable by car. In the winter time, only a truck with special tires, an ATV, a snowmobile, skis, or a foolish man with snowshoes could get anywhere near this place.

Trance came here when he had to make peace with his world, when he'd been letting problems attack his subconscious like a nest of fire ants. It was always painful—as cleansing often is. He was glad he was alone.

For a brief moment, Trance stopped to catch his breath. He wiped the slick moisture off his brow and looked slowly around. He wasn't sure just where he was, but he knew he was close.

An hour later he neared the small cabin on top of the knoll overlooking his land. He had built this place himself, from logs he'd hewn by hand with a woodsman's axe. When he saw the shelter through the trees he stopped. He took several deep breaths, closed his eyes and moved on.

She was still here—Janice. Not just her body, but her spirit, too. Trance could feel her, spreading within him like sunshine as he snapped off his skis. He could feel the warmth of her touch as he set the skis just inside the cabin door.

"I've missed you," he said softly.

Trance stepped into a pair of snowshoes and walked back outside. He made his way through the heavy snow toward the chapel he had built in a sheltered grove of pines. Thirty yards from the cabin, it was a twelve foot high structure of carved, hand smoothed oak. Two heavy bronze doors guarded the entrance. Trance dug down into the snow to clear a space so he could pry them open. Then he walked inside.

Trance shuffled toward the lone headstone. It was made of rough gray granite, with a shiny, rounded top. There was space on the front center of the stone where the rock was polished and flat. Beneath this there was a ledge, six inches deep, also polished smooth. Trance fell to his knees and pulled a bouquet of sweetheart roses from inside his coat. He set them upon the ledge; then he recited the words carved into the stone.

"JANICE TRANCE

 WHO WILL ALWAYS BE REMEMBERED AND LOVED"

Trance clasped his hands together and raised his head toward the sky. His eyes brimmed with tears but he fought them away.

"God, I wish you were here," he whispered. He drew a halting, labored breath. Man, how this hurt. "But we all must bear our burdens, hey?" Trance fumbled with the roses to spread them evenly. "Lauren and I went down to Washington a couple weeks back. There was an invitation I couldn't refuse. Then we went to New York." Trance rearranged the roses, until they lay in a neat row along the headstone.

"I know how you liked her. It's been over six years, you know. Time flies so fast." Trance closed his eyes. "I still see your face as if it were yesterday."

Trance removed a glove and gently stroked the gravestone. "I love her, you know. Besides you, she's always been my closest friend. Maybe she and I could be happy, like *we* were. You'd want that for me, I know. But could I stand the pain? What if I lost her, too?"

***

Trance could still see Janice as the young CIA recruit that had been sent to him for training. Within days he had known they would marry. It was destiny. When Janice became pregnant they'd bought this land in Vermont, so they could get away from everything—the people, the missions, the life. The CIA was no place to raise a family. The Company had no children and it left no survivors.

Trance's mind veered to that final killing conversation with Jacob Miller. He could feel it, as if it had grown roots in his brain. He was pacing in front of Miller's desk, saying, "You're not going to let me quit?"

"That's not what I said, Jack." Miller calmly cleans his nails with the tip of a letter opener. "But you and I both know the secrets you hold. And if you're out…" Miller shrugs. "…I can't protect you."

Trance smiles. "I know. I become a liability and I'm better off dead." Trance shuts his eyes and jumps into the cold. "That's okay, Jake. I'll take my chances."

"I think you'd better not."

"Consider me gone."

"Jack…"

Miller walks to the window.

"You'd kill me yourself, wouldn't you, Jake?" says Trance, knowing what is going through Miller's head—protect the country at all costs.

"I wouldn't want it; none of us would."

"What are you afraid of? Afraid I'll deal with terrorists? Afraid I'll blow the whistle on you and your boys? Tell me, Jacob. Why is it so important that I stay?"

"Don't be irrational."

"Screw you."

Miller sighs. "You know we're both pawns in this game."

Trance walks around the edge of Miller's desk. He stops only two feet away. Miller watches him, smiling nervously. Trance reaches forward with one hand and lifts Miller off his feet by the back of his neck. He pulls Miller's face against his own. "You better hope they kill me on their first try, Jake. Because if they don't, I'm coming after you."

***

It wasn't Trance who died; it was his wife. Terrorists, they said. Supposed assassins avenging the loss of their own at the hands of Trance. Identities buried beneath a labyrinth of obscured layers, each more mystifying than the last. At the top of the suspect list sat General Mu'annar Abu Hussein al-Talid. But this wasn't Talid's style. He liked things big. Big explosions, planes going down in flames, dozens or hundreds dead. They could find no direct evidence against Talid on this. Nothing clear. They could tie him to other things, yes, but not this. And Miller? Trance was never sure if Miller himself was involved, all in a plot to keep him with T-Force.

Trance stroked his wife's gravestone as he might her soft brown hair. "I turned Miller down, again. He wanted my help with something and I refused him. You see? I'm getting stronger."

Trance got off his knees and left the chapel, shutting the doors behind him.

"God, I miss you," he said, as the doors closed shut. "But I have to go on. Life goes *on*."

CHAPTER 24
PP

Brandon Copley's right hand twitched and he knew he was awake. His throat felt like he had swallowed a cocktail made with bleach and cigarette butts. His eyes, though still closed, could feel the caustic, glaring light. It was too harsh to look into, too powerful. That light would blind him; he was sure.

Then there was the pain.

Copley tried to reach for his head but his arms wouldn't move. He had to stop it, the pain. His head felt swollen, like a water-filled basketball. He had to touch it, to make sure it wasn't about to blow open and pop like a balloon. He lifted his head upward only to have it fall back against his pillow. He tried again, then again.

"Arrgghh!"

Insects danced along his skin. Hairy spiders, he could feel them. Tarantulas with thick furry legs. Scorpions, with great curved tails and stingers twitching with every step as they tried to stick him. He wriggled on his wet sheets like a slippery eel. He felt naked and cold and slimy.

He tried to slap at them, the insects in the sheets. But his arms splayed about in a spastic, uncontrolled frenzy. He couldn't stop—the pain, the bugs, and the sweat. He knew he was going to die.

It was only then that he thought about death. *Was* he dead? Maybe he *was* dead already. He couldn't remember. The last thing he remembered was Sammantha, dragging him down to the floor in a wet dream.

"Where am I?" he said. His voice was thin and scratchy, like an old Al Jolson 78 RPM record. His throat was parched. It was hot and dry, feeling like an empty pan left on a hot stove, almost ready to melt. Every swallow burned with that dry hot pain. A scorpion stung his arm. "Get them off of me! I'm going to die... I'm going to die..."

Copley pulled at the elastic strap that held his head to the bed. But he couldn't grip it with the heavy canvas balls that were now his fingers. He began beating his head against his pillow, with a slow rhythmic *thump, thump, thump,* until finally, he opened his eyes to the white, sterile ceiling and that blinding light.

"Our patient is awake," said a muffled voice, a foreign voice somewhere in the distance.

The sound came from outside the room. Copley turned his head. There was a large, rectangular window. Beyond it was a man dressed in a too-white coat with a clipboard in his hand. The man's eyes stared dispassionately at Copley through the glass. He lifted the clipboard in a mock salute and smiled.

Copley noticed another man standing beside the first. This man's coat was equally white, so white that Copley had to blink. Was he in heaven? Was this Saint Peter? Yes, it had to be heaven. Was his name on that clipboard, with a pass that let him through the pearly gates? No. The man's hands fiddled with something in front of him. Dials, thought Copley, like a pilot preflighting a plane. *Or is he controlling me?*

"Assholes," muttered Copley.

Copley heard his words echo around him. The second man leaned forward and spoke into a microphone. "Very good," Mr. President.

The man looked downward again and his fingers seemed to type at something, perhaps a keyboard of some sort. A moment later he turned to his companion. "He's in the final stages. Tomorrow we shall eliminate all alcohol from his IV. I'll sedate him now, gently. His mentor will be here soon."

"Who gives you the goddamn right—" began Copley. In mid sentence his head fell slowly back toward his pillow. He felt like he was falling into a bed of cotton balls.

"He's relaxing," said the technician.

Copley's jaw grew slack. His eyes became unfocused. His eyelids fluttered briefly, then closed.

Dr. Alexei Karov relaxed. He had been through this many times with patients from all parts of the world, mostly in Moscow, where millions of people every year were arrested by the police for public drunkenness. Most of these were released after a day or two. But some, some were forced to undergo "treatments" by men like Karov. Treatments to test new theories on how to make them well. The lucky ones recovered, some enough to return to productive society. The others? Karov didn't know what became of them, nor did he care.

Karov stepped back from the console and allowed his assistant to take over the controls. He watched Copley, like he might gaze at an interesting cloud formation, staring, then tilting his head for a better angle. He smiled. *Good*, he thought. Three weeks and he is almost weaned. Kept on the edge of consciousness with sedatives while the effects of alcohol were slowly removed from his system. Not much longer, he thought. His patient's new drug dependence would be relatively minor after this, and easily correctable. He would need far more treatment, but they wouldn't have to strap him down.

Karov sighed. He looked through the glass at the catheter stuck into Copley's right arm. *How easy it is to control and manipulate a man.* He felt a twinge of regret, a small one, just for a moment. He preferred what the Americans called "cold turkey." He liked to strap a man down and let him scream until he quit. It was easier that way. Dr. Starodubov had insisted that this patient be treated a milder way, with drugs and time. This subject would never again be in control of his life; Karov knew that. He wondered just who the poor sucker was. He had been told to call him "Mr. President." This wasn't a president, far from it. Besides, Tilson was in Washington. He'd just seen him on CNN. He looked at Copley and wondered, *Who is this man, really?*

"You will ease him into his new world gently," Starodubov had ordered. He had done that. He had done it well, just as he always did. His years of practice had brought this subject back into the world, to whatever fate Starodubov and her team of mind-benders had planned for his sorry soul.

CHAPTER **25**
PP

The edges of Jock Tilson's cheeks began to flush with pink before he was halfway through the first page of Doheny's report. "I can't believe this," he mumbled, without looking up. He scowled, looking more like a fighter preparing to step into the ring than the nation's top executive at his desk reading...eyes focused, jaw set, muscles twitching.

"This is all you've got?" Tilson crumpled the page, then set it on his desk. He began to read the next. A minute later he crumpled that page and set it beside the other. As he came to the report's concluding statements he crumpled the final page and added it to the group of others that lay strewn across the top of his desk.

Agent Doheny, standing motionless before the president, looked down at the discarded papers and grimaced. He had already figured out the purpose of the paper balls; he could read the word *BULL* spelled out clearly across the president's desk. He swallowed hard and waited for the usual harangue to begin. He chewed holes into both sides of his tongue, wishing for a stick of gum, anything so he could stop the damned biting and the blood.

Beside Doheny, agent Cramm appeared strangely calm. He stood comfortably at attention, staring off at something deep inside his mind. Doheny wondered why Cramm looked so peaceful. Then he knew, it was the kind of look men had when they had resigned themselves to failure or death, the thousand-yard stare.

Finally, Tilson spoke. His voice was soft and controlled. "With the hundreds...no...the thousands of men you have working on this case, all you come up with is this? One big fat zero?"

"It's not really a zero, sir," said Doheny. "We've eliminated most possibilities."

With a sweep of his arm Tilson knocked the paper balls to the floor. He rose to his full height and towered above his men like an angry genie. He said nothing; he just stared.

Doheny shifted his weight from leg to leg, wringing his fleshy fingers, trying to think of something positive to say. He sucked at the blood trickling along his tongue and he swallowed. Then he looked at Cramm, as if pleading for help.

Cramm stepped forward and saved him. "We actually know quite a bit, Mr. President. We think that Fallon, the Australian attaché, has fled to Costa Rica. We suspect that he was paid a sizeable—"

"Don't tell me what you suspect, Cramm. Tell me what you know." Tilson grasped a handful of hair and pulled at it. Perhaps he could relieve the tension. He counted to ten and let go. "It baffles the shit out of me that the combined forces of the CIA, the FBI, the NSA, Homeland Security, including you, plus a whole bunch of other agencies with names that look to me like alphabet soup can only draw blanks."

"Not all blanks, Mr. President," said Doheny. "As you read, there were two champagne flutes missing from the British Embassy. We surmise that one belonged to your wife."

"Two champagne flutes? That's it?" said Tilson quickly. "Do you know how many pieces of china are stolen from dinners at the White House? It's a rite of passage."

"Your new ivory hair brush and comb are missing."

"Don't give a frigging inventory list of my personal items, Doheny. That's not what I want from you and you know it." Tilson sat heavily into his chair. "I want the murderer of my wife."

"We're working on it, sir."

Doheny and Cramm exchanged worried looks. Doheny stiffened. "We're trying diplomatic channels through Costa Rica—"

"Get real," said Tilson. "I may be new at this game, but I'm not dumb."

"We could send someone in to get him," said Cramm softly.

Tilson's ears pricked and he turned slowly toward Cramm. "And break international law?"

Cramm shrugged. "How bad do you want him?"

"Bad."

"Then we'll get him, sir."

What they didn't know, at least not then, was that Fallon was already dead.

CHAPTER **26**
PP

Sammantha Starodubov checked her rearview mirror for at least the hundredth time, as she wound her way through the twisting, snow-covered roads of northern Maine. The oversized tires of her H2 hummed softly as they plowed through the accumulating snow. More than two feet were forecast, but only a few inches had fallen so far. Sammantha hoped to reach her destination before it was snowed in for the night. Otherwise, she'd have to use a snowmobile to get to the main lodge. She hated all that noise up here in the woods. Noise was supposed to vanish out here. The world stopped, and it became new.

Sammantha came to a fork in the road. The road to the right led to Moosehead Lake. The left road angled west for miles before turning north to run parallel to the water.

"Who would ever expect it here?" she murmured. Sammantha took the left fork, driving into the wilderness, where hundreds of acres often stood between the homes of the hardy souls that lived there year round. This was the perfect place; and it was all thanks to the American capitalistic system. That and American vanity, most specifically, the Andersons.

In the 1800s, Willie "Old Man" Anderson had returned from the California gold rush with trunks filled with gold. He had purchased over a million acres of untamed forest. Anderson had harvested the timber and built one of the largest family fortunes in the east. Later, Willie Anderson expanded his empire into textiles and steel, buoyed by the belief that American industry would forever dominate the world. At its zenith, Anderson Industries had employed over twenty thousand people. The Old Man had built an estate fit for a king, right along the water, surrounded by miles of private land. Anderson's legacy was now controlled by the daughter of dead Russian immigrants.

The snow-covered road dipped abruptly, and then made a wide arching turn to the left. As the road began to straighten, Sammantha slowed her Hummer and stopped beside a tall and rusted iron gate. The gate was fourteen feet high. Its two sides spanned a broad entryway with the support from two huge, marble slab pillars on the edges. The stone was old and gray. Its once-smooth finish had been pitted by years of exposure to the harsh northern elements. Now it was mottled with green moss. There was something new though. A black box the size of a small suitcase was now attached to the back base of the pillar on the right.

Sammantha pulled a transmitter out of her purse. It looked like a television channel changer. She touched a series of numbers and pressed a button that was labeled *Trans*.

Slowly the gate swung open. Sammantha started forward and carefully drove along the long, gravel road. She passed the remains of a small town, where most of the buildings had been burnt to the foundation. The few standing structures had wooden walls that looked ready to cave in with any strong breeze.

Just beyond the town, Sammantha stopped her Rover and waited. Two men dressed in puffy, camouflage-white down parkas emerged from inside one of the buildings. Each man held an automatic weapon with his gloved fingers.

"Good evening, doctor," said one of the men.

Sammantha jutted her chin and nodded stiffly. "Valya," she said.

The man smiled. "And how was your trip?"

Sammantha sneered but said nothing. She rolled up her window and began driving forward. The man's AK-47 slashed across Sammantha's windshield. A spidery crack spread along its width. Sammantha stopped the H2 abruptly and turned to face the guard. She pushed the car door open and stepped outside.

"Asshole," she said.

The guard grinned lewdly, looking first into Sammantha's eyes, then slowly down along her body. "You didn't give me the password," he said.

The man stepped back cautiously and readied his rifle.

Sammantha tore off her sweater, unbuttoned the top of her blouse and thrust her chest forward.

"How's this," she said. "Is this what you wanted?"

"I wanted nothing of the sort. I wanted only your password."

The guard looked to his companion and laughed. In that instant, Sammantha jumped forward and ripped the gun out of the guard's hand. She turned it quickly toward the second guard and yelled, "This doesn't concern you. Throw your weapon down. Now!"

The second guard hesitated, but followed Sammantha's order. He knew who she was. He wasn't going to mess with her. No frigging way.

Sammantha tossed the first guard's gun to the ground and squared her stance toward him. "You are one stupid, arrogant bastard," she said.

The guard lowered his head and shook it slowly, laughing. "No," he said in Russian. "I just know how you got here, and I'd like a little piece of it."

Sammantha spat into the man's face. He lunged toward her. As he did, Sammantha stepped to the side. She caught hold of the guard's arm as he moved past her and snapped back on his wrist until it cracked. She kept pulling until the man's arm was twisted high behind his back.

"There," she said. "Now you've had a piece of me. Wasn't that fun? You want to do it again?"

"You broke my wrist."

Sammantha pulled up on the man's arm until he groaned. "Do you want more? You want me to break an arm, too? Or have you had enough of me?"

"I'll kill you for this," muttered the guard. He struggled to stand. Sammantha let go and backed away.

Sammantha scoffed. "You'll be lucky to stay alive, because you're going to be on the next flight to Siberia, to guard the motherland against Santa Claus." Sammantha walked toward the H2's open door. When she reached it, she turned. "As Nabokov's bodyguard, I'm sure you heard stories about me, Valya. Some of them may even be true. But that was years ago." She paused. "I did what I had to do. Nothing more. You go tell Nabokov to keep his men away. I won't go easy on the next spy he sends to watch me."

The second guard walked cautiously toward Sammantha's car, only once she was back inside. Before closing the door Sammantha looked at him and said, "Don't believe everything you hear, Andre. It's liable to get you killed." Sammantha waved toward Valya. "Enjoy your physical therapy in Siberia." Sammantha slammed the door shut and drove on.

CHAPTER **27**
______________PP______________

Benjamin Anderson was sitting in bed reading a book. He was being held in one of the third story bedrooms of what was once his family's servants' residence. It was a large brick house standing three hundred feet from the main lodge. In any other setting it might have looked like a wooden palace, but next to the lodge's gargantuan spread of stone and timber it looked as insignificant as a collar on a dog. Anderson heard Sammantha's H2 as it wound closer through the woods. He walked to the window. Soon he saw the lights of the car. He followed the headlights until the car passed by his prison. He watched the taillights until the Hummer stopped at the final guard post, before disappearing into the central barn beyond the estate's main structure.

"I wish I knew who the hell you were," he muttered. Ben Anderson walked back toward the bed. He picked a half-empty glass of bourbon off a bedside table. He walked out of the bedroom and down the stairs. Once in the living room he turned on the light and walked to the room's central fireplace. Above the mantel sat a portrait of his great grandfather, Willie Anderson.

"I'm sorry, Old Man," he said to the portrait. "I had to do it. Didn't think it would end like this."

Anderson walked to the edge of the room and opened a pine cabinet door. Behind it sat several bottles of unopened Maker's Mark. Anderson removed the cork seal from one and refilled his glass. Then he returned to the painting.

"You made your fortune in gold, then timber. But you screwed up by expanding into textiles. Your son cut our losses and went into steel. Steel was good, until Japan kicked our butts. Dad waited far too long to get out." He paused. "I screwed up by thinking technology and hedge funds were the way to recoup our losses. I leveraged us to the teeth and bet it all on black. We got red. When the markets turned, our money vanished quicker than smoke. We were a billion more in debt with no way to pay it off.

"So I found us an honorable solution. A *buyer*. I found someone to pay down the debt and keep the company afloat. They even let me stay on as its CEO." Anderson took several sweet sips of his drink. "Of course, they won't let me into the company offices. They've trapped me in this place, with guards at every exit...They put a high voltage fence around the whole compound. What they do in there, I don't know. The trucks come in, with a row of logs on top and who knows what underneath. Hundreds of them, Willie. They are digging. Day and night. They think I don't hear it, but I do, in the silence of the night...Why someone would remove millions of tons of dirt, I don't know. Perhaps they're mining something. But I don't think so. No. This is what we've come to, pops, locked up in the servants quarters as impotent as a neutered choir boy."

Anderson went back to the cupboard and filled his drink for a final time. He saluted the picture with his glass, turned off the light and returned upstairs. Once he was back in bed, Anderson adjusted his horn-rimmed glasses and returned to his reading. Someday he'd find out what was behind that fence. Someday.

***

Inside the main mansion, two guards sat before a monitor, watching every move that Benjamin Anderson made.

"Do you think he knows?" said one of the men.

"That we watch him? No. He wouldn't talk like he does. Does he know what we're doing here? Or that we could kill him at any moment? Not a chance."

"Surely he must know something. What if he escapes?"

The first guard winked. "We use the best American technology. The micro-transmitter in the right frame of his glasses is undetectable. The plastic explosives in the left side are equally invisible. And the detonator? It's the size of a bb and weighs nothing. Our backup system is a small poison-tipped pin released by remote control, straight into the skull."

"Also in his glasses?"

"Convenient, eh?"

"Let's hope he doesn't switch to contacts."

"Not to worry. There are bugs everywhere in the house. He's found several, but there are others he will never find…If we need to make him gone, there is a mountain of explosives in the basement. One touch of a button will turn the old house into a shallow pond."

***

Sammantha Starodubov followed a path of packed, crunchy snow to the cathedral-sized, unpainted barn that sat a hundred yards behind the estate. The barn was built to store heavy machinery, and it was the size of a football field. Tractors, trucks and bulldozers sat around the barn like discarded sandbox toys.

Camouflaged video cameras covered every approach to the barn, just as they recorded all movement inside. Two of the cameras tracked Sammantha as she walked inside the barn door. They moved along with her as she reached for a phone on the side wall and dialed a number.

"CenCom," said a voice.

"This is Starodubov." Sammantha pressed her palm against a flat glass panel, then looked into an eyehole built into a plain, wooden railing. After her palm and retina were scanned the voice said, "Perimeter defenses deactivated."

Sammantha walked farther inside the barn. She stopped by several wooden skids that had been piled haphazardly in the center. She removed a transmitter from her back pocket and pressed a series of seven numbers. The numbers registered on a backlit screen in the floor which was hidden underneath two bales of hay. Sammantha slid the hay aside. She checked and rechecked the numbers—knowing that if she entered the wrong code she would be instantly vaporized. She punched the transmit button. Slowly, a piece of the concrete floor began to recede. Twenty seconds later Sammantha walked down a set of metal stairs, until she came to another thick, vault-like door. As she reached this door, the barn floor above her began to close.

Sammantha pressed her right eye against what looked like an eye piece to a microscope. Within seconds her retinal print had been computer matched against the one taken above and also with one stored in the databanks. Sammantha stood motionless as scanners and sensors tested the entire chamber. Ten seconds later the door swung open. Sammantha walked into another small room, where she was met by a uniformed guard who escorted her along a well-lit corridor to a suite of American-style offices. There she was greeted by a precretary seated at an expensive-looking cherry receptionist desk.

"Colonel Sammantha Starodubov," she said, flashing an ID.

The secretary scanned the ID, even though this was her boss. Then she sent word of Sammantha's arrival. A minute later, a scarecrow of a man with a chicken-like face came to greet her. He was dressed in the uniform of a three-star Russian general. Sammantha stiffened when she saw him and forced a smile.

"Hello, Colonel," said the general in a patronizing voice.

"General Popov," Sammantha said, as she dipped her forehead.

Popov turned and led Sammantha through a maze of low lighted corridors. Popov's office was deep underground. It had a side window that was connected to a pair of Solatubes that brought in natural light using connecting sets of mirrors. The window was now dark, due to the night and the storm. An entire wall opened to a salt water fish tank that would have worked well at SeaWorld. Inside the tank, Sammantha could see the images of shark fins reflecting light as they swam. The rest of the room looked like any modern American office. It had a cherry desk, along with a round conference table surrounded by six matching chairs. The art on the walls was from some modern Russian artist that Sammantha didn't know. The art looked Dali, but it had no soul or originality. It was mere parody, just like Popov.

Popov closed the door behind them and said, "Your patient is now free from his alcohol dependence."

"Then I can begin."

The general shook his head roughly, like a tiger tearing at the hide of a gazelle. "There have been misgivings about your project in the Kremlin, Colonel."

Popov sat down behind his desk. He reached into one of its drawers and pulled out a half empty pack of Camel cigarettes. He offered the pack to Sammantha. She took one and waited for Popov to light it.

Sammantha said, "You and I both know that there is just one man in the Kremlin who is fully aware of this place. He would never—"

"Your man is no longer fully in control, Sammantha. There have been developments."

"Of what sort?"

Popov opened up his hands and shrugged. "They are of no concern to you." He clasped his fingers together behind his head, leaned back and looked at Sammantha's chest with lust-filled eyes. This made his chicken face look more like one of his fish. "What our leaders must know is…can you assure them of success?"

"Of course, I can." Sammantha hesitated briefly. "The only thing that could stop us would be if our subject is…subconsciously unwilling. But he is not. It is a role he has trained for all his life. It is in his genes. His not rising to the task would be like a dog refusing to bark."

Popov rose from his desk and stubbed his cigarette into an ash tray. He walked over and leaned against Sammantha, causing his bony chest to rest squarely against hers. His breath smelled like steam from a city sewer vent. It was hot and fetid, and made Sammantha think of air escaping from a bloated, dead cow.

"We are playing a dangerous game, no?" Popov whispered.

"The benefits outweigh the risks."

Popov laughed. He reached his arms around Sammantha and drew her hips hard against his own. He could feel Sammantha recoil and then relax. She knew what she had to do. She knew the price she had to pay to achieve her revenge and avoid Russian military control. Not for much longer. She brushed her leg along the inside of Popov's thigh. Her breathing grew heavy and husky against his ear. He pressed his hands against her back and she arched against him.

Suddenly, something snapped inside Sammantha, and became severed at its core. She knew she couldn't fix it. It was over. Broken forever. She pushed Popov's face off her breasts. He just stood there panting, looking ready to drool, like one of Pavlov's dogs.

"Do you remember Alexander Khodorkovski?" she said.

Popov's eyes widened as he stared at Sammantha. She actually did see him drool.

"The would-be Oligarch?"

Sammantha nodded. "The same."

"He was an arms dealer. Trafficking in—"

"He was my fiancé," interrupted Sammantha. "Seven years ago he was murdered."

"You know what he was doing. He was a threat to us all—"

"He was not!" *He was working hard for me, for our life together. Those were bullets in my chest as much as his...*

Popov's shoulders slumped. His lust was gone. His whole body sagged, like a marionette whose strings had just been cut. He lumbered back to his desk and lit another cigarette.

"Khodorkovski and his people stole eight nuclear warheads that were in transit from Severomorsk to Andreeva Bay," he said.

"That was a rumor. No warheads were ever found."

"We didn't kill him, Sammantha. Although we would have, in time."

Sammantha walked over to Popov. She took another cigarette for herself. "It was an American that killed him. I got my revenge…against *his* wife."

Sammantha stared into Popov's eyes. They had the sort of hangdog look that appears in the face of unexpected and resounding defeat.

"You are not going to be trouble, are you?" she said.

Popov shrugged.

"I am in love with Copley. You know that, don't you?"

Popov laughed, with a deep guttural guffaw that made him choke on his cigarette smoke. He bent over to cough. When he stood back up, Sammantha had moved close beside him.

"He will be the American president soon. I must be true to him." Sammantha began to remove her blouse. Then she slipped out of her pants. "You can look and you can touch. But I won't participate. Not any longer."

Popov pulled excitedly at his belt, growing hard at the thought of Sammantha, even if he could only touch her. In his excitement he failed to notice Sammantha's repulsive sneer. As Popov began to please himself, a satisfied glow formed on Sammantha's face, as her mind drifted to the American man she had kidnapped. She thought of this man, naked and sober. She felt herself respond, if only for a moment.

"You like that, don't you?" said Popov, between panting breaths.

"Oh, yes, general. You are wonderful. More man than I could ever hope for."

Sammantha thought of Brandon Copley, sitting on his Gramercy Park bench reciting Shakespeare. She liked to watch him there, especially when he didn't know she was looking. She remembered his intelligent, gentle manner, when he was sober, his quick, biting humor and his ability to laugh at himself.

Don't go there, Samm, she said to herself. *He's got to die. They all have to die. None of you assholes know this. You think this is all a game to get control of the presidency. Only I know that it will finish with the end of this presidency, and the destruction of America as we know it. This fucking country will never be the same once I am through. My death will be worth it, and so will his.*

Sammantha didn't want to live anyway. Her eyes hardened. She pressed her hips against the Russian general's thighs, hoping to get this over with as soon as she could.

Popov slobbered along Sammantha's breasts and groaned. "This is the last time, general, even for watching. I must remain pure for the American president, my man. I must stay focused on our mission. Are we clear?"

Popov whimpered. He looked at Sammantha's naked body like a starving animal, then bit into her chest. Sammantha stiffened and let him grope her, while thinking of a small New York City park with an iron fence, and a woman sitting next to a man reciting Shakespeare while holding a pink little baby in her arms, a baby she would never see but already loved.

Soon it was over. Popov's eyes followed Sammantha as she put on her clothes. She couldn't look at him. He made her feel foul, like a whore. She was not a whore; she was an *avenger*, an avenger that would do whatever it took.

"We will complete your mission, my little vixen," Popov said. He reached for another cigarette. "When it is over, we do this right, yes?"

"I can't wait." *You sorry excuse for a human.*

CHAPTER 28

___________PP___________

Jack Trance turned off the Mass Pike at the Copley Square exit in Boston. As he wound down through the gears on his Porsche 959, the tires on the white, low slung car squealed like an ambulance siren, wailing as it hugged the wet curved road. Trance emerged from the tunnel and swung the car left onto Dartmouth Street. As he took a right onto Boylston, he glanced up at Trinity Church, a place he knew all too well. The January day was unusually warm and there was a mass of people milling in Copley Square, sitting on benches drinking coffee, walking along the sidewalks laden with shopping bags and posing for pictures in front of the old historic church.

The warmth had brought out the homeless. There was a jagged line of beggars spaced at irregular intervals across the sidewalk. One of the beggars stood listening to an iPod that was clipped to his belt. The man's eyes were closed and he rocked to the beat, oblivious of the people walking by. The man's left hand gripped a metal cane that had been wrapped with red white and blue tape to resemble an American flag. On the bottom of the cane was a rubber cup that looked like the bottom of a toilet plunger. His gloved right hand held a dented tin cup that looked like it had been repeatedly run over by cars and haphazardly bent back into shape.

There was a white-bearded man standing beside the homeless rocker. Trance recognized him as a man he had once seen, deep in the bowels of Trinity Church. The man wore the same blue hooded coat that said *BOSTON GLOBE* across the back. His hands were wandering through a green trash can near the corner. For some odd reason, the man looked up, just as Trance drove by. The two men locked eyes. Trance could see the man's teeth break into a smile beneath his beard. His hand slowly rose out of the trash to wave.

Trance pulled quickly to the sidewalk and motioned for the homeless man to come toward him. The Globe man hesitated. He looked at Trance's expensive car and remembered what its driver had told him on that day, the day a man had bitten into his own skin before dying, in that unholy place deep below the church. Was today his day to die? When the Globe man reached the Porsche, Trance rolled down the window and said, "How's it goin'?"

The man coughed into his fist and said, "Been better."

"Remember me?"

The man's eyes shadowed and he dipped his head, like a horse taking a drink from a trough. "You killed a man beneath Trinity Church."

Trance shook his head. "He killed himself. You know that." Trance stared back at the man until the man's eyes softened.

"Yeah. I remember."

"Can I buy you a meal? Rent you a room?"

The man seemed to ponder Trance's offer. Then he looked to his left, down Boylston Street. "Morton's is nice."

Trance laughed. Morton's was one of Boston's finest steak houses, not a place one could take a homeless man for a quick meal. Trance accepted the challenge and smiled. He pushed open the passenger door to his car. "Fair enough. Jump in."

Trance said, "Dial Lauren," as the Boston Globe man slid into the car. A moment later Lauren answered Trance's call.

"Hey, Jackie. I'm in a car and on my way."

"Change of plan."

"Say what?"

"Can you meet me at Morton's instead?"

Trance and the bearded man could hear Lauren Haverford's muffled voice as she told her driver the new location.

"I'll be there in a few."

"Out." Trance said, "End call," and his phone shut off.

"That you're wife, mistress or a hooker?" said the Globe man.

Trance stifled a laugh. "That was Lauren Haverford, the next president of Global Credit Financial. If I can ever get up the nerve to ask, someday she might be my wife."

"You travel in fast company."

Trance said nothing as he negotiated the streets and searched out a parking space.

After a minute or two the Globe man said, "You're never going to get me into Morton's."

"Sure, I will."

The man reached into his coat and pulled out two crumbled dollar bills and said, "Bet ya two bucks you can't."

Trance looked over to the man. "I'll pay you a thousand if I can't."

"You're on."

"Dial New York Hopewell office," said Trance.

A moment later Trance's speaker echoed with the sound of a pleasant female voice. "Hello, Jack Trance."

"Hi, Jessica. How is life in the city?"

"Ben and I are doing well. And your life, wherever you are?"

"I'm in Boston. Could you please book me a table for three at Morton's? I'm about to arrive there now. I need a private room if you can arrange it. Actually, you better insist on it."

"Sure, Jack. Oh, Jack…The president's secretary called again. Mandy says you haven't returned any of his calls. If I can be so bold, sir, I don't think that you should be ignoring phone calls from the President of the United States, you know what I mean?"

Trance sighed deeply, sinking into his seat like a poorly timed soufflé. "Tell Mandy that the president can call me on my wireless anytime today after three. I've got my secondary scrambler in the car and I'll have it attached."

The Globe man whistled. "Who the hell are you…Jack …Trance… is that what she said?

Trance nodded. "Yep. That's me."

The Globe man's eyes lit up. "I knew I'd seen you before. Before the church, I mean."

"We've met?"

"Yeah, in my old life. We met at an emerging technology conference in Oakland. Back when you were with the CIA. I used to be an engineer at EMC. Before…you know…the tech implosion. I got downsized. Couldn't get a new job. Lost my home, started drinking, lost my wife. You've heard the story, I'm sure. We've all got one."

Trance looked at the Globe man more closely. "Ah, yes. Your hair was dark then. You wore a red Hawaiian shirt…and…let me think…you were sober and you wore blue Nike running shoes. You still drink?"

"Nah. Gave that up two years ago. Got too old and too tired of pukin'." The man hesitated. "I spend a lot of nights at the Pine Street Inn…serving food and such. They don't take kindly to drinking, ya know?"

Trance found a parking meter on Exeter Street and fed it. He angled his head and said, "Let's roll."

Trance and the Globe man waited just inside the lobby of what the locals called the "Darth Vader" building. Morton's Steak House was downstairs. Soon, Lauren's limousine arrived. Trance walked out through the revolving door and caught her as she was opening the limo door from inside. Trance raised his eyebrows at the car. "Nice of you to come slumming with me."

Lauren gave an embarrassed smile, the kind a young teenage girl might give her dad if he hugged her in front of her friends. This wasn't her style. "They're forcing me to use the limo, now that they've announced my pending ascension to the throne. Seems I was the only one calling the turn in the markets. Saved our capital."

"And to think that you wanted that silly federal job."

For a brief moment, Lauren looked like a bull rider preparing for the gate, like she was ready to try ten seconds with a rope around Trance's neck.

"Sorry. Stupid remark," said Trance.

Lauren placed her arm into the crook of Trance's elbow and let him escort her into the office building. They walked around the revolving door arm-in-arm. As they emerged Lauren was still looking at Trance. She didn't notice the Globe man and bumped into him as he stood inside the door.

"Oh! Excuse me," Lauren said. She put her hand on the man's forearm and said, "I'm so sorry, I didn't see you."

"Get that a lot."

Lauren smiled. "No, it's not that." She nodded toward Trance. "My friend here was getting fresh." Lauren grinned at Trance. "He's been my only man for twenty years, so I take all I can get."

This was their running joke, except this time Trance didn't laugh. Lauren punched him in the shoulder and briefly hugged him. "I do love you so," she whispered.

Trance stretched an arm around the Globe man's shoulders and motioned toward Lauren. "This is Lauren Haverford," he said.

The man wiped his fingers on his oil stained pants. He made a slight bow and offered his hand to Lauren. "Name's Myron," he said. "Myron Drake."

Lauren looked hesitantly at Trance, then grabbed Myron's hand.

"Myron's joining us for lunch," said Trance.

"Well, that ought to be interesting." Lauren placed her hand on Myron's arm and said, "Nothing against you, Myron, but you stink."

"I bet Trance two bucks he couldn't get me in."

Lauren grinned. "That was a big mistake."

Myron shook his mangy head, and his long white beard flopped from side to side. "No, it isn't. They don't like me here…us here."

"Why not?"

Myron looked at Lauren like she'd come from some other planet. "Well, duh," he said.

Lauren put her free arm into the crook of Myron's elbow and dragged both men to the elevator.

"Well, Myron, you smell like ripe garbage. I don't think I'd invite you into *my* restaurant either."

As the three of them walked out of the elevator, an obsequious Maitre' D greeted them with a smile. He didn't give Myron Drake a second look, other than to see him as an important patron.

"Ah, Mr. Trance…Ms. Haverford…and you, sir…so nice of you to join us. Right this way. He led the trio across the main restaurant floor with his head held high. The room grew slightly hushed, as some of them recognized Lauren. A couple others pointed toward Trance and Drake.

A PDA flash went off from somewhere and the Maitre' D whimpered. He prided himself on removing guests from unwanted attention, and he had failed. He had a pained look upon his face, like he'd been caught stealing jewelry at Saks. "I'm sorry," he said. He led them to a secluded room which was set for three.

"What's up, Jack?" muttered Lauren.

After they were seated, and they were alone, Trance said, "Myron saw me kill a man."

Lauren's mouth opened and Trance held up a finger. "I really didn't kill him; he killed himself with cyanide. It was when we had that little thing over in Austria."

Lauren's face relaxed noticeably. "Trinity church?"

Both men nodded. Lauren remembered the event all too well. She also remembered how Trance had vowed to help this man once things were settled.

"Payback time?" she said.

Trance nodded. Drake looked worried.

Lauren turned to Drake. "What kind of work did you do, before all this?"

"Engineer."

"Any good?"

"Cal Berkeley. Graduated at eighteen. My doctorate's from Georgia Tech."

Lauren groaned. She looked at Trance. "You're doing it again, aren't you?"

Trance said nothing.

Lauren turned her attention back to Drake. "He offer you a job?"

Drake shook his head. "I'm not too employable, Lauren."

"Tell that to him. He does this all the time. Fancies himself as some kind of crusader. Started this crazy foundation called *Second Chances*. You up for a second chance? You better be, because this guy doesn't take 'no' for an answer."

Drake looked from Lauren to Trance, then back to Lauren.

Trance said, "I was thinking more like a *real* job for Myron. Not one with the outreach group. Maybe as an engineer with Hopewell Industries. I employ over a quarter million people in the U.S., Myron. I can probably afford one more with a brain." He looked at Drake. "How old are you?"

"Sixty-two."

"Kids?"

"Three. All grown."

"They know where you are?"

"To them I'm dead."

"Why?"

Drake closed his eyes for several long moments. When he opened them, Trance could see their pain. Drake's lips began to quiver. His body started to shake. The shaking grew until it became almost violent, like he'd been out in the winter cold for far too long.

"I abandoned them. Their mother, too. I just...I just couldn't take it anymore...not finding work...not doing what I'd done for twenty-five years...I would just...I just sat down one day in an easy chair and started to drink my life away...until it was gone...all pissed away. One day my wife walked out with the kids. Haven't seen or heard from them since."

"How many tours you do?" asked Trance.

Drake's eyes darted to Trance and he smiled, grimly. "Two."

"Nam?"

"Yeah."

That explains a lot, thought Trance. "Where are they? Your family?"

Drake shook his head and snuffed his nose. He looked down at his hands and said, "I didn't have the guts to fight for them....for my life. Ya know?"

Trance pondered what to say next. His face had the kind of look one gets when standing at the top of a daunting ski run, or high above an ocean cliff, getting ready to dive. He decided to let it go and confess. "Same thing happened to me, Myron. My wife was killed and my life spiraled…it was like falling off a cliff…everything I had was gone. I didn't escape through a bottle. I went off to Nepal. Began fighting in the kind of fights where too many innocent people die. First in far off lands as a mercenary, later in a ring where men fight bare handed to the death. Yes, Myron, I've been there. I know there is a way back, 'though it's like walking on the edge of a razor. I'm getting back to normal, in time. With Lauren's help. I want to give you a chance to change *your* life, to get your life back. You up to it? You want your life back?"

Myron Drake stared at Trance in the same way he had done before, after he'd watched that man die in Trance's arms. It was like he was in a surreal painting where everything was warped out of reality. But he saw the truth in Trance's words. This was a *real* second chance.

"Yes."

"You'll start at a hundred fifty grand a year, plus benefits. I'll conduct an employee review in six months to see if you're worth my money. If you are, we'll work out a longer term arrangement. Then, maybe, we'll try to get you back in touch with your family. That work for you?"

Drake began to cry. He put his face into his hands and wept like he'd just watched Old Yeller die.

"I'll take that as a yes."

Lauren leaned against Trance's shoulder and whispered, "You are hopeless."

"I like to think of myself as hopeful." Trance motioned for their private waiter, who was lurking in the corner of the room. "A chilled bottle of your best ginger ale, please." He turned to Drake. "After lunch we'll go down the street to Brooks Brothers to get you some clothes. I'll want you to keep your current garb, after its cleaned, of course. There may come a time, one day, when I'll ask you to wear them again. It won't be for something illegal, but it could be important."

"You mean like, undercover?"

Trance shot a quick glance toward Lauren. "Sometimes I do things for people. Who, I can't say. Sometimes, a man in your current condition can learn far more than a man like me."

"I understand."

"Deal?"

"Deal."

"Good. Let's eat. You owe me two bucks, Myron."

CHAPTER **29**
_______________PP_______________

Trance and Lauren drove out of Boston on Route 3 South. They were heading toward Lauren's parents' home. Normally they would travel to exit 12 and take Route 139 east to her parents' place above the beach in Humarock, but as they neared exit 14, Lauren said, "Let's get off here, Jack."

"Lauren…"

"Jack, please."

Trance knew what she was doing. Ever since he had known her, she'd had this obsession with a house. He called it the albatross. This was not just any home. It was a majestic, white monstrosity overlooking the Atlantic Ocean, set back from a cliff, with a long slope of manicured lawn that reached to the street. Across the road there were two Cape Cod bungalows nestled into the cliff. Neither spoiled the view from anywhere in the big home. They just added to the ambiance.

"Why do you insist on wanting something you can't have?"

Trance knew the answer. If Lauren got something in her head, something she knew deep in her heart should be different than it was, there was no way to sway her from her belief, or her perseverance. Hadn't she been that way with him? He'd given her so many reasons to let go. Yet, here she was, brightening his life like a splash of tropical sun. She put lightness into his world, a deep comforting warmth that no one else could match. Like that first electrifying kiss, a feeling so rare and so special that it defies description. While everything else faded like old soldiers, Lauren's love remained like spring flowers always on the bloom.

Lauren smiled. "You know me, Jackie. I am an incurable romantic. Can't you see us standing up there on that balcony, watching our children playing in that great expanse of lawn, while the sun shimmers down upon the water? Every time I see that house I see us together. I always have and I always will. No pressure on you, though."

Trance grinned. "Nah. None at all."

Trance guided his Porsche along Route 228 through Hingham into Hull, and then south along Jerusalem Road. Jerusalem Road was a street where people like the Hopewells and the Kennedys lived. Trance's grandparents had once owned a vacation place here. It was a pseudo castle, complete with its own tower. When Trance's father had been assigned to the Bourne Naval Base, his mother's father had offered them the home. His parents had refused it, choosing instead to buy their own more modest house in Humarock. That's how he had met Lauren, in the three years his father had been stationed in Massachusetts. A blink in Trance's childhood, a monument in his life.

Trance stopped the car along the side of the road and allowed Lauren to stare at her dream. She closed her eyes. He knew she was seeing the two of them turning into the driveway. She saw them letting their children spill out of their SUV to go frolicking on the soft grass.

"Want to drive in?" said Trance. "We'll bust through the gate and tell them we're lost."

The glow on Lauren's face faded quickly. It reminded Trance of a dying sunset, the darkening of lost dreams. She shook her head. "Don't be silly."

"If you want it, Lauren, I'll buy it, No matter what it costs."

"That's not it, Jack. You know that." Lauren looked beyond Trance, toward the slate-gray ocean shimmering behind him and sighed. "Besides, the Vanderweggens will never sell this home. They've got more money than Croesus and they have roots here like a banyan tree."

"Things change, Lauren."

"No, Jack. Some things never change."

They drove south in silence. Trance wondered what was getting into Lauren. She was always so cheerful, always joking and laughing at his imperfections, kidding him like she might a favorite nephew. Now, there was silence. Was Lauren's clock ticking that loudly? Was she beginning to think that this vision of their perfect life together might never come true?

Trance wound up Elm Street into the Humarock hills. He pulled into the Haverford's driveway and watched as Lauren's parents come rushing out to greet them. Lauren's mother was slender, with dark hair smattered with random strands of gray. She had a stylish suburban haircut dropping just to the shoulders. Her face showed little wear for its sixty years, her skin like a pebble that had been smoothed by ages in the sea and sand. Lauren's father, Max, ambled behind his wife with the gait of an old thoroughbred race horse. Confident and sure, with a reservoir of power remaining if he needed it. His hair was turning white. When he smiled, his face crinkled into oft-used mirth lines that looked like a crumpled pieces of stationery, deep and grooved, and etched with character.

"Here you are!" said Lauren's mom, Angie. "I just finished baking an apple pie. I know how you two love it hot with vanilla ice cream." She gave Lauren a long, motherly hug.

Max did the same with Trance, pulling against him like he was his own. Max murmured, "Save the world today, Jack?"

Trance smiled playfully. "Not yet, Max. But the day's still young."

Trance's Sectéra wireless began to vibrate. He looked to the screen and groaned. He looked at Lauren. "It's the White House." Trance was expecting this call, so he'd already attached a secondary encryption device to its end.

Lauren made a *well, come on,* gesture with her hands. "C'mon. Answer it," she said.

"Hello, Jock." Trance fell silent as Tilson spoke. He nodded several times and said, "Uh-huh," several more times. Then he said, "It's not that I don't want to help you find your wife's killer, sir. It's just…it's like…Yes, I know how you must feel. You feel like you are sitting on the edge of a black hole. And everything around you is trying to suck you in. You fight against it, but you keep circling around it until finally, you begin to fall inside." Trance paused and looked into Lauren's eyes. "Then, if you are lucky, you find someone to help you crawl back out, someone to bring you back into the light, to live again. I am just starting to live again, Mr.—

"Yes. Okay, Jock. But if I become involved in finding Kiki's killer, I might slip back into that hole myself. I'm not sure I'd be able to find my way out again."

Trance listened for several more minutes. Again he said, "There are hundreds of other men…Yeah…Uh-huh…Sure…I can do that."

Trance hung up the phone and drew a long, slow breath. After holding the air for several moments he let it out in a tired sigh. It was the kind of sigh a person makes at the end of a frenetic day, that bone-weary deflation when one is drained, feeling each pulse of the heart rush through the veins, waiting for just enough energy to last until bed time.

Trance said, "There's a terrorist threat against Boston. Nothing imminent, but timely. Credible sources. It might be nuclear. They don't think fission or fusion, just dirty and dangerous." Trance looked at Max and Angie. "You'll need to keep this to yourselves. Okay? If I were you, I'd take a trip somewhere. You too, Lauren."

Lauren wrapped an arm around Trance's waist. "Do you need to go?"

Trance shook his head. "They want me in Quincy tomorrow, at 10 A.M." He turned to Angie and tried to smile. "Did I hear something about pie?" Trance's eyes looked like they'd just watched a horrible tragedy on TV, like the fun had been siphoned out of them by horrific events that were now hitting home.

The weight on his shoulders was palpable, almost pulsing, weighing him down like sandbags.

***

Trance planned to take the coastal roads north to Quincy. He left early, to give himself time to think. He'd convinced Lauren to stay with her parents and not return to her Boston townhouse, just to be safe. She'd reluctantly agreed.

As Trance passed *the house* in Cohasset, he made a decision, one he had been postponing for far too long. He dialed Judy at his office in Vermont.

"Hey, slacker," Judy said.

"Good morning to you, too, dear. Hey, I need you to do something for me."

Judy remained silent on the other end of the line, waiting. Having Trance as a boss was like playing a TV game show where you choose between a door holding a million dollars and one that holds a can of soup. "Yeah?" said Judy, growing impatient. Was today the money or the soup?

"You know that house in Cohasset that Lauren can't get off her brain?"

"Jerusalem Road?"

"That's the one. I need you to buy it. I heard through the grapevine that Vanderweggen took a bath in the stock market, and that his company got clobbered in the recession. He had that thing where he'd pledged thirty million to Milton Academy for the new Vanderweggen Center. That's not happening with what I hear he's got left. Tell him you represent someone who will help him fulfill his pledge and help finance his company. Call him discreetly. Don't tell him who we are. Use one of the offshore companies. Work that out with my CEO, Art Winthrop. Please make sure it happens, Judy. I don't care what it costs. I also want you to buy the two houses across the street, as well as every other house nearby. I'll need security."

"Are we moving to Boston, Jack?"

"You okay with that?"

"Just as long as I don't have to commute."

"We'll set up an office by the water, on the South Shore."

"Is it okay if I get pregnant?"

"Excuse me?"

"Dave and I have been wanting to start a family. The schools are good down there."

"Fine with me. We can work out of your home, if you want. Why don't you look for a house where we can also have our office? I'll buy it. My treat."

Judy remained silent for several moments. "Jack, you don't need—"

"I want you to be happy, Judy. You and Dave. I'll do whatever you need."

"We've got this worked out, Jack. Really."

"Tell Dave he's got first dibs on all the new architectural work. I've got lots of plans."

"He'll be ecstatic. Count him in. When do you want this done?"

"I don't care if it takes a year. No one is to know about this, especially Lauren. Got it?"

"This is going to cost a lot of donuts, Jack. You want me to run things by you first?"

Most men wouldn't trust their assistant with tens of millions of dollars. But Judy was different. A Colby grad, she had an MBA from Wharton and a JD from Yale. Trance paid her half a million a year, ostensibly to help him practice law. He paid her more than he billed, and he gave all that to charity. What Judy did was keep his chaotic life in order. Never complaining, taking days off on short notice just as eagerly as working forty-eight hours straight.

"No, you've got a free hand…Oh, Judy?"

"Yes, Jack?"

"Would you call Charles Johns, and see if you can arrange a meeting? Boston or Florida, wherever he wants."

"The Red Sox Johns?"

"Uh-huh. Any day after tomorrow would be fine."

"How 'bout we both go to Florida? My tan is fading."

"You'll have to get your tan on the slopes, Judy. Go to Bromley. It faces south. I need you in Vermont to man the fort."

"All right, Jack. Bye."

Trance hung up the phone and turned his attention to Boston. Boston was a haven for Middle Easterners. With its host of top colleges, it was a prime destination for Arab leaders to send their privileged children. Most learned how to be better world citizens. A few learned skills that could make them dangerous in any part of the world. Many of them never left. There was a large contingent of Arab royalty in the northeast, particularly in Boston. Boston was home to princes who were known to drop a hundred thousand dollars on Newbury Street and not even notice. While most were harmless, some had ties to terrorists like Bin Laden, and the money to fund them. Yes, Boston was both haven and target. Someday it could explode.

CHAPTER **30**
PP

Sammantha Starodubov stepped out of a red-roofed rickshaw, onto the parking lot outside Beijing's Drum Tower. She gave twenty dollars to the man who had pulled the cart with his bicycle. She entered the building and took the steep stairway up to the top of the tower. She walked into an empty room and stared out over the city. The sky seemed like it had been enveloped by a Gobi sandstorm. The pollution was so thick it looked solid enough to walk on, like clouds of red concrete.

"Not much of a view today," said a voice from behind her. Sammantha didn't look at the man, but softly said, "I've seen better days."

"Then perhaps you must come again. On a clearer day."

"I will always return to this fine place. It is my home."

"We will welcome you with open arms."

After their code was complete, Sammantha turned slowly to face her contact. The man looked like the victim of intense Chinese "political reconditioning." He stood half a head shorter than she. His face was so pockmarked, it looked like it had been used as a country club doormat. The man's right eye was permanently angled to the side, while his left eye seemed to wobble in its socket, like a character out of a Harry Potter movie. The man was dressed in a faded red robe that was tied at the waist by a black rope belt. "Follow me," he said.

The man stopped outside a gnarled wooden door that looked like it had been made during the reign of Kublai Khan. There were four men guarding it, with two standing on each side. The short man knocked four times, then stood aside. The old wood moved with a grinding moan and Sammantha walked inside. There was no one near the door; it seemed to have been opened on its own by some mysterious and hidden force. Across the room, a man stood at a window, looking a hundred feet down toward a shadowy flock of tourists milling about like lost sheep. "This building was originally built during the Yuan Dynasty, in 1272," the man said.

"And your point is?"

The man turned to face Sammantha. Unlike Sammantha's earlier guide, this man was half a head taller than she, like a pro basketball player. This man was handsome, not made into a freak show performer by political correctness. His face was smooth, like caramel. His eyes looked like cultured pearls, with small black beads floating in the center of a bed of oyster white. These were eyes of death, black eyes that slackened Sammantha's knees for a sickening, paralyzing moment. Once she recovered, Sammantha peered at the man's face, seemingly unafraid.

"You like my eyes?" he said.

"I didn't notice," she lied.

The man intensified his gaze on Sammantha. She could feel the draw of their full hypnotic power. They were like Ogarkov's eyes. However, there was a darkness to these, a kind of malevolence that was sickening. The sickness built with each moment, as if he were putting something *into* her eyes, not merely looking at them. Sammantha stared back, willing herself to make him blink. Finally, she had to pull away before she fainted.

The man shrugged. "Yes, you did notice. They are my greatest asset. It is my eyes that have brought me to where I am. Many say they are the eyes of a God. Others call me a demon. Some say I'm a bit of both." The man pondered what he could see of the Beijing skyline and mused, "I am just a man with vision. My eyes see much. Today I am the second most powerful man in China. With your help, I will become the most powerful man in the world."

"Of that I have no doubt."

"What do you bring me?"

Sammantha reached beneath her long wool coat and unbuttoned her blouse. From beneath her bra she removed four photographs. They were small, just two inches square, but they showed enough. The photos showed Brandon Copley. He looked much like the American president in three of them. In one, he was wearing a dark blue business suit. A second showed him sitting in the lab as his mind was prepared for programming. The third showed him walking beside Sammantha wearing dress pants and a blue striped Oxford shirt. The final photo showed him drunk and naked, embracing an equally naked Sammantha, with his penis rising between them.

Li Zhiyang studied the photographs and smiled. "You are very attractive, Ms. Starodubov."

Sammantha reached into Li's palm and removed the pictures. She pulled a Bic lighter from her pocket and set them on fire. When the photographs had turned to ash, she said, "Can I count you as an ally?"

"You promise that you can secure the trade treaties we discussed?"

"Yes."

"The American president will help facilitate the business acquisitions we have targeted? He will relax his environmental demands?"

"Yes."

"And he will insist on meeting with me and me only, in China?"

"Yes."

Zhiyang reached into the pocket of his cashmere coat and withdrew a scrap of paper. He handed it to Sammantha. Sammantha looked down and read a series of numbers.

"These numbers will give you access to the account in Macau. As agreed, I have placed the sum of one billion U.S. dollars into this account. The money is now yours. Spend it as you will. Deliver what you have promised and I will match it. If you don't..."

Zhiyang turned away. As he reached the door, it opened eerily on its own, and then closed behind him.

"Well, screw you, too," said Sammantha, softly under her breath.

CHAPTER **31**
PP

Sammantha Starodubov pressed her eye against the final optical scanner, before being allowed into her underground laboratory, deep in the woods of Maine. She was now ready to begin the programming; the next step toward completing her plan.

Sammantha was struggling with an unexpected concoction of emotions. It was like a drug she couldn't fight, a drug that brought visions of babies and a woman walking down an aisle in a white wedding dress. She pinched herself and shook it all away.

While Sammantha had built a plan for each of the major presidential hopefuls, fate had treated her like a kindly babushka, when Tilson had emerged the victor. This would be simple, when compared to the other candidate scenarios. Tilson was the easy route to her goal, because she knew something that no one else knew about Tilson. Tilson had a twin. That made all the difference. It was like fate had delivered oils, canvass and the perfect model to a master artist. She would now create a masterpiece.

She remembered that day again, like an old movie playing over and over in her mind.

Her fiancé had been dead for years. She had taken his far reaching properties and business interests and sold them, pocketing more than a billion dollars, all to be used toward the goal. The only thing left was his Moscow home, a palace built with obscenely large rooms, manicured gardens, and too many ghosts.

Sammantha had fired most of the staff, keeping just enough to maintain appearances. She had built a secret, state-of-the-art hospital deep below the mansion. She and her team provided medical care to wealthy dictators, despotic terrorists and an endless stream of unsavory criminals seeking to change their identities.

Sammantha was watching news of the American presidential campaigns on CNN. She was wondering just how she would execute the destruction of the American government when her housemistress, Katarina, had changed everything. "I held him, when he was a baby. Tilson. His mother worked with me in America. He has a twin. But that is a secret. A secret that only I know. I held his brother, too."

"He is an only child," said Sammantha.

Sammantha had learned everything she could about the candidates, searching for any chink in their armor that would let her penetrate. This was nothing she had found, or hoped for.

Katarina shook her head. "When I was a girl, I worked in America. I worked for an important man, a wealthy man. In summer, we would all go to a house, like this one. It was in Maine. Bar Harbor it was called. They would have parties, entertain many fat men and skinny women."

Katarina fell silent. Her nose crinkled, as if she were remembering the smell of something rotten. Her head and her lips twisted into a frown, as if a bitter aftertaste had filled her mouth. And it had.

"He was a bad man, Sami. He used to take us into the bedroom, when his wife was away…sometimes two or three in one day. She went away often, his wife. She wanted a baby, and he try hard. That was their way."

"Why didn't you leave?"

Katarina's lips twisted again. "I was illegal in America. Where else I go? I needed work. But he didn't care for *me* much."

Sammantha waited while Katarina primped her hair, as if she were preparing for a date. After a few moments Katarina began again.

"They have no children, the master and his wife. Nobody knows why. But we do. The staff knows."

"Why, Katarina?"

Katarina uttered a deep, belly driven laugh that was almost a growl. "He was big man. Powerful man. He had many rich, powerful friends. But when he was in a bedroom…he was just a boy." Katarina pointed an index finger at Sammantha, then let it droop. "Like a soft, cooked noodle, at least with me."

"You weren't raped?"

"Oh, I was raped. Clothes torn off me, him humping at me like a dog on a leg, with his manhood soft as spaghetti noodle." Katarina fluffed her gray hair again and sat up, straightening her shoulders. "He would beat us then, like it was our fault."

Katarina fumbled in the pockets of her apron and pulled out a pack of cheap Russian cigarettes. She gave one to Sammantha, took one for herself and lit them both with a wooden match that she struck on her shoe.

"One day it stopped, the day we learned that Martha was pregnant."

"Tilson's mother?"

"Ya. When she delivered the boys… they were going to take both to New York. But I…" Katarina hesitated. "I was cook and I had my knives. One day I grab him by the hair and press a blade to his throat. I make him promise."

"Promise what?"

"I make him give one boy to Martha. She got one of her babies." A glow spread across Katarina's face, coloring her cheeks like she had spent a long day in the sun. Her eyes softened, then brightened as they filled with the memory. "They were beautiful, those little babies, so innocent…I used to hold them and rock them to sleep while Martha cleaned."

"They made her work?"

"Of course. She was a servant girl. But we helped, we all did…she was so tired."

"Then you left?"

"We were let go. All of us. He bought me a ticket on a tramp steamer and train ride to Moscow. He told me if I ever talked…"

"But you weren't afraid of him. You put a knife to his neck."

"I did it for Martha. Later he beat me, almost to death." Katarina unfastened her blouse and showed her back to Sammantha. Stretching its length were long white ridges of scars.

"He whipped you?"

Katarina nodded. "But, Martha…Martha, she got one of the babies for her own. He is now the American president. Good for me, yes?"

***

"Yes," whispered Sammantha, "and good for me." Sammantha cleared the final security checks and entered the compound's inner sanctum, five deep stories below the land's surface. The elevator opened into a long passageway. The walls were lined with thousands of green ceramic tiles. The floor was white marble and polished to a spit shine. Paintings hung symmetrically at ten foot intervals, copies of Audubon drawings, all showing various exotic species of birds. Chirping sounds were piped in through speakers concealed in the walls, while natural lighting filtered into the hallway, carried through more aluminum tubes and mirrors. It all made the hallway feel like a surreal jungle path, with the natural feel of the outdoors, despite being over a hundred feet underground.

Sammantha's boots squeaked against the smooth floor as she walked. With each step they squeaked like an old car's fan belt in the rain. *Screech...screech...screech.*

Sammantha carried a thin black briefcase. She clutched its handle tightly in her fist, as if it might wriggle away like a frightened frog. Sammantha grew increasingly anxious as she moved forward. The screeching shoes, the overpowering birds and the white corridor floor made her think of a sanitarium, one she might see in a nightmare, one with no way out. Her throat tightened and she felt almost sick.

After close to a hundred yards, Sammantha came to a green, metal door that lay flush against the wall. It was nearly invisible, opened only by remote, with no place for fingers to pry. Two men stood rigidly outside the door. They stared forward like Buckingham Palace guards, giving no outward notice of Sammantha as she approached.

"Step aside please," she said when she reached the men. One of the guards saluted and took two steps to the side. Sammantha pressed an eye against a keyhole and the door silently swung open.

Sammantha entered a broad, expansive area that was a far different world than the claustrophobic hallway. The floor was covered by pale green carpet that felt lush on her feet. The walls were painted in earthy, pastel colors that were soft and comforting. The room was tastefully furnished with both early and modern American pieces. They were strewn about the floor in casual groupings. Small oak tables and matching chairs were positioned around the chamber for discreet conversations. Other areas had more comfortable arrangements, with couches and overstuffed chairs.

Against the far wall, Sammantha saw a glass observation deck with fifty-foot-high, layered laminate windows. Outside the window, she could see Brandon Copley sitting in a leather chair, facing her way. There was an individual seated in front of Copley, his back to the glass wall, moving things in front of Copley's face. Two men were standing by the window, looking in while taking notes. They were dressed in white lab coats, hospital scrub pants and Birkenstock shoes. One of them turned as he heard Sammantha approaching across the expansive space.

"Oh, good." The man rushed to greet Sammantha with outstretched arms, surrounding her like a warm blanket. "How are you, my dear?"

Sammantha patted the man briefly on his shoulder. Then they both stepped back to look at each other.

"Hello, Uncle Ivan."

"Hello, precious."

Ivan was as close to family as Sammantha had. She had done a year under his tutelage, after returning from medical school in the United States. Ivan had taught Sammantha how to probe the depths of the human brain, how to understand its enormous capacities and exploit its many weaknesses.

"You're pet is nearly ready for his new studies."

Sammantha hit Ivan with a hard glance. Copley was no pet. He was a friend. No, more than a friend. A lover. Even more than a lover. Sammantha pushed those thoughts from her head. He was her *subject* now, nothing more.

"How long has the subject been awake?"

"Just an hour. We have been using a series of nano-implants, shocks, hypnosis, Propranolol, EMDR and NLP to clear the remnants of his negative programming. His axons have been mapped and his dendrites are ready for new stimulation."

"Stress issues?"

Ivan looked towards the other man and smiled. "Oh, yes. He was abused as a child. Left alone in dark closets for hours, if not days. He was beaten, his head dunked into the toilet, you name it. No outward scars, except for the drunkenness. It's taking me quite a bit of time to erase *his* flash memory."

"No problems, though?"

Ivan smiled. "Gavril, Valerik and I always succeed." Ivan looked to the man by the window. "Don't we, Valee?"

Valerik nodded. "We've seen far worse in Moscow, Sammantha. This here…Copley…He will be no problem. You should know that."

Valerik's eyes seemed to mock Sammantha, as if she were an amateur card player joining a serious professional's game.

Sammantha stepped forward and gripped Valerik firmly by the testicles. "Are you willing to stake your manhood on that, Kuznetsov? That there will be no problems?"

Valerik whimpered but said, "I am."

Sammantha let go and turned toward the other man, her mentor. "And you, Ivan? Are you willing to stake your reputation on the American?"

Ivan Novikov looked Sammantha straight in the eye and laughed. "You know that better than anyone, Sammi. We have worked with thousands of subjects, of which *you* were one. You know what we can do."

Sammantha thought to her own nightmares. Ivan had erased most of them. But, sometimes, it was like wiping chalk off a blackboard. There were those he could never hope to fully erase, fully touch, memories so indelibly etched into her brain, so deeply carved into her being that nothing short of a lobotomy would make her forget.

"So you and I both know you aren't foolproof," Sammantha said.

Ivan made a *tssk, tssk* noise with his tongue and tried to hug Sammantha again. This time she recoiled and kept her distance.

"His trauma was nothing like yours, my dear. In two more days his mind will be an empty slate, ready to record whatever you want."

"Have you drilled the holes yet?"

"Not yet."

"How many will you need?"

Ivan shrugged. He curled his lower lip in thought, stretched out his hand, palm down and waggled his fingers. "It depends upon his suggestibility, Sammi. Most likely, I will need no more than three, maybe four probes into his brain. He appears to be easily stimulated, and unusually creative. You say he was an actor?"

Sammantha nodded.

Ivan nodded back. "It makes sense, then. His right brain is rather dominant."

"I want the most sterile conditions possible. You understand? If he has an infection, I will cut off your balls with a pair of garden shears."

Ivan winced. Then he chuckled. "I believe you, my dear. I have seen you do it, remember?"

Sammantha remembered the rape. She remembered the revenge she had exacted. Frontier justice, that's all it was. Nothing more.

"Jasha deserved what I gave him. You know what he did to me."

"I understand; I do. I would never hurt you. Never."

"Tell me you're not doing this just for the money."

Ivan pondered her question, as if staring at some unseen bird in flight. "The five million U.S. dollars you have offered may have clouded the judgment of many. But not me, Sammantha Starodubov. I live like a miser, always in the lab. I have all the money I need, you know that. I am doing this for the glory. It will be our greatest achievement, perhaps the greatest achievement of all neurology. To take one man's brain and wipe it clean. Then give it the full identity and experiences of another, so much so that the man *becomes* the other. In only six months? This will embody *all* of our theories, take *all* of our experience and resources. We have worked on thousands, *destroyed* thousands of brains to get to this point.

This is the ultimate challenge, my dear. I would do it for free. I *will* do it for free, if you wish."

"No," Sammantha said softly. "You will get your money. I will double it if he asks me to marry him when we're through. Ten million, to each of you."

Ivan's jaw seemed to grow loose at its joints, grinding in a strange circular motion, as if he were rolling marbles with his molars. He looked from Sammantha, to Brandon Copley though the glass, to Valerik Kuznetsov and back to Sammantha. "You love him?"

"Don't be a fool."

"A fool, I am not. But you? Perhaps you are the fool. Don't worry, my sweet. We will give back to you a far better man than the shadow you brought us. He will love you. I will *make* him love you."

"You will *make* him president."

"Oh, yes. He will be an even better president than his brother."

"Good. "

Sammantha motioned with a flip of the hand toward one of the oblong tables that were placed around the edges of the observation deck. She started walking toward the table, waving to the two men, saying, "Come. Come and look."

When they reached the table, Sammantha withdrew several manila folders from her briefcase. She opened them slowly, one at a time, and placed them on the table beside a short stack that was already there. "Tell me what you see."

Ivan and his partner looked into the folders, turning the pages quickly, like novels they couldn't put down. From time to time they consulted the other folders that had been lying on the table before Sammantha arrived. After thirty long minutes Ivan closed the last folder and smiled. "This will be routine, Sammi."

"Nothing is routine. What are the hurdles?"

Ivan reached for one of the folders and slid it toward Sammantha. "This is a scan of Tilson's eye." He pointed at a large photo showing what looked like a 1970s pop art painting of a nest of spidery veins in psychedelic colors. "See this spot?"

"Yes."

"That's a blind spot in Tilson's left eye. One his twin does not have."

"Can we duplicate it?"

"Sure. With a laser, just take a moment."

"And will he…I mean Copley…will he lose sight?"

"Just the tiniest bit. Nothing important, unless he's trying to try to hit an inside fastball. I'm sure Tilson doesn't even know the hole is there."

Sammantha swept her hand across the folders. "What else?"

"Tilson's brain MRI shows a small flat globule on his cerebellum. Copley will need an injection into his brain. We'll take care of that when he has his liposuction. We'll need to drop his cholesterol by twenty five points. His triglycerides, too—without medications. That means a strict diet, with niacin, if he can handle it, flaxseed oil and fish oil. We'll need to up his calcium intake and lower his sodium slightly. His other levels are fine.

"There is a scar on Copley's arm that must be smoothed, and one on the left leg to be added. Nothing a little plastic surgery can't fix. A small chip of bone must be shaved off of Copley's spine."

Sammantha tilted her head but said nothing. Her eyes asked the question.

"Tilson jumped out of a hayloft as a boy and broke a small bone off his back. No other breaks to duplicate, just that small piece missing from his outer backbone, on L4."

"Where is it? The chip?"

Ivan shrugged. "Don't know. Don't care."

"What else?"

"Tilson has a scar on his right index finger where he cut himself. We'll need to give one to Copley. We'll also need to rough up his fingers. There's more wear on Tilson's prints."

"He grew up farming. Copley grew up playing piano."

"I can tell."

"Is it a problem?"

Ivan made a sound that was half laugh and half snort. "Sammantha…This is nothing….It's child's play."

"It's got to be perfect, especially the hands and face."

"You are asking me to duplicate his twin, Sammantha. God already did this for me. All I need to do is put on a little makeup."

"And verify the DNA."

Ivan nodded. "Already done. The saliva on Tilson's glass, and the hairs from his brush, are a dead DNA match for Copley." Ivan began to laugh. "A dead match…Funny, no?"

Sammantha studied Ivan like she might look at a wart, with part analysis and part distaste. She nodded. "Funny, Ivan. Real funny." *If only you knew that this would all end in fire. Then you wouldn't think it so funny.*

Sammantha reached into one of the folders and withdrew a small box. It looked much like a jeweler's box. But when she flipped it open, rather than a ring inside, it held two small metal chips. The chips were enclosed in clear plastic, and sitting upright in small slits.

"These are the GPS transponders we will need to insert into Copley. The serial numbers match the ones inside Tilson. One is for his torso. The other goes in a tooth."

"Who did you have to screw to get that?" mumbled Valerik.

Sammantha snapped the box shut with a loud *click.* She gently placed the box on the table. Then she took a quick shuffle step toward Valerik, pressed her fingers around the front of his throat and pushed upward, until Valerik was standing on his toes.

"Everything is fair in love and war, Kuznetsov. This is a war. My war. How I prosecute my war is none of your business. Like any good soldier, you do what you are told and nothing more. Do we understand each other?"

Valerik nodded. This caused him to choke. Sammantha continued to hold his neck, until his head looked like a round beet. Then she let him down slowly.

"Yes, I think we understand each other…Now get to work."

CHAPTER **32**

PP

Jack Trance maneuvered his hunter green Range Rover north, along coastal Route 3A into Quincy, Massachusetts. After clearing the Fore River bridge and the rotary, he pulled off the main road onto a small neglected street. The road ended in front of the well fortified, but highly disguised entrance to a little known facility run by the U.S. Special Operations Command. The complex was surrounded by a twelve-foot chain link fence. As Trance pulled into the decaying edge of a parking lot, he could see evidence of dogs along the edge, as well as camouflaged cameras in every direction. A man stepped out of a rickety gate house, spoke into a walkie and motioned for Trance to roll down his window. Well beyond the guard, Trance saw other people begin to stir.

"Colonel Jack Trance. Here for a meeting with General Abrams."

"ID please."

Once inside the gate, Trance was met by a camo green Humvee holding three soldiers dressed in rough street clothes. They looked more like iron workers than highly trained members of the U.S. Special Forces. Each man had an M-16A4 resting on the floor between his knees. As they drove forward, Trance noticed snipers slowly slip back into the shadows on the roof of the compound ahead.

Trance followed the Humvee toward what appeared to be an old shipyard building. They parked a good thirty yards from the entrance. The building's corrugated steel looked like it was about to crumple inward. The walls were dented and rusted. Dried grass grew waist high around the entire structure. Old ship cranes teetered above them like giant dinosaur bones, looking like they might pounce at any moment. Weeds sprouted up through the cracked and pebbled tarmac. The road crunched like popcorn under Trance's feet as he walked behind the men toward the structure.

The men ducked under the rusted remains of an outside door. The building's interior had been stripped of everything but its corrugated walls. They walked another fifty yards to the opposite end of the open shell. The far wall was made of crumbling concrete. One of the men stuck a plastic ID into a discreet card reader built into the wall. It worked like an ATM, except that the slot looked more like a crack in the concrete than a sophisticated card reader.

"This is the back entrance, general," said one of the men.

"I'm a colonel, soldier."

The guard smiled. "Right, sir. Sorry, sir."

A portion of the wall began to slide sideways. Beyond it was a dusty, concrete corridor. The man motioned Trance forward. "Most people come in from about a click away. There's an old office building, and a tunnel running three stories down."

"Sent me on the scenic route, I see?"

The soldier chuckled. "You'll find it comfortable enough inside, sir."

The men walked about twenty yards and stopped beside an old freight elevator. The elevator doors were wedged open with triangular wooden doorstops. There was no smooth wall lining this elevator shaft. It looked like something out of an *Indiana Jones* or a *National Treasure* film, just a hole dug out of pitch black dirt and packed tan sand, with a crude elevator to get them down. All four men stepped onto the platform and descended into the yawning hole.

"Keep to the middle," said one of the soldiers. "Sometimes shit flies off the walls onto the platform."

"Nice to see my taxes so hard at work," mumbled Trance.

When the elevator began to slow it was still dark in the shaft. It felt like the inside of a coffin, the space annoyingly tight, the air dank and acidic. When the platform hit bottom, a faint light came on. A gleaming metal door opened to reveal another small corridor. This corridor, however, was spotless. The floor was made of pale blue, ceramic tile and the walls were painted with a high gloss paint of the same cool color. Stainless steel lamps were built into the wall, with spiral, unshaded low-wattage bulbs spilling light every twenty feet. Trance could see the lenses of video cameras nestled into the base of each lamp.

At the end of the corridor the lead soldier put his card through another slot. Then he pressed his thumb onto a keypad. The two other soldiers did the same. When they were done, all three men turned toward Trance.

"The biometric sensor is programmed for your thumb, sir."

Trance pressed his right thumb against the keypad and the door opened.

A loud group of voices yelled, "Surprise!"

Trance could see Lauren standing before him. She was flanked by thirty or forty other men and women.

"What the—"

Lauren ran forward and gave Trance a hug. "Happy birthday, darling."

Trance blinked. This was the last thing he expected. The president had asked him to come to Quincy to help analyze an imminent terrorist threat, not attend a birthday party.

Trance saw Tilson step out from behind the crowd. His eyes looked playful when he saw the look of shock cross Trance's face.

"Got you, didn't we?"

For once in his life, Trance was speechless.

Jock Tilson motioned for Trance to walk toward him. The people parted to give him room.

"You are here for three reasons, Trance," said Tilson. "First, it *is* your birthday. Lauren actually has a cake for you, later. The second reason is your promotion."

"Promotion, sir?"

Tilson held up a set of general's stars.

"But—" said Trance.

"Third," said Tilson. "I am presenting you with a Navy Cross."

Trance shook his head. "To begin with, sir, I don't deserve any more medals. I am not 'officially' active military. So, I haven't earned those stars. There are plenty of men who've done braver things than I...And...I don't really celebrate my birthday anymore."

"Well, tough shit."

Tilson smiled. His teeth glistened a whitish gray in the intense, underground fluorescent lighting. "Since we last met, I have been checking up on you. I was pissed that you wouldn't help me find my wife's killer and I wanted to know why. I called my predecessor. He told me that you, almost single-handedly, stopped a third world war. He said you helped save millions of lives. I think that warrants a promotion and a medal." Tilson motioned to the small crowd surrounding Trance and they began to clap.

Trance's lips began to quiver. He had done what any soldier would do. He hadn't done it for a great cause or grand thoughts of *nation* or *country*. It was just that it *had* to be done. He wasn't sure why, but he felt like crying. There was a dull ache inside him, like there was something missing, some essential piece of him that had been ripped away and thrown in the gutter. Medals and promotions were an honor. But they were powerless against this feeling, the feeling that there was something else, something more. Trance looked toward Lauren. He felt a stirring inside him, something on the edge of his consciousness. It was *there*, he knew it. He couldn't put his finger on it, couldn't reach it, whatever and wherever it was.

"There are a lot of men and women who deserve medals more than I do, Mr. President. I can give you a list—"

"Not now, Trance," said Tilson. "This is your day. That's an order."

Trance began to protest, but stopped. Tilson was the Commander In Chief. He couldn't protest anymore. Not in his face.

After the ceremony, Tilson pulled Trance into a small office and said, "I had to get you alone, so I appealed to your love of country."

"Damned smart of you, sir."

Tilson smiled. He pondered his next words. "The death of my wife was a terrorist act of the highest order, General Trance. I've got hundreds, thousands of people trying to hunt down Kiki's killers and we're getting nowhere. Now, I don't need to impress upon you the magnitude of this undertaking. We are talking about national security. We are talking about national pride, our status in the world, General."

Trance winced each time the president called him by his new title. He knew what the title came with. It meant dropping into a world of gray, where there was no right and wrong, only guesses and interpretation. Kill or be killed, then pay the price because someone in an office thousands of miles away decides that your motives or intentions were not appropriate. And then…and then there were the memories…They never went away, like India ink on the fabric of the mind.

"It's not like I don't want to help, Mr. President—"

"Call me Jock."

"Yes, sir." Trance allowed a small smile to escape his lips. "It's just that the lines are so fuzzy, and the challenge too great. If I look for your wife's killer, I'll be reminded that I was not able to find the killer of my *own* wife. It will be like some horror film playing over and over inside my head. You see, I *know* how it feels…to wake up every day and know that you have *failed*…that you have failed to bring about justice…that you are letting down your wife's memory, letting down her family. Janice's family won't even talk to me. I have ruined their lives."

Tilson put his hand on Trance's shoulder. "Don't you believe in God?"

Trance chuckled. "If you only knew."

"Let your faith guide you, Jack. Know that it was for a reason. Finding Kiki's killers could put everything back into balance. Balance, Jack. Light, dark, up, down, positive, negative, yin, yang—everything has its opposite. God made it that way."

"I'm not sure God has anything to do with this, Mr. President."

"Jock."

Trance smiled. "Jock."

"Maybe they are one in the same. You ever think of that? Maybe the same person killed both of our wives."

"Impossible," said Trance.

"Is it? Why? Because you don't want to find out?"

"I can't stand the pain."

Neither can I, thought Tilson. *But we have to. We have to go on…* Tilson patted Trance's shoulder again. It felt like he was hitting casted bronze, the muscles rippled and as hard as a government building. "You just think about it, okay?"

Trance looked into Tilson's eyes. In those earnest, glassy little balls he saw a man much like himself, a man trapped by the responsibility he had chosen. His eyes had a deep, melancholy sadness that Trance could feel resting heavily within his own gut.

"I'll think about it, Jock."

"Think about how else you might serve your country, in my administration."

Trance tilted his head, looking almost sideways. "Can I ask you a question?"

Tilson nodded.

"When have we done enough?"

"When we're dead, Trance. Then we can rest as long as we like."

That was the problem, waiting for death, like it was a fine desert after a good, long meal. *Oh, were it only that easy*, thought Trance.

***

When Tilson and Trance emerged from their meeting, Lauren was standing beside a huge, rectangular birthday cake. It was decorated like a flag with candles making stars. She lit the thirty-six candles and said, "Make a wish."

Trance closed his eyes. What did he want above all else, he wondered? With his eyelids pressed tightly together and his jaw clenching like a tightened vice, Trance wished, *Today, I wish for your happiness, Lauren Haverford. That is my wish.*

Trance blew out the candles with a single blow. One of the candles flickered and then flashed back to life. Trance blew it out again and it flamed once more. Trance looked at Lauren and saw her grin. He grinned back. "Funny." Trance wet his index finger and thumb and snuffed out the wick with an audible *hiss*.

"Thank you, Lauren," whispered Trance. "Remind me to deal with you later."

"Wait 'til you see what else I've got planned."

***

Later, Trance and Lauren emerged from the dilapidated set of buildings that camouflaged one of the government's most secret anti-terrorist facilities. Trance had entered the building alone. Lauren had driven with Tilson from the airport. Now they were heading back toward Lauren's parents' home together. Trance maneuvered his Rover back onto Route 3A.

"How about The Bay Club for dinner?"

"Going to eat some raw oysters to get ready for your birthday present?"

Trance shook his head and smiled as he looked at Lauren. "How did you arrange all that?"

Lauren shrugged. "It was easy, and I needed something to do."

"However did you get Tilson to fly here?"

"Simple. He wanted to see you."

Trance's eyes flicked toward Lauren, and then back to the road as he negotiated a sweeping round rotary. They drove off the rotary onto a bridge that looked like it had been built from a massive toy erector set. The bridge's driving surface was constructed with angled steel beams that were anything but smoothly sealed. The car *thumped thumped* its way south, bouncing up and down along the bridge's series of girders.

"He wants to use me," said Trance.

"No," said Lauren. "He wants your help."

Trance drew a deep breath. He thought about how his father had raised him for this, taught him everything he would need to know so he could protect and serve. This was a burden he didn't want, not anymore. But no matter what he did—

As they neared the flattened apex of the narrow lift bridge, Trance felt something flash behind him. Bullets pinged off the Rover's bulletproof rear window. Trance looked in the mirror, just as a burst of machine gun fire erupted behind them.

"Head down, Lauren."

Trance jammed his foot on the accelerator and his car began to leap like a deer over the uneven bridge girders. The tires on the Rover squealed and thrummed with each gyration. Gunshots rang out again. Several pinged into the Range Rover's body, but it kept on racing forward, gathering too much speed. Trance saw a black Jeep Cherokee hop behind them. Two men were leaning outside the back side windows, while a third man had jammed his body up through an oversized moon roof. All three were firing AK-47s at Trance's car.

Trance opened up a sliver of space between the two vehicles, but that would be useless once they hit the traffic lights ahead. The Rover launched into the air as it sprung off the final upwardly angled girder. The car hung for several seconds, before pounding back to the flatter surface. Up ahead, Trance saw a line of cars stopped at a red traffic light beyond the bridge. He closed his eyes and swore. He couldn't lead killers into a crowd.

Trance reached below his seat and pulled a 45 caliber Glock from a custom car holster. This was a safe-action model with safeties that deactivated when its hair trigger was pulled.

"Hold on," said Trance as he neared the end of the bridge.

Trance's car launched into the air for one final time. As it bounded back onto the road, Trance hit the brakes and turned the wheel sharply to slide the car around. Then he gunned his engine. The car spun around and Trance aimed his pistol at the onrushing Jeep. He fired three quick shots. The Jeep swerved left and angled into a line of cement guard-rail blocks that were laid down like dominoes. The blocks tossed the Jeep high into the air. The car swung upward and to the left, rolling in the air like a paper plane. The car skipped against another car traveling in the opposite direction, roof against roof. Then it continued sliding across the road. The Jeep hurtled over the heavy stone fence that protected cars from the Fore River bank, which sloped steeply away from the road. The car began to roll, twisting over and over until it stopped, wheels down, on the edge of the river below.

Trance's car continued spinning. Its back wheels locked against the cement railing and it, too, went airborne. The wheels landed on the northbound side of the bridge, screeching to a stop, just as it met the oncoming bumper of a Toyota Prius. The cars barely kissed, but the Rover's bumper crumpled the front end of the Toyota until it looked like crunched up cardboard. When Trance saw that the woman driver was okay, he drove the Rover forward and stopped where the Jeep had jumped the side rail. He looked cautiously over the embankment. Far below, the Jeep's body had twisted into a large pile of rocks, as if it were molded clay.

There was a man standing outside the car, wobbling like a drunken frat pledge. There was blood flowing down his face. His left arm hung lifeless at his side. Trance raised his Glock and yelled, "U.S. Military. You are under arrest!"

The man laughed. His teeth were strikingly white against his unusually dark skin. The man aimed a gun into the passenger seat of his own car and pulled the trigger. Then he turned his gun upon himself. Before Trance could react, the final shot rang out, as the man blew a hole up under his chin and out the top of his head.

Trance leaned against the guardrail. He put his head in his hands and groaned. Lauren walked up beside him and pulled his head against her hip. Lauren's hand was fluttering like a tuning fork, while the rest of her body shook like a willow in a storm.

Her voice was trembling when she said, "Well, that was fun. You sure know how to impress a girl, Trance."

"Don't I?" Trance kept his face hidden. This was the worst of his fears come true. "See what I mean?"

"It's okay," whispered Lauren.

"But you see?"

"We're okay, Jack."

"No, we're not. This is why I can't marry you, Lauren. This is what happens to me…and to the people I love. This will happen to you. One day, it will happen to you."

"No, Jack. You *can* marry me. I like this stuff. I *live* for this stuff."

"No, Lauren. You *die* with this stuff."

"No…I…won't."

Trance shook his head. "I'm sorry, Lauren. I love you. I just can't take that chance."

CHAPTER **33**
PP

Tilson was standing by a window when his secretary led Trance into the Oval Office. He was holding back the heavy curtains with the back of his hand, staring through the thick glass out into the Rose Garden. Tilson didn't turn at first. Instead, he let his eyes wander across the subdued winter flowers, thinking how his life matched the drab contrast they made with the summer roses and tulips.

"Sir…General Trance to see you," said the president's body man.

Tilson turned around and looked at Trance. *He looks so ordinary*, he thought. Not tall. Not short. Not fat. Not thin. His face was nothing extraordinary, except maybe for that slight Oriental tinge of the eyes. Tilson looked at Trance's hands before shaking. *Those hands…those are extraordinary, like solid chunks of steel. And his body, it's like some finely tuned cyborg out of a Terminator movie…with those hard popping muscles hidden beneath that plain-looking persona and those plain, non-descript clothes. Then there is all that money. A fortune almost too big to fathom.* Tilson knew what Forbes said, in its annual list of 400, the billionaires club. But Tilson knew about other holdings, ones Trance had inherited from his uncle and his grandfather, ones even Forbes didn't know about, ones far outside view of the U.S. financial markets and regulations. *Yet, Trance acts like his money doesn't exist. He lives in that small Vermont home he built by hand and walks to work in that tiny, converted Cape house he calls an office.*

"Thank you for coming, Jack."

"Sure, Jock. Things have changed. Someone tried to take me out, again."

"Any idea who?"

"Talid's nephew was one of the shooters."

Tilson swore under his breath. Talid was already a source of frustration to his administration, just as he'd been for the two administrations before his. As a country's sovereign leader, no matter how brutally he had gotten there, Talid was untouchable, as long as he didn't start a war.

"Why would he want to kill you?"

Trance shrugged. "I had dealings with him a few months back. He was planning to kill Americans by selling tainted drugs, down in Miami. Would have been a lot of dead bodies. My team stopped him, then separated him from a hundred million dollars. All for charity, of course."

"I take it Talid wasn't feeling charitable?"

Trance shook his head. "It's more about pride than money, Jock. We've taken out a lot of his men over the years. But this…this latest attempt…Somehow, I suspect this is connected to your wife's death."

Tilson noticed a subtle, but obvious shift in Trance's demeanor. He was with him now. They were on the same team.

"You want to help?"

"I do."

"Cramm and Doheny will be here shortly. I'll have them bring you up to speed."

"I'd prefer to bring in my own people, Jock. If that's okay with you. I'll even pay them myself."

"I can't authorize that, Jack."

"I know, sir."

The two men locked eyes. Trance could do as he wished. He'd form a parallel team on his own, outside the law, while the president maintained plausible deniability for all his actions.

The president's intercom buzzed. "Agents Cramm and Doheny, Mr. President," said his assistant.

Cramm and Doheny entered the room like wary tigers, circling slowly around the office like they were afraid Trance would steal their food. Neither man offered to shake Trance's hand. Tilson laughed; he didn't blame them. What man willingly puts his hands in a tightening nutcracker?

The president's intercom buzzed again, "Jacob Miller, Mr. President."

Jacob Miller walked into the room and saluted Trance. "General."

Trance grinned and stuck out his hand. Miller grabbed it hesitantly and tried not to wince as Trance gripped on it like a Saint Bernard puppy who doesn't realize how big he is.

"Haven't seen you in a while, Jake. Cut the 'general' crap, okay? I hear congratulations are in order. Congress is going to confirm you as head of the Company?"

Miller smiled grimly. "I tried to turn the president down on the CIA. Too administrative for this ol' dog. But he convinced me; he's a persuasive man. Thank you for your recommendation, by the way. It's worth more than you can imagine."

Trance snuck an accusing glance at Tilson. "I tried to say something bad about you, Jake. I really did. But I had to do what was right for the country. So, try as I might, the bad stuff wouldn't come out. I'm glad you took the gig. Your country needs you and we'll all sleep a little better at night."

Tilson's intercom buzzed once more. "Your national security advisor, the secretary of state and the defense secretary are here, Mr. President."

"Send them in."

Trance knew each of these advisors personally, so there were no introductions made. Tilson motioned for them all to follow him to the Roosevelt Room, where the conference table had been prepared for the meeting. When they reached the room the president motioned for the group to sit, while putting Trance at the head of the table.

Tilson said, "General Trance has agreed to join our anti-terrorist team. He has also agreed to help find Kiki's killers."

What have I done? thought Trance. Tilson now had him on an anti-terrorist *team?* This was not the plan. He wanted *his* team.

"Let me clarify what Jock means," said Trance. His use of the president's first name was lost on no one. Trance smiled to himself as he watched the eyebrows rise around the table. "I will be working independently, with my own people, to help find Kiki's killers and determine if there is, indeed, a current terrorist threat to the nation." Trance turned to the president. "Isn't that about right, Jock?"

Tilson's eyes showed surprise and then anger. For a brief instant, he almost rose to Trance's taunt. Then he laughed. "My God, Trance. You are one stupid, complicated bastard."

The men at the table nodded. They had all seen Trance work, yet none of them knew what made him tick.

Trance leaned forward and looked at the group. "Tell me what you've got."

Doheny pressed his elbows against the table. He jutted his chin forward like he was waiting for a punch. "We believe that the killer was a woman going by the name of Sandra Smith. She vanished on the night of the murder."

"You sure she wasn't just an innocent witness? Has she been found?"

"No. But the man who referred her to the Brits *has* turned up, dead."

"Was *he* anywhere near the Embassy on the night of the murder?"

"No. He was in Australia. That's confirmed, without doubt. He died in Costa Rica."

"That's not helpful," muttered Trance.

"Nothing about this case is easy, general. We combed Smith's place and found nothing."

Trance frowned. "Nothing? Not a hair, a partial print, no drop of spit or a splash of urine?"

"Nada. The neighbors say they never saw her."

Typical, thought Trance. "Murder weapon?"

Poison. We found botulism and hemlock. We think they're red herrings. We found traces of what we believe to be some new synthetic neurotoxins. Exotic mojo no one has seen before."

"And?"

"That's it."

Trance stared at Cramm and Doheny. He looked to the president's other advisors. None of them wanted to meet his eyes or say a word.

"That's all you've got? What about satellite images?"

"Bad weather."

"Bank records? Dry cleaners? Restaurants? Grocery stores? Anyone else ever seen with her?"

"We've sifted through thousands of hours of video. We've picked her up in a couple places. She's always alone. No bank account. No credit cards. No car. No insurance. No movie rentals. No phone. No nothing. The woman did not exist."

"You've got video from the Embassy. No match on her face, anywhere?"

"We've had a few thousand possibles on the facial databases, but nothing's panned out."

"No fingerprints? No skin? Hair?"

"Everything wiped clean. The woman's a ghost."

"No travel records?"

"I told you. Nothing. N-O-T-H-I-N-G."

"That is simply not possible. You're not digging deep enough."

"Go fuck yourself, Trance," said Doheny.

"You didn't mean that," said Miller. "Believe me, Doheny. You did not mean that."

"Yeah, I did. He thinks he can waltz in here and find something we missed? I've got the best people in the *world* working on this. I've got profilers, forensics, chemists, biochemists, psychics, physicists…Hell, I've even got people from Social Security and the IRS burning time looking around the planet for this woman."

"Sure she's a woman?" asked Trance.

"The Embassy chef swears that, underneath her disguise, the woman was hot. We can't see it. He swears he could get a hard-on just looking at her."

"All right," said Trance. "I won't intrude on anything you've done. I think I'll backtrack on a few things, though, to see what I find."

Doheny shrugged his shoulders. "Knock yourself out."

Trance stood. He smiled and seemed to soften. "Well, Jock. Doesn't look like we've got much to go on. There's usually a loose end somewhere." Trance turned to Doheny. "Please have your people copy me on everything you've got. I mean everything, no matter how insignificant. Keep me up on all you find. Here's my condition, and this is the only way I'll work." Trance looked at Tilson. "You will share *everything* with me. If I learn something that *I* don't want to share, I will keep it from you. Not because I am trying to sabotage the investigation or show you up, but because I don't trust how you, or your people, will react. I will work with you, but I will also conduct a parallel investigation that may be outside your purview."

Doheny began to protest but Tilson interrupted him.

"Fine, Jack. Just solve the case and bring me justice."

"If it makes you feel better, Doheny," said Miller. "Trance has no use for glory; never seeks it. He hates it, in fact. He came here kicking and screaming. So, if he solves this thing, he'll be happy to give you all the kudos."

"That's not—"

"I don't care. Just get it done," interrupted Tilson. "Now, stop wasting time and get working."

CHAPTER 34

_______________PP_______________

Trance pulled his dented Range Rover to the side of the road half a mile away from his home. He plugged an encrypted laptop computer into a connection in his car and accessed his home security system via an NSA satellite uplink. With this system, Trance had a record of any and all activity on the grounds of his home, including that of any small animals. He had video feed of every room, as well as heat and weight sensing data for the home and the grounds. His computer processed this data constantly, and was programmed to alert him at the first sign of danger. He'd had no warnings.

Lauren Haverford pulled beside Trance in her BMW X6 Hybrid and waited, while Trance made an inventory of the home and the grounds. They spoke on the phone as Trance ran through his elaborate set of commands. After ten long minutes, Trance closed the computer and headed on toward the house.

"You really think you want to live like this?" said Trance.

"I thought your computers did this for you. You always this way?"

"Someone did attempt to kill us, Lauren. You think they'll stop at one try?"

"Why don't you just hire security?"

"I don't know. Privacy, I guess."

"You can't walk through your house without a camera picking up every move."

"I can turn off any camera I want."

"That's good. I'll remind you when it's time."

Trance was laughing as he pulled into his underground garage. Lauren parked beside him. Trance made one more cursory check of security before they exited their cars.

Inside, Trance grabbed a couple of Vitamin Waters from the fridge and handed one to Lauren. He plugged his PDA into a charger, kissed Lauren on the cheek and said, "I'll need about ten minutes. Then I'll turn off any monitors you wish."

"Promise?"

Trance kissed her again and walked to a cabinet built into the wall of his study. He pressed his palm against a scanner, punched a number code onto a keypad and a door to the cabinet opened. Trance then turned the tumblers on a wall safe and pulled out a phone.

"A bit elaborate, don't you think?" said Lauren.

"Makes me feel like Bond…James Bond."

Trance dialed a number and let it ring on speaker for five full minutes. He turned to Lauren and said, "Stick still won't use voicemail. This could ring for days."

Granger finally answered the phone by saying, "This better be good."

"Hello, Pirate."

"Hey, JT."

"Lauren's here, too."

"Hey, babe. You keeping our man happy?"

"When he lets me."

"When you going to marry her, Trance?"

A pained look crossed Trance's face. He said nothing. Instead, he said, "You heard about the first lady?"

"Only that she died."

"She was murdered."

"That sucks."

"Yesterday, two men tried to terminate Lauren and me. Then they killed themselves."

"You okay?"

"Yeah, but the Range Rover got a boo boo."

"What can I do?"

"I've agreed to help Tilson with this."

"Not again, Jack."

"Yes, again."

"It's summertime down here. I hope you're not asking me to fly somewhere."

"I wired some gas money this morning."

"Ah, Jack. I thought we retired. Didn't you send an email to all the bad guys telling them to shoot at someone else?"

"I think it's Talid."

"Not good, Jack."

"Tell me."

"You think he killed Tilson's wife?"

"Don't know yet."

"But you want my help?"

"No moss on your brain."

Stick sighed and whispered, "Honey, you're going to have to get off of me now. Jack wants me to fly to America."

Trance laughed, sure that Stick was goofing on them, until he heard Stick's wife say, "Hi, Jack."

"Hey, Marlee. You keeping my boy happy?"

"I was until you interrupted my grand finale."

"Knowing Stick, you'd be done by now anyway. How about if you and Junior join him? I'll put you up anywhere you want. What do you say?"

Lauren punched Trance's shoulder to get his attention. "Tell her she can stay with me," she said.

"Lauren says you can stay with her."

Trance heard murmuring on the phone. A moment later Stick said, "She says I'll have to let her go shopping."

"Can you afford that, Stick?"

Trance heard Stick say, "Honey, you're not going to buy a Mercedes or something, are you?" He came back on the phone and said, "She says she wants to shop at some woman's store. You ever heard of a place called Tiffany's?"

"Just get your ass here. I'll buy her whatever she wants."

"That's an A okay, ol' buddy. Later."

Trance dialed a second number. This time he reached Trancelike Effects, a four-hundred-employee subsidiary of a company called Trance Entertainment. Trancelike specialized in exotic special effects and computer generated graphics for the film industry.

"This is Jack. Could you find Jaxon Krautheim for me, please?"

A minute later a voice came on the phone, "This is the Jazzman. What can I do you for, boss?"

"Hey, Jazz. I emailed you a couple photos of a woman. We think she might have disguised herself. Could you give me some renderings of what she might really look like?"

"Sure, Jack. This urgent?"

"Yeah."

"Give me sixty. Back at ya."

Trance hung up the phone and looked at Lauren. "We've got an hour before Jaxon calls back. You have any suggestions on how we might use the time?"

Lauren put down her water bottle and walked over to Trance. She put her arms around his neck and said, "I think you and I might be able to think of something." She moved her hand along Trance's thigh. "Why don't we retire to the bedroom, turn off the monitors and see what you can come up with."

"That sounds like a plan to me."

Sixty minutes later Krautheim called back. Trance put him on speaker.

"Jazzman, here. I just shot off a dozen images of what your woman might look like underneath that disguise."

"Hold on," said Trance. He opened a notebook computer on his bedside table, accessed a secure website and scrolled through twelve photos of the would-be killer.

"I don't think she looks like a Wookie, Jazzman." Trance angled the computer screen so Lauren could see Sandra Smith depicted as the character from Star Wars. "Nor do I think she resembles Pee Wee Herman...or Jack Black naked."

Trance scrolled through the rest of the photos and said, "Very good, Jaxon. We might just have something here."

"She could be one hell of a looker, Jack."

"Or one ugly animal."

"I'd bet on the looker. You ever hear of something called Phi?"

"Fee what?"

"It's an artistic term, a kind of explanation for the perfect order of nature."

"You're losing me here, Jazzman."

"What I'm saying is...this woman has a perfect face. We'll get hits on models around the world when we run it through the system. Guys are going to have trouble concentrating. Be a hell of a lot easier if she was a Wookie."

"Thanks, Jazz. I owe you one."

"Remember this at bonus time."

"I already pay you far more than you're worth, Jaxon."

The Jazzman cackled like a witch and hung up the phone.

"He always like that?" said Lauren.

"The man's a genius."

"You going to invite him to film our wedding?"

Trance laughed. "Golly, you're persistent...Let's just keep you safe."

Lauren kissed Trance on the cheek. "I'll get you yet. In some moment of weakness, I'll get you yet."

CHAPTER 35
PP

Sammantha Starodubov looked like a small bug as she stood beside a monstrous wall. The wall was three hundred feet wide and twenty-five feet high. It was constructed with shiny steel girders spaced eight feet apart. Between the girders, tall glass panels opened up to a vast cavern that looked like a moonscape. The area was the size of five football fields and it stretched more than eight stories from top to bottom. There were three similar viewing platforms, each about thirty feet higher than the other. A series of catwalks stretched out from the viewing area, giving full visual access to the entire region.

Hundreds of men were manning bulldozers and cranes, moving immense amounts of dirt onto a moving track that stretched upward toward the surface. Exhaust ports from each machine were attached to long, gray hoses. Each hose was hung by heavy wires from a superstructure built into the ceiling. They all ran to a large yellow machine that rested on a platform built high above them. This, Sammantha knew, flushed the exhaust, through well-spaced outlets, into the atmosphere. The exhaust was replaced with cool blasts of fresh, clean Maine air.

On the far right side of the cavern, slightly lower than the viewing deck, a lighted area drew Sammantha's attention like a beacon. There were many rooms being built, each in a different stage of completion. Some were fully furnished, while others were still empty shells. Every room would be visible from one of the four viewing levels.

The whole area was like a huge Hollywood movie lot, with dozens of sound stages and hundreds of sets built for shooting the scenes of an epic or even multiple films. This was not a movie lot; it was more like a series of Broadway stages, where actors would ply their trade, acting out every probable situation that might befall the American president. These were the theaters where the country's future president would learn and perfect his roles.

"That…" said a man standing beside Sammantha. He pointed toward a lighted room to her right. "…is the Oval Office. It is an exact replica." Inside the yellow office they could see Brandon Copley dressed in a blue striped business suit. He was parting the window drapes with the back of his hand, while staring out at the lighted rose garden.

Sammantha turned to the engineer standing beside her. He was new and she couldn't place him. She made it a point to know everyone. "What's your name?"

"Martin Warvla."

"Oh, yes. Martin, are those real roses?"

Warvla laughed. "No. Just a good illusion. Some of our sets seem more realistic than the originals."

Sammantha turned around and motioned toward a young man who was standing about ten feet behind her. "Come on," she said. "Don't be shy. Your father and Talid helped fund all this."

Omar Karkhabi stepped forward and gaped at the expanse. "My God," he whispered. "All this…underground?"

"This is an important undertaking…"

"Of which I have no knowledge. Talid said I was to help you. What do I do?"

Sammantha smiled slyly. "You know the old saying, 'If I told you, I would have to kill you?'"

Karkhabi closed his eyes. After a moment, he slowly nodded his head. Of course he did. He'd seen it done.

"The less you know, the better. You were sent here above my protests. You know that, don't you?"

"I mean you no harm, Ms. Starodubov."

He is just a boy, thought Sammantha. *He wants nothing of this. Yet, Talid has sent him to spy and then die.* Sammantha put an arm around the thin young man, turned him around and nudged him toward the exit. "Why don't you go swim in the pool or something? Maybe catch a movie in the theater. It's going to be months before I need your services."

Sammantha looked back toward the Oval Office. Two men had just entered from the main office door. They were actors, very good actors who had been hired to play their assigned roles. Copley strode confidently toward them.

Sammantha could hear shuffling through a set of speakers above her head. Then she heard Copley say, "Hello, gentlemen. Good to see you again."

Ivan emerged from an elevator at the far end of the platform. He strode toward Sammantha and stopped at her shoulder. "Good, no? The one on the right is Boxer Henning, Secretary of Defense. The big one on the left is National Security Advisor, Jeremiah Pincenogle. Garrett Sloan should be with them any moment. Then Jacob Miller."

"How will our president know what they've discussed in prior meetings?" asked Sammantha.

"We've had psychologists analyze hundreds of men and women around the president. We've reviewed thousands upon thousands of pages of transcripts from old meetings, listened to tapes and watched videos. We've even been able to eavesdrop on conversations with planted bugs, directional microphones, internal spies and phone taps. You'd be amazed at how much is said over non-secure lines. Even the president's Sectéra Edge PDA isn't secure from everyone, especially those of us with resources."

Sammantha bit her bottom lip and looked out beyond the glass. She saw herself touch Copley's hair and caress his face. Her memories were as strong as…as strong as some of the dark ones that still clung to her like barnacles. "He looks good, doesn't he?"

"The man is a machine. He works twenty hours a day. He has a word-trap mind and an uncanny flare for faces and figures. You couldn't have chosen a better subject."

"Yes," said Sammantha. "What about his old memories?"

Ivan took a measured breath and exhaled slowly. He shrugged his shoulders and peered at Copley through the glass. "Who's to say? We are using everything—implants, hypnosis, electrical brain stimulation, hallucinogens, non-stop movies, subliminal tapes and viral injections. We've made films of every major event in Tilson's life. His wedding, graduation, college, sports—"

"Brandon told me that he struck out Tilson for the Ivy League championship, in baseball."

"He won't remember that, I'm afraid. He's going to remember *losing* the game, not winning it. Every memory in his mind will be one of Tilson's. He won't remember *anything* of *his* past."

Sammantha touched her cheek and whispered, "He'll remember me."

Ivan laughed. "You were the first thing we erased."

Sammantha stared at Ivan and then slapped him across the face. "You had no right."

Ivan fingered his reddened cheek. His eyes widened briefly, but then settled back into something more like fatherly compassion. "You said you wanted this to work."

"But…"

Ivan gently patted Sammantha's shoulder. Then he grasped it firmly. He turned Sammantha toward him, holding both her shoulders at arm's length. "Don't worry, my angel. He will fall in love with you again."

"And if he doesn't?"

"Oh, but he will. He will crave you more than he ever has. How could he not?"

CHAPTER **36**
_______________PP_______________

Jack Trance stood on the sidewalk. He gazed across the street to the crumbling tenement building that Sandra Smith had once called home. Stick Granger, Budd Doheny and Steve Cramm waited beside him. Trance didn't move. He just stared at the building, as if listening to a lover's whisper, hearing and feeling what went on inside.

Doheny said, "You'll find nothing here, Trance. We've had three separate teams process the place. It's clean. Totally clean."

Trance slowly took his eyes off the building and looked at Stick. "What do you think?"

"Bet they didn't use the *I Ching*." Granger turned to Doheny and Cramm. "You use the *I Ching?*"

"What the hell is an Eee Ching?" said Doheny.

Granger shook his head. "Bet you didn't put your ear to the floor and the walls either, did you?"

Doheny and Cramm looked at each other and held out their hands, as if to say, *What the hell...*

"What kind of shoes did you offer them?" said Trance.

Doheny said, "Shoes? What do you mean, shoes?"

"And you guys are supposed to be good?" said Stick.

Trance said, "Go get the shoes, Stick. Let's see what we find."

Stick Granger walked to Trance's Range Rover, which was parked illegally on the curb. He made sure that Trance's White House decal was showing in the window, before popping open the back hatch and pulling out a massive white mesh bag that was filled with basketball shoes. He hefted the bag onto his shoulder and hauled it back to the men.

"C'mon," said Trance. "Let's go in."

Trance led the men across the street. They walked up the three flights of stairs to the apartment where Sandra Smith had lived. Smith's door was covered with yellow crime scene tape. Trance sliced it with the blade of a Swiss Army knife and pushed the door open.

Stick peeled from the group and began knocking on doors, yelling, "I've got shoes! Nike shoes, right from the factory! Free shoes here! Who wants to be a basketball star?" Seconds later he was surrounded by a mass of children and young adults. They emerged from the walls like seagulls, coming out of nowhere to snag tossed bread.

Trance walked into the apartment and frowned at the smell. The place was clean but it smelled faintly of rat piss. Trance ran his hand along the walls, feeling for something. He read the scrawling and wondered what it must be like to live in a world like this. *Free Mandela* he read. Mandela got free, all right. Decades ago. One wish granted. Obama? Everyone knew that story. He wondered if *Gina* was still alive and if Bobby and Carmen were still together.

Trance put his ear to the walls and to the floor. He listened for that little voice inside him, the one that said, *she was here*. Doheny and Cramm watched Trance with a mixture of disdain, awe and curiosity. He was acting like no detective they had ever met. He wasn't examining things as much as he seemed to *become* them. For two hours, Trance merged with the floor and the walls. He held his hand against the small cast iron stove and heard the words *Burn Baby Burn.*

"She was here, all right. I can still feel her anger. Serious anger."

Trance stood in front of the cracked and faded mirror, the same one that had caught the broken reflection of Sammantha Starodubov. He could almost see her in the shards. He could definitely *feel* her spirit in the room.

He went to the area that would have been used as the kitchen and examined the cupboards. He ran his hands along the outside edges, feeling for remnants of Sandra. He closed his eyes and let himself drift into meditation. Trance willed his mind to merge with that of Kiki's killer, to see what she saw and feel what she felt.

She had poison. Where would she have kept it? He looked inside the low cupboards again.

"Bingo."

Trance pointed toward the bear and rat traps sitting on the floor inside the cupboard.

"You dust these for prints?"

"Yeah. Nada. We put 'em back where we found 'em."

Trance closed his eyes. He reached his hand inside the cupboard and slowly removed the largest trap. His arm began to scrape against the cupboard's edge.

"Give me a light," he said.

Doheny handed Trance a small flashlight. Trance shined it all around the inside of the space. Even though everything had been moved and replaced, there was already a thin layer of new dust forming on the bottom. Trance stuck his head inside and looked all around. Then he saw it.

Trance crawled out of the cupboard and reached for his army knife. He removed the metal tweezers from the knife's edge and stuck his head back inside. A few moments later he came back out again. He held the tweezers in front of his face and said, "These might be epithelials. You never know."

The tweezers appeared to hold a tiny spec of dried skin, with a darkened swatch of what could have been blood, all barely visible to the eye. Trance placed the skin into a fold of a Post It note and stuck it together. He put the paper into a plastic bag and zipped it shut. He pulled his PDA out of its case and punched the push-to-talk button. "What you got, Stick?"

"I've got a recliner chair. Three doors down the hall on the left."

Trance looked at Doheny and Cramm. He raised his eyebrows up and down, like Tom Selleck in the old Magnum PI. "Let's go see what we've got, boys."

Stick was waiting by the door. Inside the apartment they found a weary-looking mother. No more than twenty-five, she had six children inside, ranging from around ten years old to a baby on her hip. Every one of the kids now wore a new pair of basketball shoes. Stick held a photo of Sandra Smith in front of the woman's face.

"You say this is her?"

The woman nodded. "Uh-huh."

"And you say she left this chair?"

"Yes, sir. We didn't steal nothin'. She left the door wide open. We knew she was gone."

"We're not here to arrest you, miss," said Trance. "What is your name?"

"Angela."

"Angela, are you sure this was hers?"

"Yeah."

Trance saw the sharp springs poking though the seat of the chair. It was worth a shot. He pulled a money clip out of his pocket and peeled off five one hundred dollar bills.

"I'd like to buy this from you. Is five hundred dollars okay?"

"There's no drugs inside, mister. If that's what you're looking for."

Trance smiled. "The woman wasn't a drug dealer, Angela. But she may have committed a crime. We're trying to find out who she is. This might help."

Angela took the money and Trance took the chair.

When they were outside, Doheny said, "I'm sorry, Trance."

"For what?"

"I doubted you."

"No harm, Budd. I doubt myself sometimes. Let's go see what we've got."

When they got outside, Stick pulled Trance aside and whispered in his ear. "Angela also told us what Sandra really looks like. I showed her all of Jazzman's photos and she said that one is a dead ringer. Says she saw her like that, just one time, when Smith opened the door for a visitor."

"Not the Wookie, I hope."

"Nah, Pee Wee Herman."

"Of course. Why didn't I see it?"

"We now know who we're looking for."

"A guy wearing makeup and whacky clothes?"

Stick flashed Trance one of the pictures. "Her."

Trance smiled. "That's a start, Pirate."

Stick and Trance caught up with Doheny and Cramm on the street.

"Something you want to share, Trance?"

"Nah. We were just making dinner plans. You didn't know that Stick and I were an item?"

Doheny and Cramm grabbed the chair and began to walk it across the street to Trance's Range Rover. Trance grasped Doheny by the shoulder. "Hold it." He pulled out his modified Sectéra PDA. "Let's make sure no one's tampered with my car."

Trance's thumbs worked quickly as he accessed his car's sophisticated computer. "Dang it." Trance looked at Doheny and Cramm. "You guys toss my car while we were inside?"

Both men shook their heads.

Trance said, "Let me go first."

Trance began to walk across the street, alone. When he was halfway across he looked back and said, "Don't just stand there. Fan out and catch me a bad guy."

Trance inched cautiously toward his car. He prayed silently; he asked God that today not be his day to die. Trance was worried about a bomb, one that could be detonated from a remote location, by some unseen terrorist who didn't have the guts to show his face. Why did this always happen to him, right when he thought it was over? Why was it that he couldn't say *no* when they came calling? Why did he always have to slap a big red bull's eye on his forehead and say, "Come get me?" Hell, it had been little more than a month since he'd been kidnapped and forced to endure things no man should ever know. He ran his fingers across the arm of his coat. He could almost feel the aching, pulsing need in his veins, begging for another fix and a trip to oblivion's living room.

Trance called Stick Granger with his phone. "What you got, Beta?"

"It's *Alpha* to you, boy."

"I think *Little Man* suits you better. Or maybe *Mini Man*. What you got, Mini Man?"

Trance smiled as Stick didn't reply. He stepped back to the curb, waiting for some response. Then he heard someone yell, "Damn. There they go!" Trance heard the sound of footsteps and heavy breathing coming through his PDA. "They just drove off in a car," Stick said, between huffing breaths.

"And you're *running* after them, Mini Man? Don't you need wheels to catch a car? You know you're slower than Tom Brady."

"Funny…Beta."

Trance chuckled. "It's Alpha to you. Over."

Trance walked to his Range Rover. He dropped to the ground and looked up into the chassis until he found it. When Trance slid out from underneath the car, he was holding a block of Semtex by its edges. An explosive cap dangled from the end like a deadly snake.

"Look what I found," he said.

Trance pulled the wires out of the plastic bomb, making sure not to disturb any latent fingerprints. He handed both pieces to Doheny. "See if you can learn where this came from." Doheny took both pieces, being careful to touch just the places where Trance had held them.

Trance turned to Stick. "You get a good look at them?"

Stick didn't speak. He just stood there, looking at Trance, with a humorous twinkle in his eye.

"Well?" said Trance

"I don't want to be Mini Man."

"Oh, you're definitely Mini Man."

Stick turned to Doheny and Cramm. "You think I look like a Mini Man?"

Stick stretched to his full six-foot-four inch height and loomed over the two government agents.

"Don't I look more like an Alpha to you? You wouldn't call me Mini Man, would you?"

Doheny shook his head slowly. Cramm did the same.

Trance got into his car and said, "Come along, children. Throw the chair in the back of this thing and let's get going. We've got work to do."

CHAPTER **37**
_____________PP_____________

Stick Granger wound Trance's Porsche 959 up to 6,000 RPM before shifting gears. The engine whined and the wheels screeched as Stick slung the car along the road leading deeper into the woods. He took every corner at stomach twisting speed, punching the accelerator just enough to keep from sliding off the road.

"I don't think you're going to make it," said Trance. He looked to his watch and then back to the road. "Why don't you slow down?"

Stick pushed down on the accelerator and the car went airborne, as they crested over a minor bump in the road. The car landed with a jarring, scratching _clang_, before it scampered on its way.

"That's my car you're driving, you know," said Trance.

"You don't think I'd drive my own car like this, do you?"

A guard post came into sight. There was heavy metal gate beside it blocking the road. Stick floored the accelerator for a final sprint. Two uniformed guards walked out into the middle of the road and raised automatic weapons to their chests. Then, just before crashing into the gate and drawing a fusillade of fire, Stick jammed on the car's brakes. The Porsche came to a loud, earsplitting, wailing halt, with its front bumper barely kissing the fabric on one of the guard's pants.

Trance pressed the timer button on his watch and said, "Damn it, Granger."

"I did it, didn't I?"

Trance pulled a dollar bill off his money clip and handed it to Stick. In front of them, one of the two guards did the same with a twenty.

Trance rolled down his window and a guard poked his head inside. Trance said, "Jack Trance and Stupid Granger here to see the president."

The guard looked beyond Trance and said to Stick, "Nice driving, Pirate."

Stick turned to the guard. "I saw him give you twenty bucks. What'd you bet?"

"That the car would touch my pants before you stopped it. Got twenty to one odds on a Washington."

"God, you're a dumb ass, Perkins."

The guard smiled. "Yeah, I guess so. Just got to feel the rush."

"Sucks, don't it? All this peace and quiet."

The guard patted the car and said, "Hazard of the job."

Perkins pulled a radio receiver off his belt and said, "General Trance and Major Granger here to see Wonder Dog."

"Send 'em in."

Trance and Stick exchanged glances. Trance stuck his head out the window. "Wonder Dog? You call him Wonder Dog?"

"Nah. We call him Centurion, but I like Wonder Dog. Has a nice ring to it, don't ya think?"

"I thought you guys always use POTUS for the president?"

"Tilson didn't like it; said it sounded like a disease. He demanded a new name. We gave him two."

Stick Granger kept the car to a slow, rumbling crawl as they passed through Camp David.

Jock Tilson met them in the street and motioned them to a wooded parking space. "Put her in there, boys. Don't forget to lock up."

Stick smiled. "You have politicians on-site who might steal our things, Mr. President?"

The three men jumped into an ATV that was fitted with a set of studded snow tires. Tilson angled it up a hilly, rutted icy path.

"Glad you could make it," Tilson said. "I was getting stir crazy out here alone. They tell me it's been unusually cold for Camp David. But, being an old downeaster, this feels like fall to me. What do you guys feel like doing?"

Stick said, "I suppose tanning and scuba diving are out of the question?"

Tilson smiled. There was a hint of laughter in his eyes, a tiny glowing ember of joy that one day, with care, might actually burn again.

"Don't mind him," said Trance. "He's baked his brain cells dry in the tropics."

Tilson said, "I thought we might take a little ski, maybe shoot some trap and skeet. After busting up some targets, we'll get down to business. Work for you?"

"Have you got a Ski-Doo around here?" said Stick. "I'll break your trail."

Trance chuckled. "Stick's not too good on his feet, Jock. Put him under water or in the air and he's Mozart. Put him on his feet and he's…well…he's Stick Granger."

Stick cuffed Trance and said, "I can whip your ass at skeet."

"Not after a 10k ski, you won't."

Stick sighed, "Got a point, JT."

Tilson stopped the ATV beside a rustic wooden building and said, "You guys want to change up?"

"Sure," said Trance. "But first, let me give you this."

Trance reached into a knapsack he had brought with him from the cab. He withdrew a slab of fresh bacon that was wrapped into a tight wad of wax paper. Then he pulled out a white bag that read *Radler* on the side. "I've got a tin of Johnson's popcorn from Ocean City, New Jersey in the car, Jock. Best stuff for long meetings."

"Awfully nice of you to remember."

"Lauren reminded me."

"Ah…Lauren. I suppose she still wants that banking job?"

"Only if she deserves it."

"How about Treasury Secretary? Turns out my first two choices have tax problems."

"Good news, Jock. Lauren does her own cleaning and she doesn't have a nanny. You want me to have her call you?"

"Please do." Tilson began driving away and yelled, "Back in ten with the gear!"

***

When the men finished shooting, Stick handed Trance back his dollar, saying, "Can't beat two hundred straight."

"No wind, today," said Trance.

"Yeah. That's what you always say."

Tilson said, "He always shoot like that?"

Stick replied, "Nah, I saw him miss once."

Trance laughed. "When you goosed me."

Tilson led the men into the large living room inside the *Laurel* lodge. There was a huge fire searing the air on one side of the room, burning a stack of four foot logs. Resting on the mantelpiece was a picture of Tilson and his late wife, arms around each other, grinning at the camera like teenagers at a carnival.

Stick pointed toward the fire. "I see that you're the cause of Global Warming."

Tilson grinned. "I buy carbon offsets from Al Gore. Don't you guys know that wood saves on oil?" Tilson reached into a cabinet, pulled down a tray of glasses and set it on a round oak table. "What can I do you for?"

"I'll have a beer," said Stick.

Tilson turned to Trance. Trance shook his head.

Tilson frowned. "This is social, Jack, not business."

"You have any scotch?"

"Dewar's, Chivas and Johnnie Walker."

"Johnnie Red, Black or Blue?"

"Black."

"Black's fine. On the rocks, please."

After a moment Trance said, "You know, Jock, if you are going to be entertaining world leaders in this place, you really should have some decent scotch."

Trance grabbed his PDA and dialed his office in Vermont.

"You're lucky I came in today, Jack," Judy said. "I was going to play hooky and go ski."

"Hello to you, too," said Trance, smiling.

"Where are you?"

"Camp David."

"Last week, St. Croix. Yesterday, New York. Today, the president. You see why I can't leave this place?"

"Are you going to complain about all your free time, or are you going to ask me what I need?"

"Shoot."

"Very funny." Trance looked at Tilson. "Our president has no decent Scotch at Camp David. Would you please send him a couple bottles of Johnnie Blue and a few bottles of Macallan?"

"What year?"

Trance smiled at Tilson. "Send him the fifty. He might need it for something important some day."

"Anything else?"

"You are now done for the day, Judy. Go ski."

"Already dressed. Was only waiting for your call."

When Trance hung up his phone, Tilson said, "Am I supposed to know what this means?"

A playful smile creased Trance's face. "I'm sending you some fine blended scotch and a few bottles of fifty-year-old single malt. I suggest you save the single malt for special occasions."

"Do you happen to know what the Russian president likes to drink?"

"Ogarkov?" said Trance. "I've seen him drink Macallan and cheap vodka with equal vigor. He likes to complain about the sediment in the Macallan, just for fun. I suggest you let him have his joke. It makes him laugh."

"Sediment? In a bottle of scotch?"

"Only in the best ones, Jock."

"Learn something new every day." Tilson frowned and looked questioningly at Trance. "You know Ogarkov?"

"Sure." Trance left it at that, and so did Tilson.

Tilson took a St. Pauli Girl out of a refrigerator and handed it to Stick. Then he grabbed an ice tray from the freezer and emptied it into two squat rocks glasses. He poured them nearly full with scotch.

"We need doubles for this, Jack."

Trance looked at Tilson. He saw a kind of dark mourning drift across his face, like a stray cloud on a brilliantly sunny day. It was the look a man gets when he's beaten down, when he sure that life has passed him by, when the brass ring has always remained just beyond his grasp and it's now dropped away for good.

"It hurts something awful, doesn't it Jock?"

Tilson closed his eyes and dropped his chin into his chest. "It feels…like all the air has been sucked out of me… each and every breath is a struggle. I keep telling myself *one more minute* which turns into *one more hour* then *one more day*. That's how I get through it all, Jack, one breath at a time."

Tilson took a swallow of his drink. Trance did the same. Stick sat away from them, staring at the fire. One ear listened for them to call has name, while the other tried to block out what they said.

"It all seems pointless, now," said Tilson.

"I hear you," said Trance. "When my wife died I fell into that fire. It's a suffocating blast of life that burns away at your heart.

"I went to Tibet and Nepal. Sat high above the world on mountaintops, freezing my ass off pretending I was meditating and getting closer to the Creator. I remained filled with rage, my desire to strike back so strong that I would shake. I couldn't sleep, couldn't eat. But there is no striking back. How can you hit a ghost?"

"So, you know how I feel."

Trance looked into Tilson's eyes without speaking. He held the president's gaze for several moments, talking first without words, before saying, "I wanted to die. I started fighting, trying to lash out at the world…maybe die in the ring. I even entered a tournament, *the tournament*, where fighters come from everywhere to compete, often to die. I think I wanted to die…expected to die."

"Obviously, you didn't."

Trance chuckled. "I won thirty million dollars."

"For a fight?"

"No," whispered Trance. "For my soul. It happens every year in New York. A Chinese businessman invites sixty four of the world's best fighters. Mostly people that no one's ever heard of. They fight until only one man is standing, with people betting all the while. It costs a hundred thousand for the Internet feed. A million dollar line of credit must be secured before an individual can place a bet. Only the world's highest rollers attend. Even then, they are highly screened."

"I've never heard of this."

Trance laughed. "Actually, you have. It was mentioned, albeit obliquely, in the file you have on me. You're too noble for a world like that, Jock." Trance paused. "It's an ugly thing. The winner shares ten percent of the wager, double if he kills his opponent. Every year men die. A lot of them."

Tilson's face blanched white. His skin made Trance think of an old skull in the desert, bleached by the sun, the debris of death. Tilson took a large sip of his drink and let out a long breath. "I thought *I* had it bad."

"You're actually quite lucky. You've got a job to do, something to keep you occupied…something to siphon away the pain. I needed the fighting. You've got the country."

"I'm thinking of resigning."

"What?"

"I don't want it anymore, the responsibility. I want to quit and devote every waking hour I can to finding Kiki's killer."

Trance shook his head. "It doesn't work that way, Jock. Believe me, I've tried. And I'm a better detective than you are."

Tilson pondered his drink. He swirled the melting ice around in his glass, watching as the cubes came to a bouncing halt.

"How did you get over it, Jack?"

When Trance looked back at Tilson there were tears creeping into his lower eyelids. "I'm not sure I ever will be. Maybe if I found her killer, I'd get closure. Maybe then. But probably not."

Stick Granger stood up from his chair. He backed away from the fire and turned toward the two men.

"Man, you two are a pair of sorry asses. You can't keep holding on to the past, guys. It's like trying to catch the wind. You've got to leave your past where it is and get on with your lives. Find a good, loving woman and start over again. You've got to *live* and *breathe* and *laugh*, not mourn for eternity."

Tilson looked at Stick for several long moments, with an oddly dazed expression on his face. Then his eyes crinkled into a smile. He said, "Did you just call the President of the United States a *sorry ass?*"

"Yeah. I suppose I did."

Trance fought off a laugh and turned away.

Tilson looked at Stick, open-mouthed, before shrugging his shoulders. "I suppose you're right."

"What you need is a good island girl—"

"Stick," interrupted Trance. "That's enough."

"Well, he needs a good woman. Like you've got. And he's got to let her in, like you won't."

Trance and Tilson looked at each other, staring into one another's eyes, weighing Stick's words.

Trance said, "Maybe you're right, Stick. However, before then, I'm going to do everything I can to help my president find his peace."

CHAPTER 38
PP

Trance maneuvered the old, multi-colored car that he'd secured from *Rent a Wreck*. He guided it along 5th Avenue, then headed into the northernmost end of Manhattan. When he passed the edge of Central Park and hit 110th Street, it was almost like driving into another country. There was a distinctly different feel here, with Spanish Harlem spreading out to the right. Trance took a left and followed it toward Broadway. He could see that this area of the city was improving, with much of it being re-claimed from decades of neglect. Trance took a right onto Broadway and headed north. He saw an oc-casional Starbucks Coffee shop, a sure sign of growing affluence. Buildings that had been rescued from the dump heap were now sporting gleaming facades with newly barred windows.

Trance continued beyond Columbia University. At 125th Street, he thought to take a right and cruise past the Apollo Theater to see what was going on. He drove on instead. The air thumped with the deep bass of music coming from many of the cars. Mostly, he heard hip-hop songs. Some of them spoke about killing cops, gangs and banging women against a wall. Some of it sang about hope and love and responsibility. All of it would confuse any young child trying to decide which way to turn.

As Trance began to approach Washington Heights the music began to change. It took on more of a Latin influence. He saw the trademark red, blue and black beads of the Dominican *DDP* gang. He knew he might also find members of *The Bloods,* maybe even some *Crips*, along with a half dozen other gangs thrown in—some of them beaded, nearly all with tattoos. Trance saw what he suspected were students and businessmen. These people walked purposefully along the sidewalks, paying no heed to the occasional homeless person sprawled against a building, or to the crackheads wandering around like brain dead robots.

Trance pulled into an alley near Fort Tryon Park. He looked around to check for gang activity. See-ing none, he pulled a computer case off the car's front seat and carried it to his seedy excuse for an apart-ment. Trance unlocked three deadbolts and slipped inside. The apartment looked like a thousand others in the neighborhood. It was part of a much larger building that had fallen into disrepair before being cut into tiny pieces, with each piece rented to the highest bidder. Some resident's lived ten to a room. The floors were comprised of rotting wood that hadn't seen a coat of poly in decades. The walls were cracked and pitted, with plaster crumbling into small piles upon the floor, providing a good dusty sur-face to track the travelings of the mice and rats.

Trance had purchased the entire complex through one of his foreign companies. He had been tempted to renovate and clean up the old place. After consideration, he had decided against it. This had to be a place people feared to tread, a place he could go and disappear. He had compromised by removing all of the asbestos and the harmful molds. Then he'd rented most of the old brick structure at below-market-rates, to keep good families housed and the vagrants out. He kept three apartments for himself, for those times when he needed to get away from prying or killing eyes. He had four other such homes in Manhattan, along with his suite at the Plaza. He felt equally comfortable in any one of them.

The outside temperature was close to zero, and it was below fifty degrees inside the apartment. Trance rolled his finger against the apartment's single thermostat and turned up the heat. It wouldn't take long to warm the two-room flat. Trance removed his notebook computer from its case and plugged it into the wall. He uncoiled a fiber optic cable from off the floor and plugged it into his computer's Internet port. Trance's network here could download data at enormous speed, his bandwidth the size of a city sewer pipe. He had run his fiber optic cable through his building, then through another that he owned across the alley. This ran into a corporate office that he controlled on the next street over. The ownership of that company was buried underneath a labyrinth of foreign corporations, providing a secondary layer of anonymity to his high speed browsing. Trance's corporate network was linked to the Columbia Internet2 pipeline, as well as two other I2 sites within the city. It was unlikely that he would need such bandwidth, but he could download massive amounts of data in a very short time. This was helpful while hacking into high security sites, where it was essential to be in and out in seconds, before his intrusion was detected and traced.

Trance connected to the traditional Internet through Comcast and logged into a chat room for dog lovers. He had forwarded two of Sandra Smith's photos to his contacts. The first was Smith as the mousey, brown haired woman with blackened eyes. The other was the photo chosen by Angela, the one showing Sammantha Starodubov with silky brown hair and knee-melting beauty. Hopefully, someone had discovered who she was.

KennelClub12: *I can find no information on your rare breeding request.*

BreederMan634: *Nothing? Surely there is some way we can mate these dogs?*

KennelClub12: *We have searched every known database and we can find no way to mate your breed with the other. No hits to your Do Not Apply request.*

BreederMan634: *Please keep checking.*

KennelClub12: *Will do.*

Trance could feel his hopes drifting lower and lower, listing like a ship that had struck a reef during a storm. His chances were taking on water and the end looked inevitable; it was just a matter of when. They could not match Sammantha's photo or her DNA to any known individual. They had nothing. Maybe they never would.

Trance used his encrypted phone to call Stick Granger.

"Talk to me JT."

"No luck identifying our suspect."

"Nothing on this end either."

"Our lady is smarter than we thought."

"Yeah, a frigging genius. Nothing on the DNA?"

Trance scratched his head. "We've matched the samples from the chair to the skin fragment, so we know what she's made of. They're telling me she's from Asia, probably Russia. We just don't know who she is."

"Russia's a big country, Jack. Did you run her face through Identix?"

"I've sent the photos everywhere. I'm not hopeful. If we were backtracking a known face, it might be easier. Jazzman's rendering triggers thousands of potentials, with no high probability targets. Jazz tells me she's got proportions they call Phi, whatever that is. Something to do with beauty, I think.

"I've got nothing new from the NIST. I tracked down every math geek they could name, and I get a lot of words I don't understand. They keep saying that if she isn't in the files, we can't find her. And even if she was, our two-dimensional shots are too poor to waste time with. They're talking things like nonparametric subspace analysis and nonparametric discriminant analysis. I just want a name. I had people at the NSA burn up their Crays. They also got nothing. Ditto for our own."

"No facial match. No DNA match. That sucks," said Stick.

"You find anything in the local surveillance cameras worth pursuing?"

"Nothing. She's smoke."

"Then we're stuck. Just like Doheny and Cramm."

"Not quite."

"Come again?"
"They're still trying to kill you."
"Oh, yeah. Well, that's a silver lining."
"You get all the luck, Trance."

CHAPTER **39**
PP

Three Months Later…Spring

The winter's mammoth snow cover was just beginning to swell the nearby streams, melting them into a tumbling boil of water as it spilled into Moosehead Lake. The first signs of spring were beginning to emerge as northern Maine awoke from its winter hibernation. Flocks of Canada Geese buzzed continually overhead. Their symmetrical *V* patterns lettered the sky, while their incessant honking left no doubt that change was in the air. The ice on Moosehead Lake was morphing from a clear, crisp sheen of winter thickness, to a mix of packed morning corn, to an afternoon milky mush, then back again. It wouldn't be long before the ice cracked like thunder and the loons spilled into its wake.

Sammantha Starodubov wound her BMW through the back country roads, driving more from memory than sight, thinking of the man she was growing to love. What an odd twist of the screw, she thought, that she would find a man who not only met her visions of the ideal man, but exceeded them...just in time to die. Copley had grown from a drunken, off-Broadway actor to a man not only worthy of love, but deserving of the U.S. Presidency. He had grown in his role like De Niro, rising to the challenge of becoming the president. He would be a president that the people loved, but he would be so much more.

While Jock Tilson had shrunken into vengeful despair, obsessed with finding his wife's killer, Brandon Copley had evolved into the man that Tilson once was. Copley's wit had become laser-sharp. His acumen was growing geometrically. He absorbed the duties of the Oval Office, along with the nuances of presidential protocol and international policy, like a second skin. He learned names and faces in moments. He absorbed Tilson's memories and his personality until he became the president. As good as the original. Maybe better.

Sammantha cleared security and walked down the long, sterile corridor that led to the training center. At the end of the stark white tube, she came to an elevator and took it deep into the ground. When the door opened she crossed the cavernous viewing area to join a pair of men dressed in white lab coats. The two men stood watching her, without moving, until she halted beside them.

"Good morning, Dr. Starodubov."

Sammantha nodded, but didn't shake hands. "What's the agenda?"

"Today we are at Camp David, relaxing with friends."

The men led Sammantha toward the immense panes of glass that looked out over this level's bank of acting stages, all accessible by a series of walkway tunnels that radiated like wheel spokes from the center of the compound. They entered one of the spokes and walked deeply into the maze. "Camp David is two hundred yards down this path."

"Shouldn't he be outside?" asked Sammantha.

The lead man angled his head toward Sammantha and spoke as he walked. "We have to be careful not to show up on satellite. So, most of what we do is down here. We actually have a replica of Laurel outside, except for the roof, of course. That's made with camouflaged aluminum and covered by a canopy of White Pines. Most of our role playing takes place down here."

Sammantha nodded. She was well aware of the care they took to remain hidden. Why else would she have purchased one point five million acres in the frigging middle of nowhere? Why else would she have purchased a lumber company, whose trucks came in an out daily, carrying countless board feet of timber each month? How else would she have been able to import a small city and not be discovered? How else could she have moved millions of tons of dirt and evaded detection? Sammantha knew damned well how Brandon Copley was programmed; she had developed the protocol. She just needed to make sure that her people knew it, too.

Sammantha knew that it was far easier for a beautiful, naïve airhead to control these lower-level types than a woman of power. So she played the game.

"Oh, aren't you clever!" she said in a valley girl voice.

The technicians puffed out their chests and led her onward. After a few minutes they came to the hub of the spokes. The walls were constructed with clear layered polymer nanocomposites hung between steel beams. Their feet rested on carpet that was nailed into wooden planking that was bolted onto heavy steel girders. The rooms around them stretched out for hundreds of yards to a spoke. On one side, reaching down two stories below them and out for a hundred yards, they could see a replica of the U.S. Capitol Building. To the left was Camp David. To their right was the House Chamber, from where the president would address the nation in less than nine months. D day. Detonation day. Armageddon. The end of her quest, a new day for America, the day when Americans would bow their heads and weep for their dead nation.

Brandon Copley entered *Laurel*, the main Camp David cabin, through a door at the far end of the room. Behind him came two men.

"Who are they?" said Sammantha.

"Jack Trance and Jacob Miller."

Sammantha's eyes narrowed as she stared out at the men. There was no fucking way that she wanted Copley to meet with Trance, let alone befriend him.

Sammantha's guide said, "Trance is the only person who doesn't want something from Tilson. Naturally, the president and Trance have become good friends."

Not for long, thought Sammantha. She made a mental note to chastise Talid. After Talid's nephew, the little twerp, had died attacking Trance on the Quincy bridge, Talid had cowered like a beaten dog. Sammantha hadn't pressed the matter. She planned to deal with Trance herself, in her own time. But now…now that Trance had *her man*, it was time for him to vanish. It was bad enough that Trance had killed her fiancé. Now, to have him an arm's length from the president, her man…He would get close to Copley, too close. She couldn't have that. There was far too much at stake. Trance had to die.

CHAPTER **40**
PP

Stick Granger was back in the South Pacific, sprawled across his favorite hammock, with a paperback book resting face down upon his bronze chest. His eyes were closed and his head had drooped over the edge of the hammock, just enough that his gold anchor earring was swaying back and forth like a pendulum in the breeze. It had been a long, taxing day. Stick had been awake by seven. He and his wife had gone out on their boat and fished until noon. Then they'd come back and made love on the beach, before settling down to a lunch of yogurt and fruits. Then he'd spent two hours playing with his baby boy, before running five miles and taking a cold, outdoor shower. Only then, had Stick relaxed into his hammock to read.

Stick was snoring like a rhinoceros when a jet screamed overhead and startled him awake. He propped an eye open from underneath his aviator sunglasses, watching as the jet made a wide arc before dropping its landing gear. Stick's wife, Marlee, emerged from their large, stilted A-frame home with the baby on her hip. She shielded her eyes against the sun and waved at the jet as it touched down on Stick's private runway. She laughed as the jet's pilot turned the plane and started rolling it toward her husband. The jet stopped with its nose resting just above Stick's face, nearly touching his forehead.

"Boys," she said. "They never grow up."

A door popped open and the jet's stairs unfolded. A moment later the engines whined down to a *purr* and Trance emerged, carrying a golf bag.

"Can you tell me where I might find Marlee Granger?" said Trance. "I think I'm the father of her child."

Stick didn't open his eyes, but waved an arm toward his home. "Over there."

Trance dropped his golf bag onto the sandy grass and waved toward Marlee. "You busy, Stick?" he said.

Stick cocked an eye open and said, "I am."

"Sorry to interrupt your hard work."

"Damned rude, if you ask me. I recall you did the same thing the last time you invaded my island nation."

"I wanted to show you my new ride. What do you think?"

Stick glanced toward the jet and mumbled, "Great. Now let me sleep."

Trance waved toward the jet's cockpit. After a moment he said, "Take a closer look."

When Stick looked up for the jet, his jaw dropped open. His mouth remained wide, making it look like the opening for a carnival bean bag game. He stared at the empty space and then back at Trance. "What are you, David Copperfield?" The jet was gone.

"Pretty cool, huh? My latest trick."

Stick studied the area where he knew the jet must be, but he saw nothing, nothing but the sky and the clouds and the ocean. Then he looked down to the ground. There, resting upon the hard-packed sand stood six wheels, standing vertically in pairs. Nothing was holding them in place. They could have been coconuts fallen from a tree. "I give up."

Trance waved again and the jet reappeared. A moment later, the jet's engines shut down. Lauren emerged from inside, carrying her golf bag.

"That explains it," said Stick. "I knew you were no Copperfield."

Lauren set down her clubs and gave Stick a peck on the cheek.

"Hello, darlin'," he said.

"Like Jack's new toy?"

"What is it?"

Trance said, "A new prototype. A couple of my companies were tasked by DARPA to develop more efficient stealth technologies. Mostly for military use. This jet is part of a whole new field of science, shattering many commonly held beliefs about the behavior of matter."

Stick stepped out of his hammock and stretched. "You going to tell me how it works?"

"We've moved far beyond the B-2 and the F-22 bombers Stick. Our new metamaterials can absorb light waves and pass them through the other side of almost any object. On this side, we are seeing what is on the other side of the jet, as the light is rerouted through the plane rather than reflected off it. We do the same with radar. In the air, we can be…we are…invisible."

"Except for the wheels. You forgot about the wheels."

"The wheels retract, Stick."

"Oh, yeah. Sorry."

"We're working on other nanomaterials to make things like miniature supermicroscopes and tiny manufacturing plants. The possibilities are endless."

"You could take on the Romulans."

"Excuse me?"

"Or Harry Potter."

"Oh, you mean the cloaking?" Trance smiled. "It's scary stuff, Stick. Our main fear *now* is learning how to *detect* these things, when other countries catch on. We're about a year away from perfecting a quantum computer that will do that." Trance put his hands on his hips and began walking toward Stick's home. "But you don't want to hear about that. I know you're busy, so I'll leave you alone. I just needed to clear up this paternity thing. I won't be long."

Lauren and Trance walked toward the A-frame, stopping when they reached the broad patio that ran beneath it. The home was held aloft by a series of titanium posts that were sunk deep into the ground. They could hear shuffling on the wooden floor boards above, as Marlee prepared for their visit. "Stick didn't tell me you were coming," Marlee cried as they began climbing up the spiral staircase.

"Didn't warn him." Trance hugged Marlee. "We were just in the area."

Lauren hugged Marlee, too. "How've you been, girl?"

Marlee smiled, her teeth the color of bleached sugar against her darkly tanned face. "You wouldn't believe how peaceful this is." Then she lowered her voice, "But lonely, sometimes."

At that moment Stick loomed behind Trance. He motioned toward the baby and said, "Trance says that's his kid."

"Probably," said Marlee, winking at Trance. "Even if he has your vacant eyes."

Stick seemed to ponder the fact. "Good." He turned to Trance. "Can I manage his trust fund?" Stick spread his arms and buried Trance inside them. "Great to see you, buddy. So nice of you to call ahead."

"Figured if I called for a tee time you'd claim you were fully booked."

"You're here to play golf?"

"Sure."

"You're eight thousand miles from home."

"We like remote courses."

"Well, you're lucky the club's open. It's been closed for construction."

"You're playing preferred lies then?"

"Never. On my course, you play it where it lands, even if it's within the coils of a snake."

Stick looked back out toward Trance's turquoise jet. "That's some kind of ride, JT."

"Besides the stealth, we've also been working on the engines, the electronics and the software."

"Yeah, but how's the mileage?"

"It's a hybrid. I get a hundred miles per gallon in the city."

"That thing'll ruin a city, Trance."

"Actually, this plane was built to cruise with feathered engines, which cuts fuel consumption to forty percent of comparable jets."

"That should be a hit in Hollywood. Great mileage, and it can fool the paparazzi."

"We can also travel a thousand kilometers on batteries... which virtually eliminates the heat signature."

Stick knew what this meant. DARPA had commissioned the perfect stealth fighter, invisible to the eye and radar, with no heat signature. Trance's companies had delivered it. The question that put Stick's hair on end was, *Why is Trance here?*

Silence hung in the air like junkyard smoke, thick and heavy and not smelling very good. Nobody traveled eight thousand miles just to play golf, particularly when they showed up in a jet like this.

"Why are you here, Jack? Something up with Tilson?"

Trance shook his head. "No, but it's getting pretty sad. Just had to get away."

Stick nodded. "I've seen *you* there…where he is. It isn't pretty."

"He calls me every week and I give him nothing. I just had to escape, at least for a couple weeks. I'm still dealing with the aftermath of my kidnapping." Trance thought back to the warehouse room, where a drug dealer named Ramon Cesar had kept Trance in chains, shooting him full of enough cocaine and heroin to kill an elephant. All for little more than sport.

"Cesar was one sick bastard, Jack. He's gone. You'll be okay."

Trance smiled. "It's been months now, but Lauren still won't let me out of her sight. At least until the cravings are gone."

"Doesn't she have a job?"

Lauren said, "I said I'd quit if the board didn't let me take family leave, plus my accrued vacation time. Since I saved the bank ten or twenty billion by convincing them to limit our exposure in derivatives during the past decade, they gladly did so."

"I bet she could even walk on water," said Trance.

"As long as you're here, why don't you two get married? I'm a judge on this island. I'll do the honors."

"You, Marlee and baby Jack are the *only* residents of this island."

"Exactly. That makes me president, judge, jury, boat captain, greens keeper *and* chief bottle washer."

Trance slowly shook his head. "I love Lauren more than anything; you know that. But I'm not quite ready, not yet. There are things I need to deal with first."

"They have therapy for PTSD, Trance. That's what it is, you know. Acute *and* complex. You go through tough things and your body shuts down. Your body tries to protect you from it happening again. You've just got to work through it."

"What are you, my shrink?"

"Doesn't take a lot of specialized schooling to see what you need, Trance."

Trance smiled. "Thank you, doctor."

"Just tell me what I can do to help."

"Right now I want to kick your ass in golf."

"Not a chance, Trance. You've never played a course like this."

"You want to bet?"

Stick ran a hand across his face. He looked out over the ocean as if watching some tiny sail on the horizon. After a long moment, he smiled slyly. "The usual?"

"Uh-huh. A dollar a side and two on the total. Scotch foursome."

Stick grinned. "Bad move, JT. Marlee's been tearing it up this month."

"We'll see about that."

***

Trance looked out beyond the driving area from the first tee. Before him stretched an expanse of ocean that ended with an uphill green sitting on a tuft of land two hundred and thirty yards away. The green looked like a small splotch of paint surrounded by nothing but rough and trouble.

Trance said, "Is that a green up there or a throw rug?"

"I wanted the course to start out easy, Trance. Don't worry. It'll get challenging enough, after a few holes."

Trance pulled out a three iron and lofted a shot high into the air. His ball landed pin high but skipped thirty feet before stopping on the back edge of the putting surface. "These greens made of concrete, Granger?"

Stick said nothing. He pulled out a four iron and swung it smoothly. The ball landed off the green to the left, took a sharp kick to the right and stopped ten feet inside of Trance.

"These greens are like Augusta, Trance. You've got to play them a few dozen times to know where to hit."

"And you're not going to tell us, are you?"

Stick grinned. "Of course not."

The women's tee box was a mere twenty yards closer, a daunting shot for any female golfer, and suicide for most.

Trance chuckled. "Didn't give the women much of a handicap, did you, Granger?"

"I've got to play with Marlee. She'd kick my ass all over this course if I made it anywhere close to fair."

Marlee teed her ball, pulled a hybrid from her bag and spun the ball to a stop no more than fifteen feet from the stick. Then Lauren did the same.

"I get the feeling that the girls are going to carry us today," said Trance.

"Don't they always?" replied Stick, with a knowing grin.

Trance waved for the women to take the long, uphill walk to the green. Marlee slung her bag upon her shoulders and pushed the baby forward in a running jogger. Lauren strapped on her bag and walked beside her. Trance let them leave, before drawing Stick toward him.

"If I die…"

"Whoa, Jack."

Trance shook his head. "Listen. Someone is trying to kill me and he's getting close. If I die, I want you to make sure that Lauren is taken care of. I'm leaving her everything. You know there will be a fight, particularly from my extended family in Europe…I need you to be there for her. I've named you as my executor and trustee."

"You're scaring me, Jack. I can't handle all that stuff. I'm just a simple pilot with the body of a Greek God."

"It's Talid, Stick. You know what that means."

Stick Granger closed his eyes and drew in a long, groaning breath. He looked out over the ocean. The water was a clear blue-green and there was nothing else in sight. Not a boat, not a plane. Nothing.

Trance followed Stick's gaze and his body sagged, as if he'd thrown an ox yoke over his shoulders. "Sometimes, I just wish it would all go away. I'm tired, Stick. Tired of all this responsibility."

"The world ain't goin' nowhere, Jack. Neither is your quest, so give it a rest."

"I wish I *could* let it go."

"Come hide with us. We've got room at the other end of the island. We could stand your company, provided you promise not to sire any more kids with my wife."

Trance smiled. It was a sad smile, just a forlorn pinching of the mouth. "Talid keeps a harem of slave girls."

"Doesn't every despot?"

"He was going to buy Jaime Crandall after she was kidnapped in Miami."

"Yeah, I know."

"He's killed hundreds of thousands of his own people. He rules his country by fear and torture. He spreads hatred for America and funds schools that brainwash others into feeling the same."

"Any idea why he's trying to kill you? I mean, besides the fact that you're a shitty golfer?"

"I made his life hell with T-Force. Tompkin still does. Plus, I think he's still pissed about that hundred million we took from him and gave to SOSCADA."

"So, send him money."

"He wants revenge, not money."

"So, we take *him* out. We'll fly your jet over one of his palaces, when he's there of course, and drop a big bomb."

Trance laughed. Stick Granger would never stand for taking innocent lives. What Stick *was* saying, was that he was up to the challenge of helping Trance get to Talid.

"It's not that easy, Stick. He's a frigging dictator. You know the code. We don't kill *Heads of State*, no matter how dangerous and despotic, unless, of course, they are a target of war."

"That's an easy one. On behalf of the island nation of Stick Grangerland, I hereby declare war on Mu'annar Abu Hussein al-Talid. Will you fight with my army and help save my country?"

Trance slapped his forehead. "Why didn't I think of that?"

"It's just something that we Heads of State instinctively understand, Trance. Just being rich won't give you the keen acumen needed to think great thoughts. Only we government leaders can do things like that."

"I always thought of you more as Dorothy's Scarecrow than a world leader."

"Shows how little you know."

Trance pressed his hand against Stick's shoulder and looked him in the eye. "I don't want to kill Talid. That would just make him a martyr. But I do need to get him off my back. I can't marry Lauren with Talid hanging over our heads."

Stick slapped Trance on the back. "Well, now you're talkin'. We've got ourselves a plan."

"I was hoping you'd help."

"So, what's the plan, Jack?"

"Well, we'll have to think of one."

Stick groaned.

As the two men reached the elevated green, Stick said, "Sorry to hold you girls up. Jack and I have decided to go to Macao and gamble like despots for a few days. Then we're going to head over to New Zealand to sit on the beach and drink beer."

Marlee stood up from the crouch she was using to study the fifteen-foot putt she had left for her husband. "You mind if we finish our round first? We'll be happy to pack you dinner, after golf. You'll have to buy your own beer."

Marlee gave Stick a worried smile and drew him to the far edge of the green. She whispered, "What's going on, Stick?"

"Jack needs my help."

Marlee wrapped her arms around her husband and squeezed him tightly. "Can't you two give it a rest?"

"Not this time."

Marlee kissed her husband on the end of his nose. "Okay. Before you two go off to play, you've got a putt to make."

Granger missed his birdie putt. So did Trance. The match was square.

The second hole required a two hundred yard carry over marshland, before opening up to a small landing area of grass. There was a second landing area another two hundred yards beyond that, and an elevated green a hundred yards farther.

Trance said, "These fairways are the size of beach towels, Stick. You can't be serious?"

Stick punched Trance playfully in the shoulder and said, "This course is an architectural and ecological marvel. I do this with no electricity, with irrigation powered by windmills. All with a groundskeeper of one. Give us a little respect, Trance. I deserve a Nobel Prize."

Trance hit a four iron to the far edge of the fairway. He turned to Marlee and said, "Why don't you and Lauren go to Paris while Stick and I are gone? My treat. We'll drop you off on our way. I'll give you a card. You can buy anything you want."

Stick leaned over Trance's shoulder and said to his wife, "I need a new fishing boat, honey."

Marlee smiled. "I'm far better with jewelry, Stick. You need a Rolex or something?"

"Pick me up a Comex 1680, will you?"

Trance and Lauren exchanged amused glances. Then Lauren took Trance's hand and whispered, "I love you, Jack. Wherever you are going, be safe."

Marlee and Stick did win the match, on the third playoff hole. Dollars were exchanged. Dinner was served. By morning they were gone.

CHAPTER **41**
______________PP______________

It was well after midnight and the ancient city had long-since gone to bed. Trance maneuvered a sand colored Mercedes limousine quietly through the deserted streets. Now and then a car passed by. Not a soul was outside walking in the sultry desert air. Stick sat beside Trance, pointing a small flashlight at a map that was hand-scrawled on the back of a crumpled napkin.

"I can't read this damn thing, Trance. I feel like I'm following a maze with my eyes closed. Don't you have some kind of GPS or something?"

"Shut up and tell me where to go."

"Left at the next intersection." Stick peered closely at the napkin and continued. "Then it looks like we cross a big swatch of ketchup and take a right. Then...I think...we cross what looks like a mix of mustard and relish before turning left into a greasy driveway. These are some great directions you have here, Trance. I hope the rest of the mission is this well planned."

A few minutes later Trance pulled into the driveway of a modest, flat-roofed residence crafted with white stucco and desert mud. Trance sat inside the car and waited for a signal. He saw two flicks of a lighter come from behind a set of drapes that blackened the home's only window. "This is it."

Trance emerged from the sleek car, pulled his headdress low over his forehead and walked swiftly toward the home's front door. Trance's white Aba robe flowed behind him, glowing like a ghost in the pale moonlight. Stick walked behind him, wearing black, looking more like a tall wraith.

Trance knocked three short times against the door. There were two return knocks. Trance knocked four more times, slowly. The door opened and both men slipped inside the unlit entrance. Four men surrounded them and began to pat them down for weapons.

"I thought these were our guys, Trance?" said Stick.

"Orders," said one of the men.

The guards removed Trance's pistol and his weapons belt. They took Stick's two pistols and his hunting knife. Then they led the men into a darkened room. As the door closed behind them, the lights came on. There, seated at a square card table sat Jesse Tompkin, the leader of T-Force. Tompkin stood about six foot two. His jar-head crew cut was flattened on top, but his hair was as thick and smooth as a country club fairway. His eyes looked like those of a Siberian husky, so blue and bright that it appeared like a light was shining from inside them. He wore a desert camouflage shirt with the sleeves cut off, revealing a ripple of muscles forged by years in the weight room. Beside him sat a man named Swartz, a top ranking field officer in the Israeli Mossad. Swartz had years of hard-core experience, including some with the Israeli division known as *Bayonet*. He was of medium height, with ropes of sinewy muscle, curly black hair and eyes that were nearly as dark. His face was tanned and chocolate brown, deeply lined with irregular canyons running in haphazard directions. Too many hours in the desert sun and sand had worn his face down, so that it now looked more like a dry river bed than human skin.

The last time Trance had seen Swartz it was high in the mountains of Austria, while they were working together to prevent World War III. Swartz had requested payment from Trance, but not in money. He'd wanted something Trance could not give him, something no nation was prepared to possess. So Trance had paid him what he could, in the form of his own secret family tree, a path that would lead Swartz to billions. A small sum when compared to Trance's prize, but sufficient to reward Swartz and his nation for their sacrifice. He hadn't spoken with him since.

"Howdy, boys," said Stick. He shook hands with both men and Trance did the same.

The four men sat at the table, waiting in silence for several long moments.

"Thank you for coming," Trance began. "I know the risk you each face by being here."

"Any chance at Talid is a chance worth taking," said Swartz. "He has sworn to eliminate my nation."

Trance looked Swartz squarely in the eyes. "I'm just going to *talk* with him. That's all."

The four men stared at each other, the silence so loud it was painful.

Finally, Stick said, "Yeah, and you know what you should tell him, Trance? You should explain to him how you inherited two Ohio class ballistic missile submarines from your late grandfather, something only half a dozen *countries* have in their arsenals. I'd explain that these subs are equipped with a dozen Trident II D-5s that can turn his country of sand into a crater filled with glass. You tell him that just one of these multiple entry missiles can unleash more firepower than has been used in the entire history of warfare. And that they travel faster than his eye can see. One minute he'll be sitting on his prayer rug and the next his molecules will be spread across a hundred miles of desert air. That's what I'd tell him."

Trance smiled. "I'd rather just ask him nicely, Stick." Trance turned to Swartz. "How's that gift working out?"

Swartz's eyes narrowed but he smiled. His teeth glinted like gun metal in the low, pale light. He said, "That book should never see the light of day, Trance."

"I hope it won't."

"You risked much by giving it to me."

"The least I could do. You helped save millions of lives, perhaps even mine."

"It's been invaluable."

"Just keep me out of the spill."

Swartz grinned. "You're so resilient, Trance. Even this shit wouldn't stick on you."

"It's not me I'm worried about."

"Point taken."

The four men sat again without speaking. Each man knew what was at stake and the risks they must take. The dirty facts hung above them like a sack of leaky camel dung, threatening to douse them all in the stench.

"Tell me how I get to Talid," said Trance.

Swartz looked over at Tompkin. He looked at Stick and then back to Trance. "I want your assurances that none of this gets leaked. Not to *anybody*. Not T-Force, Tompkin. Not Miller, Trance. Not your congress, not your president. Are we clear?" Swartz paused to allow each man to nod. "We view Talid as *the* most dangerous man for Israel. He's also the most toxic for America. He is funding terrorist training camps and supporting radical schools throughout the world. He recruits jihadists like your volunteer army does. *'Be all you can be.'* Ever heard the phrase? He uses it to recruit young students for one way trips to heaven. He promises them an afterlife filled with voluptuous virgins, and money for their families here on earth. All he sows is death and destruction."

"Excuse me, Swartz," said Stick. "But we know all this."

"Most Americans don't see this as we do. Your nation cannot be destroyed in mere moments by a few short range missiles armed with nukes. You don't fight it every frigging day…the aftermath of hate." Swartz closed his eyes. "As long as we are clear…"

"We're clear," said Trance. Stick and Tompkin each said, "Ditto."

"Here's the plan…As you know, virtually every wealthy sheik keeps a harem of women, slaves, really. The wealthiest and most powerful purchase only the best. The Sultan of Brunei offers millions to beauty queens to work for him. Some say he then steals their passports and traps them in his country."

Stick said, "Yeah, I heard about that. Didn't one of them contact Trance's buddy, Trump? Some former Miss USA or something, said she was being held against her will."

"That's just the half of it."

"Where are you going with this, Swartz?" asked Trance. "We're all aware of white slavery."

"We have agents inside."

"Explain."

"We recruit women to work as Mossad agents inside the Arab palaces. They start when they are young. We give them acting lessons, plastic surgery. We enter them in beauty pageants. We give them new identities and place them in foreign countries. Then we hope they get recruited into the right places."

"And this *works* for you?" said Stick. "Sounds like a lot of wasted energy and lives."

"Most of it is," said Swartz. "You have to understand that this is not just a war for us. It is our *survival*.

"We have been able to place several women into critical positions. You'd be amazed what secrets a man will disclose to a mistress."

"No we wouldn't," said Tompkin. "Sexual spies are quite common, even in our country today."

Swartz stood from the table and began to walk around it with slow, measured steps. "We have an asset placed with Talid. She is one of his favorites. As you know, Talid never sleeps in the same palace for two nights in a row. He moves every day, usually to one of the fourteen monstrosities he has built in his capital city. He keeps a harem of twelve in each palace, and he chooses randomly among these women. Except on Thursday. Every Thursday he sleeps in the same palace, with the same woman, one of ours."

"Convenient," said Stick.

"Nothing of the sort, Granger. It took ten years of planning. She is the most skilled courtesan we have, and also the most beautiful. Talid outbid the Sultan for her services, after she was crowned Miss Galaxy. She has been in place for nearly two years, as a sleeper, waiting for the day when we ask for her services. That day has come. Her name is Roxanne Flame."

Trance chuckled. "That's original."

"More effective than Rhonda Katz, don't you think?"

"I think."

Swartz continued. "Talid travels with over four hundred people, mostly bodyguards, relatives, servants, and government hacks. Each day, before they move to the next palace, there is a catering shipment delivered to the site. Talid is cautious. There is a different caterer for each location."

"And you control the caterer to Thursday's palace?" said Trance.

"Exactly."

"Very good, Swartz."

"You may not think so after I've laid out my requirements."

"Try me."

"I can't emphasize how great an asset Roxanne is to us. I must exact a price for her complicity."

"Which is?" said Trance.

"First, you must remove any chance that Talid will suspect her."

"I won't kill her, if that's what you're asking."

Swartz shook his head. "No. But you must make it *look* like she was coerced."

Trance nodded.

"I want you to insert this."

Swartz handed Trance a small vial filled with a clear liquid. Inside it, along the bottom, was some sort of sediment, perhaps silicon or graphite shavings. Trance turned the vial over in his hands.

"I give up," Trance said.

"Nanobots. Microphone, receiver and GPS."

"This is sophisticated stuff, Swartz. Where'd you find it?"

Swartz laughed. "From one of *your* companies, Trance...based in Geneva. You really don't know about this?"

Trance shook his head. "I inherited sixty-five companies in the U.S. alone, with hundreds of subsidiaries. I've got many more worldwide. It's only been two years. I am just getting a handle on the big stuff, let alone the private and the secret. You contract for this?"

"We did." Swartz held up a second vial. Inside it floated what looked like a small chunk of #2 pencil lead. "This is a graphene based microchip connected to a graphene-based capacitor that charges off ATP in the blood."

Trance put a hand against his forehead and laughed softly, more like a forlorn, rueful sniff. He smiled. "I take it we inject this into the nasal cavity, or the ear canal?"

"Nasal cavity."

"He's going to notice this, Swartz."

"Not after you rough up his face."

Trance groaned and shook his head. "No."

"What?" said Swartz. "You have a problem with this? The man is trying to kill you and you have a problem with smacking him in the face? C'mon Trance, don't be a wuss. The man wants you dead. Got that? He wants you and your country *dead*."

"What else?"

"We want you to place bugs around the bed chamber."

"As a ruse?"

"As a ruse."

Trance looked at Stick and then at Tompkin. Stick shrugged, but Tompkin remained impassive.

"Does T-Force have a problem with this?" said Trance.

"Yeah," said Tompkin. "But they don't know I'm here. This is sort of a solo thing, strictly off the books. Personally, Trance, if you want to make sure he doesn't kill you, you make him dead."

"Not now, Jesse. I'm out of the killing business. Going to become a family man."

Tompkin grinned. "That'll be the day."

Trance jutted his chin and said, "Watch me." He looked to all three men. "Let's get this done."

CHAPTER **42**
_____________PP_____________

As Jock Tilson stepped down the stairway of Air Force One, applause spilled out across the runway. Several hundred people had turned out to greet Maine's favorite son, pressing against the ropes, waving flags and placards and holding young children in the air so they could see. Once Tilson got the go-ahead from his Secret Service detail, he walked over to the crowd and began shaking hands. It took him more than twenty minutes, but he touched every hand and kissed every baby's cheek that was offered.

Tilson smiled throughout the ordeal. It was just a reflexive baring of teeth, not a genuine pleasure, like it used to be. Tilson was dying inside, like an old tree that had begun to rot at its core. Outside, he appeared as he always had. The nation deserved a president it could respect and look up to. So he would be one. But on the inside, all the gears of his ambition had ground to a halt, and they were already rusting in place.

"Time to go, Mr. President," said one of his aides.

Tilson shrugged and shuffled back onto the tarmac. He boarded Marine One with his HMX team. Four Lockheed Martin VH-71 helicopters began to wind up their engines. One held the president, while the others would provide the standard shell game diversion. Further down the runway, several F-18 Hornets scrambled into the air. The president's two pilots set a heading for a hundred and fifty miles north, to an out of the way place known as Greenville, Maine. Two HMX crew members moved around inside the president's helicopter, making sure that all went smoothly.

Tilson was riding in one of the VH-71s that had survived Obama's order cancellation. These, along with the older VH-3Ds, were used to transport the president and vice president around the country. He liked the VH-71s because they were roomier and safer than the old 3Ds. This particular unit, along with one of the other three, had been uniquely customized to be used with the president while he was on vacation.

Besides his family, Tilson had one great passion. He loved racing speedboats in the open water, at speeds that could flatten steel. He'd been introduced to the sport by another one of Maine's favorite sons, former president, George H. W. Bush. Tilson owned two Cigarette boats, a 36' Gladiator and a 46' Rider XP Triple. During the summer he liked to scorch the edge of Moosehead Lake at more than a hundred miles an hour, usually racing against his mother.

The crew members adjusted a pair of heavy winches that had been installed in the craft. They coiled the shiny chains that were attached to the winches into metal bins just inside the cockpit doors. This gear was all for the off chance that they would have to air lift the president, or even his entire smaller boat, after an accident. Although arguably undermanned and underpowered, the Secret Service was vigilant and always prepared, for almost anything.

Tilson busied himself with his sheaf of daily briefing papers, studiously ignoring a dozen traveling staff members, who sat in two huddled groups, talking quietly.

The helicopters touched down on the front lawn of a white farmhouse nestled at the end of a dirt road off Spruce Street. As the rotors wound down Tilson stepped out of his aircraft and gazed toward a flock of vehicles, driven by the advance team of Secret Service agents that had sanitized the destination prior to his arrival. They looked like a herd of huge black cows. Tilson had the fleeting image of his mother driving them into the barn one-by-one for their morning milking. His eyes moved to a spot just outside the front door of the farmhouse, where he saw the outline of a regally tall woman dressed in a pair of blue jeans, a Harvard sweatshirt and a blue fleece vest. The woman stood unusually straight, like a marine at attention. Her shoulders were squared and her chin was thrust forward with old Yankee pride. His mother's hair was speckled with gray and tied back in a tight pony tail. Her face was lined, but still taut, showing just a fraction of her sixty-three years. Her eyes were dark green, and the springtime sun had already begun to bring out a field of Irish freckles across her cheeks.

Tilson waved and his mother began to jog toward him. She moved with the loose, loping gait of a distance runner, light on her step and long in stride. She barely slowed down before stretching her fingers around Tilson's face. She kissed both his cheeks and then tousled his hair.

"Well, hello there, Mr. President."

"Hi, Ma."

"I'm so glad you came."

"I needed a break. I'm glad you called."

"Thought you might need some cheering up." Martha Tilson stretched an arm around her son's waist and led him back toward her modest home.

Tilson pointed toward the barn, then to the horse corral that was built with sturdy, northern maple posts. "You need any help with the chores, Ma?"

"No, Jason. With the Secret Service here, I've got more help than I need."

Tilson laughed, for the first time in months. "You make your security detail work the farm?"

Martha seemed insulted that her son could ask such a question. "Why, of course I do. You don't think I'd let them sit around here all day doing nothing, do you?"

"You are not supposed to turn them into your servants, Ma."

"Servants, hell. They're my friends. We all work together. Then we run, swim, bike, skate and ski together. I think I'd like their job when I grow up. It's kind of fun."

"You'll never grow up, Ma."

"Don't I know it. And how about you, son? How are you getting on? You must miss her something terrible."

Tilson stared out to the corral, and to the three work horses that were standing along the fence, munching on the clumps of long grass that were growing beside the fence posts. He looked out to the pasture, which was spotted with cows, grazing lazily in the afternoon sun.

"We were supposed to do this together." Tilson shook his head slowly, then more vigorously, almost like a horse trying to shake off flies. "I didn't want this alone. Not alone."

Martha Tilson looked solemnly into the eyes of her son. She thought of how life could veer off course in mere moments, like the rape that brought her two sons, like the threats that had forced her to separate her boys, like the senseless assassination of her son's wife. How could she tell him that the pain would somehow pass, how unexpected joy could erupt from life's darkest places?

"Life is unfair, Jason. I've never told you otherwise."

Tilson looked to his mother. He smiled thinly. His eyes were dark, distant and angry. They reminded Martha of storm clouds ready to drench her pastures. She knew that the sun would always follow rain, eventually spilling the ground with bright warmth. This, too, shall pass. Hopefully soon.

Martha continued, "Sometimes…You know, I was never married—"

Tilson put his hand to his mother's lips. "I know about that, Ma. When I declared my candidacy for the presidency they did background checks. Deep checks. They told me…They told me that you were never married…They told me that the story of my father dying when I was just a baby was a myth. They never said who he was. They don't know."

"He *is* dead. And you should know his name—"

"I don't want to know. I have no father, you made sure of that."

"That's not fair, I—"

"No." Tilson took his mother by her shoulders and looked into her eyes. This time his eyes looked kind, understanding. "I know how good a person you are. And I know that if it was right for me to know, you would have told me. You have been the best mom and dad a son could hope for."

"Come."

Martha Tilson took her son's hand and led him toward the barn. It was a typical Maine barn, several times larger than the house and nearly twice as tall, with a shiny red aluminum roof. There were two sliding, wooden door slabs that opened into the central core. Down the left hand side was a series of stalls, built for horses, but easily used for cows and sheep as well. Along the right hand side there was a metal railing where dozens of animal leads were clipped onto steel rings that wrapped around the railing. A few pregnant cows were hitched to the leads, and were lying in clean beds of pale yellow straw. Tilson reached into a burlap bag that was hanging by a rusty nail and removed a hand full of apples. He walked down the side of the barn and greeted each cow by name. He would slice an apple, offer half with an open palm, then scratch each cow affectionately between the ears before moving on to the next.

As Tilson neared the end of the barn he turned toward the middle, to where Martha kept their two racing boats. One was painted with yellow, green and red stripes running lengthwise along the hull. It was fitted with a pair of Mercury Racing EU 662 SCi engines. The other was a collage of red, white and black splotches, looking like paint that had been splattered on a floor. It sported a single engine, a monster HP 1200 SCi. Tilson ran his hands along the two boats, feeling their smooth, sleek bulk and the lurking power that almost pulsed through his fingers.

"We going to take the boats out?" asked Martha. "I've had them both prepped."

Tilson shook his head. "Wish I could, but I don't have time. I'll be back in a month or so. We'll race then. Okay?"

"I'll be practicing."

"You'll never beat me, Ma," said Tilson with a wide smile.

"I'm not looking to beat you, Jason. I sure would love to leave my Secret Service buddies in my wake, though."

Tilson laughed. He could see his mother thrusting her boat full throttle and grinning while her protectors struggled to keep up behind her.

Tilson hesitated. He had something important to ask his mother, something vital to the national interest and to his presidency. "Would you mind giving an interview in the next week or so?"

"You know how I hate interviews."

Tilson did. His mother was one of the most intensely private people he had ever met.

"It's important to me. Important to the world."

Martha arched an eyebrow and looked closely at her son, waiting for an explanation.

"I've had a request from the Russian president. Ogarkov asked for a summit at Camp David."

"That's certainly nothing that would warrant an old broad speaking to strangers, Jason."

Tilson chuckled. "He made a bold suggestion, that we eliminate all nuclear weapons. He said that, if he and I can see eye-to-eye, he can bring every member of the club with him."

"I don't get your point."

"Ogarkov believes that every nation is composed of good people. We love our families and we love our brothers. He says that our differences become magnified, far out of proportion, by ignorance. He asked if he could send a television crew to visit with you and me, to show the softer side of American leadership, so that his nation can get over its distrust for America. I will be hosting the crew next week— at the White House and at Camp David. They are going to make a documentary to show how normal and peace loving we are, as a nation."

"Then you certainly don't want them meeting with your recluse mother. I'm more battle axe than pretty feather."

Tilson put his arm around Martha's waist and led her back toward the farmhouse. "Will you do it?"

"For you, anything."

Tilson and his mother walked through a side door of the house into the small, bright kitchen that overlooked the cow pasture. Martha reached into a cupboard and pulled two coffee mugs off the shelf.

"I made fresh coffee," she said. "Just how you like it."

"Hot?"

"Funny."

Tilson stood by the kitchen sink and looked out across the field. He smiled as he saw the blotches of cow pies littering the ground. When he was a boy, he and his friends used to shove sticks through the outer crust and get good gobs of grass-laden cow dung to throw at each other. A good pie and you could get something that would really fly. Tilson nodded, as if saying something to himself. He moved back toward his mother and sat beside her at the kitchen table.

Then he saw it. That old, faded photograph was still hanging against the wall. It was a picture taken from the first base line of a college baseball game. Jock Tilson was at the plate, with Brandon Copley on the mound. Copley had that stupid little shit-eating grin, staring him down.

"Of all the photos for you to keep in here, Ma." This was the game, the event he remembered as his single greatest failure. This photo crystallized all his fears about the presidency, and about his life. It reminded him that he was fallible. The Harvard-Yale game, the time when he had struck out against Brandon Copley. This was the moment his wife always used to kid him about, to keep him humble, she said. It was a failure that stuck to him like tar and feathers. "You know I hate thinking about that game."

"That's why I have it, honey. To keep you grounded." *And to see my two sons together.* "Lord knows you've got enough of life's trophies to fill a room. You must always remember that there's more to life than winning." Martha looked at the photo. "I think of this picture as showing both sides of you, the yin and yang, the weak and strong."

"I struck out, Ma. Three fastballs, all high and inside middle. I swear, I couldn't even see them. It was like I was powerless against him…Copley… and…I still worry that it will happen again, some time when I can least afford it."

"You won't fail, Jason. But you can't always be perfect either. To me, this photo illustrates…I see part of you in that pitcher and part in the batter."

"I don't know how you can say that. I am nothing like him. I was never that heavy and I've never worn facial hair…"

Martha smiled. It was a demure smile, a secret smile like the Mona Lisa, like there was something she was hiding and loving the mystery. Tilson didn't notice. He was too busy reliving that moment, that single moment when he had failed, like a man reaching for a handful of stars and coming up with air. If only he knew.

"That's not what I mean, Jason. When you can find peace with that photo, you will be a complete man. You need to be comfortable with all sides of yourself. I wish that it were something I could teach you. Someday, if you are lucky, you will learn that on your own."

Tilson sat sullenly, wondering just what his mother had said. After a long while he shrugged. "If you say so. Now, tell me, what's new…"

CHAPTER **43**
______________PP______________

Omar Karkhabi hovered beside Sammantha inside the observation maze, wondering what the hell he was doing there, staring for hours at what he secretly called the *theater of the absurd,* where grown men and women behaved like lab rats, acting role after role for the men up here dressed in white coats. They were like a group of circus animals, performing for treats doled out as praise spoken through a squawk box.

Karkhabi was trapped here, just like the actors. For more than six months he had been forced to watch them, scene after scene, where the former Brandon Copley interacted with every conceivable person he might face as president. Omar had witnessed play after play. He'd watched film after film made with scenes designed to burn visuals into Copley's brain. Scenes with boys growing up on a rural farm, with young men attending a high school dance, a boy having his first kiss with a girl named Kiki, telling her he would be president.

Karkhabi felt like a voyeur, watching Copley as he was strapped to a chair with wires plugged into his brain to physically sear images deep into the tissues of his psyche. Words like vector virus, stem cells, genetic reengineering, EMDR, REM, hypnosis, visualize and traumatize rattled around his brain. He had even begun to dream. He'd begun to dream that *he* was the president, with each scene playing in his brain as if it were *real*.

It was all too weird. And what was it for? Sammantha wouldn't tell him and neither would Talid. His father had just spluttered when he'd asked what they were doing, like he had swallowed a bee or something.

Karkhabi was growing stir crazy, living under the ground in the wilds of Maine, never being allowed to venture outside except to view another version of the absurd. They now had *him* taking part in these skits, playing the role of Omar, adviser to the president. Copley *thought* he knew Omar well. No. *Jock Tilson* thought he knew him well, for that's who he was now, *president Jock Tilson*. They were friends, he and Tilson. They debated the role that nuclear power should play in America's energy policy. They discussed the risks that America faced with the proliferation of nuclear technology throughout the less developed world. The president sought his guidance, as if it meant something, as if his views on Middle Eastern culture and nuclear warfare actually mattered. He was on the *team* and he did matter. Didn't he?

"Just be yourself," they told him. So he was, as strange as it seemed. He was Omar.

Omar said, "He's so close, here in Maine, less than forty miles away. The *real* president." He'd never met the man, but he knew all about him.

Sammantha Starodubov's lips spread into something approaching a smile. But there was a narrow, focused look to her eyes that seemed to brush him aside, as if he were nothing more than an annoying fruit fly.

"You are *here* with the real president, Omar. The one that's visiting Maine is just an imposter, a stand-in simply posing as president for another month or two. Don't confuse proximity with closeness. Don't mistake illusion for reality."

Omar motioned though the clear walls toward Copley. "Does *he* really believe all this?"

Sammantha nodded. "He came here thinking that he was to play a *role* as president. We told him that the real president was going to have to undergo medical procedures that would incapacitate him for months. The country needed to believe that he was still strong. The country needed Copley's help. Copley has been here for six months, Omar, so long that he forgets who he was. Of course, we've helped with that.

"The first thing we did was to wipe his mind clean, like a pencil eraser to paper. But, just like with an eraser, the paper…in this case the images in his mind…cannot be entirely removed. There is always a shadow of the past, like some faded blueprint upon which the new image is formed. Like the shadow on a hard drive, or a tape or DVR recorder that has been overused, you can record on it fine. Every now and then you get this glitch, a hiccup that mars your picture, a blip that distorts the image. Unlike a tape, though, or even a DVR, the more we program over the old stuff, the *sharper* the new image becomes.

"We do this 24/7; it never stops. When he is awake, all he sees and hears is about Tilson. When he sleeps…we shape his mind though powerful programming methods—chemical, biological, electrical and audio. Through my research I have found a way to digitize video and audio into forms that can be hardwired into the brain. Think of it as neuro linguistic programming on steroids. A virtual reality so real it can make you sweat, bleed, or even die from fright. You want a sexual experience that you will crave forever? Step into my programming chair. I can make you beg me for more, for one more twist of the dial. I can make you do or want anything.

"Everything this man's brain *hears* supports the *fact* that he is the president. He now knows that *he* is the president, that *he* had an accident and has been recovering, that the stand-in has been for *him*, not the other way around.

"Our subject remembers like the president, thinks like the president and acts like the president. He will recognize the faces of people he has never met, remember conversations he has never had. Everything about his life is Jock Tilson. Even his mother will believe he is the president. His closest aides will see no difference." Sammantha paused. "The only potential problem we had was his wife. I took care of that. Poor dear. A casualty of war."

"What is my role?" asked Omar. "Why must I take a year of my life to simply observe? You don't need another nuclear scientist here at the complex. If anything, you are overstaffed. Your reactor can almost run itself, for all you use it for. It's more like a giant battery than a power plant. What possible role could I play here?"

Sammantha patted Omar on the cheek and said, "Greenville is a *far* cry from Seboomook, even though it's just an hour's ride away. There is an ocean between the Northeast Carry and Little Squaw, just as there is between these two men. They are disparate brothers. Soon…soon they will become one. You will be asked to help with that. That is all I can tell you. You will get your chance to play a key role in a great plan."

"But what *is* my role?"

Sammantha looked at Omar. She studied his face, as if its lines could tell him what lay deep within the folds of his brain. He had been raised as a child of Islam, schooled in the strict Sunni Wahabi Madras traditions and the ways of the desert. What sympathies had he acquired during his U.S. education?

Sammantha said, "Think of this place as a desert…a desert you must cross to reach an oasis, an oasis so sweet it's like no place you have ever been. That is what your role is, Omar. You are the camel that will lead us all across the desert to the oasis."

Sammantha pondered her next words, and decided to tell a half truth. "The president will be asked to make extraordinary decisions while in office. Some of these decisions will be military or scientific, and will require an understanding of various technologies and their consequences. You are an expert in nuclear technology, including nuclear weaponry. Yes?"

Omar nodded. "My father and our great and glorious leader, Talid, made that choice for me. I had no say in what I learned in school. I was told to learn about nuclear technology, so that we could harness the atom and sell our oil. Oil is the lifeblood of our nation, our only export. So, naturally we could never use it for our own fuel. It is far too precious."

"Your country has another export, Omar. Terrorism."

Omar's eyes suddenly grew bright, like the blow of a bellows on a dwindling fire. A quick spark that rose and then died. Sammantha wondered if this was the fire of a zealot or the shame of the right-eous. "I am against terrorism," he said flatly. "It gets us nowhere."

"You like America, Omar?"

"Why should I not?"

This time it was Sammantha's eyes that glinted in the unnatural light, glowing red from her own hidden embers, embers that were searing her heart into scar. Omar was perfect.

"You should be pleased. Our plan will help put an end to terrorism, not expand it."

"Really? You see…I wasn't sure. My father and Talid grew up together as boys. They share a bond that is thicker than blood. But Talid…he says and does things…things that I…I just wasn't sure."

Sammantha took Omar's hand and placed it into her palm. His hand was cool and dry; that was good.

"Our plan is glorious, Omar. With our help, America will assume its rightful place in history. America will be reborn. It will achieve a renewal of spirit and purity that will send people singing in the streets."

"Good," said Omar. "I like America."

But you will help destroy it, thought Sammantha. She patted Omar on the shoulder and moved him toward the edge of the observation deck, to the central spoke of the complex. "C'mon," she said. "I must go see him."

Copley was on a stage built to look like a doctor's examining room. He was seated on a padded table that was covered with a white strip of paper, his legs bouncing like a child's as they dangled over the side. Sammantha entered the room wearing a white lab coat. Omar, wearing street clothes, took a seat outside. He could see inside the room through a monitor built into the wall.

"Hello, Mr. President," said Sammantha. She offered her hand to Copley and he shook it firmly.

"Hello again, Dr. Starodubov."

"You look healthy, today."

Copley grinned and patted his rippled stomach. "Been workin' on my six-pack. I feel great."

"Any problems with your training?"

"None."

"Any recurrent dreams?"

"No."

"Don't lie to me."

Copley looked like an early teenage boy who'd been discovered hiding a Playboy Magazine under his mattress, embarrassed at being caught with guilty pleasures. "Really."

Sammantha smiled at Copley. She leaned toward him like a conspiratorial grandmother sneaking extra cookies to him when no one was looking, "C'mon. Out with it."

Copley closed his eyes. Then he looked with a calm, level gaze back at Sammantha. "I dream of you."

Sammantha looked startled, but pleased. "Do you now?"

"I do."

"And what do you dream?"

"I dream that you are naked...I am holding your hand."

Sammantha's face began to flush. She turned away before Copley could notice. She grabbed a stethoscope that was hanging on a wooden peg against the wall, then began to rub it to make it warm.

"Is that all?" she said.

"Well, no. I take your hand and lead you down to the water, by the lake. Then we begin to walk across the lake. And then…and then…we make love. We make love out on the water. Above the water."

"Without sinking?"

Copley laughed. 'Strange, huh?"

"That's your only dream of me?"

"So far, yes. But I have it often."

"Nothing else? You remember nothing else?"

Copley looked puzzled. "What do you mean, remember nothing else? I remember everything."

"Do you remember Kiki?"

"Of course, I do. And I miss her. But life must go on."

"Yes, Mr. President. Life must go on."

Sammantha pressed the stethoscope against Copley's bare chest. "Maybe your dream is a past lives thing. Do you believe in past lives?"

Copley thought for a long moment. He had a vague feeling that he had lived several lives, before the accident, before his boat had crashed and he had wound up here to recuperate.

"How long have I been here?" he asked. "When can I get back to my duties as president? I think I've come a long way, don't you think? I am sufficiently healed to return, I know I am. My memory has come back in great rushing flashes, like an ocean tide that has turned. I remember all the faces now, and all the names. I am ready to resume the job to which I was elected."

Sammantha smiled. Her man *was* ready. They were all ready. *She* was ready.

Sammantha let the stethoscope slide to the floor and closed her eyes.

"Can I tell you something?" she said.

"Please."

"I dream of you, too."

Copley groaned softly. There was an ache inside him, an ache he didn't think he had ever felt. It burned in his chest and in his loins. It spread around him like a warm desert wind. He wanted to reach out to Sammantha, but she was a doctor. She was *his* doctor. How in the hell could he touch his doctor?

Sammantha gently caressed his face. "I shouldn't feel this way," she whispered.

Copley let his hand close around Sammantha's fingers. He drew her toward him. She came willingly. Then she was beside him, surrounding him. He felt her hot breath against his chest, and her hand running along his leg.

"Are you sure you want this?" said Sammantha. Her words came between husky gasps, as she placed her palm in the president's lap.

"Oh, yes," he moaned. "I have wanted this since the first time we met."

"Then you shall have me, Mr. President. You shall have all of me."

Sammantha pressed a button on a remote that was hanging off the end of the examination table. With the cameras off, she began to unbutton her blouse.

CHAPTER **44**
PP

The wailing calls to prayer began to float softly across the city as daylight approached. There was a biting chill to the early morning air, fueled by a steady, sharp wind spilling out from the desert like freezer fog. Trance and his team reached for their individual prayer rugs and laid them upon the warehouse floor. They washed their hands with moist paper towels, then placed them into small plastic bags. Each man knelt upon his rug and pressed his hands out before him in prayer. A jumble of mumbled words spilled through the open warehouse doors. The soft words mixed with the forlorn wailing, sounding like nature sounds around a small Maine pond, like the chuckle of feeding ducks and the call of loons.

After a few minutes the wailing stopped. The men stood up, wound their rugs into tight rolls and placed them side-by-side into the cab of their produce truck. They went back to work loading the daily supplies required by Talid's rolling caravan. There were huge slabs of fresh lamb. There were dates and figs. There were jars of olives and sheep's eyes. There were casks of wine, something forbidden to the holy masses, but relished daily by Talid's inner entourage. There were fruits and vegetables, oils and spices—everything for Talid's daily feasts.

When the truck was fully loaded, Jesse Tompkin pulled down the back panel, shutting Stick and Trance inside. Tompkin walked around to the front of the truck and got inside the cab. As he did, Trance bunched the bottom of his white robe into a ball and began to fold himself into an empty barrel, identical to others that were filled with rice. He checked the barrel staves to make sure they were loose enough to allow him air to breathe, but also tight enough to hold him in. Satisfied, he curled himself inside.

Stick nestled the barrel's cap over the top. He tightened a metal band around it and pounded on top with his fist.

"You going to be okay in there Trance?"

"I've been in tighter spots," came Trance's muffled reply.

"For sixteen hours?"

Trance laughed. He'd have to stay in the barrel long enough for Talid's evening help to retire. Only then could Swartz's inside people release him and lead him to Roxanne Flame. Their best guess was sixteen hours, curled together like a pretzel and squished like a sardine in a can.

As the cover sealed shut, Trance allowed himself to fall into a deep meditation, one in which he would remain until the time was right.

There was a soft tap on the top of the barrel. Trance felt it more than he heard it, deep inside the back of his mind. As he emerged from his meditation he felt a sudden rush of pain, like barbed wire wrapping around each of his joints. He ignored it.

Trance tapped six times on the side of the barrel. Then he could hear the squeak of metal, as the top band was lifted away. The barrel staves fell apart like banana peels and he was left sitting upon the floor, wrapped as tightly as an unfurled rose.

"Quick," said a man.

Trance opened his eyes and looked around. There were two men walking around him picking up the remnants of the barrel. A woman stood about twenty feet away, holding a white handbag in one fist. The woman was peering out through the crack of a slightly opened door. The room itself was dark, but light spilled in through the door as if it were aimed by a flashlight.

"Now," said the woman.

The two men lifted Trance off the floor and waited while he uncoiled himself. They handed him a keffiyeh, which he fastened around his head. He adjusted the soft leather purse that was wrapped around his waist. Then he unfolded his robe and let it fall to the floor.

"Hurry," said one of the men. He tugged on Trance's robe and pulled him to the woman by the door. Trance followed silently on the balls of his feet. The woman took Trance by the hand and began to lead him out into the hallway.

"My name is Karen," she said in Farsi.

"An unusual Arabic name," whispered Trance, also in Farsi. "You look American."

"Miss Georgia. Runner up, Miss USA, six years ago."

"Here voluntarily?"

"Are you kidding? I was offered a million dollars a year to come here. *Just to entertain my guests*, Talid had said. *No sex involved*." Karen snorted. "In that time I haven't seen a dime, other than my tips. Talid stole my passport and locked me in this godforsaken place. I've seen many a fat Arab ass in that time. European, too. Japanese, African, Chinese. Talid has many so-called *friends*." Karen paused and drew a resigned breath. "To give him credit, he makes most of them wear condoms, all but the most favored. He tests us after each encounter so that he can guarantee our purity. You get an STD they can't cure and you vanish. To where, I don't know. We work just once a week, so we stay fresh. Unless, of course, we get bruised or cut. His friends have some serious perversions…You get me out of this place and I'll kiss your feet."

Trance looked along the walls and ceiling, checking for video surveillance equipment. Surprisingly, he saw none.

Two men approached. Instead of robes, the men wore sand colored military camouflage gear. Each had an Uzi on the shoulder. One of men held up a hand and Karen stopped.

"State your business," he said.

Karen held up her white bag and offered it to the man. She said, "We needed food."

The man peered into the bag and nodded. Then he looked at Trance.

"Who is he?"

"Our great and powerful leader, General Mu'annar Abu Hussein al-Talid, asked me to entertain this important visitor."

Trance smiled at the man and said, softly, in Arabic, "Allah is good. Allah is great. And he has shown me great fortune." Trance lifted up his purse and said, "You want to see my toys?"

The man's teeth glowed white beneath his sunburned lips. He shook his head and motioned them forward. "Take her once for me," he said.

Trance smiled and waved. "Right," he mumbled under his breath.

"That was close," said Karen, once they were clear. "To get this close to Talid and fail…"

Trance interrupted. "Is that your expectation?"

Karen squeezed his hand. "I only hope that you'll slit his throat."

Trance pulled at Karen's hand and turned her toward him. He whispered, "Just so we're clear, my goal is not to kill Talid. I am here to warn him." He paused. "I *will* take you from here. Tonight, if you are ready. He might want to hunt you down; you know that?"

Karen nodded slowly, with both disappointment and fear showing in her face.

Trance said, "We'll set you up with a new identity and some funds. You okay with that?"

Karen's eyes grew focused and resolute. "Allah be praised. May seventy virgins bless your bed."

Trance snickered, "Don't thank me yet. You could just as easily die as escape tonight."

"Either fate is better than this."

"Lead on, princess."

Karen led Trance along a broad hallway floored with rough brown marble. The walls were a kind of pale yellow stucco, with thick, bullet-proof windows spaced every five paces along one side. Elaborate clusters of weaponry hung between each window. Swords of every shape and size, spears, slings, bows and arrows. There were leather breast plates fitted with dented bronze, leather wrist guards and war sandals of an enormous variety. On the opposite side of the hall was a series of doors, each of them numbered, with golden doorknobs the size of a large fist protruding like a phallus from each one. Every ten yards there were indented alcoves with prayer rugs, water bowls and statues of Muhammad blessing the faithful at each one. The hallway stretched for a good hundred and twenty yards before ending at an intersecting hallway. Trance noted one very odd thing; there still were no cameras.

"You could get lost in here," said Trance.

"Over three hundred rooms. A palace fit for a king."

"Or a psychotic despot."

"That, too."

"The alcoves…facing Mecca?"

"Yep."

"One other thing, Karen?"

"What's that?"

"Why no cameras? Surely Talid has security?"

"Talid's afraid that something will be recorded without his knowledge and then used against him. As for security…he has hundreds of guards, and he gives them extraordinary latitude. If they suspect you, they kill first and ask questions later."

"Friendly place."

"Many Arabs find that this is the only way to rule their people and keep their power."

Karen turned left. The hallway stretched for another thirty yards before ending at an ornate golden door. This time, rather than a round doorknob, there was an erect gold penis protruding upward. There were two guards standing by the door, one on each side. They stood stiffly, looking forward like statues. Karen stepped in front of one of the guards and showed the contents of her bag. He looked down and nodded. Then Karen placed her hand between his legs and massaged him until well after his pants began to bulge. Karen went to the other guard and repeated the process. After a satisfied groan the guard waved them both along, without bothering to check Trance's bag.

Karen placed her hand on the bulging gold penis and looked at Trance. "Entrance to the pleasure palace," she said in Arabic, as she pulled down on the penis. The door swung open and they went inside.

"Quite the ritual you have with the guards."

Karen smirked. "We've got them conditioned like dogs. If they ignore what or who we bring inside the chambers, we please them. If they hassle us…we kick their balls. Which would you choose?"

"Any cameras here?"

"In our chambers only. We can turn the cameras on and off at a patron's pleasure. Talid is very camera shy, particularly with his clothes off. Might have something to do with his tiny little pecker."

"That's a very good thing to know."

Karen smiled. "Some men think they're porn stars. They want a little souvenir, or something to play with once they get home. If they ask, we record our exploits and ham it up for the camera. Once I earned a million dollar tip. Took two months to recover from the beating, though. Bastard."

Trance looked watchfully about the entryway. "Isn't that a pleasant thought."

"There are some sick perverts in this world. We're forced to act out their darkest fantasies."

"Lucky you."

Karen started walking inward. "This way."

Talid's harem chamber was enormous. It was furnished like a Las Vegas whorehouse, with red flowing drapes, a pink rug and purple furniture. There were tables of mahogany and burled walnut. Erotic marble statues were standing everywhere. There were also pictures of Elvis Presley painted on velvet.

Karen stopped beside a dark wooden door. This one had no doorknob, just a black iron ring. Karen used the ring as a knocker, tapping three times in rapid succession. Someone knocked back twice. Karen knocked one more time. The door swung open and Roxanne Flame's impressive visage spilled into view.

Talid's favorite concubine stood six feet two inches tall. She had an hourglass figure, with an eighteen inch waist topped by an impressive balcony of breast. Her hips were womanly, but solid and slim. Her butt was tight. Her face looked like that of a fashion model, with big, pulpy, Angelina Jolie lips and high angular cheekbones. Her eyes were wide and the color of violets.

"Hello," she said. Her voice was deep and husky. She held out her hand for Trance to shake.

Looking at Roxanne, Trance was not sure if this was a man or a woman. She was erotically beautiful and built for a virile man's pleasure, but there was the hint of masculinity around the mouth, and a sly smile that seemed to say *I know what you're thinking and I'm not going to tell.*

Trance shook the outstretched hand. He found it firm but smooth, like a woman. Definitely female.

"Thank you for helping me," said Trance.

Roxanne's purple eyes lit playfully, as commencing an amused, but mostly hidden dance. "No," she said. "Thank *you* for helping me."

Roxanne gave Karen a quick peck on the cheek and motioned Trance inside her room.

In stark contrast to the entryway, Roxanne's suite was tastefully decorated with light earth tones. The furniture was imported from old European royalty. Elizabethan oak and walnut, with elaborate inlays and carvings. Graceful Queen Anne chairs and tables with cabriole legs and fiddle backs. There were Renaissance paintings by Raphael and Caravaggio as well as two sculptures by Bernini. Trance gazed around the room and nodded.

"Very nice."

"Not nearly as impressive as your family's collection, Mr. Trance."

Trance felt a surge of adrenaline that was almost strong enough to stop his heart. The hair along the back of his neck rose, rippled and then tingled like it was asleep.

"Who told you my name?"

"My handler, of course."

"Who?"

"Swartz."

"You sure this room isn't bugged?"

Roxanne laughed. It was a throbbing laugh, starting somewhere deep in her lungs or thighs and coming out in practiced, breathless gasps. "Talid wouldn't hear of audio or video, honey, not with the things he says and does to me."

Roxanne motioned for Trance to follow her into a much larger room, the bedroom.

"This is where I serve my country."

"Your service is a noble one."

Roxanne laughed. This was followed by a tired sigh. "We all have our God-given talents."

Trance walked to the bed and spilled the contents of his leather bag onto the fluffy silk comforter. The purse held a pack of gum, a small bottle of Scope mouthwash, a toothbrush, a large tube of toothpaste and a package of Keebler cheese and crackers. Trance split open the toothpaste tube and removed a syringe and three small vials. All three vials were filled with clear liquid. One vial had a thin layer of what looked like wine sediment on the bottom. Another held what looked like a small chunk of pencil lead floating inside. The third was only liquid. Trance cut into the side of the bag and pulled out a second syringe. This one had a much thicker, hollow point, almost the width of a crochet needle.

"Ouch," said Roxanne.

"He won't feel a thing," said Trance.

"If you say so."

"How much time?"

Roxanne looked at her watch. "An hour. Maybe two."

Trance nodded. "Good."

Roxanne was wearing a translucent silk robe over what appeared to be an outfit purchased from a Frederick's catalogue. She shifted her weight and stretched. She put a leg on the bed and leaned forward to stretch some more. The edge of her gown fell away, revealing a long, shapely leg that ended in a frilly pink thong the size of a tea bag.

"You want to kill some time before then?" she said.

Trance smiled. "I think you're beautiful, Roxanne. But, no thanks. I'm spoken for."

"You don't know what you're missing," Roxanne said in a playful, teasing voice. "This is a once-in-a-lifetime thing."

Trance could see what Talid found appealing about Roxanne. Besides the oversized proportions and the extraordinary facial lines, there was a childish playfulness in her manner, something that tugged at his manhood, but also at the boy inside him.

"I'm very good with my imagination," he said.

"I can do that, too."

Trance laughed "I bet you can."

Roxanne put her foot back upon the floor and stood facing Trance, her legs square.

"Let's get it done then," she said.

Trance pressed Roxanne gently against a wall. "Close your eyes. Keep your head against the wall and don't move."

Roxanne closed her eyes and waited for the pain.

"We have to do this," said Trance.

"I know."

"Otherwise, Talid will suspect you. He may suspect you still."

"Just beat me up good."

"Do not move, Roxanne. Remember. No matter what you feel."

Trance had years of intensive martial arts training, including a three year tutelage with the finest masters in Japan. There were times when he'd practiced ten hours a day, perfecting all that his masters demanded and more. Trance closed his eyes. He squared his stance. He centered his *Ki* and called upon the Universal forces. Then, in rapid succession, he flung his hands out with six quick strikes, hitting Roxanne three times in the face and three more in the body.

"Well?" said Roxanne. "Aren't you going to do something serious?"

Trance opened his eyes. "I already did."

Roxanne frowned. "I felt something on my face, like the tap of a feather. And then again on my chest. You need to beat the crap out of me, Trance."

Trance smiled. "Go look in the mirror."

Roxanne padded softly into the bathroom. "Holy shit."

There were crimson lumps forming above and below Roxanne's left eye. Her lip was swelling into the size of a pickle. Roxanne touched at the wounds but there was no pain, only a growing pressure. She walked back over to Trance and said, "How'd you do that?"

"I hit your outer blood vessels with a great but precise force, causing them to break and swell. I didn't hit deep enough to bruise the bone, or even damage your nerves. My gift to you. You'll look like hell for a few days. But, other than a little stiffness, you'll feel no pain."

Trance took hold of Roxanne's wrist and tapped on it with a rapid movement she couldn't see. Then he did the same to the other wrist.

"That tingles."

"Wait a second."

A moment later Roxanne closed her eyes. "I feel it."

Then, as if being blown up like a balloon, Roxanne's wrists began to swell to nearly double their size.

"That sort of hurts."

Trance shrugged. "It's going to look like hell. If you take a couple Advil you'll feel fine." Trance motioned toward the outer room. "Does he knock?"

Roxanne shook her head.

"Better lie on the bed, then. When he comes in, you'll want to look like you've been beaten and left for dead."

"That's how he leaves me sometimes. It'll save him the effort."

Trance motioned Roxanne to the bed and slid to a corner of the room. He turned the lights down to a pale glow. Now, all he could do was wait.

An hour and a half later, the door swung open with a soft squeak of its hinges. Trance watched as Talid crept quietly into the room. Then, as if waking from slumber, Roxanne turned her face toward the Arab leader.

Talid took a step backwards. He reached for the dagger in his belt, but he was too late. Trance glided across the room and ripped it out of his hand.

"Trance," said Talid.

Talid began to cry out but Trance thrust with an open palm to Talid's chest. Talid's mouth started opening and closing like a barracuda. But no words could escape his tightened airways, nor could he breathe for several long moments.

"Yes, Talid. It's me." Trance looked over toward Roxanne. In a show of apparent fear, Roxanne pushed herself as far back on the bed as she could go, pressing her spine against the headboard.

"Don't hurt me again," Roxanne whispered. "Please."

Trance winked and looked back at Talid. "I should kill you right now. But I am a peaceful man. I am here solely to give you a warning. I know that you have been trying to kill me. Why, I don't know. I want *you* to know, that if you try it again, or hurt anyone that I care about, I am going to return to your beautiful little country and pull your body apart, limb by limb. Then I am going to bring your remains to a pig farm and put them in the slop. Your body will go inside all the little pigs and you'll become one with them." Trance paused, as if thinking about his words. "You know, maybe I'll even keep a few of the pigs to slaughter and then eat when I feel like it. Then I can pass your remains out though my own bodily orifices. Doesn't that sound like fun?"

When Talid could speak, it was with a hoarse, choking whimper. "I will kill you."

Trance hit Talid's chest again. "Wrong answer. Let's try this one more time."

The air rushed out of Talid's lungs. He bent over, gasping spasmodically. Once he could breathe again, Talid said, "You think that by coming here, to my home that you can intimidate me? Intimidate me, who was brought up on the streets eating rats for food? Clawing for every small step forward?

"You, who embodies everything that I hate about this world, about the west, about America? You, who grew up with abhorrent privileges that no man should know."

"Like the ones you enjoy now, you mean?"

Talid snorted. "You can't bait me, Trance. I am on the side of Allah. Allah has called for the extermination of the west, of men like you…your sick, perverse, sex-crazed society—"

Trance pointed around the room. "Like the sex den you have here?"

Talid tried to spit in Trance's face, but the spit just dribbled down his chin. "You and your pornographic movies and websites, movie stars and your drugs."

Trance sniffed the air. He could smell the pungent scent of hashish on Talid. He also knew about Talid's penchant for pornography and kinky sex. "And you are so pure."

"Enough!"

Trance whipped his hand forward, palm up, and struck Talid's nose. Blood erupted from both nostrils. The nose remained unbroken, as Trance had planned.

"I am here in friendship," said Trance. "I want only to end the violence. I will end it with your death, if I have to. But I would rather that we both live in peace. Can you understand that?"

Talid seemed to ponder Trance's words. Then he lied, his voice growing stronger with every word. "I, too, am a peaceful man, Mr. Trance. I see that I was misinformed. My people told me that you were out to kill *me*."

"Not so. If I was, you would be dead, I assure you."

Talid spread out his hands. His eyes were sharp, even in the dull bedroom light. "Then you shall be my guest." He moved toward the exit. "Come. Come with me."

Trance whipped his hand out again. This time he struck the back of Talid's neck. Talid flopped to the floor as if his legs had turned to water.

"Is he dead?" asked Roxanne. Her voice seemed eerily, perversely concerned.

Trance could sense Roxanne's liking for this man, some rail spur off of Stockholm Syndrome, he suspected. "No. He's just out for a bit. I need him unconscious."

Trance lifted Talid and dropped him onto the bed. Then he reached for his tools. First, he took the syringe with the large needle. He used it to suck the small, dark gray chunk out of one of the vials. He plunged the needle into Talid's nasal cavity. "Believe it or not," he said. "This is a carbon based capacitor and microchip—undetectable unless its presence is already known. It recharges itself from the body, and is the control center for the nanobots I will inject into his blood."

Roxanne tilted her head as if to protest, but remained silent. Trance looked at her. "Are you okay with this?"

Roxanne nodded. "He killed my parents."

Trance pressed down on the syringe until a clear liquid ran out of one of Talid's nostrils. Once the chip was secure, Trance grasped the syringe with the smaller needle. He held up the vial with the sediment inside. "This vial contains thousands of microscopic robots. They are programmed to form themselves into several different machines, all controlled by the chip I've inserted. The machine we will use most often is a microphone. These little babies can rally around each other and created a sound so pure it could be marketed by Bose."

"Won't he know?"

Trance shook his head. "I hit him in the nose for a reason. When he wakes up, his sinuses will ache for a couple of days. He'll think that it's from the beating. After that, he'll never feel a thing, other than a little tickle now and then. The nanobots will circulate harmlessly in his blood and assemble only when called. When they are, presumably, we will be able to hear his every word, provided we've got a receiver close by."

"Damn."

Trance cocked his own head. "Problem?"

"Will Swartz be able to hear what I say?"

"Not sure. Maybe. Talid's got sophisticated electronics in his palaces, as a defense against such things."

"So, what do I do?"

"Do what you always do."

Roxanne looked at Trance as if stunned. She looked dazed for a long moment, then she laughed. "Oh, man, are they going to love this." Roxanne's eyes began to well with tears. "If they do hear me, you better make sure that nothing I say or do gets posted on the Web. Talid's a junkie for porn. He'd find it somehow."

"Your secrets are safe with us, Roxanne."

Roxanne twisted her lips into a smile and said, "My name's Rhonda Katz. Israeli Mossad. Orphaned at the age of ten and recruited to the cause."

Trance nodded and closed his eyes. "Did you know Rebecca Koppleman? She was my fiancée."

"I knew her well. She helped train me."

Trance exhaled slowly. "I loved her."

"So did I. Her death was a tragedy."

Roxanne spoke like a callous professional, or, perhaps, with the unemotional detachment of someone who had endured far too much grief. Trance couldn't decide which path had led her here.

Trance used the smaller syringe to pull liquid from the third, clear vial. "This…" he said, "…will keep Talid unconscious for the next twelve hours." Trance plunged the needle into Talid's shoulder muscle. "When he wakes up, you tell him I took pictures of his tiny little weenie. If he ever goes after me, even if he kills me, they'll get posted on his favorite websites."

Trance turned to Roxanne. "I'm going to have to tie you up and gag you. You'll need to stay that way until he wakes up. You want me to leave you awake or asleep, like him?" Trance motioned toward the prone Talid.

"He might want to kill me, no?"

"Could be."

"I'll stay awake."

Trance looked to his watch. "I'm going to remain here for another hour. I'll tie you up before I leave. I'm taking Karen with me. You sure you want to stay?"

Roxanne nodded. "My work is vital here."

"It is."

Trance extended his hand. Roxanne grabbed it and pulled Trance against her. "Thank you for doing this," she said.

"It's what we do," said Trance. He hugged Roxanne back. Then he said, "Can you call Karen?"

Roxanne nodded. "When it's time."

***

When Trance and Karen slipped out though the harem's entry door, Karen stopped to allow each guard to grope her. Then she went to work on the men, until each man grunted in pleasure. Trance waited with his faced turned away, fighting an unusually powerful urge to change the guards' *he's* into *she's*.

When Trance and Karen slipped back into the kitchen, the same two men who had helped them before were waiting by the door.

"You need to hurry. The truck is almost ready to go," said one.

Trance pointed to Karen. "She is coming with me."

Both men shook their heads at once. "We have nothing for her."

"Put her in my cask. Go get another wine or rice barrel. There are empty ones, are there not?"

"Yes, but—"

"Do it!"

One of the men hurried out of the room, waving his arms through a forest of clear plastic strips that were hanging from the ceiling. He came back a short while later carrying a smallish wine cask. "This is all we had, unless you want us to empty one from storage. There's no way you can fit—"

Trance measured the cask with his eyes and said, "How much time do we have?"

"Mere moments."

Trance looked around the kitchen. Dozens of cooking utensils were hanging off of chrome hooks that were screwed into the ceiling and the walls. Trance began grabbing at them until his hands were half full. He unhooked the top of the cask. When it popped he slipped the edge of a meat cleaver under the barrel's wooden cap and pulled it away from the barrel staves. The end of the cask came off in one, round piece. Trance quickly cleaved slivers off of three of the side staves to let in air. Then he stepped into the barrel and folded his body like a circus performer. "Seal me in and get us out of here," he said. They did, barely.

CHAPTER 45

_______________PP_______________

Jack Trance carefully lowered himself into his jet's cockpit and closed his eyes. His muscles felt like he'd been pounded with a hammer. His joints ached from being stuffed into the tiny cask like a pile of dirty laundry, especially his shoulders, which he'd been forced to pull out of their sockets just to fit inside.

Soon Trance felt the ground begin to rumble, as his prototype jet began to lift off the runway at Israel's Ben-Gurion International Airport. Trance stretched, then looked out the window. He glanced first to the rows of buildings flying by underneath. He looked to the stretch of clear blue water to the west. Then he looked to the man beside him in the pilot's seat, his faithful friend, Stick Granger.

Trance said, "That was a nice vacation, hey? Ready to get back to work?"

"I really wanted to try out one of those barrels, Trance. How come you get all the fun?"

"Lucky, I guess."

Stick didn't look at Trance. He kept his eyes moving between the instruments and the jet's windshield. "This thing is a bear to fly, JT."

Trance stared out the window to his right, letting his mind float free as the plane began to bank toward the northwest. "What do you expect from a craft built to exceed Mach 1.8?"

"I'm more the comfort type."

"Next time I'll bring my G650. She goes half the speed. You more comfy with that?"

Stick grinned and adjusted the thrusters. The jet shot forward, slapping Trance's head against the headrest.

"Ouch."

"She's a bit touchy, but she sure does fly," said Stick.

Trance grinned. "Thing of beauty, ain't she?"

"I'll say." Stick reached Mach 1.5, close to one thousand miles per hour. He put the jet on autopilot and settled back into his seat.

"You gonna tell me what we're doing with one of Talid's women?"

"She was a prisoner and she wanted out."

"She's gonna be trouble, Jack. Talid's gonna freak."

Trance pursed his lips. "Maybe."

***

As the jet prepared to land in Paris, Trance picked up an oddly shaped phone that was built into the side of the cockpit. He adjusted several knobs on the dashboard to scramble the signal, then dialed a number in Washington, D.C. It was mid morning in Paris and 3 A.M. on America's east coast. The phone rang several times before a tired voice answered.

"This better be good."

"Hello, Slow Turtle. How are you this fine morning?" Trance was speaking to Jacob Miller, his former handler at T-Force, now director of the CIA. Slow Turtle wasn't Miller's code name, but Trance often called him this, just to pull his chain.

"Asleep. Call me later, Red Dragon."

"Isn't it 3 A.M. your time? You should be awake and spooking by now." Trance paused. "I've got some good news and some bad news."

"So what's new?"

"Which do you want first?"

"Give me the bad news."

"I just liberated a woman from Desert Fang."

"Is that all?" Stealing a woman from Talid was not good. Not good at all.

"That's about it."

"So, you're telling me that I better alert Centurion that we may be at war?"

Trance laughed. "I wouldn't go that far."

"Better lay it on me, Red Dragon."

Trance explained what had happened, and how Karen, his passenger, had begged to be saved, that she was an American, and that Talid had stolen her passport.

"Let me get this straight. You entered Fang's residence illegally. You told him you were there. You beat his face in. You beat up his favorite courtesan. You drugged him. Then you took a member of his pride?"

"That sounds about right."

"What the fuck were you thinking?"

"It's okay. He won't bother us."

"You stick your face into the snake's den, an unholy reptile with enormous resources and a hair trigger for vengeance, you insult him, you beat him up, you humiliate him and he's not going to retaliate?"

"He was trying to kill me. I asked him nicely to stop."

"Why didn't you just slit his throat?"

"I'm a non-violent man. How dare you suggest such a thing? I asked him nicely to leave me alone. I expect his cooperation."

"I'm sure he'll do just what you ask. Better tell me the good news."

Trance decided not to tell Miller about the nasal nanobots, at least for now. He had to give Miller something, for Karen's sake. "I have photos."

"He doesn't give a shit about photos."

"Of his tiny little pecker? Of him lying in what looks to be a drunken stupor? The threat of embarrassment to a man like Talid is far more powerful than the threat of death."

"We'll see."

"Don't worry. It's a teeny little thing."

Miller let off a deep, tired sigh. He had a slow, raspy wheeze. Trance wondered if he was sick, or just working too hard. Probably both.

"Where are you?"

"Heading toward Paris."

"You're ETA?"

Trance lied. "Three hours, give or take."

"I'll take care of your cargo," said Miller. "You know where to bring her."

"I want her cared for. She put herself in harm's way for my benefit. I'll have my people wire funds. Make sure she gets them."

"I want you debriefed once you land."

"No can do. I'm meeting friends and dropping them off at home...in the South Pacific. We're on a tight schedule. I'll be back in a week or two or three. We'll chat then. Ciao." Trance hung up. "Well, that takes care of that."

As Stick taxied the jet off the runway toward the Hopewell hangar, a gray Bentley limousine drove out to meet them. The moment the plane was secure, a man and a woman emerged from the limo and walked to the base of the jet's stairway. Trance looked out the cockpit window and groaned. "It's Arthur R. Winthrop, III. Here to ruin my day."

Stick said, "Sure must be tough, having all those billions. A real hard life you've got there, Trance."

Trance frowned. It was the kind of look he'd give when smelling a skunk in the driveway or under the front porch—something that said, *I'd want anything else but this.*

"You want to trade?"

"No friggin' way."

"I didn't ask for this, Stick. I'd shed it all if I could."

"You mean the *saving the world* crap?"

"I wouldn't quite put it that way."

"Why don't you just live like the rest of us?"

"You know I can't do that. The Madonna would never—"

"Shhh," interrupted Stick, while making a motion to his right.

Karen had come up from her seat in the back and was standing behind them, preparing to deplane.

"How was the movie?" said Trance.

"Nice to have such a wide selection of films. Your meal service was exceptional. You want a tip?"

Trance smiled. "Not allowed on my fleet."

"I know who you are."

Trance wasn't surprised. "I know you do."

Trance motioned for Karen to step down the jet's stairs into the Paris sunshine. The day had already warmed to a comfortable seventy degrees. The sky was as smooth and blue as a robin's egg. Trance followed Stick down the stairs. The others continued toward the limousine, while Trance hung back to meet with Arthur Winthrop and his assistant.

"Where in the hell have you been, Jack?"

"Good to see you, too," said Trance. "Do you have Karen's new passport?"

Winthrop pulled an envelope out of his suit coat pocket and handed it to Trance.

"You've been gone for two weeks, Jack. You weren't answering your phone…your emails…texts…your voicemail…nothing."

"I pay you twenty million dollars a year to make decisions on your own, Art."

"But it's your money—"

Trance held up a hand. "I love you, Art; you know that. But I've got more important things to do than run this company. If you can't do it, I'll get someone who can. Until then, I need you to run things."

"Nanotel Organogenesis is in play. I know you are tight with the CEO."

Trance eyes widened and he grinned. "Ahhh." This company *was* in the center of Trance's radar, a company he needed to own. Nanotel had a huge negative cash flow but off-the-charts potential in the fields of next generation computers, electronics, batteries, capacitors, metamaterials, nanotechnology and bio medicine. Its CEO had a pet project conducting advanced research into man-made photosynthesis using quantum mechanics. Successful research could require hundreds of millions of dollars in funding, something other companies would never be willing to spend without a better chance at success. Trance would fund it to fruition.

Trance had often approached Nanotel's chairman and founder about joining forces. Yet, Trance had failed to convince him to sell to his own growing group of companies. Trance had been allowed to purchase low interest bonds that were convertible into fifteen percent of the outstanding voting stock, as insurance for its founder against a hostile takeover. So, maybe this was the day.

"What's the deal?"

"Nanotel's third tier funding fell through. There's been a two billion dollar tender for all the outstanding stock, by a new joint venture between Intel and Roche's Genentech. I'm ready to jump, but I don't want to spend that kind of money without your permission. A few hundred million and I wouldn't bother you. But three plus billion? I thought I'd better ask."

"What's our cash position?"

"Twelve billion in the U.S. Most of that is spoken for, due to all the opportunities in the markets."

"How 'bout in Europe?"

"That's why I'm here. I've been making the rounds and counting everything in the vaults. You know how long it takes to weigh all that gold and count cash? Why don't you deposit it all in banks, like most normal people?"

"You know I have my reasons. How much?"

Winthrop smiled. "I stopped at twenty billion. Didn't even get out of France. How much money do we have, really? And *how the hell* did Hopewell Industries get all that gold?"

Trance smiled. "That, my friend, is a very long story."

"I wish you'd tell me some time."

Trance turned on his PDA. He punched in the password, swiped his thumb over the biometric pad and dialed a number off his speed dial. Ten seconds later it was answered by Jerome Freeman, founder and CEO of Nanotel Organogenesis.

"Hello?" His voice was groggy.

"It's Trance."

"I've been calling you every day for two weeks, Jack. Been texting and emailing, too. Where've you been?"

Trance hadn't checked his voicemail, his texts or his email since he had arrived on Stick Granger's island. He scrolled through his PDA and found a long list of messages from Freeman.

"I've been in a remote location, Jerome. I'm sorry."

"You've heard, I take it?"

"Art just told me. We both know that Intel and Genentech are going to cut you in half and devour the remains. Neither will fund your key projects. Those will meet a sure, suffocating death."

"Nice image, Jack."

"M&A isn't pretty, Jerome."

"For once, I'm listening. I like my independence. That's why I've always held you off. Got this vision thing, you know?"

"We share the same vision, Jerome. I also owe you my life."

"And I owe you mine. Let's leave family out of this, Jack. This is a business deal and I've got investors to protect."

"Here's my proposal. You got a pen?"

"Lay it on me."

"I'll up their offer by forty percent. I'll pay cash. You get to run the company and set your own salary. You get a ten year deal with stock options on two percent of the company each year that you hit the target *you* set. I'll pay the tax. I'll also set aside a ten percent stock pool for management, with another one percent each year in shadow stock bonuses. I will fold two of my divisions *into* your subsidiary and give you control. You'll want to keep their management in place. You'll see why.

"You'll be like a kid in a candy store, Jerome, believe me. I'll give you an immediate five hundred million cash infusion and up your annual R&D budget by another two hundred million. I'll also fund every dime you need for your photosynthesis, ceramics, bio-medical and metamaterials research. I'll also let you play with my new quantum computer."

Jerome remained silent for a long time. Finally, he said, "You have a frigging quantum computer?"

"They tell me it will be operational within the year."

The phone stayed silent again. Trance could almost feel Freeman's mind at work. Then Jerome said, "What's the catch, Jack?"

"No catch, Jerome. You and I see what the future needs. We are willing to fight for it, no matter how difficult it gets. I'm willing to invest in your vision, our vision, no matter how much and how long it takes. I've got more money than I need, so why not invest in mankind?"

"Amen, brother."

"We have a deal?"

"What if they increase their tender?"

"I'll exceed it again. But don't play me, Jerome."

"Never, Jack. We've got a deal."

"Good. I'm sending Art to handle everything. He speaks for me. He'll wire the cash anywhere you please."

"I'll talk to the board, but it's a formality, since I control forty percent of the company and you can convert to fifteen. You knew it would come to this, didn't you?"

"I hoped it would, Jerome. Look, I won't be in country for another couple weeks; but I'll keep my ears on. Semper Fi."

"Semper Fi, brother."

Trance turned to Art Winthrop and said, "You get that?"

Winthrop nodded.

"Do whatever it takes." Trance motioned toward the Bentley limo. "Can we drop you anywhere?"

"We've got another car in the hanger. And Jack…"

"Yes?"

"Be careful."

"You know I never take risks." Trance stuck out his hand for his friend to take. As the two men shook, Arthur Winthrop grimaced, wilting under the power of Trance's grip. "Sorry," said Trance. "I forget."

Winthrop flapped his hand like it had been stung. "How 'bout if we hug next time?"

Trance turned and prepared to walk away. "Call me if we have a problem. Okay?"

"Sure, boss."

"Have fun, Art. This is world changing stuff and you're riding out in front."

"Yee hah."

Trance grinned. Hearing Art Winthrop say *yee hah* was as likely as hearing the Japanese emperor sing karaoke. Art Winthrop was far more comfortable with *you have a fine balance sheet, sir,* or *that was a fine shot,* than he was with anything remotely related to normal emotion. However, he was an extraordinary administrator. He drew intense loyalty and respect from his people, and from Trance. He could be trusted, to the death, although Trance hoped it would never come to that.

Trance stepped into the Bentley and allowed the driver to shut the door behind him.

"Hi, sweetheart," Lauren said, as she gave Trance a long hug. "Everything okay? Why isn't Art coming with us?"

"He's got some work to do."

"Care to share?"

"I'm buying Nanotel Organogenesis."

"Wow, Jack. When did this happen?"

"Just now."

"That was your negotiation? Two minutes on the phone?"

"You spend time under fire with someone, you get to know and trust them. Jerome and I go back a bit."

"That was still too fast. Negotiations should take weeks or months."

Trance's eyes seemed to darken, as if someone had pulled the cord on a light inside him. He didn't like what had built his company. It had been owned by his grandfather and his uncle. His uncle had betrayed his country and his president. His grandfather had nearly betrayed mankind. Both had tried to kill him…their own flesh and blood. He didn't want the company, didn't crave the money, didn't need the lifestyle or want the power. But he had been forced to take it all, not because of his grandfather's and his uncle's wills, but because of fate, his *destiny*. He had a mission to fulfill. Nanotel Organogenesis was part of that plan.

That wasn't the only reason that Trance grew somber. Jerome Freeman had already been a big part of Trance's destiny, a part he tried to keep locked in the vault of his mind, a part whose collection of dust was now being blown into the forefront of his brain. *Why not tell her?*

"Let me tell you about Jerome Freeman, Lauren." Trance paused. He closed his eyes and spoke softly. "Remember that time I was captured in Iran?"

"The time you never talk about?"

"Yeah, that time. I'm going to tell you a hypothetical story, just so you know, so that you understand that there is someone in this world that would give everything he owns to Jerome Freeman, if he would take it.

"Imagine, hypothetically, three soldiers breaking through the doors of a small prison, taking on half a dozen men, guns blazing, knives slashing. While two men haul a half-dead prisoner to his feet, the other sees that certain body parts have recently been removed from that prisoner. Fresh blood is still seeping through his pant legs. All the prisoner can do is moan, with a face so beat up that it is almost unrecognizable.

"Rather than leave with the others, this young marine goes even deeper into the prison, taking on the remaining guards, all in search of a trophy. You've got this pretty boy, the son of an orthopedic surgeon, schooled at Lawrenceville Academy and Princeton, looking like Michael Jordan with his head shaved and as shiny and black as an eight ball. The only thing Freeman can think about is finding a jar that he knows must be there. You see, that's the signature move of the butcher who tortured this hypothetical prisoner. The butcher's got…had…a collection of jars with names and dates. You get the picture? Jerome Freeman keeps looking for that name tag, knowing it must be there, refusing to leave until he has it. After several tense minutes, Freeman emerges from the prison, just as the helo is going airborne.

"When they get to Frankfurt, the visiting vascular urologist tells the men that it's virtually hopeless, trying to reattach those body parts. The former prisoner would be lucky to live through the night as it was. They've got other surgeries to perform, ones with far more chance at success."

Trance laughed. "That stupid shit, Freeman, pulls out a pistol and explains to the surgeon that he will perform that operation. He and his team will be successful or else Freeman will shoot off their nuts, so they can see how much they like it.

"Today, there is a former hypothetical prisoner who owes a great deal to Jerome Freeman. A man that…someday…maybe…might want and be able to have children. Any goodness that happens to Jerome Freeman could never pay off the debt that it owed to him."

Lauren gazed at Trance, speechless. What could she say to that? Lauren stroked Trance's cheek and kissed him. "Upon further thought, I think that's a fair deal."

Lauren knew she had to lighten the mood, so she turned to Karen and said, "Aren't you going to introduce us?"

"Sure," said Trance. "This is my new girlfriend, Karen. She was an escort for Talid. Now she's mine."

Lauren's jaw hung for a brief second. Then she said, "The more the merrier."

Karen said, "Jack spent last night with another woman, though. What was her name, Jack? Roxanne or something? She was *hot*."

Trance grinned at Lauren, saying, "Roxanne sure had fire. She didn't want to come back with me, though. Only Karen."

Karen raised her hand as if she were in a classroom. "Excuse me," she said. She looked at Lauren and then at Stick. "You both *do* know that this man is *whipped*. True to the core. He didn't blink at my ass, Roxanne's either. And Roxanne is…well…Roxanne. Everyone wants Roxanne. Except him."

Lauren stretched her hand toward Karen and smiled. "My name's Lauren Haverford. Don't worry. I'm used to having Jack pick up strays." She looked at Trance and winked.

Trance said, "Karen's not a stray. She works for the CIA. Don't you, Karen?"

For a moment, Karen looked dazed, like she'd been thumped on the forehead by a rubber hammer. But she quickly recovered. When she answered, it was softly, and with what appeared to be a touch of guilt.

"You caught me, Jack."

"Let me guess. You were sent to gain Talid's favor, like Roxanne. Then you were to pass what information you could to the Company. To help keep us all safe."

Karen nodded slowly. "It's an unconventional war."

"Only, Talid was too busy with our Israeli friend, Roxanne, to pay much attention to you."

Karen shook her head. "Roxanne is his favorite, the only one with her own suite. But she's not the only one to please him. There are twenty women in Talid's immediate, personal harem, along with a dozen at each castle. We travel with him everywhere he goes, his favorites. As you might surmise, we have a lot of free time on our hands. So…we girls talk. Whether I'm screwing him or not, I am privy to just about everything going on in his life."

"Why leave now?"

"Talid is planning something big, Jack. Just how big, I don't know. But it's big."

"Why not stay in place? Keep an ear to the ground?"

"We've all heard whispers. Talid suspects someone. Me. And now…now that I helped you into the palace…if I stayed…" Karen's words trailed, but Trance finished them.

"You would be tortured and killed. You also think that if you take the blame, Roxanne might remain safely in place."

"Correct."

Trance laughed. "Miller must have bitten his tongue when I told him I'd extracted you."

Karen chuckled. "Probably didn't know whether to cheer, scream or pee in his pants."

"That's Miller, all right." Trance lowered his voice. "You do know that he's chief dog and bottle washer now?"

"I heard. God help us."

"He thinks we're landing in three hours."

"I overheard that."

"Some kind of spy I am," said Trance. "Letting you listen in."

"You knew I was there."

"True."

Karen waved an arm around the limousine. "You are some kind of warrior, Trance. They still talk about you at Langley. Always in hushed tones, as if you're in the room. It's a kind of hero worship thing, you know? T-Force…the impossible assignments…and now, all that money. It's become a pride thing in the Company, us claiming you as one of our own. You do know this?"

Trance met Karen's eyes briefly, and then turned away.

"I'm not a hero, Karen. Don't use me as your role model." Trance stretched out his hands, fingers up, as if telling Karen to stop talking. "Let's get down to business. We'll be heading either to Paris or the Loire Valley today—wherever Lauren and Marlee want to go. Then we'll be flying to the South Pacific for a week or two, before returning to the U.S. You are welcome to tag along with us, if you want. If not, Miller is expecting you here, in three hours. How serious is this Talid situation?"

"He's bragging that he's invested billions into something that will cripple our country."

"Was he involved in Kiki Tilson's death? Was that part of his plan?"

"Don't know."

"Don't know or won't tell?"

Kiki looked to her lap. "I'm not authorized, Jack. Even for you. I've already told you more than I should…but since you saved my ass back there, I figured I owe you. Talid *was* going to kill me."

"You *do* know that the president has me working on the assassination?"

"Does he? That I don't know…"

Trance snapped open his phone and hit the speed dial. In a moment he said, "Hi, Art. Sorry to bother you. I need you to prepare one of my planes to bring my guest to Washington, ASAP."

Trance turned to Karen. "We better move quickly. I'm going to fly you home. Call me when this is over and we'll make good on the vacation. Won't we, guys?"

"Always welcome," said Lauren.

Trance dialed another number.

"Speak," said Miller.

"You didn't tell me she was one of ours."

"Need to know, Red Dragon."

"I'm sending her home on one of mine. You'll do the right thing, won't you?"

"Don't I always?"

"I'll be checking on her."

Miller mumbled, "Always the boy scout."

Trance turned to Karen. "Call me." Trance handed her a card and scribbled a number on the back. "Leave a message at this number to tell me you're okay."

"I'll call as soon as I can." Then Karen said, "Exactly *what* are you?"

Trance grinned. He looked from Lauren to Stick and back. "Just a guy, Karen. Just a regular guy that fate decided to screw with."

Trance rolled down the limo's glass partition and tapped their driver on the shoulder. "Art Winthrop is going to meet us back at the company hangar. Please take us there, Sully."

Trance looked at the deep cover CIA agent. "There *is* something big going on here, Karen. Something that took enormous brainpower and financial backing. Something even greater than Talid could execute. I am doing my best to get to the bottom of it, but it's a complex puzzle."

Karen's eyes looked surprised. "So important that you're going on vacation?"

Trance looked startled for a moment. Then he smiled. "I'm not the man I once was, Karen. I can no longer sprint for months on end." He looked to Lauren, Stick, and then Marlee. "I'm trying to accept that there is more to life than just *duty*. Otherwise, I'd just live, serve and die…There's got to be something more…There *is* something more, so I'm trying to grab it when I can, where I can. I am trying to allow myself to say *let someone else do it*. There are a lot of other warriors in our service, you know. Good ones. Great ones. I need to spend time with the people I love…Please, don't go telling everyone I've gone soft, Karen."

"I already said that you're whipped."

When Trance glanced toward Lauren, she could have sworn that he was fighting off tears.

Trance said, "Maybe so."

CHAPTER 46
_____________PP_____________

Stick Granger lowered the altitude of the Bell Jet Ranger III and began following the bends of a peaceful, winding river.

"You sure this is it for today, Trance? I mean, we've only flown four thousand miles north, only to jump in a helo and fly south."

"The girls said they were bored with Paris. You don't like the Loire Valley?"

"You've seen one castle, Trance, you've seen them all."

"You've never seen mine."

The Bell passed over the broad green lawns of Chambord, the 440 room masterpiece of King Francois I, designed by Leonardo da Vinci. The castle was surrounded by twenty miles of stone wall, a partial moat and more than a thousand acres of virgin forest.

"How 'bout that castle, Stick?" said Trance. "Just like all the others?"

Stick smiled and shrugged. The castle almost took his breath away.

They continued west toward Trance's chateau. There were rumors that da Vinci had put his hand to this one, too, although historians had never been allowed within its grounds. The chateau was less than twenty miles east of da Vinci's late life residence, in the shadows of Chateau d'Amboise. It was built with da Vinci's trademark mathematical precision, with many towers and a skyline façade. The castle had been in Trance's family since its construction, more than five hundred years before. One side of the palace was open to family and long-time employees. The other was reserved for business.

Once they descended onto the castle lawn, Lauren and Marlee stepped out of the helicopter and began to walk across the broad expanse of lawn. Stick and Trance remained behind.

"How long you had this place, Trance?"

"It belonged to my grandfather, then to my uncle, who passed it to me. It was commissioned by the family in 1490 and finished somewhere around 1515."

"Your folks were living in decadent opulence even back then, eh?"

Trance's eyes darted toward Stick. "You know why this is in the family, my friend. And you know the responsibility that comes with it."

"A nice inheritance, though, in anybody's book."

"You don't know the half of it." Trance looked to the sky, as if searching within its cirrus clouds for the right words. "This place was built as a refuge for humanism, Stick. During the late 15th century, there were religious movements afoot to destroy all art and culture. In Florence, the epicenter of the Renaissance, a Dominican priest by the name of Girolamo Savonarola began to rule, after the fall of the Medici, during the early 1490s. He was a clumsy, but charismatic preacher who said that evil could be found in false idolatry, as represented by art and literature. He gave fiery speeches about mankind's last days. Italy was enduring financial hardships, along with an outbreak of syphilis. It was easy for him to turn the masses against both art and culture. He whipped crowds into frenzies. By 1497, he had gained such a hold on the people that he sent men and boys to scour the city for artwork, books, musical instruments, dresses, fine shoes, coats, hats—anything that represented a challenge to religious purity, anything that he said represented the insane moral corruption of the day.

"They built huge bonfires, the *Bonfires of the Vanities* they were called. They burned everything they could find. Botticelli threw his own works into the fire, as did other artists. For a while, Little Bottle stopped creating anything at all."

Trance took in a deep breath and spread his hand out toward the castle. "My ancestor, along with others, worked tirelessly to save the masterpieces of Florence, along with works from other cities. Works by da Vinci, Michelangelo, Botticelli…You'll see when we get inside." Trance paused, as if debating what to say next. After a long moment, he continued. "Many surmise that da Vinci and Botticelli were Grand Masters of a secret society, one that may have created the Knights Templar."

Stick whistled softly. "The Holy Grail Templars?"

Trance shrugged. "I didn't ask for this."

"Don't tell me—"

Trance put his hand up. "That's as much as I'll say. In fact, you should forget I even mentioned it." Trance looked out across the moat, as if searching the chateau's skyline for answers. After a long moment he continued. "We run part of Hopewell Industries' European operations from here. Primarily financial. The west end of the chateau is mostly offices. The eastern half is reserved for family and staff, mainly just me, the artists and the caretakers. Entire families have worked here for generations."

"Really isn't your style, JT. Kinda gaudy, don't you think?"

"Three hundred thirty rooms." Trance smiled at the irony. He lived in a two bedroom bungalow that he had built by hand, yet he had inherited a host of places like this.

"Three hundred thirty. That all? Gee, it looks so much bigger. Are we here for business or pleasure?"

Trance hesitated. "Both."

"What is it, Trance? We're not here because the girls wanted to see a chateau. None of us knew you had this place until a few hours ago."

"I wanted to get someplace safe, someplace private. I need your help."

"Not again? Trance, when are you going to learn to look after yourself?"

"Talid's been trying to kill me every chance he gets. Who knows what he'll do, now that I've humiliated him? And there are…well, you know, others…" Trance waved an arm around the estate. "You can't imagine the security nightmare that my life has become. And now…now that I have decided to get on with my life, I'll need a qualified security team."

"That's easy. Hire a security firm. I heard Xe needs work. Or call Bo. He'll help you, I'm sure. Or Wilson. Didn't he protect your grandfather?"

"I can't have simple security. It's more complicated than that. I've got too many secrets."

Stick watched as the women were guided across the castle lawn by members of Trance's staff. "No shit."

"I need a friend."

"You've got Lauren."

"I don't want her to die. And I'm thinking…"

Stick nodded. He understood now. "Just come out with it."

Trance looked toward Lauren and Marlee. They had stopped walking and were now gazing out across the grounds. Acres of manicured gardens were spread around them like colorful islands. Beyond them, an oblong moat surrounded the tall castle, which seemed to rise out of the stone like a brilliant phoenix.

"Will you move to the States and work with me?"

Stick whistled. "America? Trance, you know how much I like solitude. America is one big-assed country. People everywhere, pushing and crowding. I just finished building my golf course. I've got to work on my game."

"Is that a 'no'?"

Stick grinned. "You are not going to believe this, Jack. But, now that Marlee and I have a kid, and another one on the way—"

"Another baby?" interrupted Trance.

"Yeah. Imagine, me, a real family man."

"You can't blame this one on me, Granger."

"Oo-rah."

"Oo-rah."

The men knocked their knuckles together and did an elaborate handshake ending up with a belly-bop.

Stick continued, "Marlee has been bugging me to leave the island lately. Says she wants the kids to grow up around other children. Doesn't want to be far from medical care, that sort of thing. Right now it's nearly an hour by puddle jumper to the grocery store. She wants to be able to drive to Stop and Shop and buy diapers when we run out, not wad up a couple of burping rags and strap them around the kid. Imagine that? I've been thinking New Zealand, but I'll see if she wants America. She grew up in Colorado, you know."

"I'd like that, Pirate."

"Just in case she asks, do you have an offer?"

"I'll pay you a quarter million a year, plus benefits. Your job will be to build and head up my personal and business security. I'll pay Marlee two million a year to keep you happy."

"She already keeps me happy."

"Should be an easy job, then."

Stick smiled. "Where will we live, Jack? I'm sorry, but I'm not going to live like you, in some tiny Hobbit hole in the middle of nowhere. Vermont is definitely out of the question."

"I thought you liked remote?"

"I love remote. But I need water. Real water. Ocean water."

"Could you stand living next to me? In your own home, of course."

Stick shrugged. "If I have to."

"Do we have a deal?"

"Why are you doing this, JT?"

"Because. Do we have a deal?"

"If Marlee wants it."

"Let's go ask her. Not a word to Lauren about the living arrangements. Our secret."

Trance and Stick ambled away from the helicopter and joined the women. Lauren and Marlee were staring up at the chateau from the near side of the water-filled stone moat.

"Jack, this is extraordinary," said Lauren. "Is this really yours?"

"That's what they tell me."

"Why don't you show us around?"

"Be happy to. It's rather interesting, as you'll see. First, Stick has something to ask Marlee."

Trance looked at his friend, then crossed his fingers behind his back.

"Jack is asking if we'll move to America."

"Stick, I've been begging to move back to America for months."

"But he wants me to work."

Marlee looked cross-eyed at her husband. "Oh, dear, Stick. You will have to work?"

"Jack wants me to head up his security. The problem is, you'll have to work, too."

"No. I am staying home with the kids."

"That's what I told Jack. But he offered to pay you two million dollars a year."

Marlee's jaw quivered. She looked sharply at Trance. "That isn't fair, Jack."

"Tell her what her job is, Trance," said Stick.

"Your job is to keep your husband happy."

"I already keep him happy."

"That's what I told him," said Stick. "He still wants to pay you."

"So, what's the catch?" said Marlee.

"The catch is, *I* only make a quarter million," said Stick.

Marlee grinned. "I like this, Jack." She turned to Lauren. "What do you think?"

Lauren gave Marlee a hug. "Maybe we could be neighbors?"

Trance uncrossed his fingers and began walking across the smooth grass. As he did, a drawbridge began to lower across the moat that guarded the chateau.

They were greeted at the entrance by two guards wearing elaborate 16th century uniforms. They were ornately elegant, if not flowery.

"Nice uniforms," said Stick. "Can I get one like that?'

'Shhh." said Trance. "These uniforms have been worn by security since the place was built."

"That's funny. They look like they were designed in the 1960s by Andy Warhol. How many you got here, Trance? Security, I mean."

"Two hundred seventy-five."

"Here? You have two hundred and seventy-five security guards here? On *this* estate?"

Trance nodded. "Thousands worldwide. And you thought your job would be easy."

Even though Trance was welcomed on sight by the guards, he was asked to press his thumb into a biometric pad. When the pad blinked green, he had to punch in a code before the group was waved inside.

"Why all the security?" asked Stick.

"I told you. We run some of our financial operations out of this location. We keep some gold and currency on the premises. Plus a few other things, which I am about to show you."

Lauren and Stick exchanged glances. For as long as they had known him, Trance had never ceased to surprise them.

The entrance to the chateau had been built to impress, with painted ceilings that were forty feet high. Smooth marble sculptures were standing on pedestals of all shapes and sizes. The walls were hung with Renaissance paintings, with virtually every known master's work in plain view. Many of the paintings had been covered by lightly tinted, climate controlled cases to protect them from the elements. Between the paintings hung a variety of tapestries, some of them inordinately large. Others were barely two feet across. They were made of every conceivable color. Some blindingly bright, while others were made with quiet earth tones.

Trance led them along a series of long hallways. The hallways were lined with weaponry—suits of armor, swords, spears, bows and arrows. Some of the weapons were surprisingly similar to ones that Talid housed in his own castle. Trance stopped beside a set of ten foot silver doors. Guarding the doors were two sentries, wearing the same, almost comical garb as the others. Trance went through the security procedures as before. Except this time he was asked to submit to an eye scan.

"You've got more security in this place than the Vatican, Trance—"

The doors opened and the words hung in Stick's mouth. Then he said, "I see why."

Before them was a single, cavernous room that was nearly two hundred feet to a side. Along the walls, paintings were hung from floor to ceiling. These paintings weren't just from the Renaissance; they represented dozens of cultures, with time periods stretching back thousands of years.

Lauren walked to one of the paintings and gasped. "This is a da Vinci, Jack."

"Yeah," said Trance. "There are a couple dozen of them here."

"No way," said Marlee. "Correct me if I'm wrong, but I thought there were only, like…eighteen verified da Vinci paintings in the world?"

Trance laughed. "There are more than that, Marlee. You just haven't seen them. There are others in my family, besides these."

Marlee blinked. Stick began to walk along the wall, gazing at the exorbitant display of unknown works by masters with household names. Stick had to weave between the sets of hand-built furniture and marble sculptures that took up nearly every square foot of the enormous, acre-sized room. Thirty feet down the wall, Stick came to a set of Japanese rice panels. They stretched deep into the room, blocking the view of what was beyond them. Stick took the detour and peered around the end of the panels. He looked back at Trance and saw him smiling. "Girls, come here," said Stick calmly.

Marlee and Lauren scurried toward the panels, while Trance walked slowly behind. When Marlee and Lauren joined Stick on the other side, they stood there speechless and motionless, looking like a still frame painting.

The first thing they saw was a marble stand. Upon the stand was a clear, bulletproof chamber that was locked in place. Inside the case was a large notebook with hundreds of brown, weathered pages. Stick was gazing at the book, which lay open in the center.

"Is this what I think it is?" Stick asked, looking at Trance.

"Don't know," said Trance. "What do you think it is?"

"I think it's another da Vinci Codex. Didn't Bill Gates pay like thirty million for the Earl of Leicester's da Vinci Codex?"

"He did."

"Then there's the…Arundel Codex…in England, right? Which is probably part of the first one. This is a second Codex?"

"You certainly know your da Vinci."

Stick laughed. "Yeah, I'm big on gay artists of the sixteenth century."

"da Vinci may have experimented with his own sex, Stick, just like he did everything else. But da Vinci didn't avoid women. He loved women."

"Like you would know."

A smile crept along Trance's lips. "I told you before, Stick. da Vinci was the Grand Master of a secret society. This society celebrated and revered Christ. They also revered womanhood. Before the Romans reshaped Christianity into the Catholic church...in the days of Constantine...around 312 AD...the sacredness of woman was as important as the teachings of Jesus. When the Romans voted to deify Christ, they set about to minimize woman and remove the female influence in their religion. Over the centuries, hundreds of thousands, if not millions of intelligent, creative, capable and assertive women were silenced, marginalized at every turn.

"da Vinci celebrated the greatness of Jesus. da Vinci also recorded, and celebrated Christianity in its early form—where man did not need a priest's blessing to get close to God. In his view, closeness to God could be most easily attained by closeness to the Sacred Feminine, a woman. These beliefs were in conflict with Rome—the pious but sometimes power hungry church. You see it all over da Vinci's art."

"Still doesn't make him straight....Not that it matters, of course."

"da Vinci had three children, Stick."

Stick laughed. "If you say so."

"One of the branches remains to this day. Would you like to meet his descendents? There are three of them living in this castle."

"Can they paint?"

"One of them is quite extraordinary. She has a studio in the far end of the castle, where the light is better."

"I don't want to know this, Trance. I like my history carved in stone."

"History is like water, Stick. It goes where we shape it."

Stick touched the top of the plastic casing and said, "Gates got screwed. This Codex has got to have a thousand pages. And this…" Stick motioned to the area beyond the codex. "This is unbelievable."

Trance smiled. "And you said all castles were alike."

Sitting upon the floor were dozens of models of da Vinci creations. Some of them, like levers he had designed to change the direction of rivers, were built to scale. Others, such as a working metal bicycle, were built to actual size.

Stick, Marlee and Lauren stared at the collection of artifacts, mouths agape at the enormity of it all.

Stick said, "I thought the bicycle wasn't invented until the 1800s?"

"Nope."

Stick did a double take when his eyes caught a scale model of a helicopter. He walked over to it and touched the metal rotor. It spun quietly and easily. "Does this thing have ball bearings?"

Trance nodded.

"But I thought…" started Stick.

"Nope. da Vinci."

There was a small, delicate couch resting beside da Vinci's Codex. Trance walked over to it. He removed a beige afghan that was covering its fabric. There was a tiny puff of dust as Trance folded the thin rug and settled down into the couch's soft seat.

"da Vinci design that, too?"

"He did. Also the guard uniforms you find so garish."

"da Vinci was a bit of a show off." Stick sat down on the couch and let out a pleasant groan. "But he did make comfortable furniture." He looked slowly around the room until his eyes stopped on Trance. "Why is this here?"

"Pretty simple, really," said Trance. "Throughout history, artists have always been at the mercy of benefactors. Van Gogh sold just one or two paintings to someone other than to his brother. Bernini and Michelangelo had the Catholic Church. da Vinci was always begging benefactors for funds so he could create. The Catholic Church hired him, but they stifled his creativity. He also felt that they manipulated religion for their own personal gain, that they were more concerned with wealth and power than with faith. You can see his disdain for them in his art, with all its hidden symbols, many of them pagan or early Christian.

"The truth is, da Vinci didn't want to part with his works, particularly the best ones. What artist does? He created paintings that would have been called blasphemous by the Church…scenes with a more recognizable Mary Magdalene at the table with Christ.…Mary holding a baby, that sort of thing. Sometimes they'd commission a work only to send it back, demanding a more 'appropriate' religious depiction. Some of the rejects ended up here, along with other works, the ones he loved.

"Also, much of what da Vinci worked on had no practical application in its day. He was so far ahead of his time it was ludicrous. Who wants to pay for ludicrous?

"My ancestor, the one who built this place, had a special fondness for da Vinci. He gave Leo everything he asked for. He paid great sums for things that nobody else wanted. I've got the sales receipts to prove it. My ancestor allowed da Vinci to create at will. He promised to store da Vinci's creations in a place where they would be preserved, while he was alive…and after he was gone.

"You have to understand the time. Religion ruled the world, but humanism and commerce were taking hold and gaining influence. Fundamentalists were attacking artists and thinkers everywhere they could. They had armies. The humanists had brushes and quills. My ancestor provided a safe haven for artists and thinkers. Not only did he pay them to create, he guaranteed that their creations would not be destroyed.

"Now, I have the responsibility of doing what I think is right. Should I share this with the world?" Trance rubbed his cheek. Then he began to massage his neck. "There are things in this room that would change the way we think of art, the way we think of mankind, of time, even God. There is a set of models, automobiles looking strangely like the cars we drive. A Silver Shadow, a Corvette, an Avanti, even a Hummer. There is a drawing of a V-Wing craft that looks much like a B-1 bomber. There are also drawings of things that could only take place in our future." Trance looked to Marlee. "Has Stick told you? Has he told you everything? About the alchemist?" Marlee nodded solemnly.

"Then you know." Trance laughed and said, "What should I do with this? I'm not sure I could spring this on the planet without consequences."

Lauren sat beside Trance on the couch and kissed him on the cheek. "I'm glad it's you and not someone else."

"I need your advice."

"I say we hang out here for a few days. Maybe then we'll know. We take Stick and Marlee home and help them pack up. Then we return to the States and make a plan."

CHAPTER 47
_________PP_________

Several weeks later:

Trance stepped out the front door of Lauren Haverford's townhouse onto Commonwealth Avenue. He turned left when he reached the sidewalk and walked to the corner. After waiting for a couple cars to pass, he shuffled across the street to the tree-lined parkway that ran between the east and west bound stretches of the road. He ambled along the walkway toward the Boston Common, nodding and smiling at an endless series of dog walkers and joggers.

It was a postcard sunny day. The air was growing warm, with an expected daytime high of seventy degrees. The sky was cloudless and there was a soft wind carrying the smell of the ocean across the Back Bay. It was an extraordinary morning and a good day to begin his therapy.

Trance walked through the public garden and took a left onto Charles Street. He ambled along the busy thoroughfare, watching the eclectic mixture of residents, students and tourists. He stopped at the Upper Crust, near Branch Street, to chat with his friend, Jordan. Jordan was standing outside the entryway, greeting guests. Trance downed a slice of Margherita pizza and continued on his way. He glanced into the window of Devonia Antiques. Seeing nothing that caught his eye, he continued on.

As Trance approached Mt. Vernon Street, he glanced at his watch. It was nearly time. He stopped to center himself before continuing on toward Louisburg Square. *I don't need to do this. I'm just fine.* Trance frowned, like a man who had bitten into a perfect-looking apple only to find that was bruised and rotten inside. If he were fine, then why was he so unsure? Why was he afraid to commit to Lauren? Why was he here?

Trance stopped before a stately brownstone and gazed up at the five story home. Not bad for a shrink on the government payroll. He wondered how many therapists had ultra top secret clearance. Not many, he was sure. Maybe only one. Trance walked slowly up the stone steps, tapped the door knocker twice and waited. After a few moments the door opened and a face appeared. Mariah Whinton. The woman looked to be in her early forties, with plain brown hair draping haphazardly over her shoulders. The brown was beginning to lace with gray, which Whinton obviously ignored. Her face was round, smooth and untroubled, with clear, narrowly set eyes. Her eyes were pale green, with a distinct look of intelligence. They should be, thought Trance. Educated at Harvard, with graduate degrees from Johns Hopkins and Columbia. She had the credentials, but did she have the stuff?

"Hello, General Trance," she said. "Do you mind if I call you Jack?"

"Please do."

"You can call me anything you like. Mariah, Dr. Whinton. My friends call me Slash."

"Slash?"

"Yeah. I grew up playing sports with older siblings. I was kind of aggressive…had to be with four brothers. I played hockey. I also did four years in the Marines. Helped put me through school."

"Then *Slash*, it is."

Whinton motioned Trance inside. The home was narrow and ornate. The ceilings were high, with elaborate wood carvings along the edges. The foyer opened to a hallway that stretched deeply into the home.

"Nice digs," said Trance.

"Isn't it great!" said Slash with almost childish enthusiasm. "I truly love this place."

"I take it you're not on military pay grade."

Whinton laughed. "Hell, no. I have a very robust private clientele who pay me enormous sums of money to be told that they're fine and healthy. It's a pretty easy gig with most. I nod, smile, tell them they're super. They hand me big checks and everybody's happy."

Trance looked closely at Whinton to see if she was serious. All he saw were those friendly green eyes, staring back at him with a semblance of both amusement and seriousness.

"The only government work I do is with brass like you. Guys and gals with big secrets they can't tell to any of the traditional schmucks that populate my profession. I'm in the reserves and this is my duty. I get paid to straighten out guys like you. Pretty cool, huh?"

Whinton curled an arm around Trance's elbow and said, "Follow me, soldier." Whinton led Trance up four steep flights of narrow stairs, then down a hallway to a final, spiral metal staircase. She walked up the staircase. Trance followed. At the top of the steps, Whinton opened a narrow door and stepped outside onto the roof of the home. Whinton's home had an expansive view of the Boston skyline. The late morning sun buffed an expanse of gray patio stones to a flinty shine. There were round white pebbles between the thick stones. An assortment of miniature trees spread throughout the patio made the roof look like a small forest.

"Thought we'd talk up here today. Okay with you?"

Trance looked at Slash's rooftop enclave and smiled. It reminded him of his own Japanese garden, the one he'd spent years perfecting.

"I like this, Slash. I really do."

Whinton walked over to a white table that had four metal frame chairs perched around it. The table was round and rested on three looping legs that set it squarely onto the patio stones. There was a black ceramic pot of coffee and two sturdy mugs upon the table. Whinton handed a mug to Trance and said, "You like Starbucks?"

"Black would be perfect."

Trance read the side of the mug and smiled. There was a cartoon picture of a woman with her hair exploding around her head. The words, *I'm going to have a nervous breakdown today. I deserve it!* were written across the bottom. Trance allowed Whinton to fill his mug and took a seat. She filled her own mug and sat beside him. Trance snuck a glance at the cup in Whinton's hand. It had a pattern of paisley flowers but no words.

"Tell me why you're here," said Whinton.

Trance took a long sip of coffee, paused, and said, "What's your clearance?"

"I can meet with anyone, including the president."

"I know things that even the president can't know."

"Does he know that?"

"Funny."

Whinton reached across the table and placed a hand on Trance's forearm.

"You can tell me anything, Jack, and I'll take it to the grave. What's your problem?"

"You don't beat around the bush, do you?"

"Life's short."

Trance took another sip of coffee. "I cried like a baby the other day…in front of friends. It made me feel weak…and confused. Plus, I've got commitment issues."

"So, let's see…you have pent-up emotions and you don't want to commit? Sounds like normal male behavior to me."

"When I love women, they die."

This time it was Whinton that drank the coffee. "Now, that's a problem. Why don't you tell me about it?"

Trance liked this woman. He didn't feel like he was talking to a therapist. It was more like she was a big sister. She didn't put on airs and she pulled no punches. So Trance let her have it.

"You know my background?"

"Miller sent me a file. He said it was complete."

"I built a secret unit for the CIA, called T-Force. While running T-Force, I got married. Then, when I was away on assignment, my wife was murdered at the Washington Mall."

Whinton's eyes softened, with a compassion that seemed to come from much farther inward than her eyes. "I am aware of that. I am sorry for your loss."

"A couple years back, my parents were assassinated in Salzburg."

"That's when you gave away the five billion dollars. I read the papers."

"Technically, I didn't give it away. I put it into a lead trust that feeds a quarter billion a year into a charitable foundation. The corpus comes back to my heirs, if I ever have any, in twenty-eight more years. My family's wealth issues are not why I'm here." Trance paused. "After my parents died, I ended up in Austria, doing things that even you can't know, let alone the president. I fell in love and got engaged." Trance stopped speaking. He let his mind look inward, seeing sights he almost couldn't bear to relive. He blinked several times. "Then my fiancée was killed."

"By Jacob Miller."

Trance nodded. "You know this?"

Whinton nodded. "I told you. He sent me your file."

"He told you about us? Jacob and me?"

Whinton nodded. "I know Jacob quite well—"

"Another patient?"

Whinton smiled again. "I happen to know that he respects you. He trusts you. And he feels enormous guilt for what happened…to both of them, your wife and your fiancée."

"You know the circumstances of my wife's death?"

"Only that Miller thought he had turned a woman who claimed she could lead him to major terrorist cells operating in this country."

"He sent my wife to die."

"Do you know who set that up that meeting, who asked Miller to send your wife?"

Trance shook his head. "It doesn't matter."

"It does matter, and I know who it was." Whinton stared at Trance for a long time without speaking. She seemed to weigh her words. "It was your late uncle, Jack. Head of the Senate Armed Services Committee."

Trance looked stunned. "It was Miller who gave the order."

"You want to blame this on Miller? Don't be an ass. You're in the fucking military, Jack. Shit happens. Orders happen. You deal with it and you move on."

Trance stared at Whinton. The blood drained from his face. He felt little drops of sweat forming along his brow, and a sinking nausea made him want to puke. He felt like he was sitting inside a ripe dumpster on a hot summer day. All he could feel was that overpowering foggy smell, swirling around his head. He closed his eyes until the feeling finally passed.

"It's my fault."

"You are not responsible and you know it. You do your duty and you take what comes. How many times have you done that?"

"Too many." Trance's eyes narrowed and he looked closely at Whinton. "Tell me, Slash. Why aren't you married?"

Whinton herself looked stunned. Her cheeks flared, with color spreading across her face as fast and furiously as a California brush fire. It took a long time for the color to subside, but Trance waited. Whinton pursed her lips, twisting them to the side as if deciding what to do. She made her decision.

"Touché, Jack. He was a stupid jarhead helo driver with NFOD."

"Not fearing death gets you killed, Slash."

"He was mort flying three wounded out of a kill zone in Afghanistan. He was the love of my life and I yearn for him daily."

"So, you know?"

"Maybe."

"The reason I'm really here is Lauren."

"Haverford? I know her."

"You *know* her?"

"You won't want to hear this, but yes, I do."

Trance closed his eyes. This was getting complicated.

"How? How do you know her?"

"We met at the Mass Biotechnology Council. I am big on biotech for its promise in medicine. She's there for the bank, to help with financing. She's a good woman, Jack."

"I've known her since I was a pup. She's my closest friend."

"So, what's the problem?"

"I don't want her to die. That's the problem."

"And you think that by *not* marrying her, you'll keep her safe? You think if you keep things informal she won't be a target?"

"That's about right."

"Don't be a fool, Jack. You can't live your life looking back over your shoulder. You've got to live it looking forward."

"I thought that shrinks were supposed to ask questions, not give orders."

"I'm a marine officer, Trance. Giving orders is second nature, even if they are to a superior."

"I…I don't know what to say."

"Say *thank you*. Your official shrink gives you permission to be happy." Whinton stuck out an open palm. "That will be six hundred bucks, please."

Trance smiled. "Put it on my tab."

"I'm serious, Jack. No guilt. No fear. Got it?"

Trance took another sip of coffee and studied the mug. "I also have this problem with death."

Whinton leaned forward and said, "Excuse me?"

Trance looked embarrassed. "In my job…they call me a lot. They call me to do things for my country, things where people get hurt, where they die. I'm tired of all the death. I tell them I'm retired, but they keep on calling."

"Who?"

"Whoever needs my services."

"Tell them to buzz off."

Trance smiled. He rubbed his hand across his forehead and pulled at his hair.

"If the president called you and asked for your help, would you tell him to buzz off?"

"Probably not."

"If a member of the Joint Chiefs, or the head of the CIA, were to come to you and tell you that a senator had been kidnapped in Rome, that ten men had died trying to set her free, and that you were the last hope, would you tell them to buzz off?"

"Depends on the senator. Democrat or Republican?"

"Funny."

"I get your point. Do you really think there's no one else they can call? Isn't the real point here that they *know* that you are someone who can never say *no*?"

Trance pondered this. There was always someone else they could call. Maybe not someone with his exact qualifications, but someone who could get the job *done*.

"You think I want to feel needed?"

"Do you?"

Trance felt the blood gurgle through his stomach, then rise into his head like hot foam. Would Slash see the blood flash on his face, like a full set of adolescent pimples sprouting all at once?

"Wow, doc. You think that's it?"

"What do *you* think? You ever feel rejected?"

Trance laughed. His mother had always been cold toward him, distant. It was like she'd been from some other planet, watching him grow like a human specimen, not her own child.

"Maybe," said Trance.

"Is this an Oedipal thing?"

"I loved my mother."

"Did she love you?"

"Yes…but she was part of a…a plan she didn't choose. Her marriage to my father was arranged. Forced upon her, actually."

"How does that make you *feel*?"

Trance yearned to feel his mother's touch, to have her wrap her arms around him like a warm towel and say, "I'm proud of you." But those words had never come, and they never would. His life had been her duty, not her passion.

"I think I get it, Slash."

"Explain."

"I was never able to please, no matter how much I did or what I accomplished."

"That really sucks, hey?"

Trance looked inwardly and nodded. Yes, it did. But it didn't hurt, not now.

"I think I'm cured, doc."

"Don't run away from it, Jack."

Trance began to breathe deeply, in through his nose and out through his mouth. He had to relax. He couldn't think about his mother, not now, not after all that had happened.

"You could never understand," he said.

"Tell me about it, then."

"I can't. Not about that."

"And why not?"

Trance thought about the Black Madonna, about the world, about time, and about the burden that lay upon his shoulders, like Sisyphus toiling with no end in sight. But he had an end. Granted, it was years in his future (Or was it his past?), but there *was* an end, an objective. Did it have to involve acquiescing to every goddamned request by his government? No. Not anymore.

"That's a long, long story. Above your pay grade and your clearance, I'm afraid."

"Bullshit. What if I told you that the Black Madonna says it's okay to love?"

Trance felt like a football coach enduring the icy shock of a Gatorade shower, the unexpected fear and suddenness spreading through him at once. How could she know about the Black Madonna? She knew. She *knew*.

"How do you know this?"

"I told you. Miller sent me your file."

"That's not in my file. Can I see that file?"

"Nope."

Trance felt his shoulders slump. Was it really okay to let down his guard, to allow the world to embrace him, and to embrace the world like some long, lost child?

"I think you are helping me, Slash."

"That's why I earn the big bucks."

"I thought it was just PTSD. It goes well beyond that."

Whinton smiled. "Always does."

Trance's eyes searched the rim of Whinton's face, as if he could see inside her mind, peeking through a side door that was barely cracked open. "I have a friend you might like."

The meat of Whinton's face seemed to shrink. Trance knew just where she had gone to hide. She was in that place you go when your life has crumbled into tiny little pieces with no visible chance of coming together again. That dark place in your heart where you sit alone and tell yourself that there is no more hope for the light.

"You'd like him. We drink fifty-year-old single malt together."

Whinton's eyes came back from the shadows. "I love a good single malt, particularly if it's Irish."

"A Bushmills girl? I prefer Macallan myself."

"To each his own."

"You'll try it then?"

"Try what?"

"My friend."

Whinton looked into Trance's eyes. It was a frosty, penetrating stare that sought to reassure both of them who was in charge. "No frigging way."

"Are you saying it is okay for me, but not for you?"

Whinton stared at Trance. After a few long moments Whinton's eyes rounded, until Trance could see Slash behind them again. "Maybe I'll think about it."

"It has been a long time for you, Slash."

"For both of us," whispered Whinton.

Trance stood and held out a hand. "This has been very enlightening."

"Yes, it has."

Trance said, "I'll talk to my friend."

Whinton stared at Trance but said nothing. She knew who he was talking about. Jock Tilson. She'd watched him in college; she'd felt his aura. But Tilson was far too close to his wife's death to seek closure, to become whole again. That took years. She and Trance were living examples of that.

"It's going to take Jock Tilson a long time to come to grips with Kiki's death, Jack. You must know that."

Trance chuckled, then smiled. "You caught me."

"He's not even ready for a therapist."

"But he's so…so lonely."

"Aren't we all?"

"His wounds are raw and infected, Slash. You can heal them, I know you can. And I also think he can heal yours."

Whinton placed a hand on Trance's forearm. "It will take him time to get over the guilt, Jack. He'll have to endure beaucoup pain before he allows himself forgiveness. It's either that or some kind of near-death experience, something where he sees…no…*feels* his own mortality, stares death in the face and emerges like a borne-again Christian, all whole and new. Maybe then. Maybe then he could let go of the pain and the guilt and begin again. But how many of us can be so lucky? So lucky as to be reborn?"

Trance place his hand over hers. "I will pray for your rebirth, Slash."

"And I for you, Jack."

CHAPTER **48**
______________PP______________

When Sammantha Starodubov dialed Martha Tilson's private home phone number, the president's mother answered it on the second ring.

"This is Martha."

"Mrs. Tilson, this is Sammantha Starodubov of Russian REN TV. I believe you are expecting my call?"

"My son did warn me."

Sammantha laughed. *Your son has no clue.* She said brightly, "As you know, President Ogarkov and your son are preparing for high level talks later this summer—"

Martha Tilson interrupted Sammantha, heeding her son's request to be discreet.

"Where are you, dear?"

"We are just approaching Bangor, Mrs. Tilson."

"You know how to get here?"

"Yes, ma'am."

"We'll talk then." Martha hung up.

About two hours later a white van pulled into Martha Tilson's driveway. The vehicle had a round white satellite dish on its top. The dish was mounted to a thick expandable arm and battened tightly against the roof with a heavy strap. Across the side of the van were written the words REN TV. Underneath this writing, in smaller block letters was written Peh TB. The van crunched to a halt on the unpaved driveway. An exotic looking blonde woman emerged from the front passenger seat. She was immediately surrounded by a group of Secret Servicemen who seemed to materialize out of nowhere. After showing ID and submitting to a detailed search of herself, the van and its other occupants, the woman walked briskly toward the house. She was followed by three men. One of the men held a shoulder mounted camera. The other two carried big green duffel bags, each with the same letters sewn onto the side—REN TV.

Martha Tilson emerged from her front door and waved. Sammantha smiled and returned the greeting.

"Mrs. Tilson…It is so nice to meet you!" said Sammantha. Sammantha emitted all the characteristics of a bubbly, southern university cheerleader. Her hair was stylishly cut, straight and flowing in the wind. Her face was perfectly smooth and radiant. Her teeth glistened in the late morning sun, like expensive white buttons on a designer's blouse. Her makeup glittered with speckled brightness, like a gymnast under performing lights. Her eyes were oddly colored. One was green and one was blue. Both looked extraordinary and beautiful.

Sammantha allowed herself to be searched by another bodyguard. Each of the three men endured the same.

"Well, aren't you the picture of beauty?" said Martha, with a wide, friendly grin.

"You as well. You look fabulous, Mrs. Tilson."

Martha Tilson looked to her ripped jeans and her washed-out flannel work shirt, then chuckled. "Laying it on a bit thick, aren't we, Ms. Starodubov?"

Sammantha stretched out a manicured hand to shake, giving no evidence that she had felt an insult.

"I mean it, really," said Sammantha. "You look the picture of health. I should know. I am a doctor."

Martha held onto Sammantha's hand and looked into her eyes. "A doctor?"

"A surgeon, actually. I started on hearts, then gravitated to the spine and brain. I do mostly brain work now."

Martha Tilson kept hold of Sammantha's hand for a moment longer, hoping to get a better sense of this woman. There was an alarm bell sounding somewhere deep in the back of her mind. She couldn't hear it, but she sensed it was there, ringing ever-so-softly.

"Trained in Russia?"

"America, actually. Harvard and Johns Hopkins. My practice is based in Russia, but I treat patients all over the world, especially children in third world countries."

Sammantha did treat patients around the world. Many of them were poor children. Most, however, were terrorists and criminals, their treatment paid for by despotic government leaders or wealthy backers of the global Jihad. This was how she had cultivated much of her financial backing, by saving the lives of people who were better dead.

When traveling, Sammantha always made a point to remain in a country after operations, to treat the poor and the young. It made her feel good. It was the only thing that made her feel good, that and her thoughts of revenge.

"So, what brings you here to see me?" asked Martha.

"The Russian president, Mr. Ogarkov, is a good man. He has great plans for Russia and fervent hopes for world peace. Ogarkov is deeply interested in caring for the Russian people, in both mind and body. We have enormous problems with alcohol and prostitution. Both are leading to grief and sickness in epidemic proportions. He is also concerned about the threat of nuclear war. My parents were both physicists. Before coming to America I studied physics and nuclear science at Lomonosov, Moscow State University. I understand the brave undertaking between our two countries on a scientific level, a level that most others could never know.

"Our president understands the importance of public opinion in advancing his noble goals. That is why he asked REN to conduct these interviews. REN is independent. That means a lot in Russia. As for me, I am a natural choice for this assignment. I speak English. I understand both medicine and physics. People tell me that I am attractive—"

"Never underestimate the power of beauty," said Martha.

Sammantha smiled briefly. "For both good and bad."

"Amen."

Martha Tilson cupped a hand around Sammantha's shoulder and led her toward the house. As she did so, the cameraman recorded the intimate gesture for political posterity. He also made a calculated swing of the first mother's protection detail lurking in the shadows.

Martha led Sammantha into her kitchen. Sammantha gazed out the broad window to the stretch of cows grazing on the grass. She turned to her cameraman. "Get a pan of that, will you?" Then she looked at Martha and said, "I would like to conduct a detailed interview with you, if that is all right?"

"Of course."

"Before we do so, I would like to introduce you to my associates." Sammantha pointed toward a dark skinned man with long, black hair and a scraggly Vandyck beard. "This is Pavel, also known as Pasha, Baranov. Please pardon his poor excuse for hair and beard. He fancies himself as an artist." She turned toward an unusually tall man with paste white skin and bulging muscles. The man's hair was cut short and he looked like military. "This is Viktor, also known as Vitya, Korovin. He is our technical specialist. If anything goes wrong, he can fix it, even if it means re-bending some of our inferior Russian equipment." Sammantha turned toward a slight, balding gentleman with a bulbous nose that was cultivating a garden of blooming blackheads. This was the man filming every move that Sammantha made.

"This man is Denis Sergeyev. Don't let his good looks fool you. He is the best cameraman in Asia. He is also a sweetheart."

Sammantha paused and locked eyes with each of her three companions. Then she turned to Martha Tilson.

"While I speak with you, would it be possible for two of my associates to take background shots for our documentary? We hope to make this a very special program, showing how much alike our two countries can be. We could add great value to this interview with images of your fields, your barn, even the president's boats."

"You've heard about our boats?"

"You are *both* famous in Russia," Sammantha lied. "Both you and your son."

Martha smiled. It was a thin smile, an almost weary smile. There was something calling her, tugging at the recesses of her mind, something she couldn't quite hear or feel. It made her uneasy. She hesitated. But this was for Jason.

"Sure," she finally said. "My son asked for this, so let them film away."

Sammantha motioned for Viktor and Pavel to leave. One of them pulled a second video camera from his duffel bag and hefted it to his shoulder. The other pulled out a soft nylon backpack with two shoulder straps, and slung it onto his back. Together they walked out the door and headed toward the barn.

Martha poured herself a mug of coffee and prepared one for Sammantha. The cup that she handed to Sammantha had colorful butterflies on its side. Sammantha had to fight hard to keep from throwing it against the wall. After a few minutes of chatting, Martha stood, walked into her living room and sat in a pale pink love seat. Sammantha followed her and settled into a brightly upholstered chair, at the perfect one-hundred-twenty-degree interviewing angle. When they were both comfortable, Sammantha nodded for her cameraman to begin rolling, then turned to Martha Tilson. "So, tell me about your son. What was he like growing up? What are some of his most memorable moments? And what is he like today?"

Martha Tilson spoke for three straight hours while Sammantha Starodubov listened.

While the two women talked, Viktor and Pavel were strolling around the grounds like vacationers, pointing often and stopping to examine the smallest details of fences, barn doors, horses and chickens. Two of the Secret Servicemen assigned to protect the Martha followed a short distance behind them, mirroring every step.

When the Russians entered the barn, one man from the protection detail entered with them. The other agent stood guard outside. The inside man took a place beside the half opened barn doors and watched. His eyes followed closely as Viktor and Pavel walked up and down the animal stalls, filming all the while.

The Secret Service agent pointed beside him to a bin of misshapen carrots that Martha Tilson received from the local grocers for free.

"You can give these carrots to the horses if you want," he called out.

Each of the two Russians grabbed a handful of carrots and began feeding them to the nearest horses. As they did so, other horse heads began to poke out from the stalls like mounted trophies. When every horse had been fed, the Russians moved toward the two cigarette boats. The Secret Service agent walked farther inside the barn, keeping a close watch on the two reporters. His orders were to give them space, but he'd be damned if he'd leave the men alone inside the barn.

The agent saw nothing unusual as Viktor walked behind one of the boats and set his bag upon the ground.

Pavel waved toward the agent and shouted, "Do you mind if we get pictures of the boats?"

"Film away," the agent said. He wanted to slip farther forward, but orders from his president to "loosen the leash" overrode his instincts and his training. He remained in place.

Viktor reached into his bag and pulled out an old Nikon SLR film camera. He reached into the bag and withdrew a plastic case filled with yellow, Kodak film canisters. He walked around to the front of the boat. He held the case aloft, along with the camera, for the guard to see—just as he had done a hundred times in drill. "I'm going to take some shots. We don't use digital. We use film, okay?"

"Shoot away."

Both men climbed into one of the boats. Pavel began filming video of the boat from stem to stern. Viktor explored the inside cabin and its compartments. Intermittent flashes of light spilled out from the small cabin. The guard didn't see Viktor crawl deep inside the V of the hull and set an explosive charge, nor did he notice when Viktor did the same to the other boat.

***

Martha Tilson was laughing with frequency now. She liked this Sammantha Starodubov. She was quick-witted and asked insightful questions, without being pushy or nosey. This was going to be an outstanding interview for her son; she was sure. Yes, when this interview was shown in Russia, its people would begin to understand that Jock Tilson was a man of character, a man who cared deeply for his country, and also for the world. They would see Americans as caring, passionate people who loved their country. They would see them as world citizens who wanted global peace.

When the interview was over, Martha Tilson gave Sammantha Starodubov an affectionate, motherly hug. It was so unexpected, and so powerful, that Sammantha felt herself pull away. Tears began to well in her eyes, sprouting from a lost childhood she could never forget. The camera caught her emotion, the grief and the painful joy. Even the cameraman felt the hairs tingle along his scalp. The camera followed Sammantha as she bent over and stifled a sniffling sob. The camera caught Martha Tilson's reaction of maternal concern, as she walked over to Sammantha and began rubbing her back.

"There, there, honey," Martha said.

"My mother died when I was young," whispered Sammantha.

"It's all right," said Martha. "I know what grief feels like. It's okay, dear. You come back here any time."

How could she let this happen? thought Sammantha. How could she let this woman touch her like that? How could she let herself *feel* like that? She didn't have that luxury, not with what she had to do. She was going to kill both of this woman's sons, perhaps even her. Sammantha straightened. She looked at Martha Tilson solemnly and nodded. Then she turned and fled.

CHAPTER **49**
PP

Jock Tilson received no answer when he dialed his mother's home phone number. He hung up and called her cell phone, which was equipped with military grade Diffie-Hellman encryption. He caught Martha in the barn, just as she was attaching teat cups onto one of her cows. As Martha answered her phone, Tilson was gazing out at the Rose Garden, which was still bathed in darkness, glowing softly under the garden night-lights.

"You're up early," Martha said.

"Hi, Ma."

"I had a most pleasant visit with REN TV yesterday."

"That's why I'm calling. The film crew is due here this morning."

"You're going to love that Sammantha lady. She would be a wonderful—"

"Ma," interrupted Tilson. "Don't go there."

Tilson walked to the Resolute desk and sat down heavily.

"I wasn't, Jason. I'm just saying that it might not be as tedious as you thought it would be."

Tilson began tapping his plastic Bic pen on a yellow pad. He crossed his legs and leaned back in his chair. "They want the whole day, Ma. Do you know how busy I am?"

"How much do you want this Russian deal?"

"It could be world-changing stuff."

"Is that worth a day?"

"How good are they? Professional or third world?"

"Professional, dear. As good as they come."

Tilson sat up in his chair and flipped through his desk calendar. "It's Sunday, so my schedule *is* light."

"Did you go to church, yet?"

Tilson laughed. "Yes, Ma. We had a White House service at four-thirty." He paused. "You really think I should give them a day? A whole day?"

"I do, dear."

"I'll take your advice, then." Never say Jock Tilson didn't listen to his mother.

***

When Sammantha Starodubov and one of her cameraman were ushered into the Oval Office, Sammantha appeared relaxed and in control. There was no sign that her heart was thumping like she had sprinted there from the Lincoln Memorial. There was no sign of sweat on her lip, although she had to fight to control her pores from leaking like rivers.

Sammantha offered a hand and looked Tilson in the eye. "Sammantha Starodubov, Mr. President. I am pleased to meet you."

Sammantha felt a deep wave spread throughout her body. This man looked exactly like Brandon Copley, right down to the small mole on his cheek and the gold band he still wore on his ring finger. Tilson's eyes had an aloof sadness, like he was Atlas, holding the weight of the world on his shoulders, but wouldn't dare ask for help. He had a firm, confident grip. Sammantha made a mental note to have

Copley practice shaking in a more forceful manner.

"I was born in America," said Sammantha.

"I know," said Tilson. "Your parents died when you were twelve. I am sorry for your loss."

"That was many years ago, Mr. President. I was raised by relatives in Russia, as you surely must know." *After you people killed my parents and left them bleeding on the kitchen floor. You've got no fucking idea how easy it has been to focus my energy and resources toward killing you and all your kind.*

Tilson shrugged. "I am sorry that your parents' death didn't draw more attention from our intelligence community, Sammantha. Perhaps we could have done a better job than the police at finding who killed them. Too many people in this world die needlessly."

And some die for a reason.

"I was well cared for. I am a surgeon now, with a highly specialized, global practice."

"And also a journalist?"

Sammantha smiled. It was a shy smile, a demure smile that disarmed Tilson at once. Tilson heard no klaxon in the back of his brain, no prick of the hair or skin, no warning signs at all.

"We all know what is at stake here, Mr. President. The Russian people will suspect that this is a propaganda piece, designed to make you and your country look good in the eyes of our citizens. The Russian people are suspicious of everything, Mr. President. It's in our history, in our DNA. The Russian president needs someone who can articulate the need for compromise in this matter, without seeming to be anyone's pawn. I am experienced, intelligent, attractive and *neutral*. I am well known for my charitable surgeries and my work with the poor. It is no secret that I earn a good living, that I live very well. I was orphaned as a child. That gives me gravitas, as your political pundits might say. What stake do I have in this deal, other than the truth?"

Tilson pondered Sammantha's face for several long moments, searching in her eyes for the truth. He thought he saw it, but he was gravely mistaken. There was no truth in those eyes, only dreams of revenge.

Two hours later, Sammantha, her cameraman and Jock Tilson boarded Marine One. As they prepared to begin the sixty mile flight to Camp David, Sammantha gawked at the nearly two hundred square feet of cabin space inside the new helicopter. Everything looked like it was designed for utility and comfort, except for two winches that seemed entirely out of place.

"This is one of the new models," said Tilson, seeing Sammantha's surprise. "Much roomier than the old ones that still make up most of the fleet."

"What are these winches and chains and cables for?'

Tilson's eyes brightened. "We're taking this unit to Maine. It's been rigged to lift a boat out of the water…just in case…"

"For when you and Mrs. Tilson race your cigarette boats? Perhaps you shouldn't do something so dangerous?"

Tilson chuckled. "When I was a young kid, my mother and I would race out on Moosehead Lake. We started with kayaks and Sunfish. As my mother got older, and I got stronger, we moved to twenty-five horse Johnsons on ten-foot aluminum skiffs. We graduated to bigger and faster boats. One day, Bush 41 allowed me to drive his cigarette boat. From the moment I felt the first thrust from the throttle I was hooked. I swore that, one day, I would own one. Now, I do. I bought one for my mother so we could race. It's our summer fun. We'll be out again soon. Next month."

Sammantha smiled. "Your mother told me the story. I think it's wonderful. You are lucky to have such a mother." *This might be easier than I thought.*

***

The helicopter touched down on one of the Camp David helipads. Tilson took command of a waiting golf cart and drove Sammantha around the grounds, showing her areas that, to this point, had been closely guarded, private sections of the retreat. Soon Russia and the world would get a much closer glimpse into the life of the American presidency.

When they passed the main lodge, Tilson said, "This place is known as *Laurel.* I spend most of my time here. I also keep an office in my personal, three room cottage, which is called *Birch.*"

When the tour was finished, Tilson guided Sammantha and her team to the fireplace that dominated the main lodge. This was where he and Trance liked to share their single malt.

"May I offer you something?" asked Tilson. "Water, soda, beer, wine, anything?"

"What do you serve your guests?" Sammantha asked.

"Whatever they want. Some don't drink alcohol. Others drink too much."

Sammantha wondered if she should risk her next question. She had debated internally for weeks about this question.

"What do *you* like to drink?"

"Depends on the guest," said Tilson, gently evading the question. It was nobody's business what he drank with his friends, family or his business associates.

"Let's say…Jack Trance, for instance. What do you and he like to drink?"

This time Tilson did feel the hair on his neck begin to rise. "Why do you ask about Trance?"

Sammantha knew she was navigating in dangerous waters, but she had to know. She was ready. "Mr. Trance is well known in Russia, Mr. President. His family has had prominent interests there for centuries—oil, real estate, mining. Perhaps you know that Trance inherited an exact replica of the American White House, except that his has larger rooms. Trance is an enormously wealthy man who lives like a recluse in a two bedroom flat, not much better than the average Russian peasant. He works for a living, as a lawyer. He is also your friend. You see, Mr. President, we have done our research, and we are trying to bring this documentary down to the people's level. We want to give them something they can relate to. A rich man, living not like an oligarch, but like Joe Six Pack is news in our country, something that will color you in a very favorable light."

Tilson relaxed. Starodubov made sense. The image of an American billionaire living like a middle class worker would go far in Russia. How could he ruin that image by telling how he and Trance shared a passion for drinking fifty-year-old single malt, costing thousands of dollars a bottle? That was bad politics. He still was a politician, after all.

"What Mr. Trance and I drink when he visits is not important, Miss Starodubov. Our bar is stocked with nearly every type of drink, from soda pop to exotic waters to rare wines, to champagne, to vodka and beer." Tilson looked into the camera. "We like to make people feel at home out here."

Well, screw you, too. thought Sammantha.

CHAPTER **50**
____________PP____________

Sammantha drove her Toyota Sequoia cautiously along Routes 6 and 15 in northern Maine. She paid little attention to the great stretches of unblemished forest. She didn't notice the varied species of white pines interspersed with spruce, or the various hardwoods, like the oaks and the drooping birches. She paid no attention to the deer standing along the sides of the road or to the elegant hawks circling across the sky. She barely missed hitting a bull moose that was standing in the middle of the road, almost cutting him off at the shoulders with her SUV. She had one thing on her mind, and one thing only—to get the job done. It was so close she could taste it, and the taste was sweet.

As Long Pond Road became Jackman, Sammantha's heart beat at an ever-quickening pace. This was close to where it would happen. Sammantha felt the urge to reconnect her car's GPS system, so that she could map her proximity to what they called the *drop site*. But she had to make sure she wasn't followed to the compound. This was her fourth car of the trip, none of them with its GPS engaged. She felt confident that no one had followed her, or had tracked her with any satellite imaging. This was so close to the day; she could afford no mistakes. Even her phone stayed off.

Sammantha turned left as she approached Moosehead Lake and headed toward Tomhegan and beyond. *The middle of frigging nowhere,* she thought. Who would have thought that she'd get this far? She had just one final tune-up of Copley's brain to complete, with fifteen hours of new digital videos. Copley would see his mother telling homespun yarns of Tilson's childhood. He would see the president himself making small talk, giving tips on how Copley should act when he takes over. Sammantha still lacked some of the intimate details between Tilson and his closest friends. But his friends would be no problem. They would not be alarmed by subtle differences between Tilson and his brother. They would chalk the inconsistencies to the accident. But Trance…Trance was trained to see such things, to analyze things. He would see the differences, no matter how small. He had the capability to act. Trance could still be a problem. He had to be stopped.

Sammantha hated Trance. He was like a wart she couldn't get rid of, marring the skin of her heart into an ugly twisted lump. She had tried to kill him, but she had failed. She had asked Talid to do it. He had botched the job. Now Talid seemed weary of the task. Why, she didn't know. She would have tried it again now, but the risk was too great and the end too near.

"He will be in Washington. He will die in the explosion," Talid had said. "It will be better that way. In the final moment he will know that we have won and he has failed."

Talid was the only person who knew her end game, the only one privy to her deepest, darkest passion—to rid America of Washington. This was Talid's mission, too. So, why had he chickened out on Trance? Something had changed. Talid had lost his balls and his swagger. No matter. Sammantha smiled. She had thought of another way to deal with Trance, as soon as Brandon became president. And oh, how fitting it would be...

Sammantha pulled her car onto the deserted dirt road that led to the Moosehead compound. She stopped before the first gate. Two guards wearing camouflage gear emerged from the woods. These guards knew what Sammantha did to men that pissed her off, so they gave her barely a glance, just a slash of eye contact and a brief check of her ID, before opening the gate to wave her on. Sammantha thought to punish the guards for their lack of security, to keep them sharp. But she knew the breach was only for her, so why rock the boat? She drove on.

Half an hour later, Sammantha walked into Popov's underground office. The general looked at her with his hungry, rheumy eyes and leered at her chest.

"You are finally here," he said. "So good to see you, my sweet."

Popov tried to hide his lust, but it was like trying to change the color of his skin. His eyes kept returning to Sammantha's honeyed chest like bees to their hive.

"Not today, Popov," Sammantha said. "Save your perversions for another time. We've got work to do."

Sammantha hefted a blue North Face Borealis day pack onto the general's desk.

"I've got the last bits of stills and video to link Copley's brain to Tilson. I've also got a valid list of the president's immunizations. We missed one, so we'll need to administer the vaccine as soon as possible. That done, their blood should match, antibodies and all."

"And the president? He has no change in plans?"

"Two weeks, general. In two weeks he comes to our front door and we take the presidency."

Popov rubbed his hands together. Then he furtively peered at Sammantha's breasts.

Sammantha closed her eyes. *I'm going to die with Brandon*, she thought. *I'll never have to feel your perverted fingers again. Maybe I'll shoot you before then, for the sake of justice. You deserve that.*

Sammantha slowly turned and began walking to where Copley was waiting. The general followed closely behind her, his eyes caressing her back side like a masseur's skilled hands.

***

Copley was seated in the middle row of a modest, but highly technical movie theater. There were nine movable rows inside the high-ceilinged room, with a movie screen measuring twenty-seven feet high and forty-eight feet wide. There were traditional speakers but also subliminal speakers. There were special headphones. There were specialized glasses. The floor and chairs could move in any direction to create the feeling of reality. There was air and water spray, like a Disney amusement ride. There were even electrical ports designed to deliver brain and body stimulation in a number of ways. Copley was sitting exactly fifty-five feet from the screen, his favorite spot.

"I see you are ready, Mr. President."

Copley turned toward Sammantha. His face broke into a smile. He stood and stretched out his arms, like he was greeting a spouse who'd just returned from a long, overseas business trip.

"Sammantha, my dear." Copley folded Sammantha into his chest. He held her briefly, kissed the top of her head, then softly stroked her cheek. "How was your trip?"

"Outstanding."

Sammantha reached into her bag and withdrew a portable hard drive. She plugged it into a computer console and watched the big screen come to life. She made a few adjustments and the new video began to play.

"This," said Sammantha, "is a recent interview with your mother. I think you will enjoy it. She has many nice things to say about you."

It took fifteen hours for Sammantha to show every image. Only once, did Copley pull his eyes from the screen. That was to go to the bathroom. He remained intensely focused on the images, reliving his youth through his mother's eyes, burning those pictures into the dark recesses of his mind. He watched his brother's interview with Sammantha at the White House, while he, the real president, was recuperating from his brain injuries.

They told him he was ready now. Ready to resume his rightful place as leader of the nation, as head of the free world. But was he really? He had forgotten so much. He'd mastered the techniques of super learning. This had helped him relearn everything, progressing from college to law school in a few short months. It was as if his brain had been wiped clean, like a freshly formatted hard drive, and everything had been reinstalled, program by program, bit by bit, memory by memory, file by file, until he was whole. But was he whole? He felt like a shadow, like a painting that was half pencil and half oil, showing promise of completion but not quite there. But duty called. He would do everything in his power to persevere. He owed that to Sammantha. He owed it to the country.

When Sammantha left Copley, he was still studying the videos, working with the fanaticism of a religious zealot to remember all the things he'd forgotten with his injury. Copley barely noticed as Sammantha pecked him on the cheek and slipped out of the room. This was a man possessed. He was ready.

As Sammantha closed the door behind her, she pulled her PDA out of its case. She pushed the talk button and said, "Are you ready?"

A moment later, Popov's voice crackled. "I will meet you in the command room. Ten minutes."

Sammantha made her way through the labyrinth of corridors, stairways and elevators. She stopped the few people she met along the way, checking their IDs and getting a status update on the various parts of the operation. After nearly ten minutes she came to a small console that was built into a white, metal wall. The console looked like an ATM machine, with a keypad, a place to swipe a card, and a camera looking out from behind tinted glass. Sammantha swiped her card and entered a code into the keypad. An opening appeared, as two sliding doors pulled away from each other and disappeared into the wall.

Beyond the opening, Sammantha could see the expanse of the control room. The room was round, with a diameter of seventy feet. There were two dozen operators sitting at computer consoles lining the circular wall. At each console was a combination HD/3-D computer screen, with a much large panel built into the wall beyond it. In the center of the chamber there was another round area. This one was raised six feet above the rest of the room. There were five desks configured in a pentagon upon the platform, each with its own computer and operator. Sammantha walked directly to the center area, climbed the six steps and stood face-to-face with Popov.

"Good morning, general."

"Good morning, my dear."

Popov glanced at Sammantha's chest. She slapped his face.

"Get your fucking head out of my pants. If you can't keep your full concentration on this mission I will castrate you and send you on a slow boat back to Russia. I am not your toy. I am not your conquest. I am not your lover. I am Sammantha Starodubov and I will have my way!"

Popov stood motionless for several long seconds. Then he began to laugh. "Oh, I love you this way, Sammi." He paused for a moment, letting his eyes wander once more. "There will be no more distractions for you to worry about."

Sammantha shook her head. Maybe she *would* castrate the son-of-a-bitch before the week was done.

Throughout Sammantha's confrontation with Popov, every computer operator remained on task. Not a single pair of eyes looked their way, although Sammantha was sure that their ears were trained on her like a baby to its mother's voice. She made a mental note to thank them all personally once this was over. Those that lived, at least.

"Are we ready?" she said to Popov.

The general touched a few icons on his computer screen and nodded.

"Good to go."

How long had Sammantha waited for this moment? How long had it been since she had pressed her face into her mother's bloodstained hair, touched her dead father's cheek and picked up the pieces of her butterfly cup? How many hours had she been dreaming of this moment, her revenge, and her payback to the country that had taken her life?

Jock Tilson would soon be joining his mother in Maine for what he thought was a vacation. One peaceful day, Tilson and his mother would board their speedboats and race into her war. She would gain control of the US presidency and put her finger on the nuclear trigger that would bring America to its knees. No, not to its knees; she would put the American government into a well-deserved grave.

Today was the test, the last dry run before Jock Tilson would become her prisoner and Brandon Copley would become America's president. Sammantha hit a black button on the central computer console. A grouping of flat panel screens descended from the ceiling. They made a semi-circle above and beyond her, leaving just enough room beneath them for Sammantha to see the backs of her computer operators.

Popov said, "We have a unit positioned at the dock where Tilson puts his speedboats into the water. Anderson Industries now owns nearly all of the land between there and here, as part of its *environment protection program*. To the outside world, this land is protected from development. For us…it gives us places to secure the cameras. We can follow every move of the president's boat, from the time he begins, to the time it erupts into flames."

"Do it," said Sammantha.

Popov gave the command. There was a flurry of movement among the computer operators and Sammantha saw the image of a ski boat form on the panels above her head.

"Commence," said Popov.

The boat on the screen began to gather speed along the shore. Sammantha watched it travel for miles, without ever losing sight of the sleek craft.

"Our submarines?" Sammantha asked.

Popov touched several points on his monitor and two new images formed on the high definition screens. The views showed murky, filmy water, with the flash of an occasional fish or weed coming into view.

"The view on the right is from the sub that will carry our divers north, after the switch. The view on the left is from the sub that will take Tilson to the safe house. Both subs are en route to our target destination. They will not surface during this exercise."

"You are sure that there is no current satellite surveillance of the lake?"

"Not at this time, we are sure. But when the president arrives we expect a satellite to be focused upon us. There may be predator drones as well."

"You are sure you can evade their signals?"

Popov gave Sammantha a mock look of surprise. "You question my capabilities?"

"I don't want mistakes."

Popov turned his wandering eyes from Sammantha's chest to her face. "I am far more worried that *you* will make a mistake."

"Me?"

"You. Sedating Copley, concussing him, burning him with boat fuel and then carrying him on the outside of a helicopter? That is far more dangerous and difficult than fooling a simple satellite and a few unmanned planes." Popov paused. "Are you sure *you* can do this?"

"Screw you."

"Any time."

Popov leered. Sammantha ignored the taunt. She thought to kick him between the legs. Instead, she looked back to the boat screaming across the lake.

Popov said, "In two more minutes we would be launching the aircraft. We won't be doing that today, but our men will simulate flying to the rendezvous point."

"It must *look* like a *missile* hit the boat," said Sammantha.

Popov looked disappointed. "Child's play, Sammantha."

"Our helicopters…it must look like *they* inflicted the damage."

"They will be shooting, Sammantha, at everything but the president. Then they will draw the Americans to the west, before going north."

"Tell them to get as far as they can before crashing. Make sure they don't hit the president's helo before going down. You are sure they are comfortable with this? Committed?"

"Talid assures me his pilots view suicide as a precious gift. They have many virgins in their futures."

"Goddamn fanatics," mumbled Sammantha.

"Seventy virgins is powerful motivation."

"They are blind."

"And you are not?"

When Sammantha looked at Popov there were tears in her eyes, tears that stained her cheeks darkly, almost to the color of blood in the underground light. "I am purely rational, general. The American government took away my life. I take away theirs."

"May God bless your tortured soul, Sammantha."

Tortured by men like you, Popov. Sammantha bit her tongue. It would all be over soon. Then she could put her tortured soul to rest, God or no God.

CHAPTER **51**
PP

Jack Trance groaned as he settled into his favorite chair. He leaned back and closed his eyes, letting his muscles settle into comfortable relaxation. Stick Granger took a seat beside him and did the same.

"That was some fine fishing, Jock," said Trance, his eyes still closed. "Never seen anybody out-fish Stick like that."

"He caught *one* more fish I did," muttered Stick. "And I'm sure he caught the same dumb largemouth at least three times. I wouldn't gloat, Trance. You were skunked. One big fat zero."

"They say you've got to think like a fish to catch a fish, Granger. Guess I don't have the brain of a fish."

Jock Tilson was returning from the bar with three glasses and a fresh bottle of Macallan. He set the glasses on the table. "Ice?"

"Not today," said Trance.

"Me neither," said Stick.

Tilson poured the rare scotch into three glasses, stopping only when they were each half full.

"Getting a little aggressive, aren't we, Jock?" said Trance, as he took the offered glass.

Tilson ignored him. "Cheers," he said. He took several big gulps.

Trance and Stick exchanged quick glances and sipped at their drinks.

Tilson gave a hearty "Ahhh." He sat back in his chair and clenched his jaw repeatedly. The tensing muscles seemed to draw dark shadows across his face, making him look like he'd aged ten years. "God, I miss her," he said.

"I know how you feel," said Trance. "Like a fish hook's been swallowed into your guts and then ripped out in one great pull. Leaving nothing but a hollowed out shell inside."

"Not the image I was thinking, Trance. But that's about it."

Trance said, "I wish we had better news. We can't find a match on Smith's DNA. There are no photo recognition hits on anything approaching a match. I had my animators run some more likely faces and circulated them around the intelligence community. We've got nothing meaningful.

"It turns out that our mysterious Ms. Smith never cashed her paychecks. She never opened a bank account, never stepped inside a bank or went to an ATM…nothing. It's like she never existed."

"None of our political prisoners can identify her?"

"Not a one."

"Nothing from any other country?"

"No."

Tilson rubbed his forehead and took another long drink.

"Drinking won't help, Jock," said Trance. "It'll just make things worse."

Tilson sank deeper into his chair and sighed. "What did you do, really, when your wife was murdered?"

Trance smiled thinly, but said nothing.

Stick said, "You know the answer to that. He tried to get himself killed; that's what. Vanished into the mountains of Tibet and Nepal, searching for Shangri-La or something."

"Roosevelt used to call *this* place Shangri-La," said Tilson.

"That explains why Trance didn't find it. When he returned, as a hollowed out shell of a man, he signed on to Robert Yang's grisly spectacle."

"What spectacle?" said Tilson.

"We talked about this before, Jock," said Trance.

"Tell me again. It's important that I know."

Trance smiled, but said nothing more.

Stick looked at Tilson and then at Trance. Trance nodded. Stick said, "I'll tell you, but you'll have to promise to forget about it."

Tilson's eyes shifted to Trance. Trance said, "It is an institution that must remain, for reasons that are hard to explain. Think of it as a place where the world's most powerful get together once a year. It's like the betting every year on March Madness or the Super Bowl. But it's also a global business summit, where some of the biggest international deals get proposed and cemented, ones that bring all our nations closer together."

Tilson nodded. "I promise to leave this intact."

Stick shifted in his seat. He turned to Trance for more reassurance and received it.

"There is a Chinese billionaire. He has this place in New York City, a brownstone on Park Avenue. Each year he invites sixty-four fighters to his home for a tournament. These are the toughest, most lethal men on the planet.

"Any spectator who attends the event must pay a fee. This fee used to be $100,000. But I hear it's gone up. The same goes for the real-time Internet feed."

Tilson frowned, but said nothing.

"This is a betting event. It's run on the same format as the annual NCAA basketball tournament. It starts with sixty-four. They fight individual matches until there are eight men, or women, left. Spectators bet on the matches. To do so they must secure line of credit of a million dollars."

"Sounds like cock fighting for billionaires," muttered Tilson.

Stick grinned. "You got it. If you don't bet, you don't get invited back." Stick looked at Trance. "Only stupid shits agree to fight in this thing. Bets are placed on each match, with the winner taking home ten percent of the money waged, twenty percent if he kills his opponent."

Tilson's face flushed red. Then the blood drained out of it, quickly, like a plug had been pulled, until his face looked more like a papier-mâché mask with bulging eyes.

"Yeah, you heard right. The betting runs into the millions, even on the preliminary matches. It rises to hundreds of millions for the final.

"The final *is* something to behold. Eight fighters are led into a steel cage fitted with razor wire, to discourage climbing. Contestants wear just a pair of spandex shorts, a concession made for the ladies, like the tight pants on pro football players. No one is allowed to carry weaponry into the ring. Once inside the cage, the combatants are allowed two minutes to collect themselves." Stick smiled. "And to prepare their weapons."

"What?" said Tilson. "You said *no* weapons."

"The fighters are not allowed to *carry* anything into the ring. Weapons make it into the ring all the same, stuffed into the various orifices…knives, knuckles, chains, even an occasional sword."

Tilson closed his eyes and shook his head. "This is barbaric."

Stick laughed. "And damned exciting. Excitement is something the rich find harder and harder to achieve, Jock. Too many women, too many toys, too many business deals, too many rounds of golf.

"They wager millions of dollars on a competition that can last mere seconds, betting on the outcome, with *life* actually in the balance. Nobody ever knows what is going to happen. It is the rawest form of human emotion you have ever seen."

Tilson looked at Trance. "You did this?"

Trance closed his eyes. "Like I told you, I have been there, where you are, Jock. Some days I still am."

"How did you survive?"

"Survive?" said Stick. "He *won* the damned thing. Walked away with over thirty million dollars. This year's winner could approach a hundred. Trance gave his winnings to charity, and none of it to me, his bestest buddy, who cheered him on, despite his lost sanity."

"Blood money anyway," said Tilson.

Trance said, "It wasn't about the money, Jock. Or the competition. It was about death. I wanted to die…Something inside made me push on, though. Something told me that things would work out, if I put my life into the hands of a greater power.

"Things have worked out. I am happier now. I'm even working up the guts to ask Lauren to marry me."

"That won't take her name out of the hat for that Federal Reserve spot, will it?" said Tilson.

Trance grinned. "I don't think so." Trance paused. He waited for Tilson to look him in the eye and said, "I did meet someone, sir. She's someone that…something tells me that she is right for you. She's been through the same thing…been pining for years. Now, I know that you might not be ready, not now. But, if you ever are, you let me know. 'Cause I don't think she's going to fall for just any old Joe. It's going to have to be someone extraordinary, someone like you."

Tilson stared at Trance. His lips began to tremble. Tilson saw the same powerful emotion flush in Trance's face. They had a quixotic, unbreakable bond, the kind that comes with sharing an experience so horrific, so unthinkable, that it welds two minds together like steel alloy. Then it binds and hardens them forever, like military fire.

"Don't do what I did, Jock," said Trance. "Find some other way. Killing yourself, day by day with scotch, isn't the answer. A drink can be a healthy thing. But drowning your sorrows in a bottle is not the answer."

Tilson slowly sealed the bottle of Macallan. "You're right. I'll save this until next time you come." He walked over to the liquor cabinet and placed the bottle deep into the back. Then he poured the rest of his drink down the sink.

Trance said, "You should take a vacation, Jock. Do some hiking, some running, something active."

"I am, Jack. I'm going to Maine to race boats with my mother. Want to come?"

Trance pondered the invitation, but said, "Thanks, but no. I've got some real estate deals to finalize. I've got architectural designs to review and approve. Then Stick and I are going to start building a new security team, for me and the company."

"Talid still at it?"

Trance frowned. "You know about Talid?"

Tilson laughed. It was a deep, hearty guffaw, with a touch of growing lightness. Tilson looked like a weight had been lifted off his chest. He looked almost happy. "Don't forget, Trance. I *am* the president."

"You are, sir."

The three men shook hands and left the cabin. They followed the meandering path back to the presidential helipads.

Once inside Marine One's cabin, Trance noticed the strange addition that had been made to this particular chopper. More than two dozen helos made up the Marine One fleet. He had ridden in many, but he had never seen a presidential transport that had two motorized winches, along with chains and cables by the doors.

"What are these for, Jock?"

Tilson smiled. "In case I crash my boat. This helo can actually lift the entire smaller craft."

"Good idea, Jock. You'll definitely want to save the boat, even if your body parts lay strewn across a hundred yards of water."

"Boating, I believe, is a lot safer than fighting for Yang, Trance."

"Just keep it that way, okay?"

"I'm better now, Jack. Somehow, I'm better."

CHAPTER **52**
PP

Sammantha had watched Tilson's first State of the Union Address so many times that she could recall every minute detail from memory—how the president was introduced to Congress by the Sergeant at Arms, how he walked through the corridor of smiling people, pressing flesh and negotiating the outstretched arms like a ski racer carving through an Olympic race course.

It seemed almost surreal to her now, as she watched Brandon Copley enter her replica of the Congressional Chamber, passing by the men dressed in blue and gray suits, and the women wearing dresses and pant suits of all colors, with some obligatory red dresses standing out like bull's eyes. She smiled as she saw Copley shake hands, hug and kiss cheeks, just as his brother had done in his first address. Sammantha looked like a proud mother watching her son speak at his college graduation. She was his creator, like Dr. Frankenstein. Except that she had sutured the pieces of his mind together rather body parts, creating order out of chaos.

This was their final dress rehearsal, mere days before Copley would assume the presidency. He was playing his part to perfection. Sammantha made one last check of the Teleprompters. Then she moved off the stage to allow Copley to stand alone before the podium.

Copley smiled toward his cabinet. He waved up toward his "family" who were seated primly in a row beside several special guests selected for the evening. He greeted the Supreme Court judges and the Joint Chiefs who were seated before him. Applause thundered as he waved and smiled toward the actors who were filling every seat throughout the grand chamber.

Copley smiled into the cameras and said, "Good evening, my fellow Americans...."

Copley spoke for fifty-eight minutes. He spoke entirely from memory, looking at his Teleprompters mostly for timing, but also to make sure of the words. His words were crisp, his inflection perfect, his conscience clear. He spoke as if this were natural, speaking to millions, perhaps billions around the world, with every sentence carrying meaning far beyond its words. He felt relaxed, like he was sitting in a Jacuzzi reading a magazine. His breathing was measured, his pulse was low. His voice was unwavering. This was the president at his best and his speech was inspirational, even if it was for actors only.

After the applause died for the final time, after Copley had walked off the stage and into the crowd, after he had left the Congressional chamber and exited through the door, Sammantha walked to the podium. She waited for the final smatter of voices and the clapping hands to silence before speaking.

"Now that..." She paused. "...was an Oscar winning performance."

The actors playing the Congressional delegation broke into spontaneous roars. Their applause was like thunder. Sammantha raised a hand and they gradually fell silent once more.

"As you all know, we started on this great journey months ago. Since then, you have all been instrumental in helping our ambitious project come to fruition. Each of you has had a role to play. You have played it well. All of you.

"Before joining this production you were sworn to secrecy. Some of you made great personal sacrifices, leaving family and friends behind. But, where else can you earn such a good living as an actor?"

There was a smattering of applause and a good deal of friendly banter. Nearly every man and woman in the room had been starving prior to joining this project.

"This film had to be made under the most secret of conditions. Even now, I cannot reveal its ultimate form or its release date. When the time comes, you will know.

"Congratulations to you all. This is our final day of shooting. You have been magnificent. You should be proud. As agreed in your contracts, we will be leaving for a three week cruise, before returning to New York."

Sammantha motioned to the side of the podium. Two men pushed mail carts onto the stage. Both carts were piled high with hundreds of thick brown envelopes.

"Each of you has received a thousand dollars per week while you have been here. These envelopes contain your bonuses. For most of you, this means twenty-five thousand dollars in cash—"

Applause erupted once more. Once it died down, Sammantha continued.

"A few of you will receive additional funds. You know who you are." She paused. She gazed out at the actors, like a candidate speaking to an adoring public. "At five o'clock tonight you should all gather at Station B with your luggage. You will board trucks that will take you to a warehouse, where you will board tour busses that will take you to our privately chartered cruise ship. Any questions?"

A man wearing a judge's robe raised his hand. "Why can't we go home now?"

"Hollywood is an intensely competitive place, George. This project has been made in secret, and it must stay that way for the next few weeks. That's why you have the cruise provision in your contracts. This will give our marketing people time to get out the trailers before any of you start talking. As hard as it is, we must all be patient."

A woman raised her hand. Sammantha pointed toward her.

The woman said, "Is this...like...a feature film? The budget had to have been...like...gigantic. So, is this...like...for worldwide release?"

Sammantha smiled warmly. "Katie, what you have done here will be remembered for generations." Sammantha signaled that the meeting was over. "You may go now."

***

Sammantha was seated at the head of a rectangular conference table. Popov sat facing her, his eyes repeatedly slipping below Sammantha's neck to her chest. Sammantha put a hand across her breasts and stuck out her middle finger. Popov laughed.

Members of Sammantha's administrative staff sat on either side of her, talking quietly. One of them leaned against Sammantha's ear and whispered. She nodded.

Sammantha's team of doctors quietly entered the room, followed closely by Omar Karkhabi. Sammantha motioned for them to be seated, but said nothing. She greeted Omar with a simple dip of the forehead.

When all were seated, Sammantha turned to Popov. "You will supervise the evacuation tonight. We will be putting the actors in the Anderson trucks with the log facades, to keep them hidden. Stagger them to avoid suspicion. We will switch them to busses inside our Portland warehouse. The busses will take them to Gloucester, where the actors will be escorted to the private ferry that will bring them to our cruise ship waiting offshore. The trucks will continue on to New Jersey.

"There will be no communications. No cell phones, no wireless computers, no PDAs. Nothing. Understand?" Sammantha glared at Popov.

"Screw you," he said.

Sammantha smiled. "Never again." She turned to her fellow doctors. "Is our subject entirely ready?"

Ivan nodded. "He is better prepared than Tilson himself."

Sammantha looked back to Popov. "I want the ship in international waters as soon as possible. Take them straight to Murmansk."

Popov nodded.

"I want them made comfortable, until it is safe."

Popov groaned. "That may take years. Why waste the money? We should kill them now."

Sammantha grimaced. "I am not a monster. I kill only when I have to, only in war. Yes, we may have to hold them for several years, but we *will* see that they remain comfortable. They will continue to get paid. I have already set aside the funds to do this. Someday, they will tell our story."

Popov clenched his jaw, but said nothing.

Sammantha continued, "I want everyone out tonight, even the cooks. Only our communications crew, our aviators and our submariners are to remain. The exchange may take place as early as tomorrow. When it does, I will create enough of a diversion for us to escape." She frowned. Then she looked directly at Omar. "All will live, except for the aviators, who have agreed to die, for the glory…and the virgins, of course."

Popov pressed his hands together, interlocking his fingers as if preparing to pray. These were good soldiers who were going to die, even if they were Arabs. Every war had its casualties, though. Their families were already taken care of. His conscience was clean.

Sammantha continued. "As soon as it happens I will open the gates to flood the complex. I will also initiate the timers. The explosions will level everything. They will find nothing here that will help them, only an empty jumble of what we now call home."

"What about nuclear contamination?" said Popov.

"I will leave the reactor intact. I want them to see all we've done. Besides, I don't want to kill the fish and the wildlife. They are innocent, unlike the Americans."

"It is a shame to leave the labs behind," said Ivan. "We have one of the best neurological facilities ever assembled."

Sammantha shrugged. "We will soon have an entire nation." She turned to Omar. "I suppose you would like me to explain your role?"

Omar stood rapidly, like a dog that has just seen its owner grab a leash. He backed away from the table and began bowing toward Sammantha. "Yes, Dr. Starodubov. Yes, I do."

"At my suggestion, the Russian president has made a remarkable proposal to the American president. Tilson and Ogarkov are planning a major summit, to bring about the worldwide elimination of nuclear weapons. The summit was to be announced next week.

"If we succeed, the president will postpone the summit, due to his questionable health. As he recovers, he will rely on you for strategic advice."

"But he doesn't know me."

Sammantha smiled. Her eyes made Omar think of a science experiment, one where crystal orbs spun beneath bright lights and he had to figure out how much light was reflecting, how much was absorbed and how much passed through. Sammantha's eyes seemed to have a light of their own, as if life itself was spawning from inside her. Hadn't she created a new Tilson from the debris of a broken man?

"He knows you quite well, Omar. In fact, you speak with him every day. You discuss global policy. You teach him nuclear physics. You let him win at gin rummy."

Realization began to coalesce around Omar like a mass of planetary gas, as everything he had seen happening for the past six months began to fall out of his mind and into an orderly orbit. All the months of watching Copley play the role of the president, of watching his doctors bend his mind to make his acting seem natural. The films, the retina scans, the fingerprints, the dental records. The mannerisms, the speech lessons, the golfing lessons. Copley wasn't going to *play* the president; he was going to *be* the president. He felt his knees grow weak. He tried to stay erect, but his body began to wobble. Everything around him seemed fuzzy. Sammantha's words felt like they were coming to him through thick wads of cotton.

"Omar. Omar! Are you all right?"

"You…this…you're going to kill the president? The President of the United States?"

"No, no, Omar. Just a simple exchange. Tilson is far too valuable to kill. We are not murderers."

Omar began to breathe in clipped, shallow heaves. How could he have missed this? He had thought it was all some big propaganda film or a plan to have Copley deliver a bogus press conference, saying things that Tilson could never take back because no one would believe it wasn't him. Kidnap the president? Kidnap the United States president? Did his father know about this? This could start a war. Did they know what they were doing? This was madness! Or was it?

Omar cocked his head and said, "How can you do this? He is guarded like the Crown Jewels."

"He is appallingly vulnerable, Omar. Soon, he will be mine."

CHAPTER 53
_______PP_______

Marine One dropped gently to the ground on Martha Tilson's front lawn. Three similar helicopters and two Apache gunships settled down around it. One limousine and three armored Bradleys were waiting for them, as well as a large contingent of security personnel. A bevy of photographers and journalists clamored behind two roped off areas

The moment Tilson's feet hit the ground he instinctively dropped his head, despite the ample rotor clearance. He sauntered toward the nearest group of reporters, searching for the face of the reporter from WABI, the local Bangor CBS affiliate. When he saw him, Tilson walked toward the reporter with an outstretched hand and a wide grin.

"Hello, Tubby," he said. "What's shakin'?"

James "Tubby" Hearns smiled at his high school classmate and said, "Nothin' much, Mr. President."

"You can still call me Jock, Tubby."

The two men briefly embraced. "How'r Sally and the kids?"

"Never better." Tubby looked toward his shoes. After a brief moment Tubby raised his head. "I'm sorry about Kiki, Jock. We all are. She was one hell of a woman. A dear friend."

Jock Tilson closed his eyes and bent his head forward. He forced a smile and slapped Tubby on the back. He lifted the rope. "C'mon inside and we'll catch up."

Tilson spent ten more minutes greeting the remaining journalists, grinning for photographs and clasping a dozen different hands before he waved them all away. Then Tilson led his old battery mate into his boyhood home. The men walked inside the kitchen and found Martha Tilson at the sink peeling carrots.

"Hello, boys," she said.

"Hello, Mrs. Tilson," said Tubby.

When Martha realized who was there, she said, "Oh! It's so good to see you, Tubby. How's Sally?"

"Fine. Thank you, ma'am."

"And how 'bout Tubby Junior? Is he going to be a catcher, like his daddy?"

Tubby grinned. "Not if I can help it. I'm teaching him to be a pitcher, like your boy. Easier on the knees."

"Who knows," said Jock. "He might just end up president."

"Golly, I hope not."

Jock motioned for Tubby to sit with him at the kitchen table. While Martha continued peeling carrots and preparing lunch, the two men caught up on the events of the past year.

After twenty minutes or so, Jock said, "So, how am I doing? What's the local reaction to my presidency, so far?"

"Aw, Jock. That's not a fair question. What, with all that happened…with Kiki."

"In other words, I'm not doing too well."

Tubby searched through the clutter of his emotions for the right answer. This was the nation's president. He was also one of his closest friends. Jock needed the truth. He also needed friendship. "It's not that nobody likes you, Jock, or has any complaints. It's just…well, it's like you're a balloon that's kinda lost all its air. What we see is just a squishy reminder of what you once were, of what you could have been. We all…the nation had such hope. And now…now it seems like you've lost your direction…moping around the White House with those sad, puppy dog eyes. You started off like a rocket and then you just sort of fizzled."

"Don't sugarcoat it, Tubby. Why don't you tell it to me straight?"

Tubby looked at his old friend as if he'd just heard Swahili. He'd told it as straight as he could. He saw that Tilson's eyes were laughing, so he laughed with him.

"If you want to make anything of the presidency, Jock, you're going to have to move on. Otherwise, get out of the way."

Tilson walked to the kitchen cupboard and pulled down a couple of coffee mugs. He pecked his mother on the cheek and poured both cups full from a fresh pot Martha had prepared.

"I'm going to do that, Tubby. I'm going to let *you* announce it to the world."

When Tubby grasped the mug from Tilson's outstretched fingers, his hand was shaking. Despite the many years of playing catch with Jock Tilson, and bossing him from behind the plate, the man *was* the president. Even if it seemed like he'd lost his way, he was a man that still subconsciously commanded respect, the man who ruled the largest economy and led the most powerful army in the world.

"I am planning a high level, two-week-long summit, late this summer at Camp David. President Ogarkov will be my sole guest for the first week. He and I will hammer out a framework on how to dismantle every nuclear warhead on the planet. I will then meet privately with the leaders of China, France and the UK, before conducting discussions with the leaders of a dozen other nuclear, or suspected nuclear states. Then we're going to sit at one table and work out something we can all live with. Ogarkov and I will then announce the treaties to the world."

Tubby's eyes rounded. He didn't blink. Sunlight shone through the window onto his face, making his eyes brighten like tiny sunbursts on water. His back seemed to liven and straighten, like a wilted plant lifting after a good rainstorm. "Wow, Jock."

"You game?"

Tubby nodded. "I'm big-time game."

"Good. You get to announce it, next week. But first, I need you to co-pilot for my mother."

"Darn it, Jock. You're not racing the boats again?"

"Sure am. I want you riding shotgun with Mama Tilson."

"But she goes so fast…"

Martha Tilson turned away from her peeling and glanced at her son. "I don't need any help to whip your butt, sonny."

"Yeah, yeah, Ma. We'll see."

CHAPTER **54**
______PP______

It was 6 A.M. and Jock Tilson had already finished his daily security briefing. He was leaning back in a chair on his mother's rear deck, working on the day's second cup of coffee and thinking about as little as possible. He watched the cows as they ambled one after another into the back pasture after their milkings. He could hear his mother barking orders to the Secret Service detail inside the old red barn, the sound carrying clearly in the crisp morning air.

"No, you don't do it that way, Hank. You gotta do it like this…You don't think that cow is going to milk itself...That's a pitchfork son, not a broom…Here, let me show you…"

Tilson smiled, as he thought of his mother. She was one of the most capable and complex people he had ever known. She could have been anything, a business mogul, a writer, a doctor, lawyer, hell even a senator or president. But she had never gone to college, choosing instead to run a small farm in a tiny town far away from any normal civilization. It was like she had tried to shelter him, keep him protected from the outside world. She'd sent him to the dinky Greenville Regional. There couldn't have been more than three hundred kids in the whole school, from kindergarten up. He'd loved it there. But it hadn't come close to preparing him for the bigness of the world.

There had never been a man in his mother's life; she'd given all she had to him and the farm. How she had gotten here, he never knew. Sometimes…sometimes he could sense a melancholy sadness creeping around the edge of her smile. She wouldn't let him anywhere close to its source. There were places he was never allowed to go, questions he could never ask. He wondered if his mother had gone to jail or something. Maybe she'd been put in witness protection. Maybe she had run away from home, perhaps after getting pregnant with him? There were times when he thought to use the full force of the FBI to find the answers. Perhaps they had a complete file, and all he need do was ask. But he allowed his mother her privacy; he owed her that.

Martha Tilson stuck her head out from the weathered barn doors. She could see the back edge of the deck and she waved at her son, as he peered around the corner to see her. Martha wiped her hands on her blue jean overalls, leaving small brown streaks of mud down the front. She kicked a piece of cow dung off the heel of one of her boots, then began to walk toward her son, the president.

Look at him, she thought. *All grown up. The most important man in the world.* She was a long way from Bar Harbor. A long way from that sixteen year old virgin who had been raped and beaten, the one who'd fought like a wounded lion to keep one of her cubs. She wondered if she'd been lucky, by choosing the right one. Was it genetics or the environment that had ruined her other son? Where was he now? Was Brandon really dead? Somehow, somewhere in the pit of her heart, she could not, would not believe that Brandon was dead.

Martha Tilson jumped up the back steps and placed a hand on her son's shoulder.

"Hello, Mr. President."

"Hey, Ma. You do know, you're not supposed to make the Secret Service do chores like that."

Martha smiled. "They love working with me. We're a team."

Tilson nodded. "I know." He paused. "Ma, can I ask you a question?"

"Sure."

"Will you tell me why you never moved from this place?"

"No."

"Will you tell me anything about my father?"

"He died before you were born, son."

"Don't bullshit me, Ma."

Martha Tilson shook her head. She looked at her son with a fierceness he had never seen before, a look that sent a cold shiver up his spine. "It really doesn't matter, Jason. Believe me."

"You know I could find out."

"Of course you can, but you won't. You'd never invade my privacy, not like that."

"I've always wondered what it is that you hide. What it was that could hurt you so."

Martha held Tilson's face within her hands. "Don't ever, for a single moment, think that I don't feel blessed in my life."

"But, deep inside, you're so sad."

"Am I? I don't think so. I just…I just wonder sometimes what might have been. That's all. Don't get me wrong, Jason. I am proud of my life. I'm so proud of you that I could burst. But…well…" Martha patted her one son on the cheek, and wondered where the other had gone. "You want some breakfast before I kick your ass on the water?"

Tilson smiled reluctantly and walked with her into the kitchen. He sat at the small table while his mother whipped up some scrambled eggs, with garlic and cheese. He stared at that disturbing photo of him playing baseball, of Copley staring him down, before shutting him down. He wondered what had ever become of the man. Perhaps one day he might track *him* down, tell him about the photo, maybe come to grips with that demon. Why did it bug him so? Was it because his mother seemed almost pleased that he'd struck out in the biggest game of his college career? She'd just laughed it off, as if it were just another game. It hadn't been just a game. Not then, at least. It had meant the world.

***

Jock Tilson sat behind the wheel of an old Ford F-150 truck. His mother rode ahead of him, sitting behind the wheel of a GMC Sierra 3500. They'd always had a good-natured competition, like Ford versus Chevy. Perhaps it came from growing up in such a remote region of the planet. They'd had to be friends, because all too often, there had been no one else around.

Martha yelled out the window. "I'll beat you there!" She stepped on the accelerator, spilling rocks and dust into the air. The 36' Gladiator hitched behind her truck bounced up and down, nearly tipping over as she jerked it out of the driveway. Martha laughed playfully at her son's open-mouthed surprise.

"Not so fast!" yelled Tilson. He rocketed off behind her with his more ponderous load. He would never catch her; that was the game. She always won this part. Always.

A school of Secret Service vehicles swam out of the driveway, while two Apache helicopters and Marine One lifted off the ground to begin pursuit.

When Martha Tilson came to the town launch she ground down heavily on the truck's gears and then jammed on the brakes. A puff of dust spilled out behind her. The dust surrounded the truck like a blizzard, as Martha turned it in a wide arc and began to back the boat into the water. Martha looked up and saw a line of familiar faces waiting for her. She waved. "Hi, Stevie," she said to the man closest to her. "Y'all coming out to watch the race?"

"Mornin', Mrs. T. Wouldn't miss it for the world. Got the text message that you was comin' down an' got right into the truck. Ya gonna beat 'im today?"

"I'm going to try."

There were already more than a dozen private boats anchored off the shore. The people inside them were waiting for the president and his mother to arrive. This was an annual event, a favorite with the townspeople. News could travel fast in these parts, especially fun news like this. The IFW Patrol Boat was also in the water, bobbing a few yards offshore, tethered to the dock with an algae covered nylon rope. It was a 26' Boston Whaler, powered by twin 225 horsepower Honda engines. It was fast by almost any standards, but no match for Martha's sleek V-shaped hull and its 1200 horses. There were two Secret Service personnel already inside the Whaler, ready to ride shotgun if needed. There was also a similar boat positioned ten miles farther up the lake.

The morning sun glistened on the water, the light dancing off it like there were a million tiny mirrors floating on its surface. The air was growing warm and the sky looked like an idyllic seaside painting.

Martha Tilson backed her truck down the boat ramp and stopped when her wheels hit the water. She motioned for Tubby Hearns and two Secret Servicemen to get into the boat. They climbed up onto the closed bow and shimmied across it into the cockpit at the back end of the craft. Martha waved off the line of Downeasters offering to help her man the winch. She began unwinding it herself until the boat slipped free into the water. The boat's yellow and green stripes bounced off the water's surface, making it look like tropical fish were darting all around the hull. Martha gave the boat a final push and it floated away from its trailer. She handed the boat's bow rope to one of the townspeople, saying, "I'll be right back." She hopped back into her truck and parked it away from the launching area. Then she waited for her son.

Jock Tilson's 46' craft rode with far less stability than his mother's smaller boat. Since he didn't have a death wish, at least not yet, he hadn't tried to match his mother's full-throttle driving speed. When he reached the dock, Tilson made a slow, wide arc with his trailer. He made sure not to hit any of the Secret Service cars that had preceded and followed him like paparazzi. He backed his boat into the water on his own, just as his mother had. He parked the truck himself. Then he ambled back down toward the small wooden dock by the water. He waved at the crowd who had come out to watch this ceremonial first race of the season.

"You going to be this slow on the water, Jason?" yelled Martha.

Laughter and playful cat calls spread through the on-looking crowd, most of them friends going back decades.

"You're a mad woman, Ma. Everyone knows it."

"You know you love this, son, just as I do. When else do you feel so free?"

"Take it easy on the water, Ma. That thing is a rocket. At high speed it could launch. Promise me you'll keep it under control."

Martha Tilson grinned. Her face softened and she touched her son's cheek. "You know I always stay under control. Don't expect me to let you win, though. You'll have to earn it, like always."

Martha Tilson began sprinting toward her speed boat. She jumped into its reach cockpit and fired up the engine. The air filled with the deep rumble of its twin engines. A small cloud of oily exhaust puffed briefly into the air. The smoke floated into nothing, tugged away by a soft breeze coming out of the west. Tilson jumped quickly into his boat, to make sure she didn't get an unfair start.

A cheer went up as the two racers backed away from the dock. Other boat engines fired up. Most of them began heading north along the western edge of the lake, just waiting for the spectacle to begin.

CHAPTER 55
_______________PP_______________

"They are about to start," said Popov.

Sammantha swiveled in her chair, atop the center platform in the compound's control center. "Prepare the president for my arrival," she said into a tiny tube microphone built into her headset.

Sammantha turned to the video panels circling above her head. She watched Tilson and his mother take off in a jet of spray.

"Greenfire One, have you made camp?" said Sammantha.

The pilot of the twenty foot, camouflaged submersible, said, "Affirmative."

"Are we a go?"

"Affirmative. We have set up camp and we are a go."

Sammantha pressed a button on her console and said, "Launch Greenfire Two."

A moment later, Sammantha heard, "Greenfire Two commencing." She watched as one of the panels showed a second submersible being launched from the shores of the compound into Moosehead Lake. Like its twin, this submarine was custom-designed to be virtually undetectable from the water's surface, or from space. It was powered by batteries and manufactured to be heat neutral. Its specialized coating made it invisible to all but the most sophisticated sonar. Each sub could travel at a speed of five knots, with a battery life of more than six hours, plenty of time to get this job done. Surrounding the second sub, Sammantha could see divers piloting Submerge underwater scooters in a trail along its hull.

Sammantha's eyes remained fixed upon the semi-circle of panel screens showing Tilson and his mother as they scorched along the lake. The boats were captured in life-like detail, by the remotely controlled cameras that Sammantha's team had assembled on their properties along the shore. The video passed from one camera to the next like the flaming Olympic torch. A camera would first show the boats coming into view from a distance. The boats would look like pleasure craft, leapfrogging each other like children playing in the back yard, until they blazed by onlookers as if they were jets. As the boats neared the camera they seemed to pick up speed, until they passed the lens in a flashing blur. The camera would turn and follow their diminishing shapes until the next one got them into view.

Sammantha followed the changing positions of the two IFW Patrol Boats. The first one fell progressively behind the Tilsons. The other meandered northward, remaining ahead of them, ready to intercept, if needed. In the sky, two Apache helicopters hovered at a distance of two miles, giving Tilson his freedom, without dramatically sacrificing his safety. Or so they thought. Marine One rode a mile behind the Apaches, hovering like a bumble bee in their wake. Sammantha was glad that there were no predators in the air. Her submarines would be safe from detection. In the distance, Sammantha _could_ see the vapor trails of several F/A-18E/F Super Hornets, as well as two F-35s. There was going to be a lot of shooting today. She hoped that nobody important got killed.

Sammantha closed her eyes and licked her lips. Her tongue felt dry and coarse, like a mouthful of dirt. This was it, that spit-sucking moment where everything mattered. She gave a brief wave to Popov and walked out of the room. She continued through the hallway for thirty yards until she came to a single elevator. She swiped her card and the door swung open. She took the elevator five stories down to a darkened tunnel area, where she jumped onto a four person monorail car. She pressed an oversized joystick to move it forward along the rail. One minute, and half a mile later, Sammantha stepped from the rail car onto a brightly lit platform. She showed her identification badge to the two armed guards standing sentry, and was allowed through a sliding metal door into a large cavern. Before her stretched an underground aircraft hangar that was the size of two football fields. There were half a dozen Harrier III jets being readied for takeoff, as well as eight AH-64A/D Apache Attack Helicopters. Pilots stood at the ready, helmets cradled in their arms. Sammantha nodded toward the pilots, but turned her attention to the door of a windowless room on the edge of the hanger.

In just a few minutes, the entire floor of the hanger would be raised five stories to the surface. The hanger's walls would slide back into the ground, so the Harriers could take off. Once airborne, they could hover in place, but getting them into the air fully loaded was far trickier. A short runway of black tarmac had been paved for this day. The planes would skate along the road beneath a canopy of white pines before shooting into the air out over the lake.

There were two guards standing at the entrance to the solitary room. Sammantha went through the same obsessive routine she had established, before being allowed into the small area.

Brandon Copley was wearing an outfit identical to the one that President Tilson had chosen for the day. A pair of LL Bean jeans, a red and white striped Polo shirt and a blue fleece vest. He was lying back in a dentist's chair, already sedated. Beside him stood Ivan Novikov.

Sammantha said, "Hello, Uncle Ivan. How long will he be out?"

"Twenty minutes. Perhaps thirty."

"And he will be okay with this, awaking as he will?"

"He has trained for this."

Sammantha's eyes narrowed. She didn't want to think about that part of the plan; it could be terrifying. "The pilots? They've all had their meal of choice?"

"By the time the Americans know what is happening, our pilots will be dead. As soon as the president is secure, we will begin moving from the bunker. We have the trucks waiting. From the sky and the ground, they will look like logging trucks. Inside, each of them can carry up to sixty of our people. Within half an hour from now, we will all be underway." He laughed. "Even if one of our trucks is stopped and inspected, it will be passed along as harmless. Our plan is flawless."

"Let's do it," whispered Sammantha. She felt her nerves spark, as if an electric current were running through her blood. She also felt a great fear lurking in the pit of her stomach. "I must give him his concussion."

"Isn't that risky?" Ivan didn't want this; he didn't trust it.

Sammantha fought the sudden urge to throw up. She closed her eyes and said, "No matter how good we are, no matter how well we have cleaned his brain of all prior memories and put the new ones in, there will be glitches—like those caused by a scratch on a record or a Blu-ray disk, or an Invalid Page Fault with a computer. When Brandon Copley wakes up as Jock Tilson, there will be a critical period of transition, before the new persona sets in and takes hold. It's like pouring cement and letting it dry. Once it hardens, we're okay. But there is going to be this netherworld where our man will be jumping from one life to the next. Before his new life sets and hardens into place, he might try to sort through his brain for some hidden files that we've missed, to regain his center, to remake the old form. That could be a disaster.

"A concussion will go a long way toward explaining his confusion. It will help him bridge the gap between Copley and Tilson, until his brain has hardened into his new identity."

Sammantha touched the chest of the prone Copley, like a woman to her lover. She placed his lolling skull into a head clamp. She screwed in the clamp's pads until Copley's head was snugly secured. She checked and rechecked the measurements she had made of the thickness of his bone. She calibrated the shiny steel machine that she'd built to deliver this calculated blow, hoping she was right. She pressed a button. There was a soft hiss, then a *crack* as a padded metal mallet crashed against the side of Copley's head. Her goal was a grade two or three concussion, but there was always a risk of serious brain injury, even death. If all went well, Copley would suffer a brief bout of post-concussion syndrome, and then return to full functionality. If it went poorly…Sammantha didn't want to think of that.

Sammantha waited for two minutes. She pulled back one of Copley's eyelids and watched the reaction of his pupil. She did the same with the second eye. Definitely concussed. Since he was already unconscious, it was anyone's guess how long he'd be out.

Sammantha felt a tear begin to well in her eye, just one. She slapped it away. "Let's finish this," she said in a low growl.

Sammantha killed Copley's sub-cutaneous GPS implant and the one in his tooth with a shock gun. Her people would do the same to Tilson's as soon as they had him. There would be no tracking of the president today, at least not by GPS. When the Americans removed the old implant, and saw that the serial numbers matched, along with everything else, they would have to accept him as Tilson.

Sammantha reached for a gasoline can containing the same 92 octane fuel that Tilson used with his boats. She opened the top and stuck the bristled end of a meat basting brush into the can. She used the brush to wipe the gasoline onto portions of Copley's exposed skin. She was careful not to get any near his face or hands, or on anything that would outwardly show. She did swipe some on the back of his neck, as well as on a tuft of hair. Then she splashed some of it on his clothing.

When Sammantha was through, she pulled three Bridela woven glass fire blankets out of a cabinet. If the water sprayers they'd filled with lake water didn't put out the flames, these would do the job.

Ivan picked up a hand sprayer and one of the blankets, while Sammantha hefted a more powerful water sprayer, one that would douse his entire body with lake water. Sammantha stood above Copley, staring at the man she had grown to love. Briefly, she thought to abort the plan. But she had come too far. She had trained too hard. *He* had trained too hard. He wanted this as much as she did. She began to cry, her tears welling up like Halloween monsters, as if to scare away all those childish years of fear. She felt rage at the nation that did this to her. Grief for the childhood that never was. Disgust for the men using her like a toy, looking at her with superior disdain and discarding her, with her mind shredded into pieces like some chewed up wooden ice cream stick. Tossed onto the refuse heap like a bag of rotten potatoes. And forgotten.

She set Brandon Copley on fire.

CHAPTER **56**
PP

Stick Granger stood on the side of Jerusalem Road in Cohasset, Massachusetts. He was facing two comparatively modest Cape Cod style homes that rested on the edge of a steep cliff overlooking the Atlantic Ocean. It was the kind of view that made him feel like he was part of the natural order of the earth, a special place sprinkled with pixie dust that brought out a kind of childish wonder at simple beauty. The water was shimmering brightly, stretching out forever, with a lighthouse in the distance and the rocky beach down below. The air was fresh and salty and clean. The sky was bright, with a touch of wispy cirrocumulus clouds high in the distance. Stick turned away from the ocean and looked across the street to an impressive stone wall. Beyond the wall, sloping upwards were acres of manicured lawn, ending with a massive, yet tastefully built, white stone mansion. At the top of the home, in its center, was a wide widow's walk, perhaps the perfect place to sit and ponder the universe, sip a cold drink, or make love to a newlywed spouse.

"Well? What do you think?" said Trance.

"Lauren likes that monstrosity?"

"I'm afraid she does."

"Probably a Cinderella complex." Stick pointed behind him toward the two multi-million dollar Capes overlooking the water. "And we're going to have to live in one of these dumps?"

"Unless you want one of the big places on either side of ours. I'm giving one to Judy, but you can have first choice."

"You bought them all?"

Trance nodded. "I had to, for security reasons. I can't let anything happen to her, Stick. I'd die, and so might the future, if you know what I mean."

"When are you going to ask her?"

"Soon."

"She knows nothing about this?"

"Not a thing."

"You better hope she says 'yes'."

Stick looked over toward Marlee, who was standing between the two waterfront homes. Marlee was gently rocking her baby while looking out over the water.

"Hey, Marlee," yelled Stick. He waved for her to join them. "What do you think?"

Marlee smiled, and then winked at Trance. "I'll make do."

"But which one do you like best?"

"Yes."

Stick crossed his arms. "Well make up your mind, girl." He turned to Trance. "I still want to know why Marlee makes all the money in this gig."

"Because you're such a dumb shit, Granger. If I asked you to do this for free, you'd do it. Correct?"

Stick's eyes narrowed. "I never said that."

"I know that if I pay Marlee my checks will get cashed."

Stick searched for a comeback that wasn't there. "Right again, Jack."

Trance stuck out his hand. "Deal?"

Stick shook Trance's hand. "Can I put our house up on stilts? I kind of got used to the sway of poles."

Marlee gave Trance a hug and whispered, "Thanks, Jack. This is extraordinary. We'll take the one on the left."

Trance reached into the back pocket of his shorts and pulled out an old leather wallet. He removed a piece of paper and handed it to Marlee. "Here."

Instinctively, Marlee grabbed at the paper. She looked down at the check written for two million dollars and gasped.

"That's a net payment," said Trance. "I've already paid your income, Medicare and Social Security taxes. I suggest you go deposit that before your husband tears it up or thinks of some childish way to waste it."

Trance's Sectéra Edge PDA began to vibrate. He frowned when he pulled it off his belt. "Oh, my God," he said.

CHAPTER 57

_____________PP_____________

Jock Tilson laughed as his mother pulled up beside him and started to pass on the right. He playfully nudged his boat toward her, before pulling away to a safer distance. Tilson lifted his face to the sun and let the wind whistle through his longish hair. This was the first time he'd had fun since Kiki's death, the first time he had felt remotely alive. He began to think that maybe, just maybe, Trance had been right. Maybe someday the pain would lift, at least enough to let him live again.

Tilson waved at two boats passing about a hundred yards beyond his mother. The boats' passengers waved back, as they continued on southward. Tilson turned his craft to meet their wakes squarely. He pulled back gently on the throttle, and was pleased to see that his mother did the same. Even so, as they hit the waves both boats went airborne, bouncing like flying fish.

Tilson heard his mother laugh and yelp. Then he heard a different sound, a sound so sickening that Tilson felt himself begin to scream. It was the sound of an explosion, and the crackling sound of his life being ripped apart. He could smell the pitchy scent of burning fiberglass. He could see the crater in the underside of his mother's boat. Her craft took one more bounce, then dug into the water like a heavy boulder. Tilson saw his mother launch into the air, followed closely by Tubby and both of her Secret Service agents. Martha flew out over the long narrow hull, her arms flailing like a bird, until she splashed against the water a good hundred feet beyond it. Tilson yanked back on his throttle, stopping his boat in mere seconds. His chest crushed against the boat's steering wheel. The air popped out of his lungs, leaving him gasping for a single gulp. His own Secret Service men flew up over his head and into the water. Tilson ignored them and forced himself to stand. He powered his boat into a turn and set out to rescue his mother.

Then Tilson heard another explosion. The bow of his own boat erupted into a shower of melted fiberglass. One of the boat's cleats flew up and whacked against his forehead. His mind began to flutter and he fought for consciousness; he had to save his mother. His shirt caught on fire and there was a sharp searing heat on the back of his neck. He smelled the sickly stench of his own burning flesh. From a distance he heard the *whupping* of helicopter blades. Missiles began exploding all around him. Through a dizzy haze, he saw several boats begin racing toward him from the distant shore. He passed out, just as his boat began to sink and water began to swell into the cockpit around his knees.

CHAPTER 58
____________PP____________

Trance closed his eyes and fought the urge to scream. He looked at Stick. "Centurion's down. No word on the outcome. They want us there." He looked toward Marlee. "Mind if I borrow your husband for a bit? We'll drop you off at Lauren's. We need to get to Maine."

Marlee muttered, "Sure," and clung tightly to her child. *Not again.*

Trance ran up the driveway and jumped into his Rover. He drove up over the grass and brought the car to a screech beside Stick and Marlee.

***

Trance dropped Marlee outside Lauren's townhouse on Commonwealth Avenue. He jumped onto Storrow Drive and took the tunnel to Logan Airport. He already had one of his company's Bell Jet Ranger IIIs fueled and ready to roll. There was no new word on the president. That was not good.

At Logan, Trance drove past a guarded gate to where the FBI was waiting to brief him on the situation.

"Get in," he said to the two agents.

"But we—"

"Get in. You can brief me on the way."

Trance got clearance from the control tower. Stick fired up the Rolls-Royce engine and they headed north toward bloody Moosehead Lake.

CHAPTER **59**
PP

As Tilson's boat began to sink into the water, a Bell UH-1Y Venom helicopter swooped down from the north and began to hover above its hull. Four scuba divers jumped into the water from inside the Bell. Behind the helicopter, several Apaches fanned out to give it cover.

Four more scuba divers approached the boat from below. They climbed up through the hole in the submerging craft and took hold of the unconscious president. One of them wrapped a full SCUBAPRO face mask around Tilson's face. The mask was attached to a hose that ran into a rebreather tank carried by one of the divers. A diver checked to make sure that Tilson was breathing. He gave a thumbs-up sign to the others. Then down they went.

The hovering helicopter dropped to within inches of the lake. The rotor wash threw the water into a swirling fog of wind and spray. Waves lashed around the helicopter skids, almost submerging the zippered black body bag that rested upon its left landing skid. The bag was fastened to the sled by a series of straps, which were flapping against the bag like freshly caught fish. After less than a minute the divers climbed back up into the Bell and they disappeared into the sky. A moment later, the president's boat erupted into a giant fireball.

As Sammantha's Bell helicopter hovered inches above the president, Marine One moved over the spot where the president's mother had gone down. This was about five hundred yards south of the president's sinking boat, but in full view of the Bell. A large green lump fell into the water, followed quickly by the jump of a solitary diver. Within moments, a life raft popped apart and began to rise from water, expanding rapidly as it filled with air.

Beside Marine One, the two US Apache helicopters hovered at bay. There was no response from their detail leader. He'd gone down with the president. The team's new head, Jesse Tompkin, assessed the situation. There was a Bell UH-1Y helicopter loitering above the president's shattered craft. Beside it hung three Apache helicopters identical to the marine choppers assigned to the president. None of them were responding to calls. The Bell was hovering only inches above the water. It was impossible to see what was happening underneath it. If they fired upon the helicopter, it could kill the president. If they fired upon the Apaches, the same could happen. Plus, they were outnumbered three to two. Should they wait for the F-18s, or did they need to go in now? This was Tompkin's dilemma.

"This is Lookout. What's your twenty, Stinger?" said Tompkin calmly. "Centurion is down. I repeat, Centurion is down. There are three Apache hostiles riding shotgun over a Bell Super Huey. The Bell is stationary over Centurion's craft. Looks like the Bell might be carrying a glad bag on its skids. We are hovering point five clicks away. Looks like we might retrieve Momma Bear, but it appears Centurion may be going airborne. Over."

"This is Stinger. Slapshot and yours truly will be there in sixty, to even this fight. Over."

"I've got no reading on Centurion's GPS, Stinger. I surmise damage in the explosion. Be careful what you shoot. Over."

As Tompkin listened, four Harrier IIIs rose out of the trees and began gliding toward the boat.

"This is Lookout. We've got a cluster fuck down here. Four jump jets just rose out of the trees." Tompkin called for Washington. "Homeboy, can you read? Over."

"Lookout, this is Homeboy," said a general's voice from the Pentagon. "Drop two divers and send them in from your twenty. Then move toward Centurion, STAT. Drop the others when you're close." The general paused. "Sorry to put a bull's eye on you, Lookout. We've got to roll in the mud."

"Roger." Tompkin motioned for two of his divers to jump into the water.

The general continued, "They may be taking out Centurion now, and everything else is for show. In that case, it's over. If they want him, they won't fire at you, Lookout. They'll bug out." He paused briefly again. "Stinger, you and Slapshot go in with hell on fire. Take out the Harriers if you can. Don't put ordinance near the Bell. We'll pick off the Apaches one by one, or wait them out. Over."

Just then, the rush of jets tore through the air like the scream of a hurricane. Fire erupted in the sky, exploding like fireworks. All four Harriers became flashes of flame, dropping to the lake like diving pelicans.

The Bell helicopter rose up from the water and began to back away, with a black body bag gleaming like wet coal on one of its skids.

"This is Lookout. The Bell is leaving the fall zone. There *is* a glad bag on its left skid. Over."

"You think it's Centurion?"

"Affirmative, sir. The Apaches are covering. You want me to engage? We sure as hell can't watch them fly away, sir."

"Negative," said the general. "Just stay with them for now, Lookout. They've nowhere to go. This is one big ass state. I'm scrambling two dozen fighters as we speak. Within minutes, our 18s and 35s will clear the skies. You shadow them until that Bell is solitary...which it will be. They won't get far. Over."

"Roger that." Tompkin looked down at the water. He saw his diver pulling a body up into the raft. The diver gave a thumbs-up sign and Tompkin waved toward him.

"Looks like Mamma Bear is safe."

Tompkin saw the two Moosehead Sea Rays converging from the north and the south. "Our pursuit boats are approaching. In a minute, we should have more divers in the water, Homeboy." He watched as the helicopter began to move rapidly away. "The Bell with Centurion is on the wing, heading west like a bat outa hell. Over."

"Bug out and shadow Centurion, Lookout. Let the others manage the lake. The enemy know they're outmanned. They may just be waiting for us to shoot them down. Assassination by friendly fire. God knows what they plan. Don't shoot, Lookout. Do not engage. You copy?"

Tompkin inhaled deeply and peered out through the viewfinder of his helmet. Then he looked to his visual display. "Ain't no friendlies goin' to take down our man. Over."

"Roger that, soldier."

The Bell UH-1Y helicopter lifted farther off the water and began to fly away. The president's boat suddenly vaporized, showering flame and debris across a hundred yards of the lake's surface. Sammantha's helicopter calmly headed west over the trees on the shore, then banked sharply north. The titanium stretcher remained balanced on its left skid, its straps still flapping in the rotor wash. There was no sign of life coming from within the black bag. Or had it become a coffin?

Three new Apache helicopters rose menacingly out from the pines, as if the loss of the Harrier IIIs had been expected, maybe even planned. Six Apaches now surrounded the Bell in a moving dance, staying within mere feet of the craft while rotating two abreast in a tight circle, so that two of them were always blocking the pursuing Americans.

Jesse Tompkin kept his own helo within a half kilometer of the Bell. Marine F-18s screamed past on chafing runs, in hopes of picking off a stray Apache. But the Apaches stayed close, too close. Tompkin pondered the problem and weighed the risks. He could launch a Hellfire missile and take out any of the Apaches. The others might fire back, but that didn't worry him. He was ready and willing to die. What did worry him was that a frag from his shot might take down the Bell and kill the President of the United

States. This was not high on his list of career goals.

Maybe that *was* what the abductors were waiting for, for one of the Americans to shoot down their president. They could all go down in one big ball. The opposition could accuse the U.S. military of taking out their own president. Yet, maybe that was their plan. To make it look like the U.S. military had killed him. All any witnesses would see would be six green U.S. built Apache helicopters surrounding a U.S. built Bell helicopter being shot down by other U.S. built Apaches or F-18s.

"What a frigging nightmare," he mumbled. Tompkin pushed a few buttons on his instrument panel and calculated the miles to the Canadian border. He looked to the range display and frowned.

"They can make Canada, Homeboy."

"Patience. They've got to land. We'll take them when they do. Over."

"You think they want us to fire, sir?"

"Anything is possible, Lookout. We've got live eyes on the way. Give them room. Over."

What a mess, thought Tompkin. Eyes on the way. They were sending goddamn camera crews to film the whole thing. Now he had to watch out for them, too. How had this happened? When had America crossed the line and become more concerned about appearances than results? Washington was afraid that no one would take their word about what happened. People would *assume* the worst—that America was at fault, unless they proved otherwise. They needed proof that Americans did not shoot down their president, proof of their innocence. Guilty 'til proven innocent. What a frigging shit ass way to fight a war—when the media treats terrorists like innocent victims, and brave warriors like ruthless killers.

The stalemate continued toward the Canadian border. Tompkin followed the Bell from a quarter mile away, while the six Apache helicopters continued their buzzing circle around the president. Overhead, a legion of U.S. fighters pasted criss-cross lines of white vapor trail across the sky, making it look like a box of hot cross buns. This was madness!

They passed over the border into Canada. There was no change in topography, no big, "Entering Canada" signs, a customs stop, or a duty-free store. There was just the kidnapped body of the U.S. president hanging in the air a thousand feet above the earth.

Below him, Tompkin could see the forests beginning to reveal more and more homes. Larger roadways began to come into view. Stretches of land were now dotted with farmhouses and fields. Soon, a broad expanse of blue water began to emerge on the horizon.

"Looks like their makin' a beeline for Quebec," said Tompkin.

"Read you, Lookout. Won't be long now. Await orders."

One of the Apaches began to wobble, slightly at first, then like a drunken sailor. It peeled out from the tight helicopter dance and began a slow, graceful plunge to the earth. There was a brief flash when the helo hit the ground, then it was gone behind them.

"One of the Apaches just pounded the ground, Homeboy. No help from us, far as I could tell. Could have run dry, or maybe it was mechanical."

Tompkin peered ahead. He could see the faint outlines of Quebec. Another Apache began to wobble. It peeled away just like the other, then dropped, nose first, toward the earth.

"I'll be damned. Another Apache down, Homeboy. Are we doing this?"

Homeboy said, "We have you coming up on Quebec City, Lookout."

"I've got visual." A third Apache fluttered and fell. "This is frigging weird. Those helos are acting like a swarm of wasps that got sprayed. Over." Tompkin wondered if the military were using an electromagnetic pulse weapon to take down the Apaches, or maybe a laser cannon. If so, it was really cool to finally see the new weaponry at work. Maybe the helos were just running out of fuel. He didn't know what to think.

Beneath Tompkin, the terrain grew progressively urban as they approached the outskirts of the city.

Tompkin could see more cars dotting the roads now. The houses began to cluster in larger and larger neighborhoods. He wondered if any more of the Apaches would go down. At that moment, the final three split away and dropped from the Bell like banana peels, leaving it completely exposed. The three helicopters fell to the earth in a grinding, horrific display, with two of them shredding houses like they were made of toothpicks.

"Just the Bell, now, Homeboy."

"Stay right on its six."

The three pursuing U.S. Apaches flew in a floating triangle, like hawks toying with a sparrow before they pounced. Above them, F-18s still criss-crossed the sky. Men in two planes were filming it all. Behind the U.S. Apaches, half a dozen Hueys were airborne and closing. They were filled with men and materials for combat. They ran with the code name, *Cleaning Crew*, with every one of them hoping there would be no mess.

The Bell veered suddenly and began to speed toward the west. Tompkin turned with it. He could see a multi-lane, highway clover-leaf beside a large industrial area filled with warehouses.

"They're going down," said Tompkin. "I'm on their six, but giving them room. Over."

"Steady as you go, Lookout."

The Bell dropped toward the freeway and buzzed above the road, less than a hundred feet in the air. It dipped farther down and flew beneath a bridge. For a moment, Tompkin lost all visual of the Bell. As he passed over the bridge he saw the Bell's rotors disappearing *into* the opened roof of a monstrous warehouse building. The Bell touched down and the roof of the warehouse began to close with surprising speed, too fast for Tompkin to follow it in.

"Damn. The Bell's dropped into a warehouse and its roof is closing like a freakin' cheetah. I've lost visual. I'm going down. Protector One and Two, do you copy? Over."

"Protector One copies that," said the pilot of one of the Apaches. "Two here," said the other. "I copy."

Tompkin thought about the combined U.S. and Canadian force that had been rapidly deployed in Quebec. They went by the name *Home Team*. He hoped that they could be on the scene before he lost the president. "Home Team, do you have our twenty? Over."

"Roger that. Four clicks out and closing fast."

"Cleaning Crew, what's your ETA?"

"Ten clicks and closing."

Not close enough, thought Tompkin. "Have we got sat coverage, Homeboy?"

"Working on that, Lookout. Our fixed wings have full visual, though. Cameras are rolling. Over."

"I'm touching down."

Even before Tompkin could land his Apache, cars began to spill away from the warehouse, spreading like a handful of tossed marbles.

"You getting this?" Tompkin felt like he was riding an elevator in free fall, with his stomach punching up into his throat. He counted ten cars flying from the warehouse, shooting like arrows. They split in every direction. Some fanned into the city streets. Others raced up onto the freeways.

"Lock all roadways, Home Team. Now! I count ten, repeat, one zero cars leaving the warehouse. Have we got pictures, Camera Boys?"

"This is Camera One," said a voice. "We count eleven cars, Lookout. Not ten."

"Home Team, do you read?"

"Roger that. Will trap and pursue."

"Cleaning Crew, I want feet on the ground. Make a five click circle around my twenty and stop everything in its tracks. Don't let those cars pass! Home Team, can you cover the roads? Over."

"Negative, Lookout. We're closing the freeways and as many side roads as we can. We don't have the manpower to cloak the city, not yet. Soon, but not yet."

Tompkin shuddered. Cleaning Crew was still too far away to be effective. Home Team was under-manned and as porous as a sieve. Their enemy was about to vanish with the president; he could feel it. "Get the police, get the fire departments, you get everybody you can to help find our man!"

Where could he be? Was Tilson in one of the eleven cars, lying in a trunk or on the floor of a van? Was he still in the warehouse? Or was he already in some safe house, stolen through some sleight of hand? Tompkin had the terrible feeling that his president was about to die, or be held for some frigging ransom that the U.S. could never pay.

CHAPTER 60

PP

Four divers took Jock Tilson fifty feet below the surface of Moosehead Lake, where two camouflaged submersible submarines sat waiting on the irregular bottom. One sub lay cradled in a grouping of boulders, its cargo bay open like a monster set of steel jaws. The divers put the unconscious president into the bay, with a face mask securely fastened. They nestled Tilson's rebreather in beside him, then shut the door. One of the divers pounded on the sub's hull with the butt of a knife. There was a soft rumble as water began to rush out of the cargo bay, while air was pumped in from an auxiliary air tank that was welded behind the bay.

The submarine began to move at a rapid pace, heading toward the eastern shore of the lake. The four divers grabbed scooters and headed in the opposite direction, followed closely by the second submarine. After the divers had traveled half a mile, the second submarine stopped and allowed the four men to climb inside. Once they were in, along with their gear, the sub began to crawl silently toward the northern end of the lake.

The sub carrying Tilson continued moving east, hugging along the lake's floor, merging with the bottom, while moving silently on its batteries. This sub was the most expensive of its kind. It was built for speed, for its long recharge distance and for its stealth. The sub passed quickly and easily through the dark lake waters, moving like a deep water bass that knew every rock and weed by heart.

Four hours later the sub nosed to a stop beneath a group of remote homes. The houses were built high above the lake and were nestled into the face of a rocky cliff. The homes were owned by Sammantha's cartel. So, no outsiders noticed as the submarine passed through the deep water before them. No one saw the sub pass through an opening that had been carved into the rocks. No one saw or heard the opening close quickly behind the sub like the mouth of a whale. No one would ever know that anything was out of the ordinary, not even a boater or diver who happened near this secluded shore. The president was gone.

The sub surfaced into a narrow underground cave. The cave's walls were chiseled out of quartz and granite. They sparkled red, white and a cold blue in the low level lights. Four men and one woman were waiting inside for the sub. The moment it surfaced all five scrambled for the cargo bay. Two of the men lifted Jock Tilson onto a stretcher. He was beginning to stir, so they cinched him down with nylon straps. Two men closed the sub's hatch. The woman began shining a light into Tilson's eyes, mumbling something in Russian after examining the second pupil.

The men carried the stretcher up two flights of creaky wooden stairs and emerged into a room that was even darker than the cave. There was a stainless steel operating table perched in the center of the room. The table looked like a stage prop, with a single spotlight shining on it from above. Upon the table, there was a simple white sheet. Beside the table, there were several instrument trays, as well as a number of surgery lights, on stands with rolling wheels that locked into place.

Sammantha Starodubov motioned for Tilson to be lowered onto the table. Then she left the room. Tilson groaned as the two men set him down and strapped him in place. The men walked out the door, leaving Tilson alone. A moment later, Sammantha returned, now wearing a full set of green scrubs.

"What you are doing?" mumbled Tilson. The president sounded groggy, like he'd had far too much to drink.

"What does it look like?"

"Looks...like you're making...a big assed...mistake."

The hint of a smile crossed Sammantha's lips. "It is you that made the mistake."

"I...I remember you, Ms. Starodubov." Tilson's eyes came more into focus, as if the adrenaline of seeing Sammantha had been an EpiPen to his brain. "Making a movie for détente? Trying to show the best side of America, so your president can hammer home a deal to end our nuclear standoff? Obviously, that was a lie. Do you think you can pull this off and not get caught? Do you seriously think that you can kidnap the U.S. president and get away with it?"

"I already have."

"They will find you within minutes."

Sammantha shook her head and laughed. There was an odd, evil glint in her eyes. "But you are not missing. Jock Tilson is being rescued by your gallant military forces. A different Jock Tilson, the new Jock Tilson. *You* are no longer president of your country. You are simply a casualty of war, a war that you started. A war I intend to finish. For now, I suggest you shut your mouth and let me attend to your wounds. You do want to live, don't you?"

Tilson let his head drop to the table and allowed Sammantha to treat him. Sammantha gave Tilson a quick, but thorough examination, checking his pulse, his blood pressure, and finally, his eyes again for concussion. She drew his blood. Then she addressed his burns.

"Are you in pain, Mr. Tilson?"

"Yes."

"Good...That is very good. The more pain, the less damage to the nerves."

Tilson and Sammantha locked eyes, but neither said a word.

Sammantha cared for Tilson's burns with the ease or a concert pianist playing Mozart. She sanitized and glued two deep slices on Tilson's arms. She cleaned and bandaged several other cuts and gashes. She gave him a handful of stitches and attached two butterfly bandages.

"All in all..." she said with clinical detachment, "...you came out of this in better shape than the president."

"I am the president."

"Not any more, you're not." Sammantha put down her suturing needle and yelled, "Ivan!"

Ivan entered the room. Sammantha motioned for him to turn on a television that was lying flat against the wall. There, in living color, Jock Tilson saw pictures of the event. What he saw was a recording. The president had already been found, but Tilson didn't need to know that, not yet.

"Turn up the sound," said Tilson. Sammantha nodded and the sound came on.

"Reliable witnesses say that the president was abducted today while he and his mother were racing their speed boats on Moosehead Lake." The local anchor turned solemnly to her co-host and then back to the screen. "Witnesses say that the president's boat exploded, before he was taken from the water by kidnappers or would-be assassins."

A series of bouncy videos came onto the screen.

"These are pictures that were sent to us by viewers, showing first the explosion, then all of the helicopters and planes that were used in this daring abduction. While the White House is not disclosing the fate of the president, there are reports that the helicopters we see in these photos took the president into Canada. There are reports that most, if not all, of these helicopters were shot out of the sky by American forces. Eye witnesses claim that the helicopter with the president may have been seen descending into a warehouse district in Quebec City. The entire city has been cordoned off, and thousands of Canadian and U.S. personnel have stopped traffic both in and out. We have learned that the military are searching every vehicle. They are also conducting massive house-to-house searches in the area where the helicopter went down. There are also unconfirmed reports that the pilot of the helicopter that was used to abduct the president has been killed. There are no reports of suspects in custody at this time…"

"I must commend you," said Tilson. "How's my mother?"

The reporter continued, "…and there are fears that the president is dead."

Tilson looked at Sammantha with a mixture of awe and anger. If they were searching for him in Canada, and if there were no suspects in custody, there was nothing to lead the military to his location. Assuming, of course, he was still in Maine.

Sammantha smiled. "We killed them, our own pilots, if that's what you are wondering. It was poison. Just like your wife. Our men died willingly. There *is* no one in custody that can help save you. Only *I* can save you." Sammantha removed her surgical mask and snapped off her latex gloves. "We'll keep you here for a few days. When we're sure that no infection has set in, and that it is safe to travel, we will bring you to your new home."

"My mother?"

"Shaken, but unharmed. She's an innocent, so she will live. So will your friend, Tubby. We are not butchers, Mr. Tilson. Just soldiers."

Tilson bared his teeth into a kind of canine snarl, his eyes narrowing into dark slits. "They will raid this house, I assure you. They will find you. They will find me."

Sammantha scoffed, "Let them come. They can look through this house all they want, but they will never find you. You are in a room that was built for this occasion. We fully expect there to be visitors. The little old lady that 'lives' here will offer them milk and cookies and send them on their way."

"You are lawless animals."

Sammantha closed her eyes. She saw the faces of her dead mother and father. No, she wasn't the animal. The Americans were the animals, and they would pay. "Do you know what it is like to lose everything, Jock? To come home and find that the world you once knew is gone? To be a girl of twelve, and…an hour after you see your parents dead on the floor…to have some…animal force his way inside you? Before you're a woman. Before you've even had your first period? Of course you don't. Yeah, so your wife is dead. Big fucking deal. You know nothing. You know *nothing* about pain, about loneliness, about hopelessness.

"I've watched you during the past six months. Watched you walking around with your head hung down like some beaten puppy, while people are killing whole families on your orders, ripping at the social fabric of the entire planet."

"We don't kill families. We stand for peace."

Sammantha snorted. "Peace? You stand for death. You took an innocent twelve-year-old girl and you destroyed her life. Is that peace?"

Tilson lowered his head. "I am sorry for your loss."

"You're going to be a hell of a lot sorrier, once I am done with you."

"Is that what this is? Revenge? For something that happened decades ago? By people that you and I don't even know? You're going to put the world at risk for that?"

Sammantha pondered Tilson's words. When he put it that way, it did seem a bit silly, maybe a tad over reactive. But it wasn't that way. This is what she *lived* for. She was fighting for everyone, the downtrodden of the world, all those who did not have a voice. She would be their voice. It would ring out across the globe. Loud and clear. *We are here!* We are somebody, not pieces of debris left along the side of the road like empty cigarette packs.

"You represent the U.S. government, no?"

Tilson nodded, trying not to grimace at the pain that was burning through his body.

"Too many people in this world have no voice. People who are simply *in the way*. In the way of *progress*. In the way of what you call *peace*. In the way of *profits*, or *strategic alliances*. In the way of *economic development.* When are you going to learn that everyone needs a voice?"

"We all have a voice, Ms. Starodubov. Sometimes voices get lost in the clamor, drowned out by every conceivable reason. That doesn't mean you have to kidnap a president to be heard. To put the world on the brink of annihilation."

Sammantha felt like a meat hook was tearing into her stomach. She tried to ignore the pain, but the memories ripped into her without fear or mercy. There was no one to hear her, no one to make it right or stop the pain. Sammantha felt the bile rise in her throat. Then she saw food spill out onto the floor like a big, chunky volcano.

"Yes," choked Sammantha. "My voice will be heard."

"You intend to kill me? Ransom me? Tell me, Ms. Starodubov. What is your plan?"

"Ivan!" yelled Sammantha, pointing at the vomit. "Clean this up."

Sammantha walked over to a sink by the edge of the room and began to wash her hands. She washed and she washed, but they wouldn't come clean. They would never come clean. She turned off the water and shook it from her hands. She stood up suddenly, straight, like a pole had been strapped against her back. He wouldn't see her bend. No one would see her bend.

"America has a new president now. Someone *I* control. Soon, he will begin to implement policies to make the world a better place. Sure, I'll have to reward my supporters, give them what they paid for. You'll help me with that. And then…and then…I get my closure. A closure that the world will remember for centuries."

"I will not help you." Tilson glared in defiance, but he knew that his words were a sad, hollow promise. There were too many ways to get a man to bend, too many ways to warp a man's brain and break him into a docile puppet.

"Yes, you will, Jock Tilson. You will help us all. Because you won't want your brother or your mother to die."

CHAPTER **61**

_______________PP_______________

Jesse Tompkin searched for a spot to land beside the warehouse where the president had been taken. Below him, two narrow roads of cracked pavement crossed into an X on the corner of the warehouse, with just enough space to clear the Apache's rotors. Tompkin dropped down toward the spot. In every direction, all he could see were massive cliffs made of corrugated steel. They looked like steep canyon walls, ready to swallow him like they had the president.

When Tompkin's Apache kissed the ground he left the GE engine running in a low whine. A second Apache hovered above him. Tompkin reached back in the cockpit and pulled out a Heckler & Koch MP7. He jammed a 40 round box magazine into the pistol grip, then put another box into an oversized pocket in a Paraclete assault vest. He cinched the vest's straps, strapped on a MICH helmet and said, "Do you read me? Over."

"Loud and clear, Lookout. Go find our man."

Tompkin checked the snap on his M1911A1 sidearm and slipped an M9 Beretta into the front of his pants. He took a quick drink from a water bottle and peered out below the helmet's visor, taking a long, calculating look around.

"You there, Homeboy?"

"Roger."

"Any intel to help me along here?"

"Negative."

"I'm going to take a look-see, Homeboy."

"Support is two clicks away. You wanna sit tight?"

"Negative. Going to taste the shit and see if I can chew it. Over."

"Enjoy the meal."

"Yeah."

Tompkin dropped to the ground in a crouch, with his rifle at the ready. He saw no one. Nothing. He felt like he was standing in the middle of Tombstone before a shootout, where everyone outside had disappeared into buildings, or high-tailed it at the first sign of trouble. To his right stretched a hundred yards of metal. No windows, just a series of three large, sliding doors spaced about thirty yards apart. The door that was closest to him was sealed shut. So was the door at the far end of the building. The door in the middle yawned open like a tiger's mouth, as if daring him to enter. Moments before, Tompkin had watched in horror as eleven cars rushed out of this building like ants fleeing a stomping boot. They'd scattered within seconds. He could only hope that they wouldn't slip their net.

It made no sense for Tompkin to follow just one of the cars, the chances too slim. He had made a snap, in-field decision to stay here, hoping that the cars had been a diversion, that Tilson was still somewhere inside.

His hopes dwindled when he stepped into the warehouse. The place looked like it had never been used. The floor was concrete, but it had been covered with some sort of polymer that made it look like Plexiglas. It was swept clean of all debris and dust. It felt almost like a museum floor, squeaking under his boots.

In the center of the mostly empty cavern, sat the Bell helicopter that had taken the president from the lake. A body bag lay open upon the helicopter's skid. All that remained in the bag was a small puddle of water. The pilot's dead body was propped against the skid's frame, sitting placidly like a rag doll in a horror film. Mouth open, eyes diffuse, with blood dripping like cherry chocolate from a hole blasted into the side of his head. The pilot's hand still held the Smith & Wesson that had sent him to hell, gripped between his white, death tightened fingers.

"One more casualty, Homeboy. The pilot's DOA. Looks like he offed himself. This leaves us nothing but stir fried shit down here. Over."

Tompkin looked around and saw nothing, no one. All he could see was a row of tall wooden boxes stacked against the wall with the letters GM plastered along the sides in big blue letters. Car parts most likely, thought Tompkin. Tompkin heard the screeching of tires outside. A moment later he saw a row of soldiers stream in through the open doors, rifles at the ready. He stepped forward and accepted the salute of the new OPR.

"Major Waddell reporting, sir."

Tompkin saluted and said, "Colonel, Tompkin. Thanks for coming."

Waddell grinned at the joke, wondering if this was praise or criticism. But he saw nothing but gratitude in the Colonel's eyes.

"Glad to be here."

"Have your men search every millimeter of this warehouse. Also every other building within a half mile radius."

"Yes, sir." Waddell turned to his men, who stood in a semi-circle awaiting orders. "You heard Colonel Tompkin. Search every damned inch of this place. Now."

Waddell glanced at the dead pilot. "He kill himself, sir?"

"Affirmative."

"That blows."

Tompkin shook his head. "This whole thing blows. Maybe I should have shot this bird on the water. Then, at least we'd have had a fighting chance of recovering Centurion. Now…" Tompkin felt his spirits sinking deeper and deeper, as if into quicksand. He felt like he'd been after the president for weeks, not hours, like he'd been paddling a canoe after a jet ski, working vainly to keep pace. And now…now his canoe was taking on water faster than he could bail. He'd sweated and swore, and second-guessed himself so many times. He felt like was struggling with a Rubik's cube. So difficult, yet so simple if you knew the pattern. There had to be some kind of pattern. He sat down beside the dead pilot and cradled his head in his hands. What a nightmare this had become. *Think*, he said to himself. Think. Where could he be?

As Tompkin leaned against the stretcher to push himself back up, a thought hit him. It was as if some hidden side of his mind had come at him like a boomerang. He looked down to the body bag and fingered the small pool of bloodied water that still lay in its bottom. He looked to the floor. He could see a few droplets of water congealing along the surface. He could also make out the faint outline of other, smaller droplets that had already evaporated in the dry heat of the warehouse. As he studied the floor, he began to follow a shadowy trail. Every few yards there was a small splattering of water, or a dry faint circle of stain.

Tompkin followed the water trail for a hundred and fifty feet. It stopped by the far wall. Tompkin slumped his shoulders and sat down against one of the wooden GM crates. The trail was gone, dried up like a desert in a drought. He let out a long, defeated sigh. His career was over. His life was over. He'd been tasked to protect the president and Tilson was gone, most likely dead. Centurion, his charge, was *dead*.

Tompkin felt a slow tingling run up his back, then up along his neck and into his temples. His head began to throb. Each beat of his heart felt like a hammer against his skull. The pressure of this day, the stress of his job all seemed to fall in on him at once, like one final knockout punch. This was it. Game, set, match. He leaned back against the wooden crate and groaned. Then he adjusted the channel knob on his radio.

"Homeboy, do you read? Over."

"Affirmative, Lookout."

"Give me something good."

"Negative."

Tompkin let his eyes stretch across the cavernous warehouse. He found it strange that everything would be so orderly, so *in place*. And the floor? What's up with a polished floor in a warehouse? Then he knew, at least he hoped he knew. He felt a slim vision of hope, rising like steam tendrils on a hot summer road, not clear, but a vision all the same.

"Somebody find me a crowbar," he said.

Tompkin looked back along the floor, following the water trail to where he now sat. Could it be? Could it possibly be? Across the room he saw a Canadian Royal Mountie running toward him holding a four foot pipe. The pipe was curved at one end, with a thick flat edge.

Tompkin took the pipe. He reached high up and wedged the end of it underneath the wooden top of the box. It wouldn't budge; he had no leverage.

He moaned. "Can you find me something to stand on?" he yelled to the Mountie.

The Mountie ran off and returned a minute later carrying a smaller wooden box. He placed this one in front of the GM box and gave Tompkin a boost. Tompkin jumped up and tried to wedge the top of the box with the crowbar. There was a creaking, splitting sound. Then he heard the high-pitched screech of nails being pulled out of wood. Tompkin had to move his perch several times before he could motion to the Mountie to join him on the box.

"Let's see what's inside this thing," he said.

The top was heavy and surprisingly well fortified. It clung to the rest of the box like strings of pumpkin seeds. With both men pulling, the top grudgingly came off the box. Tompkin looked down inside. He could see a white plastic container with a series of round, inch-wide holes punched out along the top.

"You gotta light, sir?" he said.

The Mountie, always prepared, reached into his jacket pocket and produced a key ring. Attached to the ring was a small, but powerful push light. Tompkin shined the beam through the holes and gasped. He fumbled for his radio and pressed a button.

"Homeboy, you read? Over."

"Roger that."

"Do have any spring flowers?" As Tompkin spoke the code he felt his throat tighten. He still wasn't sure if Tilson was alive or not. He just lay there inside, unconscious and motionless.

"The spring flowers have passed."

"What flowers do you have, then?"

"I recommend Mums this time of year."

"Centurion is secure, Homeboy. We need a medic, STAT."

"Roger that. Good work, Lookout. Over."

Within seconds, Tompkin could hear the wail of sirens. He began to pry at another section of the box. A minute later, two military ambulances arrived, with medics jumping out of them even before they came to a halt. By now, Tompkin had removed the wood surrounding the plastic casing that held the president. The medics cut through the plastic with power saws and the jaws of life. Soon, they had exposed the president's limp body.

Tilson was slumped in a bed of straw. His eyes were closed. The rear edge of his face and the back of his neck were oozing blood. His clothes were charred and wet. The medics unfolded him carefully and laid him on a stretcher. As they strapped him down the president groaned.

By now, soldiers were gathering in a ragged semi-circle, watching intently as the medics treated the president. They began to cheer when they heard the groan. At least he was alive.

"Centurion is alive, Homeboy," said Tompkin. He looked to the medics for some kind of sign. "How is he, men?"

"Pretty banged up, sir. Seems stable, though. I'll say that for him."

Tompkin relayed the president's status and consulted with U.S. officials about where to bring him. He handed a phone to the medics who discussed the president's condition. A decision was made. They placed the president inside a U.S. Medi-Vac chopper and rushed him back toward Maine, toward the Northern Maine Medical Center in Ft. Kent. From there, hopefully within hours, the president would be transferred down to the Eastern Maine Medical Center, in Bangor.

CHAPTER 62

PP

Jack Trance nestled his helicopter into a narrow opening in the trees, across from the spot where the president had been abducted. He powered down and walked with his head hung low beneath the still-spinning rotors. Stick Granger followed on his heels. Trance flashed an I.D. in front of two armed marines who looked barely old enough to shave. They saluted smartly and motioned the men forward.

There was a swarm of people buzzing around the shore like flies. Some were soldiers. Others were locals with access. Forty yards back from the shore, Trance could see a line of yellow crime scene tape. Half a dozen journalists were setting up tents beside it, digging in for the night.

"They're like vultures, aren't they?" said Stick.

Trance nodded. The press. A royal pain in the ass, but a bastion of any free nation. He gave a quick wave to the media and turned his attention to the chaos. Trance walked toward the water, to where a group of people stood huddled on a small strip of rocky beach.

"Can anyone tell me where I can find Major Gibbons?" said Trance.

A man peered at Trance. He stood about six-foot-five, with a hard, round belly the size of a small propane tank. "And you are?" he said.

"Jack Trance."

The man shrugged. "Is that supposed to mean something?'

Trance smiled. "And you are?"

"Buford. I'm sheriff in these parts."

Trance stuck out his hand to shake. "Pleased to meet you, Sheriff Buford. I don't have a lot of time to waste. Could you please tell me where I might find Major Gibbons?"

Buford's eyes narrowed. He had little use for folks living south of the Volvo line, particularly ones wearing jean shorts, fancy polo shirts and boat shoes without socks. He grasped Trance's hand and squeezed it. His expression changed quickly when he felt the iron fist matching his grip. He looked squarely at Trance and nodded. He squeezed harder. His expression changed again, this time to wonder, as Trance met him pound-for-pound, and then sank him to his knees with a power he had never imagined could come from a man's hand.

"It's General Trance, if you really want to know, Sheriff. The president was kidnapped and injured, and I'm in no mood for any sort of macho shit. So, how about that I let go of your hand and you politely tell me where I can find Major Gibbons?"

Trance let go. Buford began to flap his hand. "Jesus H. Christ, Trance. That was awesome!" He wrapped one of his thick hairy arms around Trance's shoulder and led him down toward the water.

"Hey, Major…General Trance here wants a word with you."

The major's head snapped up and he saluted so fast that his head wobbled like a bobble head doll. "General Trance! No one told me you were here, sir." He adjusted his headset, which had nearly fallen off his ears.

Trance extended his hand and shook without squeezing. Even so, Gibbon's frowned when he felt the hardness of Trance's grip.

"Got a call from Washington and hoofed it here from Boston. How can I help?"

Gibbons shook his head. "This is like nothing I've trained for, General Trance. Guys swooped in from over there…" Gibbons waved toward a spot farther up the lake. "…like something out of Star

Wars. They blew holes in both boats, Centurion's and Mama Bear's. Then they carted Centurion off to Quebec City. We just recovered him there. In a warehouse, I think."

Trance looked out at the water, to where several craft were picking through the remaining wreckage of the two cigarette boats. He looked at Buford and nodded toward the spot up the lake, where Gibbons had pointed.

"What's up there?" he said to Buford.

"The Anderson place. Been there for a century or so. Big ol' spread. They got a million acres of timber and more money than Oprah, I reckon."

"You check it out?"

"Yeah. No one home."

"You go inside?"

"Shit, no. They're solid people, the Andersons. Do a lot of good in this area. You're standing on a piece of their land. Donated for folks to enjoy, rather than for some big assed camp or commercial compound."

"Donated? So they can spy on you?"

"What?" Buford took off his sheriff's Stetson and scratched his sweaty scalp.

Trance pointed up into the trees. "See that camera?"

Buford looked up into the pines and shook his head. "I don't see nothin'."

"Give me your gun."

Buford took a step back and put his hand on his pistol. "The hell I will."

Gibbons stepped forward and offered his sidearm to Trance. Trance fingered it and snapped a bullet into the chamber. He took what looked to be casual aim and pulled the trigger. A moment later, a grouping of pine cones fell to the ground. Nestled inside the cones was a miniature motorized video camera. Trance picked up the cone and pulled out the lens.

"Very sophisticated, Mr. Buford. Very. I suggest that we go pay the Andersons a little visit. How 'bout it?"

Trance walked back up the shore, away from the lake, while motioning for Gibbons and Buford to follow.

"Get as many feet as you can muster, then meet me at the Anderson compound. You have an extra walkie?"

Gibbons offered him one. Trance took it, before jogging back toward his helicopter. He waved again toward the horde of media and yelled, "Nothing yet, folks!"

"You're getting awfully friendly, Trance," said Stick.

"I stay as far away from the press as I can, Stick. But I've learned that the more I try to ignore them, the more they intrude. If I avoid them, they sense a story. If it's business as usual, they leave me alone. So I wave, sometimes I even talk. Now they won't be scurrying around grumbling about how secretive I am. They'll move on to someone else."

"They're going to follow us. You know that."

Trance shook his head. "Right now they're hoping to film a dead body coming out of the lake. They won't chase after a helicopter on foot or by car. Maybe when we land they'll come. Hopefully, by then we'll have the area secure."

Trance fired up his Bell and headed north along the western shore of the lake toward the Anderson compound. They flew over the twelve-foot stone wall that surrounded the entire property. A quarter mile inside the wall they passed a second fence, a new one made of metal. This one was just as tall and it looked electrified.

"Looks like they don't encourage visitors," said Stick.

Trance passed over the fence and continued toward the main lodge. When he reached the three-story building he made a quick circle around it, before landing his helicopter in the open area between the palace-sized house and its even larger barn. No one came out to meet them; the place was deserted. They could see signs of people, hundreds of footprints in the dirt around the helicopter skids. There were fresh tire tracks where trucks had been driven in and out of the barn. But not a face anywhere.

Trance was poking around the barn's double sliding doors when he caught a glimpse of movement from a third story room in the main mansion.

"Hello," he said.

Trance motioned for Stick to follow him to the house. They walked to the main doors and rang the doorbell. No one came. Trance examined the three deadbolt locks, then scurried back to the Bell. He removed a blue gym bag and carried it to the front doors. He set the bag down and fumbled inside for a set of tools that were nestled inside a soft leather case. He selected two items. In less than a minute he had picked all three locks and the doors swung open.

"I would have just shot us in," said Stick.

"That's why you're just a major."

"Not anymore, Trance. I've got a new, important job. It's *general* to you."

"General Shit for Brains."

"You expect me to protect you? Talking to me like that?"

"That and the two million I'm paying your wife."

"There is that, I guess."

When they reached the third floor, Trance listened for movement or breathing, trying to sense where anyone might be. He motioned with his gun toward a closed, elaborately-carved door. He debated whether or not to knock. He rapped his knuckles against the cold hard wood.

"Hello?" came a tentative voice.

"U.S. military. Open the door, please."

"I can't. I'm trapped in here. You better bug out pronto before this whole place blows."

Trance pondered the man's words, then said, "What's your unit, soldier?"

"The BDO."

First Infantry, the Big Dead One, thought Trance. "Too bad for you," he said.

"Not for me, men. I lived. Now, get out of here so *you* can live. It's not safe here."

"Negative. Get away from the door."

Trance aimed a kick at the door and nearly broke his foot.

"Holy cow...." Trance hopped on his good foot, holding the other one up like he'd been bitten by a snake. "What the hell kind of door is this?" he yelled. There were no locks to pick and no knob. Trance began to ponder just how to get inside.

"Thick," yelled the man. "This place is going to blow, soldier. You need to scramble."

Trance spoke into his radio. "Gibbons, what's your twenty?"

"Nearly there, sir."

"You have any RDX?"

"Yeah."

"Bring it to the main house, will you? Third floor. North side. ASAP."

Trance knocked on the door again. "Who are you?"

"Name's Anderson."

"You own this place?"

"Not anymore. Sold out two years ago. Been trapped here ever since. I was in the old servants' house until last week. Then they moved me here."

"Hope you've got a piss-tube and shitter in there, Anderson," shouted Stick. "Otherwise we're not coming in."

"Even got a working John Wayne."

Stick nodded. "Okay then."

Gibbons arrived with the C-4. Trance shaped a small amount along the door and blasted it apart in seconds. Through the opened doorway, he saw a tall, emaciated man with a foot-long beard walking toward them. The man reached out a hand and said, "Ben Anderson. Thanks for coming."

Trance shook the man's hand warily and said, "Any idea what's going on here?"

"They've been setting explosives around this place. So, before we chew the fat, can we get out of here, please?"

Trance nudged Anderson by the shoulder toward the stairs. Anderson listed unsteadily on his feet, nearly tumbling over. Stick hefted him onto his shoulders and carried him down like a fireman. When they got outside, Anderson stretched his face toward the sky and breathed in a big gulp of air. "Man, that tastes good." He began to half walk, half hobble toward the woods. "Follow me."

Trance knew enough to believe a seasoned infantry man, so he and the others kept pace.

When they had traveled a good fifty yards Anderson stopped and said, "I heard them talking." He looked to his watch. "And if I'm correct—"

Anderson was interrupted by a low rumble deep in the ground below them. A flash of flame and smoke exploded from the central estate. At the same time, the roof also lifted off the barn, jumping into the air like a giant, startled crow. A plume of concrete and wood erupted like a volcanic burst, showering them with burning cinders and chunks of glowing stone.

"Man, that's hot," said Stick, slapping away at a slab of burning wood.

"As always, the master of understatement," said Trance. He turned to Anderson. "What happened here?"

"My family's been in the lumber business for generations. At one point we controlled nearly two million acres of prime timberland, mostly here in Maine."

"A series of bad business moves left us a couple billion in debt and hemorrhaging money like a hemophiliac."

"Why didn't you just sell some of the timber?" said Trance.

"I thought that's what I did. Before I knew it, though, the company was stripped from me, like old birch bark, and I was locked inside the servants' place."

"The locals seem to think you still own the company."

Anderson laughed. "That's my alter ego. The PR department issues statements from time to time. They publish a blog in my name, Twitter constantly and send out podcasts whenever they can get me to talk."

"Any idea who did this?"

"Russian, I think."

"You think?"

Anderson shook his head. "The place seemed to be run by some Russian general or something. There was also this blond woman. She came here often, always with a different car."

"You think she was worried about being followed?"

Anderson shrugged. "They had hundreds of people in this place. No one ever left, except for the lady. Yeah, I think she made sure no one knew she was here."

Trance had seen the footprints, made by hundreds of people. Where could they all have been?

"Where did everyone live?"

Anderson pointed to where the barn had stood. It was now a leaping pyre of flames a hundred feet high. "Under there. They carried truckloads of dirt out of here for months. In logging trucks, with logs only on the top. I'm guessing it's pretty big down there."

"You think anyone's in there now?"

"They were taking people out yesterday, like clockwork. Truck after truck, at least twenty of them, maybe a thousand people. The last ones left in cars and two trucks a few hours ago."

"What kind of trucks? What did they look like?"

Anderson laughed. "Like every other logging truck on the highway."

"How about the cars?"

"Blue and black. Chevys and Fords, I think."

"In a few hours they could be almost anywhere," mumbled Trance.

Trance shook his head and laughed. They'd never find them. These people were too smart for that. This was terrorism on a scale that no one had seen before. Billions of dollars and hundreds of people working to kidnap a president, all without a whiff of suspicion. Incredible.

"I overheard talk about flooding down there," said Anderson.

Trance winced. That would make sense. Burn the top, flood the bottom. It would take them days to get a good look at the place. By then their quarry could be anywhere in the world.

"Russian, you say?" said Trance.

"My guess."

Trance narrowed his eyes. Then he began to scratch his chin.

"Where do you have offices?"

"Bangor, Portland, Boston, Newark, Houston and Seattle. Those are the biggest places."

"What about warehouses, transfer stations, maintenance yards…anywhere that twenty of your trucks could go unnoticed?"

Anderson thought for a moment.

"We maintain our equipment in Bangor. We've got a garage with five, six bays, nothing enough to hide a twenty-truck convoy. Our Newark facility could, though. We store a lot of timber there, pending shipment. It's our eastern transfer hub. Twenty or thirty trucks would be just part of the scenery in that place."

"Lot of activity there?"

"Tons."

"Enough for that many trucks to go unnoticed?"

"No one would blink an eye."

Trance unclipped a pen from his shirt and fumbled through his wallet for a piece of paper. He handed both to Anderson. "Your address in Newark, please." Anderson scribbled the address on the paper and handed it back to Trance. Trance looked at the paper and said, "Follow me." He sprinted to his helicopter. When Anderson and Stick reached his side, Trance was saying, "Homeboy. This is Red Dragon. You read?"

"Well, hello there, Red Dragon. How's it hangin'?"

"I need you to dispatch a team to the Anderson Industries transfer facility in New Jersey." Trance gave him the address. "Whoever took Centurion had a base up here, a big one. Moved hundreds of people out last night, most likely in timber trailers.

"You'll also need to dispatch a team to the Anderson compound on Moosehead. We'll need divers, an EOD team and fireman. The place has flames a hundred feet high.

"Task a team on the infrastructure trail coming into this place. Someone was providing the supplies, maybe medical care. Let's find out whom.

"Hunt down any satellite images of the region. Maybe we'll find a needle in this haystack. Do the same for the other Anderson properties. Maybe they made a mistake, thinking we'd not catch on to them this fast. Hell, maybe we'll catch us a string of busses heading to Miami. Somehow, I don't think so, but you never know."

Trance felt himself shudder, as if a cold, frosty wind had skipped across his heart. Could he be after his own people? Was this some sort of black ops coup, engineered outside the chain of command? Was he just a pawn in this game, now marked for death?

"Confiscate every video system within five miles of Anderson's New Jersey warehouse. Same for the Turnpikes. Match photos with any sat images and find me someone to chase. By the time I get to Newark, I want somebody with answers."

Trance turned to Anderson and Stick. "Wheels up, men." He motioned for Anderson to enter the helicopter. "You're coming with us."

Trance pulled Anderson beside him into the cockpit. He checked the instrument panel and then spoke distinctly into a microphone. "Anderson Industries, Newark, New Jersey." A moment later, Trance pointed toward a backlit digital screen. "That's the address, right?"

Anderson nodded.

Trance allowed Stick to sit in the pilot's seat, while he pulled Anderson by the shirt collar to the back of the helicopter. "Now you and I are going to figure some things out."

Trance paused. Then he looked at Stick and slapped him on the shoulder. "Wait. Change of plan. We'll need to fuel in Boston. We're seven hundred miles away from Jersey. Our men will get there long before we can. Why don't we find the president and see if he can tell us anything?"

Stick powered up the helicopter and began to lift off. "Make up your mind, Trance."

"To the president."

"The president, it is."

CHAPTER **63**

______________PP______________

Trance was already leaning out the open door when his helicopter dropped onto the parking lot of the Northern Maine Medical Center. He saluted the four men that surrounded him, dressed in fatigues and carrying rifles. The men saluted back and one of them stepped forward.

"General Trance." said one. "Glad you could make it, sir."

"How's Centurion?"

"They say he's in pain, but stable. Word is, we'll be moving soon."

"Any casualties?"

"Two of ours, sir."

Trance's lips spread into a thin, white line. He nodded grimly. "The president's mother? How is Martha?"

"She's concussed and under observation. Should be okay, though. Lucky. She was doing close to a hundred MPH when it happened. Witnesses say she skipped across the water on her butt like a flat stone before digging in."

Trance motioned to Stick Granger, who was standing at his shoulder. "This is Major Granger, men. He's with me."

The men saluted and Trance began to walk beyond them toward two VH-71 Marine One helicopters and a Boeing CH-47 Chinook. A diesel generator had been stationed among them. It was growling and chugging loudly as it powered electricity for them all. Heavy, rubber-coated communications cables were slung between all three of the helicopters, connecting them into a makeshift command center with high level encryption.

Trance walked to the command helicopter and rapped on the half-opened door.

The point of a rifle nosed from the opening, followed by the alert face of a marine.

"General Trance to see Colonel Tompkin," barked Trance. The marine saluted and waved him in.

Inside, Trance saw half a dozen men sitting at computer terminals. Each operator wore a headset and every one of them was conversing, while their fingers tapped quickly onto computer keyboards.

Jesse Tompkin removed his headset and walked toward Trance with his arms outstretched. Under his shirt, Tompkin's muscles rippled like a flying flag as he moved. His neck was nearly as thick as his head, and his face seemed to rise from sinewy skin like an artist's sculpture made out of bronze-colored clay. His jaw was lean, and his head looked almost like a tan porcelain square with a bristle top.

When Tompkin wrapped his arms around Trance it was muscle on muscle. There was a distinct *thud*, almost like the clank of metal when their chests collided.

"Thanks for coming," said Tompkin.

"Didn't know you'd been assigned to Centurion, Jesse."

"Tilson insisted on a light support crew for his vacation. Didn't want to descend upon his rural home town with an army. So T-Force was pulled in to support a skeletal Service detail during his time up here. We spread out around the lake and were supposed to blend in, help only if needed. We did a piss poor job at preventing this fiasco. Damned lucky to recover him."

"Shit happens, Jesse. Let's go see him."

When Trance and Tompkin reached the area outside the president's private room, the scene was everything but peaceful. Government types were squawking into phones. A nurses' station had been confiscated by the military. Patients had been moved to make room. When Trance reached the president's door he looked in. Doctors were hovering all around the president while talking in quiet tones.

Trance spoke softly to one of the sentries standing guard, "How's he doing?"

"Bitching and moaning and swearing like a French whore."

Trance walked toward the former nurse's station, which was now operating as a temporary switchboard and command center. A man dressed in an Officer Blue Dress Delta uniform, sporting the silver leaf of a Lieutenant Colonel, was barking orders into the phone. "I don't give a rat's ass what you think is most efficient, Director Miller. The president said to get your butt up here, so that's what you'll do." The officer slammed down the phone and glared at Trance.

"What the fuck do you want?"

Before speaking, Trance studied the soldier and tried to step into his shoes. This officer was obviously called here from a formal function, probably something with his wife. She'd have to make her way home alone. This building was little more than a walk-in clinic. The president had been kidnapped and nearly killed. He was wounded. Two Americans were dead. And the president was making absurd demands of the CIA director.

"I was asked to report by the CIC," said Trance.

The Lieutenant Colonel looked closely at Trance, who was still wearing his ragged jean shorts, a faded Polo shirt and a roughed-up pair of Sebago boat shoes without socks.

"Shouldn't you be out sailing or something?"

Trance smiled and saluted. "Brigadier General Trance to see the president, Colonel."

The marine snapped to attention and saluted Trance. He remained at attention, with his eyes staring straight ahead, his cheeks coloring to a bright, reddish pink.

"Loosen your sphincter, Colonel. It's a bad day for all of us."

The marine remained rigid.

"At ease, marine."

The colonel sagged and glanced toward the ringing phone.

"I'd like to see the president when he's ready," said Trance. He nodded toward the phone. "Back to work, Colonel." Then he, Stick and Tompkin walked to the edge of the command station and sat down.

"I would have ripped him a new asshole," whispered Stick.

Trance smiled. "That's why you are a major and I'm a general."

Stick feigned disgust. "I am head of your security now, Trance. It's about time I got a new title, like general. General Granger. I like the sound of that. I want four stars, maybe a fancy uniform like those dudes in France."

"I'll start calling you *Shit for Brains* if you don't shut your trap."

"That's General Shit for Brains to you, soldier."

Soon, the president called Trance into his room. His bed was surrounded by a makeshift cocoon of clear plastic. Trance suspected it was because of the burns. Through the bubble, Trance could see that the president had several deep cuts along his face. Part of his skull had been shaved, and there was a nasty lump the size of a small mountain growing out of it. His neck and the back of his head were covered with a thin, second skin. He was hooked up to a phalanx of wires and tubes, and his face was covered by an oxygen mask. Beside him stood his chief of staff, Geoff Haley, dressed in green surgical scrubs and wearing a mask. Beside Haley stood Josh Stone, the president's body man, keeper of the gate.

"Good to see you, Jock," said Trance though an intercom.

The president looked at Trance through glazed eyes. Trance thought he saw something he hadn't seen there before. It was a look of something odd—distrust or fear, maybe both.

The president removed his mask and croaked, "What are you doing here, Trance?"

Trance frowned. "I was asked to help investigate. Seems there was a bit of a fracas."

Brandon Copley, now Jason "Jock" Tilson, tried to laugh. "Yeah, it was a hell of a show. Miller send you?"

"Among others."

"Why isn't he here?"

Trance pondered the president's words before speaking. Miller would have to coordinate with all the major intelligence agencies, as well as the military. There was too much to be done in too short a time. Far more than could be done in the air, or in a hospital room in Ft. Kent or Bangor, Maine. Anything could happen and they had to be ready.

"Pardon me, Mr. President. Perhaps you aren't thinking clearly. People had to coordinate your rescue. People had to gather intelligence from around the world, and determine the appropriate response to your kidnapping. For all we knew, this was World War III. Still might be. Now you are worrying about where the CIA director is? He is where he's most effective—in Virginia. I'm sorry sir, but we've got far greater things to worry about than Miller's twenty."

As the president stared at Trance, a brief, but strange expression seemed to cross his face. His eyes hardened at first, but then they softened and he laughed.

"It's been a hell of a day. Any idea who did this?"

"Not yet, sir," said Trance. "Do you remember anything?"

"Not a thing."

"Is there something you can think of that can help us?'

The president shook his head. "The world is one big fog, Jack."

"That's normal, Jock. We might have traced their trail to Newark. I'm on my way there now. You're in good hands. Tompkin is the best we've got."

"Tompkin got me kidnapped."

Trance's eyes widened. He counted to ten before speaking. The president had caused this to happen, by weakening the wall that protected him, by demanding privacy. "From what I hear, sir, you demanded skeletal security. There's a reason that presidents travel with a long motorcade and big advance teams."

The president closed his eyes and waved Trance away. "I'm tired, Trance. Go make yourself useful."

Trance frowned but said nothing. Technically, he was a private citizen, here only because he was asked. Now, the president was treating him like he was a petty criminal.

"If you think of anything, Mr. President, make sure to tell someone. We're on our way to New Jersey."

CHAPTER **64**
PP

Stick Granger began to descend from their cruising altitude of eight thousand feet. He spiraled down in a looping circle above the Anderson Industries Newark warehouse yard. A ten foot Hurricane fence surrounded the twelve acre complex. Its gates were spread wide, and they could see groupings of vehicles already gathered throughout the site. Many of the vehicles were painted with brown and green camouflage paint. They looked like scattered handfuls of dirt and earthworms from high above.

As they came closer to the ground they could see dozens of people scurrying around with automatic weapons and full combat gear. A man holding two bright orange signal wands motioned for Stick to land off to the side. As they touched the ground, two men rushed to the helicopter and saluted. The noise was deafening.

"At ease," yelled Trance.

Trance pointed toward Anderson and Stick. "Can you get us three brain buckets?"

One of the men nodded and gave an order through a walkie. Soon a man raced toward them carrying three Kevlar helmets. Trance grabbed one of them, put it on and began to move with the others toward the first warehouse. As they walked, one of the soldiers leaned close against Trance's ear and gave him a quick update.

When they stepped through the warehouse's thirty-foot-high doors, they were hit by the almost overpowering scent of pine pitch mixed with diesel fuel. The warehouse was five hundred feet long and over two hundred wide. It stretched out before them like a stadium, with nearly two acres of logs taking the place of arena seats.

"There was no one here, sir," said the soldier beside Trance.

Trance looked down the long warehouse. Stacks of roughly cut timber sat in tall piles along the entire right hand side. More than twenty trucks were standing side by side, with their tails backed up against the pine. Each truck appeared to be stacked with a full load of logs.

Trance walked over to one of the trucks and examined it closely. After several minutes of fingering around the wood and the metal, Trance found a hidden door. He opened it and stuck his head inside. He saw a tight seating area, big enough to squeeze fifty or sixty people inside like tennis balls in a can. The area was encased with reinforced fiberglass that still emitted a slight, telltale chemical odor. The odor was now mixed with the smell of human sweat and pine pitch. Rough timber boards had been expertly placed around the shell, so that the compartment was invisible from the side or above, and found only with the closest inspection, plus a little luck.

Trance turned to one of the men. "These guys are good. Dust these trucks for prints and swab for DNA." He turned to Anderson. "Someone's been here. Let's find out whom."

Anderson looked down to his feet and mumbled, "I am so sorry."

Trance put a hand on Anderson's shoulder. "This is no time for second guessing, Ben. Where could they be?"

"From here we load the timber into containers. We ship it by train to Houston, LA or Seattle. Or it goes onto cargo ships, heading from here to just about anywhere."

Trance motioned for one of the soldiers. "Get me a list of all current Anderson shipments on land or at sea. Now."

The man ran off. Trance walked out of the warehouse and back to his helicopter. He grabbed his phone and called the Pentagon.

"This is Homeboy."

"Red Dragon here. I'm at the Anderson warehouse. It's been abandoned. There must be twenty trucks, with enough hidden cargo space to move a thousand people. No one in sight, so they've moved on. I've got men checking for shipments out of the warehouse. You'll need to check every car, truck, boat or train that's come out of this city. What have you got from video and satellite?"

"Bupkiss. Every video camera in the area was shot out before these trucks passed by. Except for the images inside Anderson's building. It's like they were mooning us for fun.

"All we caught on tape were the drivers, wearing hats and sunglasses. People might have slid out the backs of the trucks, but they're not on video. We've got nothing good on satellite either. There's the usual array of semis coming in and out, and that's a ton. Nothing suspicious, though. No convoy. Just a steady stream of trucks. They could have left hours ago, Red Dragon. They could be two hundred miles at sea, back in Maine, or halfway across the country by now."

Trance closed his eyes. It was true. He had the sudden, sinking feeling that they would find no one today, perhaps not ever. It made him think of the old movie, *Ocean's Eleven*, the perfect con. He also thought of Newman's movie, *Butch Cassidy and the Sundance Kid*, about the intrepid, never-ending pursuit to catch Butch and the Kid, even out of the country. He wondered which of the two would win this one, the con or the capture.

"We've got to try everything. You call all the Guard units?"

"From here to California."

"We need feet on the ground and eyes in the air."

"Tell me something I don't know, Red Dragon."

Trance leaned against the side of the Bell Ranger and slumped. "I'm sorry, Homeboy. That was out of line."

"We're all a bit edgy. Say any damned thing you want."

Trance laughed. "Doesn't excuse me acting like a shitbag."

"Go find us some bad guys and leave me alone."

Trance hung up the phone. He felt like he had an anchor tied to his leg, pulling him down, down to a deep, dark underwater cave where there was no escape. He began to get into his helicopter but something made him hesitate. They had moved hundreds of people, but not from this building. Where did they go?

"To me, men!" shouted Trance.

Soldiers ran toward Trance from every direction. When a large group had gathered around him Trance said, "Hundreds of people were in these trucks. No video shows them getting out of the trucks or leaving the warehouse, so this building must lead to some other place. A storage area, a tunnel, something. Go find it."

Ten minutes later, a shout came from halfway down the warehouse.

"I've got something!"

Trance jogged toward the voice. A half dozen men were standing beside a trap door in the warehouse floor. They all looked at Trance, wondering which one of them was going to be the lead rat in the tunnel.

"Who wants to be a hero?" said Trance.

Every soldier stepped forward.

Trance grinned. "Glad to see we're still turning out heroes. Who's got a torch?"

One of the men reached into his backpack and removed a green rubber flashlight. He handed the light to Trance, along with a couple of glow sticks. Trance cracked the glow sticks, stuck them into his back pocket and moved toward the hole. He slipped his MEU pistol out from the small of his back and began to lower himself down the stairs, gun in one hand, and flashlight in the other. Trance's feet soon hit the wet concrete of a sewer tunnel about twenty feet below. There was half a foot of standing water in the tunnel, and a host of crumbling potholes where the concrete had broken apart. Trance shined his light around. The tunnel was about six feet high and it was round. The lower halves of the walls were covered with some sort of black slime or algae. The top was a mottled gray, and still in good shape. Trance could see the red beads of rat's eyes everywhere. He could hear them shuffling and squeaking, and he was glad to see them scurry away from his light.

Trance knelt to the ground and looked for signs of feet. It took only a moment for Trance to see a wet trail of footsteps moving in one direction, along the edges of the water in the pipe. He couldn't tell how many people there had been. There were just a few stray prints, as if everyone had been instructed to walk through the water only. The footprints *were* fresh, though.

"Three men down here! With lights!" yelled Trance.

Three men came down the stairs quickly. Trance pointed toward the portion of the tunnel that had no footprints. "You two, find where this leads. These prints could be a decoy." He pointed at the other man. "You, come with me." Trance began to jog along the wet tunnel, following the occasional signs of feet. The footprints continued for nearly a thousand yards before stopping by a rusted metal ladder. Trance looked at the master sergeant beside him. The man began to climb the stairs but Trance pulled him back.

"I'll go first."

Trance climbed quickly. At the top of the stairs he found a round hatch cover, much like the ones found on navy subs. There was a rusted wheel in the center. Trance turned it counter clockwise and it swung easily. After a few turns the wheel stopped moving. Trance took a breath and pushed upwards, exhaling as the hatch began to yield. Before he opened the hatch, Trance closed his eyes and let his mind feel for signs of life. There was nothing. He tossed a glow stick up through the opening. He raised his head quickly and popped it back down. Then he raised it again. No one was there.

Trance called down for the sergeant to join him, then climbed up through the opening. The hatch led to a small warehouse office. There was a green metal desk in one corner, piled high with a haphazard stack of papers. There were posters of scantily clad women holding various hand tools lining the walls, as well as photos of semi trailers with the logo AAAA Amalgamated Trucking stenciled along the side.

Trance sat down on the desk and groaned. This was probably some sort of shell company, owned for this single purpose. Who could have planned all this? What sort of organization could spend billions and years planning for a kidnapping like this? China? Iran? Then he saw the paper.

On the floor, beside the hole leading from the sewer, there was a single sheet of yellow paper. There, printed in large type was a note. It was a note that sent chills running down Trance's spine, a note that made his stomach lurch and his sphincter try to spill. It was something that he'd never expected, but somehow knew was coming.

My people were never here, Trance. Just me. You are wrong again.

I killed your wife. I killed Kiki Tilson.

We took the president. That was just foreplay. Can you guess what we'll do next?

There was date on the note. The note was dated three days earlier. He'd been played with like a toy.

CHAPTER 65

________PP________

When Trance returned to Maine, the president had been moved down state to Eastern Maine Medical in Bangor. The helicopters had also been moved. They now took up a section of the hospital parking lot. Their electrical generators were still chugging, despite a grouping of power cords that had been run out from the hospital. Several large tents had been erected, on both the parking lot and the grass beside it. The entire grouping was ringed by a crescent of Bradley Fighting Vehicles.

The president's team had taken over a floor of the hospital. One of the nurses' stations had become a de facto command post. Guards were stationed everywhere.

The president's bed was surrounded by a burn bubble. He was sitting up, looking somewhat lucid, but with a face etched in pain.

When Trance read him the note, the president closed his eyes. "Looks like some vendetta against you, Trance. Are you the cause of all this?"

Trance stared at the president, only half comprehending what he had heard. The other half of his brain was running through his memories, trying to find some rationale for what was happening, some semblance of normality, some tether to keep him centered. What *could* he tell the president? The president knew that Talid had been trying to kill him, as well as the usual mix of terrorist groups. This operation must have taken months, if not years to complete, far longer than Talid had been after his sorry ass.

"They obviously know that we're friends, Jock. I'm guessing they knew I was helping you, and they're afraid I'll get too close.

"The note has an odd juxtaposition of the words *I* and *we*. Gives me the sense that this started out as a personal vendetta, perhaps against you and me, by one person. Now it has grown into something larger, hence the use of the word, *we*. Can you make any sense of that? Can you remember anything?"

As the president looked at Trance, an odd image crept into the president's mind. It wasn't distinct, more like a cloud that was taking an odd shape. The president could almost see the outlines of the Anderson compound, like shadows seen through fog. He had never been to the place, although it wasn't far from his boyhood home. It was much like others that dotted the northern Maine landscape, built by the timber barons, their castles of wood. He had certainly seen enough places like it. That must be why he saw it so clearly as Trance described it, as if he had been there. That had to be it. He had never been there. He shook off the notion. All kinds of strange visions were passing before his eyes. No, they were passing on the *edge* of his eyes, never in front of him, always just out of reach and out of focus. That was the concussion, they said. He was lucky his mind still worked at all.

"I've got to rest now, Jack," said the president.

"Sure, Jock," said Trance, and he began to turn away.

"Jack?"

"Yeah?"

"Would you please call me *Mr. President* like everyone else? I've got to maintain respect for the office, even in private."

"Yes, Mr. President." *Well, isn't that a one-eighty?* thought Trance. Tilson had always insisted that Trance call him Jock. "A president needs a few true friends," he'd say. "If a man can't call a friend by his name then he isn't a friend."

Trance had tried to tell Tilson that the office transcended even friendship, that it stood for great things and should be treated with the highest respect by all. Now, finally, Tilson had taken Trance's advice. So, why did it feel so strange? Why did everything feel strange? This was like an Edgar Allan Poe nightmare, where reality was warped and twisted into something unrecognizable and unthinkable, where evil proved its name. Which way would the pendulum swing next? he wondered. Hopefully not across his throat.

CHAPTER 66

_____________PP____________

Sammantha Starodubov looked slowly around the Spartan, ten by twelve foot room. It was made of pine. The walls were pine. The ceiling was pine. The floor was pumpkin pine. Pictures of wooden sloops clung to the windowless walls. There was a flat TV hung among them, looking as incongruent as a scarecrow in a field. A thin green rug was thrown over the coarse, uneven floor of pumpkin pine. There was a smattering of pine furniture in the room. A rocking chair. A sitting chair with a red knitted cushion and two small tables, each with a hand-made wooden lamp purchased from the Maine Prison Store. The lamps were both lit and the room was bright. Jock Tilson was strapped in the sitting chair, ignoring the pain of his healing skin while reading a novel.

"Congratulations," Sammantha said.

Tilson looked up from his book. "Why?"

"You are leaving the hospital today."

Sammantha pulled a TV remote out of her pocket. She pressed a button and the television came to life. There, in living color, Tilson could see himself being pushed out of the hospital in a wheelchair. Once outside, the president stood and greeted the crowd with a forced smile and a half-hearted wave. His old friend, Tubby Hearns, gushed eloquently about the strength and courage being shown by America's great leader. Good old Tubby, coming through when he needed him most, just like always.

"Your imposter looks worse off than me," said Tilson.

"He has a concussion that has affected his memory. He has a couple third degree burns, but he'll recover. You think you were popular right after your election? Just wait. The country will love you now."

Tilson stared at the image of himself on the screen. "This isn't real," he said.

Sammantha laughed. She switched the television from channel to channel. Tilson was on almost every station. One network showed Tubby shaking hands with him at the hospital entrance. The imposter now had a big grin on his face. His eyes seemed to feed off the attention as if it were a drug.

"Tubby doesn't know," mumbled Tilson. "My friend doesn't know. Who is the pretender? Who is it?"

"I told you before. It's the president. Can't you see?"

"He's an imposter. Who's playing the role?"

"Your brother."

"I don't have a brother."

"Your mother never told you, then?"

"You're lying."

"Oh, no, I'm not."

Sammantha turned off the television. She sat down in the rocking chair and began to move it back and forth, like her slow moving, childhood metronome. This time she smiled, pushing off the day when she was twelve like an annoying little bug. "Your mother never told you about Brandon Copley?"

Tilson's mouth gaped open. "The baseball player? From Yale?" He'd been forced to look at that picture of Copley, striking him out at the Harvard/Yale game, for his entire adult life. Is that what it was? Was Copley his brother? It all made sense now, why his mother was so attached to that photo, the only picture she had of her two sons together. Tilson closed his eyes.

"How?" he whispered.

"The usual. She was raped by her boss. She used to work as a maid, you know. Yes, your mother, a lowly summertime maid. When she got pregnant and had twins, the Copley's wanted both. But your mother…she fought like a virago to keep you, one of you. You drew the long straw. You were the lucky one. You got all the advantages, the real ones. The Copleys paid your mother, money she used to buy that pitiful little farm of hers. In exchange, she promised never to speak of or contact them again. Your brother was sold for twenty pieces of silver, Jock. How does that make you feel?"

"How do you know this?"

Sammantha savored the moment. It was like having a cold glass of milk on a hot summer day, with Oreo cookies. It was the perfect mental snack. "I know one of the maids that worked with your mother, in Bar Harbor. My friend was a willing mistress. She tried to excite him whenever she was asked. But she was never lucky enough to draw an erection, not like your mother. No one else was. Your mother was his only conquest, the only one who fought him hard enough to arouse him. My friend *was* privy to his deepest thoughts, though, his desires and his perversions." Sammantha grinned. "Oh, yes. Your father was a pervert, and a rapist."

Tilson clenched his fists. He felt like screaming out, telling Sammantha that she had no business snooping into his life, of upsetting the careful balance that he and his mother had worked so hard to maintain. But he had no power, not now. She had it all. He was at her mercy.

"A twin?"

"An identical twin."

"How did you…how did you pull it off?"

"I had to fuck a lot of people to get here." Sammantha paused and let the words sink into Tilson's brain, as well as her own. She felt a rumbling of rage begin to bubble into the back of her mind. She closed her eyes and shut that door, like she had so many times before. She rocked some more.

Sammantha looked at Tilson, her eyes like scalpel points. Just a bit longer, she thought. Then it would all be over. "I am a neurosurgeon, Jock. I study the brain. Give me a man and enough time and I will turn him into anything I want. You want a saint? I'll give you one. A perfect soldier? Done. A mass murderer? Simpler than you think.

"I begin by erasing the mind, the *self*. We used to call this brainwashing. But that term is so outdated. The days of blinding lights, painful drugs and sensory deprivation are long behind us. Today its hormone therapy, DNA reengineering, brain manipulation and targeted drugs. Throw in some of my own concoctions, relaxation, meditation, some audio, video and sensory stimulation and you've got a clean slate, a formatted brain ready to store whatever you put there. All you need do is provide the stimulus. Pictures, mostly. The brain works in pictures and colors."

"If you did anything to my brother—"

Sammantha slapped Tilson across the face.

"Shut up and listen! I love your brother and I would never hurt him."

Tilson laughed. It was a hearty guffaw that ended in a fit of painful choking. "You love my brother? God, you've got a great way of showing it. Turning him into the biggest criminal of our generation—"

"He doesn't know, Jock. He is innocent in this. It is all me. *I* was the one who seduced him. *I* was the one that brought him here. *I* was the one that erased his mind with techniques that *I* developed.

"While your scientists experiment with crap like Propranolol to re-write traumatic memories, while they fiddle with Yoga to reduce stressful images, I have unlocked the secrets to memory. I have developed a new class of pharmaceuticals that can wipe a brain clean, like Windex on glass. I have engineered viruses to act like both janitors and jailors. I can *sever* the memory pathways, and render entire reaches of them off limits. Then I build new memories, new pathways.

"Have you ever run a computer Scandisk program, targeting the bad sectors, causing them to be completely ignored and isolated? I do the same with the brain, segmenting memories into some out of the way place. Then I erase the whole section. I construct new memories where the old ones were. Memories that are as real as the originals, only better. Perfect memories, controlled memories."

"If he is anything like me, he will fight you."

"He thinks he's saving the country, you stupid shit. He thinks *he* is the real president. He won't fight me. He loves me."

"You program that, too?"

Sammantha slapped Tilson again.

"He loved me before I changed him," she hissed.

Then he will remember you from before, thought Tilson. As he stared at Sammantha, he could see her anguish, almost taste it on his tongue. And he wondered what could have caused such rage. "But…why?"

"Revenge, of course. I am going to pay you back for what you did to me."

"We did nothing. *I* did nothing. My *brother* did nothing. You will not succeed."

Sammantha tossed her head back and laughed. She walked to the chair where Tilson was strapped, her eyes filled with some strange concoction of playfulness and hate. She lifted her skirt and pulled off her panties with an exaggerated *snap*. She sat upon Tilson's lap and brought her face against his ear. She ground against him slowly with her hips and lightly licked his neck.

I am going to detonate a nuclear warhead during your brother's State of the Union Address, thought Sammantha. *And I am going to let you watch it happen. On TV. Of course, when it happens all you will see is a brief flash, then nothing. The true beauty of my plan…the true glory…will be experienced first-hand, by the thousands that will perish, and the millions that will mourn the loss of your entire Congress.*

And I will die with your brother. It will be glorious.

Sammantha looked down at the bulge beginning to form in Tilson's pants. She knew he'd been without a woman since his wife had died. Such easy pickings. She pressed her palm against his zipper. "Why, I believe I already have succeeded in changing something," she said.

Tilson closed his eyes. He didn't want this. He had no desire for this woman. Yet, she had been able to manipulate him with the ease of a circus ringmaster.

Sammantha whispered again. "There is nothing you can do to stop me. Even your little Jack Trance will fade into an afterthought. When your brother tunes him out, as he will, your buddy will find other things to keep himself occupied, like that little bitch Haverford that he chums around with, provided I let her live."

"You are insane."

Sammantha shook her head slowly. "I've thought long and hard about that, Jock Tilson. I have concluded that I am not insane, merely angry. Actually, I'm quite rational.

"How did you feel when you watched your mother's boat explode? Now, imagine watching your parents lying dead on a floor. Imagine lying down with your lifeless mom and dad, alone in the world, tasting the blood on your tongue. A man comes into your kitchen and tells you who did it. He tells you it was America. The American government. And then…as if to seal the deal…he forces himself into you. Twelve years old, I was just a child…parents dead…Americans at fault…and some pig turns you into a whore. I fought the war you created, in the only way I could. How would you react? Huh? Tell me."

Sammantha closed her eyes and drew a long, cleansing breath. When she opened her eyes again, Jock Tilson could almost feel death surround him, folding around him like a glove. Those eyes, so dark and dangerous, so filled with rage and hate.

"Tell me," Sammantha whispered. Then she began to yell. "Tell me, Mr. Fucking President! How would you react? Would you want revenge? And how far would you go to get it?"

"What do you plan to do?"

"You're just going to have to wait and see, now. Aren't you?" Sammantha turned off the television set and walked to the corner of the room. She sat down on the floor and pulled her knees to her chest. She began to rock. Then she began to weep.

CHAPTER **67**
______________PP______________

Dr. Mariah Whinton opened the front door and motioned for Trance to enter her Beacon Hill brownstone.

"Good to see you again, Jack."

"Hello, Dr. Slash."

Whinton laughed. "Let's keep things informal, Jack. Just call me Slash."

Whinton shut the door and lead Trance up the four flights of stairs, then to the final stairway that led to the garden on her roof. It was a glorious fall day. The temperature was in the low eighties, with a spectacular grouping of high, rounded lenticular clouds in the distant sky. A cool breeze blew in from the East, giving the air a fresh whiff of salt. Unusual, thought Trance, to have the ocean breeze and still such warmth on an early September day.

"So, Jack. Coffee?"

"Of course."

Whinton poured them each a cup of coffee that was strong enough to spread on a cake.

Whinton said, "Tell me. How have you been?"

Trance looked around at the flowering garden. Dozens of roses were in bloom. Hydrangeas of the strangest colors were interspersed among them, as were dozens of other varieties of plants that Trance couldn't pretend to recognize. Some of the perennials were in bloom. Some had clearly passed, while others were still on the way.

"Place looks nice, Slash."

"Don't avoid me."

Trance chuckled. He sat back in his chair. "Everyone knows the president was kidnapped." Trance took a pensive sip of coffee. He frowned, but then smacked his lips.

Slash nodded, but said nothing. Her eyes didn't leave Trance's face. Trance stared out over the Boston skyline.

"Everyone thinks the president came out of this okay. But I was there…just afterward. And…well…I used to be good friends with him…"

"I know."

Trance spoke slowly. "It's like I don't know him anymore."

"Trauma can change a man, Jack. You, of all people, should know that."

Trance smiled sadly. "It's more than that, Slash. I'm not sure it's the same *man*."

"Are you saying it's not Tilson?"

"Oh, I can't say that. When he was recovered in Canada, we followed protocol. We checked everything. DNA, fingerprints, vocal patters, retina scans, immunization markers, his GPS serial numbers. It's Tilson, all right." Trance paused. "But…it's also *not* him."

"Can't have it both ways, Jack."

"Jesse Tompkin feels the same way I do."

Slash nodded her head slowly. "Ah…Mr. Tompkin." Slash had been seeing Tompkin and his wife for several months, trying to help Kathy deal with the stresses that came with her husband's job. Kathy wasn't doing well. Whinton suspected it was just a matter of time before she bolted.

"He a patient of yours?"

"Can't say." Strange, thought Whinton, how both men would voice the same odd concern.

"You think they could have changed him? In the short time they had him?' said Trance.

Whinton looked at Trance's hard-set jaw. Then her eyes followed a jet, dropping slowly behind Trance as it prepared to land at Logan. "Doubtful. Give me some specifics."

"It's little things. Things he doesn't remember. Things he doesn't say."

"Like what?"

"Like the fact that we drink a particular type of scotch."

Whinton scoffed. "I wouldn't hold that against him. People forget things, Jack, particularly if they're drinking."

"Even fifty-year-old single malt?"

"You have fifty-year-old single malt?"

Trance smiled. He liked this woman. She was good people. She deserved something good in her life. "I've got a case of it. You like baseball?"

Whinton blinked, as if she'd finally been caught off guard. "I was born and bred in Southie, Jack."

"Oh, yeah. Sorry." Trance grinned. "Lauren and I are hosting a little get-together at her place, before the first playoff game. Then we're going to sit in the Hopewell box and scream our hearts out."

"How many people?"

"Twenty or thirty. Give or take."

"Do I have to bring someone?"

"Do you want to?"

"No."

"Then come alone. If the president was himself, I'd try to fix you up."

Whinton seemed to search through her memories. Her eyes brightened and she said, "I used to watch him, you know."

"Who?"

"Tilson."

Trance frowned. Slash watched Tilson? How could that be? Trance felt like he couldn't find the final frustrating piece to a jigsaw puzzle, one he had been working on for months. Everything seemed out of order, misshapen somehow. But everything was interconnected. There had to be a connection somewhere.

Whinton continued, "When he was at Harvard. He was two years ahead of me. Man, could he pitch. Decent hitter. Never could hit the high inside fastball, though."

Trance nodded. "Makes sense. When we were reviewing his retina scans we found a hole in his left retina. Just a pinprick. Might be just enough to render him blind to a certain pitch. Anything else and he's fine. Hell, I doubt he even knows about the eye."

"I tried to tell him."

"Huh?"

"Oh, yeah." She laughed. "My friends and I, we were baseball crazy. Used to go to all the Harvard games. Even away games. When we needed a rally I'd turn my cap inside out and wear it sideways."

Trance smiled. "You and Lauren."

"She have a ritual, too?"

"Doesn't everybody? Sometimes Lauren claims the Sox have won just because of her. She's an incurable fan. Incurable. You were saying?"

"Oh. There was this one time…yeah, it was the Harvard/Yale game. This stud from Yale was on the mound and he was throwing gas all day. But he was tiring; we could see it. He'd struck out two and walked the bases loaded by the time Jock came to bat. He blew one by Jock, high and tight. I yelled to tell him to open up his stance, turn his face toward the mound, change his sight angle, like Johnny Damon used to do. He didn't listen. Took two more pitches. Same spot. Never got the bat off his shoulder. It was the saddest thing. They lost two to one."

"I'm sure he got over it. Someday you'll have to get over things, too, Slash. Maybe find you another jarhead."

"Like you, Trance? Like you've forgotten about *your* wife?"

Trance closed his eyes. He felt that familiar, hot anguish flush through his body. Thoughts of his dead wife, feelings of pain. It was as natural as rain. But this time, the pain somehow washed away. He smiled. "Actually, yes. Like me."

"No?" cried Whinton. She brought her hand to her mouth. "Have you asked her yet?"

Trance shook his head. "I've been trying to buy the Red Sox for a wedding gift. But Johns won't sell."

"I'm not surprised. He's in the investment business, Jack. The Sox are his meal ticket. He sells the team, he loses investors. How do you think he gets money for his hedge funds?"

Trance looked confused. Then he grinned. "New York is a far bigger place than Boston, Slash." Trance remained silent for several moments. "You thinking what I'm thinking?"

Whinton nodded. "Sure. Why don't you buy the Yankees instead? The boss has estate issues, I hear. His family's going to need the cash. Maybe you could buy the Yankees and swap them for the Sox?"

"The Yankees are worth far more than the Sox."

"To whom?"

Trance smiled. "A man would take a financial bath if he swapped the teams even up. Another would make a windfall. It would take a fool to be on the short end of that deal."

"It would take a fool to pass it up," said Slash.

"Johns would make a fortune with the Yankees."

"His cash flow would certainly improve. He'd get more investors, too."

"You are one devious woman, Slash Whinton. Remind me not to tell you any secrets."

"It will cost a fortune to buy the Yankees."

"Lucky I have one."

"Ah," said Slash. "The price of love." Whinton narrowed her eyes and peered closely at Trance. "Big change for you, after living like a miser in your Hobbit hole in Vermont."

Trance laughed. "I like things simple."

"Then don't get married."

When Trance laughed again, there was a shine to his eyes. "I *like* things simple. I *love* Lauren. Besides, she's simple too."

"Just don't get attached to them."

"To whom?"

"The Yankees, stupid."

Trance smiled. "I like their players, Slash. I even like the ownership group. But I'll never like the laundry. I'm a Red Sox fan. Always have been. Always will be."

"Never forget that."

"It's in the DNA, Slash. We can't forget."

"Amen, brother. Don't wait too long before asking Lauren, Jack. Things happen, particularly to you."

"I've had to wait a bit, because I've been renovating some properties I bought. Something she'll never expect. Even better than the Red Sox.

"This Kiki Tilson thing has kinda been keeping me busy, working surreptitiously with the boys, trying to track down her killers. It's a deeply layered labyrinth, with so many twists and turns…you wouldn't believe it. And the president's not making it easy. Not anymore."

"You'd think he'd be on that like a hound on a rabbit."

Trance bit down on his lower lip. "That's another thing that makes no sense. Ever since the kidnapping, he's lost all interest in finding Kiki's killers. He shows no interest in tracking down his kidnappers. He used to call me every week, every day sometimes. It's been a month and I hear nothing, about Kiki or the kidnappers."

"A near-death experience will change a man, Jack."

Trance knew that Slash was speaking of *him*, how he had to center his own life. He couldn't always live in fear; it wasn't healthy.

Trance tilted his head, searching for some way to cut the president some slack. "Tilson does have that nuclear summit with Ogarkov. Be a hell of a coup if he and Ogarkov could agree to disarm, and then force their will on the other nuclear nations."

"Can he succeed?"

"If desire matters. It's all he thinks about," muttered Trance. "I'd love to see it happen."

"Maybe that's a good thing, then. Don't take it personally. Lives change. Friendships change."

"He *loved* his wife. He campaigned *against* terrorism. He can't *ignore* terrorism when it hits his own family. He can't move on like it didn't happen."

"Give the man a break, Jack."

Trance's mouth opened wide and he briefly stopped breathing. Then he smiled, his white teeth reflecting the sun almost like a mirror. "You are *sweet* on him, aren't you?"

Whinton fiddled with her coffee. "I sort of had a crush on him in college."

"He never knew?"

"Nah. He was too busy running the student government to pay attention to any of us. Besides, he loved Kiki. Everybody knew that."

Whinton stood and flattened her skirt back over her knees. "That's all for today, Jack. Don't know if that was you getting the therapy or me. Let's call it a draw. No bill, today."

"You never send me a bill."

"Uncle Sam pays your tab, as they should. They owe you."

Trance shrugged. "We're all citizens, Slash. Some of us get to show it more than others."

"How many scars do you have?"

"Excuse me?"

"You heard me. How many scars?"

"Inside or outside?"

"You can't count them all, can you?"

Trance shook his head. "I lost track a long time ago, Slash."

"Carry on, soldier."

"You, too, marine."

"Do it soon, Jack. Live your life. Don't let it wither away like old fruit."

"Ditto, Slash."

Whinton smiled, but inwardly she shook her head. It was easy telling someone else to move on. It was something far different to do it herself.

CHAPTER **68**
PP

The president leaned back in his leather chair and gazed around the Oval Office. How many men had dreamed of sitting here, at the epicenter of global power, the fulcrum of mankind? How many extraordinary men had shaken in their shoes as they stood facing the man behind this desk and in this chair? He stared at the intricate woodwork of the Resolute desk. The thing weighed more than a thousand pounds. It was solid, like the presidency, like his nation.

For a brief moment, the president was overcome with the overwhelming realization that *he…was…here.* He put his feet up on the desk and clasped his hands behind his head. He could do *anything he wanted.*

The president pressed his intercom with his heel.

"Mandy?"

"Yes, Mr. President?"

"Send in Grodin."

"It's Sunday night, sir. Even the chief of staff needs a break. He's at home with his family."

"Oh. Of course."

"Mr. Stone is here," said Mandy.

The president wondered if his body man ever slept.

"No. Tell him to go home, if he has one. No more meetings today."

Sunday night and he was sitting alone in his office. He felt his mind bend, like hidden hands were pulling at his brain from either side. He could hear a voice calling from the deep recesses of his mind, from somewhere in the bowels of his darkest thoughts, where instinct and consciousness clash. *Call for her,* the voice said. Call for whom? *You are lonely. You need her. She is there for you. Call her.*

"Who?" he whispered. But he knew the answer. He could see the outline of her face; he could feel the heat of her touch against his deprived and healing skin. He called for his secretary.

"Mandy?"

"Yes, Mr. President."

"Could you come in here, please?"

A moment later, Mandy Potempkin walked stiffly and efficiently through the Oval Office door. Mandy was on the backside of fifty. She kept herself teenager thin with a strict, regimented diet of salads and protein shakes, combined with bike spinning four days a week. Her hair was gray and coiffed close to her head. Executive, but still feminine.

"Do you need something, sir?"

"Do you remember the woman who did that Russian special last summer? You remember her name?"

Mandy consulted her PDA, tapping it several times with her finger.

"Sammantha Starodubov?"

"Ah, yes. Starodubov."

"Anything else, sir?"

"Yes." The president hesitated. Was this wise? A voice inside him was calling out a warning. This wasn't wise; it was trouble. But there was another voice urging him onward, a voice he could not silence. He closed his eyes. He was the president, wasn't he? He needed relaxation, didn't he? *Too much work and not enough play will make Jock a dull boy*, he heard the voice say.

"Would you please find me her phone number? I need to prepare for my upcoming meetings with Ogarkov. I think she can help us. Help me."

Mandy smiled to herself. *Sure*, she thought. *That spider will be lots of help. She'll spin a web around you and then eat you when she's done.*

"Do you think that's wise? Politically, of course. You are going to fall under a great deal of scrutiny and criticism over the next few months. Perhaps it's better—"

"Find her."

"Yes, sir."

The president felt something stir inside him, something that made his blood run hot and his breath begin to quicken. Oh, yes. She did that, even from afar.

"Good. Very good."

CHAPTER 69

________PP________

The sound of Aerosmith's *Walk This Way* began to thrum throughout the darkly-lit night club. Strobes flashed, then an exotic dancer strutted onto a spotlighted stage and began to gyrate to the music. In the far corner of the club, three men sat at a round table with their heads huddled together above its center, ignoring the dancer's every movement.

"Do you agree that Centurion is acting strange?" said Trance, barely above the bone-jarring music.

Jacob Miller, the head of the CIA and Jesse Tompkin, leader of T-Force, pressed forehead to forehead with Trance, barely hearing his words over the din.

"Frigging strange," said Miller. "He's ordered me to stop looking for Kiki's killers *or* his kidnappers."

"Ditto," said Tompkin. "He said if I pursue this anymore, he'll slap me with an OTH."

"He's threatened you with an other-than-honorable discharge?" said Trance.

Trance looked at the CIA director. He studied the focused brown eyes hiding behind the tortoise shell glasses, the expensive haircut, the high patrician cheekbones and the thin, almost frail physique. Miller didn't look powerful, but he was. He knew where every body was buried in this town and he wielded as much power as anyone in Washington. "Who's doing this, Jake?" Trance said. "Who's neutered him?"

Miller shook his head. He didn't know. He honestly didn't know, and this tortured him to no end. He reached into his sport coat pocket and withdrew a silver drinking flask. He unscrewed the cap and took a long, pensive gulp. Then he said, "I don't know…Tilson…something happened to him out there. It's like only part of him came back. Like he's a shadow, just someone playing the role of POTUS. There is *nothing* behind the face, nothing really inside the eyes. It's like he doesn't *feel*. He doesn't take *interest* in his life. Not the same way that he used to.

"I tell him that we've got to save face. We've got to let the rest of the world know that we won't stand for terrorism on our shores, especially in the White House. We've got to deliver *justice*, to *somebody*. To tell you the truth, in a way, I don't give a shit who's guilty, as long as somebody pays. We are a fucking laughingstock now. Puts my job in Satan's kitchen.

"Tilson no longer cares who killed his wife. He doesn't give a damn who kidnapped him. All he can think about is this damned Ogarkov summit. Keeps muttering things about *global peace* or some such nonsense. Give me a frigging break. Global peace. We won't have global peace until we've blown some big holes in the ground. Country-sized holes."

Trance peered closely at Miller. "It's not you, is it, Jake? You're not behind this? Are you?"

Miller stared at Trance for a long moment. His face remained motionless, then it seemed to swell in size. Miller's whole face grew pink, as if a week's worth of his Pepto Bismol had bubbled up to its surface. "You, of all people, Trance...you know what I've sacrificed for this country. Just because…" The fight suddenly seemed to escape from Miller, his face deflating like a balloon that had been cut at the stem. His cheeks withered, until they looked like shrunken prunes in the shadowed light. He cradled his face with his hands, drooping, as if his head were growing heavier by the minute.

Trance stared at Miller, trying to get inside his mind. It had been Miller who had ordered Trance's wife to meet with the supposed informant at the Washington Mall, just days before she was due to leave the CIA, just months before she was due to deliver their first child.

For years, Trance had blamed Miller, blamed him for never revealing who had ordered him to send his wife, or revealing who it was that she had been sent there to meet. He had blamed Miller for never finding out, never telling him who had committed the murder and why.

Trance handed Miller the note he had found on the warehouse office floor.

My people were never here, Trance. Just me. You are wrong again.

I killed your wife. I killed Kiki Tilson.

We took the president. That was just foreplay. Can you guess what we'll do next?

Miller stared at the note. The color started to drain out of his face. Soon it began to look like the head of a marble statue, as lifeless and white as stone. His lips folded into a colorless, thin solid line. When he looked at Trance there was sadness in his eyes, a weary melancholy that Trance could feel in his bones. The sadness felt like a tuning fork, vibrating inside him with a low, sad hum.

"I am so sorry about Janice."

Trance shook his head. "Not a time for guilt, Jacob. Somehow, these killings are related. It's time to think. Think back to when you sent my wife to the meeting. Who's idea was it and who was she there to meet?"

Miller stared at Trance. There was an odd glint to his hardening eyes. Then they softened. "I thought you knew? Your uncle ordered the meeting, Jack."

Trance closed his eyes. His uncle, again. He'd heard the rumors, but he'd never believed it. Never wanted to. It was easier to blame Miller. "What else?"

"There was this woman. I never met her; I just talked to her on the phone."

"What did she offer?"

"She claimed to have evidence."

"Of what?"

"She claimed to have evidence that Hussein al-Talid was planning major terrorist attacks against us."

There he was again, Talid. Why did this man keep popping into his life like a cold sore? And the woman. Had this woman killed both his wife *and* Kiki Tilson? Could that be possible?

"You never met her?"

"No. I just spoke with her, or someone who claimed to be her."

"Do you have recordings? Recordings of your conversations?"

Miller shook his head. "Sorry. They were destroyed…your uncle."

Now, it was time for Trance to share.

"Talid has been trying to kill me."

Miller laughed. "No shit, Trance. I've had men watching your back for years."

Trance frowned. This was news. "You have?"

"You didn't know this?"

Trance shook his head. "When I paid that visit to Talid, earlier this year…" Trance paused.

Miller finally said, "Yes?"

"I gave him something."

Miller waited.

"I planted nanobots in his blood and a controller in his nasal cavity."

Miller's mouth widened into a grin. "That *I* didn't know."

"It's an advanced nanotechnology, developed in secrecy, somewhere in Cambridge, Massachusetts, and perfected by a homeless guy I hired off the street to work for me." Trance shrugged and smiled sheepishly. "Swartz gave me the stuff. He'd commissioned it from a Swiss holding company I didn't even know I owned."

Miller said nothing. He was aware of the labyrinth of companies that Trance's family had controlled for centuries, and of the far-reaching technological infrastructure they had built, as if they believed technology would rule the planet. Trance had access to influence and technologies that the CIA would kill to obtain. Yet even Trance was not aware of the full extent of his capacities or resources.

Trance continued. "The microphone signal is weak. It comes and goes. He jams his palaces, so we get little, if anything, from there. I've been listening to him for months now. In public, he won't talk of Centurion, as if he knows we are listening. Mostly he just drinks and screws, watches porn and Brittany Spears videos—all the things he rails about in public."

"He knows," said Miller. "He'll only talk about Centurion where he knows he's secure."

"The microphone is undetectable. The only way he might find it would be with an MRI. His nose might shred before he knew what was happening, though. The stuff is organic, virtually alive and feeding off ATP. It's so new, though, that we haven't tested how it reacts to things like highly magnetic fields."

"You think Talid is involved with this?"

"To his eyeballs. But he is smart beyond reason. So are the people he works with. They don't screw up. They leave nothing behind, nothing but a letter mocking me. Mocking us. Makes me wonder how safe we really are in this world. Makes me wonder what else we are missing."

"Such as?"

"Such as Centurion."

Trance looked to Miller and then to Jesse Tompkin. "Is this the Jock Tilson you knew?"

Both men shook their heads. Something had definitely changed about the president.

"This would make sense out of Kiki's death, wouldn't it? We might only *suspect* the man. But Kiki...she would be sure."

The three men sat in silence, while the music blared. The woman danced around the stage, stopping to make simulated love to a fire pole before squatting at the edge of the stage to accept tributes in her G string. The three men never looked her way, so she stepped off the stage and strutted to their table. She stood beside Trance and began to shimmy her chest. Trance shook his head and looked at his companions. They were laughing. Trance pulled a card out of his wallet and scribbled his initials on the back. He slipped the card into the G string on the dancer's hip. He called her to his lips. When she leaned over he said, "If you want an education, my foundation will pay for it. No strings attached."

The dancer looked at Trance and laughed. "Men have said a lot of things to get into my pants, mister. But this takes the cake."

"I'm serious."

The dancer stood upright and said, "You're serious?"

"I am."

"With no strings attached? What about my kid?"

"I ask only that you work hard and make something of yourself. Kids are no problem. They get private school and tutors. We pay for it all."

The dancer stopped dancing. She looked at Trance. He nodded. The dancer slowly walked back to the stage. They could see her thinking, with a slight hesitation in her step, almost a waver, like a candle in the wind. When she reached the stage the dancer kept walking, right through the black curtain.

Miller said, "You do that often, Trance?"

"First time in a gentlemen's club. But, yeah, all the time."

"Does it ever work?"

"More often than you'd imagine. Sometimes all people need is a chance, and belief in themselves. God blessed me with money, so I try to make it work." Trance leaned forward and said, "Where were we? Oh, yeah, Kiki's death."

"You don't really think the president is an imposter, do you, Trance?" said Miller.

"I'm going to try to find out."

"That's like putting a cobra down your pants, Jack. Tilson could bite your privates at any second, and all you'll be able to do is grab your crotch and pray for your life and your lost manhood."

"Beautiful image, Jake. I'll remember that."

Miller stuck out his hand to shake. "Good luck, Jack. Don't come to me unless you really need help. Tilson could make us all vanish in a moment. What good could we be to anyone if we're dead?"

Trance grasped Miller's hand. "I don't blame you anymore, Jake. Not for my wife. Truce?"

Miller's eyes widened. He let out an audible breath, as if he'd been holding it for years. "Truce?" he asked, not quite believing what he'd heard.

"This is beyond anything we could have imagined. Let's just hope our country doesn't rot and die from within."

"Maybe it's already started."

CHAPTER **70**

____________PP____________

One by one, people sauntered into the Situation Room in the basement of the West Wing of the White House. They had all been summoned to this spot, created for crisis management, a place built to be used by the president and his advisors when America was under attack. This was not a place for the routine preparation of a presidential summit. No, this was serious, and the significance was not lost on the men and women in the room.

Nearly every member of the president's cabinet was in attendance. The Joint Chiefs were there, as was the Chief Justice of the Supreme Court. Several members of Congress had also been asked to join, representing both parties. Garret Sloan, the president's secretary of state had not been invited. He was too persuasive, and the president didn't want someone at this meeting who was more persuasive than he was. He would have his way.

Some guests sat in tight closed circles, arguing politely. Others seemed to be staring at their own thoughts, eyes forward and unfocused. The president sat at the head of the large conference table, saying nothing.

Computer monitors were snuggled inside the table's top, looking like hard clear Jell-O. Behind the president, a wall of panel screens stretched to the ceiling. They also ringed the room like in a football stadium. Men and women fanned out beyond the president, split evenly on both sides. The room seemed to hush, as Washington's final power brokers seeped quietly into the surprisingly small room.

Guests began to stand around the cramped room's edges, until there was a solid row of them packed shoulder to shoulder, the powerful and less powerful arranged in no particular order. They did little talking now, looking more and more like lambs waiting for slaughter. This had to be serious, perhaps even war.

When all fifty guests had squeezed in, the president motioned for the doors to be closed. There was a loud *click* as the doors sealed into place, making the room feel like the inside of a vault.

The president smiled to himself. Even as a child, he had imagined running a meeting like this, with every guest wondering why they'd been called, and what he'd say.

"Thank you for coming," he said. The president's voice was strong and forceful. There was no hesitation in his words, no weakness. He was in control, every line memorized and rehearsed.

"Before we begin today's meeting, I want you to know this—if word leaks out about what is said here today, I will personally see that you lose your job and your career. I will see that you are prosecuted to the fullest extent of the law, with the charge of treason. If you cannot abide by this request, then you should leave this room, now. I consider this meeting to be crucial to our national security, and I will treat it that way." The president paused. No one moved. He turned his head toward the members of Congress. "That goes especially for you. There will be nothing but silence. No partisan politics, no comments, nothing. If you leak anything whatsoever, I will have your asses on a platter. Are we clear?"

The congressmen nend women nodded like scolded school children.

"Okay, then. You have been asked here to debate a proposal I am about to make." The president paused, and then looked from face to face. "You are encouraged to disagree with me. You can also support me. At the end of today, I am going to ask for an up or down on my proposal. If I have two thirds yea, I will press on. If I don't, I will drop my proposal. Any questions?"

There were none.

The president unscrewed the top of a plastic liter bottle of water. He took a sip and resumed talking.

"As you all know, in three weeks I am hosting a summit with the Russian president, Ogarkov."

A soft murmur spread throughout the room.

"Yes, I know that some of you disagree with my philosophy. That's why you are here.

"Ogarkov and I have had informal communications, setting the agenda for our summit. We want to make the world a safer place."

The president paused again. "Is there anyone in this room who does not want to make the world a safer place? Raise your hands. Anyone?"

No one took the bait. "Good, then. At least we agree on something."

Another murmur spread throughout the group.

"I am going to propose that the U.S. and Russia effectively eliminate our nuclear arsenals."

This time the room erupted into a rumble of voices, with everyone speaking and arguing at once.

The speaker of the house rose pompously from his seat. "Why, that is political suicide!"

The president smiled. "Thank you for your typically brilliant insight, Mr. Speaker."

The speaker gave a loud *harrumph* and sat back down.

The president's turtle-like national security adviser rose slowly from the table. "Perhaps we should discuss this in private, Mr. President?"

The president waved him off. "I called this meeting for a reason. I want your raw, unrestrained reaction to this proposal."

"Well, I think it stinks," said Pincenogle. His head seemed to wobble inside the folds of his neck, as if it were a slowly spinning top surrounded by giant flaps of skin.

"Why does it stink?"

The security advisor began to blink. "Well, because it just does."

"Does what?"

"It is a naïve proposal that will signal to the world that we've gone weak."

"Weak in what way?"

"Well, we need to be the biggest bad-assed bully on the block. No one can mess with us, or we'll blow them into the Stone Age." Pincenogle seemed to retract his head back into his shell of shoulders, then sat down with a "Humph."

"How can we ask other nations to disarm if we don't disarm ourselves?"

The security advisor lumbered back up, sputtering, "You don't *ask* them to disarm. You *make* them. Surely you are not so naïve as to think that the world is a civil place? Where everybody *believes* everybody else? Where everybody treats each other with respect and kindness?

"What good is a policeman without a weapon? You do understand that we are the world's policeman, don't you? Surely you understand this? Tell me you do."

"I appointed you, didn't I?"

"The world doesn't listen to polite requests, Mr. President. If it did, the United Nations would be effective, not just a way for corrupt politicians to make millions of dollars off the backs of their people."

"That's cynical. You see no higher purpose, no role for the U.N.?"

"Well, yeah. It provides a kind of open forum."

"Open is good."

"Open sucks when it means ganging up on America. All they do is complain about our nation. They work together and try to squeeze us for all they can."

"Point taken." The president looked around the room. "Any other dissenters?"

A woman in the back raised her hand. The president looked at her and pointed with one outstretched finger.

"Yes, Ms. Pomeroy. What does the Hoover Institution have to say on the subject?"

"While I think this is a noble undertaking, geopolitically, it has proven to be more effective to deal from a position of strength rather than from weakness. While I laud your noble objective, perhaps we should approach the goal in another way. No nuclear nation will give up that power, sacrifice what it perceives as security, unless there is a powerful incentive."

"Here's the incentive," said the president. "More and more nations are going nuclear. With each new member, the chance of major conflict increases exponentially, logarithmically. If we all can't agree on nuclear disarmament, and then enforce it, we may all perish." The president paused. He smiled and said, "What would Jesus do?"

The room grew silent, as if it were in stunned, suspended animation. Not a single person uttered a word. What the hell did Jesus have to do with national policy?

The secretary of defense finally said, "Let's not forget, Mr. President. Jesus was crucified."

At that moment, nearly every person in the room began shouting, mostly defending or attacking faith and religion. The president crossed his arms and listened, with a broad smile spreading across his face. Now he had a debate.

Six hours later, the president called for a vote, by hand.

"It is time to cast your lot," he said. "I am asking that each of you vote to allow me to propose mutual disarmament with Russia, provided we can get the rest of the nuclear world to join in. This is an open vote."

The people in the room let out a collective groan. The president touched the screen behind him. A spreadsheet emerged with each person's name highlighted in bright blue. Beside each name were two columns, with the headings *yes* and *no*. The president went from face to face, staring at each person until their vote was cast. It took nearly an hour, but at the end of that time, the president pointed to the spreadsheet's tally.

"Looks like we vote for peace."

"Or our own destruction," murmured someone at the back of the room.

CHAPTER **71**
____________PP____________

It was 10 P.M. The president was still in the Oval Office, reviewing brief after brief on the state of nuclear technology and its proliferation. All he could do was read the titles. His eyes skipped over the words like pebbles bouncing on ice. He would stare at the letters, but they just wouldn't sink in.

She was coming. He could feel her already. He'd been notified at 9:30 that she had arrived at the West Gate for processing. It took his full concentration to keep from rocking in his chair or pacing about the office.

The president could remember the interviews to the smallest detail. The first was in this office; but something was different about the desk. Had it been lighter, less dense? The feel against his leg, it felt odd. He remembered Sammantha sitting across from him, her legs spreading seductively as she asked him questions about his presidency. He could remember those legs. Soft, golden thighs with the promise of forbidden sweetness.

Earlier this week, he had called for a copy of the video. He'd watched it a dozen times. He knew he had been there. Somehow, it was as if he were watching someone else, some other president who looked just like him. It was the accident, he knew. The concussion he'd suffered had been severe, more than first thought. His PCS jumped out in the strangest ways, like today, with his memory of Sammantha Starodubov. Somewhere, stirring inside his brain, like windows behind a translucent curtain, he remembered things he was sure he couldn't have done. Sultry, steamy things. Post concussion syndrome was a bad-assed thing on the brain, he thought. It should be against the law.

"Ms. Starodubov is here, Mr. President."

"Send her in."

As Sammantha Starodubov walked into the Oval Office, the president felt as if he'd thrust a wet finger into an electrical socket. His body began to prickle with gooseflesh. He wondered if his hair was standing on end. He could feel another part of him beginning to tingle, too, as vague visions of love making leaped across his mind like naked dancers. The president steadied himself against his desk. When Sammantha was halfway toward him, he began to walk toward her, while motioning for her to sit beside him at a round conference table.

"So good to see you again, Ms. Starodubov," he croaked.

The president stretched out his hand. Sammantha shook it firmly.

"Mr. President."

The president held Sammantha's hand and stared into her eyes, as if studying a road map. After a moment he shook his head. He tried to shake away the nagging wisps of memory that swirled around the edge of his consciousness.

"As you know, I am hosting President Ogarkov at Camp David in two weeks."

"Mr. Ogarkov is looking forward to the meeting."

"I was hoping you could tell me something about the mood in Russia, something my other advisors might have missed. I was also hoping that you could help me better understand Ogarkov himself."

"Really?" Sammantha settled herself into a chair and waited, watching the president's face intently.

"Well…yes. I…You know Ogarkov personally."

"I was never his lover, if that is what you're asking."

The president's eyes grew wide, his mouth opened and he looked like he'd been goosed, which, of course, he had. Had he been so obvious? "Ah…That's not what I meant—"

"Yes, it is. But that is all right. I get that a lot. Not about him, but about others."

"I didn't mean to—"

"As I said, it's okay. Just so you know, I am a single woman who has been linked, from time to time, to powerful men. Most of this is rumor, innuendo and plain wishful thinking. My heart has been held by very few men. How else could I have found time to become a neurosurgeon at a young age? And Ogarkov? He is still very married to his late wife. I would never sleep with a married man. You haven't married since we last met, have you?"

The president fiddled with his fingers and struggled to look Sammantha in the eye. He hadn't looked at another woman since his wife's death; he was sure of it. Was it that apparent, the aching loneliness and the brooding desperation that hung around his brain like a dark curse?

"There is something you *should* know about Ogarkov. If he says something, he means it. He isn't like other politicians…He is much like you, in fact. He has a clear vision of what is right and what is wrong. He has the courage to stand by his convictions."

Sammantha shifted in her seat and smiled. "About the Russian people? The video we created has been enormously well received. It has been run thousands of times on our state-owned television stations. Video copies have been given out at the bread lines. Do not think, though, that anything you do with Russia will be viewed as genuine. Our people have learned not to trust, ourselves or other nations. It will take a pure heart, an iron will and years of persistence to make our people believe in your sincerity."

"Do you? Do you believe in my sincerity?" The president held his breath. Why was he acting this way? He hardly knew this woman.

"Of course I believe you," said Sammantha. "I love you."

The president felt his chest tighten, as if someone had wrapped a pair of long powerful arms around him from behind and was pulling tighter and tighter, almost to the point of suffocation. "I'm sorry?" he said.

"I said, *I love you.* In those hours we spent together…there was something that happened between us. Didn't you feel it? Don't you feel it now?"

The president walked to the far end of the room, moving slowly as if walking in darkness. His head felt dizzy. He was sure he was having one of his PCS attacks. Sweat broke out across his forehead and his hands began to shake. He pulled aside one of the drapes and looked out the window into the night. The Rose Garden was lit with soft-colored lights, and the roses seemed to glow like fairies. Was this real?

Sammantha said, "You do love me, don't you? Please say you do."

The president felt his throat constrict, and when he said the words they sounded like a halting, raspy echo. "I do."

"Oh, Jock."

Sammantha stood behind the president and touched his back lightly. She drew beside him, with her arm resting gently around his waist, looking out at the garden. "It's beautiful here."

The president nodded. "It is." *But lonely, oh so lonely.*

Slowly the president turned. He opened his arms and allowed Sammantha to fold inside them. Then he held her, letting the warmth of her breath and the smoothness of her skin comfort him like a baby's lullaby.

CHAPTER **72**
PP

"I have control of him now," said Sammantha. She stared down the length of the rough, wooden farmers table and waited for questions from the four men seated before her. Nikolai Ogarkov, the powerful Russian president, sat to one side of her. As she spoke, his dark unibrow dipped up and down like a yo-yo, reflecting, perhaps, some inner debate. He remained silent. Beside Ogarkov, Vasily Nabokov, head of the Russian armed forces, narrowed his eyes, nervously chewing on repeated mouthfuls of bacon. Nabokov was a vocal hawk. He too, said nothing. Boris Trotski, head of the Russian Secret Service, inhaled deeply, then exhaled with a wheezy sputtering sound. *Too much smoking*, thought Sammantha, like far too many Russian men, their clocks ticking down by the puff.

Ivan Petrovski, Russia's Prime Minister, was a mathematician by training. Brilliant and ruthless, he had made his fortune building and trading high tech weaponry. He was in his early 70s. He was still built like a tight coil of wire, thin and angular, with gold reading glasses always resting on the end of his nose. Petrovski had a long life ahead of him, one he planned to live with opulence, power and the Russian presidency—even if he had to kill his rival to attain it.

Disarming Russia's nukes would attack Petrovski's personal wealth and power, let alone weaken his nation. Unless, of course, disarmament brought about the removal of Ogarkov. A wave of public disenchantment could clear the path to Russia's highest office. He was the first to speak.

"You have control of whom, Miss Starodubov?"

"President Tilson."

Petrovski looked to Ogarkov with a questioning stare. Ogarkov subtly smiled, but again said nothing.

"I find that difficult to believe, Miss Starodubov. It is one thing to sleep with a man. It is a far different thing to control him. While I am well aware of your sexual prowess, and your willingness to use it, I don't have a Ruble's worth of faith in your political acumen." *And I don't trust you. You are cut from unpredictable cloth.*

"You are a naïve pig, Petrovski," said Sammantha. She stood up from her chair and began to walk toward the prime minister, with the full intention of breaking his scrawny little neck.

Ogarkov intervened. "Miss Starodubov has more political persuasiveness than you might think, Ivan."

Sammantha stopped beside Petrovski and patted him on the cheek. "I can do far more than screw. You want to try me?"

"I gave her two billion dollars," said Ogarkov.

Petrovski turned toward his president, his eyes wide and uncomprehending. He'd been chosen as prime minister by this man. He had his leader's deepest confidence, or so he had thought. How could Ogarkov betray him like this? Two billion dollars?

Ogarkov smiled. "Unlike you, my friend, I pay attention to what is happening here at home. I have seen Miss Starodubov work her magic with our troubled soldiers. She has developed breakthrough techniques that have turned battle scarred vegetables back into normal, productive men. She has gone into our asylums and performed miracles, even with the so-called 'incurable.' I've seen patients lost to the world for twenty years walk back into life as if they had been on nothing but an extended vacation. Insanity can vanish under her brush. Why not the fears of one man?

"When she came to me and said that she could influence the American president, I believed her. When she told me it would take a billion dollars, she got it. When she needed a billion more, she got that, too. I thought it a small price to pay for disarming the world of nuclear weapons, an investment we would recover in a matter of months."

Petrovski looked like he was developing sun stroke. His face seemed to swell with a milky red, making it look like a rotting cranberry. Veins started popping out along his neck, like throbbing purple ropes. "You have always been an idealistic baboon, Ogarkov. But now…now it may be time we discussed your retirement. In fact, I propose it now, to all here." Petrovski put a hand on his side-arm and continued, "Are you proposing that we tear down our nuclear arsenal and render our nation defenseless? The mere hint of this will cause great unrest with our people. It may even incite them to revolution. You are putting your faith in this whore? I thought you were a man beyond such weakness."

Ogarkov appeared unconcerned, even amused. "In two weeks, I will be meeting with the American president. You will see the results of my investment at that time."

"I think not," said Petrovski. He drew his pistol.

Ogarkov laughed. "Ivan, must you be so obvious? I know that you covet my job. I know that you have been fomenting unrest wherever you can. But, to try this in my home?"

Ogarkov reached into his shirt pocket and pulled out a pack of Marlboro cigarettes. He tapped the top of the pack against the rough table, withdrew one and put it in his mouth. He struck a wooden match against his shoe and took two deep drags on the filter before looking back to Petrovski.

"Put that gun away before I shove it up your ass."

The two men began to walk toward each other, until they stood chest to chest. Ogarkov, the tree trunk, and Petrovski, the sunflower. Ogarkov took another pull on his cigarette and exhaled it into Petrovski's face. Petrovski put the gun to Ogarkov's forehead, his hands trembling like a Parkinson's patient.

"Do that again and I'll put your brains against the wall," muttered Petrovski.

"Do that and my men do the same with you."

Sammantha wedged herself between the two leaders, pushing them apart like a boxing referee.

"I will settle this." Sammantha flipped open her phone and said, "Bring him here." Sammantha looked to Ogarkov. "A car will be approaching your lower gate shortly. You will let it through."

"What is this?" said Ogarkov.

"Trust me."

Ogarkov paused for a long moment before relaying Sammantha's instructions. He looked into her eyes, weighed their sincerity then nodded. They all waited, without saying another word.

After twenty minutes there was a knock upon the outside door. Ogarkov opened it.

"Hello, Mr. President." Jock Tilson was standing in the doorway, with his right hand extended.

Ogarkov looked to Sammantha. Sammantha looked to Ogarkov, then to the others. She looked like she had just tied her first shoe. There was a look of triumph, a childish satisfaction on her face that left no doubt as to who this man was.

"President Tilson?" asked Ogarkov.

"I thought you were expecting me," said Tilson.

Ogarkov shook his head. "I thought we were meeting in your country? Two weeks from now."

"Then why would you kidnap me?"

Ogarkov looked to Sammantha. "The kidnapping attempt in America…You didn't?"

Sammantha nodded. "This is President Tilson. The man in the White House is someone else, someone I've programmed to do anything I want."

Ogarkov sat down at the table and put his face into his hands. "Sammantha, what have you done?"

"I have given you the opportunity of a lifetime."

"You have brought him here? To Russia? To my retreat?"

"I smuggled him out of America from a home with a private dock in Camden, Maine. Sailed him by sloop to a motor yacht waiting twelve miles offshore. Entered him into the Motherland by boat through St. Petersburg, and then brought him here in a produce truck."

"You realize what this could do? The danger you have put us in?"

"You said that you wanted the chance to change history. You now have President Tilson's undivided attention. What did you think you would get for two billion dollars? Cookies?"

"You said that you could convince Tilson of the sincerity of my intentions."

"And I have. Wouldn't you agree?"

Ogarkov felt his stomach begin to lurch. He rushed out of the room. They could hear him retch in the nearby bathroom, three times. When Ogarkov returned, he looked like he had gargled with onion juice. His skin was a pale gray. His hair was askew. There was a look of devastation across his face and in his eyes, a hollow desperation that made Sammantha wonder if he'd last the night. When Ogarkov began to speak, it was as if his voice had been carved away, its humanism stripped, leaving just a machine that spoke in a dull, robotic monotone.

"I'm sorry. I can't send you back, Mr. President, and risk having Russia blamed for this act—"

"You did pay her," said Tilson. "If what she said was true."

"Not to harm you. Not to kidnap you. All I wanted was peace!" Ogarkov lowered his voice. "I was not the only one who paid her, you know. Oh, far from that."

Tilson looked to Sammantha. She nodded.

"That is true. There were others who funded my cause. Each with his own motives."

Tilson tried to laugh, but the sound that filled his throat sounded more like a growl. He had a mind to scream outrage, to threaten the full might of the United States against them all. But that was pointless. He was at their mercy, like some squishy amphibian they held pinned under their boot.

Tilson said, "You promised these men something you could never deliver, Miss Starodubov. The American Congress must vote on such extreme actions by the president. They won't be bamboozled by some pretender."

"You forget, Mr. Tilson. You were voted into office with the biggest mandate since Roosevelt. You campaigned for change. That's what the American people want and it's what they're going to get. Who knows? Maybe you will even bring your country some good."

"There can be no good from this, not with a fraud in the White House—"

"The question now is," interrupted Ogarkov. "What do we do with *you*?"

"That's simple. Send me home."

Ogarkov slowly shook his head. "I never wanted this. I think it is abhorrent. But I cannot undo it."

"They will find out, you know. They will come for me."

"Who's going to save you? Jack Trance?" said Sammantha. "You think Trance will come to Russia? That he even knows you're here? Do you think he can break into the Kremlin and save your sorry ass? He couldn't protect his own wife."

"The Kremlin?" said Ogarkov. His face grew pale, and his bottom lip began to twitch. He looked like a child who'd been swimming in freezing water for far too long, his skin turning a whitish blue, his eyes looking exhausted from the effort.

"Of course," said Sammantha. "Do you know someplace safer? There are hundreds of places within the Kremlin in which to hide a man. Not good enough for you, Ogarkov?"

"But, if someone finds out?"

"Who would believe them?"

The color began to flow back into Ogarkov's bleached white face. It was true. No one would, or could look for Tilson there.

Sammantha placed a comforting hand on her president's shoulder. "You should talk with him, maybe come up with suggestions I can pass along to the new American president."

"There will be no torture," said Ogarkov sternly. "There will be no mistreatment at all."

"Of course," said Sammantha. "No mistreatment at all." *But only while you stay in power, Ogarkov. If Petrovski takes over, mistreatment will be the least of our problems.*

When it was time for them to leave, Sammantha, Petrovski, Nabokov and Tilson gathered at the front door to Ogarkov's dacha. Sammantha gave Ogarkov a peck on the cheek and said, "Don't worry. This will work out."

Two Mercedes limousines were waiting outside Ogarkov's dacha. Sammantha motioned for Tilson to get inside the second car. She joined the other Russians in first. She took the seat beside Trotski, across from Petrovski and Nabokov, hiking up her skirt so she could cross her legs. "If you ever call me a whore again, Petrovski, I will cut off your dick. Do you want me to demonstrate?" Sammantha spoke the words in English, as if drawing a cultural battle line in the sand.

Petrovski smiled warily, and replied in Russian, "You surprised me."

Sammantha answered in English. "You underestimate me because I am a woman."

"No. Not because you are a woman. Because you are a beautiful woman."

"You treat me like a whore. I am not a whore."

"I apologize. I did not know of your achievements."

"This is just the beginning." Sammantha rolled her tongue across her top lip, as if savoring the sweetness of powdered sugar. "I have more planned. Far more."

"And you need my help, I suppose?"

"I do."

"What can you offer me in return?"

"For starters, you can keep your penis."

Petrovski laughed loudly. "You will never catch me unaware again, Miss Starodubov. You'll have to do better than an old man's penis to get my cooperation."

"What if I deliver Ogarkov?"

Petrovski's eyes darted to Nabokov, to Trotski and then back to Sammantha. She was offering him the presidency.

"And in return?"

"I want a weapon. A nuclear weapon."

Petrovski and Nabokov looked at each other again, this time as if weighing the proposal between them.

Sammantha continued, "Not any nuke. A suitcase nuke."

"What will you do with this?" Petrovski leaned forward, looking at Sammantha like a Cub Scout listening for the end to a ghost story, eyes wide, his breathing suspended, waiting…just waiting.

"I'm going to use it, of course."

"Don't screw with me. What for?"

"I plan to detonate it during the American president's State of the Union Address."

Petrovski blinked. He could feel his heart gain speed in his chest, until it was thumping hard, almost uncontrollably. For a moment he thought he was going to faint. He closed his eyes and calmed himself. Then he whispered, "You are going to kill the entire U.S. Congress?"

"Along with Ogarkov."

Petrovski smiled hesitantly. Then his mouth spread into a crescent nearly as wide as his face. This was brilliant. He looked to Nabokov, who signaled with a subtle nod of the head. Trotski did the same. "I admire your ambition, Miss Starodubov. Who is to know of this? That we supplied the weapon?"

"Just the three of you."

"It seems that I get the best of this bargain, Miss Starodubov. What is that you get?"

"Revenge. Simple revenge…and a final chance at peace."

CHAPTER 73
PP
____

Jack Trance, Jesse Tompkin, Stick Granger and Jacob Miller rode in silence as they approached Camp David by air. Each of them was searching for something to explain the president's odd behavior, anything, some rational explanation for how he'd tilted so far off kilter.

Trance had seen his friendship with the president wither, like a flower that had bloomed full and was now facing a slow, but inevitable death. Jesse Tompkin was working twenty-hour days to find the president's kidnappers. But every time he needed access to sensitive information, or to wiretap a foreign agency or apprehend suspected conspirators, he was blocked by the president. Miller, too, had fought the same losing battles. He had been thwarted in every attempt to share intelligence among the various domestic agencies. He was being forced to waste precious resources duplicating efforts he was sure other agencies had already made. They were all running in circles.

It was not unusual for a president to become distracted. They had all seen this before. The job came with enormous responsibilities, extraordinary pressures and wide-ranging requirements. Even the strongest man could whither under the white-hot glare of the U.S. Presidency. This was when others had to step into the breach, to stabilize a listing ship. But the president had to let them help him. He had to stop fighting them.

Stick lowered Trance's Bell Jet Ranger onto the designated helipad. The four men stepped out beneath the whirling blades and walked to a waiting Humvee, which took them to the camp's main lodge.

The president was sitting alone on a couch in front of a large, crackling fire. Along the wall, a flat panel screen was showing the preview to Monday Night Football, a much publicized game between the Colts and the Patriots. The sound was turned up and the cabin sounded like a stadium, with noise blaring from a circle of wall mounted speakers. The president held a bowl of popcorn in one hand and a TV remote in the other. He motioned with the remote for the other men to join him.

"C'mon in, men. I was just sitting down for the game. Can I fix you something to drink? What'll it be, the usual?"

In training, Brandon Copley had rehearsed this scene a dozen times. He watched it play out as expected. Each man nodded and murmured, "Sure." Copley reached into the refrigerator and pulled out a pair of Sam Adams beers for Granger and Tompkin. He handed Miller a glass filled with ice alone, which Miller filled with Pepto Bismol from a flask he pulled out of his coat. He threw some ice into a glass and poured Trance a shot of scotch, not the Macallan 1949 that Tilson kept hidden in the back cabinets of the bar. Instead, he poured from Trance's gift of Johnnie Walker Blue.

Trance closed his eyes when he saw the president forego their traditional single malt ritual. He felt the hair on his neck begin to rise and then flatten, especially when the president poured himself a club soda and spiced it with a wedge of lime. This was not normal, not good.

"Not going to join us, sir?" said Tompkin, as the president handed him his beer.

"Nah. Since the accident I haven't felt much like drinking."

The president lowered the sound on the game and motioned toward a spread of chips and dips. "You fellas want anything to eat?"

"You have any bagels?" said Trance.

"Sorry. Don't like them," said the president.

Trance frowned, knowing how Tilson loved his bagels. He didn't comment, not about that. They had more important issues to discuss. Since he was the only one not on the government payroll, Trance spoke first.

"Sir, we are very concerned about how the assassination and the kidnapping investigations are being handled. Very concerned."

The president peered closely at Trance. He seemed to weigh his words carefully, but his eyes flicked several times to the pre-game show, a distraction not lost on Trance. The president's attention was on a frigging football game, not the nation's security, his own safety or on the justice they must mete out to preserve respect. Finally, the president said, "Take that up with Doheny."

Trance said, "We need you to expand our authority."

"How so?"

"There are half a dozen agencies working independently on these investigations. No one has been authorized to share data on either event. No one has been given the teeth to get the job done. We have no wiretap authority, no subpoena authority, no search and seizure authority and no arrest authority. You are asking us to fight a war in bare feet with our hands tied behind our backs."

"I think that's a little over-the-top, Trance. Don't you?"

"Over-the-top? If I didn't know better, I'd think you were stonewalling us. I think, maybe, you don't want us to find who did this."

The president frowned, but nodded slowly. "Well, in a way, I don't."

"What?"

"You heard me. Right now I am focused on global nuclear disarmament. I think I've got a real good chance at making it work."

"That's another thing, Jock—"

"*Mr.* President."

Trance looked at his president as if he didn't know him. Something had happened to this man; he didn't know what. Had this all happened during the kidnapping? Had there been enough time for them to do something to his mind? Did they have some new weapon, some advanced controlling device, some nanotechnology that they hadn't seen before, something eerily similar to what he had inserted into Talid's head? Did they have something that could make the president an unwilling accomplice to whatever they planned?

"Yes, Mr. President. Sorry."

The president fluffed his hand. "Carry on."

"You can't meet with Ogarkov without more groundwork. A lot more. Nuclear policy changes will have dramatic effects on world security, even drastic effects."

"That's what I'm hoping for."

"We have treaties. Formal ones and unwritten ones. We have unwritten *promises*, too, promises that must be kept."

"I will keep those promises."

"You have to accept counsel, Mr. President. Put together a team of highly qualified experts—"

"I held a meeting with fifty members of this administration. They voted with me, not against me."

"We weren't there. Neither was Sloan."

"Like you all matter? I have other advisors, good ones."

Trance felt like the president had reached inside his gut, pulled out his insides, thrown them to the floor and was gleefully stomping on them. He felt a deep and palpable ache, a press against his skull, like a loud bell ringing out a warning, a warning he could feel all the way from his jaw to his toes. "Advisors? I wouldn't call that Starodubov woman an advisor—"

"You have something against her?"

"At least let us vet her, sir. She is a Russian national. She pops up out of nowhere and you won't let us do a background check? What are you, suicidal? You are making a mockery out of the presidency—"

"She was vetted before she conducted the Russian documentary."

"That was just a surface check. It wasn't made with the expectation of her sharing your bed—"

"Enough!" shouted the president. "You will not speak to me that way. I have reasons for what I do. *My* reasons. I expect you to follow orders."

"Technically, sir, I am not officially in the military, or under your direction. You can't give me orders."

"You are in the Reserves, yes or no?"

"Officially? No, sir. I have no signed contract."

"I expect you to behave as if you do."

Trance stared into the president's eyes and slowly shook his head. "I love this country, Mr. President. I have offered her my life, left pieces of my flesh on four continents, on far too many occasions. I will do so again. But I am not your slave."

"You will stand down on this matter." The president glared at Trance, and then at Tompkin and Miller. "All of you. You, too, Granger."

Trance said, "We have all sworn an oath to defend this country."

"So have I. Unless the Constitution has been changed, I believe I am in charge? Do you really think you can challenge me? Stop me?"

"If you do the wrong thing," said Trance. "We might have to."

"Like what? What are you afraid of?"

"Treason."

"Treason? You think I'm committing treason? I am planning for peace!"

"I don't know what you are doing, Mr. President. Not anymore. You are not listening to reason. You are ignoring policy that is *embedded* in our history. You are planning to meet with a man that could level this country on a whim, at least get us into another world war."

"True peace takes extraordinary measures, bold measures, ones never tried before."

"I hope you are right," said Trance. "Because, if you are not, so help me God, I will do everything I can to stop you."

"So will I," said Tompkin.

"Me, too," said Miller.

Stick Granger remained speechless, too stunned to talk.

The president smiled. It was the eerie, feral smile of a man who had gone wild, one who had lost his human core, the smile of a man that had been programmed to destroy. The president pursed his lips, and then slowly said, "I know how much you men have sacrificed for our country. So, I will not charge you now, because I know that your motives are pure. I'm going to pretend you didn't say those words. But, if you ever challenge me again, if you pursue actions to impede my efforts for peace, I will see that all four of you spend the rest of your days in Leavenworth. You got that?"

Trance and the others nodded.

"Get out of here. I have work to do."

The president turned his attention to the game and restored the sound. He didn't bother to shake hands, or even watch the men as they walked out the door.

Several minutes later, Sammantha Starodubov walked into the main room of the lodge and sat beside the president.

"Well, that went well," she said.

"Yeah."

"They don't want peace. They want only to preserve their own power."

"Right."

"But you…You are a man of extraordinary vision. A man willing to step outside the box to achieve something no man has done before. You, Mr. President…They will celebrate your name for centuries."

Sammantha snaked her arms around Copley's neck and kissed him softly. She felt him respond, so she drove her hips against him.

"I love you so," she said with a breathless purr. She was even beginning to feel that way, more than she had with any other man.

"You are my world," said the president. He pressed Sammantha into the folds of the couch and lay down beside her.

"Make love with me, Mr. President. Like there is no tomorrow."

CHAPTER 74

PP

As Trance's helicopter lifted away from Camp David, Jesse Tompkin spoke into his headset. "Well, doesn't this just suck..."

"I'm going to resign," said Miller.

"You can't," said Trance. "We need you here to protect him, to protect the country."

"Something bad is going down, JT," said Tompkin. "I can feel it."

"It was all too neat, wasn't it?" said Miller.

"Uh-huh," said Trance. "It was like they left him there for us to find. Not that you didn't do a hell of a job, Jesse, but, c'mon. A plan good enough to get the president out of the country should certainly be good enough to get him out of a warehouse."

"What did they do to him?" said Tompkin.

"It isn't Tilson," said Trance. "He's awfully good. But it's not him. Maybe someone's found a way to genetically alter a full-grown man, some cloning thing."

"Who is he, Jack?"

"I don't know, but we need to find out."

"You heard the president. If we even so much as sniff into this, he's going to have us imprisoned," said Tompkin.

"Since when does something like that stop Trance?" said Stick."

"You've got a point," said Miller.

Trance said, "Stick and I are the two civilians. Stick's got a family, so here's the deal. You all stay clear, while I investigate. Miller...Tompkin...You two have got to remain in place, so you do nothing. The nation is going to need your help. We have a deal?"

"Roger."

"Roger that."

"God help us."

CHAPTER **75**
PP

Sammantha Starodubov leaned back into the soft leather seat of her white, Lincoln Town Car limousine. Through the darkly tinted windows she could see a mass of white and black robes milling in an outdoor market. The sounds of chaotic shouting and the low growl of hundreds of people talking seemed to thump against the glass. Men and women stood in tightly packed stalls, selling everything from fresh farm produce to automobiles. There was a rope draped across one of the stalls like a clothes line. Upon it hung a string of American-made automatic weapons, along with two helmets and three flak jackets. Sammantha smiled to herself, knowing how it worked. The American forces gave out the gear to a foreign army, who gave it to their soldiers, who sold it on the street to the opposition forces, who used it to kill Americans. Generosity and capitalism in their most perverse and vile forms.

The style and quality of robes changed as the car left the market and entered a run-down tenement section. It was like day turning to night. Soon Sammantha could smell the heavy scent of raw sewage seeping through the car's air conditioning system. She inhaled it deeply and smiled with grim satisfaction. There was a time when she had lived like these sorry souls, screaming and fighting over scraps of refuse, ranting how it was all caused by the rich western world. She passed a group of lepers standing in a ragged line along a sequestered wall, as if waiting to be shot. She could see their black and deformed skin; she could feel their pain. *This is for you,* she thought. *I do this for all of us.*

The limousine stopped before a fifteen foot fence made from shiny steel. Even through the windows, Sammantha could hear the *click, click, click* of electricity as it pulsed through the woven metal mesh. Beyond the fence she saw a row of Russian T 90S tanks, each with a uniformed soldier sitting beside the driver's hatch, ever vigilant against attack. Beyond the soldiers they came to a second wall. This wall was higher and made of huge white stones. A pair of black metal gates were slung between two stone pillars leading inside the compound. The gates began to swing open as Sammantha's limo approached.

Sammantha looked to the man sitting beside her and said, "He is ready for us, Omar." Sammantha looked to the college-age boy and wondered what he was feeling inside. For almost a year he had been in her care. What an odd year it had been for him—moving to the underground bunker, his only job being to watch. That, and befriend the president-to-be. He had played his part well, gaining the new president's trust and confidence. He had learned to let the president win at cards. He had taught him to see science with a human face. Yes, Omar had done well. Now came his test.

"Are you nervous?" Sammantha asked.

Omar shook his head. "Of course not. I am coming home."

You wish, thought Sammantha. But she said nothing.

The car stopped on a driveway of hard white sand. As they walked from the car toward the palace, Sammantha could hear the sand squeak under the soles of Omar's Nike shoes. *This may be home to you,* thought Sammantha, *but to me, these are the gates to hell.*

Inside, they were led down a long corridor made with light gray marble. Omar's running shoes squeaked even louder, while Sammantha's red heels clicked like maracas on the cold polished stone. They passed several small alcoves built into the wall. Each alcove contained a rolled up prayer rug and a stone bowl. Each bowl was filled with water that flowed out from the wall. The water dripped over the edge of each bowl into pools filled with round black stones.

They were led to Talid's study. He was standing by a window, staring out over the city as intently as a star-gazer searching for the first light of night. He was wearing a white robe and a black and white head cloth fastened with a silver rope. Sammantha stopped by the door and waited for Talid to call her in. Omar stood behind her right shoulder like he was on a leash.

"Enter," said Talid. He stretched out his arms and drew Sammantha against his chest. He held her tightly and began to press his hips against hers. She responded by kissing him on the lips. Talid groaned. Then he jumped away from Sammantha and howled. Blood poured from his lower lip and he wiped it with the end of his robe.

"What's the matter, Talid? Do I play too rough for you?" Sammantha said, in fluent Arabic.

Talid grinned. "You are a truly evil woman."

"That's why we make good teammates."

Talid looked at Omar. He beamed, standing back like a proud, loving father, arms out from his sides, his eyes searching Omar from head to foot. "And look at you..." He slung his arms around Omar and pounded his back. Then he grabbed him by the shoulders to closely study his face.

"Has he behaved?" Talid said to Sammantha.

"His behavior was exemplary."

Talid turned to the young man and said with a solemn voice, "Are you ready for your next challenge?"

The muscles in Omar's face tensed. He looked to Sammantha with a questioning gaze.

"I have not told him, yet," she said. "I wanted to give you the pleasure."

Talid reached under his robe and pulled a Motorola communicator from somewhere underneath. "Send them in," he said softly.

Talid motioned toward the far end of his office. In the corner of the room, upon a gold and blue oriental rug, sat two pale yellow couches. They were separated by an oblong coffee table that was made from something that looked like sanded driftwood. Talid motioned for Omar and Sammantha to take a couch, while he remained standing. A minute later, three men walked into the office. One of the men was Omar's father, Talid's closest friend and advisor. The other was a man Sammantha had not seen before. He carried what looked to be a large Halliburton Zero attaché case. He was dressed in a pair of brown, well-worn pants with a matching brown shirt. There was a green L.L. Bean backpack strapped across his shoulders. The third man was Ivan Petrovski, the Russian Prime Minister.

Omar's father winked at him but said nothing. Karkhabi stepped back, allowing the unfamiliar man to place the suitcase upon the table.

"Guess what this is," said Talid. He looked to Omar, who stared at the suitcase and shrugged.

"I don't know. A briefcase? Luggage?"

"Think."

Omar grabbed the handle of the attaché and began to lift it. It was heavy, as if it were filled with lead. He began to shake it gently.

"I wouldn't do that," said Sammantha.

Omar put the case back on the table.

Talid looked to the stranger. "Open it."

The man grabbed a key ring that was hanging by a carabineer fastened to a loop on his pants. He removed two keys and inserted them both into the edge of the suitcase. He pressed a twelve number code into a keypad that was built into the top of the case. Then he turned the keys in unison. The man backed away without opening the top.

Talid motioned for Omar to approach the case.

Omar opened it and gasped. "Allah be praised," he whispered.

Omar had studied advanced math at Princeton. He had earned a Doctorate in nuclear science and engineering at MIT, finishing near the top in his class. He had toured nuclear reactors; he'd seen their inner cores. While at MIT, he'd done an internship at the Pilgrim nuclear plant in Plymouth, Massachusetts. But he had never laid eyes on this mythical beast, the suitcase nuke.

The device was tubular and surrounded by a pale metal shell. The tube ran from one corner of the suitcase to the opposite one. There was a digital display built into the frame, and what looked like a small microprocessor resting in one open corner of the suitcase. The other corner held a detonator, which was about six inches long. There was also a large, rectangular battery. Wires ran from it to the detonator and canister.

"Is this an RA-115? Is it hot? Will it work?"

"You like it?" said Talid, as if he were showing off a new car.

The Russian technician pulled a small motherboard out of his backpack. He slipped the motherboard into a slot inside the suitcase. He pulled a notebook computer out of his pack and set it down next to the bomb. He plugged what looked to be a firewire into his computer and then into a slot built into the bomb's frame. Petrovski took a spot beside him and crossed his arms like a sentry.

"You speak Russian? This computer in Russian. You speak?" said the Russian technician.

Omar nodded. Russians had been advising his country on military and energy matters for decades. He had been schooled in their language out of necessity.

The Russian continued, but in English. "Bomb not hot. I check today. No emission. Zero. Very safe. Now I show you how to arm weapon and set timer. Yes?"

Omar stood over the man's shoulder and watched his fingers glide along the keys with sure, quick clicks. "You see?" the man said.

The programming appeared to be a version of the old Microsoft DOS. The codes were surprisingly simple, mostly famous Russian names and simple numbers, like the Fibonacci Sequence.

"Do you have this written down? Is there a manual?" asked Omar.

The Russian laughed. "No. Must remember. You remember?"

"Yes. I'll remember."

They went through the arming procedure three times, until Omar could do it with his eyes closed.

"Once you arm bomb, you set timer. Then…" the Russian looked from each face to the other and smiled. "Boom. Timer good for up to three months, but clock runs slow. Russian made."

"How big?"

"Thirty kilo weight. Two kiloton bomb."

Omar felt a strange sensation tingle through him. It reminded him of the time when he'd taken a ride on the London Eye Ferris wheel. All had gone smoothly until the wheel had reached the top of its arc, a full four hundred and forty-three feet in the air. The wheel had stopped. He sat high above the earth, swinging back and forth in the wind, utterly powerless against the great forces of nature. He couldn't remember anything after that moment. He had awakened on the ground, his body bathed in sweat, with people standing above him and slapping his cheeks.

Omar felt a gurgle in his stomach. Something rose into his throat, like a warm, wet burp. His mouth tasted like hot chocolate at first, all warm and sweet. The aftertaste was nasty, like raw ginger, so strong he almost gagged.

Omar thought of his years in America. He thought of his friends, from countries around the world. What would they think of him now? He thought of Allah. Allah had put this gem into his hands. Two kilotons was small, less than one tenth the size of Hiroshima and Nagasaki. Even so, the mushroom cloud would rise majestically. It could kill thousands, tens of thousands. His throat began to tighten, making it almost impossible to breathe. Sweat broke out across his forehead.

"Allah is great," he choked. Omar unhooked the wires, removed the bomb's motherboard and closed the case.

Talid rested his hand on the side of the suitcase. He turned to Petrovski and then to Sammantha. "You think I will let you take this?"

Sammantha pulled Talid's hand away from the bomb. "I do."

Talid put his hand back. "Think again. I will kill you before I let you walk out with this case."

Petrovski walked over and stood beside Sammantha. "Then Russia will turn this city into a sandy parking lot."

Petrovski and Talid locked eyes, staring at each other without blinking. Sammantha watched them with an amused expression on her face. Then she said, "Calm down, boys."

Sammantha leaned against Talid's ear and whispered her plan. Talid straightened and he looked to Sammantha, and then to Petrovski with a mixture of joy and awe.

"Really?"

"Really."

"I want to be there."

"As do I," said Petrovski.

Sammantha sneered. "If either of you step foot in America, you will jeopardize the mission."

"You will not do this without me," said Talid.

"Or without me," echoed Petrovski.

Sammantha smiled slyly. "I plan to be there when it happens. Why don't you men join me? We'll have a detonation party, on our way to hell."

Talid's teeth bared. He had the grin of a growling Doberman, and his eyes stretched into slits. He reached for Sammantha's throat and began to squeeze it, tighter and tighter.

Petrovski didn't move to stop him. He was too busy wondering if he could get himself to stand near the bomb while it exploded. Of course he couldn't. Someone had to take charge after it happened. He had to be there to shape the aftermath. Let the others die. Not him. He was too important.

Sammantha's eyes began to bulge. Her face turned into a blotchy patchwork of blood and skin. She narrowed her eyes and she began to smile. She pressed her hand against Talid's robe and found his penis dangling loosely within the cotton cloth. She grabbed it and she screamed. "You will not fuck with me, Talid!" Sammantha yanked on Talid's penis, as if she were pulling a tree out of the ground. She pulled fiercely, fueled by rage, and she nearly twisted Talid off at the root.

Talid spun away from her and yelled, "Don't you fuck with me! You will see this through, in Washington. *We* will see this through. I will be there and I will join you. But not in hell. It will be in glory to Allah, with virgins for everyone."

CHAPTER **76**
_______________PP_______________

Martha Tilson parked her Ford F-150 truck in the parking lot of Greenville's Village Food Mart. She shuffled over to the black GMC Yukon with tinted windows that had stopped a discreet forty feet from her truck. She rapped against the side window.

"You boys want anything from the store?"

The window rolled down and a man wearing aviator sunglasses shook his head. "No thanks, Mrs. Tilson."

"You boys stay here. I'll be just a minute."

Martha walked into the store and grabbed a shopping basket. She gathered a loaf of bread, some frozen vegetables and stooped to pick up a half gallon of 1 ½% milk.

As she was grasping the milk's plastic handle, a voice behind her said, "Mrs. Tilson. Could I have a word with you? It's about your son."

Martha Tilson stood up and looked calmly into Trance's eyes. Too calmly. She knew something about this; he could tell.

Relief seemed to wrinkle across Martha's brow, but she tried to feign normality. "Oh, hello, Jack. It's been a while. How've you been?"

"This is not a social call, Mrs. Tilson. The president doesn't know I am here. In fact, if he knew I were here, he might lock me away to die."

"Jason wouldn't do that."

"That is correct. Jason would not. So, who is in the White House?"

Martha put the milk in her basket without looking at Trance.

"My son, of course."

"You need to tell me, Mrs. Tilson."

"No, I don't."

"What is it you're not telling us?"

When Martha Tilson looked back at Trance there were tears brimming in her eyes.

Trance patted her on the shoulder. "I'm only asking this for the good of your son. For the good of the country. Something has changed the president. If you have any information that can help us, we need to know it."

"I have two sons," said Martha. Her voice was barely audible, like the ghost of a whisper.

"Excuse me?"

"I have two sons. I had two sons."

"You'll need to explain."

When Martha looked at Trance, her face looked oddly misshapen, as if it had been broken into pieces and reassembled by a child. Her eyes were wide, almost wild. Her teeth were partially bared. Her lips were wet and red, and pulpy with pulsing blood. Martha fought against the memories. But there was so much else going on in her head. The mother in her needed to protect her sons, both of them. The girl in her needed to flush out the memories, wash them away and let them go. The patriot in her needed to tell the truth.

Part of Martha felt an enormous relief. This was a burden she had carried alone. Always strong, always stoic. She could feel a part of that strength crumbling like a cookie in milk, under Trance's gaze.

Another part of her was scared, scared that she would lose her boys, scared that she was making the wrong choice, for her family, for her country. Martha stood staring at Trance, those thoughts spinning in her brain, whirling and contorting her face into a vision of grief. Finally, the truth won out.

"Jack, I've never told anyone about this..." Martha's eyes looked to the floor, but she went on. "I never thought...I could ever speak...about this to anyone. Even Jock doesn't know...You see, Jack, well..." Martha gathered herself. She stood erect; then she looked Trance straight in the eyes. She whispered, "I was raped..."

Trance patted her shoulder. Martha swayed unsteadily. She caught herself by placing a hand on the produce counter. She stood firm again.

"I was sixteen...working the summer in Bar Harbor, as a servant girl. There was this family there...big old house on the water...must have been fifty rooms...They were the kind of people you read about in books like The Great Gatsby...More money than sense...Opulent parties with hundreds of guests...One day he asked me to take a walk through the gardens. He was a nice man, kind of cute, if you liked older guys...And...And he took me into the...There was this gazebo. It had walls around it, and closed-in windows...He threw me to the floor...And...And he ripped off my uniform...I screamed, but no one came. No one dared...And he forced me...He beat me...He raped me...I closed my eyes...And...And when it was done he grunted, getting up on his knees, buckling his belt...I stared at him, wearing that crazy smug smile on his face...And there...there, behind him, through the window I could see her...Mrs. Copley...She was watching us through the glass...with this kind of pained smile on her face...Watching...And when it was over...he walked out and he took her hand...He took her hand and they walked back to the house together...while I...while I had to clean up the blood..."

Martha Tilson's eyes pleaded with Trance, as if he could set her free. Trance waited.

"His name was Copley. Brandon Copley, from New York."

Brandon Copley...Brandon Copley, thought Trance. Where had he heard that name? Then he remembered, the Plaza Hotel. Cover of the *Times*.

"The Brandon Copley who was found dead in the Hudson?"

Martha's lower lip curled. She brought her hand to her mouth and nodded.

"I never knew him," she whispered. "But I saw him some. He went to Yale, while Jock chose Harvard. I used to watch them play baseball together. They were like gladiators."

In a strange way, this made sense. It explained a lot of things, the identical DNA, the lack of remembered details, the irrational difference in concerns, the death of Kiki Tilson.

"Could the Jock Tilson in Washington be your other son? Could he be Brandon Copley?"

"I...I don't know."

"I think you do," said Trance. He placed a hand on each of Martha's shoulders and willed her to look at him. "You do know, don't you?"

Martha nodded.

"Do you have any idea what could have happened to Jason?"

"He tells me that *he* is Jason. But I know...A mother knows."

Martha Tilson's body seemed to lose its fiber. She leaned against the milk cooler and let out a low, slow moan. Trance held her in his arms and patted her on the back.

"It's okay, Mrs. Tilson. It's not your fault, none of it is. None of it was. I'll find him. I will find your son. Someday, I promise, you will be a family. All of you."

Trance prayed that this was a promise he could keep.

CHAPTER 77
PP

Trance could hear the faint sounds of the city in the background of his mind—the occasional honking horn, the beeping of delivery trucks backing up and the bark of dogs. He glanced at his watch, then pulled a pillow over his head and rolled over in bed. He wasn't ready for the day. Not yet. He could hear the sounds of bacon sizzling and coffee percolating in an old-style coffee maker. It wouldn't be long now before Lauren brightened the day with her smiling face.

Trance replayed the conversation with Martha Tilson, rolling it over and over in his mind like a video. He thought about Brandon Copley and the president. Twins. Separated at birth. Who else could know? Someone knew. They had spent years and enormous sums of money to put that knowledge to use. For what purpose?

Trance wondered how far they had gone. Had they programmed Copley? To do what? This had to be something big. It was mere days before he was due to meet with Ogarkov. Was that the plan? Was he going to cut some treaty to sell the country short? Or was he going to pass something along? Nuclear talks. Nuclear codes? Was Copley going to give Ogarkov the country's most heavily guarded secrets? Or was he going to kill the Russian? Murder at Camp David?

"Time to get up, sleepy head," said Lauren. She plopped a breakfast tray on the bed and slipped under the covers beside Trance. "Room service with a smile. And, if you're a good boy, desert, with an even bigger smile."

Trance propped himself up in the bed and cradled Lauren under one arm. She snuggled against him.

"I love you," said Trance.

"You do?"

Trance tickled Lauren under her arms. She giggled and tried to tickle him back "You know I do," he said. Trance pulled Lauren tightly against him. "More than you know."

Maybe I'll ask her today, he thought. *Yes, today should be the day. We'll take a walk down Boylston Street to look for rings, maybe go over to Lux Bond and Green, or Tiffany in the mall. We'll do it together...*

At that moment there was a crash in the downstairs entryway of Lauren's brownstone. Trance leaped to his feet, spilling their breakfast across the room. "To the floor," he said. "Under the bed." *Like that will help*, thought Trance. *This is not good. Not good.*

Trance could already hear boots thumping up the stairway. He grabbed his Colt 32 off the night stand and snapped a bullet into the chamber. He didn't have time to put on clothes, so he stood there, naked by the door, gun at the ready.

"U.S. military!" he yelled. "Locked and loaded!" He didn't have an M16 in his hands, as the old slang suggested, but they'd know what he meant. He would come out firing.

The intruders didn't stop at the top of the stairs. Instead, they sprinted into Lauren's bedroom, wearing body armor and helmets with bulletproof shields. Trance immediately processed the data and began firing at their hands and knees and ankles. Men kept pouring into the room like a new hatch of mosquitoes. Trance got off all eight rounds before he was surrounded by more than a dozen men.

One of the men started to shout, but Trance put two knuckles into his throat. He hit another intruder across the neck with the side of his hand, as he took out another with a side kick to the chest.

Trance spun and whip-kicked a fourth man in the face. Then he felt the sting of a Taser hit his back. His body convulsed, but not enough to keep him from reaching back and ripping the prods out of his skin. Another shock hit him and he did the same. Trance fought on with agonizing fury. He took four more men down before his world went dark, as one of the men jammed edge of a rifle butt deep into the crevice between Trance's skull and his neck. Trance stood for a moment, wobbled, and then dripped to the floor in a puddle of skin.

When Trance regained consciousness he was in the back of a panel truck. His hands were pinned behind him with a pair of hinged Hiatts UL5 handcuffs. The cuffs, in turn, were fastened to the truck. There were two rows of soldiers seated upon benches that were bolted to the sides of the truck. Trance could see men attending to bleeding arms and legs. Two of the men had bones protruding through their bloodstained pants, swearing, as medics pulled at their legs to straighten them back into place. The remaining soldiers kept their assault rifles warily trained on Trance.

"Who are you?" said Trance.

"You know who we are," said one of the men.

"Who?"

Then Trance noticed a T-Force logo on the breast of one of the uniforms. A sickening dread began to form in the pit of Trance's stomach. As much as he hoped against it, he knew that the president had held true to his word. Trance had continued looking into the president's identity. This was payback. He even sent his old team. He wondered if they were going to kill him, perhaps even today.

"I'm sorry, guys," said Trance. "If I had known it was you…" He closed his eyes and groaned.

After less than half an hour, the truck glided to a halt. The rear panel slid open and bright, blinding light flooded the back of the truck. Then Trance saw him, standing outside, his hands on his hips. Jesse Tompkin.

"Hello, Jack," said Tompkin, saluting.

"Hey, Jesse."

"Sorry to have to do this."

Trance jumped down off the truck bed, with his hands still securely fastened behind him.

"The president sent T-Force after me?"

"Affirmative."

"You going to kill me, Jesse?"

"No. Just a ninety-day lockup. You'll be here for Christmas, but out for the New Year's bowl games."

"Lucky me." Trance closed his eyes and forced a laugh. Why did it always happen this way? All he ever did was try to make things right. Last year he'd been kidnapped, hooked on heroin and nearly killed. The year before that, he'd been kidnapped and shot. He spent half his life recovering. And what for? Maybe it really was time to give up and settle down.

"Is Lauren okay?"

"Affirmative."

"Your men?"

"You banged 'em up, Jack. They'll live. They're tough."

"Lauren has power of attorney for me. Tell her what happened. Tell her that I love her and that I'm okay. If you or your men need anything…Tell them I'm sorry…Have Lauren make it right. Make it right, Jesse."

"We take care of our own."

Trance laughed. "Jesse, I *am* one of your own."

"Kinda sucks, don't it?"

"You could have knocked on the door. I would have come."

"We were ordered not to. They made us do a full frontal."

"He wanted me to attack our men," whispered Trance.

"Or for you to be killed."

"There is something seriously wrong here. All I did was talk to his mother."

Tompkin leaned against Trance's ear and whispered, "Don't say anything more. Just take your ninety days and get out of here. We need you."

Trance said, "Can Lauren visit me?"

"I am authorized to let her visit once per week. No conjugal."

"Can I have a computer?"

"Word processing only. No Internet."

"NFL Network?"

Tompkin laughed. "Sorry."

"Have Lauren call Ben Johnson, to arrange a way for us to communicate. Work it out with Miller. He'll know what to do. Can you do that?"

"Affirmative."

Trance looked around. He recognized the government's secret Quincy location for counter-terrorism. They could keep him here forever and no one would know. Ninety days. He'd been lucky. He'd be out at the end of the year, provided things didn't change. But what didn't change these days?

"His name is Copley," said Trance softly. "Brandon Copley, of New York. I don't know where Tilson is. Tell Miller."

"Roger that. " Tompkin suddenly shoved Trance forward and kicked him in the butt. "You will not say another word, soldier!"

"Copley," mouthed Trance.

Tompkin led Trance inside the building, to a small solitary cell. He closed the door and locked it behind him. As Tompkin walked away, a powerful sense of fear began to form in Tompkin's mind. For some odd reason, it made him think of Frodo in *Lord of the Rings*, advancing resolutely toward the cracks of doom. And one ring to rule them all…Next time, he'd be ordered to kill Trance. And there would be a next time. Trance was a bulldog. Once he got hold of you, he wouldn't let go until you fell to your knees, or he died in the trying.

CHAPTER 78

_____________PP_____________

There was no twenty-seven car presidential motorcade to meet Nikolai Ogarkov as he emerged from his unmarked jet at Reagan National Airport. Instead, a string of non-descript, two-toned Mayflower Cabs stood waiting in the darkness. As the jet taxied to a stop by a private hanger, the cabs formed a receiving line, taking groups of four as they walked out of the plane. Ogarkov took the fifth cab, sandwiched between two units of Russian soldiers in full assault gear.

It was 11 P.M. when Ogarkov's taxi rolled through the gates of Camp David. Ogarkov smiled, thinking how fitting it was for them to meet like this, far outside the glare of camera lights. He was most comfortable this way, like at his dacha. He wondered if the fake Jock Tilson would feel the same.

The president was waiting for him, standing with his hands on his hips, wearing a pair of faded khaki pants and a blue and white, striped Oxford shirt. When Ogarkov stepped out from the cab the president rushed forward to greet him.

"Hello, Mr. President," gushed the American. "So glad to finally meet you."

The president offered an outstretched hand. As Ogarkov grasped it he carefully studied the president's features. This man looked identical to Jock Tilson. He knew that the real U.S. president was being held in the bowels of the Kremlin. Still, he found it difficult to believe that _this_ was not the American president. He looked so…presidential.

The president motioned for Ogarkov to take the passenger seat in an oversized golf cart. The cart was made with a miniature chassis of a Humvee, replete with brown and green camouflage paint. The tires spun small clouds of rocks and dust as the president jammed his foot on the accelerator, pushing it at top speed toward Birch, the president's personal cabin.

The Humvee cart skidded to a halt outside the rustic but oddly elegant, three room place that Tilson used as his second home. The president's Secret Service detail, along with Ogarkov's twelve hand-picked men, fanned around the sides and the back of the building. Four men entered inside, with rifles at the ready. Soon they declared it clear.

Sammantha Starodubov was standing just inside the front door when the two men entered. She and Ogarkov locked eyes. A smile crept across each face.

"I believe you know Sammantha Starodubov?" said the president.

Sammantha extended her hand, palm down, and Ogarkov kissed her across the knuckles.

"It is a pleasure to see you again, Miss Starodubov."

"The pleasure is mine."

Ogarkov turned to the president. "I have seen the documentary that Miss Starodubov produced on your presidency. It has been most favorably received in our country."

"She is a remarkable woman. She has been essential in helping me understand the complexities of the Russian psyche."

Ogarkov chuckled. "I do not think that even Miss Starodubov can understand the conflicted and tortured Russian mindset."

"I have been far more interested in how to deal with you," said the president bluntly.

Ogarkov's eyes rounded into a smile and his teeth gleamed yellow in the subdued light.

"In these negotiations, Mr. President—"

"Jock. Please, call me Jock."

"In these negotiations, Jock, we can only trust ourselves. You and me. No one else. Not even your mistress."

"Mistress?"

"I can see it in her eyes. She worships you. Or, at least, she pretends to."

The president grunted.

Ogarkov waved him off. "No matter. You are single man, no?"

The president nodded. "I am."

Ogarkov pointed a finger at Sammantha. "She may advise you well. But not in this. In this, we must be man to man. No outside interference."

Ogarkov had spent hours meeting with Sammantha about their subject, the new American president. She had helped him understand the American's own psyche as they developed their preferred strategy. So far, all was working according to his plan. But not hers. This was *not* what she had planned. She was to be there, at the epicenter, to keep control.

Anger seeped through Sammantha, fogging her brain like a steamy bathroom mirror. She tried to wipe her thoughts clean, to let it pass. Ogarkov could see that she was a tightly coiled spring, almost ready to snap, but he would not relent.

"I am not an interference," Sammantha said stiffly.

Ogarkov took Sammantha's hand and patted it softly. "Yes, you are, my dear. Why don't you take a walk and let these two sad widowers get to know each other?" Ogarkov squeezed her hand to make his point.

Sammantha's eyes softened. "Of course. How selfish of me." She turned to the president. "You be strong with him, Jock. Ogarkov may be honest, but he is a brutal negotiator."

Ogarkov smiled derisively. "You give me far too much credit, Miss Starodubov. I am but a simple peasant."

Sammantha looked at the American president. "Remember what we discussed. Be strong. Settle for nothing less. Nothing." She stood on her toes and kissed the president on his cheek. "You can do this," she whispered. She winked at Ogarkov and walked out of the room.

After Sammantha had left, Ogarkov turned to the president and said in a glowing voice, "What an exquisite creature. Is she really yours?"

The president nodded slowly, as if embarrassed.

"Then you are a lucky man."

The president lifted his chin. His shoulders straightened and he looked like a soldier on parade. "I most certainly am." The president sobered quickly. Suddenly this was all real. He felt his tongue go dry and his hands begin to sweat. "Why don't you speak first?"

Ogarkov ambled to a chair and sat down heavily. "I am getting far too old for this." He watched the president take a chair beside him, then said, "I will be leaving office within the next year or two." He paused. "I would like to leave a legacy. A lasting one."

"Wouldn't we all."

Ogarkov paused, then said, "Before we begin, I want to tell you a little bit about the Russian people, what we will both have to deal with to make this work.

"My people like to see themselves as victims. Most of us feel powerless. We *were* powerless against the Czar. Then came the Revolution, when we thought we would feel liberated. This turned out to be a hoax perpetrated by a few men to grab power and money in a different, more brutal way.

"Few Russians own land. Fewer feel any measure of prosperity. For most, life is a tiring grind from childhood to death. Half the women in Moscow sell themselves as prostitutes. Alcoholism runs rampant…twenty, thirty percent. Our productivity lags the world and we fall farther and farther behind our most feared enemy—China. Now that America trades with China like a neighbor, the Russian people regard America with the same suspicion.

"Our nation also has some of the world's greatest talents, in science, the arts and athletics. These are a source of pride for our people, a consolation prize, if you will. Perhaps our greatest source of self-worth comes from our military might, be it real or imagined.

"When I asked you for this meeting, I did so with the most noble of intentions. I want to bring peace and safety to the world. Just one of our multiple entry missiles can unleash more destructive power than has been used in the history of warfare. We both have hundreds of these primed and ready to fire. How can we sleep at night? How could our citizens, if they really understood their proximity to extinction?

"I want to ensure peace for Russia, in a world that is growing more and more complicated, a world in which we, as a nation, are finding it increasingly difficult to compete economically. As NATO builds a new missile shield against us, despite your claims to the contrary, it is all I can do to keep the jingoists at bay.

"If I bring something back to my people, it must appear that we have gained, not fallen farther behind. As much as I might try to extol the virtues of spending less on our military and more on our people and technology, it will not sit well with the average Ivan if I don't bring him something of value. So, if we are able to get anything done, we must, at the least, save face for Russia. That said, let us begin."

"Well spoken," murmured the president.

Ogarkov smiled ruefully. "Let us hope that you will say the same about my proposal." Ogarkov licked his lips and glanced toward the president's bar. He wanted a drink, but he said nothing. "This is what I propose. I would like both of our countries to reduce our nuclear arsenals by ninety percent. We have each bloated our capabilities to levels far in excess of what we could ever use or need. How much have we spent? Trillions? For what? To maintain a nightmare standoff?

"This reduction will leave us both with the power to defend ourselves, or blow any single nation back to the Stone Age. But, hopefully, not enough to destroy the planet. I would also like a new treaty with your country that protects Russian from China's aggression. You may have a similar agreement that protects China from Russian aggression. That way, America can referee our differences. Once these plans are in place, we can work to bring about further reductions."

The president sat for a long, quiet moment, then said, "The size of our debt owed to China does not worry you?"

Ogarkov shook his head. "Whether you realize it or not, Americans fear China just as we do. Soon your people will stop worrying about turning a green America greener. Soon, they will see China as the greatest cause of global pollution. They will lose their love affair with cheap goods and ignorant hypocrisy. No, they will see this agreement as a matter of principal, not economics."

The American president considered Ogarkov's words carefully before answering. The Russian's proposal was what Sammantha had said it would be. But this was still too limited to be an effective solution to an ever-growing problem. He stared for a long moment into Ogarkov's eyes. He saw a sadness there, but he also saw hope. So he knew that his own proposal, the one he had not discussed with Sammantha, would be well received.

"You and I have had the sobering experience of learning just how close we are to mutual destruction. Just one simple command, followed by a few keystrokes and codes and our planet could become virtually inhabitable for generations.

"Add the fact that two dozen nations have the same technology, if not our mass destruction and production capabilities, the world sits on a dry stack of firewood while we light matches every day. It's just a matter of time before one of us catches fire.

"While I applaud your proposal, I feel that it is too limited in scope. It is too centered on America and Russia, and not enough on the rest of the world. I propose that we construct a framework to drastically reduce nuclear weaponry among *all* nuclear nations, and that we reduce our own stores of these devices dramatically below what you suggest. We shall do this as equals. You think that will work in your country?"

While Ogarkov thought over his proposal, the president motioned toward the liquor cabinet. "Can I offer you something to drink?"

"You have vodka?"

"Grey Goose okay?"

"I am not used to such refined spirits. Perhaps you have a good single malt?"

The president's programming missed Ogarkov's not-so-subtle hint. "Ice? Lime?"

Ogarkov shook his head.

The president poured Ogarkov half a glass of vodka. He prepared himself a soda water with lime, before continuing, "I propose that we form a new organization that consists only of nuclear nations, The United Nuclear Nations.

"To join, each member of the organization must agree to dramatically reduce their nuclear arsenals, or face drastic sanctions. Each member shall be allowed a small cache of nuclear warheads. For defense purposes only. I recommend two.

"Russia, China and the U.S. will form a prime alliance, something similar to what you proposed. Each nation shall be allowed five multiple entry missiles. There will be an additional twenty warheads that can be used by the alliance, with approval from all three nations required to activate the warheads, and the missiles upon which they sit.

"Then, working together, we shall make sure that no other nation joins the nuclear club."

Ogarkov waited for the president to continue, but he said no more. The president's proposal was simple. It meant destroying thousands of warheads. Tens of thousands. It meant erasing his country's false security blanket—the thought that, no matter what happened, Russia had the capability to destroy the planet. That road lead to nowhere. What good was mutual destruction?

It was true. As long as the three great powers held their extraordinary nuclear arsenals, they had no moral authority over other, lesser nations. None. Other nations could justify building their weaponry unchecked, until they, too, had the world in a noose.

Could it possibly be that by emasculating Russia's arsenal he could make his country safer? In a strange way, it made sense.

"You would be willing to submit to such a proposal?" said Ogarkov.

"I would."

"It sounds so simple."

"Getting lesser nations to agree will be a challenge. We will have to force them to comply, with unprecedented and unwavering economic and public pressure."

"I worry about France, Britain, Germany, Israel and India. They may insist on joining the prime alliance."

"Let's talk with them and come up with a joint accord. Perhaps they could have a partial vote."

The president picked up the phone and dialed for his ever-present secretary.

"Yes, Mr. President?"

"Would you make arrangements for President Ogarkov and me to speak with the leaders of China, Germany, France, England, India and Israel all within the next two hours?"

"I'm sorry, sir?"

"You heard me. I want fifteen minute TelePresence conferences lined up back-to-back-to-back.

They have been alerted by Secretary Pincenogle. They should be waiting for your call. Inform them that President Ogarkov and I will be speaking with them jointly. They must have only trustworthy, senior officials in their rooms. This is Top Secret UMBRA."

"Yes, sir."

The president turned to Ogarkov. "In the next few hours you and I are going to make history. We will take the first steps toward making the world a far safer place. By this time tomorrow, we will be well on our way toward an historical treaty. I have been thinking long and hard about this.

"I plan to invite you and other nuclear leaders join me for my annual State of the Union Address. We will unveil our plan at that time, with the whole world watching.

"We shall stand on stage with a show of unity. All of us. A global accord to surpass all others in modern history. It will be a command performance. It will be glorious. The world will stand and they will cheer. People will speak of that day for centuries."

How right he was.

CHAPTER **79**

_____________PP_____________

Lauren Haverford was leaning against the headboard of her bed with the covers pulled up around her neck. Two men in fatigues and vests stood at her feet, each with an M16 cradled at the ready.

"Who are you? Where is Jack?" said Lauren. She'd asked those questions repeatedly for hours. Each time she had received the same courteous answer.

"I am not at liberty to answer that, ma'am. All I can say is that General Trance is in no present danger and neither are you. Our orders are to remain—"

At that moment they could hear muffled talking coming from the main floor below. The polite soldier grew silent, angling his head as if waiting for someone to call out. Several moments later a man appeared in the doorway.

Jesse Tompkin walked into the room and saluted.

"At ease, men. Go downstairs and wait for me."

Tompkin turned to Lauren, who was staring at him, wide-eyed and silent.

"I am sorry it had to happen this way, Lauren."

"It was you?"

"Yes. Would you like me to leave so you can get dressed?"

"Not until I've got answers. What did you do with Jack?"

"He is being held by order of the president."

"Jock Tilson would never do this."

"That is correct."

Lauren began to speak but Tompkin put a finger to his lips. He moved closer and began whispering in a hushed voice.

"Jack has been checking into the unusual circumstances surrounding the president's abduction and his recent behavior. The White House did not take kindly to Jack's actions and ordered us to contain him."

"To contain him? What, like a terrorist? He is a private citizen—"

"Not really, Lauren. Jack operates in a bureaucratic netherworld. He serves his government, but nothing is official. No paper trail. This gives the White House plausible deniability. It gives Jack less scrutiny, but also no *official* protection. Jack has the highest access to classified information, government systems, data and manpower. He also serves at the whim of the president. He takes orders. This puts him smack under military control." Tompkin smiled. "It's also allowed him to make general and earn him a chest full of medals...for all the good it does."

Tompkin closed his eyes and sighed. He leaned against the doorway, his shoulders slumping.

"It's all come unglued, Lauren. Jack was ordered to back off investigating the president's kidnapping and the murder of his wife. He saw things that didn't add up, so he kept on digging. That pissed off the president. So, Jack's got ninety days to rethink his priorities."

"Where is he?"

"He's in protective custody."

"Protective custody, my ass."

"Lauren, he injured people."

"He was defending himself! You broke into my house and attacked *him*."

"You and I know that. But the transcript will read—"

"Then you *fix* the transcript."

Tompkin shook his head. "I can't, Lauren. The president has assumed a very personal role in tracking what Jack does…what he has done. The president called me *personally*. Said he was giving Jack ninety days to think about his life and move on. Says if Jack continues his pursuit of forbidden answers he will face a general court martial and will spend the rest of his life in prison, or worse."

"I *know* Jock Tilson. This is *not* Jock Tilson. Someone has to—"

Tompkin pressed his palm against Lauren's mouth and whispered, "We can find no hard evidence. His DNA is the same, his fingerprints, dental records, his GPS serial numbers, his scans…Hell, even the scar on his scalp where he was kicked by a cow is the same."

"You know it's not him."

"But we can't prove it. And if anyone tries to…well, you see what happens. The White House wields a lot of power."

Lauren's eyes hardened. She jutted out her chin and whispered, "I am not afraid. Tell me what I can do."

"Does the name Brandon Copley mean anything to you?"

Lauren frowned. She'd heard the name before. Where had it been?

Tompkin said, "He was an actor."

"Oh, yes. He was found in the Hudson. From a wealthy family. I remember now…We were at the Plaza. Jack bought a paper from a young man and gave him his card…Told him to call Spike Jackson."

Tompkin nodded. "Jack gave me Copley's name. Before coming here I did a Lexis-Nexus search. There is incongruence; lots of it."

"What are you saying?"

"I'm saying that I can't follow up on this without ending up like Jack. Maybe *you* can. If you do it discreetly."

"Can I see Jack?"

"Once a week. He asked me to tell you that he loves you and to tell you that he's okay. He also wants you to contact Ben Johnson, to arrange a method of communication via computer."

"You holding him in Quincy?"

"He's close."

"Close, my ass. He is as far away from me as the moon." Lauren paused. "You know he won't stop, Jesse. Jack can't stop. Not when something isn't right, when it isn't *just*."

"He's got to let it go, Lauren. For his sake…for your sake. When we let him out, you'll need to take him somewhere. Somewhere far away, away from Jock Tilson, away from Washington—"

"Are you *in* on this?" interrupted Lauren, finding it hard to believe that Jesse Tompkin would ever walk away from any righteous fight, no matter what the odds.

Tompkin drew a long, solemn breath, then spoke softly. "There is a fine line between fighting and suicide, Lauren. Jack and I, and you, are far better for this world alive, than dead."

"Can you and your men leave now? I need to think."

"Are you okay?"

"Sure. Just a normal Saturday morning in the Lauren Haverford household."

"I mean, with this. With Jack's incarceration?"

"You mean, am I calling the authorities?"

Tompkin nodded.

"I thought you *were* the authorities."

"So did I."

"Go," said Lauren. "We're not doing any good sitting here. Do things your way, I'll do things mine."

"Be careful."

Lauren laughed. "You bet your ass, I'll be careful. But I won't lie down, I promise you that. I've got resources."

"Good."

Lauren kissed Tompkin on the cheek.

"I know this was hard on you, Jesse. Remember, some things are worth fighting for, even if it doesn't look that way."

"I know, Lauren. Believe me, I know."

As Tompkin turned to leave, Lauren said, "What did Jack say about your men?"

Tompkin frowned. "Sorry?"

"Jack hurt some of your men. His men. He must have said something to you about it."

"No. Not really."

"Don't bullshit me."

Tompkin grinned sheepishly.

"Thought so. How many men did he hurt?"

"Eight."

"He must be getting slow."

"They were my best."

"I will send two million for their restitution and recovery. A quarter million each."

"They were just doing their job, Lauren. You don't need to—"

"Shut up, Tompkin. I'll wire it tonight. To the Freedom account. You let me know if you need more."

"I'll find out when you can see him."

"Thanks."

CHAPTER **80**

_________PP_________

Sammantha Starodubov drove her rented Fiat Linea into a small, private parking lot near the Montenapoleone metro station in Milan. She spoke with the sketchy attendant, asking in halting Insubric if she could keep her keys. The attendant said "no," but in the end, cash won out.

It was a cool, gray morning, still early. The tightly packed city was already approaching its normal frenetic confusion. Sammantha pulled a red backpack off the passenger seat of her car. She locked the door, slid the keys into a pocket of her jeans and began walking along the narrow Via Montenapoleone. This street had yet to awaken. There was an intermittent stream of cars heading one-way toward her, but there were few pedestrians. A scattering of tourists were window shopping and a few of the local residents were walking an assortment of odd and exotic looking dogs.

Sammantha hunched forward as she walked, head down. The mostly empty street seemed to crowd against her. It was as if the sides of the road had been pinched together by some great hand, forcing the brown stone buildings closer together and higher than they were meant to be. It was invading her personal space like a claustrophobia machine.

This street was obscenely wealthy. Sammantha could feel the money here, like oil on her skin. It was oozing out into the street from the fashion and jewelry shops that were stacked one against another like runway models behind a stage.

Sammantha stopped beside a narrow door of thick, frosted glass. She rang the bell and a voice called through an intercom, in Italian. She spoke her name and the door buzzed loudly. Sammantha opened it and began climbing up a dark, steep stairway. The stairway ended at another door, this one made of steel. She looked up at two video cameras that were mounted into the ceiling. She smiled and waved. The heavy door buzzed and she entered.

She walked into a vast, open loft. The floor was wood and rounded with centuries of wear. One of the walls was glass, opening out to the vista of the narrow street. Skylights carried natural light in from the roof, making a kind of checkerboard across the ceiling.

Canvas was everywhere. New canvas, old canvas, loose canvas, stretched canvas. Canvas covered with random spots of paint, and canvas revealing the strokes of master painters. There were paintings stacked against each other along the wooden walls, some large, some small. There were marble busts and bronze sculptures. Some were lying on the floor, while others rested on pedestals like Roman Gods.

Despite the early hour, there were a dozen artists already plying their trades. Most were standing before easels or chunks of rock. In a separate, glassed in area, other artists were seated at potter's wheels, centering huge lumps of clay.

A man approached Sammantha. He would have been tall, except for a rounded hump on his right shoulder that made him walk with a pronounced stoop. His hair was black, but turning into a pleasant tone of silver, as was his Vandyck beard. His eyes were blue, weary and wary.

"Hello, Miss S." The man extended a hand that was covered with dried paint.

Sammantha grasped the man's hand and shook it firmly. "Good to see you again, Andre."

"This way."

Andre led Sammantha across the loft to a small office in the corner. He closed the door behind them and sat on a folding metal chair. He motioned for Sammantha to take a chair beside him.

"What brings you back to me, Miss Starodubov?"

"I need your help."

"Most certainly. You were pleased with my last creation?"

"Very much so."

Sammantha reached into her backpack and withdrew a tubular canister. It was slightly larger than the one housing the nuclear weapon that she would be smuggling into the U.S. She wanted enough space to provide sufficient padding and the shielding she'd need to get the weapon through customs.

"I want a bronze sculpture that will house coins kept in a container of this size. Thirty or thirty-five kilos. I will also need a separate compartment that is twenty by twenty by thirty centimeters."

Sammantha offered the empty container. Andre Fellini took the canister and turned it over in his hands.

"Not a problem. No problem at all."

Fellini had begun his career as a struggling, Czech sculptor by the name of Andre Grotkin. When a well-respected art dealer had offered to pay him an exorbitant sum to create a piece with hidden compartments, to be used to smuggle diamonds out of America, he had grudgingly complied. He'd needed the money; didn't they all? The second time it was easier. Then a career was born. Grotkin, now calling himself Fellini, had grown famous among the wealthy, known for his trustworthiness, his discretion, and for his ability to create useful sculptures that could easily spread hidden wealth across the world. Fellini also had talent, loads of talent, which was all the better.

"I want the piece to be of a woman…a woman who has endured great hardships, but has been released of her burdens. It will be a piece of exultation, a spirit rising to the heavens. Can you do it?"

"Of course."

"I will pay you two hundred thousand dollars, if it is satisfactory."

Fellini nodded. "Agreed."

"One million dollars if it moves me."

Fellini smiled. "That will be my pleasure."

Sammantha nodded. She reached into her bag and withdrew a small, black felt pouch. She tossed it to Fellini. Fellini caught it and turned it over in his palm. Four large D flawless diamonds tumbled into his fingers. He smiled and put the stones back in the bag.

"You must do this one yourself, Andre. No one is to know what it's for."

Fellini stood and stuffed the diamonds into his pocket. "When do you need this new masterpiece?"

"Sixty days. Preferably less."

Fellini whistled softly.

"That a problem?"

Fellini scratched his scalp nervously. Then he began to stroke his thin beard. He had heard things about this woman, things spoken only in whispers. He wondered how much of it was true, how ruthless she could be. He didn't want to find out.

"No problem. You must bring the actual canister to me when it is ready, along with any other materials you need inside. I will personally weld them in. You will need easy access to your wares, I presume?"

"I must be able to get to the contents within minutes. With no more than a hammer or a small torch, preferably less."

Fellini reached out his rough, workman's hand and waited for Sammantha to take it. He brought her hand to his lips, while looking into her eyes. "You wish to have an orgasm when you see this sculpture?"

"Do that and I'll give you three million."

"I could do that right now."

Sammantha pulled her hand away. Fellini laughed.

"At least I tried," he said.

"Many men have tried, Andre. Only one man has succeeded. You won't be the second."

CHAPTER 81
_______PP_______

Lauren Haverford parked her BMW hybrid SUV in the empty parking lot outside the facility where Trance was being held. A trail of dust flew up from her tires as she skidded to a halt on the loose gravel. Before her stood what looked to be a dilapidated warehouse, made of rusting metal that tilted slightly to the right. As she closed the door to her car, a plain clothed man emerged from inside the warehouse and meandered toward her.

"Ma'am?' he said.

"I'm having a problem with my car's transmission. I was told by Jason that you work cheap."

"We do. Please come inside, ma'am, and we can discuss the matter."

They passed through a squeaking door that was four inches thick. Once the door closed the man snapped two deadbolts in place, then punched a code into a keypad along the wall. He brought Lauren down a narrow dusty hallway which ended at a wall. Before the wall stood a fold-out card table, with two men sitting on either end, playing a lazy game of poker. These men were also dressed in plain work clothes, although Lauren could see the bulge of weapons beneath their un-tucked shirts. Lauren watched their eyes follow her as she and the first guard approached. Their hands also edged subtly toward their pistols.

"These two men will help you with your transmission, ma'am," said the guard. He walked halfway back down the hallway, then disappeared through a hidden door somewhere in the wall.

"We'll need you to put all your belongings on the table, ma'am," said one of the card players.

Lauren pulled a small wallet from the back pocket of her jeans and placed it on the table. She dropped her keys beside it and said, "That's it."

"Jewelry, too, ma'am."

Lauren removed her Timex Triathlon watch. She took off two rings and set them on the table.

"Earrings, too, ma'am."

Lauren sighed and removed a pair of thin gold loop earrings.

The man placed everything in a plastic box and knocked behind him. A heavy door opened and he passed the box inside. Then the man stood and passed a wand slowly along Lauren's entire frame. Half a minute later the door opened again. The two guards picked up the card table, moved it to the side, then ushered Lauren through.

The area inside looked like the entrance to a courthouse. Armed guards were standing on either side of a metal detector that looked more like an oversized, tubular MRI machine.

A guard said, "Please walk through this, ma'am. Slowly. We may ask you to stop in the middle." As Lauren began to walk through she heard, "Stop, please." Then, "Okay." When Lauren had passed through, the man said, "You can retrieve your possessions on the way out, ma'am."

Lauren smiled. She had wanted to carry Trance's communication chip inside her watch. Ben Johnson had insisted on another way, a far less ladylike way. Now she saw why.

Lauren was introduced to a woman wearing a white lab coat, who led her to a small room.

"I will be conducting your cavity search," the woman said.

"Excuse me? A cavity search? Who do you think you are? Kidnapping my…my…friend and holding him here against his will. Then stripping me naked…"

"This is high security facility, ma'am. I know nothing about your friend, only that it is my job to make sure that you don't pass anything harmful to our detainees."

The woman pointed to a small area behind an off-white curtain. "Behind there, ma'am. Please take off your clothes."

Lauren stripped and threw her clothes onto a chair. She walked back around the curtain, drew a breath and spread out her arms and legs. "Search away."

Trance was being held inside a small, Spartan cell. Through its square glass window, Lauren could see a cot along one wall. In a dark corner of the room, there was a white porcelain toilet, without a seat. Beside it stood a cracked porcelain sink. There was also a small desk and chair, with a notebook computer sitting closed upon the desk. Trance was on the floor doing pushups.

The door opened with a pneumatic hiss and Lauren stood in the doorway, looking at Trance as he jumped up and grinned.

"Hey! Like my new crib?"

Lauren ran to Trance and hugged him. Trance wrapped his arms around her and lifted her into the air.

After a long moment, Lauren said, "What is this place, really?"

"You mean other than a place for birthday parties? It's an op center, and a little detention facility. Counter terrorism, that sort of stuff."

Lauren looked up at the ceiling and saw two cameras with fluorescent green lights colored on. "Have they hurt you?"

Trance laughed. "I don't think so."

Lauren took Trance's face into her hands. "I missed you." Lauren appeared to hiccup. She let go of Trance, bent over and coughed. After a moment she stood back up. "Sorry. Where were we? Oh, yes..."

Lauren drew Trance toward her and began to kiss him deeply. She opened her mouth and he opened his. Their tongues intertwined. A small balloon passed from Lauren's throat into Trance's mouth. Trance swallowed it as quickly as he received the highly sophisticated flash drive, one detectable only by methods beyond this facility's capability.

When Trance pulled away he said, "What did you eat, onion pizza?"

Lauren poked him in the ribs. She leaned against Trance's ear and whispered, "Miller said you should read *The Art of War.*"

The Art of War, a fitting work to use with a simple book cipher. Miller was well aware of Trance's gift of memory. Trance could recite Sun Tzu's masterpiece word for word. His mind could see each page as if it were on a screen. That was all he would need to decipher Miller's message.

Lauren was allowed to remain with Trance for one hour, timed to the second. With cameras recording their every word and action, most of the time was spent with small talk—how Lauren's parents were doing, how Stick and Marlee could not compromise on a home, how they were still bunking in a rented beach home on the shore of Scituate, how Lauren was doing at the bank, and what Trance's and Lauren's other friends were up to.

"Does Judy know I'm okay?" asked Trance. He'd had no time to tell his personal assistant and unofficial law partner that he'd be AWOL for three months.

"Yes. I told her I'd continue her salary while you were gone. She told me she already signs her checks."

Trance laughed. "That woman would work for peanuts if I let her. When I rescued her from that big Boston law firm she swore eternal allegiance to me for pulling her out of the grind."

"She adores you."

"It's my animal charm."

"I don't mean that way, stupid. I mean she is a loyal employee and a good friend."

"What's that supposed to mean?"

"I like her. That's all. I'd like to be able to confide in her. Outside of Marlee, I have no one I can tell. Not even my parents."

"What are you going to tell her, that I've been detained by the president for treasonous activities?"

"You've got a point."

Trance thought for a moment. "Tell her she can take on any legal case she wants. She's a better lawyer than I am anyway."

"And far more reliable."

"That, too."

When the buzzer sounded Lauren kissed Trance one final time and left the room, feeling better.

CHAPTER **82**
____________PP____________

The president was waiting by the West Wing gate of the White House when Sammantha Starodubov and Omar Karkhabi arrived for their scheduled evening appointment. The president watched with a careful eye as the two were frisked, hand-wanded and then passed through the phalanx of other sensing devices. Omar carried a shiny suitcase in one hand. He offered it to one of the guards, who ran it through a series of inspections.

When they finally passed through the gate, Omar handed the suitcase to the president.

"This is for you," he said.

The president lifted the suitcase to eye height and examined it carefully. It looked like a Halliburton Zeroller, complete with two polyurethane wheels and a pull out handle.

"Nice," he said.

"The latest style," said Omar.

The president and Omar embraced briefly. Then the president kissed the back of Sammantha's hand. "It is so good to see you again," he said.

They entered the West Wing and went through a final search before winding their way to the corner Oval Office. The president threw off his suit coat and motioned for Omar to do the same. Omar hesitated.

"Omar, we're friends. Make yourself comfortable. Can I offer you a cigar?"

Omar politely refused. The president reached into a humidor, grabbed a fresh Cohiba and thrust it into his mouth. He caught Sammantha's hard stare and his shoulders slumped.

"Those aren't good for you," she said.

"It's only my second one—"

"No."

"But you smoke."

"Not anymore, I don't." Sammantha took the cigar out of the president's mouth and kissed him on the cheek. "I love you, dear. Please stay healthy for me."

The president pouted briefly, then smiled. He motioned toward the door that led into the president's study. "Let's sit in here. I'll get us something from the fridge." The president turned to Omar. "If I recall, you like red pepper hummus with Ritz crackers, right?"

Omar smiled shyly. "That is most thoughtful of you."

"No problem. I just ordered it from the kitchen." The president turned to Sammantha. "And for you, Caspian Sea Beluga caviar and Dom Pérignon. I'd join you, but I don't have much taste for alcohol these days. You like Poland Spring water, don't you, Omar?"

You can't drink and you know it, thought Sammantha. *Good for you. Good for me.*

The president motioned for his guests to sit at a small coffee table. It was already arranged with three settings of china. He set down the suitcase, walked into the kitchen and returned with a split bottle of Dom and two plastic bottles of Poland Spring water. He made a second trip and came back with a tray sporting various finger foods. Once they were seated he pulled a small device out of his shirt pocket and flipped a switch.

"This will distort our conversation, just in case someone is listening without my knowledge," he said softly. The president also turned on a table radio, adjusted the volume, then said, "Now, tell me about this wonderful suitcase."

Omar took hold of the case and opened it easily. "The Russians have two models of this case. One of them is twenty-four by sixteen by eight inches. This one is a bit larger, so it can carry a…" Omar lowered his voice. "…bigger payload of U-233, Plutonium. This is an actual case. As you see, the Russians took your basic Halliburton suitcase and made a few simple modifications inside."

Omar pointed out where the nuclear core, the detonator and the battery would go. "The original device had just a kiloton of yield. Today's devices can be many times that size."

"Like Hiroshima?"

"Yes. Like Hiroshima or even more."

"Good. That will make a very powerful statement."

"What, exactly, do you plan to do with this case?" asked Omar.

The president smiled. "We're going to put a model bomb inside this case. During my State of the Union Address, President Ogarkov and I will symbolically remove the detonator from the device, just as other world leaders join us on stage."

Omar looked from the president to Sammantha and back. This man had no idea what was coming. He was a willing accomplice to the destruction of Washington, along with most of the world's major leaders. Allah be praised.

Omar said, "That will certainly create a lasting impression," Mr. President.

"I thought so. I have commitments from the leaders of China, France, Britain, Germany, India and Japan to join us on stage. We will then make a pledge to the world."

"No Israel or North Korea? No Iran? And what about the other nuclear nations?"

"Israel will work with us on this. It will be a complicated arrangement, with other treaties involved. Something too complex to work out by early February. Iran…North Korea…and a few other rogue nations will have to be cajoled by public opinion and severe sanctions. Then, of course we must finalize the inspection parameters."

"Aren't you walking a political tightrope?"

The president shook his head. "I already have the support from the world's great powers. The others will fall in line. Imagine the political power of the world's major leaders all on stage together, hands united, pledging to rid the world of the threat of nuclear extinction. It will be glorious."

"Something the world will never see again," said Omar softly. "A vision for the ages."

Omar locked eyes with Sammantha. She sat quietly, smiling demurely as the two men talked.

The president said, "I will need your help over the next two months, with some of the nuclear technicalities. I want you to teach me everything, everything I'll need to know."

"Don't you have men on your staff that can do that? I—"

"This is a secret, even from them. Nothing can be kept hidden in Washington, everybody knows that. This whole endeavor succeeds or fails on its shock value. I have been given assurances from the other world leaders that this will remain a secret until that fateful day. We all know what's at stake."

Sammantha raised her glass of champagne. "To that fateful day, when the world will change forever."

The president and Omar clinked their plastic bottles along with Sammantha's glass in a toast for the ages.

The president stood up and placed a friendly arm around Omar's shoulders. "There will be rumors about your visit. That's why I had you here at night. The press will catch on; they always do. If someone asks you, tell them that you're a goodwill ambassador for your country, that you were sent by Talid and your father to discuss how we might settle our political differences peacefully. Say nothing more. At the appropriate time, I will make it known how helpful you have been in our quest for peace."

"Thank you, Mr. President. You are most kind."

The president guided Omar to the door, where Stone, his ever-present body man was waiting to escort him back through the outside gates. Once Omar was gone, the president turned to Sammantha. Soon they were falling to the floor, in a presidential sex act that did not involve infidelity or a cigar.

CHAPTER **83**

________________PP________________

Jack Trance waited until well after midnight before he climbed out of his cot and took his notebook computer to the one spot of his room that the cameras couldn't see—the toilet. Jesse Tompkin had fought to allow Trance use of the bathroom without eyes. He just hadn't told them why Trance needed privacy.

"What's he going to do, kill himself on the throne? If he does that it's his problem, not ours."

Once his computer was on, Trance regurgitated the coated balloon holding the graphene-based flash drive that Lauren had slipped to him during their kiss. He carefully untied the balloon and put it into his pocket. He'd need it again to pass the drive back to Lauren the next time she came.

It took more than an hour for Trance to deciphered Miller's full message. The CIA director had been busy. He still had nothing to help them take Copley into custody. Nor, did he know how to find Jock Tilson, assuming the real president was still alive. The message ended with:

Checked on BC. Verified. Twin. No leads on C. SS is enigma. Sketchy hist. BC home staked. Interviews. No leads. Eyes everywhere. Life sucks. How r u?

Brandon Copley was Tilson's twin. He was now in the White House. Sammantha Starodubov may be the key to the puzzle, but her life was a mystery. Copley's New York home was being watched and relevant people were being interviewed. There were no leads. Miller was being watched. He had to be careful, or he might vanish like Trance. Yeah. Life really did suck.

Trance typed a note using the same cipher and placed the flash drive back into the balloon. He opened the bottom of his computer and hid the package inside. He's swallow it when the time came.

CHAPTER 84
______________PP______________

Sammantha Starodubov made her way back along Via Montenapoleone, walking slowly, taking her time to look in every window along Italy's fashion row. She barely glanced at the elegant designs; nothing moved her. She was too focused on seeing what Andre Fellini had created. Was this to be her crowning moment, when she would see herself in full triumph over her demons, when she would throw off the crusted chains that had hung around her neck since that day? The day. The day when America had destroyed her life. Was today the day when she would break those chains and soar to freedom?

It took Sammantha three hours to make the ten minute walk to Fellini's loft. When she reached his door her heart began to beat heavily in her chest. She could feel the blood pumping through her veins, pulsing with dread and hope. She tried to steady her breathing, but it was hard. Very hard.

Why was this important to her? It was just a goddamned statue. Sure, it was her gift to Brandon Copley. Sure, it was to carry the cylinder that would lay waste to Washington D.C. and render it uninhabitable for generations. But that wasn't it, was it? No. She'd made a huge mistake, a classic mistake. She'd fallen in love with the man she was going to kill. She'd fallen in love with Copley, and it *mattered* what he thought of this statue. Would he see her for what she was? Or for what she could become, what she might have been? And then…and then…how could she give it to him, knowing that this was what would kill him, what would kill them both?

It would kill them *both*. This gave her comfort. This would end it all. She would finish her life in triumph, having avenged her parents, having avenged her life.

Sammantha rang the bell and it buzzed. She opened the door and climbed the steep stairs slowly, as if she were marching toward her execution. Andre met her in the loft and led her to the center of the room. There, in the middle of the great expanse, it stood. It was covered by a soft, cream colored tarp, but she could already feel its power.

"Are you ready?" said Andre.

Sammantha tried again to control her breathing. She wanted to pull her heart from her throat, squeeze it quiet and stuff it back into her chest. All she could do was nod and fight for air.

Andre pulled the canvas off the statue with an exaggerated flourish. He stood back, as if to say *ta dah.*

Sammantha stared upon her likeness with unfocused eyes. This was it. Somehow, Andre had pulled her lost spirit from the ether and put it into this statue. The woman stood naked, her eyes stretched to the heavens while her arms cradled…while her arms cradled….a baby. The statue wasn't a dull bronze, or even the golden bronze that was now popular. Andre had taken it upon himself to plate this entire statue in gold. The effect was radiant.

Sammantha sank to the floor and began to weep. "How could you," she mumbled.

Andre sat beside her and began to stroke her hair. "I looked deep into your pain and I found the one thing that would set you free."

When Sammantha looked into Andre's eyes, he could see through her tears that he'd been right.

"You have earned your fee," she said softly. Sammantha reached into the outer pocket of the backpack and removed a pouch with more diamonds. "No orgasm, but something better. A revelation, in fact. This is worth all of three million dollars."

How could he do this? How could he do this to her? She had asked for a woman in triumph and she got this? A mother? She had wanted this statue to help set her free, to be a tribute to her crushing those demons that had tortured her every moment. Every waking moment. Every hour of her unsettled sleep. And she got this? A baby? She had never thought of this herself. So, how could he have known?

"Do you have the materials?" said Andre.

Sammantha felt like her brain was partially frozen, dragging behind her at half speed. A baby? She reached into her backpack and struggled to remove the canister that held the two separated masses of Plutonium. She had lost her strength.

"In here," she said, and reached into her bag.

Andre hefted the canister and carried it toward the statue. "It goes in here," he said.

The statue was resting on a hollow metal platform with legs about three feet high. Andre slid himself under the statue and tried to place the canister up inside.

"A little help, here," he said with a grunting voice. "This is very heavy."

Sammantha felt her focus return. She inched herself beside Andre and helped him nestle the Plutonium into its specially designed, cushioned compartment.

When everything was safely in place, Sammantha walked to a corner of the loft. She sat upon the floor. She began to rock, back and forth without looking in the direction of the statue. But she could feel that statue, as if its eyes were upon her, seeing everything as she rocked the baby inside her.

In the next hour Andre packed the canister with special padding and heat resistant insulation. He welded the false bottom with twelve carat gold. He ground it smooth. When Andre was finished, he walked over to Sammantha and helped her up from the floor. Sammantha couldn't look at him. She reached into her jeans pocket, withdrew a sheet of paper and put it in his hands.

"Send it here. In the usual way."

Then Sammantha left for America.

CHAPTER **85**
PP

Lauren Haverford used Trance's National Arts Club key to open the gate to Gramercy Park. She walked around the small, private gassy area in the middle of New York City, finally choosing a place against a small tree across from the old Copley brownstone. She put down her L.L. Bean day pack and pulled out a book. She remained there for several hours, leaning against the pack and the tree, reading and watching. At noon she pulled a Cobb salad out of her bag and ate it with a plastic fork. No one came. By late afternoon Lauren had finished her novel, the last part completed in the dark with a reading light. She stood and stretched. Then she made her way back to Trance's suite at the Plaza.

Lauren repeated this ritual for three straight weeks. She saw no one enter the building, except for the old man who came at nine and left at five. She was sure that she spied a team of agents watching the building with her. The faces changed each day, but the locations didn't. Each morning there was someone else watching the mansion, waiting for the people who never came.

It was nearly Christmas. The air was growing progressively colder and the days had grown short, too short. Lauren felt helpless just sitting in the park, like a butterfly in a hail storm. The private detectives she had hired to find more details had found little of value.

Martha Tilson had worked as a summer maid at Copley's Bar Harbor estate. She'd been sixteen. The president's new friends, Omar Karkhabi and Sammantha Starodubov were an unlikely pair. One was a surgeon from Russia with a sketchy past. The other had been a brilliant student, the son of a leader in a Muslim country that was unfriendly to America. What were they planning? Something had to be done, and soon.

The Copley estate had yet to be probated. A corporation based in the Isle of Man was paying the mortgage. It had also paid Copley's other bills in cash. In her search, Lauren had found a curious tie between Copley and the Hopewell side of Trance's family. There had been a number of business dealings, joint ventures between the two families in the late nineteenth and early twentieth centuries. The Hopewells had purchased all the partnership interests over the years, but Copley still received an interest income on one of the notes. Among the papers, she had also found a curious photograph, of Trance's mother holding a baby. Upon the back of the photo, in a flowing script, was written, *Mama Holding Brandon Copley.*

One day, Lauren finally rose from her frosty seat in Gramercy Park and walked to the front of Copley's home. She could see the name *Copley* chiseled into the stone, like on a library or a government building. She rang the bell. No one came, so she rang it again. She began to pound on the door's brass knocker, knowing that the old man was there, willing him to appear.

After twenty minutes the man with the soft white hair poked his head through a chained door.

"May I help you?" Clyde said.

Lauren spoke the words she had rehearsed.

"Yes. I represent the Hopewell family. I need to speak with you."

"Mr. Copley is dead, miss."

"We know that. But there are things we can do to help with the estate."

"You'll need to talk with his lawyers, miss."

"I've heard he was intestate."

"What?"

"He had no will."

"That doesn't mean he had no lawyers, miss."

"My name's Lauren."

Then, inexplicably, Clyde opened the door and motioned for Lauren to step inside.

The entry hall was dark and musty, but the home reeked of old money. It reminded Lauren of the interior of an antique Rolls Royce Silver Shadow. The home was once the picture of opulent elegance, but it had faded into drabness. The expensive carpets were heavily worn. The intricately carved wooden walls needed a good sanding and new coat of stain. There was a wooden staircase that went upstairs and continued down to a basement. There was also an elevator with a tarnished brass door.

"And your name is?" said Lauren, holding out her hand.

"Clyde."

"Nice to meet you, Clyde."

Clyde looked to the floor. "I'm not supposed to let anybody inside this place. But…"

"You miss him, don't you?"

"I raised him."

"You identified the body, didn't you?"

Clyde nodded.

"It wasn't Brandon Copley, was it?"

Clyde looked at Lauren. She was sure she saw a rogue spurt of tears began to well in Clyde's eyes before he looked away. "I can't say, he mumbled."

"Well, I know it wasn't, and so do you."

At that moment they heard the creak of a door below them. A moment later, a bundled figure came shuffling up the stairs. Clyde frantically motioned for Lauren to leave, but it was too late. Sammantha Starodubov emerged from the basement carrying two cloth grocery bags.

"May I help you?" she said.

Lauren was stunned. Her brain stuttered. She blurted the first thing that came to her mind, a lie. A stupid defensive lie. "I…was lost and was asking for directions."

Sammantha looked at Lauren and then at Clyde. She pondered what she should do. If she took this woman now, she would have to do something with Clyde. He might go along with misidentifying Copley, after Copley had left written instructions asking him to do so, but he wouldn't stand for murder. Sammantha knew the house was being watched. This must be some sort of ploy.

"Where are you going?" said Sammantha.

"I'm staying at the Plaza."

"Really? You're a bit far away, aren't you?"

"I went out for a walk. I have a key to the park, from the National Arts Club. I came here to eat my lunch."

"In New York we use restaurants for that."

Lauren smiled. "Not me. I have a very peculiar diet. Allergies, you know."

"What is your name?"

Lauren suddenly felt woozy. She hadn't planned on this, not a direct attack. Then she remembered her plan.

"I'm not supposed to tell anyone but Clyde. My name is Lauren Haverford. I am representing the Hopewell family." She reached into her knapsack and withdrew a contract. "The Hopewell interests thought that Mr. Copley's heirs might want the note paid off." Lauren reached back into her knapsack and withdrew a picture. "They also thought Clyde might like this photo."

Lauren handed the photo to Sammantha. It was a picture of Trance's parents standing in front of the Copley mansion. Trance's mother was smiling, while holding the young Brandon Copley in her arms. He couldn't have been more than a year old. He was wearing a blue snow suit with a red knit cap.

Sammantha looked at the fading photo. Her face softened into an almost motherly glow. "Is that Brandon?"

Lauren nodded. "It is."

"He has so few pictures, only portraits. This is adorable."

Lauren stretched out her hand to shake. "Glad you like it. And your name is?"

Sammantha's eyes seemed to swim and she briefly looked flustered. "Smith," she said. "Sandra Smith."

This Sandra didn't look like any of Jazzman's photos—even the one identified by her neighbor in Washington. This woman was a pro, a true pro. But she had finally made a mistake.

Bingo, thought Lauren. She smiled. "Nice to meet you, Ms. Smith. Can you tell me how to get back to my hotel?"

Sammantha hesitated at first, wondering if she should kill Lauren before she caused trouble. She thought better of it. There were too many witnesses, so she told Lauren where to go.

When Lauren reached Park Avenue she took out her phone and dialed Stick Granger's number. He answered on the second ring.

He said, "You have reached the Great Protector. I don't talk directly to people anymore, due to my new, exalted position of general. Leave your name and number at the beep and I will have one of my staff get back to you within a week or two—"

"Stick, it's Lauren."

"I know that."

"I need protection, and I might need it fast."

"Something happen at the mansion that I don't know about?"

"You know about the mansion?"

Stick laughed. "JT has me watching you 24/7."

"The men in the park?"

"Ours."

"Where are the government's men? Surely they are watching the place, too?"

"Oh, yeah. They are far more sophisticated than we are. They drive around the block in cars and sit with telescopes in far away buildings. Turn around."

Lauren turned around and a man behind her waved.

"Is that you?"

"Uh-huh."

"Don't you voyeurs have anything better to do than follow single women around New York?"

"Nope."

"I adore you."

"And we adore you, sweetheart."

"Thank you, Stick."

"Have a pleasant day."

"Come see me at the hotel. I have some news."

"Will do."

CHAPTER **86**
PP

"So, where are we going?" asked the president. He folded his coat and ducked into the fortified presidential limousine known as *Cadillac One,* but affectionately called *The Beast.*

"I have a Christmas present for you," said Sammantha.

"It's Christmas? I never would have known. Is that what all those silly decorations around the White House are about?" The president laughed with the loud, hearty *guffaw* that Sammantha had grown to love. She cuddled up against him and he pulled her closer.

"I had something made, just for you. I'm bringing you to see it."

"And where is this mystery masterpiece?"

"At the Corcoran."

"We put the motorcade together to go to the Corcoran? We could have walked."

"We'll need the car."

"The Corcoran," said the president to his driver. The motorcade rolled the short distance to Seventeenth Street.

They entered through the front door, where the museum's director greeted them profusely. "Omigod. No one told us you were coming. If I had advanced—"

The president shook the director's hand and interrupted, "Even *I* didn't know I was coming here." The president began to motion toward Sammantha, but a shiny, gold-leaf sculpture caught his eye.

"Wow. Look at that," he said.

The director beamed. "Isn't it extraordinary? It came in last week, on short-term loan by its owner. It's a Fellini."

"The film maker?"

The director hid a smile. "No. He is a famous sculptor. Perhaps the best alive, when he does things himself. But like Bernini and Rubens, he has a group of technicians that complete most of his designs. This, I am told, was created by him personally. Do you like it?"

The president was not one to feel awe in front of art. An actor, maybe, but a painting or a sculpture? Hardly. But this…this one tugged at his heart. This one spoke to him, in a voice he had never heard before.

"This…is extraordinary."

"I am told that it was commissioned by a woman for the man she loves."

"Lucky man," said the president.

"Lucky woman," said Sammantha. "Merry Christmas."

The president looked from the sculpture to Sammantha and back. He looked at the woman's golden face, then to the baby in her arms. There were tears in the statue's eyes, tears of joy as she held the child to her breast. The president felt tears begin to form in his own eyes. He saw a flash in his mind's eye. It was a fleeting image of a man. It sparked briefly, like lightning in the dark, then died. He saw a man lying drunk on the floor with a woman kneeling above him. The woman of this sculpture. Was this that woman? Who was the man? Certainly not him.

The president stretched out his arms and allowed Sammantha to cuddle within them. Cameras began flashing. The president tried to hide his face. Big mistake; the tabloids were going to have a field day.

"This is…I am speechless," he said.

"So was I when I first saw it," said Sammantha.

"The baby? What is the baby?"

Sammantha turned away. How could she face him now? She had known for a month about the baby, the one that was growing inside her. There had been no baby when Fellini had created the sculpture. There had been no intention to have one, only visions of death and revenge. So, why had she stopped taking the pill? Had it somehow been the statue, calling to her like a Siren, telling her there was more to life than death?

"Sammantha. Are you all right?" The president shook her gently.

Sammantha smiled. "Never better."

"What do we do with this thing?"

"We bring it with us. Movers will put it in the trunk of the limo and ride with us to the White House."

"We can't just bring this to the White House, Sammantha."

"Why not? It can be moved with a dolly. Besides, if a president can do a flyby of New York City in Air Force One, you can certainly get a statue past security. After all, you are the president, aren't you?"

The president cocked his head. "I suppose I am. Wherever are we going to put it?"

"In your bedroom, of course."

CHAPTER **87**
PP

After Lauren closed the door to Trance's suite at the Plaza and waited in place for Stick to arrive. Within thirty seconds a knock came on the door.

"Who is it?" said Lauren playfully.

"It's the Great Protector."

Lauren opened the door and Stick stepped inside. When Stick saw the panoramic view of Central Park before him, he whistled.

"Trance told me he bought a crib here. Called it an apartment. He never said it looked like this."

"Nice, hey?"

"Money has its privileges. You think I could afford a place like this?"

"Not on two or three million a year, you can't. You have any other assets, Stick?"

"Just an island and a plane. Trance offered me a couple hundred million once, after that Austrian thing. Couldn't find any use for the money, so I turned him down."

"Having second thoughts?"

"Nah."

"Me neither. I wouldn't want his life for anything."

"But you'd marry him?"

"In a heartbeat. But that's different. I won't have the same pressure."

"Kinda sucks, being the world's caretaker."

"Spoken like a true, sensitive gentleman."

"I just tell it like it is, sister." Stick looked into Lauren's eyes. "Tell me what happened."

"I saw her."

"Who?"

"Sandra Smith."

"How do you know it was her?"

"She gave me the name."

"No frigging way."

"I think I startled her by being there. She certainly startled me. I gave her a picture of Brandon. You should have seen her face light up. When I asked her name she didn't want to say Sammantha Starodubov, so she said the first name that came to her mind."

"Big mistake. Big problem."

"Yeah. The president's girlfriend is also his wife's killer."

"Wait 'til Jack hears this one."

"Oh," said Lauren. "He's sort of suspected this all along. Couldn't get proof with the president running interference though. Her disguise was so good even Jazzman couldn't break it down."

"We do have DNA," said Stick. "We got it from the apartment where she lived."

"Where is that now?"

Stick frowned. "Dang it. We gave it to the president's people."

"So, it's probably lost by now, by presidential order."

"Is there nothing we can do?"

"Short of shooting the president?"

"Don't say that," said Stick.

"It might just come to that, you know," said Lauren. "There may be no other way to stop him, stop them."

"God help the man who takes that shot."

Lauren and Stick looked at each other as the words sank in.

"Oh, no," they both said. They knew the *one* man who would take that shot.

"I'm not going to tell Jack about this," said Lauren.

"Me neither."

CHAPTER 88

_______________PP_______________

Ivan Petrovski tossed back his head and gulped a double shot of vodka like he would a glass of water. He winced briefly, then gave a satisfying, "Ahhh." He set the glass down with a snapping _clink_. Then he walked out of his office, which was housed inside the Kremlin Arsenal. He hopped into the back of a waiting Mercedes limousine. "Novo-Ogaryovo," he said to the driver.

The driver headed west and then turned onto the Rublyovo-Uspenskoye highway. A short while later, on the outskirts of the city, the limo stopped in front of an impressive white residential structure. The building had tall circular columns in front, much like a southern Georgia mansion. This home had been built after a 19th century manor, for the daughter of the Communist, Malenkov. It was now home to a much simpler man, the Russian president.

"Ivan, so good of you to come see me," said Ogarkov.

Petrovski stood outside the large doors, looking up into the face of his country's leader.

"Thank you for inviting me, Mr. President."

Ogarkov smiled but said nothing. He turned away and began walking deeper into the house. Petrovski followed. Ogarkov stopped when they reached the main room of the mansion. The chamber was expansive, built for entertaining, with high ceilings and elongated airy windows, giving it the feel of open space.

"Sit down," Ogarkov said. "By the fire."

When the two men had settled into a pair of overstuffed chairs, Ogarkov said, "I understand that you have been meeting with Talid."

"Who told you that?"

"If I told you, you would have them killed. Wouldn't you? I am not a murderer. Are you?"

"We have advised Talid's country for years, old friend."

"We _used_ to advise his country. We stopped advising Talid when he became a terrorist, or don't you remember?"

"I…" Petrovski had to think fast. "I was told that he wanted to have you killed. I went there to warn him off."

"Really?"

Petrovski nodded. "I did."

Ogarkov stared at his political partner, also his biggest adversary. "Since I am still alive, I suppose I must thank you."

Petrovski jutted his chin. "You are welcome."

"See him again and I'll have you entombed beneath Cathedral Square."

Petrovski wasn't sure what this meant. Did Ogarkov mean the torture tower? Or did he mean the Tainitskaya Tower, where Petrovski was holding Tilson?

Petrovski stiffened. "You are my country's leader. If given the choice again, I would still choose to save your life."

Ogarkov laughed heartily. "Why is it that we Russians can never trust each other?"

"You can trust me, Mr. President."

"About as far as I can throw you. Now, go. Leave me to think. I must prepare for America."

Petrovski shook his head. "I urge you to remain at home. No good can come of this foolish pact you're concocting with the fake American president. Someday they will discover that he is an imposter, and you will look like a stupid peasant."

"I think not."

"If I were you, I would expose the lie."

"And risk forfeiting a global agreement on nuclear disarmament? Never."

"You can do the same thing with the real president."

"After we've held him here for months? I think not."

"Then kill him. Kill him and our problems are over."

"I am not a butcher."

"You should be." Petrovski paused. Then he lowered his voice. "So, what will you do? What do *we* do?"

Ogarkov shrugged his shoulders. "We do what we always do, Ivan. We press on."

CHAPTER **89**

PP

NEW YEAR'S EVE: THE WHITE HOUSE

The reception line began to cue at 5:30 P.M. By 6:00, guests began entering one at a time, to be searched before being allowed into the large Entrance Hall. From there they were escorted by male and female marine officers, wearing *Evening dress A* uniforms, to the East Room. The male marines were wearing long-sleeved evening coats with a strip collar and a white waistcoat. This was worn over plain white shirts and sky blue pants with white web belts. Down the side of the pants was a gold stripe, within that a thin red stripe. Black dress shoes and socks and white gloves finished the dress, except for medals and chest ribbons. The women wore black pumps instead of shoes, long midnight blue skirts with minia-ture medals and badges. The women were escorting all the men, while a man escorted each woman.

Upstairs, honored guests were gathered in the Yellow Oval Room to chat with the president before dinner. The president was wearing a simple, but finely made black tux, a slightly ruffled white shirt, a black cummerbund and a maroon silk bow tie. Beside him stood Sammantha Starodubov, wearing a cream silk Biagiotti dress that flowed like a second skin as she moved. The neck was open, revealing Sammantha's smooth, ample cleavage, along with a stunning set of three yellow teardrop diamonds. She wore her hair up in a French twist held by two ivory, diamond studded chop sticks. Teardrop dia-monds also hung loosely from her earlobes, matching the ones that sparkled across her neck.

The usual assortment of leading congressmen and senators were gathered, as was the all-but-for-gotten vice president and his wife, Alonea, stood alone along the wall. The head of the Supreme Court was resplendent in a designer tux, looking far more elegant than the president. His wife, though attrac-tive, paled beside the radiant, almost ethereal Sammantha.

There were business leaders and key lobbyists already working the room. They were nearly as busy as the president, who spoke with each person in the room as if they were boyhood friends.

"Thank you all for coming," said the president after forty minutes of concentrated socializing. "As most of you know, this has been a difficult year."

There was a scattering of unsure laughter. The guests all glanced to each other, wondering how to react.

"This year I had the misfortune of losing a wife to assassination. I managed to get myself kid-napped, where I was drugged, concussed and burned. All-in-all, I would say this is one year I will be glad to put behind me. There are some things I will not forget, though. My lovely wife, Kiki." The president paused for a moment of respectful silence. "And also how fragile our national safety has become. In the upcoming year, I hope to use my experience to make the world a better place. A safer place. I propose a toast."

The president held up a champagne glass filled with ginger ale. "To this great country and it's even greater citizens."

"Hear! Hear!"

"I believe we have a reception to attend before dinner, and a party to bring in the New Year. Let us all go downstairs and enjoy ourselves."

The president and Sammantha walked arm-in-arm down the grand staircase and stood at the bot-tom to greet each honored guest. After a short handshake, each person went with their military escort to the State Dining Room, where they gathered with tonight's other, less important attendees. One hundred and forty people were taken to their assigned seats, while the other one hundred guests remained in the East Room, enjoying an opulent buffet and an open bar.

Once everyone was seated and wine was served, the president stood from his place at the head table. Glasses clinked and the president waited patiently for all talk to stop.

"Thank you for coming to the first annual Jock Tilson New Year's Eve celebration. I hope you all have a good time. Before we begin, I want to go over my house rules. After careful consideration, I decided that this should be a time for us to come together and celebrate our lives in this great country.

"When you entered this house you were asked to surrender your cell phones and PDAs. I understand that this may be a hardship for some of you. Never say that this president isn't sympathetic to your text and tweet addictions. I have established a communication zone in the Green Room. This is connected to the East Room, where our party will officially commence after dinner.

"So, if any of you have managed to slip a phone or a PDA past our security, please surrender it now, so it can be safely moved to the Green Room. It will be tagged with your name and kept under guard."

The president waited while seven more devices were recovered.

"So much for White House security," he said, to a chorus of laughter. If he'd known the folly of those words, he wouldn't have laughed. He'd have cried outrage.

"Now that I have your full attention…I would like to say a few words about my first full year in office." The president took a sip of water and looked around the room. *My God*, he thought. *What an enormous concentration of intellect and influence.* Here he was, standing in front of them as their supreme representative. In a way, he felt like an actor playing the role of president, not the truly elected leader of the free world. He supposed all presidents felt that way, at one time or another.

"I ran my campaign on *change*." He paused. "Don't we all?" The president paused again to allow the laughter to subside. "I spent this first year just kind of reacting. Yes, I know the polls have my approval rating at a sixty-year presidential high. To tell you the truth, it took me six months after my wife's death to actually care again. After the kidnapping, I tried not to overreact, choosing instead to follow a steady equilibrium.

"Now that this first year is over, I plan to fulfill my promise of change. Real change. Important change. A month from now I will be giving my first full-year State of the Union Address. In that address I plan to outline a bold initiative for change. I'm talking *bold*. Some of you may think I've gone too far. Some of you might even feel some heat…" Again, the president waited for laughter to subside. Why did they laugh when he was talking about changing the world? he wondered.

"I assure you. The course I will be charting this fine, new year will be seen by history as the next big step for American greatness and world peace."

The president dropped back into his chair and absorbed the applause like an actor making a curtain call. He smiled, nodding to the rapt, expectant faces, looking like a king acknowledging his faithful subjects. Yes, he had *arrived.*

As dinner turned to coffee and desert, the military escorts began leading guests from the State Dining Room to the East Room. They walked arm in arm down the expansive, red carpeted Cross Hall, with its two great sparkling chandeliers throwing light like confetti. Inside the East Room, the rugs had been removed to reveal its smooth, polished wooden floors. A bandstand was set up beneath one of the room's chandeliers. Lights from the bandstand shot up into the crystal, making it act like a disco ball, sending greens and blues splashing around the room.

The music was in full-swing, as the first of three bands played its opening set. Along one wall, bartenders wearing white tuxedos poured drinks by the dozen. The popping of champagne corks sounded like firecrackers. A dance floor had been formed in front of the band and guests were already gyrating like it was the Roaring Twenties.

At eleven o'clock, Sammantha pulled the president off the dance floor and leaned against his ear. She squeezed his elbow, his hypnotic trigger point.

"It is time for your drink now," she said.

The president's smiling face drooped. His eyes grew suddenly slack and dull. He nodded like an emotionless drone. Sammantha fulfilled his programming by handing him a glass of champagne.

"To America," she said.

Brandon Copley lifted the glass to his lips, his eyes looking vacantly across the room. He gulped the champagne like Gatorade after a long summer run. By midnight, the president was leaning against Sammantha for support while he babbled non-stop, ordering drink after drink.

As a set of video panels showed the ball beginning to fall in Times Square, Sammantha motioned for Omar Karkhabi to take hold of Copley's other arm.

"Let's get him to the Southwest Suite," she said.

Sammantha and Omar had little trouble getting the president past his marine protection detail. Omar had been a private guest on numerous occasions. The president had informed the guards personally that Omar was helping the White House craft a new Middle East policy. The guards were well acquainted with Sammantha. They had heard her screams of sexual ecstasy, along with those of the president, as it had filtered through the bedroom door with increasing regularity.

The marine guards stepped aside as Sammantha and Omar half carried the president up to the second floor of the Executive Residence.

As they came up the stairs, one of the guards said, "Would you like some help, Mr. President?"

The president looked at the guard with glazed eyes and murmured, "Sure. Get me a drink."

Sammantha smiled forlornly. "Our resident teetotaler decided to tie one on tonight. We'll stay with him and get him into bed. You'll stay here though, won't you?"

"Of course, ma'am."

"Good. Thank you, soldier."

Sammantha and Omar half dragged, half carried Copley into the master suite. They lifted him onto his bed and removed his tuxedo and shoes. Within moments, the president was lying on his side, snoring like a Maine logger's chain saw.

Sammantha shook the president and he didn't stir. She turned to Omar and whispered, "Are you ready?"

Omar nodded. He walked to the president's walk-in closet and retrieved the Halliburton case.

Sammantha took a Swiss Army knife off of the president's night stand and walked over to the statue. She flipped open the knife's long, thin nail file with its pointed tip. She pushed the nail file in through the statue's nose and prodded for a tiny hole inside. Fellini had done much better than a torch or sledge hammer. The man was a genius. Sammantha heard a muted *clank* at the statue's feet, as a powerful spring-loaded device pushed out a piece of the statue's brass, gold-plated bottom. The statue tilted, but did not fall. They waited for a reaction from the marine guard. There was none.

Omar and Sammantha tilted the wobbling statue onto its back, with Sammantha's smooth exultant face looking upward in full frontal splendor. On the bottom of the statue, a half-inch-thick plate had popped slightly outward. They peeled back the plate, just enough to press four release levers. This allowed the entire bottom to be removed as one unit.

Omar reached into the hollow bottom and withdrew the plutonium canister. He held it to the light like sacramental bread and murmured a short prayer. He unclipped the circuit board from inside the statue, along with the rest of the bomb. When the pieces were removed, Omar turned his attention to the warhead.

Sammantha busied herself resetting the bottom of the statue, until it appeared again as one single shape. As the bottom regained its smooth surface, Sammantha made a mental note to thank Fellini for his brilliant creation, sometime before she died.

Omar fitted the canister into the bomb's case and placed the circuit board into its slot. He connected the circuit board to a notebook computer and ran a quick diagnostic of the device.

"It is working," he said.

"Good. Help me get this statue back into place."

Sammantha and Omar struggled to lift the large, heavy statue. After several tense, teetering moments, the woman snapped back into the upright position. Sammantha drew in a long, thankful breath, wiped a slick of sweat off her brow and said, "Let me know when you're done."

Sammantha shuffled to the president and sat down beside him on the bed. "I'll stay with him," she murmured, while stroking his hair.

Less than an hour later the bomb was armed. Its timer had been set to explode at 9:45 as a crescendo to the president's speech, just as he and the Russian president would mount the stage together. Omar closed the device and set a code to keep anyone from searching inside. When he was done, he went over to Sammantha by the bed.

Omar said, "Are you sure he will not want to look inside the suitcase?"

"No. His programming is too strong."

"No one will check it during the three weeks it is here?"

"The president has informed his staff that it holds documents for his eyes only. It is off limits."

"And the Secret Service? They will let him take it to the Capitol?"

Sammantha smiled. "You think we haven't thought this through? The protocol has been set. It will be chained to his wrist. His men will not ask to see what's inside. If they do, the president will inform them that he knows about their whores, then give them a choice."

"I'm sorry?"

Sammantha laughed. "The weakness of any young man is inside his pants. Even a good marine can be seduced by a beautiful woman, particularly if he thinks he's picked her up in a bar. Talid sent members of his harem to ensnare the president's guards. Most have been compromised. You should see the photos."

Omar looked at Sammantha in a way he might regard a holy Imam, with a mixture of adoration and fear, even awe.

"You have thought of everything."

"I have had a very long time to plan."

CHAPTER **90**

_____________PP____________

Jack Trance walked pensively along the edges of his prison cell. When he reached the door he leaned back against it. He looked around the cube that had been his home for the past ninety days—to the thin cot, the toilet with no seat and the cracked porcelain sink. He made peace with the image, because there was a good chance he would return here, or to someplace like it. Because, he'd be damned if he would allow the President of the United States to remain kidnapped, and he sure as hell wasn't going to allow some pretender to ruin his country.

As Trance was led down the long corridor, several men stopped to salute him. Each time Trance snapped off a precise response. It felt strange to salute men who had been holding him prisoner. But it wasn't their fault. Perhaps it wasn't even the president's fault. Maybe it was just the system. It was built to protect the office at all costs.

Trance had spent hundreds of hours thinking about the American government, the country's people, and his own place within it. Yet, he felt no closer understanding his role. He felt like a ship in a storm, with forty foot waves rising on all sides, powerless to do anything except try to steer into the wind, to steer the course. But what was his course?

Trance had been forced to accept the burdens his heritage had placed upon him—raised half West and half East, a conflict of cultures and religion that never let him feel like he fully belonged in either world. The money, the traditions, the training. The expectation of a nation…no…the world, that he be there when needed.

There was a part of him, a big part, which had enjoyed his stay in that tiny cell, where all he need do was exist. It had been like a vacation, a chance to restore some semblance of balance in his life, to renew his energy and his focus. Despite his inevitable clash with the president, and his impending battle with the full weight of the Oval Office, he felt a strange sense of anticipation, like he had been reborn and was starting fresh. Another year was beginning.

Since his incarceration, the weather had changed from New England's warm fall sunshine to the raw cold of late December. As Trance emerged from the warehouse, he was met with the full force of a Nor'easter. Snow was blowing sideways against the building. Eight foot drifts had piled up against the outer walls. Trance still wore his prison fatigues, as ordered by the president. He'd been given a final warning and sent back into the world wearing nothing but thin gray cotton with fat white stripes. He came out alone, as alone he would be for the rest of his life, if he screwed up again.

Trance braced himself against the storm. The snow hit hard against his skin, almost blinding him with a pummel of icy crystals. Lauren was waiting across the parking lot in Trance's repaired Land Rover. Stick Granger, Marlee and Jesse Tompkin sat in the back seat. As Trance emerged from the building Lauren honked the horn and began driving toward him through the heavy snow. She stopped beside Trance and he climbed in.

"Hey, cowboy," said Lauren. "Can I take you somewhere?"

"Nice to see you, too."

It had been three weeks since Lauren had been allowed to meet with Trance, and he hadn't shaved since then.

"What's with the beard?" asked Lauren.

"You like it?"

"Let me see." Lauren leaned over and kissed Trance. "Okay, I think. I'll have to test it some more, later."

Trance turned around and looked at Tompkin, Stick and Marlee.

"Hey, guys. Thanks for coming."

"I'm on your payroll," said Stick. "I had to be here."

"Lotta good you did me."

Stick grinned. "I'll do better next time. You and Lauren won't mind me sleeping between you, then? We can make a man sandwich."

"Think I'd rather die," mumbled Trance.

As Lauren began to pull out into the snow-covered street, Trance turned to Jesse Tompkin. "Anything new on Tilson?"

Tompkin shook his head. "Everything we check says that it's him in the White House. Everything lines up…just a bit off center…like a fax...but it lines up."

"What about Brandon Copley?"

"He went missing a year ago."

"Any prints? DNA? Dental records?"

Tompkin shook his head. "His dental records are missing. Anything with his DNA has been sterilized, or surgically removed from his home. Whoever did this thought of everything."

"We know who did this. Sammantha Starodubov," said Trance.

"Who just so happens to be sleeping with the president."

"Lucky us."

Tompkin shrugged. "We've got to be real careful, Jack. The president's got people watching everyone."

"He should arrest his girlfriend."

"It's a wall, Jack. An impenetrable wall. We can't touch her."

"You haven't quit, have you, Jesse?"

"Hell, no."

Trance turned to Lauren. "Honey, why don't you take us to the Harvard Club so we can get a good meal?"

Lauren pointed to a knapsack at Trance's feet. "We're having a late Christmas dinner at my parent's house. All of us. There's a change of clothes in that bag. Make yourself presentable."

Trance laughed and started taking off his pants.

"Mom and dad were very worried about you, Jack. As were we all."

Lauren dragged a sleeve across her nose, but she kept staring forward into the snow.

"I love you," said Trance.

A chorus of "Ahhhh," came from the back seat. "Isn't that sweet..."

Trance turned back toward Tompkin and Stick. "Just so you know, I don't intend to give up on this. Jock is my friend. And, in case you've forgotten, he is our CIC." Then he looked at Lauren. "I'll make this up to you."

Lauren blinked, but kept peering into the pelting snow. There wasn't another car on the road, and it was all she could do to keep the Land Rover from slipping into a ditch.

Trance said, "I'm going after Sammantha Starodubov."

"She's untouchable, Jack," said Tompkin.

"No one is untouchable."

Or so he thought.

CHAPTER 91
PP

Sammantha Starodubov left her car with an attendant at the Gramercy Park Hotel. She gave him a twenty dollar tip and began walking in the direction of the Copley mansion, approaching it from the back. The home beside Copley's had been converted to a coop in the 1970s. Sammantha had purchased a unit on its first floor. She entered the building through a back entrance and walked down the hall to her own apartment. She slipped inside, dropped her purse onto the kitchen counter and picked up a Petzl headlamp. She wrapped the elastic band around her neck, then went back into the hall and locked the door behind her.

Sammantha walked down the first floor hall to a rusted steel door that led into a musty, mold-filled, stone basement. She opened the door with a bent skeleton key, then locked it behind her once she was inside. She pulled the band of the headlamp around her head and flicked the light on. She walked down a flight of grooved stone steps that opened to something barely taller than a crawl space. The room had a six foot ceiling consisting of creosote-covered planks. The walls were rough discolored limestone, with water and rust streaks covering nearly every inch. Against the far wall there was a small, square metal door with a heavy, sliding bolt across the front. Sammantha slipped back the bolt, opened the door and climbed inside. She shut the door behind her by pulling a chain she had rigged through the door to seal it shut. She locked this door from inside with a sturdy padlock.

Sammantha squatted within a rounded concrete sewer pipe. The pipe was about five feet in diameter. The bottom was covered with a thin layer of slime, but the rest was dry. The air smelled like rotten fish. That didn't bother Sammantha; she had lived in worse conditions. It had a kind of familiarity that gave her comfort. Sammantha half walked, half crawled through the pipe until she came to another hatch-like door. She unlocked a padlock on this door and used an extended coat hanger to slide open the well-oiled bolt on the other side. It slid easily. A moment later, Sammantha climbed inside the basement of Copley's home. She took the stairs two at a time to the first floor.

"Clyde!" she called. There was no answer. Odd, but not alarming.

Sammantha shrugged and stepped into the elevator. She closed the collapsible brass gate in the front and rotated a lever that sent the contraption into a slow upward motion. Sammantha could see each floor as the elevator passed by with its *click, click, clicking* sound. When she reached the penthouse living suite, Sammantha stepped inside. She marched straight for Copley's bedroom, taking off her clothes as she walked. Blouse, bra, slacks and panties. When she reached the bedroom door, all she was wearing was a pair of short black socks. She held the rest of her clothes in a tight fist by her side.

"Hello, Sammantha," said Trance. He was sitting in a chair in the corner of the room. "Or, should I say, Sandra?"

Sammantha turned to run and Trance yelled, "Don't even think about it!"

Sammantha remained in place, as if frozen to the floor. She knew enough about Trance to believe him. She dropped her clothes and put both hands on her hips. She stared into Trance's eyes, not quite knowing what she saw there. Was it anger, hatred or fear? She waited for Trance to look from her face to her body, but he never did.

"Where is Jock Tilson?"

"He's at Camp David with Ogarkov. They're putting the final touches on that treaty. The one Jock will announce during his Address."

"Why aren't you there?"

Sammantha frowned. "Men only. I won't see him until the morning of the Address."

"I will ask you again, where is Jock Tilson?"

"I told you—"

"I know that you put Brandon Copley into the White House, Sammantha. What I don't know is…where did you put the president?"

Sammantha smiled. She reached her hands behind the back of her head and stretched, arching her back seductively. "I'll never tell," she said playfully. Sammantha dropped one hand to her breast and touched it gently, before letting her hand fall back to her side. "Can I get you some coffee? Tea? Or me?"

"Put your clothes back on, Sammantha."

"But I like you…" Sammantha began to walk toward Trance, trying to gain control of the meeting, using the one thing that had always worked in her life. Trance pulled a Colt 32 out of his waistband.

"Put…them…on, Sam."

Sammantha complied. Once she was dressed, Trance motioned with the gun for her to sit on the bed.

"You going to rape me now?"

"What?"

"Are you going to rape me now? Like every other fucking man in my life?"

Trance recoiled. He felt her pain. It was like she'd lit a match to his mind. He could almost hear it crackle and hiss, reaching into the tendrils of his most sensitive nerves. "Not all men are pigs, Sammantha. All I want is to find the president."

Sammantha scowled. "When will you leave me alone?"

"I'm sorry? I don't get—"

"You are just like them…you *are* them."

"I don't understand."

"You killed my fiancé."

"What?"

"Think, Trance. He was Russian."

Trance didn't want to think. He had killed too many men, always in self-defense, and for his country. He knew who she meant; somehow he knew. Alexander Khodorkovski.

"Khodorkovski was stealing nuclear weapons and offering to sell them to Islamic terrorists."

Sammantha shook her head. "He would never have done that."

"He did, Sammantha. You want proof? Find me a computer with Broadband and I'll show you."

Sammantha shrugged. "Doesn't matter now. I got my revenge."

Trance felt his throat begin to constrict, like a fist was being shoved down inside it. It felt like a spider was running up the back of his neck, tingling along his spine, then radiating outward. Was she the one?

"You killed Janice?"

Sammantha laughed. "It was so easy. All I had to do was funnel a request through your stupid uncle, Senator Hopewell. I had information about terrorist activities. I would only speak to a woman. I would only speak to one woman—Janice Trance."

Sammantha lay down on the bed and threw her head back. "It was so fucking easy."

Trance closed his eyes. It had been long ago, yet it seemed like yesterday, when he'd had to bury his wife and his unborn child. He had spent years searching for her killer, with a rage burning inside him like a bonfire. His wife's killer lay before him now, but he couldn't attack her; he couldn't make her pay. Not now. The president's life was at stake.

"You had no right…No reason."

"I had every right! You kill one of mine, I kill one of yours. You play the game. Isn't that the way it works? Aren't those the rules?"

"What do you want with Tilson? And why Copley?"

"You haven't guessed? No, you could never guess." Sammantha paused, as if deciding what to say next. "It is all about revenge, Jack Trance. Very simple."

"You have your revenge."

"Do I? Not hardly. Think about this for a moment. You are a girl of twelve. You are living in America. Your parents are noted Russian physicists who have been lured out of their country by the promise of American freedom and riches.

"One day this little girl comes home…home to find her parents dead on the kitchen floor. Slaughtered like cattle, bleeding everywhere. She holds her dog and her butterfly cup and she lies there with them telling her parents to wake up. Wake up!

"But they don't wake up. There's all that blood…and a butterfly cup…Then this man…he comes into your home and he tells you. He tells you who did it. The *American Government* did it. And he takes you away. Only he…only he…he has other things in mind. That day…that day when you have seen your parents murdered…twelve years old…you are forced…forced to…it…forced into things too heinous to describe or remember.

"But that is just the beginning. Oh, yes. When they get you to Russia, things get worse. Much worse. You get the picture? Do you understand why I need my revenge?

"This is war, Trance. All is fair, and I've used every weapon I could."

"You killed Kiki Tilson."

"I had to kill her. She would have known."

"You kidnapped the president."

"It was the only way."

"You brought him to Russia."

"I didn't say that."

Trance thought for a moment. "Your parents…who were they?"

"Why, Starodubov, of course."

Trance stood. "You hid in plain sight. Very good. Where's a computer? You have Internet here, I assume?"

Curious, Sammantha walked to the far end of the bedroom, into the large dressing room near the bathroom. "In here."

Sammantha turned the computer on and allowed Trance to sit down before it. Then she began to back away toward the clothes closet.

"It won't work," said Trance without looking.

"What?"

"The panic room. I disabled the door. You can't get inside and hide. So sit down and let me see what we can learn about your parents. I'm not here to hurt you. I need your help."

Although Trance had the highest government clearance, he couldn't get into high security databases through this computer. He needed specialized encryption software and hardware for that. But he could enter the government computers through his New York offices. He pulled a VPN encryption key from his pocket and plugged it into a USB port on Copley's computer. He logged onto his company Intranet and opened one of his secret files. He memorized the day's codes and shredded the file. Then he rerouted the browser into the Langley computer system. Within ten minutes he said, "Ah, hah. Your parents were physicists. Before coming to America, they worked for a businessman and KGB operative by the name of…holy shit…Ivan Petrovski. How could we have missed that?"

Trance sat back and allowed Sammantha to read through half a dozen reports. Soon, she could see that it had not been the Americans who had ordered her parents killed. Her parents were killed because they came to America to escape…to escape the employment of *Ivan Petrovski*, the future Russian prime minister.

"How do I know this isn't planted? How do I know this is real?"

"Listen to your gut. What does your gut tell you?"

"Oh, my God." Sammantha looked toward Trance. "You must let me return to Washington. I must go to the president…Copley. There is something I must do."

"I think you've already done enough."

Sammantha looked into Trance's eyes. She tried to convince herself to tell him. Maybe there was something *he* could do to stop this. But she knew better. Trance would only get himself thrown in jail, this time for life.

"Show me the files about my fiancé, Khodorkovski."

Trance sat back down. After several minutes he stood back again.

"I shouldn't be showing you this."

Sammantha gave Trance a weary smile. "I killed your wife. You owe me."

Sammantha skimmed through the file on Alexander Khodorkovski. Dear, sweet Alexander. Soon, she began to weep. The tears started as tiny drops, seeping out through the corner of her closed eyes. Then she started to moan. It was a haunting sound that made Trance think of the times that he, too, had let out that primal cry of loss. It made him want to reach out and touch Sammantha, to tell her that it would be all right. But that would be a lie, because Trance wasn't sure that it ever could be all right.

Sammantha stared at Trance through her bloodshot eyes. "I fucked up everything. My fiancé…my fiancé…he worked as an enforcer for Petrovski…a killer…That…that must be why he befriended me…to assuage his guilt…he murdered my parents…he didn't love me…he ruined…my…life."

"You can't change the past, Sammantha. But you can make this right. Let's make this right."

Sammantha looked toward Trance and focused her watery eyes. Trance took her hand, hoping to let her see into his mind, and know he spoke the truth. All he felt was a fiery heat, as if Sammantha's pain were burning into his bones.

"Tell me what you must do," he said.

"I can't. I really can't. Not yet. But I see, now. My life has been a lie. I have focused all that anger, all that hate in the wrong place." Sammantha looked at Trance. "I killed your wife. I am sorry. So sorry."

Trance weighed his options. Should he force Sammantha to go with him or let her go? He made a choice, hoping it was the right one. "Make this right." Trance handed Sammantha a card with a single phone number written across the top. "I'm going to let you go. This is my private number. You need anything, you call me."

Sammantha looked at Trance, not fully believing what he'd said. "You're not going to kill me?"

"There are things more important than revenge, Sammantha. I hope you understand that now."

Sammantha prayed she could get to Copley and undo all she had created. She had to reverse the months of programming and de-program the knee-jerk reactions that he would think as instinct. She had to undo all the things he'd rehearsed and dreamt, day after day, until they were part of his imprinting. If she couldn't, all of Washington would vanish. The world would be at war. She would be dead. So would the man she loved. And so would her baby.

CHAPTER **92**
___________PP___________

Sammantha Starodubov paced inside her room at the Washington Ritz-Carlton Hotel. It was six thirty in the morning and she was already showered and dressed. Her stomach felt like it was filled with earthworms, churning and gurgling under the strain. Her heart felt like it was beating in her throat.

The president was due back in Washington today. At 10 A.M., Marine One would land on the White House lawn. He would step out and walk to the Oval Office, shoulder to shoulder with the Russian president. Later in the day, he would step onto the back portico and give a briefing about tomorrow's State of the Union Address. She had to meet him before that briefing. She had to tell him, about everything. He had to live on. The country had to live on. The bomb had to be stopped. They were having a baby. The baby had to live on.

It felt so strange. Sammantha had planned her life for this day, tomorrow, the day the U.S Congress would be obliterated, the day Washington would be left in charred ruins like Dresden, Hiroshima and Nagasaki. And now, that day could never come. It *should* never come. Her life had been a lie. A lie…All the years seething with visions of revenge against America—working twenty-hour days in school, prostituting herself for the power and the money, with men willing to invest anything for a tiny piece of her ass…no…ownership of her soul. She had patched her life together like her butterfly cup. It was fragile and frigid, with parts of it strewn across Asia like fallen cherry blossoms, ready to break at any moment, but still able to cut deep into the toughest skin like a knife to whipped cream.

Sammantha had studied the mind. She'd learned the mind's deepest secrets. She could play a man like a maestro cellist. She could play the highest of highs and the lowest of lows. She could control and manipulate with the ease of a puppeteer. In her quest for understanding and knowledge and revenge, Sammantha had also learned to heal. She had cured thousands in her drive to perfect her craft. In parts of Russia she was hailed as a savior. She had taken men whose minds had turned to mush and she had rebuilt them like Geppetto. Yes, *resurrected* them from the *dead*, as if they were Lazarus and she were a God. And what was it for? Her life had been focused on learning how to manipulate a man. To manipulate *one* man and program him to destroy. To *destroy*, not *create*. She was a fraud.

How could she have known that she had chosen the wrong enemy? How could she have foreseen that she would fall in love with the one she was supposed to kill? She fell in *love*. After all of the pain and the anger, after all the sweating rapists and all the self-loathing, that pure, rabid hatred…after all of that, she had found someone to love. And he loved her. *Her.* He loved her, not because she had manipulated him to do so; she had avoided that. He loved her for *her*. Sammantha.

In those dreams, tomorrow always ended in fire. A beautiful, purifying fire. She would sear a black brand on the heart of America to replace her own. It would cause a dearthful mourning that would make 9/11 seem almost silly, a pall that would hover over the nation like a toxic cloud for decades. Now everything had changed. That dream had been doused, like a fire by rain.

That day could still become a day of triumph. A day when *her* man, Brandon Copley, would announce to the world a treaty so bold and so visionary as to be almost unthinkable.

Sammantha closed her eyes and shivered. She wrapped her arms around her belly, her baby belly, that little innocent life spawned by manipulation into something so pure it was heavenly. There was no way she could be with Copley to share this love. She had done too much. Killed too many. She'd been blind, blinded by a pallor so vile, so cloaked in a shadow, so pervasive as to block every source of light into her heart, or into her withered black soul. But she could still save Washington and her baby's father, the one man she had ever loved, really loved.

There was a knock on her door.

"Room service."

That would be breakfast and the paper. She didn't want to eat, but she had to; she was eating for two, now. Sammantha smiled and thought of how much her life had changed. It had been just a year since she was lying in this same hotel, wondering if she had assassinated the first lady. The first lady. She had *killed* the first lady. *How could I have done that? How could I have ever thought that killing, especially the innocent, was the answer to anything?*

Yes, she had killed the first lady. Yes, she had kidnapped the president and shipped him to the bowels of the Kremlin. Yes, she had put a pretender into the greatest seat of power in the land. But then…life had changed. She had fallen in love with the president's brother. She was carrying his child. A nuclear bomb was programmed to destroy Washington in less than forty hours. She could change that. She would change that. She had to. Today.

Sammantha opened the door and a hand shot through the opening. Sammantha tried to push the arm back out the door, but a shoe followed the hand into the breach, along with the man who wore it.

"Hello, Sammantha," said a familiar voice.

"Petrovski?" Sammantha barely recognized the Russian prime minister through his disguise. She looked beyond Petrovski and saw Talid. "And you."

"Hello, my sweet cherry. We have come to see that you don't lose your nerve."

This is not good, thought Sammantha. Not good at all. "I never lose my nerve."

"Aren't you going to invite us in?" said Petrovski, as he forced the door all the way open.

Sammantha gave way. Petrovski and Talid were followed by two bodyguards, who made a quick sweep of the suite before standing on either side of their leaders.

"You should not be here," said Sammantha. "I am meeting with the president this morning. His men will be here any moment. They cannot see you."

Petrovski nodded toward one of the bodyguards. "Then we must go," he said. The bodyguard plunged a needle into Sammantha's neck and her world went dark.

CHAPTER **93**

_____________PP_____________

Four Marine One helicopters swirled toward the White House in their traditional zig zag shell game. The air buzzed like it was filled with a swarm of locusts, as the helicopters performed their oft-practiced air ballet. When the helicopters reached the White House grounds, two of them peeled off in opposite directions, while two landed on the lawn.

The president emerged from one of the helos. As he set his feet onto the ground, he didn't raise his arms, due to an irrational fear that he couldn't control. He didn't want his fingers chopped off by the whirling blades, despite the twenty feet of clearance that made it impossible. He knew it was the PCS. It made him fear strange things, like losing his fingers or his voice. He couldn't lose his voice; it was his instrument. And Trance; he feared Trance most of all.

Ogarkov stepped out of the other craft. He raised both arms, after gauging the safe distance above his head with a more practiced and fearless eye.

A select group of reporters had been invited to witness this landing and mark the event. Cameras rolled as the two men walked toward the White House. When they reached the West Wing Rose Garden, both men turned. They locked arms and raised their hands together in a show of friendly unity.

Let them put that in their pipe and smoke it, thought the president. He could imagine the speculation now. He had spent a week at Camp David with the Russian president, then a week with other world leaders, just before delivering his State of the Union Address. It didn't take a rocket scientist to see that these events were linked, no, welded together like a car frame. The president's handlers had leaked enough to put extraordinary rumors into play. The buzz over tomorrow night's speech was reaching legendary proportions. This was going to be the most watched program in television history. It would also be the most historic.

As the president looked out from the Rose Garden, he scanned the faces, searching for Sammantha. She was supposed to meet him here, to read his speech and help him rehearse. He had missed her, more than he thought he ever could. He needed her. He wanted her beside him, for comfort and for her advice.

"Has anyone seen Miss Starodubov?" he asked Stone. "She is supposed to meet me here."

"No one has seen her, Mr. President. She was not at her hotel when our people arrived. She has not been answering texts, phone or email."

"Any note? No messages?"

"No, Mr. President."

"Any sign of struggle at the hotel?"

"Excuse me, sir?"

The president shrugged and turned away. "Never mind."

The president felt the urge to run out to the street, to sprint along the sidewalks screaming Sammantha's name. He had to see her. Had to. It was as if he were an addict and she was his drug. Something, some primal need, was compelling him to see her, as if the world would end if he didn't.

Sammantha would have to show up by tonight. Otherwise they wouldn't be able to meet until *after* his speech. His entire Tuesday was scheduled to the second. He was to meet with the Russians, Chinese, Germans, Brits and the French to review the final drafts of their agreement. They needed to practice the choreography of their carefully staged event, to rehearse it until they got it right.

Three hours before the address, he would go into the *zone*, where no one would be allowed to see him. Even his makeup artists would be banned from his sight. He would sink deep into character, letting nothing distract him from his performance. Even Sammantha. He would rehearse his lines until they were memorized to perfection. And nothing, absolutely nothing, would get in his way. He was a professional.

CHAPTER 94

_____________PP_____________

Trance and Lauren carried their own luggage up to Trance's suite at the Ritz-Carlton in Washington. Trance swiped his electronic key card. There was a buzzing noise. Rather than the door unlocking, a biometric keypad emerged out of the wall.

Trance turned to Lauren. "This is something Stick added for my security."

Trance punched in a twelve-digit code and pressed his left pinky finger against the digital reader. The door swung open and they entered. The heat fired up and the suite lights snapped on automatically. Trance flipped down a computer keyboard on the wall and typed a few keystrokes to check his security codes. He viewed the digital readout on a monitor that was flat against the wall. Satisfied, Trance pushed the computer keypad back into place.

"Getting a little paranoid, aren't we?" said Lauren. Then, thinking better of her words, she said, "I take that back."

"I don't want bodyguards shadowing our every move. So, Stick and I came to an understanding. I would follow security protocol and he would give us space. A bit excessive, you think?"

"Better safe than sorry."

"Stick and Marlee are on their way. They should be here any moment."

"Going to let them sleep on the couch?"

Trance laughed. "I thought I'd give them the guest bedroom and have _you_ sleep on the couch."

"How about if I stay in your room and _you_ sleep on the couch?"

"How about if we both stay in my room?"

Lauren bit down on her lower lip, as if thinking this one through. "Now, that's a novel idea."

"No naked balcony walking," said Trance, remembering a time, not too long ago, when Lauren had mistakenly walked naked onto a South Beach balcony, to the delight of an octogenarian nearby.

"Well, you're no fun."

Trance took Lauren into his arms. Maybe they could stay here a few days. Maybe look at rings. He was ready for marriage now. She had been ready for decades.

"I may not be much fun. But I do love you," he said.

"Prove it."

CHAPTER **95**
PP

When Sammantha Starodubov awakened, it took only a moment to realize where she was. Even before opening her eyes, she felt the familiar aura. She recognized the smell, the faint whiff of old cigar and cigarette smoke emanating from the walls, the subtle mustiness of the expensive, but worn out carpets, and the slight hint of car exhaust moving in the air from the street. She was in New York. She was in the Copley mansion. She was home.

Oh, no.

Sammantha opened her eyes. Two men were seated before her in chairs, holding rifles across their knees.

"What day is today?"

"Tuesday. You slept through the night."

"I was drugged through the night."

The Russian guards smiled. One of them was the man who had injected her. She felt like tearing out his throat. *Think.* She had missed her appointment with Copley, but there was still time.

"How did you get inside this house?"

"We knocked on the door."

Sammantha closed her eyes. Clyde. "What did you do with Clyde?"

"The old guy?"

"My *friend.*"

The Russian laughed. "We tied him up. We might even let him go after the president's speech. That is up to you."

"Where is Petrovski?" she said in English.

"He went for paper," replied the guard, in English.

"And Talid?"

"Washington. He stay there." The man laughed, with an almost childish giggle. "He took your room."

Sammantha thought, *He is in Washington to die. No doubt he will take credit for the slaughter. He's going to make himself a martyr...that bastard.*

"What are your orders?"

The men looked at each other. Then one said, "To shoot you if you move."

"How pleasant."

"For me, yes," said the guard. "For you? I don't think so."

"I need to use the bathroom and get dressed. I want to put on fresh clothes. Call Petrovski and tell him I want to shower."

One of the men withdrew a phone from his shirt pocket. Without taking his eyes off Sammantha, he called Petrovski. After a few sentences he nodded and closed his phone.

"You shower," he said. Then he smiled. "Undress here."

"No." Sammantha narrowed her eyes. She began to walk backwards toward the bathroom, never taking her eyes off of the men. "If you bother me, Petrovski will kill you." She was right and they knew it. "Assuming I haven't killed you already," she mumbled to herself.

Sammantha stepped into the glass-encased shower stall and let near-scalding water pelt down upon her. She breathed in the steam, as if it could purify her. When she finished, Sammantha walked into her clothes closet and selected a fresh pair of jeans and a cotton t-shirt. She grabbed socks and a pair of Nikes. Then she turned to see if the men were watching her. She was out of their field of vision. They hadn't moved and were guarding the door, nothing more.

Sammantha faced the clothes closet. The closet was about twenty feet across. Two shiny metal bars ran horizontally along it at eye height. The right bar held a string of dresses, blouses and pant suits belonging to Sammantha. The left bar held a bank of little-worn dress suits and shirts that were owned by Brandon Copley.

Sammantha slid the dresses and suits away from the spot where the bars met in the center of the closet. There, behind the clothes, built into the wall was a small door. Sammantha calmly pulled the door open. It was enormously heavy, nearly a foot thick, but it swung easily and noiselessly on its well oiled hinges. Sammantha stepped into the adjoining room, closed and bolted the door from inside, then slumped to the floor. Now, what should she do?

Copley had built his panic room before she had met him.

"All my friends have one," he'd said.

She had thought it a frivolous expense, like all the other stupid things he had bought with his money. Just one more thing to bring him to the edge of financial disaster. Now, she hoped this room would help save the country from an unthinkable disaster.

The area was substantial, ten feet by twenty. It had shelves stacked with a month's worth of canned goods and rows of plastic five-gallon water jugs. An electrical cable had been run through the core of the house and into the room. The cable was surrounded by a foot-thick steel pipe that would take hours to cut through. There were also backup battery packs and a hand powered generator to charge them.

The room had its own communications capabilities. It was also hard wired to a private security firm. There was a public Wi-Fi connection, plus fiber optic broadband. Phone and television cables also ran through the nearly impenetrable pipe.

Sammantha debated what she should do. She could call the police. That would create more problems than it solved. She could call the president. That, too, was a minefield she might not survive. How could she tell anyone that she had been plotting with an Arab head of state who was more terrorist than leader? How could she make them believe that the Russian Prime Minister was hell-bent on seeing his own president killed, along with the entire U.S. Congress? Impossible. Before she could get anyone to believe her, it would be too late.

Should she call Jack Trance? The man who had killed her fiancée? The man whose wife *she* had murdered with grim, gleeful pleasure? She had to. She had to call the man whose life she had ruined, all because of her warped vision of revenge.

CHAPTER **96**

______PP______

"How 'bout we go shopping?" said Trance.

"Something wrong with you?" asked Lauren.

"I thought we might do some looking…at rings."

Lauren's jaw quivered. She stared at Trance, afraid to speak. Not because he was talking of marriage, but because of what might happen, what always happened whenever they got this far.

"Nothing fancy," said Trance. "But something nice. Don't like to waste money, you know."

"I'd be happy with a ring from a Cracker Jacks box. Like the one you gave me at our senior prom. Do I understand what you're asking?"

At that moment, Trance's PDA rang. *Don't answer it,* he said to himself. When he saw the name *Copley* on the digital readout he closed his eyes and took the call.

"Sammantha?"

"I've been kidnapped, Jack. By Petrovski."

"The Russian Prime Minister?"

"Yes. I'm in Brandon's panic room. Petrovski went out, but he'll be back soon."

"How good is Copley's room?"

"Very."

"Good enough for me to get there from Washington?"

"If you're flying. We'll need to get back to Washington before the speech."

"Why?"

"I can't tell you why. Not yet."

"Something bad is happening tonight, Miss Starodubov. What is it?"

The phone went dead. Trance closed his eyes; then he looked at Lauren.

"That was Sammantha Starodubov, the president's lover. She killed Kiki Tilson and she kidnapped the president. She now claims that she's been kidnapped by the Russian Prime Minister, and is being held hostage in New York."

"And I was worried that this was something serious."

"She also killed…Janice."

"Oh, Jack." Lauren took Trance's face into her hands. Trance tried to pull away but she wouldn't let go.

Trance said, "Something unthinkable is planned for tonight; I can feel it. I don't know what it is, but she does. I've got to go to New York. I love you. We'll look for rings tomorrow. I promise."

Lauren smiled briefly as she patted Trance on the cheek. "I've been waiting twenty years, Jack. What's another day? You go fix whatever needs fixing. I'll wait here."

If only she had known.

Trance walked into his study and removed a painting from the wall. Behind it was the door to a metal safe. Trance spun the combination, pressed his finger into the biometric reader and the door swung open. He grabbed a stack of cash and a fistful of loose diamonds, which he stuffed into a black felt bag, then into his pocket. He had weapons in his helicopter. He closed the safe, kissed Lauren, called Stick out of the guest bedroom and walked out the door.

CHAPTER 97
______________PP______________

Stick Granger landed Trance's Bell helicopter on the private, rooftop helipad of the Hopewell Industries building on New York's Avenue of the Americas. It was a sixty-story structure, inherited from Trance's mother's side of the family. The building housed a dozen of the sixty-five U.S. subsidiaries that Trance now controlled.

Trance briefly waved at the group of executives that had gathered on the roof to greet him. He walked by them without stopping though, followed closely by Stick. He half sprinted for the executive elevator, which lay open awaiting their arrival, as requested. The elevator took the two men to ground level in a few dizzying seconds. They ran through the cavernous lobby, out to a BMW motorcycle that was waiting for them on the street. Trance stuffed a blue gym bag into the bike's saddlebags, jumped on and cranked it awake. He wound the engine for a second, then let it purr like a big jungle cat. Stick jumped onto the back and they sped into the street, weaving through traffic like a drunken Copley.

"You sure you don't want to call some of the guys?" yelled Stick. "This could get big time ugly."

"No time!"

Trance raced down Broadway and cut over on 23rd Street to reach the entrance to the Gramercy Park Hotel. He handed three one hundred dollar bills to the valet and said, "Would you keep this here for us? We shouldn't be long."

"Are you staying at the hotel, sir?"

"Uh, sure."

Trance tossed the key into the valet's open palm, retrieved his gym bag and began jogging toward the Copley mansion.

"What's the plan?" said Stick.

"Who said anything about a plan?"

"We've got to have a plan, JT. Everybody needs a plan."

"I thought we'd ring the doorbell."

"Uh, I hate to break it to you, but the woman's been kidnapped. Those guys will have guns."

"Oh, yeah. The bell probably won't work, huh?"

Trance slowed and made his way along the backside of the adjacent buildings, skulking through the alleyways, staying out of the line of potential snipers. He screwed a silencer onto the barrel of an M-11 pistol and held it up to his cheek.

"You think Petrovski is gone?" said Stick.

"I do."

"You think he left shooters behind?"

"I do."

"Aw, shit," said Stick. "If there's anything I hate, it's snipers. They like to shoot at you when you're not looking."

"Is that what they do?"

"With guns, Trance. Nasty ones that put big holes in your butt."

Trance smiled and motioned with his gun. "Why don't you walk ahead of me, then. That way they'll shoot you first."

"Oh, no," said Stick. "You walk first. I walked first last time."

"What *last* time? Aren't I paying you to protect me?" Trance edged his way along the side of the brownstone next to the old Copley mansion, looking everywhere, feeling everywhere.

Stick replied, "It's my wife's job to protect you. You gave her the big bucks, remember? I can't risk my life for a lousy quarter million. For a quarter million, I walk behind."

Trance laughed. "You want a raise?"

Trance motioned for Stick to stop. He pointed toward a man holding a pistol, lurking in an alley with a clear sight of the Copley mansion.

"No time for nice, nice, Trance," said Stick. "You better shoot his ass."

"I hate this," said Trance. He fired off two quick shots and the man flopped to the ground, gripping both thighs. A moment later, another man began running from the same hiding place. Trance shot him in the butt. The man clutched his left cheek and tried to shuffle away. He quickly realized that he couldn't get far, so he tossed his gun into the alley and threw up his hands.

"Go cuff the guys, will you?" said Trance. "Provided that's within your job description. We'll call an ambulance before we leave."

Trance proceeded cautiously, but he could sense no other danger. They were gone. After a few watchful moments he bounded up the stone steps of the mansion, picked the locks on the front door and stepped inside. Pistol drawn, he made a quick tour of the first floor. Then he ran up the stairs, three at a time, until he reached the top floor. He surveyed the area, then entered Copley's bedroom suite. He walked into the closet, pressed the intercom to the panic room and said, "Sammantha. You okay?"

"Who is it?"

"It's Trance. We're clear out here."

Trance backed away so the bullet-proof video cameras could get a clear picture of his face. He heard the door bolts slide and Sammantha Starodubov walked into the bedroom closet. Trance frisked her for weapons, then motioned for her to follow him into the bedroom.

Trance said, "Why was Petrovski here?"

"Because I was working with the Russians."

"Ogarkov? Is this a setup?"

"Ogarkov only wants peace. He knows nothing about the rest."

"Petrovski?"

"He wants Ogarkov dead. Talid wants everybody dead."

Trance's head snapped toward Sammantha, like it had been released by an elastic band."

"Mu'annar Abu Hussein al-Talid?"

"The very same."

"Talid is behind this?"

"To his eyeballs."

"Talid wants nothing more than to slaughter innocent American lives."

"He does not see your Congress as innocent."

Trance sighed wearily. "Where is he?"

"My room at the Ritz-Carlton. Washington."

Trance closed his eyes. It was a bad day when a country's Prime Minister tried to kill his own president on another country's national stage, or when one of the world's most dangerous terrorists even set foot in Washington. "What have you done?"

Sammantha looked down. Then she slowly met Trance's gaze.

"There is a bomb in Washington, Jack."

Trance felt his body swoon. His temples began to pound. He could feel the *whoosh, whoosh, whoosh* of blood racing through his head, then sinking into his stomach. He felt like he was about to vomit.

"Timer or trigger?"

"A timer. There's one man who can diffuse it. Only one."

"Where is the bomb? Do you know where it is?"

Sammantha thought to tell the truth, but she shook her head. If she told them where it was, if she told them it was nuclear, they would never let her see Brandon. She had to see Brandon before they took her away. She had to tell him that she loved him, no matter what they would say. No matter what kind of a monster they would make her out to be. It had all been a mistake. Her life had been a mistake, everything she had thought and all she had done. It was a lie.

"You know when it's set to detonate?"

"At 9:45 P.M."

Trance looked to his watch. "Less than four hours from now...Tell me where it is."

"I don't know. Somewhere near the Capitol Building."

"You need to tell me, Sammantha."

"I won't. You can torture me all you want. Give me any kind of drug. I won't tell you. Believe me, I've trained for this."

"What is it you want?"

"I love him. He needs to know that."

"You love him? Yet you do this?"

"I was wrong. I was blinded...I was driven by rage, misplaced rage...at America...at you...at myself."

"Let's call him. You can tell him."

"No. I need to see him."

"I can't let you do that. You are—"

"I said I love him, damn it!"

Then, an almost primordial howl came from Sammantha's lips, sounding like a mother wolf wailing into the night for her lost cubs.

Trance looked at Sammantha, at a loss for words, with visions of the nation's Capital in flames roaring through his head. This woman had a bomb in Washington, set to detonate toward the end of the president's State of the Union Address. And she wants to tell him that she loves him?

"I've got to have the president removed from Washington," said Trance.

"He won't go."

"Of course, he will."

"He's in character."

"What?"

"He's an actor, Jack. He's a performer, a great performer, now that he's sober. Three hours before every performance he gets into character, tuning everything out but his script."

"He'll listen to this."

"No, he won't. He's been programmed. It's something I did to him. Something only I can make right. That's why I need to see him."

Trance sank to the floor. "I don't believe this."

"I can stop it," said Sammantha. "I *want* to stop it. I realize now that my life was a farce. Hating the wrong people, vowing revenge on an innocent country. Killing your wife..."

"And the first lady."

"Her, too."

"So, where is the president? The real president?"

"I will tell you. But only after Copley is safe."

Trance wanted to lash out at Sammantha. He wanted to wrap his hands around her throat and make her talk. He began to yank the hair on the back of his head, as if his own pain could tell him what he needed to know. What should he do?

"You sure we can't just call the Secret Service? I can get to them. They can get to Copley."

Sammantha looked to her watch. "No, not now. They'll have orders. He won't listen."

"But *they* might. Our people can take him at any time."

"You think they will forcibly detain the president?"

Trance hesitated. "They might."

"Some of *them* have been compromised, Jack."

"Not Miller? Not Tompkin?"

"No, not Miller or Tompkin."

Trance punched his PDA. He had to talk to someone. He could call the FBI director, the National Security Advisor, or the head of the president's Secret Service detail. He had to talk to someone with enough stones to handle it. This was global, so the CIA should know.

"What, Jack?" said Jacob Miller when he answered his phone.

"Need your help."

"We're rather busy down here. In case you don't know, the president is addressing the nation tonight."

"We have a situation. Call me back, STAT."

Trance reached into his bag, pulled out an additional encryption device and attached it to his PDA. He ran through a set of codes and waited for the phone to ring. A few moments later, it did.

"What's so important, Jack?"

"There is a bomb in D.C. You need to evacuate Centurion and the Capitol Building."

"Is this credible? We've had thirty other threats, today alone."

"It's credible."

"It's not nuclear, is it?"

Trance turned to Sammantha. "Tell me this thing isn't nuclear."

Sammantha shook her head and lied. "It's not. But it's big. A MOAB, I think."

Trance's eyes widened. "That's twenty-one thousand pounds of explosive, Sammantha."

Sammantha nodded. "I know. I told you, it's big."

Trance spoke into the phone. "Should be easy to find, Jake. She says it's a MOAB."

"You've got to be fucking kidding me."

"Desert Fang is in town."

"Talid? Shit, Jack."

"I know where he is."

"I'm waiting."

"He's at the Ritz-Carlton." Trance gave Miller the room number.

Miller said, "I've got teams in the area. Are we done?"

"For now."

The phone went dead. Twelve minutes later, Miller called Trance back.

"We have Desert Fang, Jack."

"You owe me," said Trance.

"Big time. I'm a star."

"Centurion knows about the bomb?"

"He has been told."

"So, he'll listen to us?"

"I have been advised that Centurion won't talk to anyone now. Even me. His detail has closed ranks like a shell."

"You'll have to force him."

"Negative. He is the Commander in Chief, Jack. His orders trump mine. His orders are clear."

"The show must go on."

"What was that?"

"Nothing," said Trance. "He's an actor."

"Don't worry, Jack. I've already got people with sniffers, both canine and machine, combing the Capitol Building. I've got more teams coming and I'm expanding the search grid exponentially. If there's a bomb here, we'll find it."

"Call a Cabinet session. Get the House speaker, too."

"No fucking way, Jack. This is a sitting president who's done nothing wrong. We don't have a shred of evidence against him."

"He is *not* the president."

"But can you prove it? We've been over this before. The DNA, the fingerprints, yadda, yadda, yadda."

Trance looked at Sammantha. "I need proof of this bomb."

Sammantha shook her head. "Not until I've spoken with the president."

"He's not the president!"

"What?" said Miller.

"I wasn't talking to you."

Trance looked back at Sammantha. She said, "We're wasting time, Jack. The sooner we get to Washington, the sooner we can diffuse this thing."

At that moment Stick Granger lumbered into the room.

"I've been looking all around for you two...I found this old guy in the basement. He said he works here, so I untied him. He's okay—"

Trance held up a hand to stop Stick from speaking. He spoke again to Miller. "I'm coming to Washington. I'll need a team. Will you call Tompkin and have him ready when I get there?"

"Tompkin was fired, Jack. I thought you knew."

"What?"

"Last week. He went snooping around on the president. Lucky they didn't throw him in jail, like you. Just gave him a DOD and tossed him into the street."

"Who's heading T-Force?"

"Ali."

"Oh. Okay, I recruited Ali. Will you have him ready when I get there?"

"Where are you?"

"New York. I'll be airborne in twenty."

"When is this thing supposed to blow?"

"Timed for 2145. If you can't locate it, I might have someone who can tell me where it is. She won't give until she's seen the president."

"Why don't you persuade her?"

"It's a little more complicated than that, Jake. It's Starodubov."

Miller sighed. The president's mistress. "I told you she was trouble."

"Roger. Out."

Trance looked at Sammantha and Stick. "We'll have to squeeze three on the bike. Let's roll."

CHAPTER **98**
_____________PP_____________

When Trance's Jet Ranger touched down on the west lawn of the Capitol Building, it was nearly 8 P.M., just an hour from the start of the president's address. Even before Trance had a chance to unhook his harness, Jacob Miller was pacing outside the helicopter's door.

Miller looked like a starving hyena waiting for a lion's kill, moving from side to side with jerky, agitated steps. Miller knew enough about Trance to take him seriously. He also knew enough about politics to take a bomb threat in stride. As Trance slid open the door, Miller shouted, "The area is clean, Trance."

The whine of the engine and the spinning rotors drowned out the words, but Trance could read what Miller said. Trance walked away from his helicopter and away from the noise. Stick and Sammantha followed closely on his heels. When they were clear of the rotors, Sammantha grabbed Miller by the shoulder and said, "I need to see him."

Miller shook his head. "He's not talking, to anyone."

"He'll talk to me."

Miller pressed a button on a communicator attached to his hip and spoke into his headset, "This is Mad Dog. Have someone tell Centurion that Sammantha Starodubov insists that she see him. Over."

There was a short pause, before his man inside said, "He's not talking. Says he listened to us before, because you said it was a national emergency. He says a bomb threat is not a national emergency and he won't fall for it again, sir."

"This *is* a goddamn national emergency. You get him on the fucking phone!"

A minute later, Miller heard the president's agitated voice. "Put her on the phone, Miller."

Miller handed his headset to Sammantha. "Jock, darling. I need to see you."

"As soon as the speech is over."

"No. I need to see you now. It's important. Very important. Critically important." Sammantha closed her eyes and whispered, "I love you."

Brandon Copley felt something strange, a feeling that left him almost breathless. He knew that he'd been loved by his mother, almost coddled while growing up in Maine. But there was a feeling, somewhere deep inside him that felt differently. There was something calling to him, saying that all his life he had been on his own. He saw flashes of parents who were too busy to care about him, too busy to notice him. Too busy with their travels, too busy with their parties. Visions where he felt like he was an unwanted appendage, like a third leg that dragged uselessly behind his parents' lives.

Copley had been raised by Clyde Davis and a string of nannies. He was sent off to boarding school. Then it was apologies and summer camps, seeing his parents for two days at Christmas and one on Thanksgiving. That was it. Except for his 16th, 18th birthdays, as if it were a sacred duty his parents had to fulfill. At this moment, he could see all this as if it were real, although he knew it could only be his imagination.

Brandon Copley had grown up less than an orphan. Copley knew more about his parents from reading the papers than speaking with them. He had always viewed them from a distance, like he was in the middle of a lake, sitting in a boat with no motor or oars, powerless to get to shore, or even move. When his parents had died, the lawyers had taken their place, seeing how much they could suck out of him and the estate.

All of this played through the president's mind in a camera flash, like the briefest flick of light in a dark underground room, the images sparking like cave paintings in a strobe light, there to see then gone, as if they didn't exist.

And now…now…there was someone who *loved* him. He felt himself waver, as if he were being raised on a cross to be worshipped. Sammantha Starodubov loved him.

"Oh, Samm. Where were you last night? I needed to see you last night."

"I wanted to be there. I know that you're busy now. But I have to see you…now. Before they take me away."

"No one is going to take you away, Samm."

"Will you see me?"

The president paused. "I'm done rehearsing. Memorized my lines in record time. I'm ready to knock 'em dead. We're just going to tidy up, now. I'll tell them to let you through, before I go back into the *zone*."

Fifteen minutes later, Sammantha Starodubov was led to the private office where the president was prepping for his speech. He was seated before a large mirror, with a woman hovering above him, dabbing makeup on his cheeks. His chief of staff stood beside him, barking orders into his phone. Others were scuttling about the room like they were preparing for a prize fight. Stone stood in a corner of the room ready to direct the president's every move.

Copley saw Sammantha in the mirror and smiled. He raised a hand to move his makeup artist away. Then he stood. Copley turned toward Sammantha, still wearing a cloth bib over his white shirt.

"Okay!" he yelled. "Everybody take five…"

The room seemed to freeze. All heads turned toward the president.

"Leave!" he said. "Be back in five minutes."

Everyone scuttled out of the room. When the door closed behind the last person, the president spread out his arms. Sammantha walked to where he was seated and sat in his lap.

"Oh, Brandon," she said.

"What?" said the president. "What's the matter, dear?"

"It's all gone crazy. I'm so sorry."

"Sorry for what?"

"For doing this to you." Sammantha pulled away and looked into the president's eyes. "Do you know who you are?"

"I'm the president. Jock Tilson."

"No. You're Brandon Copley, the president's brother."

Copley closed his eyes. He felt confused. This couldn't be. He was President Jock Tilson, about to give the State of the Union Address to the nation. Brandon Copley was just a name. He was a baseball player, whose picture was on his mother's wall, that was all. He saw his old life flash again, but he shook it away.

Stay focused, he thought to himself. *This is your night.*

"We'll talk about all that later," he said.

"No. You need to listen to me—"

"No! You need to listen to me. In less than half an hour I am going on national television to speak to the nation. To the world. I am going to announce the first major progress in nuclear arms control in decades. You can't take that away from me. The nation needs a president. It needs a strong leader. It needs me."

"You are not the president. Listen to me."

Copley's head felt like a balloon that had been blown up beyond its capacity, with so much pressure closing in around him that he began to grow woozy.

"You are not the president."

Copley's head began to spin. It was as if Sammantha had put a pin to his blown up head, and his senses had scattered into a confused pop of air. He closed his eyes.

Calm down. Center yourself. The nation needs a president. You are the president.

"Not now," he said, shaking his head. "You must go."

The president walked to the door and opened it, preparing to push Sammantha back through it. There, standing in front of him was Jack Trance.

"You," he said.

"Hello, Mr. President."

"I told you to back off."

"I am here to protect you, Mr. President. That's all."

The president looked to Sammantha. "What have you done to her?"

"She was kidnapped. I freed her and brought her here."

"Kidnapped? By whom?"

The president looked to Sammantha and she nodded. "Ivan Petrovski."

"The Russian Prime Minister?"

"Yes. He is trying to kill both you and Ogarkov."

"No one is trying to kill me."

"They are, Brandon. There is a bomb."

"My name is not Brandon and there is no bomb!"

Sammantha tried to embrace the president but he pushed her away.

"Go," he said. "I will deal with this later. Right now, I have a show to prepare for."

"There is no show, Brandon. You have to believe me. Call for Omar. You need to get him here, now, so he can diffuse the bomb."

The president looked at Sammantha as if she were a stranger. He tilted his head and mumbled, "Omar is dead, Sammantha."

Sammantha brought her hand to her mouth. "Oh…my…God."

The president turned to Trance. "You take this woman and keep her safe until after my speech. I will not have anything deter me from my duty. Not you, not Sammantha, not Petrovski." He looked to his watch. "In twenty-two minutes I will be on stage addressing the nation. The president has to be strong. The show must go on."

"You can't do this, Brandon," begged Sammantha. "There is a bomb, a real bomb."

"I won't call off this speech. The world *needs* this speech." The president looked at Trance. "If there *is* a bomb, I suggest you go find it. But leave me alone." He took Sammantha by the shoulders and gently pushed her toward Trance. "You take her to the family section, Trance, where I can see her. This speech will not be stopped." Then he yelled, "Makeup!"

Trance took hold of Sammantha and pulled her down the office corridor, even as she fought against him. He took her past the confusion of bodies until they reached a quiet nook in the wall.

"You've had your say, Sammantha. Now, where is the bomb?"

Sammantha looked like she was plunging into shock. Her skin was growing paler by the second. Small beads of sweat were sprouting across her forehead like little drops of rain. When she spoke, her voice seemed distant, as if she weren't all there. "I don't know. Omar is dead."

"Omar Karkhabi?"

"Omar was to handle the bomb."

"Then it couldn't be large, certainly not a MOAB. If he's dead that could be good, right?"

"Probably not. Omar was to guard the case...the suitcase...once the president brought it into the Capitol Building. Now that he's dead, it could be anywhere."

Trance spoke into his headset. "Miller. You have anything? You find a suitcase?"

"The place is clean."

Trance turned to Sammantha. "There is no bomb. No MOAB and no suitcase."

Sammantha nodded numbly. *Maybe this is the end,* she thought. *Maybe this is the way it should be.* What should she do? What could she do?

At 8:55 P.M., Brandon Copley made his way into the Congressional chamber inside the Capitol Building. He passed through the corridor of people, shaking hands with the men and giving hugs and air kisses to the women. It took more than five minutes. At 9:03 the president began his speech, with a flag draped behind him, flanked by the vice president and the speaker of the house on either side. There was a titanium attaché case at his feet, beside the podium, looking like a stage prop, but ticking ever-closer down to destruction.

Sitting before the president were his joint chiefs of staff, his cabinet (except for the one designated survivor), and the members of the U.S. supreme court. The entire congress was there, except for their few chosen survivors in the event of catastrophe. Also in the audience sat many of the world's top leaders. After the applause died down, this enormously popular president began his highly-anticipated speech.

"Mr. Speaker, Vice President Kelley, members of congress, distinguished citizens and my fellow Americans. Each year, by law and custom, we gather here to review the state of the union. This year we gather in this chamber with extraordinary hope and promise..."

Sammantha Starodubov and Jack Trance were seated in the upper middle section, where the president had them in clear view. As the president began speaking, Sammantha began to envision what she had done, what was about to happen. More sweat broke out across her forehead. She began to hyper-ventilate. Her mind saw visions of a mushroom cloud. They saw Washington in flames. They saw that extraordinary statue, the one of triumph, with the mother holding her baby in her arms melting away into nothing. As the president began the second paragraph of his speech, Sammantha Starodubov slumped against Jack Trance's shoulder, deathly unconscious.

CHAPTER **99**

_____________PP_____________

Jesse Tompkin walked out through the lobby of New York's Drake Hotel and stood on the sidewalk. He stared at Park Avenue as if it were a foreign country, a place where he felt completely out of his skin. Is this what he wanted? Was it right to sell his soul, what little of it he had left? He had worked so hard for two decades, serving his country in the best way he could, putting his life on the line day after day, and for what? A dishonorable discharge, a loss of all benefits, and twenty years of pension down the tubes? All for trying to make sure that the man in the Oval Office was the man his country had elected? He should have listened to the advice he'd given Trance. *Walk away. Let it go. Live your life.*

Tompkin walked the short distance to the unmarked Park Avenue brownstone and stared up at the imposing structure. Ten stories of promise. The New York home of Robert Yang, a Chinese businessman with too much money and a healthy lust for blood, sport and profit.

This was where it happened every year, that legendary tournament. It was about to begin again, when Yang invited sixty-four men to his home to fight, often to the death. Was he ready for this? Did he really want this?

Of course he did. What did he have left? If he entered this tournament he could walk away with millions. And if he died, so what? At least it was over. His life was over anyway. A DOD and nothing in the bank? Pension gone. No woman to come home to. No employment prospects. Why the hell not?

Tompkin climbed the stairs and pressed the door buzzer.

"Speak," said a voice through an intercom.

"Number 100046, reporting as requested," he said. He'd received his first invitation and was seeded 46th in the tournament. Not a good seeding, but that didn't matter. He was in. It scared the shit out of him. The door buzzed and he walked inside.

A man greeted Tompkin at the door. The man made Tompkin think of an odd oriental coat hanger. He was so thin that he was almost translucent, with a balding head and a beak of a nose that looked like it belonged on a parrot. "This way," he said in clipped Oxford English.

Tompkin followed the man to a circular stairway made of pink Italian marble. The equally pink walls were lit by gold sconces with bright, low-energy bulbs covered by delicate Chinese lampshades. He followed the man up six flights of stairs. They turned off the stairway into a darkened hallway. The only light here came from a row of faint bulbs set deep into the recessed ceiling. The man stopped about thirty feet down the hall and opened a plain wood door.

The door led to a bright, airy room with a white floor, white ceiling and equally white walls. A large window opened to the street, with a broken view of skyline across the way. There were three people inside the room. One looked to be a doctor. He was wearing green scrubs with white shoes. What looked to be a nurse stood beside him. She was clothed in white.

A sleek looking Chinese man stood between them. He was wearing a black silk suit with a white shirt and open collar. His thick black hair was combed straight back over his scalp, with curls tumbling down his forehead like an Elvis wannabe. He looked to be about sixty, but his skin was as smooth and unblemished as a twenty-year-old model. He was close to six feet tall and built like an athlete, with a slim waist and the defined chest of a gymnast. The three of them stood huddled in a corner near the window. They were speaking Mandarin Chinese and waving their hands like animated symphony conductors. As Tompkin entered the room they turned to him, stopped gesticulating and smiled.

"Mr. Tompkin," said the well-dressed man. He extended a muscular arm and shook Tompkin's hand with exaggerated vigor. "I am so glad that you decided to participate in this year's tournament."

"Got nothing better to do."

"Yes," said Yang softly. "I heard about your dishonorable discharge. That's why I sent your invitation."

Tompkin didn't question how Yang knew something so highly classified. Yang was regarded within the intelligence community as a *person of interest,* and rumored to be on the payroll of the Chinese Army. He was in the country legally, as free as any American, with a record so lily-white it had to be sanitized.

"You asked that I report at this time, sir."

"Yes. As you know, we give all of our contestants a thorough physical exam, including tests for diseases. My clients will be betting millions upon your success and failure. I must certify your fitness to compete."

"Test away," said Tompkin.

"Please remove your clothes," said the doctor.

Tompkin stripped. The doctor motioned for Tompkin to sit upon an examination table.

Yang said, "We should have the results from your blood work tomorrow. If you are cleared to compete you will receive an email, along with one hundred thousand dollars wired to your personal account, wherever you choose."

Tompkin nodded. "Thanks."

"No. Thank *you.* I will earn over five hundred million dollars next week because of men like you, Mr. Tompkin." Yang smiled. "And you? You could earn nearly a hundred, if you win."

"You mean, if I live," mumbled Tompkin. "You lost fifteen fighters last year."

"That's why this event is so popular, Mr. Tompkin. People pay a quarter million dollars, in person or for my Internet feed, to see men fight to live."

"I thought it was a hundred thousand?"

Yang shrugged his shoulders. "That was last year." He smiled and his face seemed to emanate both warmth and a genuine kindness. "Because of the poor economy, demand is unusually high this year. People need an escape. They pay dearly to enjoy the best."

"Your competitors pay dearly with their lives."

"Come, come, Mr. Tompkin. No one is forced to be here. Besides, you don't need to win to walk out a wealthy man. Is it my fault that some choose to earn double by killing their opponents?"

"You pay for death."

"I pay for sport." Yang frowned. "Whether you admit it or not, that is why you are here. This is the ultimate test of your will. Most would have it no other way. Too bad you can't talk your friend, Red Dragon, into fighting. He was our most popular champion ever."

"He's in a far better place than fighting for you."

Yang laughed. "You are never more alive than when you are fighting for your life, Mr. Tompkin. You will see."

CHAPTER **100**
PP

Sammantha awakened to the jolt of Trance slapping her on the cheek. She was lying on the floor of a wood-paneled office outside the Capitol chamber. Trance was kneeling beside her head.

"Sammantha…" *Slap, slap, slap.* "Sammantha, are you okay?"

"Jack. I'm sorry, I…What time is it?"

Trance looked to his watch. "Ten after nine."

Sammantha looked around the room. There was no one else inside. A pained, hollow look creased her face. She exhaled softly, while saying, "The bomb is nuclear, Jack."

Trance closed his eyes. Somehow, he wasn't surprised. "How big?"

"Two megatons, I think."

Okay, thought Trance. This was devastating, but manageable. Controlling it would be like sitting on the back of the space shuttle as it launched, but it *was* manageable, if they got lucky. "Where is it?"

"I saw it on stage. That's why I fainted. It is in a Halliburton Zero Roller suitcase. Beside the president. He is using it as a prop. During his speech he is going to call president Ogarkov to the stage. Together, they plan to disarm a symbolic suitcase nuke, just as the other world leaders are asked on stage. Only this bomb is real. It can't be disarmed, not without Omar, not without his codes. If the suitcase is opened it will detonate."

"A nuclear bomb on stage, at the president's feet? Tell me you're joking."

Sammantha shook her head.

"And it is set to go off in thirty-five minutes?"

Sammantha nodded. "Before then if the case is opened."

"Shit." Trance pressed a button on his hip pack. "Miller."

"Yeah."

"The bomb is nuclear. It's at Centurion's feet. Do you see a suitcase out there?"

There was a moment of silence, then, "Fuck."

"I take that as a 'yes.' There's no time to evacuate. We'll need to get the bomb into a mine shaft or a cave. Or somewhere into water. I need you and Ali to meet me at the hall entrance. STAT. Bring Pincenogle if you can find him."

Trance turned to Sammantha. "Look at me."

Sammantha gazed into Trance's face, her eyes still struggling to focus.

"Tell me again."

Sammantha frowned and closed her eyes. "I didn't…I thought…I had to get revenge. I didn't plan to fall in love. I didn't know about Petrovski. I didn't know about my parents. I thought it was the U.S…I am so sorry."

Trance dialed the number to a tactical nuclear team. Trance had formed the elite, U.S. group while heading T-Force, with men stationed in New York, Washington, Los Angeles and Bentonville, Arkansas. They'd been assembled to diffuse a nuclear event, and to clean up after detonation. As Congress strengthened its myopic assault on defense spending, the group's funding had been one of the casualties. So Trance had funded the organization himself. Since one of his inherited companies manufactured nuclear weapons for the military, he thought this only fair. This was not the first time his men had been called, nor would it be the last.

"Gems Are Us," said the happy voice on the other line.

"This is Red Dragon," said Trance.

"You are talking to Conquistador. Where you been, man?"

"Busy. Sending." Trance punched the numbers 187*#3-++@1298337 into his phone.

"That's a big 'how are ya.' I.D. confirmed. What you got?"

"I've got a two carat diamond in Washington, D.C. that I would like to sell," said Trance.

"You want to bring it by? Or should we come to you?"

"It's hot," said Trance. "We'll need to close this deal by 2145 hours."

"Come again?"

"I want to drop this gem off somewhere by 9:45 Eastern Time. Tonight."

"Roger that. How soon can you begin transit?"

"Ten minutes, maybe."

"Can you get authority for a tunnel drop?"

"Negative. Authority is unresponsive."

"Shit. Hold a mike."

A few moments later Trance felt his PDA vibrate.

"Just sent you the GPS coordinates for the meet, Red Dragon. Best spot is the Chesapeake. Nothing on land in that time frame. At least nothing we can get access to without presidential decree or brute force. You sure we can't cool this gem down?"

"Negative."

"We'll dispatch our buyers, then."

"Roger."

"Good luck, Red Dragon. Over."

"Back at you, Conquistador."

Trance turned to Sammantha and said, "You are going to come with me."

Trance led Sammantha to the main door of the Capitol chamber. Raymond Childress, the head of the Secret Service detail, Jacob Miller and Abdul Ali, the new head of T-Force, were waiting there for them.

Trance looked at Childress and said, "Am I good to deal with this?"

Childress nodded. "This is beyond my training, Trance. Be glad to have you."

Trance turned to Ali. "Get a Marine One chopper with dive gear in front of the Capitol building, ASAP. I want Stick Granger, two pilots and two crewmembers standing by, along with Miss Starodubov, here."

"Yes, sir." Ali started barking into a walkie.

The president's national security advisor came huffing around the corner. Like always, Jeremiah Pincenogle looked like he had been squeezed into a suit that was two sizes too small, with his rounded back making him look like a big, lumbering snapping turtle. "What's this I hear about a bomb?" he said, through gasping breaths that actually sounded like a snapper's *hiss*.

Trance said, "Sir, we don't have time for detail. A suitcase nuke is set to go off at 2145. It's big enough to level a good chunk of the city. We can't evacuate. If we try, we'll jam the streets and scare the nation. Our best bet is to have Centurion interrupt his speech. That will give us the chance to retrieve the warhead and carry it out to sea, or bury it in some mine shaft somewhere. I've got coordinates to a Chesapeake drop, but I'd much rather get this thing underground. Can you get us in somewhere?"

"How soon did you say?"

"Thirty minutes."

Pincenogle groaned. "Won't happen, Trance. Budget cuts and all. Where is it?"

"At Centurion's feet."

Pincenogle's eyes began to bulge. This made him look more like a frog than a turtle. The folds of his neck seemed to roll like jelly over his shirt collar. But his voice remained calm.

"What proof do you have?"

"We don't have time for proof. You must send a message over the president's teleprompter. Tell him that he needs to excuse himself for one minute. That's all we need, maybe less. We'll remove the bomb. Then he can return to his speech. If that doesn't make him stop, you need to inform him that we have an imminent, credible bomb threat. If that doesn't work, you need to tell him it's nuclear and at his feet." Trance looked to his watch. "You need to get that done within four minutes. Mark the time and get your ass moving."

To Trance's mild surprise, Pincenogle turned and waddled quickly away.

Trance looked to Miller. "You feeling brave tonight?"

"What?"

Trance smiled. "I need you and your men to flank the president. If he pauses, you grab the suitcase and run it outside. If he goes down, you do the same and get it to Marine One. Shoot anyone who gets in your way."

"What do you mean, *if he goes down*?"

"You'll know if he does. Repeat to me what I said."

"If the president pauses or goes down, I run the suitcase that's on stage to Marine One. Shoot anybody that tries to stop me."

"Very good…my friend."

Miller stared at Trance but said nothing. After such a long-standing, contentious relationship that bordered on hatred, the last thing Miller expected was a peace offering. He knew why it was coming now. Trance expected to die.

Trance turned to Ali. "There are two Marine One helos with chains and winches for hauling the president's boat out of the water. Get me one of those, if you can. I'll need a length of free chain weighing at least two hundred pounds, and something I can use to secure it."

Trance looked at Miller. "You got a twenty on Granger?"

"Yeah. He's with ours."

"Good. Get him to Marine One. Let's do this, men. Don't screw up. We get only one chance."

Trance looked to his watch. Then he turned to Ali. "I need one of your shooters to come with me."

Ali spoke into his headset. Within thirty seconds a sharpshooter carrying a SAM-R rifle appeared beside him. "Go with General Trance," Ali told the sniper.

Trance walked calmly up the stairs of the Capitol Building, followed by the sniper sent by Ali. When Trance reached the desired spot he stopped. He moved slowly onto the edge of the balcony, while remaining in the shadows. He looked for Miller. Miller now stood to the side of the vice president. He was flanked by several other men in uniforms, standing just out of camera range. Trance could see Miller's sweat glistening under the bright stage lights and he chuckled. If he only knew what was coming.

Trance didn't have long. Time was critical and running short. He saw the president pause, ever-so-briefly, as he read the first teleprompter message. Trance saw Miller signal that the first message had been delivered. The president hesitated when the next message flashed. But he didn't stop. After the third message Trance looked to his watch. The president wasn't going to step off the stage. Time was up. Trance lifted the marksman's rifle. Without taking time to rethink his plan, he drew the rifle to his shoulder and shot the president in the chest.

CHAPTER **101**

_______________PP_______________

Lauren Haverford was alone in Trance's suite at the Ritz-Carlton, watching the president as he delivered his speech. She was propped up in bed, wearing pink pajamas and a pair of dance slippers. She was thinking how smoothly the president spoke his words when he seemed to falter. The president looked briefly confused. Then he faltered again. And then…then the president stepped back like he was about to choke. He looked down and pressed his hands to his chest. Blood began to seep through his fingers. He fell to the ground and was covered with what looked like a rugby scrum.

Lauren held her breath as a crowd descended on the stage, surrounding the president with a human shield. A news commentator's voice broke in, "The president has been shot. I repeat, president Tilson has been shot."

Lauren couldn't take her eyes off the screen, not even to blink. Nor could she breathe. The network panned to its news anchor. "We have just obtained exclusive footage that might show the president's would-be assassin." The television flashed to a shaky camera shot of someone's back as he was leaving one of the balconies. The man had a sniper's rifle in his arms and was wearing a marine officer's uniform. She couldn't see the man's face, but by the way he moved, Lauren was sure, without doubt, that the shooter was Jack Trance. She let out her breath in a long, low groan.

***

Jesse Tompkin was also watching as the events unfolded. He saw the sea of bodies surround the president. His trained eyes also saw the blur of movement, as Miller swooped in from the side of the stage and grabbed the Halliburton case.

"Oh-oh," he whispered. "Shooting the president is a big no no." This could only mean trouble.

When Tompkin saw the footage of Trance fleeing the scene, he knew, without a doubt, that their worst fears had been realized.

"Jesus, Jack. What have they made you do?"

CHAPTER **102**
PP

Jack Trance handed the SAM-R to the marine sniper and said, "Follow me."

The marine pointed his rifle at Trance, still trying to process what he had just seen the general do. "Sir..."

Trance began sprinting down the stairs three at a time, too fast for the confused sniper to consider a shot. The young man bolted along behind him.

The sniper came to the bottom of the stairs and turned into the hall, just as a group of Secret Servicemen ran past him, going upward. He turned to look for Trance but couldn't see him. Suddenly he felt exposed, like a man in the desert with nothing but sand around him. He was standing in a crowd of people, holding a gun that reeked of cordite. He slung the weapon over his shoulder and began to run outside, to where he hoped to find Marine One waiting.

Trance raced toward the grand entrance to the Capitol Building. Already, a frantic line of politicians was beginning to stream out into the main lobby. Trance launched himself like a hurdler over a screening table, ignoring shouts coming from the marines who'd been manning the post. "General Trance, men. At ease!" he yelled, hoping that his general's uniform and the words would keep them from shooting him in the back. He held his breath as he sprinted out and down the stairs. The Marine One helicopter was already winding up its engines to take off.

When Trance reached the helicopter he found Miller standing beside it. Miller was leaning over with his hands upon his knees as he gulped for air. Between Miller's legs, Trance saw the Zero Halliburton case. Miller was flanked by Stick Granger and the helo's co-pilot. Both looked ready to roll. Trance could see the pilot and two other crew members waiting farther inside the craft.

Trance nodded toward Miller, then said to the marine, "You ready to die for your country, son?"

"We are, sir. Yes, sir!"

"Then get us the hell out of here."

Trance grabbed the case from Miller. "Thanks, Jake. I owe you a dinner."

Miller started to laugh. "Jack...You shot the fucking president."

Trance shook his head. "That's not Jock Tilson. Unless I've lost my touch, there will be blood but little real damage. A clean through and through. He should be fine."

"I'll come visit you in prison, provided you live."

Trance took hold of Miller's shoulder. "I always blamed you for Janice's death. I understand now that it wasn't your fault. I'm sorry. See if you can keep everybody off my six long enough for me to get this thing out to sea."

Miller pulled away as the VH-71 began to lift off the ground. "Been nice knowing you, Jack!" he yelled, as he stretched out his hand.

Trance laughed. He grasped Miller's hand briefly, letting go as the helicopter pulled up into the air. Trance wrapped a headset over his ears, slid the door shut and sat upon the floor. He closed his eyes and let out a long, deep sigh.

"Where too, general?' he heard.

Trance said, "How long for us to reach open water?"

"Twenty to twenty-five minutes, sir."

Trance looked to his watch. This was going to be ugly. He didn't like his nuclear team's choice. But they were right; it was all they had. "Fly this thing as fast as you can east southeast, directly over Chesapeake Beach into Chesapeake Bay."

Trance got up and punched the coordinates into the helicopter's guidance system. He looked down at the map and hit a spot on it with a stylus. He looked at the pilot and said, "We need to find the closest deep water where I can carry this thing down. This should be the spot. Can you get us there before 2140?

"We'll effort that, sir."

Trance thought back to his days at the Naval Academy. He'd studied Operation Crossroads, where a twenty kiloton bomb was detonated in two hundred feet of water, causing a ninety foot wave and a mile-high Wilson vapor cloud. This nuke, he hoped, was just one tenth that size. Unfortunately, the depth of the Chesapeake was rarely more than a hundred feet, and usually less. Far less. This could be a disaster. No, it *would* be a disaster. The question was, *how severe*?

"If I may ask, sir...What is it we're carrying?"

"A live two meg nuke on a timer."

"Well, that's cool."

"Set to go off at 2145."

The pilot inhaled deeply, then said, "Oo-rah, sir." He grinned and tapped a fist on his knee. "Now this is what I call a rush."

Trance focused on Stick and Sammantha. Both were leaning back in their seats, their eyelids partially closed as if traveling on vacation. The suitcase rested between them. Trance pointed to it and said, "Bring it here, please."

He looked to the two crew members sitting toward the rear of the cabin and motioned them forward. Both men came promptly and saluted.

"At ease, men," said Trance. "Is there a thermal drysuit around here?"

"Nah. Just a three eighths wetsuit. You're gonna freeze your nuts off."

"Get it for me, please."

One of the men opened a side door, pulled out a black neoprene wetsuit and tossed it toward Trance.

"Don't suppose you've got a tank, a regulator and a head lamp?"

"Negative, sir."

Trance dropped the wetsuit down to the floor and began to strip.

"Gloves, booties, fins, mask and a dive computer?" he said.

One of the crew members tossed a pair of gloves, two fins and two booties onto the floor beside Trance. He handed Trance a mask, along with an Oceanic dive computer. Trance put on the suit and the booties. He left the gloves and mask on the floor. He crawled over and grabbed a rescue harness. He slung it over his shoulders and secured it. Then he turned his attention to a coil of heavy chain that had been thrown onto the helo's floor. There was more chain than he had asked for, but that was good. Trance tried to fit it through the handle of the suitcase, but the links were too thick. He rummaged around the chain and found several oversized carabiners beside the chain on the floor. He slipped a carabiner through the loop on the suitcase and fitted it through two links of chain. He then wrapped the chain around the suitcase until it looked like something Scrooge's Marley would carry. He fastened two more carabiners around everything to secure it. He tried to pry the chain off the suitcase, but it held fast.

The case, combined with the chain, now weighed over three hundred pounds.

"You gonna toss that overboard, Jack?" said Stick.

"I'm going to carry it down."

"All the way to the bottom?"

"That's the plan."

Stick groaned. "Aw, Jack…That means we'll have to wait."

"You can leave if you want."

Trance pointed across the cabin to the winch and cable. Then he looked at the marines. "You guys know how to work the winch?"

"Bet your friggin'A, general."

"Good."

Trance looked to his watch and winced. So little time. Beneath the wetsuit, he was beginning to perspire. Hot rivulets of sweat were already streaming along his forehead, down his chest and into his crotch.

"How're we doing on reaching the Bay?" he yelled.

"Should be getting there….right…now."

Trance slid the chopper's door open. A cutting wind carved into their faces. It felt like a blizzard was whipping in through the cabin, the wind blowing their vision into a wet blur.

"How much time 'till we reach the target?"

"No more than three minutes, sir."

"Bring us to the surface and hover when we get there," shouted Trance above the noise. He put on the booties, the fins and then the gloves. He and Stick dragged the heavy suitcase to the edge of the cabin by the door. The marines clipped the winch cable onto Trance's harness, so they could to pull him from the water if he made it. One of them pulled at the cable to make sure it was securely fastened, then gave Trance a thumbs-up.

Trance took off his dress watch and replaced it with the dive computer. He spit onto the faceplate of the old-style mask and rubbed against the glass. Not that it mattered; he'd be close to blind in the dark water anyway.

He said, "When I come up, I'll pull on the cable and signal. When I do, you bug out. This is going to be close. You get me into the craft after we're underway. Got it?"

The marines both nodded.

"If I don't make it back in time, don't wait. That's an order."

"Thirty seconds, sir!"

Trance crouched in the doorway. He put on his mask and wormed his hands into the suitcase and chain. Already, his hands were beginning to grow numb from the wind and the cold. The helicopter came to a full halt about ten feet from the surface. Trance looked to his watch. Six minutes. He hoped the bomb's clock wasn't fast. Then he jumped into the frigid, rolling waves.

CHAPTER 103

_______________PP_______________

The president lay on his back, staring up at all the shadows hovering over him. His chest felt like it was caving in. His breathing came in short painful gasps. A Secret Service EMT threw an oxygen mask over his face.

"Look at me, Mr. President. You were shot in the chest. You're going to be okay. My name is Henry, and I'm going to be riding with you to Bethesda. Don't try to talk. Just lie back and look at me. I'm going to be talking to you the whole way. Just keep looking at me."

Two other EMTs lifted the president onto a stretcher. They jogged him out toward a waiting helicopter, while Henry walked beside him. The president's personal physician caught up and jogged along, as the EMTs rushed on with the president.

"You're doing great, Mr. President." Henry took hold of the president's hand. "If you can feel my hand just blink."

The president blinked several times.

"That's good. Real good, sir."

The president was slipped inside the Marine One MedEvac chopper. Henry, the EMTs and the president's personal doctor jumped aboard and they lifted off. The EMTs worked to control the bleeding, while Henry continued his non-stop monologue. "We're just a few miles away, Mr. President. I know that you must be feeling pain right now. We're going to take care of that in just a few minutes, but not yet. I'm going to keep talking to you as we go. Your personal doctor is here with us, and he's coming in with you to the hospital.

"I was listening to that speech. That was one helluva speech, sir. I was sure wondering what you and Ogarkov were going to do with that suitcase. In case you're wondering, he's fine. You were the only one hit."

The president's eyes began to close.

"Stay with me, sir." Henry squeezed the president's hand and the president squeezed back. "You must stay awake, all the way to Bethesda. There's a trauma team waiting for us there."

A few minutes later the helicopter touched down on the hospital's helipad. A team of doctors rushed out and sped the president into the ER, where a new team of surgeons would do their best to save his life.

While the president was in surgery, the lights began to flicker. A short time after that, there was a far off _boom_ outside, like the roar of distant thunder. This was followed a brief burst of wind, before the night outside returned to what seemed like normal.

CHAPTER **104**
_________PP_________

Amidst the frenzied cacophony of sound and bodies, Jacob Miller assembled a meeting in a conference room within the Capitol Building. Seated at the table were the joint chiefs of staff, the vice president, the president's national security advisor, the heads of the FBI, the Secret Service, the NSA, Homeland Security and the speaker of the house.

Miller said, "I am told that the president is alive and in stable condition. He was shot once in the chest—"

At that moment the lights flickered off. The city went dark for one brief moment, before the power resumed as if nothing had happened. "That would be the electromagnetic pulse from the nuclear warhead," said Miller.

Stunned faces looked his way. Without a word being spoken by others, Miller continued.

"Just moments into the president's speech, we became aware that a nuclear warhead had been placed on stage. We do not know, at this time, how this happened.

"Throughout the day, the president made it clear that he could not be disturbed. Before beginning his speech, the president left orders that no one be allowed onstage with him. A perimeter guard was established and snipers were positioned throughout the Capitol hall. The president refused to wear an earpiece.

"We were sure that any attempt to go on stage with the president would cause an incident. Our orders to countermand the president would be met with force.

"The president was made aware of the warhead though his teleprompter. The president ignored three warnings. We shot him to create a diversion big enough for us to go up on stage, retrieve the nuclear device from his feet and try to take it to safety."

"*We* shot the president?" said the FBI director.

"I take full responsibility for that," said Miller. "It was the safest alternative." Miller almost laughed at the irony.

Miller checked his cell phone. It was dead. "This was a *nuclear* weapon, gentlemen, not some load of C-4, ammonium nitrate, or even a MOAB. This was enough to make this city glow for decades. The EMP has crippled my telephone service, although it looks like the power grid is intact. I don't know where it blew, how many are dead, or how many will die. It could still be that we all die. Potassium iodide pills *are* on the way for everyone.

"I am encouraged though, because we kept power. If I were to guess, I'd say they got it to water before it detonated."

"You brought it out to sea?" said the speaker of the house.

Miller shook his head. "I doubt it. Reliable intel said it would detonate at 2145. If we're lucky, they immersed the warhead in the Chesapeake."

"Good God," said the vice president. "Think of the environmental consequences."

Miller stared at the vice president, but said nothing. *What a frigging boob*, he thought. At least they were alive and the Capitol wouldn't glow.

"Any I.D. on the shooter?" said one of the Joint Chiefs.

Miller paused, as if debating what to say. In the end, he settled on the truth.

"It was Jack Trance."

The Joint Chiefs Chairman, a marine general by the name of Longboat, chuckled softly. "Figures it would be a marine."

"He started as one of ours," countered the navy's Admiral Chester.

"We can both take credit," said Longboat. "The man's got stones."

"I wouldn't be gloating, boys," said Miller. "My guess is that this president will have him hung."

"He wouldn't," said Longboat. "Trance has more guts than all the men in this room combined. He's spilled more blood for this country than—"

Miller interrupted. "You don't have to convince me, General Longboat. The president will ask why we didn't just fire a warning shot, or something more benign than a bullet to his chest. Surely we could have created a diversion in some other way?"

"Look," said Longboat. "By all accounts the president has turned into a pantywaist and a media hound. You know how hard it has been to work with the man, since the abduction, I mean. You know the rumors…that it isn't even Tilson. He certainly seems hell bent on destroying the military and anything we stand for.

"If we told Centurion that he was in danger, and he ignored it, there was no other option. You can bet your sorry ass that if we'd just fired a warning shot, the president would have raised holy hell… No. Trance did the right thing, the only thing."

"He will still face consequences," said Miller.

"Upon my resignation," said Longboat.

"And mine," said Chester.

"And mine."

"And mine."

Miller looked at each member of the Joint Chiefs of Staff and smiled grimly. "And mine."

The Speaker of the House, Benjamin Hibbleton, rose from the table. He was a towering man, built like a crane, with a sharp jaw, and an even sharper temper. "You fellas can insult the president all you want. Yeah, we've all heard the whispers; *he's not the same man.*

"Which of us would be the same man after the murder of a wife, a brutal burning and a kidnapping? Until you bring me one shred of proof that this is *not* president Tilson, you will face the full power of Congress in every move you make to try to smear his name. You all got that? And if any of you try to resign, I will make it my personal mission to destroy your name and your reputation, such that you will regret the day you tried to paint a black spot on this administration. Am I clear?"

"Yes, Mr. Speaker," said Miller.

"If Trance survived this thing, I want you to make sure he's remanded. I don't want the man who tried to assassinate the president running free, no matter what he claims were his motives. He must be held accountable, for the president's sake, for the country's sake. You got that?"

May you rot in hell, thought Miller. But he said, "Yes, Mr. Speaker."

CHAPTER **105**
______________PP______________

As Trance jumped into the cold, milky brine of the Chesapeake, he began to pray. Please let the water be deep enough. Please save the people nearby. Please save the Bay. Please let Copley be alive. Please let me find a way to rescue Tilson. Please let me see Lauren again. Please let me live.

Trance expected the chain to pull him down and deep like a great white shark. But the airtight bomb casing was surprisingly buoyant. It wanted to meander in the water like a wet log. On its own, the case and chain would drift lower, but at nowhere near the rate needed to get the bomb to the bottom in time. Trance pushed the case down, kicking furiously with his fins. They went deeper and deeper, the bomb and Trance. The bomb provided stubborn resistance, so Trance kicked harder, pushing with every bit of his strength. The cable on Trance's back felt like it was slowing him down, so he unhooked it. Still, the progress seemed painfully, dangerously slow. Trance gave up hope for saving himself. Now, his only aim was to get the bomb as deep as possible before he passed out. *Please, let us go deep*, thought Trance.

The water in the Chesapeake was often shallow, averaging less than thirty feet along most of it's nearly two hundred miles. There were spots where the glacial rocks and the currents had carved grooves and pits that could go a hundred feet down or more. He prayed for the depth indicated on his chart.

It didn't take Trance long to pass beyond the glow the helicopter's searchlights. After less than a minute he could see nothing. He kept on kicking. He had to go deep. His lungs began to burn for air. He felt the water pressure closing in on him like an elastic body wrap. If he could breathe, he would surely be strangled. Still, he kicked.

Trance finally felt the case thud against the bottom of the Bay. He tugged at the chain, to make sure that the bomb was secure. Then he pushed himself back up toward the surface and kicked as hard as he could. Stars danced before his eyes. He began to see a bright white light in the distance, like a door opening to the great beyond. A strange peace seemed to settle upon him. It looked comforting, the light. It beckoned him, like the call of love, pulling him toward it before his body could reach the surface of the Chesapeake. Trance's mind began to float, and he felt himself start to relax, to let go.

***

Stick held his body out over the water while the helicopter hovered at a height of no more than fifteen feet. There was a searchlight shining down on the black water, but all Stick could see was s swirling froth of charcoal foam.

"It's been over three minutes," said one of the marines. He brought his head up over Stick's shoulder and began to tug him back into the craft. "C'mon, sir."

"We'll wait," said Stick. He looked to his watch. It read 9:42.

"Sir, he's not coming back. He'd want us to go. He ordered us to go."

Stick ignored him and remained in place, staring into the gloom.

The marine said, "We'll wait, but you know he'd want us to protect a woman on board. That thing is going to blow any minute. Might be good for us to be away from the spray."

"We wait," said Stick.

The marine smiled. "Okay."

Good for you, thought Stick. *You poor, brave son-of-a-bitch.*

CHAPTER **106**
_____________PP_____________

The president was still conscious as he was wheeled into the ER. The trauma team lifted him off the wheeled stretcher and slid him onto a more stable operating table, this one equipped with a set of retracting wheels.

"How are you feeling, Mr. President?" said one of the surgeons, as he pulled the oxygen mask off the president's face.

"Just ducky."

The surgeon placed a new mask onto the president's face. This one was hooked to a tank attached to the table. "We're going to get some quick pics to see what you look like inside. If you can stand it, I'd rather give you just a topical for the pain right now, at least until we know what we're dealing with. You okay with that? Just blink."

The president blinked.

Minutes later, two doctors were viewing a pair of monitors, scrolling through X-ray and CT scans, while another watched a third screen as an ultrasound wand was run across the president's chest.

"You are one lucky man, Mr. President," said one of the surgeons. "Looks like the bullet passed between your lung and your subclavian artery. It also passed between your ribs, causing minimal damage there. Maybe just a nick of the cartilage, maybe. I can fix in a couple minutes if we need to. It also missed cracking your scapula. Damned lucky all around.

"In fact, I'd almost call it a miracle. I don't see any organ damage. No bone damage. Little blood vessel damage, despite the size of the round. The bullet passed cleanly out your back. It must have had a full metal jacket, 'cause the exit hole isn't much bigger than the entry. We are going to run a few more tests. But I think that all we're going to need to do is give you some fluids and stitch you up. We'll take an MRI later, just to make sure we haven't missed something. But I want to deal with this now, rather than wait."

"It hurts like a mother."

"We'll give you something for the pain. But we're going to keep you conscious, if that's okay with you?"

"Just do your thing, doc."

The lead surgeon rolled the president onto his side and they began to scrub him down. That's when the lights flickered. At the same moment, the bottom of the Chesapeake Bay began to bubble under the heat of a million degrees.

After a few quick stitches to his chest and his back, the president was allowed to lie in a more comfortable position.

"Yep," said the surgeon. "You are one lucky man."

"What is your name, doctor?"

"Oh, I'm sorry. My name is Julius Barfield, M.D., Ph.D."

"Well, Dr. Julius Barfield. I appreciate your enthusiasm about my condition. But the important issue here is that this was the second assassination attempt on my life. I tried to forget the first one and carry on with my duties as president. This time I won't rest until these killers are given their due. When do you suppose I'll be able to get out of here?"

"You could leave right now, if you forced us. I wouldn't though. We'll want to keep you here for observation, to make sure you don't bleed internally. As always, the big worry is infection. We're going to give you some class A antibiotics for the next week or two. That should prevent any major infection. But you never know. Anytime someone or something goes tickling inside your chest cavity..."

The president cut Barfield off in mid-sentence. "I get it, doc. I'm a lucky man. Will you call for my chief of staff? I've got a country to run and I'm really pissed that I didn't get to finish my speech."

Barfield looked briefly puzzled, then said, "Yes, Mr. President. Right away."

CHAPTER **107**
______________PP______________

Trance's face broke up through the water. He took in three huge gasping breaths of sweet, salty air. He was giving thanks for being alive when he realized that the men in the helicopter couldn't see him. The chopper was criss-crossing the area and they were heading away from him. With only moments to go before the explosion, they were moving away.

Trance looked to his watch. He had been underwater for over five minutes. They wouldn't look for much longer, of that he was sure. They had already stayed longer than they should have. Trance waved frantically. Marine One was drifting northward, with its searchlights panning the water below. *Damn!*

"Perhaps we should call it, sir," said the marine pilot. "It's been nearly six minutes. The general couldn't have survived underwater for that long, and we can't see a lick down there. I'd stay until hell froze over, but that thing is going to blow, sir. Any second now. The farther away we are, the better chance we've got."

Stick Granger was beginning to panic. Had Trance decided to die with the bomb? Did he simply hold it down until his lungs gave out? No, Trance wouldn't do that. He wouldn't let them die; he *knew* they would wait.

"I won't leave a marine here to die," Stick said.

One of the crew members pulled his gaze away from the open water and yelled above the noise, "We wouldn't either, sir. But it's way past the time he could have survived down there. Probably why he unhooked his tether. We do have a woman on board, sir. The general wouldn't want us all to die. Would he?"

Stick worked his way into the cockpit. He looked out through the wind screen and swore. This was like trying to find a lost earring in beach sand. He patted the pilot on the shoulder and said, "I'm going to leave this one up to you, son. I've seen Trance hold his breath for more than six minutes before. He's one of the finest SEALs the navy ever produced...Led covert operations all over the globe, including the one that just saved Washington. He doesn't deserve to die this way."

"Did you say, Trance, sir? Jack Trance?"

"I sure as hell did."

"You didn't say this was Trance. Never met him, but I've sure heard the stories."

The pilot whipped the helicopter into a tight roll and headed back toward their original drop zone. He consulted his GPS and began to guide the helicopter back to the precise location of Trance's entry into the water. "Anyone else and...well...I thought it was just some general down there...and a fool's errand to wait more than three minutes, let alone six."

They came to the spot where Trance had gone into the water. They saw nothing but night. The crewmen swept the water with their spotlights. They could only see a black swirl below. Then Stick saw movement, just beyond the reach of the searchlight, more like a moving shadow than a body. Trance was stroking rapidly toward the helicopter with a manic crawl stroke. He was barely visible in his wetsuit, just a flash of face where his mask had been.

"Over there," said Stick calmly, while pointing.

The helicopter swooped low and a crew member threw the harness back into the water. As the harness swept past Trance he grabbed it and slung it around his shoulders in one quick motion.

"Go!" yelled Stick.

The helicopter whipped up into the air and started racing away. They reeled in on the winch until Trance's hands reached the skids. Trance fought against the wind and the cold and his bulky wetsuit to climb up onto the skid below. The crewman on the winch gave him some gentle help. After a few harrowing moments, Trance flipped himself inside the cabin. He said, "You shouldn't have waited, guys. But thanks."

Trance looked to his dive watch. It was 9:46 Eastern time. He grinned. "Doesn't look like we've got much time, does it, Pirate?"

"All we need is another minute or two. How deep did you get it?"

Trance looked to his watch and read the depth history. "I made it to a hundred and nine feet before hitting bottom. Lucky as hell in these waters."

"Maybe your boys dug that hole. Think it's enough?"

Trance shrugged. He patted Stick on the shoulder. "You should have bugged back there, Granger."

Stick grinned. "And miss all the fireworks?"

"You talked them back, didn't you? You made them turn."

"Nah. They're a bunch of brave hombres. I just told 'em it was you and they knew what to do."

"Thanks."

"Don't thank me yet, Jack—"

At that moment they saw a flash of eerie light spread over the horizon. The engine on the helicopter faltered, but kicked back in, thanks to the helicopter's EMP shields. They heard a rumble beneath the bay. The water seemed to round into a bubble, before settling back down into a series of moderate waves. Nothing devastating. There was no Wilson Cloud that they could see. They'd been lucky. Damned lucky the bomb wasn't bigger or the depth more shallow. A few might die today, but not a hundred thousand. And not the President, not the Congress, the Cabinet, the Supreme Court or the world's top leaders. Trance's response team would be on the spot within minutes, doing their best to minimize the damage. This could devastate the Chesapeake, but the damage might not be irreparable; at least he hoped so.

"Thar she blows," said Stick. "Ain't it great to be alive, you sonofabitch!"

"I just wish this were the end," said Trance softly. "The property owners along this coast will suffer immeasurably. Depending upon the current, it could take years to clean this completely. And us? We've got an awful lot left to do. Assuming we get to do it at all."

CHAPTER **108**

___________PP___________

The speaker of the house rode Miller like a sadistic straw boss, threatening hell and damnation if Trance wasn't captured. He made sure that a Delta team was assembled to apprehend Trance, assuming he'd survived the detonation, he ordered Miller to stay with them.

There were reports from multiple locations of a Marine One helicopter in flight. Two came from the north, two from the south, one from the east and one from the west. The helicopter's GPS chip had been damaged or disabled in the blast, for they could find no sign of it anywhere. The ship was a mystery.

"When he comes in, you nail his ass," said the House speaker.

Miller said, "I'll take him into custody, Mr. Speaker. But he should get a hero's welcome, not charged with treason and attempted murder."

"You leave that up to others, Miller. In fact, why don't go find some spook shit to do. Find some real imminent danger, something out of my way. Get the hell out of my way."

Miller took a slow draft of Pepto from his hip flask. He let his gaze fall upon the speaker of the house. He just stared. After several awkward moments he said, "In case you're not aware of this, Mr. Speaker, the president was attacked by people from *outside* this country. When he was kidnapped he was taken *outside* this country. So, just in case you forget, as director of the CIA, I have an obligation to be here. I have a responsibility to my president and to my country, even more than you."

"Why don't you just go back to your country club, Miller? Men like you screw things up in this town. Men like you make it impossible to govern, at least properly. It's men like you that put the president in harm's way."

"Excuse me, Mr. Speaker. But, fuck you."

The speaker of the house looked calmly at Miller and smiled. In the low lights, Miller was sure he saw the speaker's eyes glint red, with the satanic pleasure of a power addict.

"I'll tell the president you said that," he said. "Now, go find me our number one terrorist, Jack Trance."

CHAPTER **109**
________PP________

"We should be back at the Capitol within fifteen minutes," said the Marine One pilot.

Trance leaned over the pilot's shoulder and said, "I need you to head toward Newark, soldier."

The pilot stared at Trance. "That's over two hundred miles out of our way, sir. I'll have to get clearance for that."

"I think not. To retrieve that bomb, I had to shoot the president."

The pilot looked at Trance but said nothing. Trance thought he saw a brief smile cross the pilot's face, but he wasn't sure in the pale cockpit light.

Trance continued, "The president gave orders against all contact before he made his speech. He surrounded himself with guards, with orders to kill. He ignored three requests to pause his speech and let us retrieve the bomb from his feet. There was no other way."

The pilot nodded. "Don't have to explain that to me, sir. I know who you are."

Sammantha Starodubov walked to the edge of the cockpit and stuck her head inside. "Did you kill Brandon?"

Trance shook his head. "He'll be fine, unless I've lost my touch."

"When I get confirmation of his safety, I'll take you to Tilson."

"Where is he?"

"Your president is out of the country. No more until I hear that Brandon's all right."

The pilot looked at Trance and then at Sammantha. "I don't think I want to hear this."

"No, soldier," said Trance. "You don't."

"Guess I better take you to Newark, then."

"Good thinking."

The pilot reached forward and fiddled with his controls. After a few moments he turned to Trance. "They're hailing us, sir."

"Ignore them and go dark."

"Dark it is."

An hour and fifteen minutes later they could see the lights of Newark ahead to the north. The air inside the cockpit began to take on the smell of refinery sulfur, like rotten eggs, despite the helicopter's filtration system.

"That's Newark ahead, sir."

"Come parallel with the highway," said Trance.

Several minutes later they could make out the bright lights of a truck stop, with its name shining brightly from a fifty foot pole.

"There, sir?" said the pilot.

"No. Not yet. In a moment, I'm going to tell you where to go."

CHAPTER **110**
_____________PP_____________

"Where the hell are they, Miller?" yelled the speaker of the house.

They were standing inside the Capitol Building, beside the team assembled to take Trance into custody when he landed.

"Probably dead."

"The president wants him in custody. Dead or alive."

"The president is an ungrateful prig and we both know it."

"Our president has been through hell!" The speaker of the house pressed his nose against Miller's forehead and began screaming. Spit started flying from his lips, as if he were a barking Saint Bernard. Drool dripped down Miller's nose and into his mouth, like a goopy hawker had been blown at him in disgust.

"When one of our own shoots down the president he's going to have to pay! Now, I assure you, Trance's trial, and his hanging, will be quick and private. But it _will_ happen. Have no doubt.

"So, you tell Trance to get his ass here before…just have him get his ass here."

"We don't know where he is, sir. I told you that. We're not even sure he's alive. In fact, knowing Trance, he probably did die, after saving Washington and your sorry ass."

"You're done, Miller. We're going to clean house after this. And you are going to be the first one out on the street."

"I'll look forward to that, Mr. Speaker."

CHAPTER **111**

_______________PP_______________

Just before Marine One reached Newark, Trance said, "Now head northwest toward Columbia."

The helo pilot banked to port. Fifteen minutes later the helicopter touched down on the outer rim of a brightly lit truck stop parking lot. Behind them, a tall aluminum pole rose into the sky, shining the letters, *TA*, so all could see. Trance saluted each of the men inside helo. Then he extended a hand to the pilot.

"You're all now part of the family," he said.

"Family, sir?"

"Yeah. You stayed when you could have run."

"We did what any marines would do, sir. Marines don't cut and run…Never leave a live man behind, not if there was any chance…"

Trance scribbled a phone number onto a piece of paper and handed it to the pilot. "You boys ever need anything…and I mean anything…you call me."

The marine took the paper and stuffed it into a pocket. As he did so, Stick Granger leaned over and whispered in his ear. "That's a get out of jail card, a get rich quick card, a business loan card, a mortgage for your home card, a job card, a send your child to college card, kid. I suggest you boys use it someday."

The young marine grinned at Trance. "It's been a kick-ass pleasure, sir. Semper Fi, sir."

"Semper Fi, soldier. And remember, you dropped us off in Philly."

By the time Trance and the others stepped onto the parking lot, the night had grown bitterly cold. Trance's damp uniform began to instantly freeze. He was already chilled to the bone from his dive and his teeth began chattering wildly. He pulled a stack of damp five hundred dollar bills out of his pocket, peeled off two and handed them to Stick.

"Would you please go in? Get us food and some discreet clothing. See what they're saying about the shooting. See if they've got my picture plastered everywhere. If so, we'll have to adjust."

Stick stared at the five hundred dollar bills. "You sure this is real money, Trance? They're going to look at me like I'm crazy, flashing these things."

"That's all I've got, Granger. Sorry. You're more than welcome to pay."

Stick laughed. "Only if I have to." Stick took the money and began walking toward the brightly lit building.

Trance watched Stick go, turned to Sammantha and said, "So, where is Tilson?"

"Moscow."

Trance groaned. "Where in Moscow?"

"The Kremlin."

Trance groaned again. "The Kremlin is a big place, Sammantha. Sixty-eight acres of impenetrable fortress. Where in the Kremlin?"

"I'm not sure. Not really, not anymore."

"Oh, great. Like we're going to fly into the Kremlin and demand our president back. Does Ogarkov know he's there?"

"He does."

"He's part of this?"

"Yes and no. He had no part in Tilson's kidnapping…except to give me cash to help fund the project.

"He thought he was funding a mission to influence the president toward nuclear disarmament, not kidnapping and murder. When Tilson showed up at his dacha, he didn't know what to do. He couldn't send him back, not without triggering a war. He wouldn't kill him. So he made sure he was safe, pending the outcome of my mission. You see, all *he* ever really wanted was a peace accord. I promised to deliver that. He didn't know that it would be with Brandon Copley as president."

"Ogarkov must have been beside himself when he found out."

"He threatened to kill us all. Then he saw the results of my plan, a president who was willing to negotiate a lasting peace accord, like no president before him."

"While all along, you were planning to kill them both?"

"Nothing personal. Ogarkov would have been collateral damage. Not part of my original plan, but expendable. Everyone is expendable in war, aren't they, Jack?"

"All this for revenge against America?"

"You could never know the pain I endured, the hell I went through. I won't make excuses, because I am guilty. Your answer is, yes. It was revenge…No, it was war."

"For something we…I mean our country…didn't do."

"I didn't know that then."

"But you know it now?"

Sammantha nodded. "I do. I wish I could make it right, but I can't. Once I've helped you get Tilson, I will submit to your authorities and pay for my crimes. I wish I could take it all back…take my whole life back…and run away with Brandon…All I ever wanted was to quiet the screams, the ones inside…inside my mind. You don't know what it was like, how inhuman…all the pawing, the slobbering, being used and abused like a cheap sex toy. For most of my life, all I've done is try to survive…for one more day, one more hour, one more minute. It was like my body was bleeding from a thousand places. All I could do to keep my body alive was to feed it more blood. That blood was revenge. That's what kept me alive, my thoughts of revenge. I deserve to pay for that."

Sammantha touched Trance on the shoulder. "I am so sorry about Janice. I thought…I thought that if I killed what you loved, I would feel better. You had taken mine, so if I took yours…"

"Now, you know you were betrayed?"

"My whole life was betrayed."

"I am sorry," said Trance.

"How can you say that, after what I did?"

"Because I have done things, too. You wouldn't believe what they've had me do, the things we all do every day in the name of freedom, in the name of country. Freedom is paid for with bullets and blood, Sammantha. I've been freedom's weapon of choice." Trance looked out to the night stars. "Sometimes I lie awake at night and wonder why we're all here. What is our purpose? What is it all for? Sometimes I wish I could just slink away to some deserted island and escape it all.

"Things that I can't control always stand in my way. I was born to money. Born to responsibilities that you could not imagine. Things that extend two thousand years back and hundreds of years into the future."

"Sometimes life just sucks," said Sammantha.

Trance laughed. "Yeah, sometimes it does."

Sammantha looked into Trance's eyes. "What's going to happen to you now?"

Trance shrugged. "Probably be court marshaled and hung as a traitor."

"You're not a traitor. You're a patriot. You saved Washington…the entire Congress."

"I shot the president, Sammantha."

"To save his life! Besides, he wasn't the president."

Trance slowly shook his head. "He thinks he is. You, of all people, Sammantha, should understand the law of unintended consequences."

"I say you should live. You will live. You will be recognized as the man you are. We are going to go find the president. We are going to bring him home. I will expose my plan and everyone will know. Then *you* will be honored as a patriot, not hung as a traitor."

Trance shook his head again. "You can't expose your plan, Sammantha."

"Why not?"

"We can't admit to the nation that we've had an imposter in the White House for half a year. An imposter signing legislation, negotiating treaties, setting U.S. policy, addressing the nation. We cannot let our people, or other nations, know that our security could be so compromised as to have a spy in the White House, or a bomb at the president's feet. If that means that I fall on my sword, so be it.

"Right now, all I want to do is find Jock Tilson. Then I'll turn myself in and let fate take it's course."

"We will find him," said Sammantha. "That, I will assure you. But you can't fall on your sword. I won't let you, not after what you've done."

"You can't control everything, Sammantha. Sometimes, no matter how good or caring or righteous you are, the world can't let you be. Look at Jesus, for God's sake. What did he do to deserve crucifixion?"

"He died for our sins," whispered Sammantha.

"Including yours," said Trance.

Stick Granger came walking toward them, carrying a yellow duffel bag over his shoulder that was filled with jeans and shirts and coats. In his hands, Stick carried a brown paper bag and a tray with three coffee cups. Stick handed the bag and the tray to Sammantha, dropped the bundle onto the ground and said, "Not the greatest stuff to choose from, JT." He pulled a pair of jeans from the pile. "These should fit you," he said, while tossing them at Trance. He reached down and pulled two long sleeved sweatshirts from the pile. "You want *I Heart New York* or *I Heart New Jersey*? It was either that or ones that said, *I'm with Stupid* and *Stupid*."

After they had eaten and changed into warmer, more comfortable clothing, Trance focused on finding a ride to New York. "Let's get closer to the entrance," he said.

They waited about thirty yards from the truck stop entrance for close to ten minutes, before Trance said, "There." He pointed toward a black man with very dark skin. He had a curly, black growth of beard. The beard had a single round patch of white in the center of his chin, like Jay Leno's hair.

Trance angled toward the man as he carried a box of french fries toward a row of big rigs. The target stopped beside a dark, midnight-blue Peterbilt truck with a shiny silver trailer.

"Excuse me, marine," said Trance. "I could use your help."

The man brought his hand to his hip and put his palm onto the grip of his KA-BAR fighting knife. "Who's asking?"

"The name is Trance. General, Jack Trance."

"You're too young to be a general."

"I'm old enough."

"You're no general, son."

Trance thought to reach into the duffel bag and retrieve his uniform. But that could raise as many questions as it answered. "I am. But you don't have to believe me."

"I do if I'm going to help you. How'd you know I was a marine?"

Trance pointed to the man's feet. "Only an ex-marine would wear such spit-shined boots and carry a KA-BAR on his hip."

The man laughed and extended his hand. "I don't believe you're a general, but the name's Jones. My friends call me Deacon."

"You play ball?"

"Football? Nah. I'm just a religious sort."

Deacon unlocked his rig and said, "You wait here for a bit, okay?"

"Please, don't tell anyone I am here."

Deacon looked at Trance for a long moment. Then he pulled a mobile phone off the cab's front seat and used the speed dial. After a few moments Trance could hear him speaking. "Yeah, I know it's late…No, I don't care what I'm interrupting…Who saved your ass…That's right. I need you to check up on someone…Yes, now…Yes, I'll wait."

Deacon turned toward Trance. "One of my buds works in admin. He'll be able to check you out. What's your full name and service number?"

Trance told him.

Deacon spoke into his phone. "His name is John Patrick Trance, Jr…Uh-huh. I'll wait."

Deacon held the phone to his ear and waited. He kept watch on Trance, who stood at a non-threatening distance, still shivering from the cold. After a few minutes the man was talking again.

"No shit? Uh-huh."

The man turned to Trance. "There are two John Patrick Trance generals in the files."

"The other was my father. He was a three star. I'm a one star."

The man spoke into his phone. "He says his father was a Lieutenant General…Uh-huh." He turned to Trance. "Where were you born?"

"On a military base in Japan."

"Who'd you serve with?"

"Became a man at Annapolis, then joined the SEALS. Was in the CIA and the marines. Called up now and then for a bunch of little things."

Deacon held up a finger while he listened to his friend on the phone. "No shit…Thanks." Deacon looked at Trance. "My man says you were awarded the Congressional Medal of Honor. That true?"

"Don't mistake that for uncommon bravery, Deacon. I'm no braver than any other warrior, just too stupid to stay out of trouble."

Deacon snapped to attention and saluted. "It is an honor, sir!"

Trance laughed. "I'm willing to pay you for your time."

Deacon pondered Trance's words briefly and said, "No need, sir."

"I insist," said Trance.

Deacon shook his head. "Sorry, General Trance. This one's on me."

Trance waved toward Stick and Sammantha. "There are three of us. We need to get to New York, where we can hide."

CHAPTER **112**
_____________PP_____________

It was just after midnight. The president pressed the nurse call button and a woman scurried quickly into the room.

"Can I help you, Mr. President?"

"I would like to speak with Geoffrey Grodin. Have someone call him, please."

"I believe he is still here, Mr. President. Why don't I go down the hallway and see?"

The nurse went to her station. She buzzed another nurse who was standing inside the hospital cafeteria.

The cafeteria had been transformed. While the vice president had taken up residence in the White House, the members of the president's administration had migrated to the hospital. They were sitting in jagged circles throughout the cafeteria. Some were speaking on phones. Others were checking their PDAs or their portable computers. Some were huddled in somber conversation. Three members of the president's cabinet were playing poker at a corner table, using packets of salt, pepper and sugar as chips. Geoff Grodin stood at the shoulder of the Secretary of Health & Human Services, advising her to bet all her sugar packets on a straight flush. Twelve of the president's policy "Czars" were sitting alone in one corner, as if they were too good for the general riff raff.

The nurse scurried over to Grodin and informed him that the president wished to see him. Some in the room looked toward Grodin with jealous eyes, but most kept busy with their appointed tasks.

The chief of staff entered the president's room wearing his usual khaki pants, blue blazer and his Harvard tie. He was wearing penny loafers without socks.

Grodin and Tilson had been roommates at Harvard. From an old-line investment banking family, Grodin didn't work for the money, or even the power. He had the luxury of serving his long-time friend, and his country, just for the fun of it. Grodin was well-built, and stood just a shade under six foot two. A former athlete, his stomach was showing just small signs of age, sagging slightly onto his belt, but not over it. His dark brown hair was thinning on the cap of his head, like a tree that's lost half its autumn leaves. He now employed an artful, but not quite obvious, comb-over. His eyes were bright, his teeth sturdy, white and straight. He could talk the ears off a priest.

"Hey, Jock. How'r ya feelin'?"

"Like crap, Geoff."

"You want me to sneak in a flask of Dewar's?"

"I gave that stuff up, remember?"

Geoff Grodin thought back to the day he and Tilson had first met. It was freshman year at Harvard, two days before classes were to begin. He had walked into his dorm room to find Jock Tilson sitting there with an unopened bottle of Dewar's Scotch sitting on their suite's coffee table. Tilson stood up from the table and introduced himself. Then he'd pointed at the scotch.

"You ever drink this stuff?" he'd said.

"Nope."

"Me neither. My mother stuck it into my bag this morning. Said I might as well get it over with, taking my first drink that is, and learn how to handle it in private before I drank in public. You want some?"

They had finished the bottle that weekend. They'd both become so blindingly sick that neither had ever gotten truly drunk again. They had learned to love their scotch though, like men intrepidly facing their greatest fears. It was one of those weird things that had bonded them for life, like a sacrament. Now, his friend had quit the stuff, which was almost as sacrilegious as quitting coffee.

"Oh, yeah. Forgot you quit."

The president sighed and leaned back in his bed. "You've known me a long time, Geoff…"

Grodin took a seat beside the president and waited for his next words.

"…I want you to tell me something, truthfully. Have I changed as much as people say I have?"

"What do you mean, Jock?"

"You think I don't hear the whispers? Or the arguments?"

"You have been through a lot, old friend. More than anyone should have to bear. It's hard enough to lose the love of your life. It's hard enough to shoulder the burdens of a nation. It's hard enough to be a hockey puck that people hit around and shoot at. But when you combine all three?"

"What should I do about the man who shot me?"

"From what I hear…this is only hearsay, I must add…it became known that there was a nuclear warhead at your feet and something had to be done."

"No one specifically told you about this, Geoff?"

"No sir. Just rumor."

The president sighed. "I learned about it was when I was giving my speech. I can't be expected to interrupt my State of the Union Address for some stupid bomb threat, can I? I mean, I can't appear scared; I must be strong. The show must go on."

"We're not acting here, Jock."

The president laughed tiredly. "It's all a big act, being president. Every time I go out in public, I'm supposed to be wearing a smile. While, behind my back, enemies are plotting against me like I'm Caesar or something. The media is searching for every piece of dirt they can find. Other countries are trying to pick my pocket every chance they get…and Congress…Well, you know what they're like."

"And to think that this is what you've wanted since you could walk."

"I can't let *him* walk."

"Who?"

"Trance. The man that shot me."

"I hear he might be dead."

"If he's not, he will be. He's got to pay."

"Pay, Jock? From what I hear, he saved Washington. I'd give the man a medal. They say he could have stayed away from the city. Instead, he chose to come to the Capitol to do whatever it took to save you, Washington, and our entire national government."

"I don't see it that way."

Grodin lowered his voice. "If word got out on this, you'd have a public relations nightmare. The man is a decorated hero, Jock. Hell, he's got more medals on his chest than any two of your Joint Chiefs. He doesn't have to work for the government; he does it because of *duty*. He did this because you left him no option. From what I hear, you ignored three warnings. So, if you are going to set an example, you better do it privately and without fanfare. Just make him vanish, Jock. Put him into some hole from which he will never emerge."

"I'll need to find him first."

"Maybe he's dead."

"For his sake, I hope he is."

CHAPTER **113**

PP

The big rig crossed the George Washington Bridge and took 181st Street to Broadway. As they passed an all night coffee shop, Deacon looked at it longingly.

"You awake?" said Trance.

"Yeah. But I sure could use a grande black coffee."

"Don't think you'll find a Starbucks here, my good man. Stop the truck, though, and let's see what we get."

Jones quickly hit his brakes, to the annoyed honking of horns behind them. Stick jumped out of the truck's cab, while Jones made a long circle around the block. After eight minutes Jones pulled back to the curb. Stick jumped inside quickly, saying, "People get mugged for coffee in this part of the world, Trance. I was holding four cups. You're lucky I'm still alive."

"Wait 'til you get to *my* neighborhood," said Trance.

Although it was the middle of the night, they could hear the thumping sounds of hip hop music reverberating through the streets. Along Broadway, they saw several crowds of teenagers standing in circles. Breakers and poppers danced on the cracked cement and on flattened cardboard boxes. Other people huddled around lighted trash cans, staring at them with vacant or wary eyes. Drug dealers sold their wares from well-defended locations, like corner gas stations without the bright lights and the glowing signs.

As they moved deeper into Washington Heights the music mix became more Latin. They began to see more beads, often the red, blue and black beads of the Dominican *DDP*. Gangs ruled territories here. They were carved out of neighborhoods like Halloween jack-o-lanterns, with boundaries as unpredictable and asymmetrical as island nations.

With the cold weather, most of the homeless had found other places to sleep, primarily shelters or alleyways that were protected from the wind.

"You live out here?" said Deacon Jones.

An amused smile crossed Trance's face. "I hide out here. I shot the president tonight, so I need to disappear."

"Figured that was you. I was watching your face, as we listened to the radio."

"I know."

Deacon snickered. "You have something to do with that nuclear thing?"

"I did. Swam the warhead to the bottom of the Chesapeake Bay."

"Going to ruin the fishing," said Jones. "Then again, it might make it easier to fish at night."

"It was the only way to save the Congress."

Deacon nodded. Having been in combat, he knew how righteous reality could take some horrific shapes.

"Now they want you for the shooting?"

"You know the way it works, Deacon. No good deed goes unpunished. I've got to do a little something before I surrender."

Trance pointed toward the alley where he usually parked, not far from Fort Tryon Park. "You can leave us off here," he said.

Deacon looked at Trance like he was crazy. "Here? At night?"

"Yeah. You have an extra flashlight?"

Deacon reached under the dash and pulled a black rubber light out of a metal clip. He flicked it on and off, then handed it to Trance. "You want some flares or something?"

Trance laughed. "Nah." He reached into his pocket and pulled out the felt pouch he had taken from his place in Washington.

"You got a woman, Deacon?"

"Been married twenty-two years. To a fine lady. Yes, sir."

Trance pulled three diamonds out of the bag and pressed them into Jones's hand.

"These are worth forty grand apiece. Bring them to my office at Hopewell Industries, here in New York. Ask for Art Winthrop. He'll give you cash for these, no questions asked."

"How will he know they're from you?"

"They are laser etched with markings they will recognize."

Deacon shrugged and put the stones into his shirt pocket. "You didn't need to do that, general. But I've got two girls who want to go to college."

"Do you, now? Are they smart, like their daddy?"

Deacon laughed and shook his head. "Fortunately, they take after their mother. Her parents naturalized here from Mexico, legally I might add. My wife's mother cared for some rich politician's kids, while her father did odd jobs, most janitorial. She got a Ph.D."

"I'd like to pay for their education," said Trance. He wrote his personal phone number on Deacon's dash clipboard. Then he wrote a short note and signed it.

"C'mon?"

"I have a foundation that funds education for people with special circumstances. I probably won't be around after this, so you'll need to make an appointment with my secretary, Sarah. She will have someone meet with you and the kids. If your kids are anything like you, I'd be honored to pay for their education. I'm serious. You help me, I help you." Trance paused. "If I'm dead, you still call Sarah. Have her get you in touch with my trustee, Lauren Haverford." Trance wrote down the name. "Tell her about tonight, show her that note and she'll make things right. Understand? Stick will vouch for you."

"I don't know what to say," said Deacon.

"I'm saying *thanks* to you. So you say, *you're welcome.*"

Trance heard Deacon sniff in the darkness. Then the man did something that seemed completely out of character. Deacon hugged him.

"You be safe now, you hear?" said Deacon.

"We'll try."

Trance hollered to Stick and Sammantha, who were lying back in the sleeping compartment. They set down their cups of charred coffee and jumped out of the truck with Trance.

Trance made a quick survey of the street to check for gangs. There was a group of young men loitering on the corner, but they seemed tame. The alley was a black hole. Light from the street cast dim shadows for only about fifty feet. Beyond that, it was like walking into a cave, with the only light coming from a dim, quarter moon. Up ahead, Trance could see rats picking through a Waste Management dumpster. Besides rats, Trance saw nothing but clumps of trash. He shined the flashlight farther into the alley. Several cat-sized rodents scampered into the shadows. Trance began walking into the alley, while Stick and Sammantha followed behind.

As Trance neared the door to his apartment a shuffle of footsteps turned the corner and began heading quickly toward them. A wedge of young men came down the alley at a near-run. So much for safety.

"We got suckered," said Trance. He rushed to unlock the three deadbolts in his door. Then they heard another shuffling sound, this one from the opposite direction, and much closer.

"Seems we have some uninvited visitors to our neighborhood," said a loud, clear voice.

Trance looked to the source of the words, a very tall man wearing red, blue and black beads. He wore a kind of brown cape over a pair of torn and washed-out jeans.

"We have no quarrel with you," said Trance.

"Yeah. But we have one with you, mon. And your lady? She look like fun."

"Touch her and I'll break your neck," said Trance.

By this time, more than a dozen gang members were standing in a loose semi-circle around Trance and the others.

"And I'll break it again," said Stick.

"You protect Sammantha, Stick," said Trance. "Let me deal with this."

The tall man laughed. "You don't seem to understand the situation, mon. We are going to *take* the lady from you. Then we gonna break *your* neck."

"Let's see if we can figure some way out of this," said Trance. "How 'bout if I pay you some money?"

"We already going to take your money."

"I could bring you more. Say, a million dollars?"

"That means you be worth twice that for ransom. So, maybe we won't break your neck, maybe just your knees."

Money wouldn't work with this gang, so Trance tried the next best thing, pride.

"I bet I can fight every one of you. You want to make a bet?"

"What kind of bet?"

"A quarter million dollars against our freedom. I fight you and your men one at a time. If I'm the last man standing, I win. If I'm not, you win and I give you a quarter million."

The tall man took a tiny step backwards. He spoke softly to the members of his gang. Every one of them was holding some sort of weapon—a knife, a pipe, a blackjack. Not a gun in sight. Guns got you in jail.

"One rule," said Trance. "If you come at me with a weapon I will use it against you, and I won't guarantee that you will live. Fight me fair, and you will walk away from this."

Trance began to walk toward the leader with his unblinking eyes leveled against him.

Trance said, "You're not scared of me, are you?"

The man stood his ground. Trance stopped an arm's length away.

"You want to go first, big man?" said Trance.

The tall man hesitated. He wasn't feeling quite so brave on his own. Like most gang members, thought Trance. Trance removed his *I Heart New York* shirt and faced his would-be killer with his chest laid bare. His muscles flexed and jumped as if they were being sparked by electric shocks. The dragon tattoo upon his back looked almost alive. The tatoo was partially disfigured by scars from bullets that had riddled Trance's chest over the years. Two men behind Trance began talking in low voices. They began to slowly back away.

"Where you going, mon?" said the gang leader.

"See the tattoo, the red dragon tattoo?" said one of the retreating men. "And all thos scars?"

"I don't give a shit about scars and no tattoo. You come back here."

The two men continued backing away. "You crazy to fight Red Dragon, Dewan. I see you later, mon."

The gang leader had dug himself into a dangerous hole. He couldn't walk away and keep his gang's respect. It was a fool's errand to fight the mythical Red Dragon alone, assuming this was the real Red Dragon. So he changed the deal. He pulled a six inch knife from under his cape and got into a fighting crouch. He looked to his remaining gang and said, "Let's filet this sucka and leave him to bleed—"

Trance lunged forward and drove his fingers into Dewan's throat. Dewan's words turned into a gurgle and he flopped against Trance like a paper doll. The rest of the gang began to close in around them. Trance looked for the strongest link and charged. He led with flashing hands, followed by two quick foot strikes. By the time he had broken through the circle, two more men lay on the ground, groaning.

"It is time for you all to go," said Trance. "Why don't we call this a draw?"

The group, sensing blood, charged as one. Trance grabbed the lead man's wrist. He snapped it back until it cracked, while snatching his knife in the process. Trance held the knife in his fist, blade down, and began to wind his arms in a circular motion. Two men attacked him, one with a heavy chain, the other with a black steel pipe. Trance caught the chain and pulled it out of the attacker's hand. In the same motion, he used the chain to flick the pipe out of the other man's grip. He lunged forward, faster than the eye could see, and he drove the knife across the outstretched arms of both men.

That's when it hit him. A tire iron slammed into Trance's chest, swung with a force that felt like a wrecking ball. Trance staggered and fought for breath. How had he missed this? Trance lashed out with a side kick that crumpled his attacker's face. Then he turned to the remaining four men. They showed no signs of fear, as if this were a game they played every night.

"You started with a dozen or so…and now…you have four," said Trance, between choking breaths. Trance put his hands on his knees like a tired athlete. "You can't like those odds. Why don't we call it a day? Okay?"

One of the remaining four men struck toward Trance with a knife. Trance let him lunge, then used the attacker's momentum to turn the knife back on himself. The man stopped in mid stride and looked down at the hilt of his knife, which was now buried deep in his side.

"I don't want to do this," choked Trance.

Trance fought hard to breathe. There was fire in his lungs. He felt like he had inhaled a rose bush. There was a great weight pressing against his chest, so hard that it felt like a giant boulder had rolled off one of the buildings and pinned him to the ground. How could he have been so stupid? To let a man blindside him like that?

Trance needed to end this fight before he passed out, so he took the offensive. In just twelve seconds, the remaining three men lay writhing and groaning on the ground. Trance looked to Stick Granger. Granger pressed a button on his sports watch and said, "Three minutes and twenty-eight seconds. You are definitely losing it, Jack. One of them even hit you."

Trance smiled grimly. "I'm out of practice, Stick. I'm hoping it stays that way."

Trance motioned toward the injured group of men and spoke softly, but firmly. "Party's over guys. Get your butts out of here. And don't come back."

The gang members began to skulk away. Some were walking on their own, while others needed help from comrades.

Trance shuffled to the door to his apartment.

"That was impressive," Sammantha said.

"But not fun," said Trance.

"What's with the Red Dragon?" said Sammantha. She lightly touched the red tattoo emblazoned across Trance's back.

"When I was a kid in Japan, they tried to force me into a Yakuza...what we call gokudō... gang. When I refused, they beat me close to death and tattooed me with the dragon."

"It's beautiful. Is that why you keep it?"

Trance entered the apartment, bolting the door after the others had come in behind him. "I wear the tattoo as a reminder, Sammantha, that there is evil in this world."

"Evil, like me," Sammantha whispered.

"You're not evil, Sammantha. Just terribly misguided."

"We're going to get him, you know. We are going to find the president and bring him home. That's the only way they'll let you live."

"And maybe even save your life," said Trance.

"I don't deserve to live. In fact, I *want* to die."

"There is lot of good that needs doing, Sammantha. And far better solutions than death. "

"Solutions? How could I live with such blood on my hands? I killed his wife. I killed *your* wife. How can you even look at me?"

Trance let himself sink to the dusty wooden floor. "I have seen far too much death in my time. I've done too many dark things to judge someone else. We do all we can to reason with people like terrorists, do everything in our power to resolve issues peacefully. But when someone is killing your family, or threatening your life or your country, you've got to make a choice. Do you turn the other way and accept death, or do you fight to protect and preserve what is right and just? Then it gets ugly, when you are forced to respond. You do things you would never think to do, not in your wildest dreams, but you have to, to preserve and protect what is right. Often that is something so revolting it makes you puke. But it is right. It is necessary. It is just."

"But you do it for your country. I did it for revenge."

"War is war. You will have to live with that...like we all do."

"I can't. I won't."

Trance got up slowly from the floor. "C'mon. They'll be back soon. The police might even show up. We can't let them find us here."

Trance reached into a fuse box against the wall and pressed several switches. Bright lights jumped on inside the apartment, looking like small, powerful suns after the blackness outside. Trance walked over to one of the apartment walls and moved his hands along the broken plaster. He stuck his finger into one of the holes and waited ten full seconds. They heard a soft humming sound. The wall began to pull out into the middle of the room. It appeared to be made of thick steel. After a few seconds the humming stopped, revealing a crack where the wall used to be.

"Follow me," said Trance.

Trance turned sideways and walked through the wall opening. The others followed behind him before it closed. Beyond the wall they came to a bedroom suitable for any fine mansion. The lights turned on automatically, glowing softly when they entered the room.

"Nice digs, JT," said Stick.

"This is the apartment next door. I own the whole block, so I made what modifications I deemed necessary."

Trance pointed to one of the walls. "There is a family living on the other side of that wall. You'd never know they were there, just as they have no idea what's here."

Stick said, "Does their place look like this, too?"

Trance walked to an intricately carved wooden cabinet. He rummaged through it for a minute or so. He came back holding a blue gym bag that had been filled with an assortment of tools.

"How many blue bags have you got, Trance?" said Stick.

"Got a bunch of them once, on sale at BJ's."

Trance walked to the far end of the room and motioned for the others to follow. There was a brass light fixture built into the wall, with the tips of several brass screws sticking out from the base like nubs of corn. Trance pulled out all of the screws except for one. Then he twisted the lamp ninety degrees to the right. The wall began to slide open, revealing a set of stairs going downward. Trance put the lamp back into its original position and replaced the screws.

"This way,"Trance said.

Once they were in the stairway, Trance pulled a small lever and the door slid back into place. This area became bathed in red light. There were two flights of stairs going down. They ended in a small, square room, with a rusted two-door bulkhead on the cement floor. Trance unlocked a padlock that was fitted into the bulkhead handles. He opened one of the heavy doors. Hot, moist air began to spill into the room

"Man, does that smell," said Stick.

"We're going into the sewer system," said Trance.

"Not me, Kimosabe," said Stick.

"And I thought you wanted to live."

"Well, if you put it that way."

Trance turned toward Sammantha. "This should seem perfectly normal to you."

Sammantha's lips twitched. It was much like the sewer tunnel she'd used to pass unseen into Copley mansion, also the one she'd traveled beneath Anderson's warehouse in New Jersey.

Trance slowly climbed down twelve rotted, wooden steps, shining a flashlight as he descended. The stairs ended in a cement tunnel that had a foot of putrid water lying stagnant on the bottom.

"Roll up your pant cuffs. We've got to walk about two hundred yards down this tunnel."

Trance moved quickly, squishing through the foul water like it was a tiny wading pool. They came to a *T* in the tunnel, where it branched to the right and left. Trance took fifteen steps to the right and stopped. He inserted an oversized skeleton key into the wall and pulled open a hidden door. Beyond the door, there was another door. This one had a shiny, ceramic face. Trance inserted two keys into the deadbolt locks, then punched a code into a small keypad.

"Must have been hell to get the building permits for all this," said Stick.

Trance laughed, then opened the door. They entered a square room similar to the one in the other building, except this one had a mini-shower and disinfectant for them to clean their legs and feet, along with rows of padded Japanese slippers and soft moccasins. Soon they were standing inside a luxuriously furnished apartment.

"They won't find us here," said Trance. "They can bomb or burn the other place. The police or the NYFD can enter it for any reason, but they're not going to find us here."

Trance looked to his watch and noted the time. He reached into his blue bag and withdrew what looked to be a shiny steel bracelet. He opened it, and then closed it around one of Sammantha's wrists.

"You have done a lot to help us, Sammantha. But I still don't know how far to trust you. This will keep you inside the building, just in case you're able to decipher my codes and fool my biometrics. Be advised that the phone and Internet here are highly encrypted and password protected. So, don't try to contact anyone outside."

"I'm on your side now. We want the same thing."

Trance looked into Sammantha's eyes, reading her for truth or guile. Satisfied, he said, "I am going to see what I can dig up on the Kremlin. Why don't you guys go take showers and relax?"

Stick went off in search of a shower, while Trance sat down at a desk and turned on a computer.

"I can help you with that," said Sammantha. "I can get you blueprints of every building inside the Kremlin."

Trance smiled. "Thanks. I've got resources, too."

Stick poked his head back around the corner. "What Trance really means is that he has access to Google. With luck he can get us driving directions to Moscow from Paris."

"Actually, I'm hoping to pull a subterranean map of the Kremlin out of the NSA Echelon system.

Or maybe an infrared or MRI shot from one of the Hopewell Telstars. If memory serves me, there is a lot of limestone in that area. Limestone tends to hold heat. So, an infrared taken late in the afternoon might just show any tunnels or caverns between the river and the Kremlin. Now, get out of here and leave me alone." Trance chuckled as he began setting up the series of global links to hide his computer's IP address and location, before hacking through back doors into the CIA, NRO and the NSA data archives.

CHAPTER **114**
_________PP_________

The weather was turning colder by the minute, as a massive high pressure system was plunging into New York from Canada. The day dawned bright and clear, with thin, tufted clouds spotting only the upper atmosphere.

Thick oak boards had been nailed over the metal bars of Trance's tenement windows. So there was no outside light to brighten the rooms. The air inside the apartment felt oddly stale, with the faint odor of last night's sewer sludge mixing with dust from the termite-ridden walls. Trance rolled out of bed and winced. He felt like he had been branded on the chest. He looked down and saw a long, black and blue ridge along his chest where the tire iron had slashed from his left nipple deep into the cavity of his chest. Trance also felt a shiver of bone-chilling cold. With all of last night's distractions, especially the gnawing pain in his chest, Trance had forgotten to turn on the apartment's heat. He walked to the wall and turned on the roof mounted heat pump. This would clean and warm the air inside the apartment in mere minutes.

Trance shuffled through the hallway wearing a pair of flannel shorts, a T-shirt and a fleece vest. He knocked softly, then stuck his head inside the second bedroom. Sammantha Starodubov still asleep. He walked by Stick Granger who had his six foot four inch frame crunched into a couch. Stick was snoring so loudly that Trance felt a playful urge to cover his mouth and startle him awake. He might have done so, except that any small movement of his arms set his chest on fire.

Trance padded into the kitchen and started a pot of Kenya Roast coffee. He turned on a computer that was built into the kitchen counter, with its screen and touch keyboard forming the smooth tabletop. The screen flashed to life the moment Trance touched it. Trance perused the _Financial Times_, the _New York Times_ and the _Washington Post_. Then he took a peek at the _Wall Street Journal_, before hitting CNN and Fox News. Nowhere, did he find mention of his name.

The news reports did speculate, from "reliable anonymous sources," about the rumored capture of a major terrorist cell near in Washington. Again, no names were mentioned.

The news was all about the assassination attempt and the nuclear detonation under the Chesapeake Bay. The computer flashed with scenes of the president going down in slow motion, from multiple angles, like a Sunday football game. The talking heads were in their glory, wielding dueling telestrators like light sabers, and talking through the replays like football analysts.

Stick Granger ambled into the kitchen and sloshed some coffee into a cup.

"I had a fun day yesterday," he said. "How 'bout you, Trance? Anything exciting going on in your life?"

Trance motioned toward the refrigerator. "There are some bagels and English muffins in the freezer. There's also some frozen cream cheese. I'd recommend the peanut butter, though. It was a very good year."

Stick didn't move. He just savored his coffee with his eyes closed. "Makes you feel alive, don't it, Jack? I mean, now that you've got the heat turned up."

Trance turned off the computer and put a couple frozen bagels into a microwave. After thirty seconds he cut them both in two and dropped them into a toaster. He wondered if this was one of the last normal things he would ever do. "Thanks again for yesterday," he said.

Stick shrugged his shoulders. "Heck, all I did was take a couple helo rides."

Trance sat stiffly onto a barstool beside an island in the middle of the kitchen, cradled his head in his hands and groaned.

"What's up with you, Trance?"

"I need Jesse Tompkin."

"We can do without him."

An amused, half smile crept across Trance's face. "How's your Russian?"

"Sehr gut," said Stick.

"That's German."

"Sounds the same to me."

"I need someone I can trust, someone who is good with weapons and hand-to-hand combat, someone who speaks flawless Russian."

"That would be me," said Sammantha. She was walking into the kitchen wearing a Pat Tillman football jersey pulled over a pair of rolled up jeans.

"Someone besides you," said Trance. "I'll need you, too."

"I take it you know where to find Tompkin?" said Stick.

"That's the problem. I bet he's here in New York."

"That's good, then. Isn't it?"

"No. It's not good."

Stick frowned. "Would seem to me that it's good news. He's out of a job. His wife left him. Probably needs some money…Uh-oh…" Stick's jaw hung open and he shook his head. "He didn't? Tell me he hasn't gone to Yang."

Trance shrugged. "A DOD sort of limits your job prospects."

"That would explain his attempt at suicide. We'll have to find someone else, Jack."

"I wish we could."

"This is not good. I know what you're thinking."

The bagels popped up. Trance layered the four slices with chunky peanut butter, keeping one for himself, while handing one to Sammantha and two to Stick.

When breakfast was over, Trance led the others to his media room. He had several still cameras mounted on tripods, as well as two studio quality video recorders. There were two graphics computers, two high resolution scanners, three laminating machines, three high end printers, a magnetic coding machine and a wall for hanging various backgrounds. There was even a latex molding machine connected to one of the computers.

"We'll need new identities," said Trance.

"I want to be a general," said Stick.

"General Goodfornothing?"

"General Goodwitheverything."

"The only general I've got in stock is General Shitforbrains."

"I already own that ID."

By the end of the day they had new identities, and disguises that would get them past any curious border security. Trance hoped it wouldn't come to that, but they couldn't take chances. Trance also prepared a set of IDs for Jesse Tompkin, using stock photos he had of him in the computers.

After dinner Trance said, "We go tomorrow morning."

"Where're we going?" asked Stick.

"To get Jesse."

"Aw, Jack. Let's not do this, not again."

"What are you two talking about?" asked Sammantha.

"Jesse Tompkin," they both said.

"I know that, but where is he?"

"Unfortunately, you're about to find out," said Trance. His voice carried a wistful softness. For some odd reason, it made Sammantha think of riding horses as a child.

Trance went into his bedroom. He came back holding something in his hand. Sammantha tried to see what it was, but Trance kept it hidden inside his palm. Trance brought the item to the kitchen sink and washed it with dish soap. He went into one of the kitchen drawers and withdrew something that looked like a thick, oval balloon, almost like a condom. Trance rolled back the latex. He took the item, rolled the balloon around it, then set it on the counter. All Sammantha could see now was a round lump. Trance secured the balloon-like container with a tight rubber band. Then he put it in his pocket.

"What are you doing?" asked Sammantha.

"Can't you see he's getting ready?" said Stick. "Just in case."

"Just in case, what?"

"Hopefully, you won't have to see."

CHAPTER **115**
________PP________

Dawn had yet to break when Trance nudged his rusted, gray 1995 Mercedes E250 Turbo Diesel out of a dilapidated garage that was several doors down from his safe house. Trance drove the car to a garage near Park Avenue, where he surrendered it for a ticket. He accepted the valet's obvious disdain for his dented car with a 'what can you do' kind of shrug. His eyes narrowed protectively, as he saw the valet's hungry eyes undress Sammantha. He thought of how hard it must be for her to befriend anyone, with men ogling her for her looks at every turn. He couldn't understand the strange attraction that men seemed to have for her. Whatever it was, he didn't feel it. To him she was a woman, no more, no less than any other. Women deserved respect, not abuse.

"You sure you want to do this?" said Stick, as the three of them walked out onto the street. "I remember last time, Jack. It wasn't pretty. People die in there."

"I don't plan to fight, Stick, or die. At least not yet."

"Why'd you swallow the thing?"

"What thing?"

"The thing thing."

"I didn't swallow any thing thing."

"I saw you swallow the thing back at the house. I know you did. You're preparing to fight."

"I won't unless I have to."

"Just tell them you can't. Tell them the fate of the world is at stake. Tell them you need Jesse to help you rescue the president from the Kremlin."

"That'll work."

"Then offer him money—Yang likes money."

They walked down Park Avenue and stopped in front of the ponderous, but subdued brownstone that was owned by Robert Yang. Even at this early hour, there was a line of people queuing near the wide stone steps. There were three men dressed in black tuxedos. A fourth man was a well-known musician wearing patched up jeans, lizard skin cowboy boots, a white shirt and a green beret. From the look of the man's eyes, Trance was sure he hadn't slept in days. There were four women wearing expensive looking shoes and long fur coats.

Trance recognized one of the men as a hedge fund manager who'd made a fortune selling stocks short during the mortgage meltdown, then going long before the stock rebound. The woman with him was not his wife, but a supermodel best known for her work with Victoria's Secret. Trance couldn't place her, but he knew he'd seen her face.

It was still dark outside. Even the well-lighted streets couldn't draw these people out of the back shadows, which was where they wanted to be. Guilty pleasures were best enjoyed in private.

Trance wasn't concerned about being recognized. He wasn't expected here, nor was anyone on the lookout for someone matching his new look of spiked blond hair and Goth-black eye shadow.

Sammantha said, "If this thing doesn't start until afternoon, why are people here already?"

Stick replied softly, "Yang rents out rooms. Some are used for rest. Others are for more salacious activities. You'll see once we get inside. There's another entrance in the back, where most people come...more discreet."

There was a man at the door, checking IDs and speaking quietly with each of the guests.

"So good to see you again, Mr. and Mrs. B. We have received your attendance fee of five hundred thousand U.S. dollars and secured your line of credit for…" The greeter checked a clipboard. "…two million U.S. for the competition. Should you desire a room, please let me know. Because of the increased attendance fee, the room price is just fifty thousand this year. Please step inside."

The man at the door checked in the other couples, the lone female and the rock star, before looking at Trance. The man frowned, staring at Trance's *I Love NY* sweatshirt. "I am sorry, sir, but this is a private residence."

"Would you please tell Mr. Yang that Red Dragon is here to see him?"

The man raised an eyebrow and gazed closely at Trance. Then he bowed deeply.

"Just one moment, Mr. Red Dragon, sir."

Trance reached to the back of his neck. He unclipped a gold necklace that held two clear amulets with a bluish liquid shimmering inside. He looked at the amulets briefly, almost reverently, and then handed the necklace to Granger. "Please keep this stuff safe, Stick."

A few minutes later, Yang came to the door. He extended his hand toward Trance and pulled him inside, while motioning for Stick and Sammantha to join them.

"What a pleasure it is to see you again, Red Dragon! You have been ignoring my requests for years. Have you come to fight?"

Trance bowed. "Most honorable Yang, I wish only to speak with one of your fighters." Trance knew this was impossible—Yang would never let him inside to talk with Jesse. He would let him inside to fight, but it would have to be Yang's idea. Trance couldn't ask, not at this stage; he would have to be invited. He would have to play Yang, just as Yang would play him.

"The competitors have been in seclusion since yesterday, Red Dragon. You know the rules. Only other fighters are allowed in their presence until the competition concludes."

"I respectfully request that you alter your fine tradition for a matter of great international importance. I am willing to pay you well for my intrusion, perhaps a hundred million?"

Yang scoffed at the mention of money. To him, this was more for sport and honor than money, despite his substantial profits. The competition must remain pure.

"I cannot do that, Red Dragon. The competitors have been announced. You will need to wait until the competition concludes to speak with your friend."

"That may be too late." Jesse Tompkin was good, but he was not that good. He might make the final. There, he would be defeated early, and quite possibly killed, to prevent distraction.

Yang shrugged. "Every man has agreed by contract. They have each received one hundred thousand dollars that I cannot recover. I do not break contracts. My clients demand honor. If I allow impurities in the fighting, my clients will lose faith in me, and in this competition.

"Besides, we both know that as the competition nears, some men inside this building will have second thoughts. They will want to beg for release from their agreements. If I let fighters leave, my competition will lose its edge and its harmonic balance."

"What if I were to compete?" said Trance.

"It is too late. I have my sixty-four."

"You just told me that fighters want out."

Yang smiled. "I was merely making a point, Red Dragon."

"But there *are* some who wish to withdraw?"

Yang nodded. "From time to time."

"Then let me take someone's place."

Yang smiled; he had just gotten his way.

"If you insist, Red Dragon. You may join the others in meditation."

Trance looked at Stick and shrugged.

"I warned you, Trance," Stick said.

Trance took a deep, painful breath. He removed his watch and placed it into Stick's opened palm.

Yang said, "You know the rules. You may carry nothing into the ring."

"I am aware of the rules, most honorable Yang."

"You must also pass my doctor's inspection. That is also a rule."

"Inspect away."

Trance followed Yang down a hallway, where he vanished behind a pale oak door.

Stick and Sammantha were led to a large open space, much like an indoor sports stadium. Rather than a basketball court or a hockey rink, in the middle there was an area that looked like a boxing ring. The area was larger than a traditional fighting ring, with borders made with six elasticized ropes stretching around it. Recessed into the floor, surrounding the ring on all four sides, were grooves in the floor about three inches wide, with strips of brushed steel inside.

Above them, circling the room were recessed lounges that looked like mannequin displays. Half naked men and women were standing in various poses, looking out over the ring. Soft spotlights shone upon them in muted earth colors of red and brown.

Stick nodded toward the lounges. "A rented room comes with your choice from a lizard lounge."

"Sick," said Sammantha, shaking her head.

"Look who's talking."

Sammantha laughed. "Touché, Granger." Her smile dropped and she said, "I've been encaged like that, but never by my own choosing."

Trance was led upstairs to a sterile white room. A doctor drew blood and examined his body carefully, both inside and out. "What did you do to your chest?" the doctor asked. He pointed at the spot where the tire iron had nearly crushed Trance's ribs.

"I fell on some ice. It's fine."

Without warning, the doctor punched Trance in the discolored spot. This was no ordinary doctor, but a man highly trained in the martial arts. Trance was ready for the blow. He showed no reaction. He simply let the doctor hit him, with a bored expression on his face. Pain rushed through his chest. Trance had visions of jalapeno peppers dripping and burning blisters into his flesh. He wanted to scream. He wanted to bend over to walk off the pain. Instead, he stood his ground like an impassive rock.

Satisfied, the doctor nodded. "I will have the results of your blood work shortly."

"It will be clean," said Trance.

"I am sure. But our patrons demand integrity."

"Then let it be so."

Trance was led back downstairs, to an area that looked like the main workout room at a gym club. It was more than seventy feet to a side. Along one wall there was a set of mirrors, with a cluster of free weights and a loop of Cybex exercise machines. There were stationery bikes and treadmills, all with monitors mounted in front. There were three massage tables, where burly masseurs were digging their vice-like fingers into the backs of relaxing fighters.

A murmur spread across the room as Trance entered the chamber. He could hear the whispers, *Red Dragon.* Trance ignored the stares and walked along the perimeter of the room, until he reached Jesse Tompkin.

"Mind if I sit down?" Trance said.

Tompkin looked up and grinned. "Hey, bud. Bet I know what brought you here."

"I came for you.'

"Uh-huh."

"I need your help with the president."

"The one you shot?"

"No," whispered Trance. "The other one."

"You know where he is?"

"Moscow."

"Oo-rah." Tompkin fell silent. He looked across the room. He leaned forward and began to take great interest in his bare feet. "There's just one problem," Tompkin said softly.

"And that is?"

"We're both here. We'll have to fight our way out."

"Whatever possessed you to do this?" said Trance. "Why?"

"You, of all people, should not have to ask that question, Trance."

"You didn't need this, Jesse."

Tompkin stared at Trance for a long time. At first his eyes were hard and accusing. Then they softened into a mirthful, almost happy glow. "I seem to recall saying those same words to you, Jack. After Janice died. When you held your own life in shattered pieces.

"Well, right now my life is in the shitter. I caught my wife sleeping with a non-com. The president gave me a DOD. I lost twenty years of pension. How the hell am I going to get a job with a dishonorable discharge from the Marines? All I did was try to serve my country. I got screwed everywhere I turned. Retirement gone. Wife gone. Future gone. Branded as a loser.

"This time it's for me. If I die here, so be it. If I don't, maybe I walk away with a new life, maybe a fresh start."

"Come work with me. I'll pay you whatever you want."

Tompkin shook his head. "It's not the money, Jack. And I don't want charity."

"This won't do it, Jesse. Believe me, I know."

"Maybe I'll get lucky and end up dead."

Trance grinned. "Not with me here riding shotgun."

"I don't want your help, Trance. You save your own skin. That'll be tough enough."

"It's not my skin I'm trying to save."

"You mean the president?"

"The country deserves its true leader, Jesse."

"Semper Fidelis. Sometimes I think that's a four letter word, Jack."

"It is who we are Jesse. We carry on."

"Let's just hope we don't get carried *out*."

CHAPTER **116**
PP

A hulking Chinese man suddenly filled the entrance to the gym. The man made Trance think of a dark cloud passing in front of the sun. He looked like Yao Ming on steroids, looming above them and shading light like a tree. He looked as comfortable in his black tuxedo as a senator caught wearing a bra and panties in a public restroom. Behind him stood six other men holding M16s.

"As I call your number, you shall come with me…Competitors one, two and three. Competitors sixty-two, sixty-three and sixty-four."

Trance stood up.

Tompkin said, "Got a bad seeding, huh, Red Dragon? What are you, sixty-four?"

Trance smiled. "The good news is I'm odd. You're even. We won't fight until the final. If you get hurt, stay down. No macho bullshit. I'll drop out as soon as you do."

"Break a leg, Red Dragon."

Trance shook his friend's hand. "Stay within yourself, Jesse. I need you. Your country needs you."

As Trance walked along the dimly lit corridor toward the fighting ring, he felt like a gladiator being led to the lions. With millions to be earned with just one victory, Yang's competition fielded only the best. Every man, from one to sixty-four was a deadly killer. The way the rules were written, a drawn-out kill was the most profitable result. Like Trance, many of the competitors would choose honor over money. But there were some who would gladly collect the bounty for a dead man's skin.

Trance stood at the base of the ring and scanned the crowd for Stick and Sammantha. They were sitting just three rows back from the ropes, in a place of honor. Behind them, the stadium rose high into the rafters, with thousands of people waiting to watch him die.

"Good evening honored guests," said Yang from the center of the ring.

Yang was dressed in a white tuxedo with black and white snakeskin shoes. He didn't hold a microphone. Instead, he wore a rock-star headset, with a small, pea sized black dot on a tube that sucked up his every word. High above the ring, four twenty-foot screens displayed his image in high definition, 3-D color.

"I am pleased to welcome you to the world's most exciting athletic competition. To the seven thousand people here, and to our worldwide audience, I say, *let the games begin!*"

The crowd erupted into a strange but elegant mixture of applause and friendly cat calls.

"This year I am most happy to announce the return of…Red Dragon!"

This time the applause was thunderous.

"As many of you know, Red Dragon once electrified our audience with his split second knockouts and his unequaled display of strength, quickness and acrobatic skill in our final. I have talked him out of retirement and he is joining us here today, as our number one seed."

Trance stepped into the ring and bowed toward the crowd in all four directions. He was wearing the required fighting uniform of a simple pair of black Lycra briefs. The red dragon tattoo looked like a flag flying in the wind, as Trance's muscles rippled and twitched across his back.

"Red Dragon's first opponent today is Adnan de la Cruz. de la Cruz comes to us from the Philippines, where the martial arts are part of their national culture. He is one of their most decorated fighters."

de la Cruz entered the ring and bowed to the crowd.

"The rules of this competition are simple. No man may carry anything on his body into the ring. Competitors will fight until one man dies, a man surrenders by tapping out, or our referee declares a winner. Each fighter is allowed to compete in any manner he sees fit, with no gloves and no shoes..." Yang motioned each man to a corner. "...As per our tradition, each competitor shall have two minutes to center himself before he fights."

Trance stood in a corner and watched as de la Cruz regurgitated a six inch knife, still within its scabbard. The crowd began to roar as they watched de la Cruz pull the blade free and hold it high. Trance didn't bother to call upon his own weapon of choice, not yet. Although he did regurgitate it and swallow it again, just to keep it near the surface. He would regurgitate the weapon completely before he slept, so its coating wouldn't disintegrate. This would also prevent the weapon from passing into his system. He felt no need for his weapon now. If he wanted de la Cruz's knife, he would take it from him.

After two minutes the fighters were called into the center of the ring. As the two men shook hands, de la Cruz feinted with his knife. Trance smiled, but didn't flinch.

"And now," said Yang. "We begin!"

Trance and de la Cruz began to circle the ring. de la Cruz made several jabbing motions, trying to see which way Trance might move. Trance remained square on his feet, centered, and careful not to give away his strategy. Soon it became apparent that Trance was going to wait for de la Cruz to attack. His opponent had the same idea, but Trance wouldn't take the bait.

The men circled for several minutes before de la Cruz grew impatient. He grasped the knife in his fist, with the blade extending out from his pinky finger side. He began to wave the knife back and forth, lunging slightly from time to time, waiting to catch Trance in between strides.

Then, with a quick flurry, de la Cruz slashed forward, aiming his knife toward Trance's neck. Trance was ready. As the knife came toward him, Trance grasped de la Cruz's arm with both of his hands. He stepped to the side and used his opponent's momentum against him. Before anyone could see what had happened, de la Cruz was standing with his eyes wide, staring down at the blade sticking out from his shoulder.

Trance moved to a corner to allow de la Cruz to stop the fight. Instead, his opponent pulled the knife from his bone and lunged toward Trance again. Trance stepped to the side and pushed de la Cruz to the ground with an open palm. Trance stood above him and said, "Stop this, Adnan, before you die."

After several tense moments, de la Cruz tapped the mat three successive times. Doctors jumped into the ring and began attending to de la Cruz's wound. Others scampered inside to clean the blood and spit off the canvas floor. Trance walked over and grasped de la Cruz's hand. Then he patted de la Cruz's good shoulder.

"Sorry about that, Adnan. I hope you're okay."

While de la Cruz grunted, Trance walked into the center of the ring and raised his arms.

"Dragon...Dragon...Dragon..." shouted the crowd. Red Dragon was back.

Trance easily won his second match of the day. Jesse Tompkin also won both of his.

Just before midnight, the two were able to sit together in the gym holding cell, awaiting rubdowns, before being turning in for the night.

"How'r you doing?" asked Trance.

Jesse Tompkin's fighting style was more grappling than karate. He had been a member of the U.S. Judo Olympic team, taking a silver medal in the event. He'd also been a national champion college wrestler at 235 pounds. He was a fifth degree black belt in Kung Fu, but that wouldn't help him against these fighters. They could take on someone with his karate skills with their eyes closed.

Grapplers usually hold the advantage over strikers in this type of event, because once a hitter is caught, he loses his edge. Trance could do both. He preferred to strike when he could. Striking was easy and took less energy, particularly against a weak non-striker. He could escape a grappling big man, but it was far more difficult for him to hold one down for a tap out.

"I'm doing well enough to kick your ass," said Tompkin.

Trance laughed. "That's good. Stay confident, Jesse. But know this, the final is nothing you can prepare for. There will be eight of us in the ring. That will neutralize *everyone's* advantage. A hitter can take you down with a kick or punch, and you won't see it coming. You could be about to break a man's arm, but then find your head in a lock from someone else, or pulling a knife from your side.

"Keep your head on a swivel. Don't get entangled with anyone early. Because that will leave you open for a cheap, kill shot."

Trance leaned toward Tompkin and lowered his voice. "They will gang up on me first, Jesse. I am going to need your help during that first onslaught. After that, I can protect you."

"I don't need protection, Trance."

Trance laughed. "Man, you don't know what's coming."

Later, the hulking Chinese man came to bring the final sixteen competitors to their rooms for the night.

Trance was led to a sixth floor bedroom overlooking Park Avenue. He stared through the barred windows toward the street, wondering how it had come to this.

Why had his father raised him for the military? Why had his family heritage put such requirements on him? Why was there so much guilt if he didn't serve? All he ever did was the right thing. And what was his thanks? An impending court martial and a hanging? All for trying to save Washington?

Trance thought of Lauren. She had waited for him for twenty years. Didn't she deserve happiness, too?

What about Tilson? What was he doing at this moment? Was he being tortured? Was his brain being harvested for every scrap of information it contained? Was death his best option for release? Or did Trance actually have a chance to save him?

Then there was Sammantha Starodubov. She had killed his wife. She had killed the president's wife. She had engineered the kidnapping of the U.S. president and the programming of his imposter brother. What should he do with her? She should be the one that was hanged. But, was she a victim here, too? Even more than he? Trance couldn't imagine coming home at age twelve and finding his parents dead. It had been tough on him when *his* parents had been assassinated, but he'd been far older, not a fragile, young flower just beginning its stretch toward the sky.

What would it be like to be orphaned at twelve? To be forced to act like a circus animal just to survive? Prostituting herself to every man that claimed he could save her. It was those men who should be punished. Not, perhaps, the victim of their crimes.

Trance moved away from the window and sat upon the bed. He spit up the balloon he'd swallowed that morning. He had upchucked the damned thing into his throat a dozen times during the day, to keep the stomach acid from breaking through the latex, and to keep it from passing into his bowels. He let it fall into his palm and examined the balloon for wear. Satisfied that it would survive the next day, he placed the balloon under his pillow and fell quickly to sleep.

Breakfast came to his room at eight. They wouldn't bring him to the ring until afternoon, so he ate everything on his plate. After eating, Trance spent half an hour stretching. Then he went back to sleep.

The knock came at twelve thirty.

"You fight now," said a voice.

Trance swallowed his balloon. The door swung open, and the Chinese bodyguard escorted him back to the large gym holding cell.

He said, "You have thirty minutes to stretch and prepare."

Trance's opponent today had come to America from Hong Kong. He was well known for his Hollywood action films. He was a master in karate, but also in the arts of acting and deception, having trained at the China Drama Academy in Hong Kong.

As the two minute signal was given, Trance watched his opponent closely. The man turned away, bent over and pulled a piece of rope out of his throat. He tied a large knot in the center of the rope and popped it several times with his fists. Trance saw no need to use his own weapon yet. He would need it to survive the final match, provided he made it that far. But not now.

The two men circled each other, feinting to test reaction speed and tendencies. Trance didn't want to hurt this opponent; he knew him too well. He respected his work. Trance's film production company had produced two of his movies, and had plans to do more. The two men began to circle warily around the ring.

"Hello, Charlie," said Trance in Cantonese. "Taking a vacation from acting, are we?"

"So, you are the famous Red Dragon," said Charlie, also in Cantonese.

"I am just a man."

"And I thought you just had money and liked being around actors."

"Looks can be deceiving, my friend."

"You have always shown great respect for my skills."

"I have great respect for your skills, Charlie."

"Ah, but you lied to me. You are Red Dragon. My skills pale to yours."

Trance continued to circle, waiting for Charlie to make the first move. "Look, Charlie. I'm not here by choice. You know I don't need money. And I don't want to fight. I am here to protect a friend. This is a matter of national security."

"Was that you who shot the president?" Charlie grinned. His eyes showed only professional curiosity, no anger, no shock. "I could tell on the television that it was a Sensei, by the way he moved."

"I would never shoot the president," said Trance. He looked at Charlie with a questioning expression on his face. How could Charlie know it was he? Then he knew. Charlie was military, too. Red Chinese Army or one of ours? he wondered. It didn't matter. Their contracts with Yang, plus their own personal code, forbid them from using information gained here on the outside. He now saw Charlie as something more than an actor who could fight, the pieces tumbling into place like loaded dice. They were more alike than he had thought.

Charlie tossed his rope to the side and said, "Let's get it on, Jack." He launched himself toward Trance with a fury of kicks and punches that were as impressive as his films.

Trance blocked each kick and punch, except for a strike that snaked though and caught him in the chest. Trance felt a blistering pain shoot through him. He couldn't move. It was like he'd been stung by a giant sea creature. The strike sent him into an electric spasm, his nerves shooting stuttering sparks like downed power lines after a hurricane. Sensing victory, Charlie moved in for the kill. He did his trademark somersault, with his feet arching up into the air, aiming down at Trance's head. Trance dodged the blow, but remained on his hands and knees, still fighting for breath.

You can't give up, he said to himself. Trance willed himself to stand. He staggered slightly and then steadied. Charlie paused, deciding what to do next. This gave Trance just enough time to recover. He roared. It was a primal shriek, brought mostly by the excruciating pain. It was something one might have expected from a Cro-Magnon cave dweller as he his leg was shredded by a lion's claws. Charlie still didn't move. That was his mistake.

Trance attacked Charlie with even greater quickness. He hit him with fists to the chest and then the face. As Charlie stood, stunned, Trance caught him with two quick kicks, one from the right, the second from the left. Then he hit him with a sidekick that sent him falling back against the ropes. Charlie remained standing, but he drifted from side-to-side, like seaweed in the ocean surf.

Trance didn't like to leave his feet, but this was a show. It was entertainment, so he let them have it. Trance threw himself into his own summersault, landing with his knees on either side of Charlie's head. This pulled Charlie to the ground, with his head twisting precariously between Trance's legs.

"You don't want to die, Charlie," Trance said. "All I need to do is turn…I wouldn't want to do that. We have more movies to make. I'll pay twice your usual fee."

Charlie tapped the mat. The crowd roared. They had just watched America's karate film superstar showing he was as good as his reputation. He had lost to a former champion, a man who was even faster and stronger. Half the audience looked to the computer displays at their seats to view their winnings. The other half gave off a long chorus of boos and counted their losses. Above them all, the four big screens replayed different parts of the match in slow, high-definition motion.

***

Jesse Tompkin entered the ring and stared at his gargantuan opponent. The man standing before him had to be seven and a half feet tall. He was built like a weightlifter, or a WWF wrestler, tipping the scales at four hundred pounds of solid, steaming steroidal muscle.

The man roared to excite the crowd, as they waited for the two minute buildup to elapse. Tompkin bent over and spit out a pair of brass knuckles. "Lotta good these are going to do," he muttered. He doubted that he could even reach his opponent's chin.

Until now, Tompkin had advanced because of his size, strength and his quickness. He'd had the speed to grab his opponents first, and the strength to take them down. This was a man he couldn't grab, not if he didn't want to be broken like a potato chip. This was not good.

Tompkin slipped the brass knuckles onto his right hand. "All right," he mumbled. "Let's see how quick you are."

The two men circled, with the giant man smiling like he was about to eat a rare, gourmet steak. He moved well for a big man. He was not as fast as Tompkin, but he was quick. This was not good. Not good.

The giant lunged toward Tompkin. Tompkin ducked under his fist and hit him on the knee with his knuckles. The man laughed and came back at him. Tompkin hit the giant again in the same spot. The giant smiled once more. But he began to limp as he walked in a slow circle around Tompkin.

"C'mon, big fella," said Tompkin. "Let's see if we can do this one more time."

The man lunged at Tompkin, this time keeping his center and his knees slightly behind him. Tompkin swung at the giant's jaw. His hand bounced off it like he had hit an anvil. Before Tompkin could dart away, one of the giant's arms wrapped around his waist. A moment later he was airborne.

The big man tossed Tompkin across the room like a pillow. Tompkin crashed into a corner, with his legs in the air. The giant came at him again. Before Tompkin could right himself, he felt himself going airborne once more. As he passed by the giant's face Tompkin took a wild, almost pitiful swing at the man's huge head. Tompkin's fist caught the edge of the big man's temple.

The giant staggered and the crowd roared. Tompkin wobbled to his feet and stood facing his foe. The giant looked like a distorted monster through his hazy eyes. Tompkin dove at the man's legs and lifted him up, just enough to send the man tipping down to the canvas, slowly, like a tall tree. Tompkin began to hack at the man's knee. On his third strike he heard something *pop*. The big man roared. He picked Tompkin up and tossed him to the side with one hand, like he might a stuffed toy.

Tompkin landed on his head the corner. He tried to clear his vision. He rolled over and just sat. He blinked his eyes as the giant limped toward him, dragging his leg behind him like a slab of beef. Blood was dripping down the big man's leg, but not enough to slow him down or weaken him.

If the giant caught hold of Tompkin again, he was done. Tompkin was so dizzy he could barely stand. He willed himself to his feet. Tompkin began to circle around the big man, being careful not to let himself get pinned against the ropes. He kicked forward with a front kick and hit the giant's good leg in the knee. The giant nearly buckled, before reaching out toward Tompkin. The man got a weak grip on Tompkin's shoulder. Tompkin ripped it away, losing a gash of skin, but nothing serious.

Tompkin kicked the man again. This time the giant fell to the floor. Tompkin stood above him and kicked his good leg with all his weight. He heard a *crack* and stood back.

"What was I thinking?" he mumbled to himself. This was *crazy*. Trance had been right. This was *not* the answer. This was barbaric.

The giant tried to crawl toward Tompkin, but Tompkin was too fast. Tompkin continued jumping out of the man's reach. Meanwhile, the canvass was becoming streaked with blood from the giant's broken knees. Finally, seeing that Tompkin refused to go in for the kill, the referee stopped the fight.

Tompkin acknowledged the crowd with a brief, tired wave and limped out of the ring.

***

"You made it," said Trance, as Jesse Tompkin crumpled down beside him in the gym.

"You were right, Trance. This is no answer to the anger."

"Amen, brother."

"I don't even want to win this thing anymore. I've spent my life protecting people, not killing them."

Trance arched an eye in Tompkin's direction, as if to say *what?*

"Okay," said Tompkin. "I've killed people. But I've killed only bad people. People who wanted to kill good people, people who wanted to kill Americans."

"Sometimes the world just stinks," said Trance.

"I'll say."

"So, here's what we do," said Trance. And he told him.

CHAPTER **117**

_______________PP_______________

Lauren Haverford waited for twenty-four hours before taking a jet back to Boston. Visions of the president going down in a heap still played through her head like a grade B horror film. In black and white, with jagged, jerking movements, the victim lying limp as a cloth doll. Miller had come to her room and told her what happened. Trance had done it again. He had stuck his nose into the middle of a bee hive and shaken his head. The whole hive was after him now. All she could do was be home if he called. *If* he called.

Lauren was sitting at her office desk in her home on Commonwealth Ave. She had opened more than a hundred emails, hoping one of them was from Trance. She had only glanced at her business messages. Instead, she had combed through her personal account, particularly her junk mail, scanning it carefully for something meaningful.

Lauren stared at the phone, willing it to ring.

An email hit her account and her PDA vibrated. She could attain blissful happiness through the use of rare Japanese herbs. She walked to her desktop computer and opened the password-protected file. She right clicked on the attached PSD file and saved it to her computer. She then opened the file in Adobe Photoshop.

She unlocked the layers using another prearranged password. Then she saw it. Inside a white space in the ninth layer of the photo, there was a text box with white, invisible lettering. Lauren clicked on the text box and selected the invisible white text. She changed the color to black and read the note.

Doing well. Will contact soon. Have the big boat ready.

"Big boat? What big boat?"

Lauren dialed Arthur R. Winthrop, III, the CEO of Hopewell Industries.

"Art, this is Lauren. Where are you?"

Winthrop said, "Do you know where Jack is? I've had hundreds of calls from people looking for him. Including the FBI and Homeland Security. Do you know anything about this?"

"Where are you, Art?"

"I'm in Boston, for today only."

"How about lunch?"

"I have an appointment for lunch, Lauren. How about dinner?"

"Lunch, Artie. Legal Seafoods, at the mall on Boylston, up from Exeter. You know the place?"

"Yeah."

"What are you wearing?"

"Navy suit. Crimson tie."

"You are so predictable, Artie. I love that about you. Thirty minutes. Wait at the entrance to Legal holding a folded *Boston Globe* in your left hand."

Lauren hung up the phone. *The big boat? What the hell is the big boat?*

Lauren left her townhouse and began walking toward the mall. She had no intention of eating at Legal Seafoods, however good the chowder might taste. This was a logical place for a meet. There was enough noise in the mall, particularly in the nearby food court, to mask most listening devices the government might try to use.

Lauren looked to see if she was followed, but she saw no one. She knew they were watching her.

They must have gone to the mall to set up shop. Perfect. Their mistake.

When Lauren reached Newbury Street, she looked at her watch. It was nearly time. She hailed a cab and said, "Drive around the block and stop in front of the mall on Boylston, please." She swiped her credit card and then slipped the driver a one hundred dollar bill.

In a few minutes Lauren's cab was approaching the mall. She dialed Art Winthrop's mobile phone. When he answered, she said, "Sprint down the stairs to Boylston Street. As fast as you can. I'll be waiting on the street in a Yellow Cab."

Lauren laughed as she saw the always staid and proper Arthur Winthrop, III come running across the sidewalk with his crimson tie flipped up over his shoulder and his white mane of hair flowing back over his scalp. She opened the cab door and Winthrop jumped in.

"Hit it, please," Lauren said to the cab driver. She turned to Winthrop and whispered in his ear. "We don't have much time. Jack needs our help. You can't repeat this to anyone, even the FBI. Are we clear?"

Winthrop nodded.

"If you told the FBI, it would ruin Jack's life. So, I would make it my personal mission to ruin yours. Are we still clear?"

"I know more about Jack than you might think, Lauren," Winthrop whispered back.

Lauren hesitated. Of course, he would. "Sorry."

"What is it, dear?"

"Jack needs the big boat. Do you have any idea what that means?"

"Of course, I do."

"Can you clue me in?"

"He means the *Lauren*."

"The *Lauren*? What the hell is that?"

"It's Jack's yacht."

"Yacht? Jack doesn't have a yacht. He's got sailboats only, stripped down for racing."

"His uncle had a yacht. Now it belongs to Jack."

Lauren slapped the side of her head. "Who knows about this?"

"Just Jack and me and the captain, I guess. She's based in Grand Bahama Island. Registered under a series of dummy corporations."

"Does Jack use this thing?"

"It's a *her*, not a thing. No. Not yet. But he plans to."

"Whatever for?"

Winthrop ducked the question. "When does Jack need the *Lauren*?"

"I'm not sure. Soon."

"I'll have her fully fueled, staffed and ready within two days."

"Did Senator Hopewell call it the *Lauren*?"

"No. He called it *Global Dominance*."

"Fitting. How big is this thing?"

"Oh, two hundred fifty feet or so. We squeeze her in over at Charleston. Anything else you want to tell me, Lauren? Like what's going on?"

"Oh, Artie. It has to do with shooting the president, a nuclear detonation and a kidnapping."

"The usual stuff, then."

Lauren smiled, and so did Artie.

"Well," said Artie. "Let's hope the ol' cat can land on his feet one more time."

"Let's hope so."

CHAPTER **118**

_______PP_______

The president was sitting in bed watching the Bogart classic, *Casablanca,* when Jacob Miller was brought to his room. The president's initial urge to leave the hospital and pursue Trance had been replaced by the odd, unexpected desire to withdraw from the glare. Now, hidden within the black and white world of yester-year, he felt strangely comfortable, as if he were a caught fish returned to the water.

The president motioned for the CIA director to be seated, while putting a finger to his lips for silence. He mouthed the words with Bogey, "Where I'm going you can't follow. What I've got to do you can't be any part of. Ilsa, I'm no good at being noble, but it doesn't take much to see that the problems of three little people don't amount to a hill of beans in this crazy world. Someday you'll understand that. Now, now . . . Here's looking at you, kid."

When the scene was over, the president paused the film.

"I didn't know you liked old movies, sir," said Miller.

"What is that supposed to mean?"

"Well, I like the old movies, too. Can even recite Bogey's words like you. *Where I'm going you can't follow. What I've got to do you can't be any part of. Ilsa, I'm no good at being noble, but it doesn't take much to see that the problems of three little people don't amount to a hill of beans in this crazy world. Someday you'll understand that. Now, now . . . Here's looking at you, kid.*"

The president laughed. "Can you do *The Maltese Falcon?*"

"Well, if you get a good break, you'll be out in 20 years and you can come back to me then. I hope they don't hang you, precious, by that sweet neck."

"*The Caine Mutiny?*"

Miller stood at attention. "And so today you are full-fledged ensigns. Three short months ago you assembled here from all parts of the nation, from all walks of life: field, factory, office and college campus. Each of you knew what the fighting was about, or you wouldn't have volunteered..."

"Well, well..." The president crossed his arms and looked upon Miller with newfound respect. Here was a man who knew his movies.

"People have been asking what your plans are, sir," Miller said.

"I want Trance captured and hung. It's that simple."

"Your plans about resuming your duties as president, sir."

"I have resumed my duties as president."

"Ah, I don't mean to sound rude, Mr. President. But you have been in the hospital for close to a week. All you have been doing is watching old movies."

"I was shot, Miller. I am recovering."

"I'm not implying that you don't need recovery, sir. It's just...well, people everywhere are asking questions. People are thinking *Kennedy.* The public needs to *see* that you are okay. Foreign leaders need to *see* that you're okay. The least you should do is address the nation, if only for a few seconds. That would be helpful."

"I want to finish my speech. I had a great speech and I was in the zone. I was just getting ready for my finale when that asshole Trance ruined it."

"There was a nuclear bomb, sir."

"Which he dropped into Chesapeake Bay. He ruined the environment there for years."

"That's a hell of a lot better than Washington, sir."

"Is it?"

Miller's jaw tightened and he closed his eyes. He wasn't hearing this. He couldn't be hearing this. Did the president have a death wish?

"Perhaps you should seek help, sir."

The president chuckled. Then he peered closely at Miller. "Do you love someone?"

Miller looked to the floor. For years, he'd been too busy chasing enemies to have anything more than occasional sexual encounters. "Not since my wife died. But I loved her with a passion so strong, so deep that I still ache." Miller held out his bottle of Pepto Bismol. "Why do you think I drink this?"

"I feel the same way, and I can't find her."

"Kiki's dead, sir. You have to accept that. A year is too long to mourn publicly when you're the president. You must be bold...decisive...not moping around, simply going through the motions."

The president stared back at Miller. He wanted to explain that it wasn't Kiki he missed. Samman-tha Starodubov had vanished with no trace. Without her, his life felt utterly, unbearably empty. Then his programming took over. "It's been a tough year...a long couple of days."

"Will you think about addressing the nation?"

"I want to finish my State of the Union Address."

"The time has passed for that, sir."

The president thought about it and nodded. He would give a new speech, an even better speech. "Get me my script writers, will you?" He smiled. "Yes, I'll speak to the nation. I'll give 'em hell."

CHAPTER **119**
PP

The Chinese hulk with the tight fitting suit returned with his guards. His flat, cratered face looked almost like the surface of the moon. It was pale and mottled in shadow. His eyes looked as sharp as Talid's daggers. He bowed respectfully.

"The remaining eight champions shall follow me now."

The men were led back to the fighting ring where they were placed into a semi-circle. Outside the ring, Yang's guards kept order, with rifles ready.

Yang spoke to the crowd through his microphone. "We now come to the championship round of our competition. Before you...stand our eight finalists..."

Trance assessed the six other fighters besides Tompkin. He had performed an exhibition with one of them in Okinawa. He knew his fighting style well, and the extent of his skill. The man stood there confident and unblemished, with reason. He was that good. He was also an honorable man—samurai. Another of the fighters was a man known as Black Dragon. It was Black Dragon who had put the red dragon tattoo on Trance's back. He led a Japanese gang known for its brutality, a gang where this kind of fighting was routine. The third man was known to Trance by reputation only. The third man had earned the name, The Executioner, since he had not left a man alive behind him in the ring.

Trance didn't know the fourth competitor. He had a field of purple bruises on his body where he'd been hit. He still looked fairly strong, so Trance didn't know what to expect from him.

The final two fighters shouldn't have been there. They were Trance's friends, from his grandmother's village in Japan. *They must have a great need for money*, thought Trance. He could think of no other reason for them to be there.

Looking at these fighters, Trance knew that his chances of saving Jesse from harm were slim. Trance could barely breathe. Tompkin was overmatched and untrained for what was to come. Trance prayed this didn't mean they were going to die here, or that Tilson was going to rot in captivity in some dark and dank Moscow dungeon. Trance looked upward and called upon the Universal Force and the Creator, so that he might find the strength and good fortune to see another day.

Yang droned on. "Each of these men has won three matches to get to this point. Combined they have earned nearly one hundred million dollars, thanks to you, our generous patrons."

The crowd cheered. Many began to chant their favorite's name.

"In a few moments we will have our final fight. In the end, only one man will remain standing. Only one man will leave here as Grand Champion."

Again, the crowd began to cheer. Yang stepped out of the ring.

"The cage, please!"

A four-sided cage of steel bars emerged from within the flooring, rising to a height of twenty-five feet above the ring. Thick bars stretched horizontally, forming rectangles with the vertical struts rising from inside the floor. The bars were covered with razor wire to prevent climbing by the fighters. A top to the cage descended. the ceiling to seal them in. It was a mesh of heavy steel, but was not laced with sharp wire.

"Two minutes!" cried Yang.

One of the men that Trance knew spit out a full-length samurai Hachiwari helmet splitter. It was a sleek and curved sword, with a small, nasty hook near the base of the handle. Another man disgorged a sheathed throwing knife and three spring-loaded throwing stars. Poison was strictly forbidden. Trance hoped the star thrower was playing by the rules.

Trance calmly spit out the balloon he had been hiding. He split the latex open, to reveal a small pair of gloves, with hard metal finger tips that could resist the razor wire. Trance pulled these carefully onto his hands, making sure the metal rested on the finger joints. There were also flexible Kevlar tubes, which he wrapped around his four biggest toes.

"Those sure look deadly, Red Dragon," said Tompkin, as he pounded his brass knuckles into a palm.

Trance smiled. "Remember. When this starts, they will all come after me."

"Fighters….Begin!" yelled Yang.

All of the fighters raced toward Trance, seeking to take out their greatest threat together. Trance scurried up the wire like a chimpanzee until he reached the top of the cage. He turned, just as the throwing knife came toward his face. Trance grabbed it by the handle in mid-air. It would just get in the way, so he pressed it through one of the holes in the cage. It clanked harmlessly to the ground. Then came the throwing stars, one after the other. Trance caught the first one with his left hand. He used this star to deflect the other two. Then he tossed his star out of the cage.

By then, the fighters had turned upon themselves. Trance looked down toward Tompkin. He was standing face-to-face with The Executioner. Trance cursed himself for not keeping the knife, or even a star. That way he could just throw something at The Executioner and remain in place. Unfortunately, Trance had to do something to keep Jesse alive. The president's life was at stake. Maybe the entire nation. He launched himself from his perch twenty feet in the air and landed with his knees around The Executioner's head. He twisted and The Executioner's neck made a crunching, grinding sound. He would awake in an hour or two, unharmed, but with a headache from hell. The Executioner slumped slowly to the ground, softening Trance's landing to a graceful, gentle stand. Trance fought off a quick parry from the fighter with all the bruises. He caught the man in the throat with two extended fingers and sent him home for the day.

Trance scrambled back up the cage and hovered above Tompkin. He had to keep him alive and unharmed. He also had to conserve his strength, for what he knew was to come.

One of Trance's old friends turned on Tompkin with the Hachiwari. Tompkin was no match for this man's skill, or his weapon. Tompkin could be killed in seconds. Trance hated being airborne; it was the place of maximum vulnerability. He saw no other choice, so he pounced again. Trance landed upon the shoulder of his friend's sword arm. The sword dropped to the ground. The man wobbled unsteadily. Tompkin picked up the sword and stood guard, while Trance put one hand under the man's arm, locking the hand at his neck. Trance quickly did the same with his other arm, completing a full Nelson hold. Trance put his back to the ropes, so he could see all the other fighters. Then he said, "Hello, old friend. I wish you no harm. But I must do this." Trance began to crank his hands against the man's neck, putting unbearable pressure on the man's spinal cord. The man tried to wiggle free, but it was useless. He tapped out, just before he lost consciousness. The fighter slowly stood and faced Trance. The two men clasped their fists in front of their chests. They bowed toward each other in a friendly and respectful way, while speaking soft words in Japanese.

Only four were left in the competition—Tompkin, Trance, Trance's other childhood friend and his old nemesis, Black Dragon.

Tompkin watched curiously as Trance and one of the fighters bowed toward each other, with their hands clasped against their chests. Black Dragon was bent over in a corner, recovering from a kick to his chest. The muscles on his thick shoulders twitched with each breath, looking like thick ropes beneath his tattooed skin. Trance and his old friend locked eyes and smiled. They both turned toward Black Dragon as one. Tompkin still held the sword, but he backed out of the way.

"Want a sword, Trance?" he said, offering Trance the helmet splitter.

Trance shook his head.

"You?" Tompkin offered the sword to Trance's friend, who also shook his head. This was obviously personal.

"You back for more, little red dragon?" Black Dragon said to Trance, in their Japanese village dialect.

Trance narrowed his eyes. "You will give no tattoos today, Black Dragon."

Trance and his friend began to circle the gang member.

"He has to die," said Trance's friend.

"I will not kill him," said Trance.

"His soul rests in your hands, Red Dragon."

"I do not kill out of hate. It stains the heart."

"I do not hate him, Red Dragon."

"That is very good, my friend. His life is in your hands, then."

Trance and his friend attacked, while Tompkin watched on. The crowd began shouting and screaming and waving their hands. They shouted bets to men with electronic pads. They entered them furiously into their computers. Tote boards on the walls updated the odds with equal fury.

Black Dragon was good, but not good enough to take on both Trance and his friend. Trance expected him to tap out, to live to fight another day. But he didn't. Trance and his friend took turns attacking, until Black Dragon began to tire. Trance's friend began an attack that the gang leader couldn't counter. A blow to his chest sent Black Dragon staggering to the floor.

"Swear on your honor that you will no longer prey upon the people of our village," said Trance's friend, as Black Dragon lay panting on all fours.

"Never." The gang member stuck out his head and bared his neck.

"Is that your choice?"

"You are a spineless dog. You don't have the will. Too bad, because I will kill you the next time we're alone."

Trance's friend drew high with his fist. He paused. He looked at Trance. Then he dropped the blade of his hand down through the gang member's neck, driving him hard into the mat.

Trance's friend looked at him sadly and said, "He has been a scourge to our village, Red Dragon, spreading death like so many lotus blossoms. If he didn't die, many others from our village surely would."

"He made his own choice. You showed him honor."

"He did not deserve honor."

"He will kill no longer, my friend," said Trance.

Trance's friend smiled. "Are you ready to spar? Like the old days?"

"In a moment, Shingen" said Trance. "First, tell me, cousin. Why are you here?"

Shingen and Trance began to circle around each other, while speaking softly to themselves, in their village dialect.

"We have a great need for money in our village, Red Dragon. They will soon put a new highway through its heart, unless we pay to have it routed around the valley."

"You were sent here to earn money? How much money is this?"

"More than one hundred million dollars."

"Why didn't you call me? I would be happy to pay this."

"It was a matter of honor."

Trance laughed. Honor was a very strange thing, especially in Japan. "You will not earn one hundred million here, Shingen."

"I will if I kill you."

Trance laughed. "Are you so desperate, that you would kill a brother?"

"After more than a thousand years, our village will die, unless we pay their blood money. Tell me. Why are you here, Red Dragon?"

Trance motioned toward Tompkin, who was standing in the corner, sword in hand, waiting.

"I am here to save him."

"You are not here to win?"

"I do not fight for glory or for money," said Trance. "*He* wanted to win. I need him for something else, something greater."

"We are all just pieces in the Creator's game of Go."

"We were both sent here by the Creator," said Trance.

"We are here to help each other."

"It is as He wills."

Both men nodded.

Trance backed away. Trance's friend, Shingen, turned toward Tompkin. Tompkin saw a sudden flash of movement, but he was too late. He tried to lift his sword but Shingen hit it out of his hands. Then Shingen came toward him. He thought that he parried Shingen's blows. He felt just a series of small stings in his arms from Shingen's knuckles and thumb. Suddenly, his arms felt numb. He tried to lift them, but they wouldn't respond. Shingen came at him again, this time kicking his exposed face with a calloused foot. Tompkin staggered backwards. Shingen hit him across the neck with the side of his hand. Then Tompkin's world went dark.

Shingen turned toward Trance and Trance bowed.

"Thank you for being gentle," said Trance.

Shingen smiled. "It is now between us, as it always has been."

"I have what I came for," said Trance. "The money is yours." Trance began to bow out, but Shingen stopped him.

"You must honor me, Red Dragon. You must fight."

"Then you must honor me, Shingen."

The two men walked around each other in a circle, still speaking softly in their village dialect.

"If I fight..." said Trance, "...you will help me save my president. Agreed?"

Shingen pressed his right fist into his left hand and bowed. Then Trance did the same.

"Let's give the fans their money's worth," said Trance.

Without notice, Trance attacked Shingen with a flurry of fists. Shingen blocked them expertly, almost with ease. Then he came at Trance with the same intensity. Trance stood his ground, blocking each strike in the same perfunctory manner.

Trance countered with a series of kicks. First to Shingen's head, and then to his knees. Shingen countered with a driving side kick. Trance launched himself backwards in a somersault, landing squarely and ready for more.

The crowd roared. It was almost deafening in the tightly enclosed stadium.

Trance wavered, as a deep, breath-sucking pain began to radiate through his chest.

Not now, he thought. Not now.

Shingen sensed his advantage. He came toward Trance, driving him into a corner. He began pummelling at Trance, with several blows striking him hard. Trance countered and caught Shingen with a palm to the nose. Blood began spurting over Shingen's lips. He laughed.

"You broke my nose again, Red Dragon. Why do you always break my nose?"

"Some things never change."

"Yes, they do. Today I shall beat you."

The men fought on for several more minutes. Trance's chest began to burn as if there were a fire inside it. Each punch he threw or received just seemed to fan the flames. Trance's strength began to waver. He took a roundhouse kick to the side of his face and staggered. Then he dropped his hands and let Shingen hit him one last time.

CHAPTER **120**

_______________PP_______________

"And the winner is…Shingen Takeda HARUnobu!" yelled Robert Yang, using Shingen's proper samurai name.

The crowd was on its feet. Some were chanting Shingen…Shingen…Shingen!

Others were shouting Dragon…Dragon…Dragon!

Trance staggered to the center of the ring and bowed toward his friend. Then he walked over and put an arm around Jesse Tompkin.

"Why didn't you stop him?" said Tompkin.

"I thought you wanted to win on your own? I asked him to go easy on you."

"Easy, yeah. What I wanted was the chance to beat your ass."

Trance managed a smile. "Never happen, Jesse."

Robert Yang held Shingen's arm aloft and said, "As is our custom, we will now announce the winnings of each participant.

"Our winner, Shingen, has earned…" Yang looked down to a piece of paper in his hand. "…seventy-eight million dollars. Our second place finisher, Red Dragon, has earned twenty-seven million dollars. Our third place finisher, The Babe, has earned fourteen million dollars…"

Trance turned toward Tompkin and said, "The Babe?"

Tompkin grinned sheepishly. "I like baseball."

"By the way," said Trance. "Before this thing started, I arranged for my winnings to be paid to you. It is part of my contract with Yang, so I can't change it. Congratulations, you now have forty-one million dollars, twenty-five million after taxes, if paid on-shore."

"Guess I'm going to Disney World."

Trance shuffled over to Shingen, with the crowd still chanting. He lifted Shingen's arm in the air. _Shingen…Shingen…Shingen…_ shouted the crowd.

"You ready to earn the rest of what we need for our village?" Trance said, his voice laboring between rapid, shallow breaths.

"Is your cause just?"

"Oh, yeah."

"Brother Kenshin and I will both be honored to help you."

Trance looked to his other old friend, who was still seated where Trance had taken him down. He bowed toward Kenshin, then turned back to Shingen.

"We became men together," said Shingen, speaking of their samurai genpuku ceremony, at the early age of fourteen. "We will always be brothers."

"You might not feel that way when you learn what we need to do."

CHAPTER **121**

_______________PP_______________

No one took notice of the eclectic group of passengers inside the old Mercedes diesel as it chugged along Broadway. Trance pulled off the road and drove into the alley between his safe houses in Washington Heights. He aimed the car into a dilapidated garage and shut off the engine, waiting as it chugged for several more seconds before coughing into silence. Trance stepped out of the car, followed by Tompkin and Stick, Sammantha and the two samurai. Trance negotiated the security system and they all went inside.

Stick went straight for the refrigerator, pulled out a six pack of Sam Adams Winter Ale and waved it in the air. "Who wants a beer?" he yelled.

Everyone did, except for Trance. Trance fell into a blue couch and leaned sideways against a fat pillow that was resting beside the couch's arm.

"Are you okay?" asked Tompkin.

"Just a little tired, that's all."

Sammantha looked at Trance. She could see sweat breaking out in rivers across his face. His color had grown oddly pallid, as pale as a freshly scrubbed potato. His breathing came in soft irregular gasps. Sammantha went over and took his pulse, then took a look at his eyes.

"You're going into shock, Jack. Lie down and put your feet up."

Trance murmured that he was fine, but he allowed Sammantha to remove the pillow and put it beneath his legs.

"Tell me what hurts."

"It's nothing, Sammantha. I just need a little rest."

"Take off your shirt. I want to listen to your chest."

"I'm fine—"

Sammantha looked at the two samurai and said, "Please take Jack's shirt off of him."

Trance tried to protest, but he didn't have the strength to stop his friends.

Sammantha put her ear to Trance's chest. She tapped several places along it, then pressed her hands against Trance's rib cage above his heart. Trance winced and pushed himself farther back against the couch.

"Jack, we should get you to a hospital."

"I'm fine, Sam. Nothing's wrong. I'm just a little sore, that's all."

"Sore, my ass. You've got pericardial effusion in your chest cavity. It is constricting your heart, and it could kill you. Plus, you've got broken ribs. Don't tell me you don't because I can tell. This is not something to mess with, Jack. Don't you have someone you could call?"

"With the whole world after me? I don't think so. I just need time to rest." Trance stood up slowly. "I'm going to go take a bath and lie in the tub."

"Not without icing your chest, you're not."

Trance nodded wearily.

"Don't drown yourself, Trance," said Stick. "I've had a hard day and I'm in no mood to clean up another one of your messes."

"Perhaps you should—" began Shingen, but Trance put a finger to his lips.

"Jesse," said Trance. "Could you send a message to Lauren? Tell her that I will also need my legacy."

"Your legacy?"

"She'll know what I mean. Tell her we'll need the big boat tomorrow after midnight. She's to meet us there. She can't be followed. She'll know who to call and what to do to shake her tails."

Tompkin walked over to a computer. He logged into an online video game and searched for Lauren's gamer tag. He found her and invited her into a private chat room. He gave her Trance's coded request, told her all was well and signed off.

Trance hobbled into the kitchen. He pulled an ice pack out of the freezer, showed it to Sammantha, then shuffled into his bedroom and closed the door.

Trance reached for the necklace he had recovered from Stick after the fight. Two clear amulets were dangling from a heavy gold chain, the light dancing off them like cold blue flame. Trance pulled one of the amulets off the chain. He snapped open the glass top and sucked down the sparkling blue liquid. He sat on his bed and allowed the hot, tingling family Elixir to flow through him, like St. Elmo's fire.

After a few minutes Trance got down on his knees. There was a deep sense of foreboding shadowing his mind, and he prayed for the strength to rescue the president. He prayed that he wouldn't be captured and hung before then. He prayed for Lauren. He prayed that one day she would find a man to love, someone who could make her happy for many years, someone who wouldn't bring death to her doorstep every chance he could, someone who wouldn't die.

CHAPTER **122**
PP
____

President Jock Tilson sat on the cold stone floor of his hidden cell beneath the Kremlin's Tainitskaya Tower. The walls of his prison were carved out of white limestone. Thin layers of iron ran through the stone, rusting in chaotic lines, making the walls look like a 1970s tie dyed T-shirt. Tilson rested with his back against a wall and his feet outstretched. Across from him sat a cot made with dented aluminum and ripping canvas. Beside that stood a makeshift port-a-potty that had been brought in for his use. On the floor, beside Tilson, sat a tray holding the remains of the greasy Borsch soup he had eaten for lunch.

"What a life," he mumbled.

Tilson was beginning to think that this was the only life he would ever know again. He had lost track of the days, with no windows, no watch, and no regular eating schedule. He wasn't sure if he had been here for six months, a year, or three. He could barely remember who he was, who he had been. He was The President of the United States. He laughed at the irony. *I am the most powerful man in the world.* Later today he would beg for a second serving of beans with his dinner. Yeah, he was powerful all right.

Tilson heard the bolt on the outer door slide open, and then the ominous squeak of its rusty hinges. *Not again*, he thought. He was getting tired of this. Tired of the subtle torture, never knowing when he would get to eat or bathe, or when they would pull him into a room and stick him full of needles. Or shock him. Or shine those scorching lights into his eyes. He tried to shrink into the floor, maybe vanish, as he heard the footsteps come toward him.

"Hello, again," came the voice. Petrovski. The goddamn Russian prime minister.

Tilson didn't look up.

"Today we are going to have a little conversation."

Tilson bowed his head but didn't speak. The whip came. He heard it crack like a gunshot beside his ear. If he didn't speak the next one would take a chunk from some random part of his body.

"I have nothing to say."

Crack. The whip's leather dug into Tilson's shoulder like the bite of a wolverine.

"What do you want?" said Tilson.

"Tell me about Jack Trance."

"Who?"

Again, the whip.

"What about him?" said Tilson.

"He just shot your president."

For the first time in months, Tilson laughed. "Did he now?"

"Where would he go? Where would Trance go?"

"What do you mean, where would Trance go?"

"If he were to hide, where would he go?"

"Beats me," mumbled Tilson. Then he smiled. "Maybe he'll come here."

The whip slashed into Tilson's collar bone, leaving a jagged, bloody line across his skin.

"How the hell should I know? Yes, Trance is a friend of mine. But you know his family. A man with that kind of global infrastructure could go anywhere. Combined with his training, he could be anyone or anything. Even you."

Petrovski sat down beside Tilson and sighed. "If you were shot while giving your State of the Union

Address, what would you do?"

"Is that what time of year it is?"

"What would you do, Mr. President?"

"How bad am I hurt?"

"Just a flesh wound. In the chest. It looks worse than it is."

"I'd want to find the man who did it."

"What if it was Trance?"

"Trance wouldn't shoot me."

"He just did."

Tilson brushed his hands across his body. "I'm sorry. I don't see any bullet holes, Petrovski. Just scars from your whip."

"What would you do if a nuclear bomb went off in your country?"

"You assholes! Were many killed?"

"Let's assume that it detonated deep within the Chesapeake Bay, and that no one was directly harmed."

"I'd say that I would hunt you down and have you shot."

Petrovski laughed. "The explosion is being blamed on your friend, Trance."

"You are a very sick man, Petrovski."

"I love my country, Mr. President. I do what I have to do."

"Why don't you kill me and be done with it?"

Petrovski shook his head. "There is still too much you can do to help me."

"Don't count on it."

Petrovski laughed.

CHAPTER **123**
PP

Trance drove his cranky Mercedes along Boston's Tremont Street until he passed within sight of the Bunker Hill Monument. It was just after midnight, and the lighted obelisk stood like a lonely soldier guarding the water in the clear night sky. Trance continued on, passing beneath the Tobin Bridge until he came to the Shipyard Quarters Marina. Even at this hour, in the middle of winter, there were still a few cars on the roads. There was even one hardy couple walking along the street. Trance used a cloned key card to enter the inner marina. He stopped the car in a parking lot and looked around, before shutting off the engine. Again, the intrepid motor refused to quit for several long seconds, before finally chugging to a wheezing halt.

"If we're going to get caught, this is the place," said Trance. He looked out across the water toward the Boston Navy Yard in Charlestown, knowing it was teeming with far too many warriors for him to stop.

"Depends on how hard they want to find you, Trance," said Tompkin.

"The president sure wants his ass," said Stick.

"While everyone else cheers him on. They know it's not Tilson. Deep down...everybody knows."

Trance stepped out of the car and closed the door. He pulled out a blue gym bag, along with a large attaché packed with cash. "Let's do this," he said.

Trance limped toward the end of the marina, to the deep water slips. He stopped when he reached the bow of a floating leviathan riding high in the water.

"You never told me you had one of these," said Stick.

"It belonged to my uncle."

Stick whistled. "This is some kind of ride, JT. You got an LZ on this thing?"

"Sure. Got a helicopter, too."

"Pool? Jacuzzi?"

"This isn't a vacation, Granger. But, yes."

"Just checking. This cruise could take a while. I want to make sure I'm comfortable."

At that moment Lauren Haverford began to walk down the rolling gangway that lead from the ship to the dock.

Stick said, "I see that you keep beautiful women here, too."

Trance remained in place as Lauren walked down the stairs. He felt tears begin to well in his eyes. Tears for the lost years. Tears for today. Tears for a tomorrow that might not come. He was dying; he could feel it.

"Hello, baby," said Lauren. She kissed Trance on the cheek. Then she held him at arm's length, assessing his bleach blond, spiked hair and his goth-black makeup. "Nice look." Lauren waved to the group that stood behind Trance. "I see we've been picking up strays again." Lauren gave brief hugs and cheek kisses to Stick and Tompkin. Then she introduced herself to Sammantha. "Hi, I'm Lauren Haverford. Remember me?"

"I am sorry for the pain I have caused you and your friends."

Lauren frowned but said nothing. She looked at the two Japanese men, and then at Trance. "Well?"

Trance rested an arm on Lauren's shoulder. He spoke to his old friends in their Japanese village dialect. "This is the woman I love, Lauren Haverford. She is a most honorable lady who deserves the greatest respect we can give her."

The two men bowed toward Lauren.

"What did you tell them?" Lauren asked. She knew the gist of what he'd said, as her Japanese was good enough to understand much of this strange dialect.

"I told them you were my concubine."

"Is that your fantasy, Jack?" Lauren turned toward the two Japanese samurai and spoke to them in Japanese. "What names have you taken?"

They told her their samurai names and she bowed.

"Shingen and Kenshin are from my grandmother's village in Japan," said Trance. "We became samurai together, a bond that can never be broken. We are also distant cousins, as are all from our ancient village."

Lauren studied the bruises on their faces. "Where did you meet them, Jack, at a fight club?"

"In the city."

"What city? They look like they've been mugged."

"They were at Yang's."

Lauren's face seemed to fall. She drew a quick breath. With the low light and Trance's disguise, Lauren hadn't noticed the cut lip and growing shiner around Trance's eye. Nor could she see the massive black stain spreading across his chest like the plague. "Tell me you didn't fight again."

"I didn't want to."

Lauren turned to the others and said, "Excuse me." She pulled Trance aside and said, "Let me see if I have this right. First you shoot the president. You swim a nuclear warhead into the Chesapeake. Then you go fighting at Yang's. Are you going through some kind of mid-life crisis, Jack?"

Trance looked over at his friends. He could see them laughing. He almost laughed himself.

"It's a long story."

"I've got time. Let's hear it."

"Well…I had to stop the bomb, didn't I?"

"So, you shoot the president?"

"Well, yeah. I had to. Besides, he isn't the president. We all know that."

"And then the fighting? How come the fighting? You promised me there would be no more fighting."

"I told you, I had to."

"You didn't have to."

"I had to save Jesse."

Lauren looked toward Tompkin. "Jesse went there to fight?"

Tompkin nodded.

"Well, that was flat-out stupid, Jesse."

"I needed him," said Trance.

"Needed him for what?"

"Never mind."

Stick drew Tompkin to the side and whispered in his ear. "She's acting like she's his wife."

"She loves him."

"I think he kinda likes it. Won't be long now. Provided he lives, of course."

Lauren said, "I want to know what you have planned before I let you take my boat."

"Your boat?" said Trance.

"Yes. My boat. Go look at the back of it. What name do you see painted in big gold letters? *Lauren*, that's what you see. It's *my* boat."

Trance looked around the area. He nudged Lauren with a pinch of the shoulder and softly said, "We better go inside."

Trance led them up and across the deck, then down toward the inner cabins. The inner rooms were protected by thick walls and elaborate security gear. Once they got inside, they could see why. Like the chateau in France, the walls of the yacht were hung with rare paintings from all of the great masters. As they walked along the hallways, Trance ignored the paintings, as did the others.

Trance led the group to a conference room that was fitted with a bolted, wooden table that could seat twenty-four. Built into the table's top there were computer monitors at every seat. There was also a large whiteboard behind the head of the table.

"Sit," said Trance. He pressed the intercom and said, "Could you bring refreshments to the main conference room, please?"

Trance turned to Lauren. "Is Art here?"

"He's with the captain."

Trance pressed the intercom again. "Would Art and the ship's captain please come join us?"

Trance touched a few spots on the conference table, while Lauren glared at him with a slight smile upon her face.

A huge, slightly curved flat panel, 3-D screen, far larger than the whiteboard, slid up from the floor behind Trance. It was already showing the output from his computer. The Kremlin.

"This is where we are going, men."

"Aw, shit, Jack," said Stick. "I was thinking the Bahamas. You know how cold it is in Moscow right now?"

"I didn't choose the spot, Granger. That's where the president is, so that's where we go."

"At least let's wait until summer. Moscow's okay in the summer. He's been there a while already; what's a few more months? I get cold just thinking about Moscow."

Trance turned to Sammantha. "Where was he last?"

"Tainitskaya Tower."

"The secret tower?" said Tompkin. "I've heard bad things about that place, Jack. Like it's cursed or something."

"Why would Petrovski keep Tilson there?" asked Trance.

"To keep him from Ogarkov."

"But Ogarkov has full run of the Kremlin."

"Not anymore. Petrovski has grabbed much of the power now, with his ex-KGB thugs and all."

"Why the Tainitskaya?"

"Because of its symbolism. It was a place built for the Czars to escape the Kremlin. Tilson can't escape. Petrovski feeds off the irony." Sammantha paused, as if deciding how much to tell. "The tower has underground passageways that were built in case of attack. During one of the tower reconstructions, some of the passages were found and sealed, while the men that worked on them went missing. Only a few of us know they are still there."

"How do you know?"

Sammantha smiled. "Men will say anything to impress a woman, particularly if they want to get her in bed. But even I don't know their precise location, at least outside."

"Can you get us inside the tower?"

"Conventionally? Never. You'll have to get in from a tunnel."

Trance walked to where Sammantha was sitting. He took the seat beside her. Then he looked into her eyes. "Do you love Brandon Copley?"

"I do."

"Do you want a life with him?"

"We're beyond that now."

"Perhaps. Then again, maybe not. He is Tilson's brother."

"I do not deserve Brandon Copley, or happiness, not after all I've done."

"Others will be the judge of that, Sammantha. Right now, you need to help us find Jock Tilson. You have to help us get him out of your country." Trance began to walk around the conference room. When he got to the opposite side he stopped and looked across to Sammantha. "The secret tower…If memory serves me, it is the tower closest to the river?"

At that moment, Art and the ship's captain came into the room. The captain looked to be of Mediterranean descent, possibly Greek. He was a big man, a head taller than Trance, and half again as broad. He had dark, swarthy skin that was carpeted with thick, curly black hair. His only smooth skin was around his eyes, which were surrounded by two white sunglass circles. The rest of his face was whiskered and bumpy, and as weathered as an old oak.

"Hello, captain," said Trance. He extended a hand, and was pleased at the captain's strong grip.

"So, you are the one they speak of," said the captain. "My name is Nicholas. People call me Nikko."

"People call me, Jack."

"Among other things," mumbled Stick.

Trance looked at Stick, smiled, but said nothing.

"Nikko, can you bring us to Helsinki without refueling?"

"But, of course. We have a range of seven thousand nautical miles."

"At what speed?"

"That depends. This ship was built for a top cruising speed of forty-five knots."

Trance frowned. This was counter to all his navy training. "That can't be correct. The speed of a displacement monohull tops out at one point three times the square root of the length. Which should give us a max speed of…" Trance did the calculations in his head. "…about twenty-one knots, give or take."

Nikko grinned. "To reach forty-five knots, we will have to engage the ship's trimaran feature."

"Explain."

"This ship is equipped with extendable, wave-piercing sidehulls. We also have a narrower hull extension that slides out from the main hull to help us plane. We can get to Helsinki in four days. Five days max."

Trance looked at Winthrop. His company CEO nodded. "One of your companies built this, Jack. It is highly experimental, but enormously effective. We have bigger prototypes in development for the navy."

"Why don't you tell me these things, Art? I don't know half the things we do and make."

Winthrop chuckled. "You're never around, always too busy doing whatever you do. Hell, even I don't know all of the things we have in development, Jack."

Trance stared at Winthrop for several long seconds. Then he nodded. Art was right, there had to be thousands of projects underway. Maybe tens of thousands. Trance shrugged and looked at Nikko. "I'd like to learn more about this, later. Will you prepare to weigh anchor?"

"We are ready any time you say."

Trance turned toward Art and then Lauren. "You two should head back now."

Art stepped forward and clasped Trance by the shoulders. "Good luck, Jack."

Lauren squared her stance and put her hands on her hips. Trance wouldn't look in her eyes. Lauren didn't move.

"Okay, okay," said Trance. "You can come. But not to Moscow. Finland is as far as you go."

CHAPTER **124**
_______PP_______

The *Lauren* passed through the Baltic Sea without incident. They cruised along the edge of the main shipping lanes through the Gulf of Finland, passing container ships from time to time. In the distance they could see a few fishing trawlers, but there were few pleasure craft in these cold waters.

It was after midnight when they neared Helsinki. Nikko wormed his way through the final scattering of islands. They could see occasional patches of lights along the coast, from smallish settlements that were separated by dark spots of dense forest. They rounded a final peninsula and came upon the main city. Even at night, Helsinki's waterfront was bathed in bright dancing lights. Groupings of commercial vessels were anchored offshore. Along the shore, rows of docks moored vessels of all size and nationality.

Hopewell Industries had several subsidiaries operating in the region. The *Lauren* was able to dock near the heart of the city, with only a cursory attention from customs officials.

Trance was conducting a final meeting in the ship's conference room. Across the grouping of wide video panels, Trance displayed a plot plan of the Kremlin.

"This is a highly fortified complex in the heart of Moscow," Trance said. "There are four separate palaces and as many cathedrals, plus a host of other buildings. The complex is surrounded by a triangular wall that is more than a mile long. This wall is thick and at least fifteen feet high. Often higher. There are twenty towers along this wall, built to protect the Czars from invasion. They can be used against *us* now.

"To the east, just outside the wall, you can see Red Square. The Tainitskaya Tower is here."

Trance pointed to a modest brick structure along the southern wall. He tapped his computer console and another image filled the screen. This showed a detailed 3-D blueprint of the building. Trance showed several versions of the same blueprint, stopping on one that showed a labyrinth of underground passageways.

"This…" Trance moved the red dot of a laser pointer along the architectural drawing. "…is a tunnel that runs from the tower to the Moscow River. The tunnel does not lead directly to the river. It runs parallel to the water at first, branching out many times and dead-ending in every place but one—the river chamber. Years back, the riverbank was fortified with a wall of heavy stone slabs. So, the river chamber now lies behind tons of rock. This is rock we are going to have to secretly move, if we are to have any chance at rescuing the president."

"Why don't we just scale the walls and slip in through a window?" asked Stick. "That would be easy. We'll get you one of those ATLAS rope ascenders, Trance. You won't even have to stress your heart."

Trance laughed. He loved the way Stick was able to lighten any mood, and help take the fear out of risk. "This is the Kremlin, guys. The Kremlin is one of the most fortified places in the world. Our president is heavily guarded. If, by some odd twist of fate, we can actually recover Tilson, we will then have to take him across hundreds of miles of open space, with the Russian army on our tails."

"I should have gone to Disney World," muttered Tompkin. He raised his voice. "I'm out of the military, Trance. Remember?"

Trance grinned. "Isn't this great, though?"

Lauren cleared her throat. The smile fell off of Trance's face.

"I mean, isn't it great that we're rescuing the president?" Trance turned toward Tompkin. "You have any operatives here we can trust?"

"As long as you pay them."

Trance nodded. "It has been cold as hell in America. But it has grown unusually warm in Russia, historically warm. Climate change. Go figure. The one time we need the Moscow River to be frozen solid, it's melting like ice cream in the summertime. It was like this in 2006, when the ice didn't start to form until the end of January. Then it was just for a couple weeks. I'm betting that it'll get cold and the river will freeze back up. If so, we'll need a Snow Cat and six snowmobiles, fast ones. I'll also want a truck with tundra tires that we can outfit as a State-owned vehicle.

"If it remains warm and the river runs free, I'll need two boats. Something fast and something forgettable, preferably a tug. We'll need geophysical radar and infrared scanners sensitive enough to pinpoint the river cavern. I want to make sure it's where we think it is, before we start pulling slabs off the river bottom. That data, combined with what I've got from space, should help us target the cavern within a couple feet.

"My company has oil interests in Russia and the Ukraine. I've summoned some of our geo guys. They should be here by tomorrow. If the tunnel cavern is there, they'll find just where it is."

Tompkin laughed. "You really think you can do this."

"Of course I do." Trance hefted an attaché case onto the conference table and laid it open. He looked at Tompkin. "This is two million dollars. I've got more cash in the ship's safe. I can also supply funds in Rubles or Eurodollars if that's their preference, by wire or paper. We can deal in gems or rare coins. Hell, we could even deal in art.

"We're going to need a panel truck. I'd also prefer one of those hollowed out Rosneft oil tanker trucks to get us across the country. We have any of those in the region?"

Tompkin said, "I'll check the inventory, but that shouldn't be a problem. The boats? Those I will have to work on."

Trance handed Tompkin a brown accordion folder that was secured with a burnt orange elastic band. "Art Winthrop prepared a list of my family's interests in the region. My grandfather was heavily invested in Russia, even before the revolution. When he and Verushkin died, everything was left to me. For all I know, I've got boats sitting here in Moscow. Check into it and see what you can find."

Trance turned to Shingen and Kenshin. "Have you been able to communicate with the village?"

"Yes, Red Dragon," said Shingen.

"Have they received the transfer?"

"They say you sent fifty million, not twenty-five. There was no need—"

Trance held up a hand. "You will need even more funds, I assure you. I did some checking. The authorities never expected that you could raise such money to redirect the road. They will ask for more. But they are now honor bound to accept your cash."

Both of the samurai bowed and remained silent.

Trance motioned toward Lauren, who was standing at the back of the conference table. She approached Trance hefting an old, lightly-oiled leather roll-up case. Trance took the case and laid it on the conference table. He unfurled the leather to reveal an assortment of ancient Japanese weapons. There was a gleaming samurai Katana sword, with a jewel encrusted scabbard, and a longer Tachi sword. Both were family heirlooms, passed through the generations, dating from the 14th century. There was a matching wakizashi short sword, and a second Hachiwari. A pouch held a cluster of throwing stars. Another housed a matching set of ornate daggers.

Trance said to the two samurai, "These are the weapons of my family. Use them as if they were your own."

Shingen and Kenshin touched the weapons, as if they were priceless Ming china, running their fingers lightly along the shining steel.

"We are most honored," said Shingen.

Stick raised his hand and waved it like a fifth grade student who knew the answer to a challenging class problem.

"Yes, Stick?" said Trance.

"Why don't we just steal a tank and blow a hole in the tower wall? Or maybe use a Tomahawk missile. Then we could walk in and out without all this underground tunnel stuff. I hate going underground. I just hate it. Cold water is worse."

Trance said, "Why don't we invite the Russian Army for a break-out party? I'm sure they'd understand."

"There you go," said Stick. "I knew we could make this simple."

"I want to finish this operation within two weeks," said Trance. "Anyone think we can't get it done?"

Trance looked around the room, but heard only silence.

"Good."

Trance turned to Sammantha. "You think you can make up with Petrovski?"

Sammantha shook her head. "If I saw him, I'd kill him."

"How about Ogarkov?"

"He might support us, but we can't be sure. He's Russian, you know."

"This would be a hell of a lot easier with his help."

"He could have sent Tilson home at any time. But has he? No. Ogarkov can't tip the fragile balance of power. Russia has been teetering back toward communism and totalitarianism ever since Putin put his clamps on the presidency. Ogarkov has been trying to pull the country back from the precipice. A scandal involving the American president would kill him, politically, if not personally."

"What if he pinned it on Petrovski?"

Sammantha shook her head. "It still happened under Ogarkov's watch."

Trance thought for a moment. "Can we count on his neutrality, if not his support?"

"Probably. But who is to know?"

Trance looked closely at Sammantha, as if trying to see beyond her eyes to a place inside that could tell him who she was, what she believed, whom she hated and whom she loved.

"Tell me," he said. "What do you think of our plan?"

"I think you are a fool to let me hear it."

Trance closed his eyes and smiled. "I have learned that my gut is a better judge than my brain. My gut tells me that, deep inside, you are a good and honorable person."

"I do not deserve honor, not after what I've done." Sammantha's eyes began to glaze. She looked like she'd been peeling an onion, not quite enough to make her tear, but enough draw out the red. Dry tears, as if all of life's juice had been sucked out of her, a kind of white flag waving when all hope was lost.

"If you behave with honor," said Trance. "You earn honor."

"How can you say that? I killed Kiki Tilson. I killed your wife. I *killed* your unborn child! I am a murderer. There can be no honor for me. I deserve to die. I want to die. After this is over, I fully expect you to arrest me, try me, and shoot me as the terrorist I am."

"The terrorist you *were*."

Sammantha dropped her head to the table. Lauren Haverford walked to Sammantha's side and placed a hand upon her shoulder. "He does this all the time, Sammantha. It's in his genes. It's also in

America's DNA, that rare and beautiful ability to forgive. America is a forgiving country."

"It can't be that forgiving, not for someone like me."

"What about Copley? Doesn't he deserve his life back? Who is going to give him his life back if you are gone? I'll tell you, no one. There is no one else that can glue his pieces together and make him whole."

"Like a butterfly cup," whispered Sammantha. "Like a butterfly cup."

Sammantha thought back to that day, that horrific day, when her parents had died, when she'd been branded inside like some barnyard animal. She also remembered that little girl with the butterfly cup full of milk…and Oreo cookies…looking out at the pond, sitting in the sunlight with her mother, laughing and dreaming. She could still feel that girl, that innocent child inside her, as if she'd been hiding in a dark corner closet. She was here. She was *here*. Trapped, but still here.

"You *can* trust me to do what is right," Sammantha said. She turned to Lauren. "You are extraordinary. And you have an extraordinary man."

Lauren nodded. "I do have an extraordinary man. You can be extraordinary, too, Sammantha. Choose that path and you can do it. Good luck and Godspeed in Moscow."

CHAPTER **125**
_________PP_________

The seven hundred miles from Helsinki to Moscow were uneventful. Their papers held and they were cleared through Russian customs, at a cost of just two D-flawless diamonds from Trance's pouch.

Trance was traveling as a prosperous Dutch diamond merchant. Sammantha, dressed as Miss Smith, was Trance's assistant. Stick, Tompkin and the samurai traveled separately, posing as representatives of a multi-national chemical concern that was in negotiations with the Russian government. Tompkin was the only one who spoke Russian, so he was their leader.

Trance and Sammantha checked into the Hotel Baltschug Kempinski, with its panoramic view of St. Basil's Cathedral and their target, the Kremlin. The others checked into the more pedestrian Tourist Hotel on Selskohozaystvennaya Street.

The weather remained unseasonably warm, the warmest winter in more than a century. The Moscow River continued to flow, despite its slow pace and its relatively shallow depth. Reluctantly, Trance put the backup plan into play.

Trance was piloting a small red tugboat up the Moscow River. The boat's old diesel engine clattered and clanked as it pulled a barge laden with a mountain of black coal. It was early morning and the sun had yet to brighten the eastern horizon. The boat's progress was grindingly slow, little more than walking pace, snailing its way innocuously against the slow current. In the pale shimmer of dawning light, no one noticed as two divers wearing black thermal drysuits flipped into the frigid, murky water, or saw the large black bag that went over the side with them.

At this point the river was less than twenty feet deep. The divers were forced to hug the bottom with their load. Shingen and Kenshin allowed the river to pull them downstream to the GPS coordinates that Trance's team had pinpointed as the secret river cavern. It was over two hundred yards downstream from where a direct tunnel from the Kremlin would have met the river. Hopefully, this was far enough to give them the head start they would need, if they ever got that far.

When the two samurai reached the appointed spot, Shingen put a harpoon gun to his shoulder and fired an explosive tipped bolt into the base of the stone river sidewall. Attached to the bolt was a metal ring, which he used to clip the black bag in place. Shingen fired another ringed bolt into the wall. He and Kenshin fastened themselves to it, by clipping straps attached to harnesses they had slung around their chests.

The men pulled battery-powered underwater drills from the bag and began to grind into the cement holding the stones of the wall together. After two hours, despite their thermal dry suits and their extreme physical effort, the divers were so cold they could barely move. They had Nitrox left in their rebreathers, they had more batteries in their bag, but they could no longer function with any kind of strength. Shingen sent what looked like a small plastic fishing bobber to the surface of the river. The bobber was attached to a thin, rubber coated wire that carried a signal back to Trance. It was time to retrieve the two men.

Trance had offloaded his coal barge at a depot two miles upstream. Then he had parked the tug to wait, with a second barge containing machinery in large wooden boxes, ready to be taken downstream. When the signal came, Trance maneuvered his tug back into the river. As he drifted by the Kremlin, Trance waved furtively toward a Mosenergo Utilities that was parked on the street between the Kremlin and the river. Stick and Tompkin waved back and gave a subtle thumbs-up sign. All was clear and on task.

Shingen and Kenshin grabbed a pair of chains that were dragging behind the slow-moving barge. They clipped themselves and their bag to the chains and drifted behind the barge for another thirty minutes, bouncing along the treacherous river bottom. When the barge slowed to a stop, the two men unhooked themselves and swam to shore.

They repeated this process again the next morning, with new air, fresh batteries and warmer suits. They would do so until they had either been discovered, or they had broken through the wall and found the hidden cavern.

Over the next week, Shingen and Kenshin removed a grouping of the flat slabs of stone that were lining the side of the river. They did this by levering the stones with two man-sized crowbars, and come-alongs screwed to other stone slabs in the river lining. When they had created enough room for several men to tunnel through, provided they had the right spot, the samurai began digging through the sandy mud of the riverbank. The work was tedious, wielding shovels while holding a battery powered vacuum hose in place, particularly when they had to stop every few minutes to remove the endless series of rotted logs and small boulders that got in their way.

On the seventh day it happened. Shingen was driving forward with a shovel when it nearly lurched out of his hands. He dug at the edges of the hole until he made a space large enough for a man and a rebreather tank to fit through. He swam into the narrow tunnel and came to a large pool of water. Kenshin followed. Together they swam upward, breaking the surface of the water about ten feet above them.

The men emerged into a dark, carved out cavern. In front of them was a small wooden platform, sitting just above water level. The men tested the platform and found it marginally, but suitably solid. They threw their fifty pound tanks onto the wood and climbed out. The ceiling of the cave was no more than seven feet high. Beyond the platform they could see a square room about fifteen feet to a side. Beyond the room, there was a roundish tunnel stretching off into the blackness. The floor of the tunnel was made from chipped limestone, while the walls and ceiling appeared to be edged with thick, tar-treated planks, perhaps railroad ties, or something even older than the first locomotive. Along the side of the walls they saw a row of unlit torches sticking out from the wood. Shingen touched the ceiling above his head and found it solid.

The two men looked at each other, smiled and bowed with their hands clasped near their chests. This was their version of a high five and a chest bump. They jumped back into the water, created more space around the river opening and sent up the plastic bobber for one final time.

CHAPTER **126**

______________PP______________

Trance checked out of the Kempinski and paid cash, with Euros, for a new suite at the Tourist Hotel. The Tourist complex was large, boasting more than five hundred renovated rooms spread across six buildings. It catered to the business traveler, so it was a good place to blend. Trance took the stairs to his third floor suite and was soon joined by the other members of his group. Tompkin pulled a wand from a briefcase and swept the room for bugs. He found two. He also found a small video camera disguised as the glass top to a table lamp in the bedroom.

"So much for privacy," Stick said, after he'd jammed each bug and thrown a hat over the camera. "Now I know how they get all that steamy Russian porn."

"What do you know about Russian porn?" joked Trance.

"You didn't know I was a Moscow film star? Not by my own choosing, mind you. But greatness always finds a way—"

"Sure, Stick. You're a real Johnny Depp. Enough about your *rising* film career. Let's wrap this up. We go tomorrow. Everyone sure of their duties?"

His team all nodded.

"Tompkin, tell me your role."

"I drive the truck. I wait downstream at the appointed place, with the people we've hired to take your place on the boat. At approximately 10 A.M. you will call me, as you approach from up river. I will have my people ready at the water. You will come to me with the president and I am to drive slowly through the streets to your place in the warehouse district."

"And what if I am not with them?"

"If I have the president, I am to drive on without you."

"Stick?"

"I pilot the barge and drop you and the gear into the river. Then I go upstream and wait with the speedboat. I have its canopy in place and the uniforms ready. When you call me I race in to save the day, picking you up a thousand yards downstream from the tower. I bring us to the bridge, swap drivers and get in the truck."

"Sammantha?"

"I come with you. If we meet anyone along the way, I am to detain and distract them if I can, and kill them if I can't."

"Shingen and Kenshin?"

"We go with you into the tunnels. We light the tunnels so you can see. We set the explosive charges and detonate them once you have passed each marker. Then we swim with you downstream and wait for the boat."

"Once we get into the truck," said Trance. "We will be taken to the warehouse. There, we will get into the hollow cabin of a Rosneft tanker. This will take us across this beautiful, snow-cursed countryside back to Helsinki, where we will toast with champagne and eat something better than this god-awful Russian food."

Trance shook hands with them all. "Good luck everyone. This should be fun."

How wrong he was.

CHAPTER 127
_____________PP_____________

It was not yet dawn when Stick slowed the barge to a near stall as they passed the Kremlin. Trance released the cable that was pulling gear in their wake, including four Seadoo water scooters. Then Trance, Sammantha, Shingen and Kenshin slipped overboard. They each grabbed a scooter and maneuvered them toward the opening in the river wall. They clipped the scooters onto bolts drilled into the wall by the samurai. Then they swam inside.

When they reached the river cavern, Trance and Shingen lifted two black waterproof bags onto the platform. Trance pulled a Full Spectrum Battle Equipment Amphibious Quick-Release Assault Vest out of his bag and handed it to Sammantha. He fitted it with body armor, then placed a 9mm Beretta with two clips into the vest. He slipped a KA-BAR into a side sheath and took Sammantha by the shoulders. He looked her in the eyes. "You can do this."

Trance pulled out a vest for himself. He adjusted the light armor plates and put extra ones in a couple spots, particularly the area above his heart. He slipped an M9 pistol into the vest along with several 15-round double-stack magazines. He also slipped in his old Colt 32, with several fresh clips. He added a samurai short sword, before putting on a lightweight ballistic helmet. He blew into the mic to test it. Trance threw four XM84 stun grenades into side pockets. He added four Mk 2 "pineapple" grenades, two Power Bars, and a bottle of water. He was ready.

Trance's samurai brothers chose not to wear armor. Instead, they each hoisted a knapsack holding explosives and a samurai short sword onto their shoulders. They'd be better off that way, Trance thought. The vests would just slow them down. Speed and mobility were their critical assets.

"Ready?" said Trance.

Trance hefted his black bag and led them onward, using a SureFire M3 CombatLight. Although bulky, Trance liked this light because it made a good club, if it came to that.

The tunnel was clear. It didn't take long to cover the few hundred yards to the edge of the Tainit-skaya Tower wall.

Trance spoke through his headset to Shingen. "Tell me when you have set the charges."

Several minutes later, he heard, "We are ready, Red Dragon."

Trance hoped that Sammantha's intel was accurate. He tapped lightly on the wall with the hilt of his KA-BAR. A moment later he heard a light return tap. Trance wasn't sure if the president understood Morse code, but he tried it anyway.

"This is Trance." he tapped.

"You bring single malt?" came the tapped-out reply from Tilson's butter knife.

"Forgot," said Trance.

"Pity."

"Alone?"

"Yes."

"Guards?"

"No. Want me check?"

"Yes."

Trance waited for a moment, until he heard, "None."

"Close?"

"Upstairs."

"You mobile?"

"Bet your ass."

"Distance from wall?"

"Fifteen feet."

"Prepare. When I say."

Trance reached into his bag and removed some small blocks of C-4 explosive. He shaped them into several places on the wall and wired it all to a detonator. He tapped on the wall. Then he grabbed his gear and began walking back through the tunnel.

"Come with me," he said to Sammantha.

When they had moved a good way down the tunnel Trance pressed the detonation switch. The tunnel wall exploded. The sound was deafening, like standing inside thunder. Limestone and rock dust filled the air for several dragging moments. It looked like a night-time blizzard, with everything so dark it seemed like they were surrounded by black ink. Trance looked for the president, hoping he would be running toward them. But he wasn't.

Trance ran through the rocky debris to the wall. There was a hole there now, but it was barely the size of a watermelon. Trance stuck his head through the hole to his shoulders and looked for the president. Tilson was standing with his hands on his hips, his face covered with rock dust, laughing.

"Is that the best you can do, Trance?"

"Didn't want to kill you with the blast, Jock."

Trance stepped back and launched a sidekick into a crust of stone that was hanging from the edge. It barely crumbled beneath his boot. He kicked again, as hard as he could, but the rock wouldn't give.

"Ouch!" yelled Trance. "Shit…shit…shit." He shook his right leg while jumping up and down on his left.

"You're not supposed to kick solid rock, Jack. You'll break your leg that way."

"You got a better plan?"

"How about more C-4? Perhaps a grenade?"

"Too dangerous."

"How 'bout a pick axe?"

"Didn't bring one."

"Don't you plan these things, Trance?"

"Close your trap and let me concentrate."

Trance sat upon the floor and collected his *chi*. After twenty long seconds he stood. Trance closed his eyes and launched a donkey back kick that was so powerful, so violent that the earth shook around them. A large chunk of the wall tumbled down.

"Can you run?" Trance said, wondering if he could run himself. The pounding nerves of his right leg made it feel like it was partially frozen. He could sense his knee and his foot, but that was all. It was as if there were nothing solid there at all. There was just a memory, a memory that might or might not respond to his brain.

"I've been sitting for six months," said Tilson, as he ducked under the opening in the wall. "But I've done what I could to keep fit."

At that moment the door to the president's cell swung open.

Trance pulled Tilson through the hole. "Move!" he shouted. "Sammantha, take Tilson!"

Trance stepped into the chamber and triggered a volley of gunfire. The Russians scampered behind the dungeon door. Trance glanced back quickly to make sure Tilson was gone. As he turned, a Russian soldier jumped across the door opening and fired two wild shots. One of them hit Trance in the chest. His body armor stopped the blow, but the pain was extraordinary. It felt like he'd swallowed molten ball bearings, the pain radiating through him like a sunburst. Trance fell backward. He felt the world begin to close in around his eyes, like a shade being drawn against the light. He shook his head and willed his body to move. He put a bullet between the advancing Russian's eyes. He fired three more shots into the doorway, before turning to hobble back through the tunnel.

After fifty yards Trance saw Shingen waiting for him with a plunger in his hands. As Trance passed him, Shingen drove the handle down. A bone-jarring blast rocked the tunnel. The walls shook, and chunks of the ceiling began to rattle to the ground. Behind Trance, the tunnel seemed to be swallowed by rock and splintered wood. Another wave of rock dust flooded through the tunnel. Trance and Shingen outran the cloud, barely, as if it were a dog, nipping at their heels.

Forty yards ahead, Kenshin was waiting with a second plunger. He set off another explosion. Chunks of wood and gritty stone whooshed through the tunnel like arrows. Behind the debris came a dry, windy heat that sucked everything from their lungs. This was followed by another billow of heavy rock dust. It obscured their vision for a few long moments, before it settled onto the floor like volcanic ash.

"That's enough!" shouted Trance. "Come!"

They raced down the tunnel, catching up with Sammantha and Tilson at the river cavern. Tilson had already thrown on a drysuit and was strapping a rebreather tank onto his back. When Trance reached the cavern he leaned over and put his hands on his knees, wobbling like a marathoner who had succumbed to the heat.

Between breaths, Trance said, "You…dive before…Jock?" Trance worked hard to control his breathing, but it was like trying to relax in the middle of a tornado. He could feel his heart trying to grind to a halting, stuttering stop, as if it were rusting in place. The world spun around his eyes, growing red, like strawberries in a blender. His blood felt like cooling bacon grease, getting harder and harder to push through his veins, his limbs growing dull and heavier by the second. Every heartbeat came with a stuttering thud. Trance wondered if he could go on. He had to go on. He looked at his president.

"Never gone diving like this," said Tilson. "In the cold and the dark with people gunning for my ass."

"It'll…be… a piece… of cake." Trance pointed to the water pool below them. He took a deep gulp of air and willed his breathing to slow. "We're going to swim through…a small opening…down there into the Moscow River. We've got four Seadoos waiting at the opening. They are…tethered to each other, so we won't get separated. You're going to…ride behind...me."

Trance clipped the tied end of a rope to his belt and clipped the other end onto Tilson's rebreather harness. "All you'll need to do is…hold onto…me. Got it?"

Tilson nodded. "You okay, Jack?"

Trance grimaced, but tried to make it look like a smile. "We're…going to surface…about a thousand yards…downstream. There may be some shooting…so keep your…head down."

Trance looked around the cavern to the others and gave the thumbs-up sign. "Let's roll, guys."

Trance flipped on a light that was part of his dive mask. He took hold of the president's shoulder and jumped with him into the water. He felt the president recoil as the thirty-four degree water settled around his dive suit. Tilson wouldn't feel cold at once, like with a wetsuit. He wouldn't get numb for a good while. But Tilson *would* feel the icy, dark water lurking outside like a hungry wolf. Trance was already sweating from running in his suit, so the coolness surrounding his drysuit came almost as a relief. He felt his heart shudder again, as if anticipating the coldness of death. His testicles rolled up inside him like dried grapes.

Trance grabbed hold of a Seadoo and banged the butt of his dive knife on its side. *Clunk, clunk, clunk.* When the others did the same, Trance released a floating device that was attached to his harness.

The device rose to the surface and began emitting the *ready* signal to Stick Granger.

Trance patted the president's leg and the president hit him back. He was ready. Trance powered his Seadoo and began heading down river. The river's winter flow speed was just a tenth of a meter per second, only fifteen feet per minute. The Seadoos could travel at about three and a half miles per hour, or ninety yards a minute. Combined, they were traveling at a rate of barely a hundred yards a minute. Far too slow for Trance's taste. He had to balance the risk of being shot from the Kremlin towers versus the risk of getting caught by pursuers on land. The longer they stayed beneath the water, the farther they got from the Kremlin. But it could take mere minutes for the Russians to send scouts along the river to hunt them down.

Sammantha had assured Trance that Tilson's incarceration was a closely guarded secret, known only to a few of Petrovski's handpicked guards. A general call to arms would require an explanation. Petrovski wouldn't risk that kind of exposure, unless he wanted to try to lay the blame on Ogarkov. That was unlikely, though, since they were still politically joined at the hip.

Trance was betting that Petrovski's guards would spend the first few minutes trying to pursue them through the tunnel. Only then would they move to the surface. Petrovski would be notified, but it could take time for him to act.

Trance waited just three minutes. They surfaced five hundred yards downstream of the Tainitskaya Tower. Stick was waiting two hundred yards beyond them, looking frantically across the surface of the water. Trance waved an arm in the air. Stick powered the boat toward them and stopped with the boat facing the Tower, shielding Trance and the others from potential gunfire on the downstream side of the boat. He threw a climbing ladder over the side and the others scrambled into the back of boat.

The Kremlin was eerily silent. There was no gunfire from the Kremlin walls. They could see no one rushing toward them along the banks of the river. Stick powered the boat downstream and jammed it full throttle. He pointed to a pile of Mosenergo Utilities uniforms that were neatly folded and stacked on the boat's floorboards.

"Get dressed, guys. There's work to be done."

As they pulled off their dive suits and got into the Mosenergo uniforms, Trance began to think that, maybe…just maybe…their plan might work. There was also a foreboding feeling that radiated from deep within Trance's chest. Something was about to go terribly, irreversibly wrong. He just knew it.

CHAPTER **128**
_____________PP_____________

Jesse Tompkin stopped the Mosenergo Utilities truck beside a bridge about ten miles west of the Kremlin. He raised the truck's cherry picker toward the overhanging set of utility cables. This was a busy industrial area and most of the vehicles passing were commercial. No one gave the truck a second glance.

The escape boat would have to travel south along the canal before almost doubling back to the north and west to reach the rendezvous point. It could be a good twenty minutes before they arrived. A lot could happen before then. If the authorities stopped to question him, he would tell them that he was checking a transformer over the bridge. Tompkin had the uniform; he looked the part. His Russian was good, if not perfect. He'd pretend he had a cold.

Tompkin placed several reflective orange triangles and two cones onto the road behind the truck. After ten minutes Trance called him.

"Bluebird, are you in the tree?"

"I am in the tree and ready to fly."

Tompkin noticed the weak waver in Trance's voice and said, "How is everybody?"

"We're good."

"How about Red Dragon? How's he holding up?"

Trance closed his eyes. He tried to control his breathing once more. It was impossible. His heart was thumping rapidly in its constricted space, like a compressed snare drum, with shafts of pain shooting through his chest with every aborted beat. He would need a long rest when this was over, that's for sure.

"Ready to kick back...when we see you...In about ten...Over."

Tompkin slid open the door that led into the back of the truck and walked inside. The spacious compartment was filled with an assortment of electrical equipment—coils of wire, boxes of tools, clamps and heavy wire cutters. There were two deep throated metal shovels to be used for clearing spaces through the traditionally tall piles of snow along Moscow's roads.

Two opposing steel benches seated a Russian family of six. Tompkin smiled at the Russians as he reached into his pocket. He pulled out a stack of Rubles and counted out sixty thousand for each of them. He pressed the money into their palms, saying, "Thank you," in Russian, to each one of them. "You are doing a great deed for your country."

It was not much money, about two thousand dollars each. But it was a fortune to these poor people. Russians are easy to bribe, so deep is their need for cash. But their loyalty is fickle. These people could turn on them in a heartbeat if they thought there was more money to be made by turning them in. Or, if they thought the authorities had any inkling of their dealings. This was a serious payday. Was it too much money, though? Enough to raise the warning flags, telling these people that it was something worth telling the authorities? Tompkin hoped not. He prayed not. These people were going out for a weekend spin in a nice new boat, a boat that would soon be theirs. They were also employed by one of Trance's companies, not that it mattered much. Loyalty for sale almost always went to the highest bidder.

Tompkin continued in Russian, "You will walk down to the base of this bridge and get into the boat. You will ride the boat downstream for thirty minutes, before turning back toward Moscow." Tompkin held up a set of car keys. "These are the keys to your new truck. It will be waiting at the boat dock, along with your new trailer."

Ten minutes later, Trance called again.

"Hey, bud…you should be able…to see us…now. Over."

Trance's voice sounded soft and reedy, like it was coming from cancer-filled lungs. Tompkin said nothing; there was too much to be done.

"Okay," Tompkin said to the Russians. "Follow me."

Tompkin slipped through the opening he had dug in the dwindling snow bank. They walked down a steep, slippery path to the concrete abutment underneath the bridge. The Russian family followed him and gathered in a tight group when they reached the bottom. The wind was blowing and the air was moist with impending snow. Tompkin could see the boat approaching, but Stick Granger was the only person in sight. The rest were huddling beneath the boat's small canopy.

Stick angled the boat toward the bridge's concrete base and reversed the engines. The boat slowed and gently kissed the side. Trance and the others jumped out of the boat, while the Russian family jumped in. The exchange took only moments. Soon the Russians sped off downriver. Tompkin led the group up the steep embankment and herded them into the back of the truck.

Trance was the last to arrive. As he stepped into the truck Tompkin looked into his eyes. Tompkin began to say something, but Trance silenced him with a wave of the hand.

"Get us out of here, marine," whispered Trance.

Tompkin closed the door and jumped into the driver's seat. He ground the truck into gear and started toward the warehouse.

Tilson sat between Sammantha and Stick Granger. Shingen and Kenshin sat on the opposite bench. Trance took a place beside them.

The president was feeling something like a drug-induced high. It was brought on by his new freedom, combined with the adrenaline rush from their escape. He began to babble. "Man that was cool. I don't know what to say. I was beginning to believe that I would never be free again when…"

As the president spoke, Trance leaned back against the side of the truck, groaned, closed his eyes, and died.

CHAPTER 129

_____________PP____________

Petrovski was eating breakfast in the airy kitchen of his palatial Moscow home when the call came in.

"The prisoner has escaped."

The blood drained from Petrovski's face. He felt like he was going to pass out, as stars began to dance in front of his eyes. This was bad. This was worse than bad. This could lead to war, a World War, or something worse, his removal from office. "When?"

"Just now, Prime Minister. Through a tunnel. We think to the river."

"You think? You don't know where they are?"

"They sealed the tunnel. There were only three of us, sir. What do you want us to do?"

"Have Yuri go to the top of the tower with a rifle, to see where they come out. You and Dimitri take a car and cover the area between the tower and the river. Look downstream."

"Yuri is dead, sir."

"Well...do something! Go find them."

Petrovski hung up the phone and dialed the president. This was something he couldn't handle alone. He reached the president's secretary.

"I am sorry, sir. But the president is in a meeting."

"Get him out of the meeting or I'll have you shot."

A minute or so later, Ogarkov came to the phone. "This better be good."

"Tilson has escaped."

Ogarkov remained silent. Then he began to laugh. This was his worst nightmare coming true. Everything he had worked for, everything he had tried to do for Russia was about to come to an explosive halt. It could be mere moments before missiles were in the air. Was his country on the brink of extinction?

"How did this happen?"

"I don't know. The only other person that knew the location was—"

"Starodubov?"

"Starodubov."

"No one has seen her, not since your murderous bombing of Washington."

"That was Talid alone," lied Petrovski. "I was there to stop the bombing."

"Shut up and stop lying!" shouted Ogarkov. "Think. Where would they go?"

"They could be anywhere."

"Anywhere is a very big place."

"We must seal the borders."

Ogarkov laughed. Seal the Russian border? The Russian border was 57,000 kilometers, 30,000 miles, in length. "You are kidding? No?"

"You have a better plan?"

"Think."

"We don't have time to think!"

"If you were Starodubov, where would you go?" said Ogarkov.

"Surely she wouldn't go home? Not to that obscene place left to her by that murdering thug?"

"He was her fiancé, not a murderer."

"He was stealing nuclear weapons and selling them to terrorists."

"True," said Ogarkov. "But tell me, my dear Prime Minister, what would those terrorists have done with such a weapon? Nothing worse than what you have done, I am sure."

"This is no time to argue."

"Then we should go to the one place that they might be."

CHAPTER **130**

__________PP__________

"Trance, how in the hell did you come up with a plan like this?" said Tilson, laughing. Trance didn't respond.

"Trance? Trance?"

Sammantha jumped from her seat and pressed her fingers against the side of Trance's neck.

"His heart has stopped," Sammantha said. She shook her head, cursing to herself. "I knew this might happen. Actually, I expected it sooner."

"Do something!" shouted Tilson.

"Well," said Sammantha. "Let's talk about this."

"Don't talk. Do something…Save him."

Sammantha looked Tilson in the eye and said, "I am willing to risk my life to save his. Are you?"

"What do you mean?"

"He has a fatal case of Pericarditis, caused by repeated trauma to his chest. His ribs are broken. They may have collapsed a lung. They may have bruised, perhaps even sheared his heart muscle."

"Can't you give him CPR? Revive him?"

Sammantha shook her head. "I'll need to insert a catheter into his chest to remove fluid before his heart will beat. I could use a pen casing right here; that could ease the fluid pressure. But he is well beyond that. I'm sure his heart is damaged, perhaps irreparably. I told him to slow down, but is a very stubborn man."

"Was," said Tilson. "He *was* a stubborn man."

"I didn't say I can't revive him."

"Then, do it."

"The chances are small. He may be a vegetable."

"Well, do it anyway."

"It will mean turning around. It may mean recapture. Are you prepared for that, Mr. President?"

Sammantha stared at Tilson, willing him to say *yes.*

Jock Tilson straightened and squared his shoulders. "Yes…I…am. You do whatever it takes to save him."

Sammantha ran to the front cab and yelled "Stop the truck!"

Tompkin jammed on the brakes and the truck screeched to a swishing halt on the side of the highway. To their left, there was a steel median, with another road heading in the opposite direction beyond it. To their right was a wooded area, with a metal fence running along the length of the road about ten yards in. The forest began about twenty-five yards beyond that.

Sammantha pointed at the truck's two shovels and calmly said, "Bring me snow." The two samurai responded instantly.

Sammantha began stripping the clothes off of Trance. When she pulled off his shirt she gasped. Trance's chest was almost completely black. There was a massive purple lump that looked like a large eggplant growing out of his skin.

"Definitely needs a pericardiectomy," she said.

"What's that?" said Tilson.

"We remove the pericardium, of course."

"But his heart isn't beating. Don't you need to start his heart to keep him alive?"

Sammantha puffed air through her cheeks. Then she laughed softly. She felt like she was speaking to a dunce, not the leader of the free world.

"Calm down Mr. Tilson. Surely you've heard stories about drownings in cold water, where people have been revived hours after death?

"If we keep him cold, his cells will remain intact. Death after resuscitation often comes from too much oxygen, not time. Too much oxygen causes the cells to implode on their own, with a protective, but deadly response.

"Beginning in the late 1800s, Russian doctors performed open heart surgery without the use of heart-lung machines. Surgeons would immerse their patients in ice, preserving them like a butcher's meat, for hours, if required.

"Mortality rates were high, but patients were known to survive. I, myself, have used this technique with brain surgery."

Shingen appeared outside the truck with a shovel full of snow.

"Drop it on him," said Sammantha. "You, too, Kenshin."

After several minutes, Trance's body was resting within a blanket of snow, looking like a dead fish for sale. When satisfied, Sammantha took the seat beside Tompkin. "Back to Moscow."

***

Tompkin whistled as they approached Sammantha's Moscow home, "This yours?"

"It belonged to my fiancé."

"Nice," said Tompkin.

"After Trance killed him, it became mine."

Tompkin looked over at Sammantha and tried to guess what was going through her head. As if she understood his thoughts, Sammantha said, "He deserved it. I know that now."

Sammantha directed them to a parking spot in the back of the estate.

"Stay here," she said.

Sammantha ran to a back door and let herself inside. Moments later, a large garage-type door began to rise. Sammantha motioned for Tompkin to back the truck into the cavernous opening, which had once served as the palace stables. Once the truck was inside, Sammantha closed the outside door. She walked through another door and came back wheeling a gurney.

"Where did that come from?" asked Stick.

Sammantha smiled grimly. "I've run a private hospital here for years. Not for Russians, but for others. We charge very high prices to people who don't want to be found. You understand?"

"Not really."

"It doesn't matter. Everyone who works here lives here. That is my rule."

"Won't they come after us? Petrovski?"

Sammantha shook her head. "I think not. The Russian authorities don't know of this hospital, not even Ogarkov. They may come looking, but my house manager will send them away."

Sammantha wheeled Trance's body to an elevator. She inserted a key and pressed a button that sent the elevator deep underground. The door opened to a broad, open area of white and chrome. It looked like a cross between a nurse's station and a command center. There was a small rotunda in the middle of the room, with a series of desks set into a circle. Above the desks there was a grouping of monitors, all of them unlit.

"I have not been operating here for months. But I have kept my two surgeons and three nurses on staff. Hopefully they are not upstairs drinking vodka, at least not for long."

"It is not even noon," said Stick.

"Apparently, you do not know Russia, Mr. Granger."

Jesse Tompkin made a quick tour of the rooms, with weapon in hand. He was accompanied by Shingen and Kenshin. They each held a Heckler and Koch MP7 in their arms, with Japanese swords slipped into their belts.

Sammantha walked to an intercom on the wall and pressed a button. She spoke forcefully in Russian.

"This is Starodubov. I want all available physicians and staff to report to operating room A. Now, please." Then she said, "Katarina?"

A moment later the intercom squawked, "Yes, miss?"

"If anyone comes for me, I am not here. Do you understand?"

"Yes, miss."

Sammantha turned to Tompkin and Stick. "She can be trusted. We've done this before." Sammantha motioned toward a line of darkened rooms. "I'm going to turn down the temperature in the operating rooms. Don't be alarmed when the air cools. It's going to get cold."

Sammantha wheeled Trance's gurney into one of the operating rooms and adjusted the thermostat down. She put on a pair surgical gloves and made a quick inventory through a grouping of stainless steel drawers. When Sammantha stepped out of the room, the air was already growing cold. Sammantha looked at Tompkin and pointed to a spot down the hall. There was a narrow set of stairs leading to a loft that stretched around the circumference of the room. The loft was encased in glass. "You men can't go inside with Trance, but you can watch from up there. Bring Tilson with you. Most of our clients will not leave sight of their bodyguards. I built that catwalk to let them watch."

Sammantha walked into another room and began to scrub down. She was soon joined by two other men and three women. Once scrubbed, they each put on cotton surgical clothing and scrubbed again.

Sammantha directed one of the men, a male nurse, to where Trance's body lay, as if in state. The nurse put on a fresh pair of latex gloves and began to run a spray of water across Trance's body. As the water hit the cold floor, it began to ice. After dousing Trance with water, the man began to spray him with an orange liquid, while scrubbing his chest with a yellow sponge. Soon, he was joined by a female nurse who was now in full scrubs. When Trance's body was fully sanitized, they lifted it onto a second gurney. The woman wheeled Trance into another room and repeated the cleansing the process. The male nurse left. Soon he entered the new room, fully dressed for surgery.

One of the nurses walked into the viewing area. She motioned to Tilson and said, "If you want to scrub, you can join us in surgery."

Tilson blinked. Then he nodded vigorously, not quite sure why. Perhaps it was because he felt like he was attending Trance's funeral. Trance deserved someone there. "I'll come. But I'll just sit inside, if that's okay with you."

The nurse held up a heavy down parka. "You wear this," she said. "It is cold. This is..." She searched her memory for the English word. "...sanitized. You put on only after you scrub and change. Yes?"

Tilson nodded. "Yes."

Trance was wheeled into a large room filled with diagnostic equipment. They ran him through a quick set of X-Rays, a CT scan and an ultrasound. They placed him into a concave, ice-lined operating table, while Sammantha and two other doctors hovered above him. A final disinfecting was done, before Sammantha made an incision between two of Trance's ribs. There was little bleeding, with Trance's body already looking like an aging gray cadaver. As Sammantha cut into Trance, the other female doctor projected his pictures onto a high definition wall screen and studied them closely.

Sammantha pondered inserting a visual probe inside Trance's heart, but decided against it. She was going to hold that heart in her hand; that would tell her all she needed to know.

The other female doctor stepped away from the lighted panels and looked over Sammantha's shoulder.

"Well, Arina?" said Sammantha, speaking Russian.

"Two ribs are broken."

"Can you fix them without damaging his heart?"

"I am an artist, Sammi. I could do this in my sleep, especially while he is dead. One of the breaks is clean. The other is comminuted, breaking inward like a green stick. Most likely, it is stabbing his heart. I can fix the bones, but can you mend his heart?"

"I really don't know yet."

"He will need good bone above his heart. I will cut this portion of rib and replace it with good bone from a less vulnerable place. I will grind the damaged bone down, plate it and put it where we harvested the replacement piece. I would feel better if you let me do this before you remove the pericardium. Also, please give his heart some protection."

Sammantha covered Trance's heart with a layer of latex. Then she stepped away.

One the nurses handed Arina a grinding device. In her hands, the nurse held a small sprayer and a suction tube. Arina quickly smoothed out the first broken bone. Then she secured a plate with screws to keep it solidly in place.

Arina looked to a nurse who was standing along the wall, as if waiting for a command. "Music!" Arina shouted.

The nurse flipped a switch and the Rolling Stones began to reverberate throughout the room.

The second rib was a nightmare. Arina viewed this as a welcome challenge, and she began to sing happily with the music. She cut the rib clean on each side of the break, leaving a four-inch hole above Trance's heart. She dropped the bone into a beaker that was filled with a clear, sterilizing liquid. She quickly ground the sharp edges off the remaining bone and measured the space with a digital device. She then did so by hand. After three careful measurements, Arina sawed off a piece of one of Trance's lower ribs. She drilled holes into each end of the new bone shard and attached a plate to each side. She took this piece and gently nestled it into the ribs above Trance's heart. Satisfied, she fastened the new rib piece with stainless clamps. She drilled through the rib plate's holes, so that a few well placed screws would secure the new piece to both sides of Trance's remaining rib. When complete, Trance's chest protection would be as good as new, maybe better. She'd smooth out the shattered bone while Sammantha operated. She would then attach this piece to the spot where she'd harvested the new bone once Sammantha had revived the patient.

All the while, Arina's head was rocking along with Mick Jagger, making her look like Jackson Pollock slapping paint on a canvass with her hair, not the master orthopedic surgeon that she was. She sang, "I can't get no…satisfaction…"

When Arina was sure that the new rib piece would fit perfectly, she yelled "Ready!"

Arina stepped back and Sammantha stepped forward. Sammantha nodded toward the nurse by the wall. The loud music ceased. It was instantly replaced by a Bach concerto in soothing 4/4 time.

Sammantha placed a spreader between Trance's ribs and twisted a lever to push Trance's ribs farther apart. She carefully removed the layer of protective latex that she had placed over Trance's heart. Then she stared at his pericardium. It had been torn into strips by his broken bone. This was tricky. Sometimes the sac would be attached to the heart like it had been sealed with Gorilla Glue. Other times, it would pull away like waxed paper. Thankfully, Trance's pericardium pulled easily off of Trance's heart muscle. Even so, Sammantha removed it with excruciating care.

When Trance's sac was fully removed, Sammantha closely studied Trance's heart. After just a moment, she closed her eyes. This looked hopeless. Sammantha looked over to Jock Tilson, then to the viewing area. She shook her head slowly. Trance's right ventricle looked like it had been beaten with a meat tenderizer. How would these shreds of muscle ever be able to pump blood into Trance's aorta?

CHAPTER **131**
_____________PP_____________

"Where is she?"

Petrovski pushed his way through the half opened doorway into Sammantha's home. Katarina Karov stared impassively at the Prime Minister. She shrugged her shoulders and told the truth. "Do you mean Dr. Starodubov? I haven't seen her for weeks."

Ogarkov followed Petrovski into the main entryway of the mansion and looked around. The house was furnished with an eclectic mix of Czarist furniture. Much of it was Russian, including three Fabergé eggs that were sitting in a delicate glass case. Other pieces appeared to be French and English, circa seventeenth and eighteenth century. The rooms were large and airy. They were so tidy and ordered that the place looked almost uninhabited.

A dozen Russian soldiers entered the house behind Ogarkov. They wore infantry vests and carried an assortment of assault weapons, mostly AK-47s. They began a methodical search of the home. Petrovski walked across the marble entryway to Katarina, his heels clicking like tap shoes on the smooth stone floor.

"Don't cross me, woman. I will splay your guts across this room if I have to."

"I haven't seen her. Really. I haven't seen her." Technically, this was the truth. She hadn't seen Sammantha when she'd entered the mansion. Sammantha had come in below, through the old stables.

Petrovski walked to one of his soldiers and pulled a knife from a scabbard on his hip. He motioned with the knife to Katarina. "Go. Sit over there."

Katarina walked to where Petrovski was pointing. She sat down in a high-backed chair with wooden arm rests and then. There was a determined look of defiance in her eyes.

Petrovski smirked. He said, "Give me your hand." Petrovski spread Katarina's palm across the rounded end of the arm rest. He held it down with his left hand while raising his right.

Ogarkov looked away as Petrovski drove the knife through Katarina's palm. Katarina screamed and began to whimper. She looked down at the knife, which stuck out of the wood, pinning her hand to the chair. "No..." she moaned.

"Let's agree that you haven't seen Miss Starodubov. If she were hiding somewhere in this place, where would that be?"

"I don't know."

Petrovski raised a second knife to strike the other hand.

"Perhaps...she might be in the basement..."

"Where are the stairs?"

"You can't get there, not without a key."

"Then get me a key, woman."

Petrovski followed Katarina and her trail of dripping blood down a long hallway. They continued through several more rooms before reaching the kitchen. Katarina removed a round key from a hook and held it out for Petrovski.

"You must stick this into the elevator door. Only then can you go down to the hospital."

"Hospital?"

Katarina nodded.

"Show me."

CHAPTER **132**
PP

Jack Trance found himself walking slowly along a beach. The sand was soft and as white as cane sugar. The sun was setting to the west. Thin, wispy clouds were turning pink and purple. The air was warm, and the sun gave off a soft, gentle glow as it fell slowly into the sea. Trance looked around and he saw his father walking beside him. His father was wearing a pair of tan khaki shorts, a Boston Red Sox T-Shirt and tattered leather sandals. Trance was wearing similar pants, but he wore no shoes. His bare chest was covered by a flak jacket.

"Hello, father," said Trance.

"It is good to see you again, my son."

"How is mom?"

"She misses her son. You were her duty; you know that. But now you fill her heart. And you? How are you?"

"I've been under a little stress lately."

"Stress comes from within, Jack."

Trance laughed weakly. He didn't have the energy to debate.

His father continued, "You must allow the Creator to work His will as he sees fit."

"I think, sometimes, that He asks too much of me."

Trance's father shook his head slowly, his eyes somewhat patronizing, like a museum docent greeting dotty old ladies for a tour. "The Creator never gives us more than we can manage."

"Sometimes it is just so hard."

"That is because you fight your destiny."

"I'm fighting a hell of a lot more than my destiny, pop." Trance unzipped the flak jacket and pulled it away from his chest. "Look."

Trance's father looked at Trance's chest and smiled. There was no black stain spread across it like old motor oil. There was just a pale yellow glow, like the sun.

"It is not your time, my son. You have much left to do. New quests to begin. Great quests that will change the world, if you have faith."

CHAPTER **133**

PP

The elevator door opened. Ivan Petrovski sauntered into the downstairs hospital as if he'd wandered into a nicknack store to buy something for his living room. His hands traced along the room, fingering the edge of a gurney, a utensil cart and the top of a Formica desk that was strewn with papers. He was followed by the Russian president and a platoon of soldiers that skittered across the room like water beetles. Petrovski swept his eyes upward. He saw Stick and Tompkin standing in the loft, looking down through the glass at Trance's opened chest. He continued scanning the room, until his eyes stopped upon the two samurai sitting cross-legged in the corner. He raised an eyebrow, but said nothing.

Stick and Tompkin looked down, but calmly ignored Petrovski and his men. They trained their attention back on Trance.

A clear plastic mask was now covering Trance's face. A white hose ran from the mask to a boxlike machine. The machine was attached to a grouping of bottles of compressed compounds, most notably oxygen, carbon dioxide and nitrogen, mixing them into Sammantha's secret breathing blend, a blend she hoped would preserve Trance's cells, provided his heart ever beat again.

Sammantha had finished applying glue and a series of painstakingly small sutures to close the major fissures in Trance's heart. She hoped it was enough to restore integrity to the muscle, but she wouldn't know until the heart beat again, if it ever did.

Sammantha looked at one of the nurses beside her and said, "Warm water, please."

The nurse adjusted a spillway to the shallow tub that held Trance. Trance's icy bath began to flow into a fat hose that emptied into a trough in the floor. When the ice was gone, the nurse readjusted the spillway. She punched numbers into a digital display to regulate the temperature in the tub. Then she reached for a faucet handle that was resting beside it. She turned the knob, while reading a digital temperature gauge built into the water pipe. When the water reached the desired temperature she backed away, looked at Sammantha and nodded. Sammantha pressed a button that started a timer. She adjusted the room's thermostat. Then she sat down to wait. Petrovski stood beside a window peering into the room like a cat watching a wild songbird, waiting for the best time to pounce.

Sammantha was preparing her first attempt to revive Trance when the door to the operating room flew open and Petrovski strode in.

"Get out of here!" screamed Sammantha. "You murdering pig."

Petrovski ignored Sammantha and turned toward Tilson. He lifted his pistol and pointed it squarely at the American president's forehead. "You shouldn't have tried to escape, Mr. President. In our country, prisoners have a way of getting shot when they do such a stupid thing."

Sammantha reached down to an operating utensil tray and picked up a scalpel. She placed it into her palm, as she had thousands of time before, to her throwing spot, that place where her mind would take her as she practiced killing her parents' killer. In her mind she had always seen Trance. That had been wrong, terribly wrong. This was the man that had killed her parents. This was the man that deserved to die.

Sammantha drew her hand back behind her ear, as if she were going to primp her hair into place. Then she calmly launched the scalpel into the air. It hit the side of Petrovski's head and dug deeply into his temple, a clean slice through his temporal lobe. Petrovski's knees buckled and he slumped to the floor. Sammantha looked to Tilson's wide eyes and waited for him to talk. Tilson said nothing. Sammantha's destroyer was dead. She gave a subtle nod to Tilson. He smiled briefly and nodded back. This was a battlefield and death was expected.

"Now, where was I?" said Sammantha. "Oh, yes. Ready to restart a life."

Sammantha reached a hand up and said, "Syringe."

A nurse slapped one into her hand. Sammantha made several small injections into the tissues surrounding Trance's heart, using a combination of epinephrine and fructose-1 6-diphosphate. She waited for a minute, then sent a jolt of electricity through Trance's chest. Nothing happened. She blew a small amount of her own air into Trance's lungs and put the mask back over his head. She charged his heart again. Nothing. Sammantha turned off the breathing bellows and adjusted a dial on the boxy machine. She removed her gloves and snapped on a fresh, sterile pair. Sammantha pressed her palms together. She said a prayer, something she hadn't done with any sense of belief since she was a little girl, a girl of twelve. She could feel something spread through her, as if light were streaming into the darkness of her heart. She tapped lightly on Trance's heart with her index finger. The muscle blipped slightly, then blipped again. It was an almost imperceptible squeeze, but it kept on, getting stronger, then stronger.

"Warmer water," she said calmly. "Sixteen degrees Celsius."

Sammantha kept her eyes on the breathing box, adjusting the mixture continually with a practiced hand. After several minutes Sammantha smiled and said to Tilson, "I don't know how, but his heart is beating. He may have brain damage; his heart might still fail. But for now, he is alive and I am guardedly hopeful."

Sammantha changed her gloves again. Now all that was left was the bone. Sammantha placed the new piece of rib into the hole over Trance's heart. She had to work it in, the measuring so precise. But the fit was perfect. Sammantha screwed the plates into the holes that Arina had drilled. She pulled a flap of Trance's skin over the bone. Then she sewed a small drain into Trance's chest. She sutured around the drain with a mosaic of delicate stitches. She used a tiny bit of glue and gave it a few more stitches. She adjusted the shunt one final time, then finished the job.

Sammantha walked out of the operating room, leaving Arina to patch Trance's other rib. Two doctors and a nurse remained to watch over Trance. Sammantha didn't even glance at Petrovski's body as she took off her mask. She stared at Ogarkov, who was standing outside the door. She looked from Ogarkov to the soldiers and shrugged.

"Now you now know my secret," she said.

Ogarkov looked around the room. "You mean this place? Or that you risked everything to save Trance's life?"

"He's the one who removed the bomb from the Capital in Washington."

"Then Trance saved my life."

Ogarkov walked over to the window and peered into the operating room.

"He doesn't look like much, now, does he? Certainly not the man I know, lying there like that. He looks so...normal."

Sammantha's mouth opened as if to speak. She closed it, as Jock Tilson walked over to join them.

"That...was extraordinary," Tilson stammered. "I didn't think it was possible—"

Sammantha angled her head toward Ogarkov. "Lot of good it will do."

"What?" said Ogarkov. "You think Trance is going to die?"

Sammantha looked to her feet and mumbled, "What does it matter? We're all dead now, anyway."

Ogarkov took Sammantha by the shoulders and forced her to look at him. "Some very terrible things have happened this year. If there were any way to undo the wrongs and make them right..." Ogarkov dropped his hand and let his shoulders slump. "You are all free to go. I will help you in any way I can." He looked at Tilson. "You know I never wanted this. But I will accept the fate you choose for me and for Russia."

CHAPTER **134**
PP

Lauren Haverford was sitting by the phone when the call came in.

"Hi, sweetheart," said Trance. His voice was a soft, almost ethereal whisper.

"Jack? Is that you? We have a bad connection."

"I love you very much."

"Oh, baby. I love you, too."

"There's been a change in plans. I want *you* to fly to France, to the chateau. Have Nikko bring the ship down to La Havre and wait for us there."

"Jack, I can barely hear you. Is everything okay?"

"Everything is fine. We have the president. He'll need to heal a bit before we bring him home. He's had some surgery.

"We'll need to have some medical equipment brought to the chateau. Hold, for just a second." Trance put down the phone and gathered his strength. He called upon his *chi,* the great universal force, before speaking again. "Would you call Sophie's son…you know the one…the chief surgeon down in Miami. Have him help you obtain whatever equipment we need. Jock had a pericardiectomy. He also has a little bruising of his heart. Tell Sophie's son that money is no object and that speed is critical. He should come here ASAP, to be with the president."

"Sure, Jack. I'll have it done by tomorrow, even if it means buying a hospital. What about the president's doctors? Shouldn't they—"

"No," interrupted Trance. "Not yet." He closed his eyes. He loved this woman. Why had he made her wait so long? Trance took several slow, deep breaths, then continued. "Please arrange for an air ambulance to fly to Moscow, in two days. We'll take it to Paris and then MedFlight flight from there to the chateau. Could you call me when you have it arranged?"

"I'll have it done within the hour."

"I love you. See you in two days then."

***

Trance turned toward Sammantha as he placed the phone back into its cradle. He said softly, "Would you please tell President Ogarkov that we would like an escort to Moscow Sheremetyevo Airport in two days?"

"Are you sure you should move that soon?"

"What are you, my doctor?"

Sammantha looked at Trance and covered her face with her hands. "Yes, I am." When she finally looked at Trance her eyes were red and wet. "Do you know what it is like to have hate consume you? And then to find out that you were hating the wrong thing? And then…and then you want to love those things that you once hated…but you are sure that you're not worthy?"

Trance reached out a weak hand and Sammantha grasped it.

"I forgive you," Trance said. He began to weep. He wept for the people he had lost. He wept for the love and the life. And he wept for what he had…a new start, a fresh start, a second chance. "Would you have Jock Tilson come see me, please?"

The president came into the room and grasped Trance's outstretched hand.

"Thank you for staying, Jock," whispered Trance.

"You're my ticket out of here."

"You were home free, but you stayed."

"It was a no-brainer, Trance. Besides, it's not like I can just waltz in and take my job back. They might thing that *I* am the imposter and throw me in jail, like they did to you."

"He might still try, Jock. I think I know a way to fix this, though. But first, we need to discuss Sammantha and your brother."

"They sure did open a big can of worms."

"She loves him, you know."

Tilson nodded. "I know."

"He used to be a drunken actor who lost his family's fortune. Your family's fortune. Now he's passing as the president."

"Doesn't change the facts, Jack."

"Can I make a suggestion?"

"Hmm," said Tilson. "Let me see. You saved Washington from a nuclear meltdown. You found my wife's killer. You rescued me from the bowels of the Kremlin. I guess I might listen to a suggestion."

"She killed my wife, too, Jock."

"Your point is?"

"To her it was war. People do terrible things in war. Good people, Jock. Good people can be forced into terrible things. In your job, you'll see, I assure you."

"You want me to forget that she killed Kiki?"

"Of course not. You can't forget. I want you to *forgive* her. It will be better for *you* that way."

"I'm a Christian, Jack. But I'm not a saint. Have *you* forgiven her?"

Trance smiled weakly. "Actually, I have. In a way, that set me free. I feel like I can start my life over again. Fresh."

"It's been just a year for me. The pain is too—"

"You are going to have to believe me here, Jock. I have *been* where she was. It was the *war* that killed Janice and Kiki. In her mind, she was just a soldier." Trance paused. "Now, you know where I stand on terrorism. I will look for any peaceful settlement to violence. I will bend, I will turn my cheek. But if someone threatens the safety of my family and my country, if someone presents a clear and present danger, I will lead the charge. I will defend and not think twice. I know the cost of freedom. It's bullets and blood. I've taken the bullets. I've spilled the blood. And I have certainly done my share of shooting.

"Sammantha was in a war, but that war is over. She no longer represents a danger to anyone but herself. You need to see that and you need to deal with it...Besides, she is the only one that can put your brother's life back together. He needs her and she needs him."

Tilson closed his eyes. He began to moan softly. He moaned for the loss of his wife and for the loss of hope. He cried out for his country, and for all those who had died trying to keep her free. God, it was a complicated thing, right versus wrong, good versus evil.

"I will try, Jack, because you asked."

"Talk with her. Get to know her. If she'll give you a glimpse of her world, you will understand. Believe me, you will. We will get her therapy, lots of it. I know just the person."

Jock Tilson stood. He shook hands with Jack Trance and walked out of the room. When he entered the hallway he saw Sammantha standing off to the side, waiting to get back to her patient.

"Come here," Tilson said.

Sammantha walked warily toward the president. Tilson opened his arms and spread them around her. "We will get through this, Sammantha. Somehow, we will get through this."

"I am so sorry. I…am…so…sorry for what I did. I am a monster. I can't be trusted. I can't believe I—"

Tilson interrupted her forcefully. "The past is behind us, now."

But it wasn't. As Tilson felt the heat of Sammantha's damp skin soaking into his chest, he began to see visions—visions of Kiki, as she sat in the grass. She was just a child, accepting Jock's silly marriage proposal as solemnly as if she were a grown-up. He saw Kiki standing naked in the White House, just hours before she died, laughing with him, teasing him, filling him with a joy so strong that he thought he would burst. He saw his children, being pushed by their mother in the swing set they had built together out of wood in the back yard. He saw his wife's body, as it lay in state, eyes closed, hands upon her chest as if she were asleep. Finally, he saw Sammantha sitting upon his lap after he was captured, laughing at him as his penis grew hard, despite his anger and his shame.

And the rage returned, boiling inside him—hot streaks of red shooting across his brain like molten lava, pressing against the hard cap of shell he'd created, until the pressure became too great to resist. The anger overtook him, like some great carnal wind, roaring out of a stygian blackness in his soul, as if on the wings of a demon's dragon, hell-bent on revenge. His arms began to burn. His vision grew dark, pinpointing into a single black spot, spreading across the backside of his mind until he went blind. He felt his hands begin to close around Sammantha's neck. He couldn't see her, couldn't really even feel her. There was just rage, pushing him into a place he never thought could exist—a place where reason fell prey to emotion, where sanity melted into a puddle to be stepped in and kicked, until it evaporated into thin air.

Sammantha felt Jock's arms stretch around her neck and thought, *Good. Let it be over*. Finally, she would have her peace. Her instinct was to jam a fist into Tilson's thyroid cartilage, or bring her fingers up into his groin and squeeze him to his knees. But she stood limp, staring into his unseeing gaze. She felt tears begin to well into her eyes, tears of unbearable sadness, an anguish so strong she wanted to moan. God, she had been so wrong. She had fought a war that didn't exist, creating an enemy out of a friend, doing everything in her power to destroy this man and his nation. She deserved what was coming, welcomed it with open arms, begged for its release.

"Thank…you…I'm…sorry…" Sammantha choked. She felt her eyelids flutter, then nothing. Darkness fell down on her life, like the snuffing of a candle, until she was no more.

Tilson blinked. His mind came floating back, drifting like a soap bubble in the wind. He felt something pop, heard Sammantha's last gasp and the heavy weight of her corpse in his hands. He looked down to his fingers. What had he done? He peered at Sammantha's dead body, just a collection of skin and bone and blood now. She looked peaceful, curled up like a baby. She had thanked him. She had apologized…and she had thanked him, for death.

"Oh…my…God," whispered Tilson. "Oh…my…God."

Tilson knelt down beside Sammantha and tried to shake her awake. "Sammantha…Sammantha!" He shook her again. "Oh, my God. What have I done?"

"Doesn't feel very good, does it?" said Trance.

Tilson looked up and saw Trance standing above him. He seemed to shimmer, coming in and out of focus, like an apparition standing in a dense fog.

"What have I done, Jack?"

"You killed her."

"I couldn't have. I didn't…I couldn't have. That's not me…Something…How did this happen?"

"It was a war, Jock. We do things in war that we would never otherwise do. You responded like any human. Now, it's over."

"It can't be. It's not right…I didn't mean—"

"She killed your wife, Jock. She deserved to pay."

"But…But…"

"You ended the war. Move on. It's over."

"I…I wanted to forgive her…But something came over me, something dark, something inhuman."

"We change in war, Jock. We have to. Ask any battle-scarred soldier. Do you understand now? Do you understand her war? To her, America had taken everything—her parents, her life, her childhood, her innocence."

Tilson began to shake. His eyes rolled up into the folds of his skull, as if he could turn away from what he'd done. But there was no turning away. There is no turning away, not from war. It eats into your skin like acid, burning your brain until you want to scream, making you do all you must to make it stop.

"Save her, Jack. She doesn't deserve this. Somehow…bring her back, Jack. Please."

"Why? She killed Kiki."

"I didn't mean to! I'm not a killer…I just…"

"Then get out of the way, Jock."

Trance knelt beside Sammantha's lifeless body. He ran his fingers along her throat, checking to see if anything was broken. He tipped Sammantha's head back and breathed into her mouth. He did this three times, allowing the air to escape in a soft hiss. Then her centered his fist above her chest and hit her with a hard thump. She didn't respond.

Trance looked up to Tilson and frowned. Tilson had his hands covering his face, and there were tears dripping along his wrists.

"If we save her, Jock…What are you going to do?"

Tilson spread his hands and stared down at Sammantha. He looked at Trance and smiled, weakly, but it was a smile.

Trance said, "She thought we killed her parents…Destroyed her childhood…Sent her into sexual slavery at the age of twelve…Made her do all those things…just to survive…"

"I forgive her, Jack. I understand, now. I do. I really do."

Trance blew into Sammantha's mouth. Then he thumped her again, this time harder.

Sammantha's body bounced slightly. Then her shoulders arched and her body heaved upward, as a breath came rushing into her lungs.

"*Huhhh.*"

Sammantha took several breaths, but didn't open her eyes. Instead, she shook her head slowly. Then she rasped, "Why did you do this, Jack? Why did you bring me back? I'd found peace...the light. I saw the light."

"We want you to live," said Trance.

Sammantha looked up and laughed softly. "Payback's a bitch. Hey, Jack?"

"Sometimes, it's even worth it."

Tilson knelt down beside Sammantha. He closed his eyes, his jaw hanging open, the words clutching to his throat. How could he tell her that he understood it now? That he had felt his whole being swept like a boat in a hurricane, tossed around as if it were a tiny match stick, powerless against some primordial storm.

"I'm sorry," he said. "I want to make this right. Somehow, we can make this right."

"It can never be right," said Sammantha.

Tilson nodded. "Yes, it can. It will never be perfect. We can never forget what we've done. But we can be a family. Let's just see if we can be a family."

"Not possible."

"Yes, it is. You, Brandon, me. We will be a family. You have a family now."

"I am not worthy."

"Neither am I. But, we'll get through it. We have to."

CHAPTER **135**
_____________PP_____________

Day was gently waning as the medical helicopter touched down on Trance's chateau helipad. A yellow-orange glow was sinking into the peaceful French valley in the cool, late winter afternoon. The air had a rosy, buff shine and the castle gleamed like silver under the sun's late rays.

Lauren Haverford rushed beneath the spinning rotors, even before the door to the helicopter slid open. Behind her ran the doctor that had treated Trance after he had been kidnapped in Miami and hooked on drugs, barely a year before. His medical team stood back on the edge of the helipad. Lauren's parents waited beside them, along with Stick's wife, Marlee, with a child on her hip and a "bun in the oven," as Stick liked to say.

Two medics removed Trance's stretcher from the air ambulance, careful not to disturb the saline bag that was swinging from a chrome pole, or the long plastic tube that was running into Trance's arm.

"I knew it," said Lauren, when she saw Trance's sheepish grin. "I just knew it." She leaned over and kissed Trance on the cheek. "Are you okay, you big dufus?"

"Just need a few days to catch up on my sleep."

Lauren dabbed at her face and turned away. "Are you ever going to learn?"

"Probably not."

Trance waved toward Lauren's parents. He was surprised to see them, knowing how it normally took something approaching an act of Congress to get them to leave Boston's South Shore. "Why are they here?"

"They were worried about you."

"Guess I'm not too good at secrets."

Marlee jumped into Stick's embrace the moment he cleared the rotors. Stick grabbed hold of her with one arm and his boy with the other. He swung them both in a wide, arching circle.

"Da da!" said the baby.

Stick hugged his boy. "Yes, my son. I am your daddy, and I love you as big as the moon."

Stick put Marlee down and began blowing into his boy's belly, making big slurping sounds, while the child screamed and giggled.

Marlee walked over to Trance. "Guess we did a pretty poor job of protecting you, Jack."

Trance smiled. "Au contraire. I came out of this alive. Your boy is a bona fide hero. I might even give him a raise, provided I'm not hung, of course."

Marlee placed a hand against Trance's cheek. "Glad you're okay."

***

Lauren wheeled Trance into the chateau's main art room. She rolled him to the da Vinci area, where a group of medical machines had already been moved into place among da Vinci's creations. Sammantha followed behind them, visibly awed by the legacy that surrounded her.

"Why are we here?" said Trance.

Lauren said, "I thought this might help you ponder the imponderable. I think you need that."

Behind Lauren, Sammantha continued to gawk around the room. "What is this place?" she whispered. After a brief hesitation Sammantha shook her head. She walked to Trance's bed and surveyed the equipment.

"Very good, Lauren. How did you get this so fast?"

"It's amazing what cash can buy."

Sammantha looked around the room again and said, "I'll say."

"Money can't buy what's most important," said Trance. "And sometimes wealth comes with burdens that are far more ponderous than its benefits. Don't be awed by all this. You wouldn't want what came with it."

Sammantha plugged Trance's IV into the appropriate bags and hooked him into the monitors. Then she began to look around the room again.

"Is this what I think it is?" she asked.

"Not even close," said Lauren, winking at Trance.

"This is da Vinci?"

Trance said, "My family ancestors commissioned works from da Vinci. Unlike the Catholic Church, they let him create whatever he wanted. He spent a lot of his later years here, thinking and creating extraordinary things."

"I see."

"I'll give you the grand tour in a few days, okay? After I've had some time to sort things out."

Sammantha began to move around the room, walking slowly, feeling breathless at almost every step. "Extraordinary."

"Could you bring Jack's medical team up to speed with his condition?" said Lauren.

"Sure," said Sammantha. She walked back to Trance's side and patted him on the shoulder. "There's nothing much to worry about now, mostly just infection…Never had a staph problem in my hospital, and I don't plan to start now." Sammantha squeezed Trance's shoulder. "I don't know how you lived through this, Jack. I really don't."

Trance smiled. "Perhaps someday I'll explain. Make yourself at home. The opposite wing is used by my company, Hopewell Industries. This side is personal. You're welcome to take a tour, if you wish. Lauren can help you with that. The back extension was roped off and sealed by my grandfather. Even I don't know what's there. Don't really want to know. There are a hundred and sixty rooms in this wing. They're all furnished. Find a room you like and tell the staff. They'll tidy it up."

Lauren said, "Tell me if you need anything, Sammantha, and I'll see that you get it."

"Thanks," said Sammantha. "For everything."

"Thank you," said Trance. "For saving my life."

Sammantha looked to the floor and mumbled, "It never should have come to this."

Trance chuckled. "You did pose a challenge. Like everything else, we'll deal with it."

"How can we make things right?"

"It's going to be delicate, but we'll do it."

"We could lose Brandon, you know. His mind could snap."

"Have faith, Sammantha. I have faith, in you."

Sammantha closed her eyes. "I'm not sure I can do this."

"Of course you can," said Lauren. "You're not alone."

"I…I don't deserve this."

Trance pointed to a spot beyond the da Vinci area, to a place along the wall that was stacked from floor to ceiling with books. There were thousands of volumes packed tightly into massive bookcases. Some of them were bound in leather. Others were held together with simple string. In front of the bookcases, there were a number of volumes sitting much like the da Vinci Codex, as if waiting to be read.

"See that book over there?" said Trance, pointing a finger at a volume that was encased in glass.

"Go get it, please."

Sammantha walked over and pulled the book out of its case. It was thick and heavy. It smelled of age and wisdom. She handed the book to Trance.

"This is a rare copy of the *Hypnerotomachia Poliphili.* Know the story?"

Sammantha shook her head.

"It is a romance, entitled *Strife of Love in a Dream.* It is a story about Poliphilo. Our poor hero has been shunned by the woman he loves. He has dreams within dreams, moving through his bizarre dreamland, encountering obstacle after obstacle, demon after demon. There are more than one hundred and fifty woodcuts in the book, illustrating everything from art to science to mythology. This book is unique. It was written over five hundred years ago, Sammantha. It switches between half a dozen languages, as if it were meant to be understood only by someone with the proper training and intellect. It is cryptic, enigmatic, confusing, complicated, elegant, beautiful, brutal and ornate. This book is about you and your life.

"Yours is not a new story, Sammantha. Like Poliphilo, we all face burdens. We all overcome challenges and demons. We are part of a species that is brutal, animalistic and self-serving. We are its survivors. You have been living in a reality far different than most. You have been forced to endure horrors that few of us ever face. You have created some of these horrors. You can also create goodness. That's what you will do.

"I give this book to you. Take it as a reminder that life has always been both dream and reality, good and evil. It is up to us to decide what part of life rules us. It is up to you to decide what will rule *you.* That is your choice, Sammantha.

"You have chosen to save my life. You have chosen to save the president. Now you must choose to save yourself. Do that, and you can spend the rest of your life spreading goodness. Can you do that?"

"I…don't know if I know how."

"You do it with the help of a family."

"I don't..."

"Yes, you do," said Trance. "You save my life, you get to be part of the family. It's one of my rules. You're part of our family. It's a big one. We will love and support you."

"I don't deserve love, or a family."

"Then earn it," said Trance.

"How?"

"I've got a plan."

"I could never undo what I have done."

"True," said Trance. "But you can fix *some* things. First, you will return all of the Anderson Industries facilities, plus five hundred thousand acres of timberland, to Benjamin Anderson. The balance of the acreage will go to a non-profit foundation that I run. This foundation is building a legacy for mankind. We have good use for the land. Anderson can work the timber. That will give him the fresh start he deserves. I will tell you what the rest is for, sometime later, when you're ready.

"You will work for one of my foundations, called *Second Chances.* You will head a division I'm creating to help rebuild the lives of America's veterans. I am donating several of my family's old homes, which we will use to house vets and their families as our heroes receive treatment. We'll start with Newport, Martha's Vineyard, Hyde Park and Oahu. Adjacent to these homes, we will construct the finest rehab centers the world has ever seen. Your sole focus will be to see that these brave men and women get the best chance to heal their bodies and their minds. I want them happy and productive. I have seen your work. I expect nothing but miracles and I will fund whatever you require.

"Later, you can expand the foundation to treat victims of abuse, as I know you can."

Sammantha stared at Trance. He lips began to quiver. "I do not deserve this."

"Are you saying you can't get this done?"

"No, I can do this…But…such an opportunity should go to someone who has earned it. I…I should be shot, not rewarded with the chance of a lifetime."

"Who better to help damaged people than someone who has walked in their shoes? Besides, this is my choice, not yours. You will serve your penance and not complain."

"Penance should be painful, not a joy."

"After what you have been through, Sammantha, a little joy wouldn't hurt."

Sammantha sank to the floor. She brought her knees to her chest and began to rock. *Tick, tock…*she could hear the slow-moving metronome, the one that sat on the piano when she was a child, the one that used to help her play to perfection. This was where she felt safe, the one place that had always healed her, just enough to get her through one more day.

"Sammantha?"

Sammantha looked at Trance.

"That part of your life is over. You don't need that anymore. Stand up and let yourself be renewed."

Sammantha closed her eyes. Slowly, she stood. As she did, she could feel herself grow lighter, as if she were shedding a cocoon of steel. She felt like wings were lifting her into the air toward freedom, as if in a dream, like the book that Trance had given her. She looked at Trance. She had tried to kill this man. And she *had* killed his wife. Now, he was offering *her* redemption. No, she thought. He was offering her the *chance* for redemption. The rest was up to her. She would have to earn it; redemption only came from within. She could do this. She would do this. She would help give others back their lives.

"I can do this," she said.

Sammantha stood straight. For the first time in years, she smiled. She really smiled. She felt warmth spread through her. It was like a winter campfire, thawing the frozen dreams of a twelve-year-old girl, a child who had never had a chance to live and be free. "Thank you," she said. "I will not let you down."

"I know you won't." Trance slapped his forehead. "Oh, I almost forgot. I had my people do some checking. They found this old horse that was abandoned, about twenty-five years ago, when a young girl went missing. Seems the girl had a very good friend by the name of Sandra Smith whose mother just couldn't let that horse get taken away. The horse's name was Starr, I believe. He became quite a show horse, I hear. I think I've got the address somewhere. You want me to get it for you?"

Sammantha's face grew suddenly pale. Her head seemed to drift to one side. She stared at Trance with an odd, quizzical look. After a moment the color began to rush back into her face. Sammantha brought her hand to her mouth. "Starr? You found Starr?"

"Everyone deserves a childhood, Sammantha. Yours was snuffed out too early. I've talked with your old friend, Sandra. She misses you. She wants to see you. She wants you to know that she's been keeping Starr for you. She and Starr are there whenever you need them. I suggest you go grab that little piece of your childhood, Sammantha. Youth has powers that can heal the greatest of wounds. So does happiness."

***

That night, Lauren climbed into Trance's bed and cuddled against him.

"I like this," she said. "Having you powerless against me."

"We still have to look for rings," said Trance. "I do owe you that."

Lauren snuggled closer, being careful not to press against the shunt in Trance's chest.

"I don't need marriage, Jack. I just need you."

Trance soon drifted to sleep and began to snore. Lauren adjusted his covers, kissed him on the forehead and walked out of the room. She followed the maze of hallways to the main kitchen, where the rest of the group was gathered. Seated with them was a woman of indeterminate age. She had coffee colored skin and long, curly black hair. Beside her sat a man with the same golden toned skin and a closely cropped beard. Beside him sat his wife.

Lauren turned to Tilson and said, "I see you have met the Black Madonna. You might think that the U.S. president is the most powerful person in the world, Jock. But there are those of us who know better."

Tilson frowned. He began to question, but Lauren put a hand against his lips. "That's all you want to know. Believe me."

"How is Jack?" said the Black Madonna.

Lauren sighed. She seemed to shrink, as if something had grabbed hold of her skin and pulled it inward—weariness, perhaps, or maybe lost hope. She spoke softly. "He is putting on a good face, even though he's still weak. It's like a part of him is gone somehow, some crucial piece of his soul, the essence that gave him his fire. It's like his fire's gone out."

The Madonna smiled. "Give him time, Lauren. He will be fine."

"Do you want to see him?"

"Not yet. Let's wait a few days. He'll be ready then."

"Ready for what?"

The Madonna's eyes reflected the light briefly, brightly, almost like a mirror. She smiled and said, "We'll see."

CHAPTER **136**
PP

Jock Tilson was seated beside Trance's bed, balancing on a three-legged, sixteenth century milking stool.

"What is this place?" Tilson asked.

"My family has been powerful since the days of Caesar. This place belonged to my grandfather, who was the family patriarch. He gave it to my uncle, just before he died, who left it to me.

"As you know, when my parents died, I put their assets into a charitable lead trust. People told me I was nuts to pass on ten billion dollars. What did I need all that money for?

"Then my grandfather and my uncle died. They had even bigger estates, with me as their sole beneficiary. Because of some issues I couldn't control, I had to keep this money, for things we can't really discuss. At least not yet. This is a part of the legacy."

"You own the greatest private art collection in the world, Jack."

"We never own things like this, Jock. I'm just a caretaker. Although few people ever heard his name, my grandfather was the most powerful man in the world. In fact, he almost destroyed it."

"Does that make you the most powerful man?"

Trance shrugged, as if it didn't matter. "I'm just a man, Jock."

Tilson spread his arm across the room. "Is this all da Vinci?"

"This section, yes. But there is more, a lot more…What I own doesn't matter, Jock. What matters is this: What do we do about the presidency?"

"Any ideas?"

"It's a hornet's nest; that's for sure. The easiest solution is to switch you back with your brother. Privately. If you challenge him publicly it could cause a national crisis, let alone bring up the burden of proof."

"Possession is nine tenths of the law, you mean? You think he'll go willingly?"

Trance nodded. "Actually, I do. There is a piece of him that seems overwhelmed by the job. I don't think he remembers who he was. If we do this right, perhaps he'll want his old life back."

"On this one, Jack, I defer to you."

"The good news is that your brother hasn't screwed up the country. He has veered to the left, politically. What actor wouldn't? Nothing you can't fix, if you want to. You've become quite popular. And this nuclear treaty? Sheer brilliance. I think he was just too naive to think it couldn't be done. With the bomb going off in the Chesapeake, Congress seems ready to sign it into law."

Tilson pursed his lips and waited before speaking. "I don't care about popularity, just what is right. If the treaty is good, I'll support it…But the country deserves its true, elected leader."

"You are going to *have* to support the treaty, Jock, regardless of what you think of it. You're brother took what you started with Ogarkov and finished it. There are many nations involved. Papers are signed. You can't undo them. You won't want to."

"I can't deal with Ogarkov. Not anymore."

"Ogarkov set you free."

"He kept me in prison, Jack. For over half a year."

"He was sitting on a political tinderbox."

"He negotiated and signed treaties with an impostor, someone he helped put in my place. Are you siding with him?"

Trance shook his head. "Things got convoluted. He did what he thought he needed to do, to prevent war, inside and outside his country. When Sammantha killed Petrovski, everything changed."

Tilson breathed a heavy sigh. He didn't like it, but Trance was probably right. He said, "Speaking of Sammantha…I am actually beginning to like her. I don't want to, but I am."

"Then the *healing* has started."

"A near-death experience will do things to you, Jack. And you? What about you?"

Trance fell back into his pillow. "I'm not sure I'll ever fully heal. My heart doesn't seem to have the strength anymore. I'm tired. I'm just tired of it all."

"Sammantha told me that you never should have lived. You'd been out too long and your heart was in shreds. She said you were either too damn stubborn to die, or you had divine intervention. She says you're a walking miracle."

Trance laughed softly. "Sometimes I think the Creator has one twisted sense of humor."

There was a soft knock at the entrance to the chamber. Lauren stuck her head inside and said, "Jack, you called for my parents? When you're ready, they are here. Sorry to interrupt."

Trance turned to Tilson. "We shouldn't be much more than a week, Jock. Then we put it all back together." He stuck out his hand. "Deal?"

Tilson grasped Trance's hand tightly. "That's a deal, my good friend."

As Lauren led her parents into the great chamber, Lauren's mother began making a series of odd chirping noises. She sounded like she was either on her deathbed, having great sex or giving birth.

"That stuff looks like da Vinci," she said. "And Botticelli, Bernini, Rembrandt, Renoir, Degas, van Gogh. Jack, what is this place?"

"I can't find a single thing by Klee," said Trance. "Picasso either."

Lauren poked Trance in his good ribs with an elbow. She looked at her parents and then back at Trance. "It will be good for my parents to understand the pressure you're under." Lauren spread her arm around the room and looked at her mother and father. "These are but a small piece of the legacy that was left to Jack. That, and a quest that neither of you would ever want to believe."

Trance took Lauren by the shoulders. He looked into her eyes, as if searching for something precious, something he'd lost deep in their darkness. "This is not a burden, it is my journey…Could you leave me alone with your parents, for a few short minutes?"

As Lauren left the room, Trance motioned for her parents to edge toward him. He grasped the hand of Lauren's mother. "Angie, you have always been like a mother to me, even more than my own. You know that, don't you?"

Angie's face seemed to scrunch and she nodded her head. "I love you like a son. You know that."

"And you, Max," said Trance, turning toward Lauren's father. "You have always been like a second dad."

Max tousled Trance's hair. "And you *are* my only son."

Trance felt tears begin to form in his eyes, but he made no attempt to hide them.

"I was wondering, Max…" stammered Trance. "…Would it be okay if I asked your daughter for her hand in marriage?"

Angie brought her hands to her face. Max turned toward her and wrapped her deeply into his arms.

"Hell, yeah," said Max, his voice barely a croak.

"I want it to be a surprise. A day that she will never forget."

"What can we do?" said Angie. Trance told them.

CHAPTER **137**
PP

The Black Madonna and her son entered the da Vinci chamber and walked with slow measured steps toward Trance. The old woman began to nod her head in a slow, bobbing motion, while peering around the room.

"Ah, I remember this room. Leo threw a fit the first time it was built—something about the movement of the air. He was fussy one. Made the builders tear down the whole thing and start again from scratch. Came out okay, I guess. Leo was happy. I prefer the Michelangelo room myself."

Trance looked at the Madonna, then to her son, his half-cousin, who was standing at her shoulder. "I am not aware of any Michelangelo room."

"Your grandfather had it sealed. The room housed many of his favorite books and manuscripts. There's a bunch of jewelry, and his collection of cars, of course. You like cars, Jack?"

Trance smiled weakly, then nodded. "As long as they're well broken in."

"It is also where he kept a lot of his gold." The Madonna sat on one side of the bed. Her son sat upon the other. "We will take you there. But first, we must help you heal. You've got to heal, Jack."

"I'm fine."

"No, you're not."

"I'm not sure I can heal. I feel too tired, like I've got a leak somewhere and my spirit is slowly draining away."

The Madonna withdrew a leather flask from a pocket of her black dress. She handed it to Trance. "Drink. No protest."

Trance drank the shimmering blue contents without complaint. Then the Madonna and her son laid their hands upon his chest. Trance could feel a kind of white-hot heat spread from their fingers. The dull beating ache in Trance's chest seemed to burn away, like baptism by fire. The Madonna began to mumble words that even Trance couldn't understand. Then her son joined in. After a few minutes they pulled their hands away and the Madonna said, "Walk."

"I don't have the strength."

"Get up and walk, Jack. *Now.*"

Trance closed his eyes and stepped hesitantly onto the floor. He took a few tentative steps. He waited for the pain in his chest to take hold, to bring him to his knees, but it never came. Instead, Trance felt a pressing weight break free, like a balloon being released from its tether.

The Madonna and her son were known for their healing touch. But this was something different. This was not a healing. It was more like…rebirth.

"You must still go easy," said the Madonna. "But soon you will be healed. Your heart will stronger than ever, along with your will...your spirit."

The Madonna stepped away from the bed and began to walk out of the room. "Come," she said, without looking back.

Trance and her son followed. The Madonna led them through a series of long hallways. After several minutes they came to a door that was covered with so many layers of nailed boards that it looked like a Halloween decoration.

"Behind here you will find the next part of your destiny," said the Madonna. "There is more besides this, Jack. You are not ready for that. Not yet."

The Madonna located two spots on the wall and pressed her fingers against the stone. A piece of the wall vanished and a small lever popped out from inside. The Madonna pressed the lever down and the entire entrance to the room began to open, including the boards that were nailed across it. The door itself, was made from a single stone that was over three feet thick.

"Clever," said Trance.

"Don't be fooled by the ease it took to get inside, Jack. The wall and the lever respond to you, your curator and to me only. If anyone else tries…you don't want to know."

When the door opened, the Madonna stepped aside, allowing Trance to enter the room before her. The right side of the room was stacked with bars of gleaming metal.

"More gold?" said Trance.

"Along with other metals, many of them rare. There is a good representation from the platinum group, which has many industrial applications. As you see, some of it is kept inside plastic and metal casings, because of toxicity issues.

"This is where your grandfather kept much of his wealth."

Trance gazed at the long mountain of shiny metal. "How much is there?"

"Who is to know?" said the Madonna. "Last I knew he had somewhere between ten and twenty million kilos of gold. Perhaps that much of the others. Some of the other metals are very rare, worth far more than gold or platinum."

"That's got to be worth billions."

"No, Jack. Hundreds of billions."

Trance suddenly noticed the ceiling. Across the near expanse of space there was a painting that looked eerily like Christ's Last Supper. Beyond that, there were many others, covering the ceiling as far as Trance could see.

"These paintings," said the Madonna, as she waved her arm across the room. "...are Michelangelo's greatest achievements."

The Black Madonna pointed along the left wall of the room. Stretching the length of the chamber, for well over two hundred yards, were sculptures and paintings of every shape and size. There were dozens, if not hundreds, of glass cases holding pottery, ancient texts and jewelry. Beyond that, for what looked like another quarter mile, stretched hundreds of antique cars and stacks upon stacks of books and scrolls.

"Now..." said the Madonna softly. "...The fun part of your life begins. Your next quest."

"What might that be?" said Trance.

"You will know, Jack. It will come to you and you will know."

CHAPTER **138**
PP

That night, after everyone but the night patrols had gone to sleep, Trance rolled over and shook Lauren awake.

"Wha…"

"I need to show you something."

"Can't it wait 'til morning?"

"Negative."

Trance slipped out of bed and stood on the floor.

Lauren gasped. "Jack, what are you doing?"

"It's okay. I can do this."

Trance led Lauren along the dark, empty hallways. He stopped before the boarded wing at the back of the chateau. He found the two spots on the wall and the hidden lever that opened the door to the golden, Michelangelo chamber. He flicked a switch and recessed lighting brought the room to life.

"Wow," said Lauren. "Look at that ceiling. Is that who I think it is?"

"The artist? Or the man with the wooden chalice?"

Lauren walked along the left side of the room, staring at piece after piece of the priceless art and jewelry.

"You're going to have to build a new museum, Jack. This needs to be shared."

Lauren walked along the row of glass cases that held countless artifacts stretching back thousands of years. There was gold and silver jewelry. There were precious stones, some the size of fists. There were ritual masks, totems, tiaras and all sorts of ceremonial clothing. The items were grouped by period and by region. Many were marked with hand-drawn signs made with a curator's skilled hand. Lauren spent a great deal of time before the cases of Egyptian gold, particularly those of Cleopatra. She fell speechless when she came to the Hopewell collection of gemstones and jewelry that had been fashioned for European royalty over the past millennium. She stopped before a case that was labeled Elizabeth I. Inside the large case, resting upon purple velvet, were crowns, tiaras, rings and necklaces of all sorts. Never once did Lauren look toward the hulking stacks of metal gleaming along the opposite wall.

"Did you see the bullion?" asked Trance.

"Jack, I've seen enough bullion to last a lifetime. You've seen one stack, you've seen 'em all…I am far more interested in Cleopatra's rings."

"The bullion is worth hundreds of billions."

"That's nice." Lauren looked out toward the sculpture area, gazing from one extraordinary statue to the next. "This is too much to handle, Jack."

"This is going to help change the world."

"The art world, at least." Lauren looked farther down the hall toward the books and the cars. "And the rare book and auto worlds, I suppose."

"I mean the metal."

"How much gold do you need, Trance? After a few million, what does money matter, except as a game?"

"That's not what I mean. The Madonna told me I have a new quest, in addition to the old one. At the time, I didn't know what it meant. Now I think I do."

"Not again, Jack."

"We just might save the world, Lauren."

"Oh, Jack..."

"This time it is different."

"Sure."

Trance stretched an arm across Lauren's shoulders and spread the other out toward the precious metals.

"What you see here, my dear, is the money and materials it will take to make the first big steps toward ridding the world's dependence on fossil fuels.

"I have always wondered why our government didn't create a national program, like the Manhattan Project, to develop clean, cold power. With all this talk about climate change and global pollution, doesn't it make sense?

"It's not something that energy companies could risk huge amounts of capital on, a technology that is twenty, thirty or forty years away. Our Congress is paid to look the other way, by too many lobbyists with too much money invested in the status quo.

"This kind of money will help us start something on a massive scale, without government interference, without the need to show short-term profits to our shareholders. With this money I can build particle accelerators, super-colliders that can help us unlock the secrets of the atom. It will give us the funds to develop cold fusion and hot fusion, where energy is safe and the by-products can be used to breathe or water your lawn. Maybe we can engineer photosynthesis in the lab, to replace carbon dioxide with oxygen to give us clean coal, thereby saving the oceans…With this we can someday deliver cheap, clean, *cold* energy for the entire planet."

Trance spread his arms across the room. "This…is mankind's future."

Lauren felt a knot begin to form in the pit of her stomach. Was she losing Trance again, this time to a dream that would take him decades? Had she waited all these years to follow nothing but another quest?

"Will you run it for me, Lauren?"

"Run what?"

"The company. The company we will form. A company with hundreds of billions in capital, one that doesn't have to answer to anyone except our Creator."

"What does God have to do with this?"

"Nothing and everything."

"You want me to devote the next thirty years to a pipe dream?"

"You've already spent twenty waiting for me."

Lauren laughed. "Are you saying that I'm the *champion of lost causes*?"

"No," said Trance. He took Lauren's face in his hands and kissed her softly. "I am saying that only someone with your unique abilities could ever see this through."

"God, you're full of shit."

"I'm serious."

Lauren thought about that, while studying Trance's face. "Will you do this with me?"

"Every step of the way."

"No more risking your life for other people?"

"This should be dangerous enough."

"What do you mean?"

"When we announce our plans there may be those who will try to stop us."

"Jack…Jack…Jack…Can't we just move somewhere…far away…and let the world live on without us?"

"That is not what we do, Lauren. Is it?"

Lauren smiled. She shook her head slowly. "I guess not."

"Somebody has to do the heavy lifting."

"Certainly not you, with that heart of yours."

"My heart's just fine. It will be stronger than ever. You just wait."

CHAPTER **139**

______________PP______________

As the *Lauren* was making its transatlantic return, Trance attended to the many details of getting Jock Tilson back into the White House. The first thing he did was to call Tilson's mother.

"Martha. This is Jack Trance."

"I am not supposed to talk to you."

"Then talk with your son."

Trance handed the phone to Jock Tilson.

"Hello, Ma."

"Oh, Jock! Where have you been? I knew you were alive…I just knew it…I just knew it."

"How is Brandon doing, as president?"

"You know about your brother?"

"Did you know about this? Before it happened?"

"Of course not. And I've spent every day praying that you were okay. Can we fix all this?"

"I am going to try for that, but it won't be easy. I need your help."

"Anything, son. I am so glad to hear your voice. I have missed you so…"

***

Trance made a call to Charles Johns, the semi-reclusive billionaire who managed hedge funds for wealthy investors, a man who also happened to own the Boston Red Sox.

"Just name your price," said Trance.

"I'm sorry, Jack. The Sox aren't for sale. I love baseball. I love this team, you know that. They are also critical to my business."

Trance was aware of John's previous failed attempts at purchasing the New York Yankees, before he had bought the Sox. Since that time, the enmity between the two teams' owners had grown almost as legendary as the rivalry between the teams.

"What if we trade?"

"Don't want to trade."

"There is one trade you would make, isn't there? Even up?"

Johns answered slowly. "There is one, Jack. Only one."

"I'll have my lawyers call your lawyers to draw up the papers. Keep this quiet."

"You'll lose your shirt. You know that, Trance."

"Lucky I've got a big wardrobe."

Trance hung up the phone. He made another call, this time to the aging owner of the fabled New York Yankees. There were rumors that estate tax issues were forcing the boss to seek liquidity, even to the point of selling the team.

"Sir, I was hoping that I might meet with you for lunch…" said Trance. "…say, in three days? Any place you choose. I'd like to overpay you for the Yankees."

"You ever come to Florida?"

"I've got some properties there."

"Tuesday. Noon. My place."

"Could you have your lawyers present, sir? I'll pay for their time."

"It'll cost you a friggin' fortune, Trance."

"Just have them ready, sir."

***

On their final night on board the ship, Trance pulled Lauren to his chest.

"Doesn't that hurt?" she whispered.

"My shunt has been removed. I think I can manage, provided you don't want to walk on my back."

"Sounds promising." Lauren nuzzled her face against Trance's neck and made him laugh.

"I am going to show you just how promising," he said.

"You think you should?"

"Sweetheart, I *know* I should."

"I ran out of pills on this trip, Jack. Be forewarned, this would be risky."

"That is a risk I am willing to take, sweetheart," said Trance.

Lauren looked into Trance's eyes. She saw something there, something she wasn't sure she had ever seen before. It was a softness, a kind of acceptance of the world as it is. His eyes had taken on an unusual look of carefree pleasure, as if this were the only moment that mattered. Lauren smiled and said, "If you insist."

"I do."

CHAPTER **140**
PP

Martha Tilson was sitting on her back porch with her Secret Service detail. When she heard the Marine One helicopters begin their weaving approach, Martha looked over to the men who had been guarding her for the past year and a half. She smiled wanly. These men had become her closest friends. They smiled back to give her encouragement. They knew what she was about to attempt, including the risks for them all.

The president's own advance detail had left the house. Agents were now standing in a semi-circle around the landing helicopters, while others had spaced themselves strategically throughout the grounds.

"Here we go," Martha said to her friends.

Martha shuffled into the house. She walked down into her basement and unlocked the door to a musty, cobweb-filled root cellar. *Some kind of protection*, she thought, thinking how the president's men had never once bothered to look inside this little hiding place.

"Out you go," she said to Jock, Trance, Lauren and Sammantha.

Trance and the others climbed the stairs and settled into the living room, while Martha Tilson walked back outside to meet her son. The air was mild. The sky was pewter gray with a light mist hanging in the air like fine dust. A few patches of grass were beginning to peek out from the melting snow. Water was collecting into small rivulets that ran from the yard into the driveway, making the gravel drive look like a river delta in a drought.

There was an odd look on Copley's face when he stepped out of the helicopter, as if he knew something was amiss. His mother had insisted on this meeting, but she wouldn't tell him what it was for.

"I've got a country to run, Mom," he'd said.

"Just get your butt up here," she'd said. So he came.

Martha Tilson confused Brandon Copley. She was supposed to be his mother. But every memory he had of his childhood was like a cardboard cutout, something he could see, but not *feel*. It was as if she were an understudy to his real mother, the mother he knew was lurking somewhere in the shadows of his mind, one he could never see.

As Copley stepped away from the helicopter, Martha took her son's head between her palms and kissed him on both cheeks.

"Mom," protested Copley. But the heat of her love flowed through him like a gulp of brandy. This, too, was a feeling he couldn't remember as a boy. It was something new and delicious. He felt almost guilty at the pleasure he felt in her embrace.

"Hello, my son," she said.

Martha took Copley by the hand. She led him through a squishy, wet path in the snow to the farmhouse. They stopped in the kitchen and sat down at the small table.

"Coffee?" said Martha.

"No, thanks. Had all I could stand on the flight over."

"Mind if I have a cup?"

Copley smiled. "Tis a nectar from which every hardy soul should partake, Mom. Help yourself."

The president turned to his picture with Brandon Copley at the Harvard-Yale game. He was standing at bat, about to strike out. This wasn't the way he remembered this scene. Somewhere deep in his mind, like a filmy shadow, he could remember that game. But he remembered it differently. He remembered himself as the pitcher, not the batter.

"I hate that photo," Brandon said.

"Why would you say that?"

"I don't know. There's something wrong, something almost sinister about it."

Martha took a sip from her coffee cup and set it down on the table. "There is something you need to see."

Martha began to move out of the kitchen. "Follow me, son."

Martha walked to her living room and stood by the entrance, allowing her son to enter the room before her. Copley made it three steps inside before freezing. There, sitting across from him in a chair, he saw himself.

"Who are you?" Copley said.

"I am the president."

"No you're not. *I* am the president."

"No," said Jock. "You are Brandon Copley. You are my brother."

Copley grew wide-eyed and looked to his mother. Then he yelled, "Guards! To me!"

The president's Secret Service detail flocked to the house like pigeons on tossed bread. Within moments, a dozen men were pointing their weapons about the room.

"Arrest these people!" shouted Copley.

The men turned their weapons toward Trance and the others. Then they hesitated.

"This man," said Jock Tilson, calmly pointing toward Copley from his chair, "is not the president. I am." Tilson appeared relaxed and in control, while Copley's face was beginning to break into a sweat.

The guards looked from Copley to Tilson and back. Then they looked to Martha for guidance.

"Which man is the president, ma'am?"

Martha looked to Jock and then to Brandon, her two sons reunited. "Why don't we settle this as a family, before it gets out of hand." Martha faced the president's security detail and tried to shoo them out of the room. They stood firm.

"Please leave the room," said Tilson. He looked to Copley, who nodded and said, "Please, do."

This was so far outside the box that the Secret Service didn't know what to do. The team leader looked to Copley and then to Jock Tilson. He shook his head. There was no protocol. He was stumped.

"It's okay," said Martha Tilson. "Give us ten minutes and everything will be fine."

"Yes. Go," said Tilson.

"Go," said Copley.

The men did understand a direct order, from whichever man was the president. So they left.

Jock Tilson turned to his brother. "How are you, Brandon?"

Copley frowned. "*I* am Jock Tilson. I am the president."

"No, you're not, sweetheart," said Martha. "You were taken from me at birth. Your father was Brandon Copley. You were raised by the Copley's, in New York."

Copley's knees began to grow weak. He searched for a chair and took one beside his brother. "This can't be," he mumbled. He turned to Sammantha. "I thought you left me."

Sammantha walked over to Copley and dropped to her knees. She took his hand and pressed it against her cheek. "I would never leave you, Brandon. I love you. Don't you remember? Gramercy Park? You were an actor. A star."

"But…" Copley shook his head, confused. His mind was spinning with a mix of images, both real and fabricated, like an out-of-control slide show running as fast as the eye could see. "Help me, Sammantha. Please, help me."

Sammantha sat on the side of Copley's chair and kissed him on the top of his head. "I love you

Brandon. We are going to make everything okay. You just wait."

"Who…" said Copley, pointing at Tilson. "…is this?"

"That's Jock Tilson. He was kidnapped and you took his place. You were a hero and you took his place, so the country wouldn't fall into war."

"I did?"

"Absolutely," said Tilson. "You rose far above the call of duty. You left your acting career and jumped in like a fearless marine to serve your country."

"I…I don't remember very much about that. All I remember is…being Jock Tilson."

Sammantha said, "That was for your own protection, Brandon. For the country's protection. You agreed to let us alter your memories so you could become more like the president. No, so you could *become* the president. You did an extraordinary job."

"Maybe better than I could have done," said Tilson. "I spoke with Ogarkov about your nuclear talks. I wouldn't have had the balls to propose what you did, and then get it done. I mean that."

"Who…who am I?" said Copley. He felt like a superhero that had just lost his disguise, somehow lessened and searching for solid ground, for roots to hold him in place.

"You are my son," said Martha. "Oh, how I have waited for this day…I can't tell you how many hours I have lain awake at night praying that one day we would all be together."

"You…are my mother? My *real* mother?"

"I am, sweetheart," said Martha. She stretched out her arms. "Come and hug your mother, who loves you to the ends of the earth."

Copley stood uncertainly, then shuffled to his mother's side. He allowed her to embrace him, still unwilling to let himself believe, really believe, that he wasn't the president. He felt like he was in some surreal stage play, where any moment he could look up and see that his mother was his imagination playing tricks, nothing more than a luring fiction. After a long moment, he relaxed into his mother's arms. This was his real mother; it had to be. He could feel it.

Jock Tilson looked toward Trance. Trance angled his head toward Martha and his brother. Taking the hint, Tilson got out of his chair and joined them. First, he put his arms around the two of them. Then he peeled Brandon Copley away, embraced him and slapped him solidly on the back.

"I think I always felt it, Brandon. Ma kept that stupid photo of us playing baseball, like it was some kind of trophy or something. I'll never forget you striking me out that day, particularly when she rubs it in my face."

"I did strike you out? That wasn't *me* at bat?"

Tilson nodded. "No. You were the pitcher."

"I knew it! Did we win?"

"Yes. *You* won."

"But I'm not president?"

"No. I am."

Copley's shoulders slumped and he let out a long, weary sigh. It was more like a *ha* or an *ugh*, some guttural expiration that came out of him on its own. Then Copley began to laugh. "Man, that's great. I was beginning to think I was crazy. I kept having these flashes of me in a different life, a life I somehow wanted back. The only thing I liked about this job was being on stage. I was always on stage." Copley hesitated. "Well, that and the travel conditions…I like the private planes…and the food…and the White House, of course…and the servants…and the respect…I liked winning the Nobel Peace Prize."

"Sure beats six months in prison," said Tilson.

"Or three," mumbled Trance.

Copley turned toward Trance. "You shot me."

Trance smiled. "I did."

"Why?"

Trance laughed heartily. "Well, Brandon, it had something to do with that nuclear bomb you wouldn't let anyone touch. If I had just shot in the air, you would have raised holy hell. I had to shoot you in a way that would cause panic, but not hurt you."

"That really *was* the bomb?"

Copley looked toward Sammantha. "Were you part of that? Did you plant that bomb?"

Sammantha began to answer, but Tilson cut her off.

"No. It was Talid. Sammantha was working for us. She helped save you. She helped save Washington."

Sammantha looked to Tilson and then at Trance. Her eyes seemed to say *thank you.* Then she took hold of Copley. "You don't know how much I love you," she whispered. "You could never know how much…You are my…my salvation."

She might tell him later, she thought. She wanted to tell him later, once he was ready. He deserved to know the truth. About the baby, too.

CHAPTER **141**
_______________PP_______________

General Mu'annar Abu Hussein al-Talid was standing outside, mingling with a group of other terrorists in a sandy prison yard. They were surrounded by palm trees, and the air smelled of fish and salt.

Trance stood in one of the guard towers, hidden from view. Beside him stood Byron Drake, perfector of the nano microphone/receiver that Trance had injected into Talid's nasal cavity.

"This thing didn't work a damn as a microphone," said Trance. "Wasn't powerful enough to work in Talid's palaces. But it sure kicks butt as a receiver. Watch this." Trance lifted a microphone, turned it on and whispered, "al-Talid."

Talid stiffened and began to look around.

"This is Allah," whispered Trance, in Arabic.

Talid walked over to a group of men and began talking and gesturing with his arms.

"They cannot hear me, al-Talid. Only you can hear me."

Talid snapped his head around, as if looking for someone who was tapping him on the shoulder and then hiding.

"I am not pleased with you," whispered Trance. Then he yelled. "Can you hear me?"

Talid jumped and looked around again. He said something to three other men, who shook their heads.

"Do not speak. I want you to listen. Listen to me well. You have been lying to the Americans. I want you to tell them the truth. No more lying, only the truth. Get down on your knees."

Talid fell down to the sand.

"Now pray. Pray for my mercy. Mercy you will never know if you continue with your lies. If you do not tell the truth I shall smite you with my wrath. I said pray!"

Talid reached out with his hands and began bowing low to the ground. Trance switched the transmitter off and turned to Drake.

"How are things at home?"

The white-bearded man smiled. "I'm back with my wife."

"That's great, Byron. And your kids?"

"We're good. Better than I could have hoped...And my grandkids...doesn't get any better than that, Trance."

"I've got an extra place in Cohasset. I'm looking for someone to live in it. It's on the water. You interested?"

"For how long?"

"I'm moving there and I need people around me I can trust. You can stay as long as you like. The view is a killer, by the way."

"My wife has always wanted..." Drake looked up at Trance and said, "Why did you do this?"

"Do what?"

"Why...why did you save me?"

"I didn't save you, Byron. You saved yourself. I just gave you the chance. Like so many others, all you needed was a chance, someone to believe in you. Believe me, I've been there."

"I will ask my wife, but I know what she'll say. She thinks you're a saint, by the way."

"I'm no saint, Byron. Just a man with resources...Tell me, what do you think about global warming?"

"I think the earth's temperature is cyclical. I mean, the planet was far warmer and the seas were twenty feet higher a hundred and thirty thousand years ago. Don't think man-made gasses caused warming back then. Don't think it's causing much now, at least not yet. CO2 levels in the atmosphere have risen from about 280 parts per million to 380 ppm over the last couple decades, and it's rising every year. If we're the cause, which we probably are, it's just a matter of time before we affect the environment in ways we can't predict. Man will ultimately affect the planet's temperature, particularly as world population grows. With two percent population growth, we'd have forty billion people on the planet a hundred years from now. Put that in your pipe and smoke it."

"Heat isn't what bothers me, Trance. What scares me is pollution. We are polluting the hell out of the planet, particularly the oceans. The oceans are filled with plankton. If we kill off the plankton, we kill off mankind, because it provides about eighty percent of the world's oxygen. I wish we spent more time talking about temperature and spend more time talking about survival of the species."

"You want to do something about it?"

Drake laughed. "I'm not sure there's much I can do, in the short run except maybe buy American, rather than goods from China.

"In the long run...mankind is one adaptive creature. We'll find ways to adjust. We'll develop technologies to convert CO2, deliver clean electrons. I'm just not sure we'll do it in time."

"What if I were to tell you that I am willing to spend whatever it takes to produce clean, cold energy? What if I were to put extraordinary pressure on the world's biggest polluters? What if I were to vow to clean up the land, the air and the seas?"

"You'd be a poor man long before you were done. Probably dead, too."

"You think a few hundred billion could do the job?"

Drake pulled on his beard and pondered the problem. "Might be a start, Trance. You got that kind of money?"

"Yeah. And I think I could raise a trillion or two or three from investors."

"No shit?"

"No shit," said Trance.

"Then you just might help preserve the planet, son."

"All we can do is try. You up for it, Drake?"

"Damned straight."

"I'm increasing your salary to five million, starting today."

"Are you serious?"

"Ever hear of Jerome Freeman?"

"Of course. He's a god in my world."

"I'm going to have you work with him."

"That..." said Drake, "...will be an honor."

The two men shook hands. Then Drake looked down on Talid.

"What's your plan with him?"

Trance took a slow deep breath and sighed. "I hear he was behind the president's kidnapping and the bombing in Washington. He was already on our Most Wanted List, despite his position as a world leader. He'll go on trial soon. All I want from him is the truth."

"What if he implicates others?"

"You know something I don't?" asked Trance.

"He couldn't have acted alone."

"The president can protect whom he needs to, with pardons. He's already done so. I'm thinking that with your little device, we might help Talid tell the truth. Maybe enough to help us get some real bad guys and put them away."

Drake patted Trance on the shoulder. "I'm glad it's you in charge of this, Trance. You'll see that justice is done."

"Justice is a funny thing, Drake. A funny thing. I'll try to do what's legal and what's right, then leave it at that."

"That's all we ever can do."

"Let's get home. We've got a world to change."

CHAPTER **142**
______PP______

Jack Trance stepped wearily out of his cross country skis. He arched his back to stretch the knots of muscle that were digging into his spine. He'd been skiing for hours, pushing himself to the limit of his endurance. Once the spasms in his back loosened, Trance wiped the collar of ice granules off the bottom of his pants. He jammed the back end of his skis through the snow's thick crust, so that they stood up on their own. He did the same with his poles. Then he pulled a Swiss Army knife out of his pocket and used its leather punch to chip away at the pond of soft ice that had collected below the doors to his late wife's shrine.

It was mid April. The snow cover was slowly vanishing, melting by day and freezing by night, the net being a steady dwindling of winter and the first signs of spring. The squirrels were leaping about on the snow, chasing each other's tails in a fight for dominance, setting the stage for the year's mating rituals. The birds were chirping more loudly now, flitting about the woods like dancers in search for food.

Trance opened the bronze doors as far as they would go. He unhooked the wooden shutters on the windows, allowing the light to pierce the darkness. Dust floated in the sunlight, looking like a cloud of newborn krill drifting in the sea. It made Trance think of life, in its most basic form, the simple the act of survival. He wondered how far up the evolutionary chain mankind had really progressed.

Trance pulled a dozen sweetheart roses from within his jacket and arranged them on Janice's headstone. He laid them side by side, in careful order, as if this could help him make sense of his life.

"Life's been strange," he said. "I found your murderer and I couldn't pull the trigger. I couldn't make her pay for what she'd done…because she'd paid too much already.

"It's funny, how you can spend years wishing for something, and when it finally happens, it is so far removed from what you expected that your world gets turned upside down. I spent years hating your killer, wishing I could find him and bring him to justice. But justice is a funny thing, Jan. It's like a cloud, shifting its formation with every passing moment, never the same, never as you saw it before. Our *he* became a *she*, and nothing like the cold-blooded assassin I thought she'd be.

"I realized something…I realized that the world is different for everybody. We see the same things and interpret them through our own prism, a prism that is coded by genetics, but shaped by experience. A U.S. soldier is seen as a patriot from our side of the ocean, and as an invading mercenary by our enemy. Our enemy, when seen by his children, could be a loving, doting father, a man willing to do anything to preserve what he sees as right, even if it means being a ruthless terrorist.

"I saw your killer as someone evil, someone who had to be brought to justice, no matter what the price. But she was an enemy combatant, seeking retribution for crimes she thought had been committed against her. Her world was so different from the one I saw from my side. She has to pay; I'll make her pay. Justice must be done.

"God, it's so screwed up. You do all you can to protect and preserve, sacrifice everything, risk anything to save the life you love. And then…and then…"

Trance heard the high-pitched rumble of a snowmobile below him in the valley. He listened carefully. He could hear that the vehicle was coming his way. Trance got off his knees and stood by the door, listening as the noise moved closer. Two minutes later he saw a snowmobile crest the final ridge to the property and head toward him.

"Damn," mumbled Trance.

Trance could see Janice's father piloting a Yamaha Apex MTX. Behind him sat Janice's mother. They were dressed in ski clothes. They had wind gear zipped up to their necks and heavy mittens on their hands. George Fitzgerald stopped and waved when he saw Trance standing in the doorway. He guided the Apex to a spot beside Trance's upright skis. He sat for a long moment after turning off the engine, as if thinking about what he was going to say. Janice's mother hopped off the back and began walking toward Trance with long, purposeful strides. No one said a word. When Marybeth Fitzgerald was two strides away from Trance she opened up her arms. She took the final two steps, pressed her cheek against Trance's chest and pulled him tightly toward her.

"It's so good to see you, Jack."

Trance draped his arms weakly around Janice's mother, feeling a guilt so strong he thought his heart might stop.

Janice's father came up behind Trance and wrapped his arms around him, so that Trance was surrounded by both parents like an egg in a carton, a support strong enough to protect him from nearly any hard fall.

"Hello, son," said George.

"I'm so sorry," said Trance.

When Marybeth pulled away from Trance, there were tears in her eyes.

"For gosh sakes, Jack, it wasn't your fault. You can't keep avoiding us forever. Janice loved you. She would want you to be happy, you know that."

"I got her killed."

"No, Jack," said George. "You gave her life." He laughed. "You know, from the time she was this little kid, all Jan ever wanted was be a spy. It was the damndest thing. She started with those Nancy Drew books, seeing herself as a mystery solver. Then it was the Hardy Boys. From there she moved on to spy novels by le Carré, Mailer, Griffin, DeMille, Morrell, Forsyth, Francis and MacDonald, She couldn't get enough of it. She read all the Sherlock Holmes stories. Dressed herself up just like him for awhile. She always had us buying things like magnifying glasses, lock picks and high tech doodads of all sorts. She wasn't but ten years old when she begged us for this plastic flower. She could pin it to her blouse and use it to take pictures. The damn thing had this remote control switch that snapped off photos at whim. Why anyone would wear such a stupid flower never crossed her mind, or the fact that each photo came with such an audible *click* that everybody knew had to be from a camera. No, she thought it was the coolest thing in the world.

"When she went off to 'Spook U,' as we all called it, she was like a kid who had inherited the candy store. And you…you, Jack…you were her knight in shining armor. You were everything she'd dreamed about in those books. You gave her a life that was better than what she'd imagined. She loved you with a passion so fierce…"

George's words trailed off. They all stood in silence for a long minute. Then George continued, "You can't give up on life, Jack, even when it deals you a losing hand. We don't blame you, never have. We have always been here for you, always will be. You've got to let go and move on."

Trance looked at Janice's parents. He'd tried to forgive himself, as they had. It was the hardest thing he had ever tried. He was almost there, almost. But not quite. Maybe he never would be.

Trance motioned for them to join him inside the shrine. The spring sun was shining on Janice's headstone like a rainbow. The room was bright and airy. A painter's easel stood in the corner with a fresh canvas, the light so perfect that the spot screamed out for a painter.

"It's beautiful here," said Marybeth. "We come here often."

Trance frowned. Janice's parents lived in Virginia, not Vermont. "You do?"

"Sure," said George. "We retired here, late last year."

"Oh."

"We can watch over her now," said George. "This can't be your ball and chain forever, Jack."

"This has never been a ball and—"

Marybeth put her hand on Trance's lips. "We know, dear. We also know Janice would want you to move on. She would want you to be happy. She would want you to let go, to live your life. She knows you will never forget her. She knows that the love you had will always remain, like one of those little scenes in a snow globe, with everything perfect, the unspoiled virgin snow so smooth and unblemished that you can almost feel it in your fingers.

"She would want you to *live* and *laugh* and *be happy*. We want that for you, too, Jack. More than you know."

Trance sat down upon the floor. He pulled his knees up into his chest and began to rock, slowly. He thought of those days with his wife, their lives so filled with promise. Their lives had not been simple, not as he wanted to pretend they were. There was the CIA, there was duty, there was country. Life never got easy, it just moved on.

"Thank you," whispered Trance.

CHAPTER **143**
________________PP________________

It was a clear, cloudless morning in the middle of May. The daytime temperature was predicted at a warm, eighty degrees. Trance and Lauren were driving along Boston's South Shore, off to spend the day with Lauren's parents.

"Let's drive by the house," said Lauren.

"What house?" said Trance.

Lauren punched Trance in the arm. "You know. *The* house."

"Not again."

"Again."

When they came to the white mansion at the north end of Jerusalem Road, Lauren gasped. There was a Coldwell Banker *For Sale* sign on the outside of the fence near the road. There was also a *Sold* marker angled across its top. Trance stopped his car and Lauren stared.

"Oh, my God. I can't believe this," said Lauren. "The place got sold and we never knew about it."

"Who would ever want that place anyway?" said Trance. "Think of the upkeep. It would be monster to heat."

Tears were beginning to drip down Lauren's cheeks. "I always…sort of…thought that we might end up in that house. Even when we were in high school, I used to dream about us living in that house, having kids and raising a family."

"I'm not sure I'm the settling down type, Lauren," said Trance. "Things always seem to get in the way."

"You don't say."

Trance pointed. "The gate's open. Why don't we go inside?"

"We can't just go inside," said Lauren. "That's trespassing."

But Trance had already started driving his Porsche through the open front gates and up the long drive. Lauren noticed that the Vanderweggens big brass letter Vs had been removed from the front gates. She wondered what new letter they would be sporting soon. The home began to loom before them. Several additions had been made to the place. The paint on the outside walls looked and smelled fresh. The most radical change was a round tower that jutted up from its center. It looked almost like a lighthouse, with a pointed cap roof above an open area looking out to the sea.

"Look at that," said Lauren. "That's so cool."

"Let's go inside."

"We can't go inside, Jack."

"I'll call Coldwell Banker."

Trance pulled out his PDA, dialed the local number to Coldwell Banker and began to speak. A minute later he hung up his phone and said, "We are free to look around. The key is under a round, white rock in the garden."

Lauren shook her head. "I don't want to."

"What do you mean? You've always wanted to go in this place." Trance searched the garden for the rock until he found it.

"That's when I had a dream, Jack. I've just given up on that dream."

"Let's go inside anyway."

Trance walked to the side door of the mansion and unlocked it. The door opened to a mud room that was attached to the home's large rear kitchen. This, too, had been recently renovated.

"Oh, isn't this beautiful!" cried Lauren. She began to walk around the spacious room. "Wow…Look at this, Jack…Oh, isn't this clever…Look at his triple stove…Oh, I love this floor…"

They moved from room to room, with Lauren complimenting the new and old owners on their imagination and taste. Even the antique furnishings seemed to please Lauren's discerning eye.

They heard a rumble of trucks outside. Trance poked his head out a window and said, "Looks like catering trucks."

"We should go, then," said Lauren.

"Let's try the tower first," said Trance. "It must be over here."

Trance took the stairs to the second floor, then walked through the house until he came to the circular staircase that wound up toward the sky. Even from below, the staircase radiated a warm glow of soothing light.

"Oh, isn't this *sweet*," said Lauren. She began running up the stairs, to a wide open space that was enclosed by glass. Two Adirondack chairs sat facing the water, looking like a Cialis commercial. They could see the Cohasset lighthouse off to the right and the Boston skyline looming to the left. Between them, the ocean stretched before them like blue glass.

"Wow," said Lauren. "Wow…wow…wow."

Trance pressed a switch on the wall and the windows slid down into the floor, until the entire space was open to the air.

"Oh, my God," said Lauren. "This is *so* cool."

Lauren looked out toward the water, where a large private yacht was motoring in the distance, traveling south from Boston. Lauren turned to say something to Trance, but he was down on one knee.

"What are you doing?" she said.

"Lauren, I know that I am not the easiest man to love. I have some hang-ups, and I do things that put your life into chaos. But, I love you and I would like to marry you. Will you marry me?"

Lauren stared at Trance and felt her knees begin to swim. "That's the first time you've actually asked…I can't believe this…"

Trance reached into his pocket and pulled out a ring. "I know that we were supposed to go out looking, but is seems that every time we try…So I had this one made, from some used stuff I took from the chateau. The gold band was worn by Cleopatra. I saw you eyeing it, and don't deny it. The two diamonds and the center emerald came from the Elizabeth section of the British Crown Jewels. They've been in my family for four hundred years. So England won't be missing them."

Lauren sank to her knees and kissed Trance. It was a strong kiss, a long kiss. When she stopped she leaned her face on Trance's shoulder. "Are you sure you want this?"

Trance smiled. "Never more sure."

"Make love with me. Right here. Right now."

"But the caterers—"

"Just do what I tell you, Trance."

"If you insist."

Later, Lauren settled into one of the chairs and sighed, "At least we'll have a good memory of this house. Don't you think?"

"Yeah. When do you want to get married?"

"Knowing you, Trance…today."

"That would be awfully tough."

"No, it wouldn't," said Lauren. "My parents are at home expecting us for lunch. Stick and Marlee are supposed to join us. Let's do it today. We'll find a Justice of the Peace and get married today, before something else happens."

"Aw, Lauren. That's asking a lot."

"Since when do I ask a lot?"

Trance looked at Lauren and smiled. It was a sly, mischievous grin. "Today?"

"Today."

"You're sure?"

"Never more so."

Trance pulled his PDA out of its case and thumbed a quick text message.

"What are you doing?"

Trance pointed toward the big luxury yacht that was beginning to turn and head their way. "That look familiar to you?"

Lauren stared out toward the ocean and squinted. "Is that the *Lauren*?"

"I thought you might want to get this marriage thing out of the way. So, I made a few preparations."

"Preparations? You made preparations without telling me?"

Trance laughed. "I still wear pants."

"When I let you."

"True. But I know you, at least I think I do."

Realization began to spread through Lauren. She could feel her jaw go slack and her knees cry for support. She began to laugh.

"This house?" she asked.

"A wedding present."

"The boat?"

"The wedding party."

"The dress?"

"Your mother's. They are on their way."

"Oh, Jack. You are such a shit."

"I know."

Lauren buried her face into her hands. All those years of waiting, and here it was. It was better than she had imagined, like a princess in a young girl's dream.

"I have another gift for you, later," said Trance.

"I bet you do."

Trance smiled. "Not that. Something else."

"Jack. I don't need anything else."

Trance shrugged. "Can't change it now."

Trance reached out with a hand. "Are you ready?"

Lauren shook her head. "First, I need to tell you something."

Trance's eyes narrowed.

Lauren continued, "You remember that night on the ship?"

"What ship?"

"The *Lauren,* stupid."

"What night?"

"*The* night."

"What *the* night?"

"The night night."

"Oh, the night night."

"Yeah. Well, remember I warned you?"

Trance cocked his head. "About what? You may recall that I wasn't quite right then. I had that little health issue, you know, with my heart?"

"Other parts were working just fine. You owe a big oo-rah to Jerome Freeman."

"No?" Trance's lips began to twist. He told himself to get a grip. *Get a grip on your life, Trance.*

"I'm pregnant, Jack. Twins, like the Black Madonna predicted."

Lauren didn't know what to expect. She'd played this moment a hundred times in her head. She'd tried to tell him, but the words just wouldn't come. They were too jumbled with visions of Trance in prison, with his future being carried by Jerome Freeman in a glass jar, of Trance lying near death in half a dozen countries around the world, of him lying listlessly in bed, surrounded by da Vinci in France. Would Trance give thanks for his blessings, or would he fear for his children, worry that he may never live to see them? Would he worry that they, too, would become targets? What Trance did was something she had never seen in her mind, nothing she had dared to hope for.

Trance let out a scream. Not just any scream, a scream so loud that Lauren thought her ears might pop. Then Trance began to jump up and down like a game show contestant.

"I'm going to be a dad?"

"Yes, Jack."

"And you're going to be a mom?"

"That would be anatomically correct."

"And we're going to be a family?"

"God, you're quick."

"Lauren, this is the best moment of my life." Trance knelt down and placed his hand against Lauren's womb. He gave it a gentle kiss, then wrapped his arms around her. He held her, with a tenderness Lauren had never seen in him, didn't know was there. She knelt down beside him and kissed him softly on the face.

Trance whispered, "Sometimes, if you try hard enough, and work long enough, dreams do come true."

The doorbell rang. Trance and Lauren stood together. They held hands and began to walk down the stairs. When they reached the living room, Trance opened the front door.

"Surprise!" shouted Lauren's mother. In her hand she held an intricately embroidered white wedding dress, the one she had worn herself as a bride.

"You were in on this?" said Lauren.

"Of course, darling."

Lauren's father walked through the door and hugged his daughter, patting her gently on the back. "Good for you, baby girl," he said. "We are so happy."

"Oh, daddy."

"Where should I put this stuff?" Stick Granger was approaching the door with a mound of gift-wrapped packages in his hands. Lauren ran to his side and began to tickle his defenseless underarms.

"You came to the wrong place," she said.

"I live next door lady," he said. "These are house warming gifts. I heard someone new was moving in."

Lauren looked questioningly at Trance, who nodded. "He does live next door. For safety reasons, I bought every house in the area. Against my better judgment, I gave one of those houses to General SFB."

"SFB?" said Lauren.

"Just call me 'general'," said Stick. He leaned over and kissed Lauren on the cheek. "Finally tied the old bastard down, eh?"

"Not yet. The day's still young."

The whir of helicopter rotors began to sound in the distance. Soon the noise began to rattle the windows, as three helicopters came to rest on the front lawn.

Jock Tilson stepped out from Marine One and walked purposefully across the lawn. He stepped inside the door and kissed Lauren on both cheeks.

"You look radiant," he said.

"Thank you, Mr. President."

"Call me Jock, Lauren," he said. "I owe you and Jack my life." Tilson looked around. "Where's Trance?"

Trance came around a corner holding a crystal vase in each arm. Both were filled with flowers.

"For me?" said Tilson.

"Don't be a wise guy," said Trance. "*Someone* has to prepare for this wedding."

"Somehow, Trance, you don't strike me as the wedding-planner type. Want some help?"

Trance grinned and handed a vase to the president. "Sure. Make yourself useful." He turned toward Lauren. "You up for this?"

Lauren's face was actually glowing. Trance remembered seeing her this way once before. It had been the night of their high school senior prom, when she'd walked down those stairs wearing that pretty pink dress, with makeup splashed on her face by such untrained fingers, her eyes so innocent and filled with…love. Even back then, they had been filled with love.

"Thank you for this, Jack."

"We should have done this years ago."

"No, Jack. Today is perfect."

The loud honk of a boat horn sounded. Then the sound of Jimmy Buffet's melodious voice began to float up off the water.

"That would be the guests," said Trance. He turned toward the president. "We better get cracking, Jock."

***

Two hours later, underneath a spotless blue sky, over a thousand guests sat watching Lauren Haverford. She stood at the end of a long aisle that had been made between folding chairs. Max Haverford stood beside her, grinning like a he'd won the lottery. A stringed quartet began playing Pachelbel's *Canon* and Lauren began to slowly walk. As her shaking legs carried her unsteadily forward, Lauren thought of all the years she had spent dreaming of this moment, the times she had held Trance in her arms, just a hair's breadth away from death. She felt the cool sea breeze drift across her face, as if it could blow away all the pain she'd endured during those years. They were alive. They were together.

Trance was dressed in his full Marine dress uniform. Beside him stood Stick Granger, looking entirely out of place in his own dress blues. Flanked beside Granger stood Jock Tilson, Jesse Tompkin, Trance's Uncle Tony, Spike Jackson, Art Winthrop, Jerome Freeman and Jacob Miller. As Lauren glided forward, she saw many old friends sitting on Trance's side of the aisle. There was the expected assortment of leading U.S. politicians, world leaders, company employees, actors, musicians and famous athletes. Jock Tilson's children and his grandchildren were there. Martha Tilson was there, sitting beside her old friend, Katarina. Sammantha and Copley stood arm-in-arm. Shingen and Kenshin were there. Janice's parents stood with misty smiles. Sophie, Millie, Muffy, Hutch and Gumbo were there. Gumbo was wearing his famous white suit. Pat Crawford, Tony Trance's wife, smiled while rocking her new baby in her arms. Cubie Drake, Wilson, Swartz and Breitfuss stood looking around, wide-eyed, as if waiting for something to happen. Smokey Jones stood with a fine looking young man at her side. Her daughter, Hope, wearing a pink dress and pigtails, walked ahead of Lauren, tossing rose petals. Byron Drake stood beside his wife, holding her hand like a young child grasping his binky. His face was cleanly shaved. He had a look of such radiance across his eyes that when Lauren saw him, she grinned even more. Lauren passed the New York City boy, Jabar, to whom Trance had given his card. Spike Jackson had his arm around the boy, in that relaxed and protective manner that only a father can have. Copley's butler, Clyde, was there, seated beside his grandson who was now re-enrolled at Columbia. Deacon Jones was beaming, standing beside his wife and his two teenage daughters.

Lauren looked to her own side of the aisle. It was equally full, with a large grouping of business leaders, friends, family and colleagues. The head of the Federal Reserve Board was there. Lauren's friend, Slash Whinton, was standing as one of her bridesmaids. When Slash met Lauren's eye, Lauren began to plot how she might introduce her to Jock Tilson.

As Lauren reached the end of the aisle, she looked into the eyes of Jack Trance. He wore the biggest smile she had ever seen. It was as if someone had stretched a coat hanger inside his mouth to push it as far as it would go. His eyes were bright and playful, but there was something else.

As Lauren stood trembling, she remembered Trance on the night of their senior prom. She remembered how she had walked down those stairs. She had seen that same childish look of wonder in his eyes, that awe and just a little touch of fear, fear of having it all snatched away by some random twist of the screw, even then. How many times had they come close, only to have something happen to split them apart? She looked to the Black Madonna and to her son, who had flown in from Switzerland to perform the ceremony. The Madonna, sitting in the front aisle, winked at Lauren and mouthed, "I told you."

At that moment there was a deafening roar overhead. Trance threw himself over Lauren and pushed her to the ground, pulling out his Colt as he did. Stick drew a huge, Desert Eagle pistol from somewhere under his coat and began waving it around like a war club. The crowd gasped, as five blue F/A-18 jets flew overhead in formation.

"Aw, it's just the Blue Angels," said Stick.

The president laughed, and said, "My bad."

The jets arched into the air. Then a yellow double-winger flew up from beneath the cliff and began letting off smoke. Two of the Blue Angels veered out and up, and then came back towards each other to make a perfect heart in the sky. Another jet began a slow roll, while the double-winger spelled out huge letters across the sky. FINALLY! The guests began to clap.

At the end of the ceremony, their minister, Trance's cousin, held aloft a wooden chalice that was filled with wine. The chalice was plain and smooth, with a delicate, five petal rose carved into its side. He offered the chalice to Trance and then to Lauren. They each drank from the cup of Christ.

"Do you, Lauren Haverford, take this man…"

"I do," said Lauren. "I really do."

"I now pronounce you husband and wife."

***

Trance and Lauren found Dr. Mariah Whinton standing near the garage, talking to a group of T-Force members.

"I'll bet you twenty bucks, I can," she was saying.

"You're on, lady," said a young, jarhead marine.

Whinton pulled a hockey stick from inside the garage and tossed a puck onto the driveway. "Let's see it," she said.

The marine wound up for a slap shot and sent the puck flying far across the back of the property. It landed half way across the wide yard, about twenty yards short of a tall oak tree.

"That all you got?" said Whinton. She tossed a second puck to the same shooting spot. She hiked up her dress and let her own shot fly. Whinton's puck hit the oak squarely in the center of the trunk.

"Well, I'll be damned," said the muscular marine. He reached down into his pocket and removed a twenty dollar bill. He slapped it into Whinton's hand and said, "Double or nothing?"

"Dr. Whinton?" interrupted Trance. "Could we see you over here for a moment?"

The marine snapped to attention and saluted Trance. His jaw grew slack. "You said your name was Slash," he said, with a look of bewilderment spreading across his face. "You're a doctor?"

"Yeah, so what?" said Whinton. "You ought to see me arm wrestle."

Slash turned toward Trance and Lauren, laughing. "I made a lot of money doing that down at Quantico."

"I just wanted to say 'thank you'," said Trance. Trance looked at Lauren. "Slash helped me work through some things. She helped get me here."

Whinton shook her head. "Nah, Jack. All I did was feed you strong coffee. You did everything else on your own."

Trance smiled. "It is time for payback."

"No, Jack. I—"

"C'mon. You promised."

Trance pulled Whinton by the hand and led her through the crowd until they reached the president. Jock Tilson was standing with Lauren's parents, Copley and Sammantha. In his hand he held a glass of scotch, with no ice.

"I see we found the Macallan," said Trance.

"I sure missed this stuff in prison."

Trance looked to Brandon Copley, who was sipping spring water with lime. "How are you doing, Brandon?"

"Better every day, thanks."

Trance paused. Then he said, "When you're up to it, my media company is planning to make a film. We're going to call it *The Presidential Pretender*. It's about a president who gets kidnapped and his twin steps into the Oval Office."

Copley chuckled. "No one would believe it."

"I'm serious," said Trance. "Your brother and I thought it was the best way to tell the story. It's going to be a hell of a flick. I'd like you to play the lead, if that's okay. Twenty-five million for the part, plus points."

Copley squeezed Sammantha's hand. He looked at her and asked, "Am I ready for this?"

Sammantha mouthed, "Thank you," to Trance. She took Copley's hand and said, "Honey, you are a star."

Copley said, "On one condition."

"A condition?" said Trance. "We're giving conditions?"

"You hire the actors that worked with me at Moosehead."

"The ones we rescued off that ship in Russia?"

"Yeah. They deserve this."

Trance nodded. "They do. I've seen the films you all made. I've already started the arrangements. Anything else?"

Copley stared at Trance. A lump that felt like a turkey leg began growing in his throat. A shower of images spattered across his mind—his parents, Clyde, baseball, Copley manor, Maine, the bathroom floor with Sammantha—it all made him dizzy. The confusion passed. A peaceful calm spread through him, like the jolt from a shot of tequila or Wild Turkey, something he would never taste again. He was whole now. He had a life. He had a family, and a baby on the way. "Thank you, Jack," he said.

Trance shrugged. "Sure." He turned to the president. "Jock, I would like you to meet a good friend of mine, Dr. Mariah Whinton."

Jock Tilson extended his hand and said, "It is very nice to meet you."

"Thank you, Mr. President."

Tilson's eyes narrowed. "Haven't I seen you before?"

"I doubt it, sir."

"No, let me think." Tilson put his hand to his forehead and turned in a circle. He said, "You used to come to the Harvard baseball games…You had that rally cap thing, inside out and backwards, or to the side, with a Red Sox hat. You did this thing with your hands…"

"The rally dance," said Whinton.

"You also used to yell at me when I was batting."

"I did."

"I could never really hear you. What were you saying?"

Whinton glanced at Copley and said, "Not while he's listening. I'll tell you later."

Tilson looked at Trance, who only smiled. "And now you're a doctor?" Tilson said.

"Yeah. I used to be Trance's shrink."

Tilson looked at Trance.

Trance shrugged. "I had commitment issues."

Tilson laughed and looked back at Whinton. "You did your job well, I'd say." Tilson snuck a quick look at Whinton's left hand. "You're not married?"

Slash blushed. "Widowed. Eight years."

Tilson's eyes softened. "I'm sorry."

"I feel sorry for you, Mr. President. Kiki was a great woman."

"You knew her?"

"We all envied her. I knew her, a little."

There was an awkward silence, while Jock and Whinton studied each other with furtive glances.

"Please, call me Jock."

"Call me Slash."

As the two of them shook hands for a second time, Trance began to back away. "We've got to go mingle. Slash, would you stay here and keep Jock company?"

"If he wants me to."

"I do," said Tilson, just a bit too quickly.

Trance and Lauren exchanged glances. Mission accomplished.

"Wait 'til they find they've been seated together," mumbled Trance, as he and Lauren walked away.

"They'll know they've been conned."

"Facilitated," said Trance. "They're both lonely. They'll make good friends." He took Lauren by the hand and led her through a series of introductions.

When they came to Deacon Jones and his family, Trance gave Deacon a hug. "Hey, soldier."

Deacon introduced his wife, Juanita, and his two daughters.

Trance looked at the girls and said, "Your dad says you two are smart. Is that true, or is he pulling my leg?"

The girls looked unsteadily at their father. "Go on," he said. "Tell him the truth. Always tell the truth."

"We get straight A's said the oldest one."

"Good," said Trance. "Where do you want to go to college?"

"Harvard," they both said at once.

"Harvard?" said Trance. "Why in the world would you want to go to Harvard?"

"Dad says that you went there," said the oldest.

Trance glanced at Deacon, then back to the girls. "Just to the law school. I went to the Naval Academy before that. Maybe you'd like to go there, join the military?"

The girls shook their heads.

Trance laughed. "It's not for everybody. Don't blame you. You're both set on Harvard?"

The girls nodded. Trance looked at Deacon, and then to Juanita. "You mind if I borrow these fine young ladies for a few minutes?"

Trance led Deacon's daughters through the crowd until they came to a middle aged man with thinning hair and gold wire-rimmed glasses. The man was wearing a tweed sport coat with a plaid bow tie.

"Jimmy," said Trance. "These ladies want to go to Harvard and I want to pay for it. Jock Tilson will be writing their recommendation and their dad is a bona fide hero. I've given you far too much money, and I wouldn't want to stop. Would you please talk to them?"

Jimmy looked at Trance, then to the girls. He laughed. "You never quit, do you, Trance?"

"Nope."

Jimmy stretched out an arm and led the teenagers toward a white gazebo with an empty wooden bench.

Trance returned to Lauren, who was still chatting with Deacon and his wife.

"Where'd you take them, Jack?" said Deacon.

"For an interview with Harvard."

Lauren laughed. "You bring them to see Jimmy?"

Trance nodded.

"Jimmy? Who's Jimmy?" asked Juanita.

Lauren said, "A friend, who also happens to be the president of Harvard."

Trance pointed toward a man who was standing about fifty feet away. "Let's go see the *boss*."

"Are you kidding?" said Lauren. "He owns the New York Yankees. He's the *enemy*, Jack. Who invited him, anyway?"

"I did."

"Whatever for?"

"The Yankees are in town. He's a friend of mine."

Trance dragged Lauren toward the owner of the Yankees. The closer they got, the harder she fought him. By the time they reached the boss, Lauren was actually digging in her heels.

"Ah, Trance," said the boss.

Trance offered his hand. "Mr. Steinhousen."

Steinhousen grasped Trance's hand and shook it vigorously.

Trance said, "I would like to introduce you to my wife, Lauren."

"It is such a pleasure." When Steinhousen took Lauren's hand and smiled, it made her think of the ocean. There was a vitality there that she'd never seen on the television screen, an energy and a zest for life that she could actually feel. Instantly, Lauren began to fear that she might actually like this man. After all the years of hating his laundry.

"Are you ready?" said Trance.

"Everything set with the league?"

"Yep."

Steinhousen reached into the breast pocket of his jacket and withdrew a folder full of papers. Trance did the same. The two men swapped folders and shook hands again.

"Have you seen the president?" said Steinhousen. "I've got to ask him something."

Trance said, "Right now he's a little busy. I'll bring you to see him in a bit, though. Work for you?"

"Thanks."

Steinhousen smiled at Lauren. It was an odd smile, a playful smile, maybe a sneaky smile. It reminded Lauren of the look that some executives get when they speak before Congress. There was something not quite honest and forthcoming, as if he were guarding the truth.

"Are you coming to the game tonight?" Steinhousen asked Lauren.

Lauren looked at Trance. "We were planning on it. But then this marriage thing came up."

"We're all going," said Trance. "Many of us, anyway. After lunch."

"What are you up to?" said Lauren, as they walked away. "You can't have tickets for hundreds of people. This is Boston versus New York, Jack. How'd you get that many tickets?"

"I have connections and I planned ahead. A lot of people will be staying here for the concerts. Others will stay on the boat. Now, come with me."

Trance led Lauren through the house and up into the tower. When they reached the top, he looked out to the ocean and inhaled a deep breath of fresh sea air.

"Isn't this great?" he said.

"You still haven't told me why Steinhousen is at our wedding, Jack. He owns the *Yankees*. It's giving me indigestion."

"No dear," said Trance. "He doesn't own the Yankees." Trance took the folder out of his pocket and placed it into Lauren's hand. "You do."

"What?"

"Johns wouldn't sell me the Red Sox. So I bought the next best thing."

Lauren opened the folder and read through the papers. She was holding all of the partnership shares to the New York Yankees. "I can't take this. I don't *want* this. What will I say to my friends? They will disown me!"

"We'll move to New York. We'll get new friends."

"Jack. How could you do this? On our wedding day, no less. This is…this is like…this is…" Lauren began to laugh. "This is like a kick in the butt."

Trance looked hurt. He began to pace around the top of the tower. "Didn't you tell me I should buy something big? Didn't you tell me I should buy a baseball team?"

"Well…maybe I did, once or twice. But I meant the Red Sox. Not the Yankees. I'd rather own a sweat shop in a third world country, Jack."

"I told you, Johns won't sell the Red Sox. You'll have to settle for the Yankees. Don't worry. You'll learn to like them."

"I won't root for them. The players are okay. Some are good role models. They do the charity thing. But I can't root for them, not the Yankees. I grew up a Red Sox fan and I'll die one. Sorry. You can go ahead and cheer for the Yankees. But don't expect me, or your children, to ever sit with you."

Lauren handed the papers back to Trance. "I love you, Jack. But not this much. The team is yours." Lauren shook her head, chuckling again. "And you even put him at the head table. The owner of the New York Yankees at the head table on my wedding day."

"Former owner." Trance took back the papers and put them into his jacket pocket. "I own the team."

"Maybe I'll put *you* at a different table. Let's get back to the party. I need a drink."

***

As dinner was served, Stick Granger began to clink his glass. "As the best man here, I need to say something.

"Today we have come together to witness the union of two extraordinary people. I've got nothing bad to say about Lauren. Trance, well, that's a different story. How much time do we have?"

The crowd ruffled with laughter.

"Today, though, all I want to say is 'It's about time, Trance!'"

Jock Tilson stood and waited for the cheers to die before speaking. "Most of you know that Jack, Lauren and I are good friends. What most of you don't know, is that General Jack Trance recently helped save Washington D.C. from nuclear annihilation. He put his life into great danger to save my life, as well as many of those in our government. For that, I am pleased to announce that I am giving him his second general's star. Congress has also awarded him *another* Medal of Honor."

Trance's whole body seemed to turn red at once. He looked like he'd run through a fraternity initiation tunnel where everyone slapped everything they could. The crowd began to clap and cheer. Trance's face became a darker, Harvard crimson. His red face, sitting on top of his dress blue uniform and his white shirt, gave Trance all the colors of a human flag.

"I am awarding a Navy Cross to my friend, Jesse Tompkin. He is also receiving a promotion. The same goes to two brave pilots and two crew members of a Marine One helo. The U.S. Medal of Freedom is hereby given to my brother, Brandon Copley, to his fiancée, Sammantha Starodubov, to Stick Granger and to Trance's friends Shingen and Kenshin, from Japan.

"In addition, in lieu of my original request for a national day of recognition for Trance and his friends, we have agreed that August 15th will be a national day of recognition. We want to thank all of our nation's servicemen who have been wounded and served in battle. Trance and I have been working with the owners of major league teams around the nation to provide free tickets to vets. We will be asking season ticket holders to donate their seats for this great occasion, with wounded vets getting the best seats possible.

"This is one small way for us to say 'thanks', to all the brave men and woman who have spilled their blood to keep us free."

Trance waited for the applause to die down, before standing himself.

"I want to thank you all for keeping this event a secret, so that it would be a surprise for my wonderful bride, Lauren. I apologize to my politician friends for not letting you in on the plan. But you are not known for your discretion.

"Lauren and I have been close for more than twenty years. During that time she has always been there for me. She was there when my first wife was killed. She was there when my parents were murdered in Austria. She's been there when I've been wounded. She's nursed me back to health on too many occasions.

"Lauren has always been there when I've needed a friend or a good laugh. I can think of no finer person with whom to spend the rest of my life. I hope to always be worthy of her love and her respect."

Lauren stood up and raised a glass to her parents. "Mom, I love you…Daddy, you know how much I love you. And you both know how much I love Jack. You always told me to wait for the right man to come around. Who would have thought we'd have to wait over twenty years? But here we are and I couldn't be happier."

Lauren seemed to hesitate, but then continued. "I understand that I will now be subjected to the increased scrutiny that comes with Jack's kind of wealth. Before the paparazzi start their engines, there are a couple of things I need to say, so that the air is clean."

Lauren smiled and raised her glass to Trance. "My husband has recently purchased the New York Yankees. I assure you, that even though this is traumatic for me, it will not damage our marriage."

Trance laughed and raised his glass. There was a roar of applause and a good deal of animated talking over this. Lauren saw several people reach for their mobile devices, trying to be the first to break the news.

"The other thing is, when we have children, which we expect will be soon, we want them to grow up in a fairly normal household. Jack and I do not seek publicity. We hope that you will respect our decision to try to live private lives."

Trance stood once more and turned to Jock Tilson. "All of you know that the president is our nation's Commander In Chief. What you don't know is that President Tilson recently showed unusual courage in the face of danger. For his heroism, I am pleased to announce that, at my recommendation, Jason Tilson has been awarded the Navy Cross. This medal is for extreme gallantry and risk of life in actual combat with an armed enemy force. The president's actions have been witnessed first hand and have been deemed to be such a high degree as to be above those required for all other U.S. combat decorations."

President Jock Tilson was overcome with a strange mixture of surprise, anguish and joy. After six months as a captive in a waterlogged, stone basement. After watching Trance die and return to life like Lazarus. After watching his mother's boat explode, not knowing if she were alive. After finding out that he had a brother, and that his brother had unwittingly become part of a global plot to destroy the country. After learning that his brother had almost killed the man who had saved him…He turned to Slash Whinton and pressed his face against her shoulder. Slash patted him on the back and said, "It's okay, Jock. Everything is going to be okay."

Trance motioned for Tilson to approach him. He held up the medal for everyone to see, before pinning onto the president's chest.

"Thank you for your courage and service to your country," said Trance.

After the applause died down, Trance said, "The silent auction for the da Vinci painting will continue for another two hours. All proceeds will go to my 501(c)(3) foundation, Second Chances. You should know that I have already bid one hundred million dollars on behalf of the Clark Art Museum. I have lawyers standing by if any of you wish to pool your resources and form partnerships or LLCs to buy this thing." Trance paused. "All right, everybody. It is time to make a choice of where to be.

"You are all welcome to stay here at the house. Guys named Mick and Bruce, and gals named Celine, Carrie and Taylor will be here to entertain you." Trance motioned toward a large man with dark, graying hair and piercingly intelligent blue eyes who was sitting up at the head table. "In exchange for my well-spent donation to the Northern and Eastern Maine Medical Centers, my friend Stephen has agreed to allow me to ruin his opening act by playing along for a bit." Trance gestured out toward the ocean. "If you want to party with Jimmy, you should come with us on the boat. Those of you continuing on to the ballpark will find limos waiting for you at Rowes Wharf. Limos will be leaving from here and returning here as well."

"Why are you in such a hurry to get to Fenway?" asked Lauren, when Trance sat back down. "The game won't be starting for hours."

"I've got something planned," said Trance. "A celebrity baseball game."

"Today?"

"Before the game. As we speak, announcements are going out on the radio. It's a charity event. People can donate whatever they want to the Red Sox Foundation. The food and drinks are free, compliments of Hopewell Industries. The president is going to play. So is his brother. A bunch of the Hollywood types, some politicians and a number of athletes are going to join us. You can play, too, if you want. It's going to be fun."

"Are you going to play?"

Trance smiled and shook his head. "Nah. I'm going to umpire."

"Good. We wouldn't want you stress that heart. At least not until later tonight."

Lauren drew Trance away by the shoulder. She said, "I have a wedding present for you, too, Jack."

"Really?"

"I do. It's not quite ready yet. I thought I might have a little more notice. I have been saving it for our wedding day..." Lauren looked at Trance and began to blink. She looked away. "I never lost hope, Jack. Never." Lauren sniffed and straightened her shoulders. "I worked on this whenever I could." Lauren led Trance over toward the garage. "Dad's been helping me for years, so he knew to bring it along with him to the wedding." When Lauren reached the three car garage she pulled open the left bay door. Inside it was a 1945 Packard. Most of it had been restored, except for the rear bumper, which was still covered with burnt orange rust.

"A '45 Packard," said Trance. He laughed. "You know, I was conceived in one of these."

"No, Jack. You were conceived in this car. This is where your life began."

"This is the actual car?"

"It took me two years to find it, but yes. It was sitting in a barn in Idaho."

Trance opened the driver's door and sat inside. "Want to try it out?"

"Later. I've got lots of plans for us later, Jack."

Trance grew serious. "This is perfect, you know. Just like you."

CHAPTER **144**

_______________PP_______________

When they reached Fenway, the old ballpark was already beginning to fill. Lauren had changed into a pair of jeans and a Red Sox jersey. Trance wore a Naval Academy sweatshirt, jeans and a Yankees cap.

Lauren stood in the Loge section behind home plate, staring out over the ballpark. She felt the same excited anticipation she felt before every baseball game, something that reminded her of childhood, when life was innocent and uncomplicated. "I love this place," she said to Trance. "Too bad we can't sit together."

"You're not serious?"

Lauren kissed Trance on the end of his nose. "I will never sit with you while you're wearing that cap."

A voice came over the loud speaker system. "Would Jack and Lauren Trance please report to the owner's box... Jack and Lauren Trance, please report to the owner's box."

"That would be us," said Trance. "Got to go place my dollar bet with Johns."

When they entered the Red Sox owner's box, Charles Johns was standing by the window, staring out at the emerald field. He stood for just a moment longer, looking across at the Green Monster, before turning to greet his guests.

"Glad you two could make it," he said.

"I'm not with him," said Lauren, playfully. "Jack's gone to the dark side."

"So, I hear."

Lauren said, "Whatever do you think could possess him to buy the Yankees?"

Johns looked to Trance. "You haven't told her?"

Trance shook his head.

Johns laughed.

"Told me what?" Lauren looked at Trance and then to Johns. "Why is everybody so weird today?"

Trance looked to Johns and said, "You ready?"

Johns nodded. "I am."

Trance reached into his back pocket and pulled out a brown manila envelope. Johns walked over to a white-clothed banquet table and removed a sheath of papers that had been rolled up and tied with a red string. The two men walked toward each other and met in the center of the suite. Trance offered his folder with one hand and took the papers with the other.

"Your lawyers happy?" said Trance.

Johns nodded. "Yours?"

Trance nodded.

The two men shook hands. Then Trance walked to the window and began to look out over the field. Lauren stood by his side. "Isn't it beautiful?" she said.

Trance began to blink, but he said nothing. He handed the rolled paper to his wife and said, "Happy wedding day."

Lauren looked at Johns, who shrugged. She looked at the rolled up paper. "What's this?"

"I don't know," said Trance. He nodded toward Johns. "He gave it to me, as a wedding gift, I think. So, I give it to you."

Lauren pulled the red string off of the roll and unfurled the papers. She dropped them to the floor and jumped into Trance's arms. He caught her lightly and swung her around the room.

Trance said, "I told you that Johns wouldn't *sell* the team. The only thing he'd do was *trade* for them, the Yankees only."

"So you don't own the Yankees?"

"Not anymore."

"You own the Red Sox?"

"No. You do."

"I do? I own the Red Sox?"

"Yes, dear. After all those years of steadfast love and loyalty, you've earned this."

Lauren began to jump up and down. She looked more like a teenager at a rock concert than the owner of a baseball team. "Oh, this is so exciting! This is so….exciting…" She ran out of the room, yelling, "Mom! Dad! Guess what…"

Trance turned to Johns. "Think she's excited?"

"She better be, Trance. You took a two billion dollar bath in this deal."

"No," said Trance. "This was the best deal I've ever made."

CHAPTER **145**
_____________PP_____________

The score was six to three. It was the bottom of the sixth inning, the final frame. Brandon Copley was on the mound, throwing gas. There were runners on first and second, with two out. The crane-like speaker of the house was up at bat, while President Jock Tilson waited on deck. Slash Whinton stood beside Tilson looking like a coach.

Whinton said, "You want to know what I used to say? Back when you were at Harvard?"

"If it would help me, now would be a good time."

"You have a blind spot."

"I do?"

"Yeah. You have a small hole in your retina. Trance confirmed it."

"How would he know?"

"He learned about it when comparing you with your brother, looking for evidence that you were missing."

"So?"

"You can't see all of a high inside fastball. You've got to open your stance, just a bit, like Johnny Damon used to do. That way you won't be hitting blind."

"That's what you used to tell me?"

"It was always obvious to me."

"Ball four," yelled Trance. "Based loaded. Next batter."

Jock Tilson stepped to the plate. He looked out to his brother. "Like déjà vu all over again," he mumbled, echoing the old Yogi Berra saying.

Tilson looked down the first base line and saw his mother taking a picture. "Give it your best, boys!" she yelled. Both sons waved to her and smiled.

Tilson stepped into the batter's box and dug in his feet. Tubby Smith was crouching behind the plate, pounding his fist into the catcher's mitt.

"Good luck, Jock," he said. He called for a fastball, but Copley waved him off until Tubby called for a curve ball, starting high and tight.

Brandon Copley reared back and threw the ball inside at the letters. Tilson jumped out of the way, thinking the ball was going to hit him, just as the ball darted down and over the back edge of the plate.

"Strike one!" yelled Trance. "Sorry, Jock. Gotta call 'em as I see 'em."

Tilson looked to Slash Whinton. She was still standing next to the on-deck circle. She made a motion for Tilson to open his stance. Stubbornly, Tilson shook her off.

Copley wasted two pitches, hoping Tilson would chase one. The count stood at two balls and one strike, when Copley came inside again. This time is was a fastball. Tilson saw the ball at the last minute and waved at it anemically.

"Two and two, Jock," said Trance.

Tilson looked over to Whinton. He looked to his mother. He thought back to that day, the Harvard-Yale game, with the bases loaded and two outs. Copley had come at him three times in a row with high middle-in fastballs. He had swung at each pitch, never coming close. All because of a tiny macular hole in his retina? No, he had choked. He'd be damned if he'd choke again.

Tilson watched as Copley shook off two signs from Tubby. Tilson looked one last time at Whin ton, before sliding his front foot back away from the plate, like Johnny Damon used to do. With his open stance, Jock Tilson saw the ball come toward him. He could see the rotation; he could feel the speed. He stepped forward and swung the bat, while keeping his shoulder in so he didn't pull off the ball. He met the fastball squarely and it launched. He stood in place as the ball arched high into the air. The ball traveled up into the outgoing breeze. It seemed to ride the wind like a wave. The ball landed in the first row of monster seats, just above the tall, green left field wall. The crowd cheered wildly, as if Yaz or Rice or Manny had come back for an encore, or Papi had hit one in his glory days. Jock Tilson looked to his mother. She was clapping and cheering with the rest of the fans. He looked to Slash Whinton. She was screaming and doing an Irish jig. This gave him a jolt, like the turning of some inner switch, telling him that he had found someone. He had found a woman who might work away that deep ache in his gut, someone who could help fill that hollow emptiness he felt when he closed his eyes at night. His life could never be the same, not like it was with Kiki. But he could go on, maybe even be happy, in time. Tilson flipped the bat and accepted high-fives from Trance and Tubby, before heading into a slow home run trot. His brother stood on the mound with a smile on his face. He was clapping, too.

There was a crowd at home plate. When Tilson jumped down he was mobbed, as if his team had just won the World Series. And after what they'd been through, he felt like they had.

EPILOGUE I

It was nearly game time. Trance finished showering and returned to the owner's box. The place was packed with wedding guests standing around an open bar and a line of buffet tables. Lauren had changed into a light fleece jacket. She was standing alone, staring out at the field, still trying to process the events of the day. The day was supposed to have been a simple lunch, followed by a late afternoon run along the Nantasket beach. Then they were to have dinner by the sea. Now she found herself married, with a new home and a baseball team.

"Penny for your thoughts," said Trance, as he came up behind her.

Lauren pulled Trance's hand around her waist. She looked out over Fenway and glow of the city beyond it.

"I was thinking how fragile and unpredictable life can be," Lauren said softly.

"Yeah." Trance squeezed her gently, making sure not to press too hard on the babies.

"To think that you were dead...What would I have done?"

"Do I look dead to you?"

Lauren closed her eyes. "I was thinking how happy I am, but how easily all this could have changed. What if the bomb's timer had been early, rather than late? What if Tilson had not turned back? What if Sammantha had not been able to start your heart? What if Petrovski had succeeded? What if the truck had a flat tire on the way to the hospital? What if—"

Trance pressed a hand against Lauren's lips. "We can only play the cards we're dealt, sweetheart, as best we can. There are powers far greater than us. We are at their whim."

Lauren regarded Trance, from his feet to his head. He was dressed in a pair of old Levis, a washed-out Red Sox T-shirt and a pair of Mizuno running shoes. He pulled a lopsided Red Sox cap out of the back pocket of his pants and fastened it onto his head. He held up two tickets and said, "I've got bleacher seats."

Lauren laughed. "Oh, my, Trance. You are really *on* today. You've thought of everything."

"Took me years to figure things out."

"You're a slow learner, but I think I'll keep you."

Trance walked out of the Bleacher Bar into the stands carrying a tray of chili dogs and four bottled waters.

"You see how much they charge for this stuff?" he said to Lauren. "This junk cost me as much as our wedding. I'm going to have to bring this up with the owner."

"That's not junk. It is baseball cuisine. And the owner of this team knows enough to stay out of the way and let management do its job. You don't like the prices, bring it up with them. I'm just a fan here, enjoying the game."

When they reached the aisle, Lauren saw a yellow bow tied across a seat that was painted red.

"Is that what I think it is?" said Lauren. "Is that the Ted Williams seat?"

"Yes, dear. That is one very expensive seat."

"Five hundred two feet away from home and worth every penny."

They settled into their chairs, in front of two familiar looking nuns wearing black and white habits.

"Hello, dear," said one of the nuns. "Good to see you again."

Lauren laughed. "Isn't this great?"

The nuns nodded knowingly. One of them said, "I think if God had one game, this would be it."

A voice came over the ballpark loud speakers. "Good evening, ladies and gentlemen, boys and girls. And welcome to Fenway Park…Before President Tilson throws out tonight's first pitch, we would like to introduce you to the new owner of the Boston Red Sox..." The voice paused, allowing the news to sink in. The crowd grew unusually quiet, as if time had been suspended. "…Mrs. Lauren Trance…Just married today."

The camera zoomed in on Lauren sitting out in the bleachers. She was in the midst of chewing down a chili dog. She raised her hot dog to the crowd and mumbled, "Go Sox!"

When the crowd saw Lauren on the center field screen they began to cheer, standing everywhere around her. They started giving her high fives, ignoring her husband. Trance liked it that way. He smiled, as he watched Lauren's face glow with a carefree excitement.

When Lauren sat back down she grew solemn. She looked to her husband and said, "I love you, Jack."

"And I will always love you."

Lauren shook her head, smiling. "My God, Trance. I think you're catching on to this game." Lauren winked that the nuns who still stood behind them. Then she turned toward home plate and yelled, "C'mon, Jock. Show us what you've got!"

EPILOGUE II

Sammantha's hand was shaking uncontrollably as she pressed the tarnished brass key into the door lock. She felt her heart rise up into her throat, squeezing the breath out of her like an assassin's hands.

"It's okay," said Trance from behind her. "You can do this."

Sammantha turned the key and opened the door. She could see herself running across that living room floor, a big smile upon her face, ready to turn the corner and race to the sunny alcove where she would eat Oreo cookies and drink milk with her mother. She could see her parents lying dead on the other side of the wall, with blood trickling from their heads and her puppy licking the floor, whining like a…like someone who had lost his way.

Sammantha took slow, tentative steps until she reached the edge of the room, knowing that the other side of that opening held a memory so treacherous that it might stop her dead.

Sammantha felt Brandon Copley grasp her hand. She felt a hot tingle run along her arm. She looked into his eyes. She wasn't alone, not anymore.

"You can do this," he said.

Sammantha looked at Trance. She looked at Lauren. She looked to Slash Whinton, her therapist, who nodded with encouragement. They were here to support her. After all she had done, after all the pain she had created, they were here for her.

Sammantha edged around the corner. She looked down to the floor. The tile was clean and shiny. Light was pouring in from the windows and the room was bright, so bright she thought she might go blind. There were no bodies on this floor. There was no blood. That was a memory, a mere memory. It was only in her mind. So why did she shake? Why was her stomach in her throat? Why couldn't she swallow? Why couldn't she breathe?

Sammantha took a halting step into the room. She looked over to the alcove. There were three place settings—three small plates and three empty glasses. Sammantha remembered now, how Sandra Smith would join them there. Sometimes Sandra would come in with her, and her mother would set an extra place. They would sit there and laugh, eating cookies and drinking that cold, sweet milk. This had been the apex of Sammantha's life, the daily ritual that stood out in her memory like a rock, an anchor that kept her sane, the vision that reminded her that carefree happiness was possible.

Sammantha walked to the table and set her butterfly cup upon it. The cup tilted and wobbled, its pieces glued together in so many haphazard places. But it was there, as it used to be, waiting for her to fill it with milk.

Sammantha looked to the old yellow refrigerator, where her mother would keep the milk, that building block of life. Milk and cookies, the foundation of Sammantha's past. The refrigerator was tattooed with white envelopes. They were held onto it with playful-looking magnets colored with things like *Sesame Street* characters, *Wild Things* and *Hannah Montana*. Sammantha walked closer. She saw that each one of the envelopes had a date written in the corner. June 8, 1995…1996…1997. Always on June 8th, the day it all had happened. June 8th, today.

Sammantha removed the earliest envelope, the one dated exactly one year after she had gone missing. She reached inside and removed three pages of white lined paper torn out from a notebook.

"Dear Sammantha," it began. *"I am writing this letter to tell you that I miss you. I want you to know that I am taking care of Starr until you come home. Mom says that there is some kind of trust or something that is going to keep this house for you until you come back. They say we can keep Starr here for as long as we want. So I come here every day to give him food and try to teach him. I don't know much*

about horses, but I am learning. Mom pays for a guy to come in from Tyson's Corner to show me what to do. I'm not really good with horses, but I'm getting better I think. Maybe someday you can come and ride him in the shows like you hoped.

"I don't know where you are or how long you will be gone. But I know I really miss you. I feel like a part of me is gone. You were my bestest friend and I think you always will be."

They heard a soft knock upon the front door, then a tentative, "Hello?"

There was a louder knock. "Hello!"

Sammantha stood frozen in place. Trance went to meet the guest. A few moments later he walked back into the kitchen. Behind him waddled Sandra Smith. She held a white envelope in her hand, with the date printed neatly in the corner.

"Sandra?" said Sammantha.

"Sammantha?"

The two women ran to each other and hugged. They did an elaborate pat-a-cake, ending with a double hip bump.

"I knew you would come back," said Sandra. "I knew it."

"You…you look great," said Sammantha. "Very pregnant, and really, really great."

Sandra patted her baby belly. "My first. You'll need to meet Dave. He's a great guy."

Sammantha ran her hand across her own growing womb and smiled. She turned to Brandon Copley. "This is my husband, Brandon Copley."

"He looks just like the president."

"Doesn't he?"

Copley kissed Sandra on the cheek. "You don't know how great it is to meet you," he said. He pointed toward the envelopes on the refrigerator. "Are all those from you?"

"I leave one every year on this day. It was such a tragedy and I…" Sandra's eyes brightened. She jumped up and down, and began clapping her hands. She took Sammantha by the elbow. "Oh, my, it's so good to see you…Come!"

Sandra pulled Sammantha out the back door in a kind of pregnant canter, too excited to slow down. Trance, Lauren, Copley and Slash followed close behind. Sandra opened the door to the big red barn and walked down its center aisle until she came to a horse's stall. There was a loud whinny, then a couple snorts, before a horse poked its head over the stall door. There was an unmistakable white star emblazoned on the horse's forehead.

"It's Starr," whispered Sammantha. She walked hesitantly toward her old horse, as if afraid he might vanish in a dream.

"Careful, he bites," said Sandra.

Starr didn't bite. His ears perked forward and he allowed Sammantha to scratch his forehead and then stoke his neck.

"He remembers you."

"He looks fabulous," Sammantha said.

"Yeah, but he's become a crotchety old thing."

"You must love him."

Sandra blinked. "He means a lot."

"Will you share him?"

Sandra blinked again. "He's your horse. No sharing needed."

"No," said Sammantha. "He's your horse now, my dear, dear friend. I would love to share him with you, if that's okay."

"Oh, Samm…We all missed you so."

Sammantha turned to Trance. She looked at him for a long moment. She thought of herself sitting on the floor, rocking, praying just to get through to the next moment. She thought of all the death in the wake of her life. Then she thought of her baby, and the new life stretching out before her. She thought of Second Chances, of the men and women she hoped to heal in the upcoming years, as she tried to earn redemption. She felt renewed, reborn. *Life is not what happens to you,* she thought. *It is what you do with your life when things happen to it. Life is not easy; it never is. But you can be worthy of it, Sammantha. Make yourself worthy.*

"Thank you, Jack."

The End

Author's Note:

I hope you enjoyed *The Presidential Pretender*. This is part of a series of books. The story begins with *The Alchemist Conspiracy*. It is continues with *The Varicose Vigilantes* and *The Varicose Vigilantes II - Hedge Money*. You can order these books through your favorite bookstore and online at major retailers. You can learn more about them through my websites, www.lumbert.com and www.jaylumbert.com. You should also visit the Shaksper Books website at www.shaksperbooks.com.

Please feel free to contact me directly. You can do this easily through my websites. My direct email is jay@lumbert.com. Because of security and spam filters, it would be helpful if you added a book title to the subject heading of your email.

I enjoy hearing from readers. Don't be a stranger. Let me know what you think.

Life is what you make it… Enjoy!

**Please note that Jay Lumbert's books are available
through local bookstores everywhere.
They can be purchased at all major online bookstores, such as
Amazon.com, BarnesAndNoble.com and Borders.com.**

You can send an email to Jay Lumbert through his websites.
www.lumbert.com   www.jaylumbert.com

If you have difficulty going through his websites, Jay's direct
email address is
jay@lumbert.com.

Because of security and spam filters, it would be helpful if you added the title to one of his books to the Subject heading of your email.

www.ingramcontent.com/pod-product-compliance
Lightning Source LLC
Chambersburg PA
CBHW082051090726
47909CB00010B/3006